"Trust me when I say you'll like this novel..."*

TRUST NO ONE

"The final twists and turns of the plot are among Krentz's best."

—*The Seattle Times*

"Clever plotting, complex pacing and a compelling cast of characters propel *Trust No One* to its dynamite finish."

—*Booklist* (starred review)

"You can count on Krentz to deliver a good story with twists and turns and memorable characters."

—**The News-Gazette*

The author of *River Road* and *Dream Eyes* delivers another masterpiece of romantic suspense . . .

When Grace Elland finds her boss, motivational speaker Sprague Witherspoon, murdered, a vodka bottle on his nightstand is a terrifying reminder of the horrors of her past—one that can be no coincidence.

To regroup, Grace retreats to her childhood home, Cloud Lake, where she meets venture capitalist Julius Arkwright, a man who lives to make money by any means necessary. But the intense former Marine has skills that Grace can use—to figure out her future. And he's the perfect man to help Grace when it becomes clear she is being stalked.

As Witherspoon's financial empire continues to crumble around them, taking a deadly toll, Julius will walk Grace step by step into her past to uncover a devious plan to destroy not only Grace but everyone around her as well . . .

"An intriguing, textured mystery that perfectly layers humor, suspense and romance." —***Kirkus Reviews*** **(starred review)**

"[A] flawlessly executed novel of romantic suspense from one of the genre's most reliable literary stars."

—***Booklist*** **(starred review)**

"Two appealing protagonists, a mysterious enemy and a twisty plot provide all the necessary ingredients for a satisfying story." —***Publishers Weekly***

"Descriptive narrative sustains the suspense while providing a good feel for time and place. Fans will enjoy reading *Trust No One*." **—Fresh Fiction**

"Zingy dialogue, superb sensuality and a pair of protagonists meant for each other drive the twisted plot of this clever page-turner to its gratifying conclusion." —***Library Journal***

continued . . .

Praise for Jayne Ann Krentz and her novels

"A joy to read." —*USA Today*

"There's a reason Jayne Ann Krentz sells so many books . . . [She] continues to exhibit a fine knack for entertaining her readers." —*Fort Worth Star-Telegram*

"Incendiary . . . evocative." —*The Seattle Times*

"Jayne Ann Krentz neatly infuses her special brand of sexy romantic suspense with a generous soupçon of psychic thrills and sharp wit." —*Chicago Tribune*

"A master of romantic mystery and suspense novels." —*The Columbus Dispatch*

"Romantic tension sizzles . . . Tightly plotted . . . fully developed characters and crafty plot twists." —*The Philadelphia Inquirer*

"Will surely keep the sandman at bay . . . Terrific." —*The Roanoke (VA) Times*

"Simply irresistible." —*Booklist* (starred review)

"Intriguing suspense and captivating romance expertly crafted." —*The (Columbia, SC) State*

"Fast, steamy and wildly entertaining." —*Publishers Weekly*

"Pure adventure and romance the Krentz way." —Examiner.com

Titles by Jayne Ann Krentz

SECRET SISTERS
TRUST NO ONE
RIVER ROAD
DREAM EYES
COPPER BEACH
IN TOO DEEP
FIRED UP
RUNNING HOT
SIZZLE AND BURN
WHITE LIES
ALL NIGHT LONG
FALLING AWAKE
TRUTH OR DARE
LIGHT IN SHADOW
SUMMER IN ECLIPSE BAY
TOGETHER IN ECLIPSE BAY
SMOKE IN MIRRORS
LOST & FOUND
DAWN IN ECLIPSE BAY
SOFT FOCUS
ECLIPSE BAY
EYE OF THE BEHOLDER
FLASH
SHARP EDGES
DEEP WATERS
ABSOLUTELY, POSITIVELY
TRUST ME
GRAND PASSION
HIDDEN TALENTS
WILDEST HEARTS
FAMILY MAN
PERFECT PARTNERS
SWEET FORTUNE
SILVER LININGS
THE GOLDEN CHANCE

Titles by Jayne Ann Krentz writing as Amanda Quick

GARDEN OF LIES
OTHERWISE ENGAGED
THE MYSTERY WOMAN
CRYSTAL GARDENS
QUICKSILVER
BURNING LAMP
THE PERFECT POISON
THE THIRD CIRCLE
THE RIVER KNOWS
SECOND SIGHT
LIE BY MOONLIGHT
THE PAID COMPANION
WAIT UNTIL MIDNIGHT
LATE FOR THE WEDDING
DON'T LOOK BACK
SLIGHTLY SHADY
WICKED WIDOW
I THEE WED
WITH THIS RING
AFFAIR
MISCHIEF
MYSTIQUE
MISTRESS
DECEPTION
DESIRE
DANGEROUS
RECKLESS
RAVISHED
RENDEZVOUS
SCANDAL
SURRENDER
SEDUCTION

Titles by Jayne Ann Krentz writing as Jayne Castle

SIREN'S CALL
THE HOT ZONE
DECEPTION COVE
THE LOST NIGHT
CANYONS OF NIGHT
MIDNIGHT CRYSTAL
OBSIDIAN PREY
DARK LIGHT
SILVER MASTER
GHOST HUNTER
AFTER GLOW
AFTER DARK
AMARYLLIS
ZINNIA
ORCHID

The Guinevere Jones Titles

Desperate and Deceptive
The Guinevere Jones Collection, Volume 1
THE DESPERATE GAME
THE CHILLING DECEPTION

Sinister and Fatal
The Guinevere Jones Collection, Volume 2
THE SINISTER TOUCH
THE FATAL FORTUNE

Specials

THE SCARGILL COVE CASE FILES
BRIDAL JITTERS
(writing as Jayne Castle)

Anthologies

CHARMED
(with Julie Beard, Lori Foster, and Eileen Wilks)

Titles written by Jayne Ann Krentz and Jayne Castle

NO GOING BACK

TRUST NO ONE

Jayne Ann Krentz

Jove Books
New York

JOVE
An imprint of Penguin Random House LLC
375 Hudson Street, New York, New York 10014

TRUST NO ONE

A Jove Book / published by arrangement with the author

ISBN: 978-0-515-15581-5

PUBLISHING HISTORY
G. P. Putnam's Sons hardcover edition / January 2015
Jove mass-market edition / January 2016

PRINTED IN THE UNITED STATES OF AMERICA

10 9 8 7 6 5 4 3 2 1

Cover photo of woman © Elisabeth Ansley/Trevillion Images;
abstract colorful background © adistock/Shutterstock.
Cover design by Rita Frangie.

Penguin
Random
House

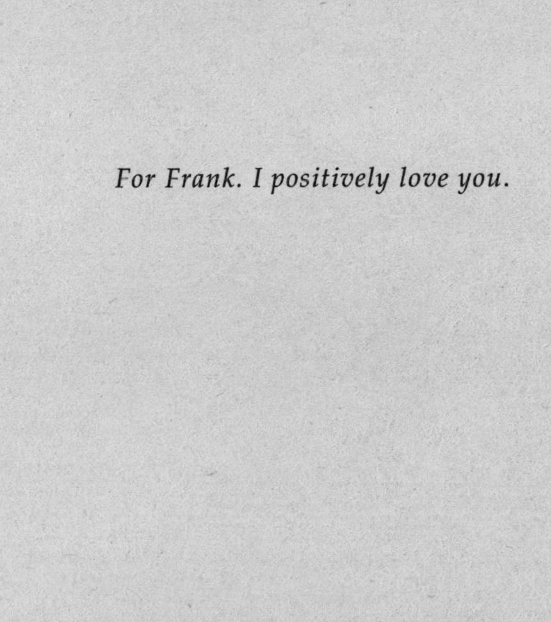

For Frank. I positively love you.

TRUST NO ONE

One

The note pinned to the front of the dead man's silk pajamas was a one-sentence email printed out from a computer: *Make Today a Great Day the Witherspoon Way.*

Grace Elland leaned over the blood-soaked sheets and forced herself to touch the cold skin of Sprague Witherspoon's throat. His blue eyes, once so brilliant and compelling, were open. He stared sightlessly at the bedroom ceiling. A robust, square-jawed man with a mane of silver hair, he had always seemed larger than life. But death had shrunk him. All of the charm and electrifying charisma that had captivated the Witherspoon Way seminar audiences across the country had been drained away.

She was certain that he had been gone for several hours but she thought she detected a faint, accusing question in his unseeing eyes. Shattering memories splintered through her. At the age of sixteen she had seen the same question in the eyes of a dead woman. *Why didn't you get here in time to save me?*

She looked away from the dead eyes—and saw the unopened bottle of vodka on the nightstand.

For a terrible moment past and present merged there in the bedroom. She heard the echo of heavy footsteps on old floorboards. Panic threatened to choke her. This could not be happening, not again. It's the old dream, she thought. You're in the middle of a nightmare but you're awake. Breathe. Focus, damn it, and breathe.

Breathe.

The mantra broke the panic-induced trance. The echoing footsteps faded into the past. Ice-cold adrenaline splashed through her veins, bringing with it an intense clarity. This was not a dream. She was in a room with a dead man, and although she was almost certain that the footsteps had been summoned up from her nightmare, there was still the very real possibility that the killer was still around.

She grabbed the nearest available weapon—the vodka bottle—and moved to the doorway. There she paused to listen intently. The big house felt empty. Perhaps the footsteps had been an auditory illusion generated by the panicky memories. Or not. Either way, the smart thing to do was get out of the mansion and call 911.

She moved into the hallway, trying to make as little noise as possible. A fog of shadows darkened the big house. There were elegant potted plants everywhere—vibrant green bamboo, palms and ferns. Sprague had firmly believed that the abundant foliage not only improved indoor air quality but enhanced the positive energy in the atmosphere.

The curtains that covered the windows had been closed for the night. No one had been alive to draw them back that morning. Not that it would have done much good. The Seattle winter dawn had arrived with a low, overcast sky and now rain was tapping at the windows. On days like this, most people turned on a few lights.

No one rushed out of a doorway to confront her. Gripping the neck of the vodka bottle very tightly, she went down the broad staircase. When she reached the bottom, she flew across the grand living room.

She knew her way around the first floor of the house because Sprague Witherspoon had entertained lavishly and often. He always invited Grace and the other members of the Witherspoon Way staff to his catered affairs.

The vast great room had been furnished and decorated with those events in mind. The chairs, cushioned benches and tables were arranged in what designers called conversational groupings. There was a lot of expensive art on the walls.

Sprague Witherspoon had lived the lifestyle he had tried to teach in his seminars, and the motivational business had been good to him. With Sprague it had been all about positive thinking and an optimistic attitude.

But now someone had murdered him.

She whipped through the front door and out into the beautifully manicured gardens. She did not stop to pull up the hood of her jacket. By the time she reached her little compact waiting in the sweeping circular driveway, her hair and face were soaked.

She got behind the wheel, locked all of the doors, put the vodka bottle on the floor and gunned the engine. She drove through the high steel gates that guarded the Queen Anne mansion and out onto the quiet residential street.

Once outside the grounds she brought the car to a halt and reached into her cross-body bag for her phone. It proved amazingly difficult to enter 911 because her hands were shaking so hard. When she finally got through to the operator she had to close her eyes in order to concentrate on getting the facts straight.

Breathe.

"Sprague Witherspoon is dead." She watched the big gates while she rattled off the address. "At least, I think he's dead. I couldn't find a pulse. It looks like he's been shot. There is . . . a lot of blood."

More memories flashed through her head. A man with a face rendered into a bloody mask. Blood raining down on her. Blood everywhere.

"Is there anyone else in the house, ma'am?" The male operator's voice was sharp and urgent. "Are you in danger?"

"I don't think so. I'm outside now. A few minutes ago I went in to check on Mr. Witherspoon because he didn't show up at the office this morning. The gates were open and the front door was unlocked. The alarm was off. I didn't think anything about it because I assumed he was out in the gardens. When I couldn't find him outside, I went into the house. I called out to him. When he didn't respond I worried that he had fallen or become ill. He lives alone, you see, and—"

Shut up, Grace. You're rambling. You must stay focused. You can have a panic attack later.

"Stay outside," the operator said. "I've got responders on the way."

"Yes, all right."

Grace ended the connection and listened to the sirens in the distance.

It wasn't until the first vehicle bearing the logo of the Seattle Police Department came to a stop in front of her car that she remembered a fact that everyone who watched television crime dramas knew well. When it came to suspects, cops always looked hard at the person who found the body.

She had a feeling that the investigators would look even more closely at a suspect who had a history of stumbling over dead bodies.

Breathe.

She looked down at the bottle sitting on the floor of her car. Dread iced her blood.

Don't panic. A lot of people drink vodka.

But the only things she had ever seen Sprague drink were green tea and expensive white wine.

She found a tissue in her bag and used it to pick up the bottle. Not that it mattered much now. Her fingerprints were all over it.

Two

"I suppose the three of us can only be thankful that we've all got reasonably good alibis," Millicent Chartwell said. She sank languidly against the back of the booth and regarded her martini with a forlorn expression. "I didn't like the way that cute detective was watching me today when I gave my statement."

"He wasn't exactly smiling at me," Grace said. She took a sip of her white wine. "In fact, if I weren't the optimistic type, I'd say he was looking for an excuse to arrest me for Sprague's murder."

Kristy Forsyth put down her wineglass. Tears glittered in her eyes. "I can't believe Mr. Witherspoon is gone. I keep thinking there must have been a horrible case of mistaken identity and that he'll come striding through the door of the office tomorrow morning the way he always does, with some fresh-baked scones or doughnuts for us."

"There was no mistake," Grace said. "I saw him. And Nyla Witherspoon identified her father's body. I was still at the house talking to the police when she arrived on the scene. She was seriously distraught. In tears. Shaky. Honestly, I thought she was going to faint."

It was just after five o'clock. The three of them were exhausted and, Grace knew, still dazed. A close encounter with murder had an unnerving effect on most people. She and her office colleagues had not only lost a great boss, they had just lost their jobs. They were all of the opinion that working for the Witherspoon Way had been the best thing that had ever happened to them, career-wise. Their lives had been turned upside down by Sprague's murder.

After giving their statements, Millicent had suggested going for a drink. There was unanimous agreement. They were now seated in a booth in their favorite after-work spot, a cozy tavern and café near the Pike Place Market.

The day was ending the way it had begun, with rain and gloom. The winter solstice had passed a few weeks earlier. The days were becoming perceptibly longer—Seattleites were keen observers of the nuances in the ever-changing patterns of sunlight—but the early evening twilight made it seem as if it were still December on the calendar.

Millicent sipped her martini and narrowed her

eyes. "If I were the police, the first suspect on my list would be Nyla Witherspoon."

As Sprague's bookkeeper and financial manager, Millicent had a tendency to go straight to the bottom line, regardless of the subject. She was a vivacious, curvy redhead with a taste for martinis and the occasional bar hookup.

Millicent had been working for Sprague for nearly a year before Grace had joined the Witherspoon Way team. On the surface, she seemed to have it all—film star–level glamour and a computer for a brain. She had used both to make her way in the world. What Millicent did not have was a family. Her past was murky. She did not like to discuss it. But she had once said that she'd left home at the age of sixteen and had no intention of ever returning. She was a survivor. In spite of the odds against her, she had landed adroitly on her stiletto heels.

Kristy blinked away a few more tears. "Nyla does have the most to gain from Sprague's death, doesn't she? But she's his daughter, for heaven's sake. We all know that she had issues with him. It was a troubled relationship. Still, murdering her father?"

Kristy was the most recent member of the Witherspoon team. Born and raised in a small town in Idaho, she had moved to Seattle in search of adventure and—as she had explained to Grace and Millicent—more options in husbands. With her light brown hair, warm eyes and pretty features, she was attractive in a sweet, wholesome way that went down well with the Witherspoon clients.

Unlike Millicent, Kristy was close to her family. Although she had confided to her coworkers that she did not want to marry a farmer, it was clear that she had a deep and abiding affection for the bucolic world she had left behind. She was forever regaling the office staff with humorous stories about growing up on a farm.

Grace and Millicent had privately speculated that Sprague had felt sorry for Kristy, who had found herself struggling in the big city. Perhaps giving her a job had been, in part, an act of kindness back at the beginning. But somewhat to everyone's amazement, Kristy had quickly displayed an invaluable flair for travel logistics and an ability to charm clients. As the demand for Witherspoon Way seminars had grown, so had the work involved in coordinating Sprague's busy schedule. Business had been so brisk lately that Sprague had been on the verge of hiring an assistant for Kristy.

"It wouldn't be the first time an heir has hurried things along," Millicent pointed out. "Besides, we know that Nyla was furious with Sprague. They argued constantly. Things between them only got worse when Mr. Perfect came along. Sprague didn't approve of him, and that just made Nyla angrier. I think she was ready to do just about anything to get her hands on her inheritance. She hated Sprague for putting her on an allowance."

"Well, she is an adult, not a child," Grace pointed out.

"If you ask me, she decided she didn't want to wait

any longer for the money," Millicent said. She swallowed some more of her martini, lowered the glass and fixed Grace and Kristy with a grim expression. "I think there's something else we should keep in mind."

Kristy frowned. "What?"

Millicent plucked the little plastic spear out of the martini and munched the olive. "It's true that Nyla had issues with her father but she wasn't very fond of the three of us, either. We had better watch our backs."

Kristy's eyes widened. "Jeez, you're serious, aren't you?"

"Oh, yeah," Millicent said.

Grace picked up her glass and took a sip. The wine was starting to soften the edgy sensation that had been riding her hard all day but she knew from experience that the effects would not last. She told herself to think positive but she had a bad feeling that the old dream would return that night.

She studied Millicent. "Do you really think Nyla is a threat?"

Millicent shrugged. "I'm just saying it would be a good idea to be careful for a while. I'm telling you, Nyla Witherspoon is unstable. She and Sprague had what can only be called a fraught relationship but the capper was the new fiancé."

"Burke Marrick," Kristy said. She made a face. "Aka Mr. Perfect."

"You know what?" Millicent said. "Burke Marrick was Sprague's worst nightmare. Sprague was always worried that some good-looking, fast-talking con man would come along and sweep Nyla off her feet.

Why do you think Sprague insisted on paying her bills and keeping her on an allowance? He was trying to protect her."

Kristy sniffed. "Small countries could live on Nyla's allowance."

"The actual amount is beside the point." Millicent aimed the olive spear at Kristy. "If there's one thing I know, it's money, and I know how people react to it. Trust me, no one ever thinks they have enough. Nyla couldn't stand the thought that the bulk of her inheritance was tied up in a special trust that she could not access until her father's death. And I've got a hunch Mr. Perfect was pushing her hard to get ahold of the money."

A grim silence settled on the table. Grace reflected on the fact that they had all had their run-ins with Sprague's temperamental daughter. Nyla had seemed jealous of the three of them. Now she would have her inheritance to go with her charming fiancé. From a certain perspective, life was suddenly looking quite rosy for Nyla. And for Mr. Perfect.

Grace cleared her throat. "You do realize what you're saying, Millicent. If you're right, that means that Burke Marrick is also a suspect."

Kristy put her glass down very quickly. "What if Nyla and Burke planned Sprague's murder together?"

Millicent shrugged. "Wouldn't surprise me."

"I think we had better hold off on the conspiracy theories," Grace said. "If you're going to make a list of suspects, you'll need a really big sheet of paper."

Kristy and Millicent looked at her.

"What do you mean?" Kristy asked. "Sprague was so nice. So generous."

Understanding gleamed in Millicent's eyes. "You're right, Grace. After Nyla and Marrick, the next name on the list just has to be Larson Rayner."

"We all know there was not a lot of positive energy lost between Larson and Sprague," Grace said. "Nothing like a falling-out between business partners to create motive."

"That's true," Kristy said. "Remember how Larson stormed into the office last month and accused Sprague of stealing his clients?"

"Professional envy and a strong dose of jealousy, not to mention a decline in revenues." Millicent smiled. Her green eyes gleamed. "Great motives for murder." She looked at Grace. "I wonder if Larson realizes that you're the reason why Sprague's business took off a year and a half ago."

Grace felt herself turning pink. "That is a gross exaggeration. I had a few ideas and Sprague let me run with them, that's all."

"Bullshit," Millicent said cheerfully. "Before you came along, Sprague Witherspoon was just another motivational speaker in a very crowded field. You're the one who launched the business into the big time."

"Millicent is right," Kristy said. "If poor Sprague hadn't been murdered last night, he would have become the number one self-help guru in the country within a few months, thanks to you."

"The Witherspoon Way was doing well before you came along," Millicent said. "But the really big money didn't start rolling in until after the cookbook was published. The affirmation-of-the-day blog caught fire after that. During the past few months, Kristy couldn't confirm speaking engagements and seminars fast enough. Isn't that right, Kristy?"

"Yes." Kristy smiled reminiscently. "Sprague was on the road every week. I don't know how he did it. But he never complained when I booked back-to-back seminars."

"He loved it," Grace said. "He thrived on the travel and the crowds. He had so much charisma and such an incredible ability to communicate with an audience."

Kristy nodded sagely. "But it was the cookbook and the affirmation blog that put the Witherspoon Way over the top. You're the one who came up with both projects."

"The cookbook and blog would never have worked if they hadn't been done under the Witherspoon name," Grace said. "All I did was dream up some marketing ideas that suited Sprague's approach to positive thinking."

"It's called branding," Millicent said. "I wouldn't be surprised if you get a call from Larson Rayner soon making you an offer you can't refuse."

Kristy brightened. "Maybe he'll offer all three of us positions in his firm. We are, or rather, we *were* Sprague's team. Larson must realize that we've got exactly the qualifications he needs to take him to the top."

"True," Grace said. "But you might want to rethink that career path if it turns out that Larson Rayner is a suspect in Sprague's murder. Could be tough to book future seminars for him."

Kristy winced. "There is that little problem."

"As for that list of suspects we were talking about," Grace said, "it doesn't end with Nyla, Burke and Larson Rayner. You'll have to add those odd and disgruntled seminar attendees—the folks who emailed Sprague to complain because their lives did not undergo a dramatic change after they started practicing the Witherspoon Way."

"Well, shit," Millicent said. "You're right, Grace. That would make for a very long list."

Kristy sighed. "It may be sort of tacky under the circumstances but I can't help noticing that if Larson Rayner is on the suspect list, our pool of potential employers is going to be extremely small. I don't imagine there are a lot of folks out there looking for people who possess the skills required to manage the office of a motivational speaker."

"On the other hand," Millicent said, going very thoughtful, "if Rayner is cleared as a suspect, he's going to need us. I wonder if he knows that?"

Grace picked up her wine. "Time for some serious positive thinking, as Sprague would say."

"We need a Witherspoon affirmation for successful job hunting," Kristy announced. She gave Grace a misty smile. "You're the affirmation writer in the crowd. Got one for us?"

Millicent laughed. "Well, Grace? What would be a good Witherspoon Way saying for those of us who find ourselves suddenly unemployed?"

Grace ran one fingertip around the rim of her wineglass and gave the problem some thought.

"If Sprague were here he would remind us that no one finds an interesting future by staying indoors and waiting for a sunny day," she said. *"To discover your future you must go outdoors and take a walk in the rain."*

"That sounds about right," Kristy said. Her warm eyes turned somber and serious. "Don't know about the rest of you, but working for the Witherspoon Way really did change my life." She raised her wineglass. "Here's to Sprague Witherspoon."

"To Sprague," Millicent said.

"To Sprague," Grace said.

Millicent downed the last of her martini and signaled the waiter for another round.

"I probably shouldn't say this," she said, "given how much money I made working for the Witherspoon Way, and absolutely no offense intended toward you, Grace, but I have to tell you that I really detest those dumbass Witherspoon Way affirmations."

Three

The dream was lying in wait for her . . .

. . . The wind shrieking through the old abandoned asylum caught the door at the top of the stairs and slammed it shut.

The darkness of the basement closed in around her. It was suddenly hard to breathe. She knew she could not allow her own fear to show. She had to stay strong for the boy. He was unnaturally calm, the way people are in dreams. He clung to her hand and looked up at her.

She knew that he was waiting to see if she would save him. That was what adults were supposed to do—save little kids. She wanted to tell him that she wasn't a real grown-up. She was only sixteen years old.

"He's coming back," the boy said. "He hurt that lady and he's going to hurt us, too."

She aimed the cell phone flashlight at the long bundle on

the floor. Her first thought was that someone had left an unrolled sleeping bag in the basement. But it wasn't a sleeping bag. The eyes of the dead woman stared up at her through the thick layers of plastic.

Heavy footsteps thudded on the wooden floor overhead. Hurriedly she switched off the flashlight.

"Hide," she said to the boy in the language of dreams.

The door at the top of the steps opened. The entrance to the basement was once again illuminated with an empty gray light. Soon the monster would appear.

"It's too late," the boy said. "He's here now."

There was a small prescription medication container on the floor near the dead woman. Next to it was a liquor bottle. She could not see the brand on the bottle but she could make out the word vodka.

The only way out was through the door at the top of the stairs . . .

The ping of the email alert brought her out of the nightmare on a rush of adrenaline that tightened her throat and iced her blood. For a few seconds her heart pounded to the dark rhythm of the killer's footsteps. She hovered in the murky terrain between the dream state and the waking state.

Breathe.

It had been a while since the dream had haunted her nights but she had long ago made the breathing exercises a daily routine. It was one of three rituals that she practiced regularly. All were related to the nightmare of the past.

She sat up quickly on the edge of the bed and focused on her breath. But the edgy, fight-or-flight sensation threatened to overwhelm her. She could not sit quietly so she got up, went out into the living room and started to pace. Sometimes it took a few minutes to calm her nerves.

The gentle glow of night-lights illuminated every room in the small apartment. In addition, the drapes were open to allow the city lights to pour in through her fifteenth-floor window. She did not turn on any of the regular lamps and ceiling fixtures because she did not want to further stimulate her already overstimulated senses.

Breathe.

The images of the dream flashed and flared, clawing at her awareness in an attempt to drag her down into the dark, seething pit of raw panic. Her skin prickled. Her pulse pounded.

As she paced, she made the promise that she always made to herself during a bad attack. If she did not get things under control she would take a dose of the antianxiety medication the doctor had prescribed. In the past few years that vow, combined with the breathing exercises, was usually sufficient to get through even the worst episodes.

Just give the breathing exercises a chance to work. The meds are in the drawer. Don't worry, you can have one if you really need it. You knew tonight would probably be a bad night.

Breathe.

She needed to go through the door. She had to get outside.

She unlocked the slider. Cold damp air swirled into

the room. She stepped out onto the balcony. The rain had stopped. The jeweled cityscape of Seattle sparkled around her. The Space Needle glowed reassuringly, a giant torch against the darkness.

She focused on the exercises.

The thud-thud-thud of the killer's footsteps faded back into memory.

Gradually her pulse steadied and her breathing returned to normal.

When she was sure she was back in control she returned to the living room. She closed and locked the slider.

"Crap," she said aloud to the silent room.

And everyone wondered why she had never married, why she never let any man spend the night. Panic attacks were like earthquakes. It wasn't a matter of *if* there would be another one. It was only a question of when it would strike. She had discovered the hard way that it might be weeks, months or even years between attacks. Or it could be tomorrow night. How did a woman explain that to a potential lover?

Maybe, if her social life ever progressed beyond the short-term-relationship pattern she had developed, she might find a man she could entrust with her secrets. But somehow that had not yet happened.

She had overcome the shivery jitters but she knew she would not be able to go back to sleep, at least not for some time. On the other hand, there was no job waiting for her in the morning, she reminded herself. She was free to sleep late. Now that was a truly depressing thought because she always got up early, even after a bad night. She was doomed to be a morning person.

She went to stand at the window. Although there were a number of condo towers, apartments and office buildings scattered around her, she could see a wide slice of the Queen Anne neighborhood. The hillside was dotted with the lights of the exclusive residences that had been built there to take advantage of the views. Tonight one of the big houses was dark and empty. Sprague Witherspoon's body was probably in cold storage in the medical examiner's office, waiting to be autopsied. The hunt for his killer had begun.

She thought about the vodka bottle that she had found at the scene. Another wave of anxiety whispered through her nerves. It had to be a coincidence. There was no other explanation.

She suddenly remembered the ping that had shattered the nightmare. She went back into the bedroom and picked up the phone. When she saw the sender's name she almost plunged straight into another full-blown panic attack. For a few beats she simply stared at the screen in stunned disbelief. This could not be happening.

Sprague Witherspoon had sent her an email from beyond the grave. The message was a macabre twist on one of the Witherspoon Way affirmations:

Each day brings us another opportunity to change the future.
Congratulations, your future will soon be very different.

Four

Well, that was the most awkward evening I've spent in some time," Grace said. "And I include the night of my high school prom, during which I discovered that my date was deeply depressed because the girl he had wanted to be with had turned him down."

"You want awkward?" Julius Arkwright asked. "Try the annual business dinner and charity auction I'm scheduled to attend later this week."

Grace gave that some consideration. "I don't think that qualifies as awkward. A business dinner and charity auction sound boring, not awkward."

"Yeah, boring, too," Julius agreed. "I will have to make casual conversation with a bunch of people who are as dull as I am. But the really awkward part comes later, when I deliver the most boring after-dinner speech ever written. The charity auction isn't so bad. I'll be stuck buying a piece of art that I don't want but that isn't exactly awkward. That's just costly."

He didn't seem to care about the financial cost of the event, she noticed. Interesting.

She had been introduced to Julius for the first time that evening. She barely knew him but she was already certain that he ranked as the least boring man she had ever met. That was, however, beside the point, she told herself. They were talking awkward, not boring, and she doubted that any business dinner could have been as unnerving as the blind date that she and Julius had just endured.

And the date was not over—not until she got back to the lake house. To get there she had to clamber into the front seat of Julius's gleaming black SUV. She hated SUVs. They were not designed for women who were frequently obliged to shop in the petite department.

She tucked her trench coat around herself and tried to discreetly raise the hem of her pencil-slim skirt so that she could position her left high-heeled sandal on the floorboard of the vehicle. Reaching up, she grasped the handhold inside the cab and prepared to haul her body weight up into the passenger seat.

There was no hope of negotiating the business gracefully. Even if she had been wearing jeans and athletic shoes she would have had a problem. Dressed in a snug-fitting little black dress and heels, the best she could hope for was to make it up and into the seat on the first try with as little bounce as possible.

She tightened her grip on the handhold and pushed off with her right foot.

"Watch your head," Julius said.

Before she realized what he intended she felt his hands close around her waist. He lifted her as easily as if she were a sack of groceries and plopped her on the passenger seat.

She tried to control her trajectory and landing but she bounced, anyway. Her coat fell open, exposing a lot of inner thigh. By the time she got things under control Julius was closing the door.

Crap.

The awkward night was not showing any signs of improving. There was probably an affirmation for a blind date gone bad but what she really wanted was a therapeutic glass of wine.

She watched Julius round the front of the SUV. For a moment his hard profile and broad shoulders were silhouetted against the porch lights of the Nakamura house. In spite of all the warnings she had been giving herself that evening, an unfamiliar and decidedly dangerous sense of anticipation sparkled through her. For the duration of the short drive home she was going to be alone with Julius. That was probably not a good idea.

He opened the door and climbed behind the wheel. She watched him angle himself into the seat with the easy grace of a large hunting cat settling into high grass to wait for prey.

Well, of course he had made the process look easy.

It wasn't as if someone had literally tossed him up into the seat.

He closed the door. An ominous but rather exciting sense of intimacy seethed in the dark interior of the SUV. At least it seemed ominous and exciting to her. Julius appeared blissfully unaware of the edgy vibe. He was no doubt eager to dump her on her doorstep.

She focused her attention on their hosts for the evening. Irene and Devlin Nakamura waved cheerfully from the front porch of their home.

Irene was a tall, attractive blonde who could trace her heritage back to some of the many Norwegians who had settled in the Pacific Northwest at the end of the nineteenth century. She was the kind of woman who could handle being the wife of a man who worked in law enforcement. She was also a very sharp businesswoman with a fast-rising local company that specialized in high-end cookware.

Devlin Nakamura bore the unmistakable stamp of a man others looked to in a crisis. Which was a good thing in a police officer, Grace told herself—unless he was looking at you. He radiated determination and a stern will, and he had cop eyes. It was easy to imagine him kicking down a door, or reading you your rights. If you were a criminal, he was not the investigator you wanted on your trail. Grace shivered. She had not been surprised to discover that Devlin and Julius Arkwright had once served together in the Marines.

"I'm sure Irene and Devlin meant well," she said.

Julius fired up the SUV's big engine. "Do you always

say things like that after someone has ambushed you with a blind date?"

"Don't be so melodramatic. It wasn't that bad. Just . . . awkward."

Grace was certain that Irene's motives had been well-intentioned. She and Irene had grown up together. They had been close friends since kindergarten.

Devlin's motives, however, were questionable. He was relatively new in Irene's life. The pair had met shortly after Devlin moved to Cloud Lake a year ago to become the town's new chief of police. Grace had been Irene's maid of honor at the wedding.

Grace liked Devlin and she sensed that he was a committed husband. But tonight she'd had the uneasy impression that he was watching her with the same cold speculation that she had seen in the eyes of the Seattle homicide detective who had questioned her after Sprague's murder ten days earlier.

"Okay," Julius said. "We'll go with awkward as a description of the date. For now."

The amusement that etched his dark, deep, deceptively easygoing voice sent another chill across her nerve endings. She glanced at him. In the otherworldly glow of the car's interior lights his face was unreadable but his eyes were a little tight at the outer corners, as if he were preparing to pull the trigger of a rifle.

Not that she knew much about guns or the type of person who used them, she thought. The only man of her acquaintance who actually carried one was Devlin.

But given his job, she supposed that he had some business doing so.

She had to admit that she was probably at least partially responsible for the atmosphere of impending doom that had hung over the small dinner party that evening. The problem was that she was not doing a really great job of thinking positive these days.

Stumbling onto a murder scene was bound to have some unpleasant repercussions. Still, it had been ten days since she'd discovered Witherspoon's body and the darkness was not lifting. It hovered at the edge of her consciousness during the day. At night it swept in like the tide. In spite of a lot of meditation and positive self-talk and the three rituals, the bad energy seemed to be getting worse, affecting her thoughts and her dreams. Both were growing darker and more unsettling.

And the disturbing emails from a dead man were still arriving every evening.

Julius eased the SUV out of the driveway and onto Lake Circle Road with the cool, competent control that seemed to be at the very core of his character. The man would make a really good friend or a very bad enemy, she thought. She doubted that he was the positive-thinking type—more likely a tactical strategist.

She refused to contemplate what kind of lover he would be.

Whatever you do, don't go there, she thought.

She had been too tense—too aware—of Julius all evening to consider the reasons why he disturbed her senses. The best she could come up with was the old warning about icebergs—the most dangerous part was hidden under the surface. Her feminine intuition told her that Julius Arkwright had a lot going on under the surface. So what? The same could be said of everyone. There was no reason to dwell on Julius's concealed issues. She had her own issues these days.

The only hard facts that she knew about Julius were the bits and pieces that had come out in the course of conversation that evening. He was a venture capitalist—a very successful venture capitalist, according to Irene. Other investors routinely entrusted gazillions of dollars to Julius to invest on their behalf.

Not that she had anything against making money, Grace thought. As it happened, figuring out how to generate some future income was right at the top of her to-do list at the moment. Nothing like losing a job to make a person appreciate the value of steady employment. She should know—she'd lost count of the number of jobs she'd had since leaving college to find herself.

The position at the Witherspoon Way headquarters had lasted longer than any of her previous careers—a full eighteen months. She knew her mother and sister had begun to hope that her ever-precarious job situation had finally stabilized. She'd had a few expectations that might be the case, as well.

Julius drove at a surprisingly low rate of speed along the narrow, two-lane road that circled the jagged edge of Cloud Lake. The surface of the deep water was a dark mirror that reflected the cold silver light of the moon.

The silence in the front seat became oppressive. Grace searched for a way to end it.

"Thank you for driving me back to my place," she said. She struggled to assume a polite tone but she knew she sounded a little gruff.

"No problem," Julius said. "It's on my way."

That much was true. The lakefront cottage that Julius had recently purchased was less than half a mile beyond the house in which Grace had been raised. Nevertheless, she hadn't anticipated the ride home with him. She had fully intended to drive herself to the Nakamuras' that evening but Devlin had offered to pick her up. She had assumed that he would be the one to take her home. But when Julius had pointed out that he would be going right past the Elland house and said it would be no trouble to give Grace a lift, there had been no gracious way to refuse—not with Irene and Devlin both nodding encouragingly.

Dinner would not have been nearly so uncomfortable, Grace thought, if it hadn't been so obvious that Irene had been trying her hand at matchmaking.

Oddly enough, now that she found herself alone with Julius, she could almost see the humor of the situation. Almost. She settled deeper into the seat.

"Did you know ahead of time that Irene and Devlin were setting us up?" she asked.

"I was told there would be another guest." Julius's mouth edged upward at the corner. "Like you said, they meant well."

"Now that it's over, I suppose it's sort of funny."

"Think so?"

"I'm used to people trying to set me up with blind dates," Grace said. "My mother and my sister have made something of a hobby out of doing that in the past couple of years. Now Irene appears to be giving it a whirl. Between you and me, they're all getting desperate."

"But you're not interested?"

"Oh, I'm usually interested," Grace said.

"Just not tonight, is that it? Got a problem with the fact that I'm divorced?"

His tone was a little too neutral. So much for making light conversation. This was getting more awkward by the moment.

She tried to sidestep.

"Nothing personal, really," she said. "It's just that I've got a few other priorities at the moment. I'm trying to come up with a new career path and that requires my full attention."

Julius did not appear interested in her job issues.

"Any idea why things haven't worked out with any of your other dates?" he asked.

She was starting to get the deer-in-the-headlights feeling.

"It's just that nothing has ever clicked," she said, very cautious now. "My fault, according to Irene and my family."

"Why is it your fault?"

"They tell me that I have a bad habit of trying to fix people. If I'm successful, I send them on their way and I move on, too."

"And if you can't fix them?"

She tapped one finger on the console that separated the seats. "Same outcome. I send them on their way and I move on."

"So, you're a serial heartbreaker?"

She did laugh then. "Good grief, no. I'm pretty sure I've never broken any man's heart. Men tend to think of me as a friend. They tell me their troubles. We talk about their problems. I offer suggestions. And then they go off and date the next cute blonde they meet in a bar or the good-looking coworker at the office."

Julius gave her a short, sharp look. "Has your heart ever been broken?"

"Not since college. And in hindsight, it's a good thing he did break my heart because the relationship was a disaster for both of us. Lots of storm and drama but no substance."

Julius was quiet for a moment. "Looking back, I don't think there was any storm and drama in my marriage."

"Not even at the very end?"

"We were both relieved that it was all over, as I recall."

That was hard to believe, Grace thought, but the last thing she wanted to do was dig into the subject of his failed marriage. She was not going to try to fix Julius Arkwright.

"Mmm," she said instead.

"Don't worry, I won't spend the rest of the drive to your place unloading on you. You don't want to hear about my divorce and I don't want to talk about it."

"Whew." Grace pretended to wipe her brow. "Good to know."

Julius laughed.

Some of the tension went out of the atmosphere. She relaxed a little more and searched for a neutral topic.

"How long will you be staying here in Cloud Lake?" she asked.

"I plan to use the house year-round. I have a condo in Seattle but most of my work is done online. With some exceptions, I can work here as well as I can at my office. Cloud Lake is only an hour from the city. I'll commute a couple of times a week to make sure things stay on track."

She reminded herself that Julius was a very *successful* venture capitalist. He probably bought lakeside cottages and city condos the way she bought new shoes and dresses. Not that you would know that to look at him, she thought. In recent years the Pacific Northwest had proven fertile ground for start-ups and the savvy investors, like Julius, who funded the businesses that hit big. There was a lot of new money walking around the region these days and very little of it gave off a flashy, rich vibe. Most of it blended in very well with the crowd that shopped for deals at Costco and bought mountain bikes and all-weather gear at REI.

Grace was quite certain that Julius's money was not the old kind. He had the edge of a self-made man—the kind of man who was accustomed to fighting for what he wanted.

"The house you bought used to be owned by your neighbor, Harley Montoya," she said. "I was surprised to hear that he had sold it. He's owned that property and the house he lives in for nearly a decade."

"Harley says it's time to downsize. What about you? Planning to stick around Cloud Lake?"

"For a while. Now that I'm unemployed I need to watch every penny. Mom kept the lake house after she and Kirk retired but they only use it during the summer. They suggested that I save rent money by living here until I figure out my new career path."

"Where do they live now?" Julius asked.

"They moved to Scottsdale a couple of years ago. Mom sold her gift shop here in Cloud Lake and Kirk turned over his insurance business to his sons. At the moment Mom and Kirk are on a world cruise."

"And you said you have a sister?"

"Alison, yes. She's a lawyer in Portland."

"So you intend to stay here in Cloud Lake only until you get your act together?"

"That's the plan," Grace said.

"What's your strategy?"

She blinked. "I thought I just explained my plan."

Julius shot her an amused glance. "I'm talking about your strategy for finding a new career path."

"Oh, that." She flushed. "I'm still working on it."

She didn't owe him any explanations, she reminded herself.

"You must have some thoughts on the subject," he said.

"Actually, no, I don't," she said, going for a frosty,

back-off tone. "My life has been somewhat complicated lately."

"I know. Must have been tough finding the body of your boss the way you did."

She hesitated, not sure she wanted to go down that particular conversational path.

"I try not to think about it," she said coolly.

"The Witherspoon Way will collapse without Witherspoon at the helm."

She crossed her arms and gazed fixedly at the pavement through the windshield.

"Trust me, all of us who worked for Sprague Witherspoon are aware of that," she said.

"You need a job. Sounds like your problem is pretty straightforward."

"Is that right? And just when, exactly, was the last time you found yourself out of work?"

To her surprise he pondered that briefly.

"It's been a while," he admitted.

She gave him a steely smile. "In other words, you really have no idea whatsoever about the current job market, let alone how complicated my particular situation might be."

"How did you find the job with Witherspoon?"

The question caught her off guard. "I sort of stumbled into it. That's usually how I find a new job."

"You stumbled into working for a motivational speaker?"

"Well, yes. A year and a half ago I was looking for a new direction. I decided to attend a Witherspoon Way seminar hoping to get some ideas. After Sprague

Witherspoon talked to the audience I waited around to speak to him."

"About what?" Julius sounded genuinely curious.

"While Sprague was giving his seminar on positive thinking, I came up with some ideas about how he could take his concepts in different directions." She unfolded her arms and spread her hands. "To my surprise, he listened to me. The next thing I knew, he was offering me a job. Once I was on board he let me have free rein. Working for the Witherspoon Way was the best job I've ever had."

"Just how many jobs have you had?"

"A lot." She sighed. "It's embarrassing, to tell you the truth. And it makes for a sketchy résumé. Some job-hopping is okay but beyond a certain point it makes you look—"

"Flighty. Unreliable. Undependable."

She winced. "All of the above. My sister knew that she wanted to be a lawyer by the time she was a senior in high school. But here I am, still searching for a career path that will last longer than eighteen months."

"You've got a problem," Julius said. "You need a business plan."

She stared at him. "A business plan for landing a job?"

"As far as I can tell, everything in life works better if you have a good, well-thought-out plan."

It was all she could do not to laugh. He sounded so serious.

"Are you talking about a five-year plan?" she asked

lightly. "Because I don't think Mom will give me free rent for five years."

"Not a five-year plan—not for finding a career. More like a three-months-at-the-outside strategy. If you're serious about this you need to set goals and meet them."

"I've never been much of a long-term planner," she said.

"No kidding. I would not have guessed that."

She gave him a cold smile. "Sprague Witherspoon said that one of my assets was that I think outside the box."

"There's thinking outside the box and then there's failing to be able to find the box in the first place. You can't appreciate the new model until you understand the old one and why it isn't working anymore."

Irritation sparkled through her. "Gosh, maybe you should go into the self-help business. That sounds a lot like one of the Witherspoon Way affirmations."

"What's an affirmation?"

"It's a shortcut to positive thinking. A good affirmation helps focus the mind in a productive, optimistic way."

"Give me an example," Julius said.

"Well, say you had a bad day at work—"

"Let's go with something more concrete. Say you found yourself at a dinner party with friends who set you up with a boring blind date. What kind of affirmation would you use to help you think positive about the situation?"

She went very still. "Probably better not to get too concrete."

"I'm a businessman. I deal in concrete facts."

"Fine," she shot back. "You want an affirmation for this date? How about, *Things are always darkest before the dawn*? Will that work for you?"

"I don't think that's a Witherspoon Way affirmation. Pretty sure it's been around for a while."

"Got a better one?"

"I don't do affirmations. I've got a couple of rules that I never break but neither of them fits our current situation."

"Here's my place," she said quickly.

But he was already slowing for the turn into the tree-lined driveway that led to the small, neat house at the edge of the lake. He brought the SUV to a halt in front of the wraparound porch and shut down the engine.

The lights were still on in Agnes Gilroy's house next door. The drapes were pulled but Grace was certain that Agnes was peering through the curtains. Agnes possessed a deep and abiding interest in the doings of her neighbors. She was bound to have heard the unfamiliar rumble of the car in the driveway.

"Thanks for the ride home," Grace said. She unbuckled her safety belt and reached for the door handle. "Nice meeting you. I'm sure we'll run into each other in town. Don't bother getting out of the car. I can manage just fine on my own."

She could tell that he was not paying attention to her less-than-sparkling chatter. He sat, unmoving, his strong, competent hands resting on the wheel, and contemplated the house as if he had never seen one.

"I had a career plan by the time I was eleven years old," he said.

"Yep, I'm not surprised." She got the car door open, grabbed the edges of the trench coat and prepared to jump down to the ground. "I had you pegged as one of those."

"One of those what?"

"One of those folks who always knows where he's going." She gripped the handhold and plunged off the seat. For an instant she hovered precariously in midair. Relief shot through her when she landed on both feet. She turned and looked back at him. "Must be nice."

He popped open his own door, uncoiled from behind the wheel and circled the front of the vehicle. He got to her before she reached the porch steps.

"It helps to know what you want," he said. "It clarifies choices and streamlines the decision matrix."

The cool, calculating way he watched her sent a little chill down her spine. Or was it a thrill? The possibility made her catch her breath. *Wrong time and probably the wrong man. Send him on his way.*

"What was your career plan at eleven?" she said instead.

"I wanted to get rich."

She paused to search his face in the porch light. "Why?"

"Because I figured out that money gives a man power."

"Over others?"

He considered that and then shrugged. "Maybe. Depending on the situation. But that wasn't why I wanted to get rich."

She watched him closely. "You wanted control over your own life."

"Yeah, that about sums it up."

"That's a perfectly reasonable objective. It seems to have worked out well for you. Congratulations. Good night, Julius."

She hitched the strap of her purse over her shoulder and walked quickly toward the front porch steps. The relentless crunch of gravel behind her made her stop in mid-stride. When she turned to confront him, he stopped, too.

"It's okay," she said briskly. "You don't need to see me to my door."

"I said I'd take you home. You're not home until you're inside the house."

For some reason, anger crackled through her. "I'm not your responsibility."

"You are until you're home." He waited.

She gripped her keys very tightly. "I can't believe I just snapped at you because you're trying to do the gentlemanly thing. I apologize. Jeez. Where are my manners? Sorry. I'm a little tense these days. Thank you."

"You're welcome." He stood there in the moonlight as if he were willing to wait until dawn for her to make the next move.

"Right," she said. "The door."

She turned again and hurried up the steps. Julius

followed her across the front porch, keeping a little distance between them, careful not to crowd her.

She dug the keys out of her purse, got the door open, stepped across the threshold and flipped the wall switch. Two lamps came up, revealing the warm, casually comfortable space. Her mother had been in what Grace and Alison referred to as her Rustic Retreat phase when she last redecorated.

The wooden floors were burnished with age. Two overstuffed chairs and a deep sofa upholstered in dark brown leather were positioned on a honey-colored area rug. A large brass basket on the stone hearth held kindling for the cold, dark fireplace.

Several landscapes featuring quaint cottages, wooden docks and old boathouses around the shores of Cloud Lake hung on the walls. Visitors rarely noticed that there was no painting of the most picturesque structure on the lake, the long-abandoned Cloud Lake Inn.

Grace turned around a second time to confront Julius. In the glare of the front porch light his gold-brown eyes were heavily shadowed. She could see that he was drinking in every detail of the living room behind her. She searched for a word to describe what she thought she detected in his expression and came up with *hungry*.

Don't go there, she told herself. If you feed him he might hang around. This was not a good time for her to be taking in strays. She was not here to fix Julius Arkwright. If she did, he would probably walk away like all the others.

And this man just might be the one she would regret setting free.

She opened her mouth to thank him politely and bid him good night.

"Would you like to come in for some herbal tea?" she heard herself say instead.

Five

"Thanks," he said. He moved across the threshold and closed the door. "I don't think I've ever had herbal tea. Sounds . . . interesting."

For a few seconds she could only stand there, shocked at what she had just done. When she realized that he was watching her, waiting for her to make the next move, she pulled herself together. She hadn't offered to feed him, she thought. It was just tea.

"Tea," she said. She turned on her heel. "Kitchen."

She dropped her purse on one of the overstuffed chairs and went into the big, old-fashioned kitchen. Through the airy curtains she could see the moonstruck surface of the water. Here and there the lights of some of the lakefront houses glittered in the trees. A long necklace of low lamps marked the footpath that circled the lake.

She discovered she had to concentrate just to remember how to boil the water in the kettle.

She switched on the gas burner and reminded herself again that it was just tea. The fact that for some reason she was feeling a little rush of edgy exhilaration was probably going to be a problem later. But at that moment she did not care.

Julius lounged against the tiled countertop and folded his arms. He somehow managed to make it look as if he were entirely at home in her kitchen—as if he were in the habit of spending a lot of time there. He watched her pluck two tea bags out of a glass canister.

"What's in that tea you're fixing?" he asked.

"Chamomile," she said. "It's supposed to promote restful sleep."

"I usually use a medicinal dose of whiskey."

She smiled. "I've been known to resort to that particular medication on occasion, myself."

"Had some bad nights recently?"

Very deliberately she positioned the tea bags in two mugs.

"A few," she conceded. "You were right. Finding my employer's body was a shock."

"I followed some of the reports in the media," he said. "The story caught my attention because the Witherspoon Way was a rising star in the Pacific Northwest business world."

She shook her head. "And now it's all gone. Everything that Sprague built will soon disappear."

"That's the problem with any business that is founded on a personality rather than a product. Celebrities, athletes, actors—same story. They might rake in millions while they're working but if something happens to them, the whole company implodes."

The teakettle whistled. Grace switched off the burner and poured the hot water into the mugs.

"When it comes to the motivational seminar business, it's definitely all about the charisma of the person at the top," she said.

"So you're unemployed."

"Again." She put one of the mugs down on the counter next to Julius. "I'm an underachiever. No other word for it. It's time I got my act together. I just wish I knew what I really wanted to do in life. Every time I get a glimmer of a career path, something happens to make me swerve in another direction."

"Like the closing down of the Witherspoon Way?"

"Well, yes."

"I planned out a future once."

"You said you knew where you were going from the age of eleven." She blew on her tea. "You wanted to be rich. What set you on that career path?"

"My parents split up. Dad remarried and moved across the country. Never saw much of him after that, except once, years later, when he came around asking for a loan. My mother worked hard to keep a roof over our heads. She sacrificed everything for me during those years."

Grace nodded. "That's when you realized that money could make a huge difference. It could buy you the kind of power you needed to change your mother's life."

Julius smiled faintly. "Are you trying to analyze me? Because if so, I'd like to change the subject."

"Irene said that you are a very successful venture capitalist. She told me that in Pacific Northwest business circles they call you Arkwright the Alchemist because when it comes to investments, you can turn lead into gold."

"I'm good," Julius said. "But I'm not that good."

"Good enough to get very rich, though, right?"

"Rich enough."

"I assume your mother is doing okay?"

"Mom's fine. After money was no longer an issue she did what she always wanted to do—she went back to school to finish getting her B.A. Wound up marrying one of her professors. They live in Northern California. Doug teaches at a community college. Mom works in the counseling office. They're going to retire soon. I manage their investments."

She smiled. "I assume they will both enjoy comfortable retirements?"

He shrugged that off as if it were no big deal. "Sure."

She raised her eyebrows. "Are you satisfied with your current financial status?"

"I've got all the money I'll ever need and then some. How many shirts can one man wear? How many cars can he drive? How many houses does he really want to maintain? Yes, Grace, I'm rich enough."

She studied him for a moment.

"Do you know, I don't think I've ever heard anyone say that he had enough money," she said. "Granted, I've never met many truly wealthy people. But I was under the impression that after a certain point people use money as a way to keep score."

"That works." Julius cautiously swallowed some of the chamomile tea and lowered the mug. "For a while."

She raised her brows. "Would you rather go back to being non-rich?"

He smiled slowly. "No."

"But it would be no big deal if you lost it all tomorrow. In fact, I'll bet you would find the situation interesting."

"Interesting?"

"As in, not boring. Starting over would be a challenge for you."

"Maybe," he said. "For me. But I'm no longer the only one involved. If I lost everything tomorrow, several small, promising start-ups would crash and burn. A lot of people who work for those little companies would be unemployed and so would the folks who work directly or indirectly for me. And that's not counting the people who trust me to invest their money, like my mother."

She leaned back against the counter beside him and took another sip of the tea. "You're right, of course. You're riding the tiger. You don't have the option of choosing to get off. If you do, you'll be okay but a lot of other people will get eaten."

"You didn't expect me to consider that aspect of the situation?"

"Now, on that front, you're wrong. I would absolutely expect you to consider your responsibilities as an employer. Irene has been my best friend since kindergarten.

I know her well enough to know that she wouldn't have tried to set me up with you if she didn't think you were a good man."

Julius's mouth twitched at the corner. "I could give you a list of people who would disagree with that opinion."

"Oh, I don't doubt but that you've made a few enemies along the way."

"Making enemies doesn't make me a bad person?"

"Depends on the enemies," she said.

A muffled ping sounded from the front room. She froze. Julius looked at her and then glanced toward the doorway.

She took a steadying breath. And then she took another. The jittery sensation receded.

"My phone," she said quickly. "Just email. I'll deal with it later."

He nodded once and swallowed more of the tea.

"Now I've got a question for you," he said.

"About my nonexistent career plans?"

"It's a little more specific. Did you kill Sprague Witherspoon?"

She stared at him, utterly blindsided. Her brain went blank. Words failed her. First the email ping and now this.

She heard the crash when the mug she had been holding hit the floor but she could not make sense of the sound for a few heartbeats.

Julius watched her the way an entomologist might watch a butterfly in a glass jar.

"Get out," she whispered, her voice hoarse with anger. "Now."

"All right," he said.

He set his unfinished tea down calmly, as though he had just remarked on the weather. He walked across the kitchen and went into the living room. She pushed herself away from the counter and pursued him, literally chasing him out of the house.

At the door he paused to look back at her over his shoulder.

"Good night," he said. "It's been an interesting evening. I don't get a lot of those."

"No shit," she said. "I think I can tell you why."

"I already know the answer." He opened the door and moved out onto the porch. "I'm pretty boring when you get to know me. Hell, sometimes I even bore myself. Don't forget to lock your door."

He went down the porch steps.

Infuriated, she crossed the porch and gripped the railing with both hands. "I didn't kill Witherspoon."

"I believe you." He opened the SUV door. "Got any idea who did?"

"No. For heaven's sake, if I did, I would have told the police."

"According to Dev's information, the Seattle police have an oversupply of suspects, including an angry adult daughter, the daughter's fiancé and a few pissed-off seminar folks who don't think they got their money's worth from the Witherspoon Way. Then there are Witherspoon's employees."

"Why would any of us murder our employer? We were all making a lot of money working for the Witherspoon Way."

"Dev says that there is reason to believe that someone involved in the Witherspoon Way was siphoning off a hefty amount of the profits and using phony investment statements to cover up the missing money."

"*What?* Are you serious?"

"Ask Dev. He says he got the news from the Seattle cops this morning. There's a lot of money missing. In my world, that counts as a motive."

She stared at him, outraged. "Are you implying that I embezzled money from the Witherspoon Way?"

"No. I had a few questions earlier in the evening but I doubt very much that you're an embezzler."

"Why not? Because I'm not a financial wizard like you?"

He smiled. "This may come as a shock but it doesn't take a lot of financial wizardry to figure out how to skim a great deal of money off the top of a successful business like the Witherspoon Way. In fact, it's dead easy—especially if no one is paying close attention."

"That is insulting on several levels."

"I didn't mean it that way," he said. "Just stating facts."

"Here's a fact you can take to the bank—this blind date is officially over." Out of the corner of her eye Grace saw the curtains twitch in Agnes Gilroy's living room window. "Crap."

She turned on her heel, stalked back inside the house and slammed the door. She whirled around and shot the new dead bolt. Then she secured the chain lock.

For a moment or two she stood listening to the sound of the SUV rumbling back down the drive toward Lake Circle Road.

When she knew that Julius was gone she exhaled slowly. Then she went into the kitchen and grabbed a wad of paper towels off the roll that sat on the counter next to the stove.

She wiped up the spilled chamomile tea and contemplated the possibility that someone had been draining off the profits of the Witherspoon Way. Even if that turned out to be true—and given that Devlin was a cop there was no reason to think his information wasn't accurate—how did that relate to Sprague's murder?

Unless Sprague had uncovered the embezzlement and confronted the embezzler.

She finished mopping up the tea and collected the pieces of the broken mug. She got to her feet and dumped the wet paper towels and the bits of pottery into the trash.

Earlier that day she had done her breathing meditation. It was time for one of the other three rituals that helped her deal with the nightmares over the years.

She walked methodically through the house, checking the shiny new locks she had installed on the doors and windows. Next she looked inside the closets and every cupboard that was large enough to conceal a person. She was annoyed with herself, as usual, when she got down on her knees and looked under the beds in the three small bedrooms. She had no idea what she would do if she actually did find someone hiding in a closet or underneath a bed but she knew she couldn't sleep until she had verified that she was the only one in the house.

When she had completed the walk-through, she poured herself a glass of wine, sat down in one of the big chairs and took her phone out of her purse. She opened her email with the same degree of reluctance she would have felt reaching into a terrarium to pick up a snake.

The email was waiting for her. Another night, another note from a dead man. The first line was familiar.

A positive attitude is like a flashlight in a dark room.

But whoever had sent the email had altered the second line.

You can use it to see who's waiting for you in the shadows.

Six

Congratulations, Arkwright. You really know how to screw up a date.

Julius brought the SUV to a halt in the driveway in front of his house. He shut down the engine and sat for a moment, contemplating the darkened cottage and the mystery of Grace Elland.

The cottage was modest but it was infused with the comfortable patina that only several generations of occupation could impart. It held a few very nice surprises, such as the brilliant view of the lake and the extraordinarily lush gardens. A man could be content with a house like this for the rest of his life.

Grace Elland held a few surprises, too. It was difficult to believe that any intelligent individual could take seriously all that nonsense about positive thinking and the power of affirmations. It was one thing to do a good job. He didn't blame her for working for a self-help guru. A job was a job. You did what you had to do. He admired competence and hard work regardless of the nature of that work. But tonight he'd gotten the impression that Grace had really bought into the Witherspoon Way fantasy. She actually did seem to believe that positive energy was a force for good in the world.

Either she was for real or she was one of the most clever con artists he had ever met—and in his line, he'd encountered some very good ones.

Mentally he cataloged his impressions of her. She was on the small side. Even in the ridiculously high, incredibly sexy high-heeled shoes she'd worn tonight she barely topped out at a point just a little above his shoulder. But she moved like a dancer. There was something light and graceful about her—and a subtle strength, as well. He'd felt the feminine power in her when he'd lifted her up into the passenger seat of the SUV. The memory of holding her for that brief moment stirred his senses.

Her hair was the color of aged whiskey. Tonight she'd twisted it into a knot high on her head, probably in an effort to give the illusion of height. The style enhanced her eyes, which were an interesting shade of amber and green. When she looked at him he got the unsettling sensation that she could see a lot more than he wanted her or anyone else to see, things that he kept hidden from the world.

Theoretically she was the kind of woman you didn't look twice at on the street. But tonight he had definitely looked twice—more than twice—and he wanted to look at her—be near her—again. There were questions hanging in the air between them. He would not be satisfied until he got answers.

Some alchemist. He had turned a golden blind date into lead. Now he was stuck with the problem of figuring out how to reverse the process.

He opened the door and climbed out of the vehicle. Harley Montoya emerged from the neighboring house and came out onto the porch.

"How'd the big date go?" Harley bellowed.

There was no need to raise his voice. The two houses sat side by side, separated only by the narrow drive that Harley used to haul his beloved boat out of the water for maintenance. Sound carried well in the stillness of the winter night. But Harley was going deaf in one ear and he tended to assume that everyone else was hard of hearing as well.

As far as anyone knew, his first name was a Montoya family name that had been bestowed on him by his parents. But back in the day when he had made his fortune in the construction and development business the rumors circulated that the name was derived from a certain brand of motorcycle. There was no getting around the fact that he was constructed along the lines of a Harley-Davidson. He was in his eighties now and had softened somewhat over the years but he still possessed the solid, muscular build that brought to mind images of the famous bike.

"It was a blind date," Julius said. He closed the door of the SUV. "It didn't go well. They rarely do. And is everyone in Cloud Lake aware that Grace and I were set up tonight?"

"Pretty much," Harley said. "You're home early. Figured you'd screwed up. What went wrong?"

"I made the mistake of asking her if she murdered Witherspoon. She got pissed."

"No kidding." Harley snorted. "Why in the name of hell did you have to go and ask her a thing like that?"

"I was curious to see what her reaction would be."

"I guess you got that question answered. I told you Gracc Elland was no killer. You're an idiot when it comes to women."

"I'm aware of that."

"Well, don't worry too much about screwing up," Harley said. "Looks like you and Grace will both be in town for a while. Play your cards right and you'll get another chance."

"In other words, I should try to think positive, is that it?"

"Hell, no." Harley snorted. "I'm talking about smart strategy, not that positive-thinking bullshit. Strategy and planning are your strengths, son. Use your natural-born talents."

"Thanks for the advice. I'll keep it in mind."

"You do that."

Julius walked across the lawn and went through the small gate. He moved out into the narrow rutted lane that separated the two houses.

"You weren't living here in Cloud Lake at the time of the Trager murder, were you?" he asked.

"No," Harley said. "Still too busy making money

in those days. Most of what I know about it and about Grace Elland comes from Agnes."

"A bad scene like that would sure as hell leave a few scars, especially on a girl who was only in her teens at the time."

"What are you gettin' at?" Harley asked.

"Just wondering why Grace never married, that's all."

"They say a lot of young women are waiting longer to get married these days, if they marry at all."

"Wow. You're an expert on modern social trends?"

"Nope, but Agnes keeps me up to date," Harley said. "She says Grace has just been waitin' for the right man to come along. We were both sort of hopin' you might be him."

"What the hell made anyone think I might be the right man?" Julius asked, genuinely surprised.

"No idea, come to think of it."

"Were you and Agnes Gilroy coconspirators with Irene and Dev when it came to planning the blind date?"

"Course not." Harley sounded affronted. "Do I look like a matchmaker to you? It was Irene Nakamura's idea. She and Grace have been friends since they were little kids. I hear your old buddy Dev went along with the notion. Go blame him if you want to blame someone."

"Thanks. I'll do that." Julius started walking down the lane toward the dock and the boathouse. "Good night, Harley."

"Don't give up, son. I think Grace is the kind of woman who would give a man a second chance."

Julius paused and looked back at Harley. "Are you sure you haven't fallen into the clutches of some motivational guru?"

"Are you laughing?" Harley demanded.

"Trust me, I'm not laughing."

Julius walked to the end of the lane and stepped out onto the floating dock. Water lapped gently at the planks. Cloud Lake didn't reflect clouds at night, just moonlight—at least it did on a night when the moon was out, like it was tonight. The water was a sheet of black glass streaked with silver under the cold, starry sky.

The weathered boathouse loomed on his left. He moved past it and came to a halt at the end of the dock. Although the trees crowded close to the water's edge, the lights of some of the houses and cottages could be seen from where he stood.

The Elland house was only about a quarter of a mile away if you drew a straight line from point to point across the lake. He could see the lights of the kitchen and back porch. As he watched, one window went dark but another suddenly illuminated. The bedroom, probably. Grace was going to bed. It was, he discovered, an unsettling thought; the kind of thought that could keep a man awake at night.

He took out his phone. Devlin answered on the fourth or fifth ring. He sounded irritated.

"This had better be important," he said. "We keep early hours here in Cloud Lake. This isn't the big city."

"You said you wanted my impressions of Grace Elland."

"Hang on."

There was some rustling. Julius heard Devlin mutter something about business—probably speaking to Irene—and then a door closed.

"Okay," Devlin said. He kept his voice low. "I'm in the kitchen getting a glass of water. Talk fast."

"For what it's worth, I don't think Grace killed Witherspoon."

"Good to know that you and Irene agree on that. Grace does have a fairly good alibi."

"Not ironclad?"

"In my experience there are very, very few ironclad alibis. My contact at the Seattle PD confirmed that the video from Grace's apartment garage camera shows that she arrived home at seven o'clock that evening and did not leave until seven thirty the following morning. The ME said Witherspoon was murdered shortly after midnight."

"Curiosity compels me to ask, what would you accept as an ironclad alibi?"

"If the suspect could prove that he or she was dead when the victim was killed I might go for it. But even then I'd look at the alibi real hard. It's not that difficult to come up with a scenario that has someone setting up a murder-suicide in which the suicide takes place before the murder."

Julius thought about it for a moment, intrigued by the problem. "I can imagine a couple of other ways a dead man could commit murder. A delayed-action weapon like slow poison, for example."

"I've told you before, you think like a cop."

"Pay is better in my line."

"Can't argue with that," Devlin said. "All right, let's say for the sake of argument that you and Irene are right when you tell me that Grace couldn't have killed Sprague Witherspoon—"

"I never said she couldn't have done it. I said I don't think she did it."

There was a short pause on the other end of the connection.

"You really think she's capable of murder?" Devlin asked finally. He sounded curious.

"You're the cop. As I recall you have told me on more than one occasion that everyone is capable of committing murder under the right circumstances."

"There is that," Devlin conceded.

"Don't underestimate Grace Elland. Underneath that optimistic, glass-half-full exterior, there's a tough streak."

"No doubt about it. I'm the one who told you the story of what happened here in Cloud Lake all those years ago, remember?"

Julius watched the lights of the Elland house. "I remember."

"Grace is something of a local legend in this town. It's one of the reasons I asked for your take on her. You're an outsider. I knew you wouldn't be swayed by the story from her past."

"She says she's here to think about her future and make some decisions regarding a career path."

"Yeah, Irene explained that Grace has spent the past

few years hopping from one job to another," Devlin said.

"I'll tell you one thing," Julius said. "When Grace finally does decide what she wants in life, I would not want to be the one standing in her way."

Unless I'm what she decides she wants.

The thought came out of nowhere, startling him so badly that he almost dropped the phone.

"Damn," he said.

He said it very softly but Devlin heard him.

"You okay?" Devlin asked.

"Yeah, fine. Just a little phone issue."

"So, how did the date go tonight?"

"It went swell up to a point. Got asked in for tea."

"Tea?" Devlin's tone suggested that he had never heard of the substance.

"Some kind of herbal stuff."

"I guess that sounds promising. What went wrong?"

"What makes you think something went wrong?"

"You obviously got home early," Devlin said patiently. "You're talking to me on your phone so, ace detective that I am, I deduced that you were no longer with Grace."

"You're good. You're also right in your deductions. The date ended somewhat abruptly when I asked Grace if she killed Witherspoon."

"You asked her?" Devlin repeated in a neutral tone.

"Yep."

"Point-blank?"

"Uh-huh."

"You're an idiot."

"Harley said something along the same lines."

"I assume she denied it?" Devlin said.

"Sure. That's when she kicked me out of the house. But here's the thing, Dev, there's something really wrong with this picture. She's scared."

"Of what?"

"Damned if I know. But I saw what I'm sure are brand-new locks on the front and back doors of the house. While we were in the kitchen the email alert pinged on her phone. She jumped. Make that flinched."

"She's a woman living alone," Devlin said. "Good locks make sense. As for the email alert, I've been known to flinch when I hear mine ping, too."

"There's something else going on, Dev. I can feel it."

"As Irene keeps reminding me, finding a dead body is bound to be a traumatic experience for someone who isn't in the business of finding them."

"You're in that line."

Devlin exhaled heavily. "You know as well as I do that for those of us who do stumble across dead bodies every so often in the course of our jobs, it's never routine."

"That attitude is what makes you a good cop."

"Why do you think I took this nice, cushy job here in Cloud Lake? I got tired of finding dead bodies in the big city."

"I know," Julius said.

There was silence at both ends of the connection for a few seconds.

"All right, back to Grace Elland," Devlin said finally. "Here's what the Seattle people have: She walked into her boss's house and found him dead in bed, shot twice with a handgun that was reported stolen."

"Someone bought it on the street to use on Witherspoon. Grace doesn't strike me as the kind of woman who would know how to buy a gun in a back alley."

"Got news for you, it's not that hard to buy a stolen gun," Devlin said. "Nothing was stolen from the house. It was not a burglary gone bad. As I was saying, the SPD people figure the most likely scenario is that the killer is probably someone connected to Witherspoon. Grace knows that. So if she's innocent—"

"She is."

"Then she's probably coping with the fact that at some point her path crossed with that of the killer," Devlin concluded. "It's not surprising that she might decide to take a few extra precautions with her own personal safety now."

"But flinching just because she got an email?"

"Could be a million reasons why it startled her," Devlin said. "She might have been anticipating a note from a boyfriend—maybe an old one she doesn't want to hear from or a new one she's hoping will call. And there you were, standing in her kitchen, when she got the ping. Maybe it was your presence that made her tense."

"She's tense, all right, the question is why. Okay, that's my report. I'm going to do some work on the computer and then I'm going to bed. Thanks for dinner, and tell Irene she doesn't need to set me up with any more blind dates. One is more than enough."

Devlin cleared his throat. "There is the little matter of the money that somehow disappeared from the

Witherspoon accounts. Setting aside the question of murder, do you think it's possible that Grace is the embezzler?"

"I considered it but if she was sitting on a big pile of money, why would she be holed up here in Cloud Lake trying to figure out how to get another job?"

"Always assuming that's why she's here."

There was another short silence.

"So," Devlin continued, "you got as far as the kitchen, right? I can tell Irene that much?"

"I'm going to hang up now, Dev."

"Hard to see you drinking herbal tea. Was there any chanting or incense involved?"

Julius cut the connection.

Seven

He stood at the end of the dock, watching the moonlight on the water and thinking about how Grace had flinched when the email alert sounded. Then he thought some more about the new locks on the doors.

He checked the Elland house. The lights were still on.

What the hell. Nothing to lose. He'd already screwed up the evening.

He opened the phone again and hit the newest name on his short list of personal contacts.

Grace answered on the first ring. "Who is this?"

The tension in her voice made him go very cold. He realized she probably hadn't recognized his number.

"It's Julius. Sorry. Didn't mean to scare you. Just wanted to make sure everything was okay."

There was a brief pause. "I'm fine. What made you think I might not be okay?"

"Four new locks on your doors."

Another pause. Longer this time.

"Very observant of you," she said.

"You sound surprised."

"I decided to upgrade the locks because I'll probably be here for a while and I'm living alone. Cloud Lake is no longer the small, sleepy little town it once was."

"According to what I heard, it wasn't the safest place on the planet back when you werc a kid."

The moment of silence hummed with tension.

"Someone told you about what happened at the old Cloud Lake asylum," Grace said eventually.

It wasn't a question. She sounded resigned.

"Harley Montoya and Dev both mentioned it," Julius said. "I was curious so I pulled up a few of the newspaper stories from that time. But according to Harley, Dev and the reports, it happened at the old Cloud Lake Inn up at the north end of the lake, not an asylum."

"The inn was originally built as a private hospital for the mentally ill. That was back in the late nineteen hundreds. After the asylum was closed, it went through several different owners who all tried to turn it into a hotel or resort. The last owner named it the Cloud Lake Inn. The place has been boarded up for years."

"The story I heard is that you stumbled onto a murder in the basement of the place when you were sixteen. You confronted the killer."

There was another long silence on the other end of the connection.

"Just how much research did you do?" she asked, clearly wary.

"You rescued a little kid. Damn near got yourself killed in the process. But it was the killer who died."

"It was a long time ago," Grace said. "I try not to think about it."

"Is that what you positive-thinker types do? Try to forget the bad stuff?"

"Yes," she said very firmly. "Where are you going with this?"

"Ten days ago you came across another murder scene."

"So?"

"Finding Witherspoon's body must have dredged up a lot of unpleasant memories. And in Witherspoon's case, the killer is still at large, so I'm guessing you're having a hard time trying not to think about the past."

"What's going on here?" Grace asked. "Are you the one playing analyst now?"

"Just looking at facts," Julius said. "Connecting dots."

"You don't need to remind me of any of it, believe me."

"You're scared."

Another silence stretched across the distance between them. For a moment Julius wondered if Grace would deny her fear.

"I'm . . . uneasy," Grace said eventually. "I didn't think I would be so nervous, not here in Cloud Lake."

"Because you're not in Seattle, where the murder occurred? I get the logic. But it's deeply flawed and, therefore, not working. Want to tell me why you jumped as if you'd touched a live electric wire when your phone pinged you about a new email?"

"I did not jump."

"You flinched and not in a good way."

"There's a good way to flinch?" Grace asked coldly.

"Let's use your word. Uneasy. The ping made you uneasy." He decided to try out one of the theories that Devlin had mentioned. "Old boyfriend giving you trouble?"

"Oh, no, nothing like that," Grace said.

She said it so matter-of-factly and with such assurance that he was inclined to believe her. But it also brought questions. There must be a few old boyfriends scattered about in her past.

"Someone else who is bothering you?" he pressed.

There was another short pause.

"I've been getting weird emails at night," Grace said finally. "The messages are short, just snide little variations of the affirmations taken from the Witherspoon cookbook and the blog. I would say it was just some disgruntled client but the creepy part is that they're all coming from Sprague's personal account."

A chill went through him, heightening all of his senses in the old, unpleasant way. He was acutely aware of the crisp night air, the featureless surface of the lake and the soft rustle of tree branches. You had to assume that the enemy could be anywhere.

"You're right," he said. "That is very creepy."

"There's something else," Grace said. "The day I found Sprague's body, there was an affirmation pinned to his pajamas. Someone, presumably the killer, had printed it out from a computer."

He got the feeling that now that she had blurted out the truth she wanted to keep going.

"You told the cops about the affirmation at the scene?" he asked.

"They saw it for themselves," Grace said. "I didn't touch it."

"Did you report the emails that you've been receiving?"

"Of course," Grace said. "I was told that someone would look into the matter. Every time I get one I forward it to the detective in charge of the investigation but I think he believes I might be sending them to myself."

"Motive?"

"To enhance my appearance of innocence." Grace exhaled deeply. "The bottom line is that the cops haven't come up with anything so far."

"Do you have any idea who is sending the emails?"

"Maybe," Grace said. She was speaking more slowly now, choosing her words. "Sprague did not have a good relationship with his adult daughter, Nyla Witherspoon. In her own weird way I think she was jealous of those of us who worked in the Witherspoon offices—especially me."

"Why you in particular?"

"It's . . . complicated."

Julius felt as if he had just fallen off the dock into the cold, dark waters of the lake.

"You were having an affair with Witherspoon?" he asked without inflection.

"Good grief, no." Grace sounded astonished, not offended. "What in the world would make you think that?"

"Gosh, I dunno. Not like there's any history of bosses sleeping with the women on their office staff."

"Are you speaking from personal experience?" she asked. This time there was an edge on the words.

The lady had claws. Julius smiled, oddly satisfied. Good to know she hadn't been sleeping with Witherspoon. Good to know she could draw blood if you pushed her too far.

"No," he said. "A long time ago I was warned not to get personally involved with the people who work for me. *That way madness lies.*"

Grace startled him with a burble of laughter. "Oh, wow, you get your affirmations from Shakespeare. Not sure the Witherspoon Way affirmations can compete."

"It's a strict policy, not an affirmation, and I didn't get it from Shakespeare. I got it from my next-door neighbor."

"Harley Montoya? What does he know about the dangers of office relationships? I thought he was devoted to his fishing and his garden. He and my neighbor, Agnes, have been rivals in the annual Cloud Lake Garden Club competition ever since he moved to town."

"Harley wasn't always retired."

"Of course not," Grace said. "Sometimes I forget that he was a successful businessman before he moved here."

"The quote about the dangers of getting involved with employees isn't an affirmation, just a realistic assessment of the potential risks. I don't do affirmations. I have a couple of rules instead."

"Really?" She sounded intrigued. "What are they?"

"Rule Number Two is *Everyone has a hidden agenda*."

"I'll bet that's a hard rule to live by."

"Actually, it's pretty damn useful. You can't be successful in my world unless you know what is really motivating your clients, your competition and the people who work for you. When it comes to closing the deal, you need to know everyone's real agenda."

"I thought money was at the top of the list for people in your world."

"Everyone involved will certainly tell you that," he said. "People like to think they base their high-stakes business decisions on rational financial logic. But that's not true. They make decisions based on emotion, every damn time. Afterward they can always find the logic and reason they need to back up the decisions."

"And you take advantage of that insight to make lots of money, is that what you're telling me?"

"I don't always win but I usually know when to cut my losses." Time to change the subject. "You said you think Nyla Witherspoon might have been jealous of you and the other members of Witherspoon's staff. Are your colleagues receiving those emails?"

"I asked Millicent and Kristy that question. Neither of them has received the emails but they agreed that Nyla is the most likely culprit."

"Did you get anything from Witherspoon's estate?"

"Heavens no," Grace said. "No one on the staff was in Sprague's will. He paid us all very well but he left his entire estate to Nyla."

"And now a large chunk of it has gone missing."

"It's news to me but if you and Devlin know that, then it's safe to say that Nyla is also aware of the embezzlement by now. But I started getting the emails immediately after Sprague was murdered—before anyone realized that someone had been stealing from the Witherspoon Way accounts."

"If she started emailing you because she wanted to take out some of her anger and jealousy on you, then the missing money would have served to enrage her all the more."

"A cheerful thought. You really are not a glass-half-full kind of man, are you?"

He watched the moonlight ripple on the jewel-black lake for a moment.

"Have you talked to Dev about the case?" he asked.

"Some," Grace said. "But I haven't gone into great detail. The thing is, I don't know Devlin very well. Between you and me, I think he has some doubts about my innocence."

Julius decided that it was not a good time to confirm her theory.

"Does Dev know you've got a stalker?" he said instead.

"I haven't told him about the emails, if that's what you mean."

"Yes, it's exactly what I mean."

"This isn't his case," Grace said. She sounded defensive.

"Did you mention them to Irene?"

"No. I don't want to make her any more concerned than she is already."

"Dev is the chief of police in this town. He needs to know what's going on. Talk to him tomorrow morning."

Grace hesitated. "Okay. But there really isn't anything Devlin can do about this."

"Dev's a good cop. He might have some ideas. Meanwhile, try to get some sleep."

"Oh, sure, easy for you to say."

He couldn't think of a response to that. He had a feeling he wouldn't get a lot of sleep, either.

"Good night," he said.

"Hang on, I've got a question. You said that your father came around asking for money after you got rich."

Should have kept my mouth shut, he thought.

"That's right," he said. "So?"

"Did you give him the loan?"

"He and I both knew it wouldn't have been a loan because he would never have repaid it."

"Did you give him the money?" Grace asked quietly.

Julius looked out over the water. "What do you think?"

"I think you did a deal based on emotion. You gave

him the money, and I have a hunch it was never repaid."

Julius's mouth twitched at the corner. "Right on both counts. It was the worst investment I ever made. Still don't know why I did it."

"The why is easy," Grace said. "He was your dad. You broke Rule Number Two for him."

"No surprise that it turned out badly."

"You did what you had to do."

"Good night," he said again.

"Wait, what's Rule Number One?" she asked.

"Trust no one."

He ended the connection and clipped the phone to his belt. He stood at the end of the dock for a while longer, meditating on the conversation.

It hadn't really been phone sex, he decided. But talking to Grace had seemed a lot more intimate than any of the sexual encounters he'd had since his divorce.

He was right about one thing—sleep was hard to come by. At two fifteen he got up, pulled on his jeans and a jacket and went outside into the cold night. He walked to the end of the dock and looked across the expanse of dark water toward the Elland house.

The back porch light was still on and a weak glow illuminated the curtains in all the windows. He knew the night-lights would still be on at dawn when he went past the house on his morning run. They had been lit up all night, every night since Grace had arrived in Cloud Lake.

Eight

The phone rang just as Grace dropped a slice of multigrain bread into the toaster. She glanced at the screen, saw her sister's name and took the call.

"Are you calling to tell me that you're pregnant again?" she asked. "If so, congratulations."

"I'm calling," Alison said, "because I just saw the news about the embezzlement at the Witherspoon Way Corporation. Are you all right?"

Alison was using her crisp, no-nonsense lawyer voice. That was never a good sign.

"Word travels fast," Grace said. "And, yes, I'm fine."

Phone in hand, she walked to the window. It was her favorite time of day. The late winter sun was not yet up, but there was enough early light in the sky to transform the surface of the lake into a steel mirror. As she watched, a man dressed in gray sweats came into view. He was running at an easy, steady pace, as if he could run forever. He followed the public path that traced the shoreline. The lights were on in her kitchen. She knew that if he looked at the house he would see her. She waved.

Julius raised one hand, acknowledging the greeting. For a few seconds she could have sworn he actually broke stride, perhaps even considered pausing to say good morning. But he kept going.

She had been living in the lake house for nearly a week. Although she had met Julius for the first time last night, she already knew his running schedule. He went past her place every other morning just before dawn. This was the first morning that she had waved at him. Until last night he had been an interesting stranger. Today he was a man with whom she had shared some secrets.

"I'm worried about this new development," Alison said. "Embezzlement is dangerous territory. There's a strong possibility that it was the reason for Witherspoon's murder."

Grace watched Julius until he was out of sight. When he was gone she switched the phone to speaker mode and put the device down on the counter. She reached for the jar of peanut butter and a knife.

"In a horrible way it would be almost reassuring to know that there was a logical motive like money involved," she said. "Otherwise Sprague's death makes no sense."

She glanced at the clock. The early morning call was unlike Alison, who lived a well-scheduled, well-organized life that revolved around home and work. Even the birth of her first child a year earlier had done little to disturb the efficient household. She balanced career and family with an aplomb that made other women marvel.

Grace knew that at that moment Alison was putting the finishing touches on breakfast, after which she would dress in one of her tailored business suits before heading to her office. Alison looked great in a sharp suit. Actually, she looked terrific in just about anything, Grace thought. Her older sister was tall and willowy. But as a successful lawyer who specialized in estate planning, Alison elected to project a conservative air. She wore her dark hair pulled back in a strict twist that emphasized her classic profile. Sleek, serious glasses framed her eyes.

"The problem with the embezzlement motive is that it points to someone who was working directly for Witherspoon," Alison said grimly.

"That had occurred to me." Grace took the lid off the jar of peanut butter. "You're worried that the cops will think I was the one doing the embezzling, aren't you?"

"You're the one who made Witherspoon so successful."

"That's not true," Grace said. "Why do I have to keep explaining that Sprague Witherspoon was the genuine article—a man who truly wanted to do good. And, yes, he had been doing very well financially in the past eighteen months. But that's just it. Why on earth would I want to kill him? Why would any of us in the office want to murder him? He was making himself and everyone around him quite wealthy. Besides, we both know I wouldn't have a clue how to go about constructing an embezzlement scheme."

"Embezzlement is a lot easier than most people think," Alison said. "There are so many ways to siphon off money from a successful business like the Witherspoon Way."

"Oddly enough you are not the first person to mention that to me lately."

"I can't believe you walked in on another murder," Alison said. "Statistically speaking, the odds of a person who isn't in law enforcement or connected to the criminal world stumbling into two different homicide scenes must be vanishingly small."

"Statistics was never my best subject. I keep reminding myself that coincidences do happen. That's why they invented the word."

"How are things going there in Cloud Lake?" Alison asked.

"Okay. I'm not making much progress on finding a new career path, though."

"Give yourself some time. It's not like you haven't had a couple of major shocks lately, what with the murder and then finding yourself unemployed."

"Tell me about it," Grace said. The toast popped up in the toaster. She removed it, set it on a plate and spread some peanut butter on it. "But as much as I'd like to blame my lack of momentum on those things, I don't think that's the real problem."

"What is the real problem?"

Grace hesitated, unsure of how much to confide to Alison. There was nothing her sister could do except worry. But they were family, after all. They had never kept secrets from each other, at least not for long.

"The dream is back, Alison. And so are the anxiety attacks."

"Damn. I was afraid the trauma of Witherspoon's death might drag everything to the surface again. Maybe you should make an appointment with Dr. Peterson."

"I already know what she would say. She would remind me to practice rewriting the dream script before I go to bed and to remember to use the breathing exercises and meditation techniques on a regular basis and, if necessary, take the meds. I'm doing all of that. It's just that—"

A small amount of peanut butter dropped off the knife and landed on the counter.

"Hang on," Grace said. She reached for a paper towel.

"It's just what?" Alison pressed.

Grace used the towel to wipe up the peanut butter. "It's just that I can't shake this weird feeling that there's some connection between Witherspoon's death and the Trager murder."

There was silence from Alison's end.

"It's the bottle of vodka, isn't it?" she said finally.

"Yes."

"Perfectly understandable, given what happened in

the past. But you said that the police found a charge for it on one of Witherspoon's credit card statements. Sprague Witherspoon bought that bottle of vodka a few days before he was murdered."

"He didn't drink vodka, Alison."

"Maybe not, but he entertained frequently, right?"

"That's true," Grace said. "The police did say that there was a large selection of liquor bottles in his kitchen. But I told you, this particular bottle of vodka was sitting on the nightstand beside the bed where I found the body."

There was a long silence on the other end of the line. Grace took a bite out of the slice of toast that she had just slathered in peanut butter.

"Grace, do you want to come and stay with Ethan and Harry and me for a while?" Alison said after a moment. "You can work on your résumé here in Portland."

"Thanks, but I really need to stay focused on my job hunting in the Seattle area. I can't do that from Portland."

"Have you got any idea what you might want to do next?"

"Zip." Grace ate some more toast. "I've been told I should come up with a business plan for finding my next career."

"A business plan for job hunting? I suppose there's some logic to that. Who gave you that advice?"

"A man I met on a blind date that Irene arranged for me last night."

"The two of you wound up discussing business

plans?" Alison chuckled. "Sounds like a typical blind-date disaster."

"His name is Julius and he was a lot more interesting than anyone else I've dated recently."

"That isn't saying much, is it? Your social life hasn't exactly been the stuff of legend lately."

"Let's face it, my social life has never been legendary."

"Your own fault," Alison said. "You're going to have to stop sending out vibes that attract men who are looking for a sister or a best friend."

"I'll work on that as soon as I get a new job."

"Mom's worrying about you again," Alison said. "She thinks you're too old to be ricocheting from one job to another trying to find yourself. She's right."

"I found myself a long time ago. It's finding a career that is giving me problems. I've got to tell you, the job at the Witherspoon Way was the best position I've ever had. I would have been happy to stay there."

"Well, that's not an option now, is it?"

"Careful, you're starting to sound like Mom."

"I'm just doing my job as your older sister," Alison said. "You know that as far as Mom and I are concerned, Sprague Witherspoon took advantage of you."

"That's not true. He gave me opportunities."

"You wrote that cookbook and blog that took him to the top of the self-help-guru world but it was his name on both."

"I've explained to you that it is not unusual for successful people to pay others to write their books and blogs," Grace said.

This was not the first time Alison had raised this

particular argument. Grace decided that she did not have the patience for it this morning. She was working on a plan that had popped into her head a few minutes earlier when Julius had run past the house. Time was of the essence.

"Sorry," she said, "I've got to go."

"Where are you going at this hour of the morning?"

"I'm going to focus on the first stage of my new career plan. Inspiration just struck."

"You sound serious," Alison said. "I'm impressed. And, may I say, it's about time you settled on a realistic career path. I was starting to worry that you would end up working as a mime out in front of Nordstrom."

"Thanks, Big Sister. You do know how to motivate a person. Now I really do have to hang up and get busy."

"Doing what, exactly?"

"I told you, my date last night suggested that I build a business plan designed to help me find a career path. He just went past the house on his morning run."

"So?"

"He'll turn around at the southern end of the lake where the path ends at the marina."

"I'm not following you."

"That means he'll be coming back this way in a few minutes. I'm going to intercept him."

"Why?" Alison asked.

"I'm going to ask him if he will consult for me."

"On what?"

Alison sounded dumbfounded now.

"On a business plan," Grace said. "Evidently he's

an expert on business strategy and stuff like that. Talk to you later."

"Wait, don't hang up. What do you know about this man you're going to intercept?"

"Not nearly enough," Grace said.

Nine

Grace ended the call and glanced at the clock. Given Julius's pace and his adherence to his running routine she thought she had about ten minutes left to prepare. She opened the refrigerator and took out two hard-boiled eggs and a bottle of spring water. Next she went into the pantry and found the old wicker picnic basket.

Eight minutes later she was ready. She bundled up in her down jacket, picked up the picnic basket and went out onto the sheltered back porch. A light rain was falling. She pulled up the hood of the coat.

She crossed the porch, went down the steps and hurried through the simple winter garden. Now that her mother and Kirk were spending a good portion of the year in sunny locales, the landscaping around the house had been reduced to the basics. The hardy shrubs and the trees that remained made a stark contrast to the glorious greenery that surrounded Agnes Gilroy's pretty little house. But then, Agnes was a serious Pacific Northwest gardener.

As if she had been alerted by a psychic intercept, Agnes came out onto her back porch and waved.

"Good morning, dear," she sang out. "Lovely day, isn't it?"

Agnes had always been one of Grace's favorite people. Agnes was a relentless optimist but Grace's mother had observed on more than one occasion that beneath her cheery exterior the older woman was not only smart, she was also a shrewd judge of character.

She wore her long gray hair in a bun at the nape of her neck and dressed mostly in baggy denim jeans, flannel shirts and gardening clogs. She had been born a free spirit and had evidently lived the lifestyle. A botanist by training, she had traveled widely in her younger days, collecting plant specimens for academic and pharmaceutical research. If her stories were to be believed, she had also gathered numerous lovers along the way. Grace found Agnes's reminiscences entirely credible.

After retiring Agnes had devoted herself to competitive gardening in Cloud Lake. She had never married and had made it clear that she preferred to live alone. But shortly after Harley Montoya had moved to town, that situation had been somewhat modified.

The competition between Agnes and Harley had led, perhaps inevitably, to a discreet, long-term affair. Without fail, Harley's truck was seen parked in

Agnes's driveway every Wednesday and Saturday night. It was always gone before dawn.

"It's risky to let men spend the entire night, dear," Agnes had once explained to Grace. "It gives them the notion that you're going to start cooking and cleaning for them."

Grace paused halfway across the garden. "Hi, Agnes. Yes, it's a great day."

The rain was getting heavier but Grace knew that neither of them was going to mention that little fact. There was some natural, built-in competition between positive thinkers, just as there was between gardeners.

"Going to waylay Mr. Arkwright, dear?" Agnes asked. "I saw him go past a while ago."

"I thought I'd give it a whirl," Grace said.

"I take it the blind date went well, then." Agnes sounded gratified. "I was pretty sure it had when I heard you chase him out of the house last night. That sort of activity early on is always a sign of a promising start in a relationship."

"Does everyone in town know about my blind date with Julius?" Grace asked.

"I expect there are a few folks who haven't been paying attention," Agnes said, "but for the most part I think it's safe to say it's common knowledge. You're rather famous around here, dear, at least among those of us who have lived in Cloud Lake for a while. Have a wonderful day, dear."

Agnes went back inside. The door banged shut behind her.

The little wrought iron garden gate was designed to be decorative. It was not a security device. Grace unlatched it and stepped out onto the path. Her timing was perfect. She could see Julius coming toward her.

When he saw her he slowed his pace. By the time he was a few yards away he was walking.

He came to a halt in front of her and smiled a slow, wicked smile that was reflected in his eyes. He suddenly looked younger and almost carefree.

"Well, if it isn't Little Red Riding Hood." His smile widened into a wolfish grin. "And to think I never believed in fairy tales."

Grace glanced down at her red jacket. She felt the heat rise in her cheeks.

"Okay, the red coat and hood thing is sheer coincidence," she said.

"If you say so."

Julius was drenched with sweat and rain. The front of his gray pullover was soaked. His hair was plastered to his head. Rivulets of water mixed with perspiration streamed down his face.

Normally she was not keen on sweaty men. She knew some women were attracted to males who looked as if they had just emerged from a cage fight but she was not one of them. But Julius Arkwright drenched in sweat was an altogether different beast. Standing this close to him aroused something primal deep inside.

Focus, woman.

"You probably wonder why I'm out here in the rain, barring your path," she said.

"I'm going to take a flying leap and say the picnic basket has some significance."

"Yes, it does," she said. "Here's another clue. I am not on my way to Grandma's house."

"That leaves us with a high probability that you have deliberately intercepted me."

"A very strong possibility," she agreed.

He glanced at the closed lid of the wicker basket with an expression of deep interest. "What have you got in there?"

"A bribe."

"Who do you plan to bribe?"

"A consultant, I hope."

He raised his brows. "You are in need of a consultant?"

"Apparently so."

"What do you want the consultant to do for you?" Julius asked.

"Help me work up a business plan that will enable me to find a new career, one that I will find challenging, exciting and fulfilling—preferably a career that will last longer than eighteen months. I want to find my true calling."

"I thought you were just trying to find a job."

"My aspirations are actually somewhat more aspirational. I have my work at the Witherspoon Way to thank for that, I suppose. I'm sure that the right career for me is out there somewhere, waiting for me to find it."

Julius studied the basket. "Am I to assume that in exchange for assisting you in finding your dream job the consultant gets whatever is in that basket?"

"Right," she said briskly. "Do we have a deal?"

"You want me to agree to the deal before I see the nature of the bribe?"

"I suppose I could give you a peek."

She raised the lid of the basket very briefly to reveal the items neatly packed inside—two hard-boiled eggs, an orange, two chunky slices of multigrain bread, a little plastic canister filled with peanut butter, a bottle of spring water and a thermos.

"It's a picnic breakfast," she explained. She snapped the lid of the basket closed to keep out the rain. "There's coffee in the thermos."

"Huh. I don't know about this. With the exception of the coffee and the peanut butter, it all looked sort of healthy."

"It's *all* very healthy. The coffee is fair-trade organic and the peanut butter is not only organic, it is unadulterated with sweeteners or stabilizers."

"That picnic also appeared to be very vegetarian."

"Is that a problem?" she challenged.

"Nope. Food is food." He plucked the picnic basket from her arm with a quick, deft motion. "You've got yourself a consultant. When do you want to start?"

"How about this morning?"

"Let's make it lunch. Your morning is already booked."

"It is?"

"You're having your little chat with Dev about those stalker emails, remember?"

"Oh, yeah, right."

"See you for lunch."

Julius loped off with the picnic basket. She stood there in the falling rain and watched him until he vanished from sight around a wooded bend. He made a very interesting Big Bad Wolf.

It's just a business arrangement, she told herself.

But it was possible that wasn't the whole truth. It was, in fact, conceivable that an objective observer would describe the situation in an entirely different way.

Some people—the unenlightened type—might say that she was flirting with the Big Bad Wolf.

Ten

Satisfied with her first serious move toward finding her calling, Grace went back inside the house. She took off her coat and hung it on a hook in the small closet off the kitchen that served as a mudroom. It was a good time to practice her third ritual. She needed to fortify herself for the coming interview with Chief Nakamura. It was hard to think of him as Devlin when he was in uniform.

She locked the doors, changed into her workout clothes and unrolled the exercise mat. She stood at the end of the mat for a time, composing herself from head to toe—mind and body—as she had been taught.

When she was ready she took the first step in the fluid moves of the ancient system of physical meditation that, together with the evening house-check and the breathing exercises, kept the nightmares and panic attacks under some semblance of control.

Eleven

"You should have told Devlin about those emails you've been receiving from Witherspoon's account," Irene said.

"There didn't seem to be much point," Grace said. "There isn't anything he can do. Besides, there have only been a few of them."

She spoke mostly into her mug of coffee because she knew what was coming next. Talk about easy predictions, she thought. Maybe she should consider a career as a psychic.

"You've only received a *few* emails from some demented stalker?" Irene yelped. "Listen to yourself, woman. Someone is harassing you and all you can say is, well, there have only been a few scary emails."

"Okay, okay, maybe I'm feeling a tad defensive because everyone is on my case this morning about those emails. I don't think I'm being stalked. Not exactly. And would you please keep your voice down? It's bad enough that my friends, family and Julius Arkwright think I'm a naive idiot. I would appreciate it if you didn't broadcast the news to your customers as well."

They were sitting at a table in Irene's office. Grace had headed straight to Cloud Lake Kitchenware as soon as she finished talking to Devlin at the Cloud Lake Police Department headquarters two blocks away. Julius had insisted on accompanying her to the tense interview. By the time it was over she had felt utterly drained and in need of a friendly ear. But all she had gotten from Irene thus far was more lecturing.

The door between the office and the sales floor of the gourmet cookware store was closed but there was a long window. Grace could see most of the front of the shop. It was not yet noon but Cloud Lake Kitchenware was bustling with customers who were browsing the cookbook collection, admiring bouquets of colorful silicon spatulas and examining the gleaming pots and pans.

The employees, dressed in dark green aprons stamped with the shop's logo, were busy but that did not mean they could not overhear a private conversation in the office—not if Irene's voice rose any higher.

Irene cleared her throat and lowered her voice. "I can't help but notice that you put Julius into a third category."

Grace frowned. "What?"

"You said friends, family and Julius Arkwright thought you were a naive idiot," Irene reminded her. "You placed Julius in a special category."

"Well, he's not family and he's not exactly a friend."

"What is he, then?"

"I'm not sure how to describe him," Grace admitted.

"But you're sure he thinks you're a naive idiot?" Irene asked, evidently intrigued by the possibility. "He actually said that?"

Grace slumped back in her chair. "He didn't use those exact words but it's not hard to tell that's what he's thinking. It appears to be a commonly held assumption."

"That's not true. Your friends and family and, I'm sure, Julius, as well, are just worried about you, that's all."

"Yes, I know. And deep down I appreciate it, really I do. But in spite of appearances, I'm not entirely incapable of taking care of myself."

"We know that."

"Yeah, sure you do." Grace drank some of her coffee. "Be honest. You think I'm a naive idiot."

Irene's eyes narrowed in sudden comprehension. "You know who is sending those emails, don't you?"

"I'm not positive but I suspect that the sender is probably Nyla Witherspoon." Grace set the mug down on the desk. "I'll bet she came across the password for Sprague's email account. It's not like Sprague treated it as top secret."

"Now she's pissed and sending you those emails

because she thinks you embezzled money from Sprague Witherspoon that should have come to her."

"Assuming Nyla is behind the emails, I need to remind everyone that she started sending them *before* it was discovered that a lot of money was missing. She was jealous of Sprague's office staff because we worked so closely with her father. But she fixated on me."

"Because you were the one who did the most to elevate his career," Irene said calmly.

"People keep saying that, but it's not true."

"There's no maybe about it. Your cookbook and the blog are what put Witherspoon into the big time."

"I keep trying to explain that it was Sprague Witherspoon, himself, who was the force behind his own success. I just helped him market his concepts."

"Bull," Irene said. "It was the cookbook and the related blog with all those dippy daily affirmations that made him famous in the motivational guru business. You're the one who wrote all of that stuff."

Grace raised her brows. "Dippy daily affirmations?"

"Sorry." Irene winced. "As a branding technique those affirmations were nothing short of brilliant. But getting back to the emails, who else might have the password to Witherspoon's account?"

"Any number of people, including me," Grace said morosely.

"I'll bet Nyla or whoever is behind the emails is hoping the cops will assume that you are sending those emails to yourself."

"That possibility has occurred to me," Grace said.

"Why do you think I didn't mention them to Devlin? I figured he would jump to that conclusion."

"No," Irene said. She said it very firmly.

"Whoever is emailing me from Sprague's account has been very careful to make sure the contents are not overtly threatening. I think that indicates that the sender doesn't want the cops to look too hard in that direction."

"But the emails are definitely intended to rattle your nerves," Irene said.

"Oh, sure." Grace drank some more coffee and lowered the mug. "I must admit the sender has had some success in that regard. I'm not sleeping well these days."

"I wouldn't be sleeping well, either, under the circumstances," Irene said. She paused a beat and then softened her tone. "Do you really believe that Julius thinks you're naive and maybe not too bright?"

Grace started to say yes but she hesitated and then shrugged. "Maybe. But he's hard to read. I also have to face the fact that there is another possibility."

"What's that?"

"He might still be wondering if I did kill Sprague Witherspoon."

Irene set her mug down with a bang that reverberated through the office. "I'm sure he doesn't believe that."

"Do you know him well enough to be able to tell what he's thinking?"

"Well, no. As you just said, he's hard to read. But Julius and Dev have been friends for years. I'm sure Dev would never have gone along with the dinner date last night if he wasn't convinced that you and Julius made a good match."

Grace managed a grim smile. "And everyone thinks I'm naive."

Irene glared. "I beg your pardon?"

"Get real. You know me well enough to trust me but Devlin doesn't. Furthermore, he's a cop—one who happens to have an old pal in town, someone whose instincts he probably does trust. So he goes along with your little matchmaking scheme because he figures it will give him the perfect opportunity to get Julius's take on me."

Irene opened her mouth to protest but after a few seconds she closed it again. She drummed her fingers on the desktop.

"Hmm," she said.

"Don't worry, I'm not taking Devlin's distrust personally," Grace said.

Irene's brows rose. "That's very gracious of you."

"I'm serious. Dev's first priority is to protect you. I can see it in his eyes every time he looks at you. The possibility that your best friend might be a murderer—and/or an embezzler—is naturally of considerable interest to him."

"I'm sure he doesn't believe that you killed Witherspoon or stole the money."

"I didn't say he believed all that stuff. I just said he's concerned—in part because I'm now living in his town but mostly because of you. He's a good cop. He's also a good husband. He'll do what he thinks he has to do to protect you."

"Yes, but I still can't believe that he went so far as to ask Julius for his take on you," Irene said.

"Seems like a logical move, when you think about it."

Irene eyed her keenly. "You know, some people might be quite annoyed upon discovering that what they thought was an innocent blind date was actually an undercover sting operation."

"Turns out I've got bigger problems," Grace said. "As we at the Witherspoon Way would say, *Today I will focus on priorities and ignore the unimportant crap.*"

Irene looked pained. "You just made up that affirmation on the spot, didn't you?"

"Yep. Has a certain ring to it, don't you think?"

They drank their coffee quietly for a time. The silence between them was the kind that could be generated only by a long friendship. After a while Irene stirred in her chair.

"Let's reverse this process," she said. "What's your take on Julius Arkwright?"

"He's bored," Grace said.

"What?" Irene stared at her, startled. "Devlin and I have been wondering if Julius is sinking into some kind of low-grade depression. He hasn't even dated very much since his divorce a couple of years ago."

Grace shrugged. "He's drifting. With some people, boredom can look a lot like depression."

"When did you get a degree in psychology?"

"Okay, you've got me there. But if you will recall, Mom made me spend a lot of time with a shrink after the crap that happened up at the old asylum. I learned a lot. What made you and Devlin think that Julius was depressed?"

"Dev told me that Julius is thinking very seriously about selling his venture capital company," Irene said slowly.

"So? A lot of people build companies and then sell them. It's a dream come true for most businesspeople."

"Dev says he doesn't think that's the case with Julius."

"Why not?"

"Julius built Arkwright Ventures from scratch," Irene said. "He poured his heart and soul into it, according to Dev. Julius loves the venture capital business or at least he did at one time. He's made a fortune because he's very good at what he does. But about two years ago his wife left him for another man."

Grace squared her shoulders. "I repeat, so?"

"Wow." Irene blinked. "Aren't you the hard-hearted woman today?"

Grace tightened her grip on her mug. "Don't look at me like that. Divorce happens."

"Well, yes, but you're usually a little more sympathetic about such things."

"Maybe Julius poured a little too much of his heart and soul into his business," Grace said. "Maybe he should have saved some for his wife."

Irene nodded slowly. "You may be right. Dev did say that Julius was married to his company. It's entirely possible that the wife felt neglected. But, really, she didn't have to run off with Julius's vice president and trusted friend."

Grace thought about that. "Okay, you're right, that's cold."

"Dev says Julius has seemed sort of numb since then, like he's running on autopilot. He keeps making money but the thrill is gone."

"There are problems in the world and then there are problems," Grace said evenly. "Frankly, the ability to make money without even trying doesn't strike me as a huge burden to bear."

Irene smiled briefly. "You really are not inclined to be sympathetic to Julius Arkwright today, are you?"

"He doesn't need sympathy. But if it makes you feel better, I can tell you that this morning I hired him to consult for me."

Irene's mouth fell open. "You *what*?"

"Last night when he took me home he told me that I needed to draw up a strategy designed to help me find a new career. This morning I hired him to show me how to go about making the plan."

"You hired him?" Irene said. Now she looked blank.

"Technically speaking, it was a bribe."

"Either way, you're joking. You can't afford Julius Arkwright."

"I already gave him the bribe. He took it. We have a deal."

Irene's eyes widened. "Please don't tell me you're sleeping with him. At least not yet. I like Julius, yes. I think the two of you would make an interesting couple. But it's way too soon—especially for you. We both know that jumping into bed with a man on the first date is not your style."

"No, of course I'm not sleeping with Julius Arkwright." Grace brushed that aside with a wide, sweeping motion of her hand and beetled her brows at Irene—making it clear that she had no intention of hopping into bed with Julius. Unfortunately she could not be sure if she was trying to reassure Irene or herself. "But I think he's got a point about me needing some kind of career path plan," she continued hastily.

"You do?"

"I'm certainly not getting anywhere on my own. I can't seem to focus. He appears to be an expert on planning and strategy. So, when he ran by my house this morning I intercepted him with a picnic basket full of breakfast goodies and told him it was a bribe for his services as a consultant. He accepted."

"Did he?" Irene tapped the pen lightly on the desktop. "So the blind date was not a complete disaster."

"Not if it keeps me from ending up as a street mime out in front of Nordstrom."

Irene looked at her. "Well, at least you'd be working in front of Nordstrom. You wouldn't be just any street mime."

"You know what I mean. I want to find out what it is that I am meant to do in life, Irene. My calling. My passion. I haven't had any luck with the online questionnaires that are supposed to guide you to an appropriate career path. So I figure I have nothing left to lose by getting some planning advice from an expert."

"In other words, you do like Julius," Irene said with a smug air. "At least enough to ask for his advice."

Grace smiled a crafty smile. "Some people would say I'm using him."

Amusement lit Irene's eyes. "I seriously doubt that Julius would let anyone use him. He has been known to do the occasional favor, however."

"Really?"

"Who do you think arranged the financing I needed to start Cloud Lake Kitchenware? Who do you think helped me find a website designer to take the business online? Who do you think guided me through the tax and accounting issues and taught me how to do a profit-and-loss statement?"

"Ah," Grace said. "I see."

Irene's expression turned serious. "Like I said, I'm rather fond of Julius and grateful to him. Furthermore, I know that Dev would trust him with his life. In fact, that is what happened when they served together in a war zone a few years ago. Dev also trusts Julius with our retirement fund investments. But if you're going to get involved with Julius Arkwright, I think there is something you should know about him."

"I'm listening."

"The vice president who married Julius's ex is Edward Hastings. He's one of the Seattle-real-estate-empire Hastingses. Fourth-generation land developers. His family's company owns a huge chunk of downtown Seattle real estate, including a few office towers."

Grace considered the information briefly and then raised one shoulder in a dismissive little shrug.

"Why does that matter to me?" she asked.

"Shortly after Edward Hastings left Arkwright Ventures he not only married Julius's ex, he also became the president and CEO of the Hastings family empire."

"Still waiting for the other shoe to drop, Irene."

"There are rumors that under Edward Hastings's control the firm has stumbled a few times in the past eighteen months. Major deals have slipped away to competitors."

Grace watched Irene over the rim of the coffee mug. "What does that have to do with Julius?"

"I'm a small-business person who swims in a very small pond here in Cloud Lake. I admit that I don't know a lot about the shark pool in which Julius does his hunting. But I try to keep up with the Pacific Northwest business news, and because of Dev's friendship with Julius, I sometimes hear bits and pieces of gossip."

"What have you heard that is worrying you?" Grace asked.

Irene leaned forward and folded her arms on the desk. "Hastings is in real trouble. Some people are predicting that under Edward Hastings's leadership we will see the downfall of a family-held company that has been around for nearly a century. The business world is like a small town—once a rumor starts, it can easily become a self-fulfilling prophecy."

Grace reflected briefly. "What does this have to do with Julius?"

"The gossip is that the downward slide of the

Hastings family empire has been caused by one man—Julius Arkwright."

"They think he's out for revenge? That he's somehow sabotaging Hastings?"

"Yes."

Grace gave that some thought. "And this has been going on for how long?"

"Nearly two years. The timing is significant."

"Because it coincides with the timing of Julius's divorce?"

"People are saying that Julius intends to destroy Hastings. Dev tells me that when Julius sets his sights on a goal, he doesn't quit. Like a heat-seeking missile, he just keeps going until he reaches his target."

"I can't believe you set me up on a blind date with a man you feel compelled to describe in military terms."

"That's Dev's description," Irene said. "I just wanted you to know about the rumors before you got any more involved with Julius. If it's true that he's plotting revenge, there may be collateral damage."

"You're the one who set up the blind date. Now you're trying to warn me about Julius?"

"I really do think that you and Julius would be good together. But I will admit that Dev and I were also hoping that if you two hit it off, Julius might be . . . distracted from whatever it is he's doing to Hastings."

"Stop trying to make me feel sorry for Julius Arkwright."

Irene blinked. "That is not exactly what I'm trying to accomplish here."

"Yes, it is. You're trying to make me think that he's depressed and obsessed with revenge and in need of fixing. But as far as I can tell, Julius is more than capable of taking care of himself. I just told you, I have other priorities at the moment. I'm trying to get a life, remember?"

"Right. A life." Irene sat back in her chair. "And you've hired Julius Arkwright to help you come up with a plan to get said life."

"That's it," Grace said smoothly. "Just a business transaction. You can move along. Nothing to see here."

"Don't give me that. What happened when Julius took you home last night?"

Grace pursed her lips. "Among other things, he asked me flat-out if I murdered Witherspoon."

"Oh, jeez," Irene groaned. "Not exactly a great conversation starter."

"Nope. But it sure was a fine way to end one, which is what happened. Sort of. I kicked him out of the house. On his way out the door he assured me that he believed me."

"But you kicked him out, anyway."

"Of course." Grace swallowed some coffee and lowered the mug. "But then he called me."

"Did he, now?" Irene said very softly.

"I ended up telling him about the weird emails and the next thing I knew, he was ordering me to tell Devlin about the emails, which is why I went to Devlin's office today, et cetera, et cetera. And there you have it. A complete portrait of a blind date gone bad but possibly a good sign for the future of my career planning."

Irene tapped the pen on the desk again, very thoughtful now. "Is there any way that call last night could be described as phone sex?"

"Absolutely not."

Talking to Julius on the phone had been a strangely intimate experience, Grace thought. But she refused to describe it as phone sex. Not that she'd ever had phone sex. It was simply that, after getting hit with the latest email from the stalker, she had felt a need to confide in someone. It just so happened that Julius had been the one to call her at that moment. Serendipity. Or coincidence. Or chaos theory. Something like that probably explained everything.

"I'm not sure what to say." Irene shook her head. "Like Dev, Julius is a little deep in places."

"Now there's a startling revelation."

Irene ignored her. "I guess it comes down to the fact that I think you can trust him. And, like I said, he's the kind of man who will do favors for friends. He took a chance on me when no one else would."

"Any investment is a risk but you and Cloud Lake Kitchenware are as close as it gets to a sure thing."

"Cloud Lake Kitchenware is working," Irene said. Pride and satisfaction brightened her expression. "It's actually going to turn a nice profit this year. But it will never make the kind of money that Julius is accustomed to raking in with his big investments. This particular project is petty cash for him."

"As it happens, Julius told me that he's got enough money."

Surprise lit Irene's eyes. Then she smiled. "Did he say that?"

"Yes."

"Don't think I've ever heard anyone actually say that before."

"I told you, what Julius Arkwright is looking for these days is a way to escape boredom."

"Considering the fact that you met Julius less than twenty-four hours ago, you sure seem to know a lot about him."

"He's hard to read but not impossible." Grace drank the rest of her coffee and set the mug down. "I know you meant well, but promise me you won't set me up with any more blind dates, at least not until I get my life together." She rose to her feet. "I'd better be on my way. I have to do some grocery shopping and then I am scheduled to meet my consultant for a luncheon meeting. We are supposed to start building my business plan."

"What will you do if you don't come up with a strategy that leads you to your personal calling?"

"Fire my consultant."

Twelve

The rain had stopped by the time Grace finished her shopping and got behind the wheel to drive back to the lake house. The high cloud cover remained, however, infusing the atmosphere with the peculiar glary gray light that made sunglasses a necessity, even in winter.

She did not recognize the expensive-looking silver sedan parked in front of the lake house but she knew the blonde in the front seat all too well. Nyla Witherspoon.

First a visit with the local chief of police and now Nyla had decided to pay a call on her. The day was not improving markedly, Grace decided. She tried to come up with an affirmation that applied to the situation. Nothing sprang to mind.

She brought her car to a halt and mentally braced herself for the encounter. Nyla erupted from the front seat of the sedan.

She was a thin, sharp-faced woman who, if she smiled more, would have been quite attractive in a chic, elfin way. But when she was not smiling—which was most of the time as far as Grace could tell—she looked like all she needed was a broomstick and a pointed hat to complete her ensemble. The bitterness and anger that simmered in her eyes seemed to bubble up from someplace deep inside.

She stalked over to the compact, arriving just as Grace got the door open.

"Did you think you could hide here in Cloud Lake?" Nyla's sunglasses made it impossible to read her eyes but her voice was tight with rage. "Did you think I wouldn't find you?"

"I didn't know you were looking for me," Grace said. She took off her own shades. "You could have called. What do you want, Nyla?"

"You know why I'm here. I want my father's money—the money that should have come to me."

"I've told you before, I don't have it."

"You're lying. You embezzled it from my father's corporation. You've probably got it hidden in some offshore account."

Grace closed her eyes for a couple of seconds and reminded herself that Nyla had some serious issues.

"I don't know anything about the missing money," she said. She tried to pitch her voice to a soothing level.

"By the way, I told the police about those emails you've been sending to me from your father's account. It amounts to stalking, you know."

"What are you talking about? What emails?"

"Nyla, if you're the one who has been emailing me, it has got to stop. The cops are trying to catch your father's killer. They need your help. Focusing your rage on me won't do any good."

Nyla's sharp features tightened. "A lot of people, including the police, think that you might be the one who murdered my father."

Grace spread her hands. "Why would I kill my employer and cut off the cash flow? Think about it, Nyla. Sprague was the one who brought in the money, not me. It was his name on the blog and on the cookbook. I was just his assistant. Trust me, with your father gone, the cash flow will dry up fast."

"You shot him because he found out that you were stealing his money. He probably confronted you, maybe threatened to report you to the police. You had to get rid of him."

"That simply is not true," Grace said. "I was home the night your father was murdered."

"Your so-called alibi won't hold water. Yes, I know they say the security video shows your car parked in the apartment garage that night but that doesn't mean you didn't leave the building. You could have slipped out and taken a cab to my father's house on Queen Anne."

"You can't prove that. No one can prove it, because it never happened."

"Your prints were at the scene." But Nyla sounded less certain now.

"My prints were at the scene because I'm the one who found the body," Grace said, struggling to hold on to her patience. "Get real, Nyla. That's not proof."

"Someone must have seen you leave your apartment that night," Nyla wailed.

"I'm not lying," Grace said, trying to de-escalate the situation. "When the cops find your father's killer, I'm sure they'll find the money, too."

But Nyla was no longer looking at her. She was staring past Grace's shoulder. Uncertainty flashed across her face. She switched her attention back to Grace.

"I'm willing to negotiate," Nyla said quickly. "I'll give you a percentage. We can call it a finder's fee or a commission. I swear you won't walk away empty handed. Return the money and I won't press embezzlement charges. Think about it. I'll give you forty-eight hours."

Without waiting for a response, she swung around and went swiftly toward her car.

Curious to see who or what had distracted Nyla and inspired her to quit the scene, Grace turned and saw Julius coming around the side of the house. She realized he had used the footpath to walk from his place to hers.

He did not appear to be in a rush but he was covering a lot of ground in an efficient manner. He was dressed in jeans, a khaki shirt, low boots and a black leather bomber jacket. A pair of wraparound sunglasses glinted ominously in the grayish light. The overall effect was rather menacing. Grace understood why Nyla had decided to depart in a hurry.

Julius reached Grace's side seconds before Nyla sped past, tires spitting out gravel. He seized Grace's arm and hauled her out of the way of the small bits of flying rock.

"Was that, by any chance, Witherspoon's daughter?" Julius asked.

"Good guess. Nyla Witherspoon." Grace tried to gently extricate her arm from Julius's hand. He seemed to have forgotten that he was holding on to her. "She's convinced I stole her father's money and murdered him. But the interesting thing is that she offered me a deal."

Julius finally noticed that she was attempting to wriggle free of his fingers. He released her. "What kind of deal?"

Grace pondered her answer while she opened the rear door of the compact and took out a sack of groceries. "She wants the money so badly she offered to give me a finder's fee if I return it. No questions asked. She promised she wouldn't press embezzlement charges."

Julius took the groceries from her, holding the heavy sack easily in one arm.

"Did she say anything else?" he asked.

"She seems to think that my alibi for the night of Sprague's murder is weak. She reminded me that my prints are at the scene of the crime."

"But all she cares about is getting her hands on the money?"

"It's all she has left of her father," Grace explained. "I think she's grieving the loss of a relationship she never had. She thinks the money will somehow compensate."

"Do you know the source of her issues?"

"Oh, yes. All of us who worked in the office were aware that Nyla blamed her father for her mother's suicide years ago."

Grace opened the front door. Julius followed her inside and into the kitchen.

"It feels chilly in here, doesn't it?" Grace said.

She went to the thermostat on the wall and checked the setting. The controls were set to the usual daytime temperature.

"This is not good," she said. "Looks like there may be a problem with the heating system. I'll give the repair company a call after lunch. Luckily I've got the fireplace for backup."

"Try rebooting the system first," Julius said.

"Oh, yeah, like I know how to reboot an HVAC system."

"I'll take a look at the controls after lunch."

She glanced at him. "Thanks."

"No guarantees."

He set the groceries on the kitchen table and took off his sunglasses. Dropping the glasses into the pocket of his jacket, he watched Grace remove the free-range eggs and a bag of organically grown red peppers from the sack. She set them on the counter next to the refrigerator and returned to the table.

"Back to Nyla Witherspoon," he said. "Your theory is that she is more interested in the money now than in finding her father's killer?"

"I think the money is important to her for emotional as well as financial reasons. But I wouldn't be surprised if she's also being pressured to get her hands on her inheritance."

"What kind of pressure?" Julius's eyes sharpened. "Is she in debt?"

"Not that I know of," Grace said. She reached into the sack and took out the almonds, sunflower seeds and hazelnuts she planned to use for a batch of homemade granola. "Got a hunch her fiancé may be pushing her to find the money."

"Dev mentioned a fiancé."

"His name is Burke Marrick. Sprague did not approve of him. Kristy, Millicent and I had our doubts about him, too. Marrick showed up in Nyla's life a few months ago and swept her off her feet. It was a whirlwind courtship. They got engaged within weeks. She thinks he's Mr. Perfect."

Julius got a knowing look in his eyes. "But you and your friends think that Marrick wants to marry Nyla for the traditional reason—her money."

Grace opened a cupboard and stored the nuts and seeds on a shelf. "You're not much of a romantic, are you?"

"I'm a realist."

"Whatever." Grace removed the Brussels sprouts from the sack and set them on the counter next to the other items she was going to store in the refrigerator.

She paused for a moment and met Julius's eyes. "Here's what I think—Nyla is afraid that if she loses the money, she'll lose Mr. Perfect, too. That possibility, coming on the heels of her father's murder, it's just too much for her. She's falling apart—consumed with anger, resentment and a deep sense of loss. Internally she's probably a cauldron of seething emotion so she's lashing out."

"People who are lashing out are dangerous, Grace."

"I know."

Julius went silent for a moment. She studied him covertly while she removed the last items from the grocery sack. She could almost see the computer in his head doing its thing, processing a lot of ones and zeroes. Arkwright the Alchemist was calculating; probably working on a strategy. She wasn't sure that was a good thing. True, she had invited him into her life with the breakfast picnic bribe but she knew that she had to tread cautiously. Men like Julius tended to take charge in a hurry. It was their nature.

Out of nowhere, one of the Witherspoon affirmations brightened with the intensity of a halogen bulb in her mind. *Embrace the unknown. It is the only certainty.*

"What are you thinking?" she asked.

"About the missing Witherspoon money." Julius looked out the window at the gray surface of the lake as if it were a divining mirror that reflected answers. "It seems to be one of the keys to whatever is going on here. You're the expert on pithy sayings. I'll bet you know the one that applies in this instance."

"Follow the money?"

"That's one affirmation I do believe in," he said. He met her eyes. "It never lets me down."

"I'm sure the cops believe in it, too," Grace said. "They probably watch television, just like the rest of us."

"They may be looking into the money angle but it won't hurt to have someone from our side take a look as well."

She stilled. "Someone from our side?"

His brows rose. His eyes glittered with dark amusement. "If there's one thing Arkwright Ventures can provide here, it's financial expertise. There are people on my staff who are very, very good at following the money."

"I see," she said. She was not certain where to go with that.

"Now, about lunch and your business plan," he said.

"Whoa." Grace held up a hand, palm out. "Stop. Just a second, here. I need to think about your offer."

Julius somehow managed to look bewildered and possibly a bit hurt. "You don't want me to look into the money angle?"

"It's not that." She paused, trying to come up with a reasonable explanation for her objections. The reality was that her impulsive reaction had been emotional, not logical.

"What is the problem?" Julius asked.

It was a reasonable question.

"I know you mean well and I appreciate your good intentions," she said carefully. "Really I do."

"This isn't a matter of good intentions. It's a simple, logical approach to a problem." He looked around the kitchen. "What were you planning for lunch?"

"Forget lunch," she said, putting a little steel into the words.

If he had appeared bewildered and a little hurt a moment ago, he was downright crushed now.

"I thought there would be lunch," he said.

"Pay attention, Arkwright. This isn't a corporation I'm running here and no one elected you CEO. This is my life, my future. If you're going to do stuff that impacts one or both of those things, you need to discuss it with me first. You do not just waltz into my house and announce that you're going to appoint someone I've never even met to examine the finances of a man some people think I may have murdered. It may be a good idea or it may not. The point is, I need to be involved in the conversation. Is that clear?"

There was a charged silence in the kitchen while Julius considered her declaration of independence. Then he evidently came to a conclusion.

"Okay," he said.

She eyed him with deep suspicion. "Okay? That's it? Just okay?"

Julius's expression was one of polite bewilderment. "Should there be more?"

"No, I guess not."

"So," Julius said. "What do you think about having one of the Arkwright financial wizards try to trace the embezzled Witherspoon money?"

She raised her eyes to the ceiling. "There are privacy issues, for heaven's sake. Not to mention legal issues."

"Not a problem," Julius said.

"I beg your pardon?"

"It won't be the first time that Arkwright Ventures has offered its professional expertise to the police for the purposes of some forensic accounting work. I'll talk to Dev. He'll coordinate with his contacts at the Seattle PD. He's worked with them before on cases that spilled over the city limits."

"I see." She thought about that for a moment. "Well, okay, then."

"Excellent. I'll get right on it after lunch." Julius cleared his throat. "I would remind you that I did not waltz into your kitchen. I just walked in. Carrying the groceries for you."

"Whatever." She pushed herself away from the counter. "All right, we have an understanding. *New day, new opportunities to shape the future.*"

"Is that one of the Witherspoon affirmations?"

"Yes, it is, as a matter of fact. It accompanied the recipe for granola in the Witherspoon Way cookbook." She paused, trying to decide what to do next. Julius was standing in the middle of her kitchen and showing no signs of going anywhere. She needed to do something with him. "Where were we?"

"Lunch," he said, looking hopeful.

"Right. Lunch." She headed toward the refrigerator, grateful for something concrete to do. "And then my career plan."

"We'll start by making a detailed list of your skill set. But first I have another, off-topic question for you."

"What's that?" she asked. She reached for the handle of the refrigerator door.

"I need a date for tomorrow night," Julius said. He did not take his eyes off her. "I have to attend that thoroughly boring business dinner and charity auction that I mentioned to you. I also have to deliver the thoroughly boring after-dinner talk on the thoroughly boring subject of the Pacific Northwest investment climate. Would you consider going with me so that I don't have to sit at the head table alone? You might be able to keep me from dozing off."

She opened the refrigerator, trying to process the invitation.

All rational thought winked out of existence when she saw the things sitting on the center shelf.

For a few seconds she just stood there. Her mind refused to accept the reality of what she was seeing. It had to be a hallucination.

But it was not a dream.

She screamed, dropped the carton of eggs and slammed the door closed.

"Not exactly the response I was hoping for," Julius said.

He was at her side in the blink of an eye. He opened the refrigerator door. Together they both looked at the dead rat lying on the serving platter. It was surrounded by sprigs of parsley. There was a slice of lemon in its mouth. Next to the platter stood an unopened bottle of vodka.

"That settles it," Julius said. "Someone really is stalking you."

Thirteen

"At least it wasn't cooked," Grace said. She shuddered. "Although whoever put it in my refrigerator went to the trouble of making that poor rat look like it was ready to serve for dinner."

Devlin looked up from his notebook. "Poor rat?"

"I'm no more fond of rats than anyone else," Grace said. "But it's really bad karma to kill an innocent creature just so that it can be used to stage some kind of sick revenge fantasy."

"Something tells me whoever left that thing in your refrigerator is not overly concerned with karma," Julius said.

The three of them were in the kitchen. Julius had called Devlin immediately after the discovery of the dead rat. Devlin and one of his officers, a sympathetic, competent woman named Linda Brown, had done the usual cop workup, including photographs of the rat and the bottle of vodka, but it was clear no one expected to find any clues.

As Officer Brown had pointed out, even if the perp hadn't had the presence of mind to think about fingerprints, most people possessed enough common sense to use gloves to handle a dead rat. She had taken the vodka, the rat, the platter and the culinary trimmings away in evidence bags.

Watching the process from the far side of the kitchen, Grace had decided to cross off a career in law enforcement. Handling dead rats was probably one of the less unpleasant jobs a police officer confronted.

She was now seated in a chair at the kitchen table, her hands folded tightly in her lap. She was unnerved. She could think of no other word to describe the shaky, edgy sensation that sent icy chills through her at intermittent intervals.

Breathe.

The refrigerator would have to be cleaned and disinfected from top to bottom, she decided. All the food inside would have to be tossed out. She couldn't bear the thought of eating anything that had shared the same space with the dead rat.

No, she concluded, simply sanitizing the refrigerator would not be enough. It would have to be replaced. She wondered how much new refrigerators cost.

And then there was the issue of the broken window in the guest bedroom. There had been nothing high-tech about the intruder's technique. Whoever it was had simply smashed the glass and climbed through the opening. That explained why the house had felt so chilly when she and Julius walked in, Grace thought.

Julius had told her that he would pick up some plywood at the hardware store and cover the opening. Ralph Johnson at the glass shop had assured her he could have a replacement ready the following day.

Buying a new refrigerator and replacing the window would put a serious dent in her savings but there was no other option. She had drawn the stalker into her mother's house. She had caused this mess. She would clean it up.

Devlin stood in the center of the room, legs braced slightly apart, and continued making notes.

"Earlier today when we discussed the emails, you told me that the stalking has been going on since the day that Witherspoon was found murdered, right?" he said.

"The emails started that night but I hadn't really considered it stalking until today," Grace said. She wrapped her arms around herself. "Until now it's just been the emails. As I explained, they were not actually threatening. I thought perhaps Sprague Witherspoon's daughter was sending them. But I honestly can't see her dealing with a dead rat."

Julius, who was lounging against a counter, arms folded across his chest, shook his head. He didn't actually say anything, but then, he didn't have to say anything, she thought. She was pretty sure she knew what he was thinking. And maybe he had cause. Maybe she had been a little naive.

"Julius is right, this incident officially makes it

stalking," Devlin said in his flat cop voice. "Tell me about your relationship with Witherspoon's daughter."

Grace went through it again, even though she had given him most of it that morning.

"That's all I can tell you," she said when she was finished. "She showed up at my door today, demanding that I give her the money she thinks I embezzled from the Witherspoon Way. She accused me of scamming her father and murdering him. She offered to keep quiet if I returned the money. She left when Julius arrived. Next thing I know there's a dead rat in my refrigerator."

"And the bottle of vodka," Julius reminded her quietly.

Her mouth tightened. "Yes. And, yes, before you ask, Devlin, it's the same brand of vodka that I found in Sprague's bedroom."

Devlin watched her for a long moment. "What's with the vodka?"

"I don't know," Grace said. "But there was a liquor bottle in the basement of the old asylum the day I found Mrs. Trager's body. I remember that it was a bottle of vodka. I didn't notice the brand but I think the label was green and gold like the label on the bottle in Sprague's bedroom and the one that was left in my refrigerator. That day, when I found Mrs. Trager and Mark, I used the bottle to—"

She broke off. No one tried to fill in the missing blanks.

Devlin frowned. "You mean you found the bottle in the basement of the Cloud Lake Inn, don't you?"

"Irene and I and everyone else back then usually referred to the place as the asylum," she said. "It was a hospital for the mentally ill at one time."

"You stumbled onto that murder when you were in your teens, according to Irene," Devlin said.

"I was sixteen," Grace said.

Another bad night coming up, she thought. No escaping this one. Might as well not even go to bed. Crap.

"According to the file, Trager had gone home for lunch that day." Devlin glanced down at his notes. "There was evidently an argument. Trager murdered his wife sometime around noon. The boy was a witness. The kid told the police that Trager wrapped up the body before loading it into his truck. He needed to hide it until he could dispose of it. And then there was the problem of the boy. Trager transported the body and Mark to the inn—the asylum—and left both in the basement. He didn't dare dump the bodies until after dark."

"Meanwhile, he had to go back to work," Grace said.

"He would have needed a boat to take the bodies out onto the lake," Julius said.

Devlin looked up again. "Trager owned a small outboard that he used for fishing. He had stored it in his garage for the winter. He probably planned to get it after dark and haul it down to the lake. He could have put it into the water at the asylum. There's an old dock there."

"But he got nervous waiting for nightfall," Grace said.

"It's a common problem for killers," Devlin explained. "Lot of truth in that old saying about the bad guys returning to the scene of the crime. They can't help themselves."

Julius nodded. "They go back to make sure they haven't made any mistakes."

"In this case Trager returned to the scene of the crime that afternoon and found Grace and the boy," Devlin said.

"Mark Ramshaw," Grace said. She squeezed her hands tighter in her lap. "Mrs. Trager sometimes looked after him while his mother worked. Mr. Trager wouldn't allow his wife to go out of the house to work but he let her make a little money watching the Ramshaw boy. Mark was just six years old."

"Why did Trager leave the kid alive in the basement?" Julius asked.

"Presumably Trager didn't murder Mark right away because he wanted the boy's death to look like an accident," Devlin said. "If he had strangled the kid or crushed the boy's skull, the autopsy would have shown results not consistent with death by drowning."

"How did he plan to explain Mrs. Trager's death?" Julius asked.

"The investigators concluded that, given the vodka and the meds at the scene, Trager intended to make it appear that his wife was a suicide. She downed some pills and a lot of booze and took the family boat out on the lake and went overboard. It happens."

"What about the injuries from the beating he gave her that day?" Julius asked.

Devlin shrugged. "I'm guessing here, but I've heard

more than one bastard tell me with a straight face that his wife got banged up when she fell down a flight of stairs."

Grace looked at him. "You did some research into the Trager case, didn't you?"

"Right after the Witherspoon murder," Devlin said. He did not sound apologetic. "Sorry, Grace. You're Irene's best friend. I had to look into your past."

Grace sighed. "I understand."

Julius moved to stand behind her chair. He rested one hand lightly on her shoulder. It felt good to have him touching her, she thought; comforting.

Devlin went back to his notes. "Trager confronted you when you tried to escape with the boy. There was a struggle. Trager fell down the basement steps and broke his neck. You and little Mark ran for help. Your mom and sister weren't home that day so you went to Agnes Gilroy's house for help. She took you in and called the police. According to her statement, there was a lot of blood on your clothes. At first she thought it was yours."

"It was Trager's blood." Grace looked down at her clasped hands. "I used the vodka bottle, you see. When I tried to follow Mark up the basement steps, Trager came after me. He grabbed the back of my jacket. I smashed the bottle on the railing, turned and . . . and slashed at him with the jagged edges of glass. There was . . . a lot of blood."

Julius's hand tightened on her shoulder. She fell silent. For a moment no one spoke.

It would definitely be a very bad night.

Julius studied Devlin. "I want to talk to you before you contact the Seattle police. Arkwright Ventures would like to offer its forensic accounting services to the authorities."

Devlin considered that briefly and then nodded. "Tell me what you want to do. I'll clear it with Seattle." He turned back to Grace. For the first time the mask of his professional demeanor slipped. "Damn it, Grace. I'm sorry to have to take you through it all again. But we need to figure out what the hell is going on here. Your boss was murdered. Someone is stalking you. There's a lot of money missing. This is a big puzzle and none of the pieces fit together."

She nodded wearily. "I know. It's okay. You need information."

For a moment no one spoke.

"Got any ideas?" Devlin asked eventually. "I could use some guidance here."

Grace looked at the refrigerator. A dark tide of revulsion rose inside her. She looked away.

"As far as the rat is concerned, I suppose Nyla is the obvious suspect," she said. "But as I told you, I can't imagine her handling a dead animal of any kind, let alone a rat. But then, I have a hard time imagining anyone deliberately putting a dead rat on a platter and sticking it inside a refrigerator." She paused. "Well, maybe in a lab setting. A lot of rats are used in scientific experiments."

"That was no lab rat," Julius said. "That one came straight out of an alley."

Grace looked up at him. "Guess that means we can

cross off any scientists or lab techs on the suspect list. Unfortunately, there weren't any there in the first place."

"Plenty of suspects left on that list," Julius said quietly.

"Too many." Devlin closed his notebook. "I'm going to call the Seattle police and talk to the investigator in charge of your case. Maybe if we compare notes we can sort out some of the people involved in this thing."

"Thanks," Grace said. She tried hard to project some positive energy and enthusiasm, but judging by the looks on the faces of the two men she didn't think she was succeeding.

"You never know." Devlin stuffed the notebook back into his jacket. "What are you going to do now?"

She gazed dolefully at the offending appliance. "Throw out all the food in the refrigerator and then go shop for a new one."

Devlin eyed the refrigerator. "This one looks almost new."

"Mom bought it less than a year ago," Grace said. "It's probably still under warranty. But I could never again eat anything that came out of that refrigerator."

"I understand that you want to clean it out," Devlin said. "But there's nothing wrong with the appliance."

Julius squeezed Grace's shoulder. "I'll help you dump the food. When we're finished we'll shop for a new one."

Fourteen

Julius studied the ranks of gleaming appliances arrayed on the sales floor. It was a bit like walking into an arms dealer's showroom. All the polished hard surface reminded him of so much high-tech military armor.

"Who knew there were so many different kinds of refrigerators?" he said.

For the first time since the discovery of the dead rat and the vodka bottle, Grace looked wanly amused. He was surprised by the wave of relief that whispered through him when she smiled.

Watching her stoically respond to Dev's interrogation had been one of the harder things he'd done in his life. He had wanted to carry her away to someplace safe where no one could ask her any more questions; a place where she could forget the past. He was still dealing with the mental image of her as a teenager covered in the blood of the man who had tried to murder her.

"I take it you haven't done this kind of shopping before?" Grace asked.

"No," he admitted. "The interior designer selected the appliances for my condo in Seattle. The house I bought from Harley came with all the stuff I needed, including the refrigerator."

Shopping for a refrigerator now topped his list of Most Unusual Second Dates, he decided.

"You didn't have to come with me," Grace said. "It wasn't necessary, really."

"Yeah, it was," he said. He watched the salesman approach. "But I admit I'm out of my depth here. Do you have any idea of what you want in a refrigerator?"

"We'll just ask for the latest version of the same model that Mom bought." Grace drew a deep breath. "Although it's going to put a very big hole in my bank account."

He thought about offering to buy the refrigerator for her but he kept his mouth shut. He knew she would refuse.

Grace gave him a sidelong glance. "Thanks."

"For what?"

"For understanding why I have to replace the refrigerator."

"I get it," he said.

No amount of scrubbing or disinfectant would remove the memory of the dead rat.

"I know you get it," she said. "I appreciate that."

"Doesn't mean you can't sell the old one, though. You could probably recover a few hundred bucks."

She smiled again. "Good point. I'll have it moved out onto the back porch until I can sell it."

"I doubt if this store is going to be able to deliver your new refrigerator today," Julius said. "It's nearly five now. What do you say we go out to dinner?"

She hesitated. "Thanks, but I really don't feel like going out. I'll just grab some takeout on the way home."

"Takeout sounds good," he said.

She eyed him. "Did you just invite yourself over for dinner?"

"I never got lunch, remember?"

"I never got my first consulting appointment."

"You're not going to want to be alone this evening, not after what happened today," he said. "Do you mind if I join you for takeout?"

"I'm pretty much vegetarian," she warned.

"I'm sure I'll survive."

She gave that a moment's close thought and then nodded once. "Okay. Thanks. It's very kind of you to offer to keep me company."

"I'm not known for my kindness."

"What are you known for?"

Julius watched the salesman start to circle. "Making money."

"That's a very cool gift," Grace said. Her eyes warmed with amusement again. "Most people would give anything to possess it."

The salesman was closing in now.

"Look," Julius said, "I'm good at investing but what I know about buying refrigerators wouldn't even fill a small shot glass."

"Don't worry," Grace said. She moved forward to intercept the salesman. "I've got this."

Fifteen

They were back in Grace's kitchen by six thirty. The salesman had promised to expedite the delivery of the new refrigerator. Julius occupied himself with opening the bottle of Columbia Valley Syrah that he had selected while Grace was making her takeout selections at the gourmet grocery store in town.

The little domestic scene in the kitchen would have been very comfortable and cozy, he concluded, if not for the edgy heat of the smoldering arousal that kept him restless and semi-erect. It was as if he were walking a tightrope without a net. *Don't screw this up again, Arkwright.*

He was old enough and sufficiently experienced to be able to control the sexual side of the situation. But what he was feeling around Grace was different in ways he could not explain. He wasn't sure what to do about the sensation but he did know one thing—he wanted to stay as close to her as possible until he figured out what the hell was going on between the two of them.

He poured the wine into two glasses and turned around just in time to see Grace bend over to close the oven door. She was still wearing the jeans and the deep blue, loose-fitting pullover she'd had on that morning. He took a moment to admire the way the denim hugged her nicely rounded rear.

She closed the door and straightened, using one hand to push her whiskey-brown hair back behind her ear. He knew from the faint tilt of her eyebrows that she'd caught him watching her.

"What?" she asked.

"Nothing." He handed her one of the glasses. "Here you go. Medicinal purposes only."

"Definitely," she said. She took a healthy swallow of wine and dropped into one of the wooden chairs. "Thanks. I needed that."

Julius lowered himself into the chair across from her. "You live an eventful life, Miss Elland."

"I will admit that lately my life has been somewhat out of the ordinary." She drank some more wine.

"No Witherspoon affirmation for the current state of affairs?"

She reflected briefly and then shook her head. "No, but I'm sure one will come to me."

"So, in spite of all that power-of-positive-thinking

stuff and those Witherspoon affirmations, you do see a role for the occasional dose of reality?"

"Hell, yes."

"Good to know." He saluted her with the wineglass. "What's for dinner?"

"Tofu satay and seaweed salad." She leaned back in her chair, stretched out her legs and closed her eyes. "I'll bet you're excited about the menu, aren't you?"

"My favorites," he assured her.

She opened her eyes, amused. "I did warn you."

"I don't have any problem with the menu. But what with one thing and another, I don't believe you ever got around to answering my question this afternoon."

He waited to see if she would pretend to have forgotten. But this was Grace, who was probably too honest for her own good.

"Do you really need a date for tomorrow night?" she asked.

He moved one hand slightly. "I can handle it on my own. Wouldn't be the first time. But I'd rather have you sitting at my side at the head table. I hate making conversation at those kinds of events. No one ever has anything interesting to say, including me. Not that you could have a meaningful conversation with ten people sitting at a table under those circumstances. And then there is the entertainment for the evening, courtesy of yours truly, who will deliver what is known far and wide as the Speech from Hell."

Grace erupted in laughter. The wine sloshed precariously in her glass.

"Are you certain it will be that bad?" she asked when she got the laughter under control.

"My after-dinner talk? I know it will be bad."

She searched his face. "How can you be so sure?"

"Because I am not without experience."

Grace watched him thoughtfully now. "This is a talk you've given before?"

"I've given variations of it so many times during the past few years, I've lost count. I get asked to speak to investor groups, business associations and the occasional MBA class. I have no idea why anyone invites me back a second time. Public speaking is not my forte, believe me."

She put down her glass and folded her arms on the table. "Let's hear it."

"What?"

"Your speech. Give me the talk that you plan to deliver tomorrow evening."

He realized she was serious.

"Forget it," he said. "Delivering the Speech from Hell is the very last thing I want to do tonight."

"Here's the deal I'm willing to make, Arkwright. If you want me to attend that business and charity affair with you tomorrow night, I insist that you preview your after-dinner talk for me now."

He watched her closely, trying to decide whether or not she was joking. But there was no amusement in her eyes.

"Why do you want to hear the SFH?" he asked.

"Plain old curiosity, I guess."

He thought about it. "I'll let you read it, will that do? I've got twenty bucks says you won't be able to make it more than halfway through."

"Twenty bucks?" She grinned. "And here I thought you were a big-time player."

"Twenty bucks—twenty thousand bucks." He shrugged. "What difference does it make?"

"You really are bored with the subject of money, aren't you? But you're right. A wager is a wager. And since I can't put up twenty grand, I'll go with the twenty bucks. Where's the SFH?"

"I store it online. If you really want to do this, I can pull it up on your computer."

"I really want to do this," she said.

He groaned. "Fine. It won't take long for your eyes to glaze over. Fire up your laptop. And get ready to pay me twenty dollars. No IOUs, by the way. Cash only."

"Understood."

She got up from the table and disappeared into the front room. When she returned she had her laptop as well as a notepad and a pen. She set the computer down on the table in front of him.

Reluctantly he went online and downloaded the Speech from Hell. Without a word he turned the computer around so that she could see the document.

She whistled. "Lot of data here."

"It's a business talk, remember?"

She started reading with an alarming degree of concentration.

"It's not the Great American Novel," he warned.

"There is no Great American Novel," she said absently. "This nation is too big and too diverse to produce only one great book. We've got lots of them and there will be more written in the future. Art doesn't stand still."

He decided there was no good response to that, so he poured himself another glass of wine and sat back to await the settling of the wager.

At some point in the process Grace reached for her notepad and pen. A sense of doom settled on him. Just how bad was the Speech from Hell? On the bright side, she would be going to the reception with him. Cheered at the thought, he lounged deeper in the chair. He entertained himself with a pleasant little fantasy that involved Grace spending the night with him in his Seattle condo. After all, the event would not be over until quite late and it would be an hour's drive back to Cloud Lake. It only made sense to stay the night at his place and drive back the following morning.

The more Grace read of the SFH, the more he immersed himself in his daydream. He was strategizing ways to broach the subject to her when she finally looked up from the screen. She reached for her glass of wine.

"Okay," she said. "Somewhere in this speech there's a very good after-dinner talk."

He raised his brows. "Think so?"

"It's too long and loaded with way too many facts and figures. That might work for a formal business presentation but you said this was an after-dinner talk."

"So?"

"You told me that business decisions are usually made on the basis of emotion. Well, after-dinner talks are all about emotion. Heck, every speech is about emotion."

He went blank. "Emotion."

"Right. But I do see a thread in here that will work. If we refocus on the emotional takeaway buried below all the details, you'll be brilliant tomorrow night."

"I know my limitations. I'm brilliant at making money. I am not brilliant at giving after-dinner talks." He glanced at her notepad. "What the hell do you mean about an emotional takeaway?"

"Studies show that audiences never remember the facts and figures of a talk—they remember the emotions the speech generated," she said. "You can't infuse too many emotions into an after-dinner talk about the current business climate, so we will concentrate on one."

He narrowed his eyes. "I double-dare you to find a single emotional element in that talk."

She gave him a smug smile and aimed the tip of her pen at one of her notes. "It's right here, the reference to your mentor."

"What mentor?" He stopped. "You mean the guy who gave me my first job after I left the Marines?"

"You said that individual gave you a break and taught you how to read a spreadsheet and a profit-and-loss statement."

Julius smiled slowly, amused for the first time since the discussion had turned to the topic of the Speech from Hell.

"My first employer was a Marine," he said. "He knew that it wasn't easy starting a new life in a civilian career, especially if, like me, you had a very limited skill set. He hired me as his driver. I learned a lot listening to him talk business in the back of the car. Eventually I became his fixer."

Grace's eyes lit with curiosity. "What did you fix?"

"Anything and everything that was a problem for him. The job covered a lot of territory."

She tapped a finger on the table and gave the subject a moment's thought.

"I think we'll change that job title for this talk," she said. "Fixer sounds a bit shady. Mob bosses and sleazy government officials have fixers."

He studied her over the rim of his glass. "Got a better word for fixer?"

"Executive administrative assistant works. Like fixer, it covers a lot of territory." She smiled a little, satisfied. "Out of curiosity, how did you apply for that first job?"

"I sent my résumé to the HR department of the company. Got no response. So I went to the president's office and sat there all day, every day, for a week until he got tired of walking past me and agreed to give me an interview."

Grace glowed with approval.

"That's it," she said. Her eyes were bright with enthusiasm. "That's your story. I love it. You're going to inspire everyone in your audience."

"I am?"

"You're going to tell them to look around and find at least one person who won't be able to get a foot in the door the traditional way and help that individual do what your mentor did—open the door a little wider."

An icy chill shot down his spine. "You want me to give a motivational talk?"

"You can think of it that way."

"You are out of your mind," he said, enunciating each word with great precision. "The audience tomorrow night will be composed of businesspeople and their significant others. It is not, I repeat, not a motivational seminar."

"An audience is an audience. You're going for an emotional hit. Your job is to make people leave feeling good about themselves. You want them to be inspired by their better angels."

"If you gathered up all the better angels in the audience tomorrow night, you wouldn't have to worry about how many of them could dance on the head of a pin because you wouldn't have a single dancing angel. Trust me on this."

"I disagree," Grace said. "I'm sure there will be a sprinkling of self-absorbed narcissists in the crowd. And, statistically speaking, there will be a few sociopaths—hopefully the nonviolent type. But I think most will be folks who at least want to think of themselves as good people. Your job is to remind them to heed the call of their better natures."

"So that they can feel good about themselves?"

"No, because it's a matter of personal honor for each individual in that crowd. Your job is to remind them of that fact."

"We're talking about businesspeople, Grace. All they care about is the bottom line."

"I understand that's important to them." Grace assumed a patient air. "And there is nothing wrong with making money. You evidently do that rather well. But I also know that honor matters to you. It will matter to a lot of those in your audience. If nothing else, you can remind them that they have a golden opportunity to leave a legacy. That legacy will be in the form of the people they mentored along the way."

"What makes you think that I care all that much about honor?"

She smiled. "You're a Marine. Everyone knows there are no ex-Marines."

He could not think of a response to that, so he looked at the notepad. "You're living in fantasyland. I wouldn't even know where to begin to write a talk like the one you're suggesting."

"We'll start with your own personal story. Tell them how you got that first job with the man who became your mentor. Trust me on this. I helped Sprague write his motivational talks. I know what I'm doing here. I guarantee you that you'll have the audience eating out of the palm of your hand."

"So I give them a feel-good story," he said. "How the hell do I end it?"

"Think like a Marine. Give your audience a mission and send them out to fulfill it. They'll feel great about themselves after you finish, and that's the whole point here."

He contemplated her in silence for a moment.

"How did you learn about Marines?" he asked finally.

"My father was a Marine." She smiled a misty smile. "He was killed in a helicopter crash when I was a baby. I never got the chance to know him. But Mom told me a lot about him. That's how I know what I know."

Julius considered that for a while.

"Okay," he said, "I'll try the speech your way. But I'm warning you, it will probably be an even bigger disaster than my old Speech from Hell. I'm not into this motivational crap."

"That's the spirit. Think positive."

"Actually, there is a silver lining in this situation," he said.

"What's that?"

He smiled slowly. "You'll be there to witness the fiasco. Later I will get to say *I told you so*. Everyone likes to say that, right?"

"The new version of your speech will work." She got to her feet and crossed the room to open the oven door. "By the way, you never told me the name of your first employer—the man who became your mentor."

"Harley Montoya."

"Harley?" Grace turned around quickly, shocked. "Your next-door neighbor? The man who sold you the house here in Cloud Lake?"

"That Harley."

Grace smiled, pleased. "That is sort of sweet."

"'Sweet' is generally not the first word that comes to mind when people describe Harley."

Sixteen

They worked on the Speech from Hell until sometime after nine, with a break along the way to eat the tofu satay and seaweed salad. Julius decided that tofu and seaweed tasted surprisingly good, at least as long as Grace was sitting on the other side of the table.

"That should do it," Grace said. She hit save on the computer. "Your audience will love it."

He studied the notes he had made on the notepad. "I don't know that anyone will love it, but it certainly won't be the speech they'll be expecting from me."

"There's nothing like the element of surprise to wake up an audience." She got to her feet. "I need some exercise. The rain has stopped. Want to go for a walk?"

He looked out the window. "It's cold out there."

"It's not that bad."

"And dark."

"The moon is out, there are lamps along the footpath and we can take flashlights for backup."

A moonlight walk with Grace suddenly sounded like an excellent plan, Julius thought. It would give him an excuse to stick around a little longer, maybe come up with a way to present his grand plan for staying the night in the city at his place.

He felt better already. Maybe there was something to the positive-thinking nonsense.

"You're right," he said. "After all that speech writing, I could use some exercise, too."

She bundled herself up in the jacket that he would always think of as her Little Red Riding Hood coat. He took his leather jacket off the back of the chair and pulled it on. Together they went out onto the back porch. Grace paused to lock the door.

The night air was well chilled. They went down to the water's edge. He waited to see which way she would go. Turning right was the route into town. It ended at the public marina. Left would take them past his house. Beyond that, at the top of the lake, heavily shrouded in trees and night, was the old asylum.

He was not surprised when Grace chose to walk toward the lights of town. He fell into step beside her. Neither of them spoke for a while but the silence felt comfortable, at least it did to him. Silver moonlight gleamed on the surface of the lake. The low footpath lamps created a string of fairy lights. They did not need the flashlights.

"Thanks for the help with the SFH tonight," he said after a while.

"You're welcome. By the way, you owe me twenty bucks."

"I always pay my debts."

"Thanks for understanding why I had to buy a new refrigerator." She paused. "We're even, right?"

"Even?"

"You know, a favor for a favor."

"Oh, yeah. Got it." He came to a halt. "Do you have a problem with owing someone a favor? Or is it just me?"

Grace stopped, too. "Not exactly. Okay. Maybe it's just you. I'm not sure yet."

"You're not making things any more clear."

"It's just that I don't want you to think of me as some kind of hobby," she said.

He tried to wrap his brain around that. And failed. "What?" he asked.

"You heard me." She turned her head slightly to look at him. The hood of the jacket shadowed her face, making it impossible to read her eyes. "I think you're just bored. I don't want you to get the idea that involving yourself in my current problems would be an interesting way to . . . distract yourself."

He stared at her, a slow-burning anger heating his blood.

"That is the dumbest reasoning I've ever heard," he rasped. "No wonder your track record with relationships is so bad."

"My track record?" Her voice rose in outrage. "You're the one with a failed marriage behind you and no visible signs of a serious interest in dating since your divorce."

"Who told you that?" he demanded.

"Irene is my friend, remember? I told her the blind date hadn't gone well but that I had hired you to consult for me. I think she panicked. She thought I ought to know a little more about you."

"We're a real pair, aren't we?" He gripped her shoulders with both hands. "Just to clarify, I am not getting involved in your problems because I'm looking for a way to distract myself."

"No? Why, then?"

"Damned if I know."

He pulled her close and crushed her mouth beneath his own before she could say anything else.

He wasn't looking for a distraction but he was looking for something, and since he could not put a name to it, he was willing to settle for sex—as long as it was sex with Grace.

As far as he was concerned, the kiss had been waiting to happen since she walked through Devlin and Irene's front door the previous night. But it seemed to catch Grace by surprise. She went still.

For three of the longest seconds of his life he wondered if he had made a terrible mistake by misreading the heat in the atmosphere between them.

But on the fourth beat of his heart he felt a shudder go through Grace's supple body. She braced her gloved hands against the front of his leather jacket.

And then she was kissing him back. It was a tentative response at first, as if she wasn't sure it would be a good thing to go down this road with him. He moved his mouth across hers, trying to persuade her that he was worth the risk.

She pressed closer and made a soft, urgent little sound in the back of her throat. In the next moment she was responding with a hungry, sexy energy that sent lightning through him.

He moved his hands from her shoulders down to the front of her coat. He got the garment unfastened and slipped inside, settling his palms on the lush, feminine curve of her hips. He was tight, hard, intensely aroused and intensely aware of everything about Grace. Her scent dazzled him. Her gentle curves made him desperate to touch her more intimately.

No wonder he hadn't been interested in dating anyone else for so long. He'd been waiting for this woman. He just hadn't realized it until now.

Grace's arms moved up to circle his neck. She leaned into him and opened her mouth a little. He was suddenly lost in the sweet, hot, aching need.

The muffled sound of a cell phone ping shattered the crystalline atmosphere. Grace froze. So did he.

"Damn it to hell," he said softly.

Grace pulled away and took a sharp breath.

They both looked down at the pocket of her jacket. Slowly Grace took out her phone and studied the screen.

"An email from Sprague Witherspoon's account," she whispered. "Nyla is not giving up easily."

"Assuming the crazy emailer is Nyla Witherspoon." A cold fury splashed through him. "What does it say this time?"

Grace opened the email and read it aloud in a flat, emotionless voice. *"Savor the present because it is all that is certain."*

"One of those damned Witherspoon affirmations?" Julius asked, knowing the answer.

"Yes, but there's more this time." There was a faint shiver in Grace's words now. *"Thirty-nine hours and counting."*

"Sounds like Nyla's counting down the forty-eight hours she gave you earlier today," Julius said. "Let me see your phone."

Grace handed it to him without a word. He studied the email, searching for any clue in the format, but to all appearances it had come from Sprague Witherspoon.

"That settles it," he said. "Looks like I'll be spending the night with you."

"What?"

The shock in the single word was not particularly heartening but he told himself that he had handled tougher negotiations.

"Nyla Witherspoon, or someone posing as her dead father, seems to be determined to scare the hell out of you. I don't think it's a good idea for you to be alone—not at night."

"Julius, I appreciate the offer," she said, very earnest now. "But there are some things you don't know about me. I'm not a sound sleeper, especially when I'm stressed. And I have problems with nightmares, especially lately. Sometimes I get up and walk around the house in the middle of the night. People find it . . . unsettling."

"What people?"

"Look, I'd rather not go into the details, all right?"

"Sure. But just so you know, I'm okay with you walking around the house in the middle of the night. I do that, myself, on occasion."

She stared at him, uncomprehending. "You do?"

"Yes," he said. "I do. We'll stop by my place first. I need to pick up a few things."

She held up a finger. "Just to be clear, if you stay at my house, you're sleeping in the guest bedroom."

"Understood."

He waited, but she did not seem to know where to go after that, so he took her arm and piloted her back along the footpath.

Seventeen

They walked past her house, past Agnes Gilroy's place and on around the little cove to Julius's house.

Julius went up the back porch steps and opened the kitchen door. He flipped on the lights and stood aside, waiting for her to enter first. She got an odd, tingly feeling when she stepped into his kitchen. A deep sense of curiosity infused her senses.

Kitchens were very personal, in her opinion. They said a lot about an individual. This one had a retro vibe. The old appliances, cupboards and tile countertops had been caught in a time warp. But everything, from the old-fashioned gas range and the chrome toaster to the ancient coffeemaker, appeared to be clean, in good repair and ready for action.

A Marine lived here, she thought, biting back a smile. Electrical cords were neatly secured. Canisters were lined up against the backsplash in strict order—short to tall. Even the saltshaker and the pepper mill seemed to be standing at attention. She suspected that Julius's office and his condo in Seattle probably radiated the same sense of order and discipline.

"I'll throw some things in a bag and get my shaving gear," Julius said. "Wait here. This won't take long."

She walked slowly around the kitchen, taking in the feel of the space. Everything whispered Julius's secret to her—he was a man who had long ago learned to live alone.

He reappeared at the entrance to the kitchen, a black leather duffel in one hand.

"Ready," he said.

She looked at him. "You really don't have to babysit me tonight. I mean, it's very nice of you and I appreciate it but—"

He crossed the distance between them in two long strides and silenced her with a straight-to-the-point, no-nonsense kiss. When he raised his head, his eyes were dark and intent.

"Yes," he said. "I do have to do this. Think of it as part of the consulting services that you hired me to provide."

"That's a stretch. How many times have you spent the night with one of your clients?"

He smiled the slow, wicked smile that made her pulse kick up, but in a good way. Arkwright the Alchemist.

"Every job has unique requirements," he said. "I try to be flexible and adaptable."

Neither of them should be thinking about sex, she told herself. But she knew that the subject was burning in the background, a smoldering fire that would flash out of control if she wasn't very careful. Too soon. Too many unknowns.

They went out onto the back porch. Julius locked up. The back door of the neighboring house banged open as they went down the steps. Harley Montoya's bald head gleamed in the porch light. He was wearing a pair of khaki pants and a faded sweater. He moved to the edge of the porch and gripped the railing.

"Thought I heard someone out here," he roared. "'Evenin', Grace. What are you two doing? Little late for a stroll around the lake, isn't it?"

"It's never too late for a walk around the lake," Julius said.

"Don't give me that bullshit," Harley said. "Pardon my language, Grace. That's a duffel bag you're carryin', Julius. You two are fixin' to spend the night together at the Elland house."

"That's the plan," Julius said. "You've probably heard by now that someone is stalking Grace."

"Yep." Harley peered at Grace. "Agnes told me about the rat in your refrigerator. Some real sick people out there. But don't worry, Julius will take good care of you."

"Julius very kindly offered to stay with me tonight so that I won't have to be alone in the house," she said.

"It's gonna be all over town tomorrow, you know," Harley warned.

Grace opened her mouth to say *He's going to sleep in the guest bedroom,* but that sounded defensive so she decided to shut up. Harley probably wouldn't believe it, anyway. Tomorrow morning no one in town would believe it, either.

"I'm planning to put in an alarm system and maybe get a dog," she said instead.

Harley snorted. "You'll be fine with Julius. In my experience, he's about as good as an alarm system and a dog."

"Thanks," Julius said. "I'll treasure your words of high praise."

"You do that," Harley said. "Take good care of Grace. See you tomorrow."

Harley went back inside his house. The door banged shut behind him.

Julius took Grace's arm. They walked through the garden to the gate that opened onto the path.

Grace glanced around at the lush landscaping. "Is this your work?"

"Of course not," Julius said. "Harley takes care of my garden and his own."

They started back toward Grace's house.

"Harley was right," Grace said after a moment. "The fact that you spent the night at my place will be all over Cloud Lake by noon tomorrow."

"Got a problem with that?"

She gave it some thought. "No, I don't have a

problem with it. I've got a problem with finding dead rats and bottles of vodka in my refrigerator, and I've got a problem with someone sending me creepy emails, but no, I don't have a problem with you spending the night in my spare bedroom."

"I like a woman who knows how to keep her priorities straight."

When they reached her house, Grace pulled some fresh linens out of a closet. Together she and Julius made up the bed in the guest bedroom.

Earlier Julius had tacked up a sheet of plywood to cover the opening left by the smashed pane of glass. The second pane was still in place, so the room was not completely shuttered. Grace could see clouds moving across the night sky, obscuring the moon. Another storm was on the way.

Getting the bed ready proved to be an unnervingly intimate process, at least on her side. By the time she had finished stuffing the pillow into the pillowcase she could have sworn that the atmosphere in the room was charged with electricity.

Julius made himself at home with the ease of a stray cat—or a man who was accustomed to living out of a suitcase. She looked at him across the expanse of the freshly made bed.

"The guest bath is just down the hall," she said, determined to adopt the same casual attitude toward the situation that Julius was exhibiting. "There are some sesame seed crackers if you get hungry."

"Thanks," he said.

She went toward the door. "I'll say good night, then."

Julius followed her as far as the doorway.

"Good night," he said.

She hesitated, aware that something more needed to be said. But she did not know how to bring up the subject of the hot kiss in the icy moonlight.

She turned away and went down the hall. She could feel Julius's eyes on her until she escaped into the relative safety of her bedroom.

She undressed, changed into her nightgown, robe and slippers, and went into the master bath to brush her teeth.

When she emerged a short time later, the door to Julius's room stood slightly open but the lights were off. She waited a moment. When she heard no sound from the guest bedroom, she hurried through the ritual of securing the house.

At least it was only a partial ritual that night, she thought. She did not have to check the closets or look under the bed in Julius's room. Something told her that if there was a monster hiding there, Julius could deal with the problem.

Eventually she turned off the lamps. The night-lights that she had placed strategically throughout the house came up, infusing each space with the exception of Julius's room with a reassuring glow. Julius must have unplugged the little night-light in his room.

She went back to her room and sat on the edge of the bed for a while, doing her breathing exercises. During the meditation process thoughts always swirled and intruded. The trick was to return the focus again and again to the breath.

When she was finished she crawled under the covers and gazed up at the shadowy ceiling and brooded on her decision to allow Julius to spend the night in the guest bedroom. One moment she managed to convince herself that there was no harm in letting him stay; the next moment she was forced to conclude that it might not have been one of her brighter ideas. She was violating one of her own rules.

But it was good to know that tonight she would not be alone if the monster came out from the darkness.

In the end she opted to go with a Witherspoon affirmation: *Meet challenges with creativity.* She had no idea what that meant in regard to Julius, but it sounded reassuring.

Julius stretched out on the bed, his hands folded behind his head, and contemplated the ceiling of the guest bedroom. He thought about how Grace had walked through the house, not only double-checking all the locks that he had secured earlier but opening and closing cupboards and closets. It all sounded methodical, as if it were a nightly routine.

Some people might have considered the detailed security check a tad obsessive, but he understood. The enemy could be anywhere.

Eighteen

A soft rustling sound brought her out of a restless sleep and vaguely menacing dreams. She woke up breathless, her pulse skittering. It took her a few seconds to center herself.

You are the eye of the storm—you are calm and in control.

She had left the bedroom door partway open. As she watched, a dark shadow moved along the hallway. Panic shivered through her. She sat up quickly and pushed the covers aside, instinct warning her to get on her feet so that she could choose fight or flight.

Reason took over. It was Julius out there in the hall. It had to be Julius. Perhaps something had awakened him.

Her pulse rate steadied and her breathing calmed. The problem was that she was not accustomed to having a man in the house—not at this hour, at any rate.

She reached for her robe, slid her feet into the slippers and went out into the hall.

The front room lay in unexpectedly deep shadows. It took her a few seconds to realize that the night-light in that room was no longer illuminated. The bulb must have burned out, she thought. She made a note to change it in the morning.

Then she saw Julius. He stood at the window watching the night through a crack in the curtains. He was wearing a dark crew-necked T-shirt and the khakis he'd had on earlier in the evening. His feet were bare.

"What is it?" she asked quietly. She moved farther into the room. "Do you see something?"

"No," Julius said. He turned back to the window. "I just had a feeling—"

"That someone was watching?"

Julius shrugged. "Something woke me. Probably a car going past on the road. It's pretty damn quiet out here at night."

"You turned off the night-light in this room, didn't you?"

"Didn't want to be silhouetted against it. I'll switch it on when I go back to bed." He glanced at her. "Is that okay?"

"Yes, certainly." Grace hugged herself. "I've had a creepy feeling that someone was watching every night since I started receiving those damned emails. I've been telling myself it's just my imagination."

"Someone *is* watching you—we just don't know if that person is here in Cloud Lake or at some other location. When we find out why, we'll know the identity of the watcher."

Julius walked across the room and came to a halt in front of her. He kissed her forehead.

"Go back to bed," he said. "You're not alone tonight."

"I know. Thanks."

The atmosphere was once again charged with edgy tendrils of anticipation. It was as if she were standing on a high cliff above a crashing sea, she thought. She longed to take the dive into the deep, mysterious waters, but she was very sure now that becoming involved in an affair with Julius would be a high-risk endeavor.

The silence between them lengthened. It was as if they were both waiting for something momentous to happen.

It was then she realized that she was the one who would have to make the first move. Julius was leaving the decision up to her. He knew how to wait for what he wanted. He possessed the patience of a hunter.

This man is different. Not another stray. You need to think about this.

She pulled herself together.

"I'll see you in the morning," she said.

"I'll be here."

It was a promise.

Grace made herself go back down the hall to her bedroom. This time when she climbed into bed she fell into a dreamless sleep. Julius was standing guard against the monsters tonight.

Nineteen

It was cold and the dampness in the night air warned of rain but the watcher in the shadows was not quite ready to leave the cover of the trees.

The night-lights in the lake house had shifted a few minutes ago. Someone had gotten out of bed—Grace, probably. She was finally becoming aware that she was being stalked. It had been fun watching her dash out to buy a new refrigerator today. Bonus points for that move. Talk about an overreaction. The woman's nerves must be shredded now.

The hunt had gone according to plan until recently. Who knew that the game would prove to be so addictive?

Julius Arkwright was an unforeseen complication, but a minor one. He was what the military described as a soft target.

Grace would be an even softer target.

Twenty

The muffled crunch of gravel announced the arrival of a car in the drive. Grace hit save on the keyboard. Following the instructions of her new consultant, she had been attempting to create a skill-set list. She had been working diligently ever since Julius had left that morning but she had not made much progress. She was afraid that there were not many employers who would leap at the opportunity to hire someone whose chief skill was the ability to write affirmation-themed cookbooks and blogs.

There had been other obstacles to productivity that morning as well. Memories of breakfast with Julius kept interrupting her attempts to focus on her project.

She had found the experience of waking up to a man in her kitchen—one who was making coffee, no less—disconcerting. She had always told herself that when the right man came along, she would reconsider her policy of not allowing a man to spend the night, but somehow that had never happened.

That morning, however, she had been confronted with the reality of Julius, and she still could not decide if he was the right man or the wrong one.

For his part, Julius had not exhibited any such uncertainties. He had settled in as if he got up and made coffee for the two of them every day of his life. Due to the empty refrigerator, breakfast had consisted of toast and peanut butter and a couple of oranges. Eating the meal with Julius had been an unexpectedly gratifying experience. She wondered if she ought to be worried about that.

There had been no way to handle his departure discreetly. Agnes was an early riser. She had come out onto her back porch to wave cheerfully at Julius when he left to take the footpath to his place. Grace had watched from the kitchen window as he stopped and chatted briefly with Agnes. Everyone involved had acted as if it was all very routine.

Grace had known then that Harley Montoya was right. The news that Julius had spent the night at the Elland house would be all over town by noon. Sure enough, shortly after nine, Agnes had departed in her tiny, fuel-efficient car. She liked to run her errands early in the day.

She had returned from her mission an hour ago.

Grace got to her feet and went to the window. It had rained early that morning but the storm front had passed and the clouds had broken up. The forecast promised more rain that afternoon but for now there was some winter sunlight.

She watched the BMW come to a halt in the drive. She did not recognize the vehicle but when she saw the man who climbed out from behind the wheel, a frisson of uncertainty made her catch her breath.

"Crap," she said aloud to the empty room.

No, she thought in the next breath, she ought to take a much more positive attitude toward her visitor. He was probably the only potential employer she knew who might be interested in her unique skill set.

Larson Rayner was also a suspect in Sprague's murder.

She opened the door just as he reached out to stab the doorbell with one elegantly buffed nail.

Larson smiled at her with his patented I-can-make-your-life-better-in-ten-easy-steps smile. Blue eyed and dark haired, with a lean, athletic build, a square-jawed profile, very white teeth, a touch of gray at the temples and a sincere, straightforward manner, he was perfectly cast for the role he played in real life. He had been born to be a motivational speaker.

"Hello, Grace," he said.

Sprague had mentioned that Larson had taken elocution lessons at the start of his career. The results had paid off in a warm, resonant voice that worked as well in person as it did with a microphone.

"I wasn't expecting you, Larson," she said.

"Great to see you again." His eyes warmed with deep concern. "How are you holding up? I've been very concerned. You went through a traumatic experience."

"I'm doing fine, thanks," she said. She infused her voice with all the perky, upbeat energy she could summon.

The front door of Agnes's house opened. Agnes stepped out onto her porch with a pair of pruning shears in hand. Grace made a point of waving at her enthusiastically. Agnes returned the greeting, the big shears gleaming in the sunlight. She smiled cheerfully and went down the steps to go about her gardening tasks.

Grace had a hunch that Agnes would be heading back into town that afternoon to run a few more errands. Two male visitors at the Elland house in less than twenty-four hours was bound to stir up interest.

It occurred to Grace that she might as well take advantage of Agnes's curiosity. It was hard to imagine Larson as a killer but one thing was certain: there had been no love lost between Larson and Sprague. The rivalry between the two men was long standing. It was not inconceivable that Larson might have been driven to murder. The idea of being alone with him raised a few red flags. Agnes made a very convenient witness.

Grace went out onto the porch, allowing the door to close behind her. She moved to the railing.

"Agnes," she called, "I'd like you to meet Larson Rayner. You may have heard of him. He's a very popular motivational speaker. Larson, this is Agnes Gilroy."

"How exciting," Agnes said. She bustled through the garden to the hedge that served as a fence. "I've seen you on TV, Mr. Rayner. Such a nice-looking man.

You are just as handsome in real life. A pleasure to meet you."

Impatience glittered in Larson's eyes but there was no hint of it in his warm voice.

"The pleasure is all mine, Ms. Gilroy," he said.

"Oh, do call me Agnes. How nice of you to come all this way to see our Grace."

"I consider Grace a colleague," Larson said. "She's had a terrible shock, as I'm sure you're aware. I wanted to see how she was getting on."

"That is so thoughtful of you," Agnes said. She chuckled and winked at Grace. "So many interesting gentlemen looking after you these days, dear. Take advantage of it while you can. The older you get, the leaner the pickings."

Grace felt the heat rise in her cheeks.

"Thanks for the advice, Agnes," she said. She turned to Larson and lowered her voice. "Just to clarify, I think that if you had been deeply concerned about me, you would have shown up here sooner. So why don't you come inside and tell me the real reason for your visit today?"

Larson blinked, evidently both surprised and deeply hurt by the casual manner in which she had brushed aside the possibility that his intentions were of a friendly nature. Tiny creases appeared briefly at the corners of his eyes and his jaw tightened, but he followed her into the house.

She led the way into the kitchen and set about making coffee.

"Have a seat," she said.

Larson hesitated and then lowered himself into a chair on the far side of the table.

"Coffee?" she asked.

"Thanks," he said. "I could use a cup. Long drive from Seattle. Traffic was bad this morning. There was an accident on the interstate."

"I hope you don't take cream in your coffee," she said. She watched his face while she ran water into the glass pot. "The refrigerator is no longer functioning. I've got a new one coming this afternoon. Meanwhile, I had to toss out all of the food that was inside this one."

"I don't use cream or sugar," Larson said. He glanced at the refrigerator. "It looks fairly new."

"I'm going to sell it," she said, avoiding the question of warranties.

She paid close attention but as far as she could tell, Larson immediately lost interest in the refrigerator. Dead rats didn't seem like his thing, anyway, she thought. She poured the water into the machine, measured the coffee and hit the On switch.

"I'll come straight to the point," Larson said. "I'm here because I want to offer you a position on my staff."

Her first real job offer and she hadn't even finished her business plan. She couldn't wait to tell Julius.

"I see," she said. "I'm flattered, of course, but I've been doing a lot of thinking and I'm not sure I want to stay in the motivational field. It might be time to move on to something different."

"I agree," Larson said.

"You do?"

Determination gleamed in his eyes. "Look, I had my differences with Witherspoon but I have nothing but admiration for you and your abilities. You were an invaluable asset to the operation but Sprague didn't give you the credit you deserved. Furthermore, I'm sure he also underpaid you. I guarantee you that I'll double your salary."

It was Larson's air of desperation more than the offer of a better salary that piqued her curiosity. In her experience, he had always been supremely confident and sure of his own charisma.

"That's very generous of you," she said. "But the thing is, I'm considering another career path entirely. I really don't think that I'm cut out to be an assistant to a motivational coach for the rest of my life. *Life is enhanced when we seek fresh challenges,* as we in the Witherspoon Way like to say."

That clearly irritated Larson but he kept the sincerity vibe going.

"It's natural that you would want to consider all your options," he said. "But I disagree with your negative analysis of your own potential."

"I wasn't being negative." She folded her arms and lounged against the counter next to the coffeepot. "I said I'm looking for fresh challenges."

"Your talents lie in the motivational field. The problem is that you haven't had a chance to fully explore the opportunities. That was Witherspoon's fault. I knew him better than anyone else did. He was slick,

I'll give him that. But he used people. What's more, he did it so well, most of them never realized how they had been used until it was too late."

"That sounds personal," she said coolly.

Larson grimaced. "I admit that I'm one of the people he used on his way up. Look, I know that you and everyone else in the Witherspoon office heard that last argument I had with Witherspoon. Losing the McCormick seminar was the final straw. It was the fifth time in six months that I'd had a call from a client informing me that a certain firm would not be doing any more business with my company. On each occasion I found out that the Witherspoon Way was booked instead."

"You think Sprague somehow stole those contracts from you?" Grace asked.

Larson's right hand clamped into a fist on the kitchen table. He seemed unaware of the small action.

"I *know* he stole those seminars from me," he said.

Footsteps sounded on the back porch, startling Grace. She glanced out the window and saw Julius. He opened the door and entered the kitchen with the air of a man who had every right to be there. He crossed the floor to where Grace stood, gave her a quick, proprietary kiss and then turned to Larson.

"You've got company," he said to Grace.

But Larson was already on his feet, smiling broadly. The hand that had been curled into a fist was now extended in greeting. "Larson Rayner. Grace and I are colleagues."

"Not quite," Grace said.

But she could tell that neither man was listening to her. They were too busy circling each other, metaphorically speaking. There was a lot of testosterone in the atmosphere. Julius and Larson were assessing each other the way men did when there was only one woman in the vicinity and they both wanted to lay claim to her.

It would have been more flattering, she thought, if Julius and Larson had been vying to carry her off into a hidden bower to ravish her. But she knew that each man had a somewhat different agenda. Larson wanted to take advantage of her rather eclectic skill set. As for Julius, she was pretty sure his protective instincts had been aroused.

"Julius Arkwright," Julius said.

The men shook hands briefly. The gesture was short and brusque.

A gleam of interest sharpened Larson's expression. "Arkwright Ventures?"

"That's right," Julius said.

He said it easily, as if everyone owned a thriving venture capital business that raked in millions. But there was something else infused into the words—a quiet possessiveness that made it clear he could and would protect what was his. He might be a bored lion but he was, nevertheless, a lion.

Larson's smile widened and his eyes brightened with what was probably intended to look like admiration. Grace thought the expression bore a striking resemblance to that of a shrewd salesman who has spotted a potential client.

"I'm very pleased to meet you," he said. "I'm a fan. I admire what you've done with your company. You've got a major talent for spotting up-and-coming markets and trends."

"I've got good people working with me," Julius said.

Larson nodded sagely. "A good leader gives credit to his people." He switched his polished smile to Grace. "I'm here today because I fully respect Grace's abilities. I'm hoping to add her to my own staff."

Julius's eyes went a couple of degrees below freezing. "Is that so?"

She shot him a warning frown. "Larson came to see me today to offer me a job."

"Doing what?" Julius asked.

"I was in the process of describing the position to Grace when you arrived," Larson said. He smiled at Grace. "I hope you will consider joining Team Rayner."

"I'm really not much of a team player," Grace said.

"You'll have your own office and all the freedom and support you need to give free rein to your creativity," Larson said. He was very earnest now. "I repeat, I will double whatever Witherspoon paid you. What's more, if you guarantee me a minimum of one year of service, I'll give you a commission on all of the seminars that you book."

"That's a very generous offer," Grace said. "But I really do need to think about it. I've got a lot of things going on in my life at the moment and I have this feeling that it's time for me to move on to another career."

Larson's smile lost some of its sparkle. "I understand that you're ready for a new challenge. I'm in a position to make that happen for you. If you aren't ready to join my team as a full-time member of my staff, will you consider consulting for me?"

"What kind of consulting?" she asked. "You're a leader in your field. Actually, now that Sprague is gone, you'll probably become the premier motivational speaker in the Pacific Northwest—maybe the whole West Coast. I don't think you need me."

"Ah, now there you are mistaken." Larson held up a hand, palm out. "No need to be modest. I know for a fact that you were the one who wrote that cookbook and the Witherspoon Way blog. You made Sprague a media sensation. But he never gave you any of the credit, did he? I'll bet he didn't give you a percentage of the take on those seminars, either."

Grace stilled. Julius regarded her with a thoughtful expression. She was learning to interpret that particular look and she was fairly certain it never boded well. But she gave him credit for having the good sense not to say anything.

"Where are you going with this, Larson?" she asked quietly.

Larson shoved his fingers through his hair. "Isn't it obvious? I want you to take over my social media. In addition, I'd like to take that cookbook idea of yours and expand it into a full lifestyle series based on the theme of positive thinking and your affirmations. Yes, I know you were the one who came up with those, too."

"In other words, you are offering me a position as a ghostwriter for both your blog and your books."

"Well, yes," he said. "We both know that it's the Rayner Seminars brand that will sell the blog and the books. But I promise you that you will be well paid, and I will see to it that your contribution is acknowledged at every step of the way."

"Like I said, I'll think about it," she said.

"What's holding you back?" Larson glanced skeptically at Julius and then turned back to Grace. "Has someone made you a better offer?"

"No," she admitted. "I'm still trying to find my path forward."

"Might as well earn some good money while you work on finding that path," Larson said. He paused for emphasis. "One more thing you should know."

"Yes?"

"I'm making similar offers to your former coworkers, Kristy Forsyth and Millicent Chartwell. I want the whole team. I guarantee that all of you will be able to name your own price."

Grace looked at him. "Aren't you afraid that one of us might be an embezzler?"

To her amazement, Larson chuckled. "Haven't you heard the latest news on the case? Sprague was the embezzler."

Grace stared at him, dumbfounded. "I don't understand."

Julius went to the coffee machine. "Rayner may be right. I came here to give you the news. According to the investigators who are examining the financial records, it appears that Sprague Witherspoon may have been skimming off the money."

"But it was Sprague's money," Grace said. "Why would he hide the theft?"

"Could have been a couple of reasons," Larson offered. "One was that he was using the money for purposes he wanted to keep secret."

"Such as?" Grace challenged.

Larson shrugged. "There are rumors that he may have had a gambling addiction."

"That's . . . almost impossible to believe," Grace said, stunned.

Julius poured himself a cup of coffee. "There are other reasons why a successful entrepreneur would want to hide a lot of cash. The experts are still looking into the records."

She shot him a curious glance. They both knew that by "experts" he meant his wizards at Arkwright Ventures.

"The embezzlement issue has gone away," Larson said. He took out a card and handed it to Grace. "I think it's safe to say that when the police finally solve Witherspoon's murder, the killer will turn out to be someone connected to his gambling addiction. It's a dangerous world. Here's my private line. Call me with any questions, night or day. I'll check back with you soon."

"Okay," Grace said. She didn't know what else to say. She was still grappling with the news of Sprague's gaming addiction.

"You were born for the motivational world, Grace."

Larson smiled. "You just need a chance to shine." He glanced at his watch. "I'd better get going. I've got an appointment back in Seattle."

"You never got your coffee," Grace said.

"Some other time, thanks," Larson said. "A pleasure to meet you, Julius. I would be happy to sit down with you at your convenience to discuss what Rayner Seminars can do for you. Good-bye, Grace. Call soon. I don't know how long I can keep this offer open."

He walked out of the kitchen and across the living room. Grace trailed after him and opened the door.

Larson went down the porch steps and got into his car. Julius came to stand behind Grace. Together they watched Larson drive out to the main road and disappear.

"He seems a little desperate," Julius said.

"I think he's just very enthusiastic about moving his company forward," Grace said.

"No, that was desperation I saw in Larson Rayner. He wants you very, very badly. You must have been damn good at the positive-thinking business."

"I did have a flair for affirmations, and the cookbook was one of my better ideas," Grace said. "But I'm not sure that I can work for Larson."

"Why not?"

"Because I don't think he's sincere about the power of positive thinking," she said. "I'm not saying he's a phony, but he's not committed the way Sprague was committed. Sprague genuinely wanted to help people. His belief in positive energy was real. He inspired me."

Julius's brows rose. "Larson doesn't inspire you?"

"Nope."

"Here's a little inside job-hunting tip—if you're only willing to work for people who inspire you, you're going to discover that you're looking at a very small group of potential employers."

She sighed. "That has occurred to me."

Twenty-One

She led the way back into the kitchen and turned to face Julius.

"Are the investigators really convinced that Sprague may have used company money to cover up his gambling losses?" she asked.

"It's still a theory at this point. I'm told that there are some strong indications that may be the case. But I'm not buying that story, not yet. I told the wizards to look deeper."

"It's almost impossible to believe that Sprague was a gambler. But if it's true, it changes a lot of things, including the pool of suspects in the murder."

"No," Julius said. "It doesn't affect the suspect pool. There is still the little matter of the vodka bottle. No professional assassin employed by a mob boss would have gone to the trouble of researching your past to come up with that little bit of incriminating information. There was no need to do that. Pros almost always get away with murder, literally. I think the murder was a lot more personal. And there's still the issue of the stalker."

"This is getting more confusing by the day."

"No, I think we're finally starting to see a pattern. But meanwhile, I'm glad you're not jumping on Rayner's offer of a job, because I'm not enthusiastic about the idea of you going to work for him."

"Why not?"

"Something about that guy feels off."

"He's a professional motivational speaker," she said. "We know how you feel about the business."

"What he's got is a talent for sales," Julius said. "And as far as I'm concerned, he's still on the suspect list when it comes to Witherspoon's murder."

"Sprague and Larson argued furiously shortly before Sprague was killed," Grace said. "The quarrel happened in Sprague's private office, but Millicent and Kristy and I were working in the outer office at the time. We heard the shouting."

"What were they fighting about?" Julius asked.

"Sprague had just received a contract for a major speaking engagement in Los Angeles. Larson felt the contract should have been his. He accused Sprague of sabotaging him. He was sure that Sprague had used his connections to tell the client that Rayner Seminars was in trouble financially."

"Why would that have mattered to the people who wanted to hire a motivational speaker?" Julius asked.

"Seems like financial troubles would just make a motivational guru all the more motivated."

She gave him a quelling look. "That is not funny. As I recall, the topic of the seminar was 'A Positive-Thinking Approach to Wealth Management.'"

Julius grinned briefly. "Okay, I can see the problem there."

"You wouldn't want to book a motivational seminar on that subject with a speaker whose own company was heading for bankruptcy."

Julius turned thoughtful. "Is it true that Rayner is having financial troubles?"

"The rumors started circulating a few months ago. Whether or not they are true, I can't say."

"I take it Rayner and Witherspoon had a history?" Julius said.

"Oh, yeah," Grace said. She led the way back into the kitchen. "They started out as partners and there was some kind of blowup. Rumors of the feud have circulated in the motivational world ever since the breakup."

Julius was briefly distracted. "There's a motivational world?"

"Yep, and it's a small one—at least it is at the level Sprague and Larson occupied."

"Any idea what caused the falling-out between the two?"

"There was a woman involved," Grace said. "Sprague's second wife, not Nyla's mother. I'm told the second Mrs. Witherspoon was about thirty years younger and quite attractive. Evidently Larson had an affair with her. I've heard that—for men—there are only two things worth fighting over: money and women."

"I've heard that old saying, too," Julius said. "I wouldn't put too much stock in it, though."

"No?" She watched him closely. "Why not?"

"I'm not saying men don't fight over money and women. I'm just saying that there's not much point fighting over a woman who doesn't want you, and when it comes to money, there's always more out there. Why risk prison for either reason?"

"Beats me," Grace said, amused. "But people seem willing to do just that all the time. Prison is full of people who shot other people for cold hard cash or drugs. And there are also a lot of people in prison who murdered other people in a jealous rage."

"Can't argue with that," Julius said. "I'm just saying those aren't good reasons to kill."

She watched him drink his coffee.

"That's very Zen," she said.

"More like common sense." Julius went to stand at the window. "The other problem with that old saying is that it leaves out a couple of other viable motives for murder."

She filled her own mug. "Such as?"

"Power and revenge."

She leaned back against the counter. "Okay. But both of those motives could have been at work in a scenario that features Larson killing Sprague."

Julius tried a sip of his coffee. "When did Larson Rayner have the affair with Sprague Witherspoon's wife?"

"Long before I was hired. Maybe four or five years ago."

"Did Rayner marry Witherspoon's ex?"

"No. I gather she did well out of the divorce but as far as I know she moved on."

"That probably makes jealousy an even more unlikely motive," Julius said. "So we're back to money. Did Witherspoon steal some of Rayner's clients?"

She raised her chin. "I honestly don't think Sprague did anything underhanded. But some of Larson's clients did switch their business to Witherspoon."

Julius nodded thoughtfully. "Thanks to you."

"I was able to leverage some ideas that worked out well for the firm," she said, going for modesty. "My skill set is somewhat limited but I do have a few tools in the box."

"And now Larson Rayner wants you and your skills," Julius said. "No surprise there. When an ambitious politician loses a race, one of the first things he does is try to hire the winner's campaign manager. Same holds true in the business world."

Grace waved one hand. "Good grief, I am not some sort of motivational gun for hire."

"You've got to admit it would look interesting on a business card: *Positive Thinking Gun for Hire. Affirmations for the up-and-coming motivational guru.*"

"Sometimes I think you go out of your way to try to impress me with your cynicism," Grace said.

"I'm a pragmatic man."

"Bullshit."

Julius's brows rose. "Bullshit?"

"What? You didn't think I knew the word?"

He smiled. "I hadn't considered the question until now. The subject hasn't arisen."

"I assure you I have a wide-ranging vocabulary, but generally speaking I reserve it for the appropriate occasions."

"Me calling myself a pragmatist qualifies as an occasion that requires the use of the word 'bullshit'?" Julius asked. He didn't sound offended, merely curious.

"Yes, I do believe 'bullshit' is the appropriate word here," Grace said firmly. "You probably think of yourself as pragmatic because you can make the hard decisions when necessary. You get to the bottom line before anyone else, and you see no point dwelling on the emotions involved in arriving at your destination."

Julius nodded thoughtfully. "I'd say that's a fair summary of my personal philosophy."

"Here's the thing, Julius—you wouldn't throw an innocent person under the bus just to close a deal or achieve your goals. You may be cynical, but you have your own code and you stick to it."

He shook his head, clearly perplexed by her naiveté. "What makes you so sure of that?"

She smiled. "If you had chosen to be a bad guy, you would do a much better job of playing the role."

Twenty-Two

The new refrigerator arrived forty-five minutes after Larson Rayner left. The deliverymen obligingly disconnected the old one and moved it out onto the sheltered back porch. They wrapped it in heavy sheets of plastic to protect it from the elements until Grace could sell it.

Julius could see the relief in her eyes when the offending appliance was finally gone from the kitchen. He understood.

The new window was installed an hour later. Following that, Grace insisted on going grocery shopping to restock her gleaming new appliance.

What with one thing and another, it was nearly one o'clock before Julius was able to settle down to the business of explaining a few of the facts of business life to his new client.

"Let's get this straight," he said. "A talent for writing cheery little feel-good affirmations is not considered a useful skill in most high-powered, high-paying industries."

"Maybe I need a low-powered industry," Grace said.

"Not a lot of those left," Julius said. "And what about the low pay that usually goes with the few that might still be out there?"

"Good point," she said.

"We need to find a different way to describe your skills."

"How many ways are there to say that I can write optimistic affirmations?" Grace asked.

"I don't know yet," Julius said. "But let's try to think positive, shall we?"

She glared at him. "That is not amusing."

"Right. Back to work, then."

The rain returned but there was a fire in the fireplace and Julius thought that the little house felt cozy and comfortable. The work on Grace's résumé was not going well but he had already concluded that he would be content to labor over it for a very long time if it meant he could remain close to Grace.

The phone rang just as she got up to make a pot of tea. Julius saw her flinch a little, even though it was a regular call, not an email alert.

Grace took the call. The conversation was brief.

"Yes," she said. "Yes, of course." She glanced at the clock. "I can be there by two thirty or three if the traffic isn't bad."

She ended the call and looked at Julius.

"That was someone from the Seattle Police Department," she said. "Evidently there was a break-in at the Witherspoon Way office. The police aren't sure when the burglary occurred and they can't tell if anything of value was stolen. But because the incident may be linked to Sprague's death, we've been asked to go to the office and see if we can figure out what was taken."

"We?" Julius repeated.

"The three of us who worked for Sprague," Grace explained. "Millicent and Kristy have also been asked to come in and take a look."

"Well, it's not like we weren't planning on driving into the city this afternoon for that damn dinner and charity auction tonight," Julius said. "I'll take care of a few things at my office while you and your friends talk to the police."

"Okay," she said.

"So, about tonight," he said.

Everything inside her tightened a couple more notches. "Yes?"

"Looks like I'm more or less going to be keeping you company in the evenings until this stalker problem is resolved."

"Yes?" she said again.

"What do you say we spend the night in the city? I'm thinking there's no point making the long drive back here at midnight. I've got a guest bedroom at my condo."

She gave that some thought. He was right. One way or another they would be spending the evening under the same roof. What did it matter if they drove back to Cloud Lake or stayed in Seattle?

"I'll pack a bag," she said.

Julius smiled and for a moment she once again pondered the risks of flirting with the Big Bad Wolf.

Twenty-Three

The bastard wrecked the place," Millicent announced. "Whoever did this must have been really pissed off when he couldn't find whatever it was he thought Sprague had hidden here."

"The cops aren't sure the intruder had any connection with the murder," Grace reminded her. "You heard the officer. They think this may have been random. They said it's quite possible that someone looking for drug money realized the office had been empty for a while."

"The only things missing are the laptops," Kristy said. "They're always prime targets in this kind of thing."

The three of them were standing in the reception area of the Witherspoon offices. A police officer had taken the inventory of missing items and left a short time ago. Afterward, the management firm that leased the space to the Witherspoon Way had authorized all former employees to pick up any personal possessions they had left behind. A representative of the management company was waiting outside in the hallway to lock up when they were finished.

It was the first time any of them had been allowed back into the office since the day Grace discovered Sprague's body. Kristy and Grace had brought small cardboard boxes to collect the few things they had left behind in their desks. Millicent had brought along a shiny, hard-sided roll-aboard suitcase.

The yellow crime scene tape had been removed but the office looked as if it had been hit by a whirlwind. Millicent was right, Grace thought. Whoever had ransacked the place must have been furious that there wasn't more worth stealing.

Sprague had overseen the interior design of his office environment. He had insisted that the space reflect the serene and harmonious inner balance that he urged others to seek. To that end he had hired a designer who had gone all in on a minimalist approach. The palette ran the gamut from gray to off-white. The only touches of color had been the brilliant flowers in the glass vases. Kristy had been assigned the task of replacing the blooms as needed. Sprague had often noted that she had a way with greenery.

The desks in the individual offices were state of the art, designed to conceal the high-tech necessities of the modern corporate world. One swipe at the small control screen on each desktop and the computer, phones and other machines vanished beneath a Zen-smooth surface.

To finish the look, Sprague had brought in a feng shui expert to arrange the furniture so that it was properly oriented. The all-important grounding touches like the little fountain in the corner had also been installed by the expert. The fountain no longer gurgled.

"I wonder why Nyla Witherspoon didn't remove the laptops herself," Millicent said.

"What would she do with them?" Kristy asked. "I can't see her selling them on eBay."

"I've got a feeling that Nyla has been focused on other things lately," Grace said.

Kristy hugged herself and shook her head. "I think the cops are right. There probably isn't a connection between this break-in and what happened to poor Sprague. Grace, I remember you said that there was no sign that the killer took anything from Sprague's home the night the murder was committed."

"That's true," Grace said. "Although I have to tell you, I did not take the time to look around. I got out of the house as quickly as possible."

Millicent sniffed. "A very wise move."

"Still, I don't recall that anything appeared to have been disturbed," Grace said. "And there was nothing in the papers about robbery having been a possible motive. If the killer was the same person who ransacked this place, you'd think he would have stolen some of Sprague's personal valuables, too."

"As far as I'm concerned, the missing laptops are

Nyla's problem," Millicent announced. "I assume you heard the rumors about Witherspoon's little gambling problem?"

"Yes," Grace said. "But it's hard to believe he was paying off gambling debts."

"I can't believe it, either," Kristy said.

"Well, I do believe it, and it explains a lot," Millicent said. "It's also a huge relief to me, I can tell you that. As the company bookkeeper, I was afraid I was at the top of the suspect list when it came to the embezzlement thing. My issues now revolve around job-hunting. I assume you both got the call from Larson Rayner?"

"Yes," Kristy said. "I'm thinking about it but I'm going to stall until we find out for certain that Larson is cleared of any connection with the murder of Sprague."

"Larson drove to Cloud Lake to talk to me about a position at Rayner Seminars," Grace said. "I'm not sure what I'm going to do. Kristy's right, it will be easier to make a decision once we know who killed Sprague."

Millicent laughed. "Unlike you two, I'm not nearly so fussy when it comes to employers. I need a job and Rayner Seminars is set to take over the motivational business in our region. I'm going to grab Larson's offer."

Kristy looked down at a heap of dead flowers that had been yanked out of the vase on her desk and dumped on the floor. "What, exactly, are we supposed to do besides collect our own belongings? I hope they don't expect us to clean up the place."

The reception desk had once been Kristy's

command post and she had occupied it brilliantly, handling the media as well as the Witherspoon bookings.

"Don't know about you two," Millicent said, heading toward her office with the little suitcase, "but if anyone thinks I'm going to tidy up here, they've got a surprise coming. The burglar was responsible for the damage, not me. I'm going to clean out my desk."

She disappeared into her office.

"This is all just so sad," Kristy said.

She sank into the high-tech office chair and picked up the framed photo of her family that had been knocked facedown on top of the desk. Very carefully she put the picture into her cardboard box.

"Got an affirmation for us, Grace?" Millicent called from the other room.

"How about *Today I will be open to new possibilities*?" Grace suggested. "I used it with the roasted fennel recipe in the cookbook."

"I hate fennel," Millicent yelled back.

More drawers banged.

Kristy made a face and angled her head in the general direction of Millicent's office.

"She'll do all right," Kristy said very softly.

Grace smiled. "Probably. Meanwhile, you and I need to remember that, thanks to Sprague, we've got a lot of unique skills to sell to our next employer."

"Please don't recite any more Witherspoon affirmations. I want to savor my gloom."

"Okay," Grace said.

She went to the doorway of her office and contemplated the chaotic scene. Files had been yanked out of drawers and dumped on the floor. There wasn't a lot to retrieve, she thought. She had never kept much in the way of personal items in her workplace. There wasn't room for that sort of thing in a minimalist environment.

She set the cardboard box on the desk and started to pack up her few personal possessions—the large coffee mug emblazoned with the Witherspoon Way logo, the blue wrap that she kept in the bottom desk drawer for those days when the building HVAC system wasn't working well, a pair of sneakers that she wore on her lunch break when she went to the nearby dog park to eat her lunch and watch city canines frolic.

She was in the process of putting her selection of herbal tea bags into the box when she heard the familiar brittle voice in the outer office.

"Don't touch anything," Nyla Witherspoon said fiercely. "Not a damn thing. This was my father's office. If any of you take so much as a pen, I'll report you to the police."

"Take it easy, honey. I'm sure they just came back for their personal things. You heard the security guard out in the hall. He's keeping an eye on the office."

Grace recognized Burke Marrick's voice. Rich and resonant, it would have taken him far in the motivational speaking world.

She went back to the doorway of her office. Nyla

was standing in the center of the reception area, vibrating with rage. Her sharp features were twisted with anger. She looked more than ever like the Wicked Witch of the West.

Burke put one hand on her shoulder as if he thought he might need to restrain her from taking a swing at Kristy.

There was no question but that Nyla had landed herself an impressive trophy fiancé. Burke had certainly hit the genetic lottery when it came to his looks. And he knew how to dress to make the most of his startling green eyes, gleaming dark hair and well-toned physique. Somehow a woman knew just by looking at him that he would be very skilled in bed.

"Get out of here, all of you," Nyla hissed. "You have no right to be here."

"The police called us in today and the building manager told us that we were free to pick up our personal things," Kristy said calmly. "Don't worry, there's nothing of value left to steal except the chairs and the desks. Good luck selling them on the used-office-furniture market."

Nyla clenched her fingers around the strap of her designer purse. "I said get out. Now. Everything in here—everything that belonged to my father—is mine now. I'm the sole heir, in case you weren't paying attention. Leave now or I will call the police and have all three of you arrested for theft."

Millicent appeared in the doorway of her office. "Don't worry, Nyla, we were just leaving." She looked at Kristy and Grace. "Right?"

Kristy sighed and picked up her cardboard box. "Right."

Grace went back to her desk, grabbed her box and carried it into the outer office. The three of them marched toward the door.

"Wait," Nyla yelped. "Let me see what you've got in those boxes."

Burke touched her shoulder again, a little more firmly this time. "Don't worry about it, Nyla. I'm sure they are just taking the things that belonged to them."

"Damn it, I don't trust any of them," Nyla wailed. "Don't you understand? One of them murdered my father."

There was a hushed silence. Grace moved first. She walked toward Nyla and held out the box.

"Take a good look," she said. "A lovely mug and some herbal tea. You're welcome to both. You can't have the wrap, though. My sister gave it to me for my birthday."

Nyla glanced into the box. Her mouth tightened.

Kristy followed with her box. "Here you go, Nyla. Help yourself. A box of tissues and a photo of my family."

"I can't believe we're doing this," Millicent grumbled. She crouched in her stilettos and opened the roll-aboard to reveal a couple of designer scarves, another pair of stilettos and a coffee mug. "I don't think the scarves are your color, Nyla. You're better in black, don't you think?"

"Leave," Nyla whispered. "All of you. And don't come back."

"Good idea," Millicent said.

She straightened and rolled her suitcase toward the door. Grace and Kristy followed. The three of them walked to the elevator in silence. Millicent stabbed the button.

"That woman is a real case," she said.

"We all know that she harbored a lot of resentment toward her father," Grace reminded them. "Now that he's gone, she's dealing with the fact that she won't ever be able to fix that relationship. She's grieving."

Kristy snorted softly. "Give me a break. She never tried to reconcile with her father. Heaven knows he wanted to bond with her. But I swear she enjoyed nursing her so-called grievances. I'm telling you, she's the one who murdered Sprague."

"I wouldn't be surprised," Millicent said. She stabbed the elevator button again and glanced back down the hall toward the office. "She is the sole heir, isn't she?"

Grace followed her gaze. "Got a feeling Mr. Perfect has other ideas."

Millicent's smile was cold. "I agree with Kristy. I wouldn't be surprised if they planned the murder together."

"Serves them right that the money disappeared," Kristy said.

Twenty-Four

That was my journey. I would not be here tonight if not for the things Harley Montoya taught me. Many of us can look back and name the people who gave us not only a chance but the guidance and direction that we needed at a crucial moment in our lives . . ."

Grace finally allowed herself to breathe. Julius was doing well on the podium. Granted, he might not make it in the motivational speakers' world or on the campaign trail. But he was delivering the new version of the Speech from Hell with a conviction that was resonating with the audience.

Nothing grabbed people's attention like a strong dose of passion, and Julius had communicated more than enough to rivet the crowd. The darkened ballroom had been hushed from the outset when it became clear that the after-dinner talk was not going to involve a lot of dull facts and figures. There hadn't been so much as a clinked glass or the clatter of a spoon on a dish since Julius had launched into the speech. Even the waiters had stopped to listen at the back of the room.

". . . Those of us who have achieved success in the business world now find ourselves with an opportunity to wield some real power—the kind that leaves a lasting legacy, the kind that can change lives.

"Look around and find at least one other person who reminds you of yourself when you were starting out. Figure out what you did right and what you did wrong along the way. Focus on the things that you can reflect back on with a sense of pride because you know you did the right thing, the honorable thing, even if it cost you some money or a contract at the time. Offer those lessons to that individual who reminds you of yourself, the one who is still trying to decide what kind of person he or she wants to be. Your mission is to help shape the future."

Julius swept up the notecards, turned and walked across the raised dais. It took a couple of beats for the audience to realize that the speech had ended. A good sign, Grace thought, satisfied. Always leave them wanting more.

The applause exploded across the banquet room just as Julius started down the steps. By the time he got to the floor, half the people were on their feet. By the time he reached the round table where Grace stood with the others, clapping madly, the rest of the audience was standing.

Grace knew that she was practically glowing. She smiled at Julius.

"That was wonderful," she said beneath the roar of applause. "You were brilliant."

"Don't know about brilliant," he said. "But at least they didn't fall asleep this time."

Without warning, he pulled her into his arms and kissed her. It wasn't a long, involved embrace—just a short, sure, triumphant kiss that sent the unmistakable impression of intimacy. It was the sort of kiss lovers exchanged.

The crowd loved it. Possibly even more than they loved the speech, Grace thought.

By the time the kiss was over she was flushed and breathless and intensely aware that everyone around her was smiling.

Julius held her chair for her.

"Thanks," he said so that only she could hear. "I owe you."

"No," she said quickly.

"Yes," he whispered. He gripped the back of her chair. "Sit down. Please. No one else can sit until you do."

"Oh, right." She looked around the room. People were still on their feet but the clapping was fading. Definitely time to sit.

She dropped into her chair. Julius guided it back into position and sat down beside her. Everyone else sank back into their seats.

A murmur of congratulations broke out around the

head table. A banker sitting two place settings away wanted to know Julius's opinion of some pending financial regulations. Grace reached for her water glass—and nearly dropped it when she felt Julius's hand close over hers under the table.

He squeezed her fingers gently. The small action seemed as intimate as the kiss, perhaps more so. *He's just thanking you for saving him from the Speech from Hell. He's relieved it's over. He's grateful for your suggestions. Don't read too much into a little squeeze of the hand.*

The master of ceremonies resumed control of the audience, thanked Julius for the talk and moved on to the next item on the evening's agenda, the closing remarks and the reminder that the auction would start in twenty minutes in the main wing of the museum. Last-minute bids were being accepted.

Once again everyone stood. A group quickly gathered around Julius. It seemed as if half the room was eager to engage him in conversation. Many of the people looked vaguely familiar. Grace knew she had seen their faces in the newspapers and on local television.

She started to ease out of the way so that the others could get closer to Julius. He did not look around but he reached back and captured her wrist.

She stopped and leaned in close so that she could speak directly into his ear.

"Ladies' room," she whispered.

At that he broke off a discussion on the subject of the lack of government funding for high-tech research and looked at her.

"I'll wait for you in the lobby," he said. He released her.

"I won't be long," she promised.

She slipped off through the crowd, aware of a few curious gazes cast her way before she escaped into the calm of an empty hallway. She paused to get her bearings, spotted the *Ladies* sign at the end of the hall and headed in that direction.

There were three other women at the long row of sinks when she entered. They nodded as if they knew her and smiled. She was quite sure she had never met any of them in her life but she smiled back and headed for a stall. This was what came of being attached to Julius's side that evening, she thought. Back in Cloud Lake it was easy to forget his position in the Pacific Northwest business community.

By the time she exited the stall the other women had left. She breathed a sigh of relief at finding herself alone and opened her clutch to take out a lipstick. The door swung open again just as she was using a tissue to blot the extra color off her mouth.

The newcomer was a striking woman in her early thirties. Her blond hair was pulled back in an elegant chignon. She wore a sleek, black-and-white cocktail dress and a pair of black heels.

There was recognition in her eyes, just as there had been in the eyes of the three women Grace had encountered when she entered the room. But this woman was not smiling.

"You're with Julius tonight," the newcomer said. There was a thread of grim determination in her voice, as if she were confronting an enemy and was prepared to fight.

"He invited me to accompany him this evening," Grace said.

The tension in the atmosphere was disturbing. She waited, uncertain what to do next. The woman was blocking the route to the door, perhaps by accident but maybe by design.

"I'm Diana Hastings," Diana said. There was a husky edge on the words, as if she were trying to suppress some fierce emotion. "Julius's ex-wife."

"I see." Grace looked at the door. The uneasy sensation was transitioning to red-alert status. She needed to escape as quickly as possible. Whatever this was about, she was sure it was not going to end well. "I'm Grace Elland. A pleasure to meet you. If you don't mind, I need to get back to the lobby. Someone is waiting."

"Julius. You're going to meet Julius."

"Well, yes."

"So you're the new girlfriend." Diana looked bemused. "You're not exactly his type, are you?

"I have no idea and you're mistaken. Julius and I are just friends. He's advising me on how to build a business plan."

That was sort of true, Grace thought. Kisses had been exchanged but she and Julius were not sleeping together. And the part about the business plan was fairly accurate.

"Julius doesn't kiss his friends the way he kissed you in front of the audience tonight," Diana said. "No man kisses a woman like that unless he wants to make sure that everyone around him knows that he's sleeping with her."

"Oh, for pity's sake, Mrs. Hastings—Diana. Julius and I only met recently. It was a blind date arranged through friends. I'm just doing Julius a favor tonight. He needed a companion for this event and I was—uh—convenient."

"No." Diana shook her head with great certainty and moved farther into the room. "Oh, I don't doubt that he finds you convenient. Julius is very good at manipulating people to get what he wants. But I know that you two are sleeping together. That was obvious tonight."

Grace felt her temper start to flare. "Not true, but even if it was, it wouldn't be any of your business, now, would it?"

Diana's fingers tightened around her gold leather evening purse. "I don't give a damn if you're sleeping with him. I suppose I should feel some sympathy. You must be as naive as I was when I married him. But do you know something? I can't even feel sorry for you. I just don't *care* if you two are having an affair. Is that clear?"

The situation was escalating. Diana's face was flushed, her eyes a little wild. Instinctively Grace softened her own voice.

"Very clear," she said. "You've made your point, so if you don't mind, I'll be leaving now."

She started forward, intending to circle around Diana and make a break for the door.

"No, I haven't made my point." Diana did not move.

"You're welcome to him, as far as I'm concerned. Julius is cold, ruthless and calculating, but that's your problem, not mine. I want you to take a message to him."

"If you've got something to say to him, I suggest you speak to him yourself. You can do it right now. He's waiting in the lobby. Do you mind getting out of the way?"

Diana did not budge. She was gripping her little purse so tightly her knuckles were white.

"Tell that bastard that I know what he's doing," she said. "Tell him everyone in Seattle knows."

Grace debated her chances of getting past Diana without physical contact. They didn't look good. She felt her temper start to slip again.

"Do I look like a messenger pigeon?" she asked.

"Tell Julius that I know he wants revenge. I get that. But he should take it out on me—not my husband and my husband's family. They are innocent. What Julius is doing is so unfair. And pointless. It's not as if I ever meant anything to him. I was just one more transaction, an entry in his portfolio. I know he never truly loved me. Tell him that even in my nightmares I never believed that he would be this cruel."

"What?" Grace was so shocked she could not think of how to follow up, so she just stared at Diana.

The door of the ladies' room swung open without warning, forcing Diana to move aside. She did so but she seemed unaware of the two women who walked into the room behind her. She was focused utterly on Grace.

"Julius is deliberately trying to destroy my husband's company," Diana said, her voice tight with fury and frustration. "It's common knowledge. Julius wants to exact vengeance on me because I left him. He can't abide losing. He's Arkwright the Alchemist. He always wins."

The two women who had just entered the room watched the scene with hushed fascination. Diana ignored them.

Grace assessed her options. There were now three people blocking the room's only escape route. A Witherspoon Way affirmation flashed through her mind. *Be the eye of the storm. It is the only way to control the chaos around you.*

It took everything she had to smile at Diana, but she managed the feat.

"It's all a huge misunderstanding, Mrs. Hastings," she said. "The rumors are wrong. I can assure you that Julius is not out to destroy your husband's company."

Tears sparked in Diana's eyes. "Tonight that son of a bitch gave a very nice, very noble speech about the importance of legacies and honor and making a difference. But what he's doing to Edward and the Hastings family makes Julius a complete hypocrite. You tell him that, damn it."

"If you know Julius as well as you think you do," Grace said, "then there is something else you should know."

Diana frowned. "What?"

"Julius is very, very good when it comes to business. You said it yourself. They call him Arkwright the Alchemist."

"You don't have to tell me." Diana dashed the back of her hand across her eyes, smearing her makeup. "Believe me, I'm well aware that he's a legend in the business world."

"Then stop and think about this for a minute," Grace said. "If Julius Arkwright actually had set out to destroy your husband's company, Hastings would have filed for bankruptcy months ago. The firm would be in smoking ruins. Julius doesn't mess around. I would have thought you would remember that aspect of his character."

It was Diana's turn to stare. She did not say a word. The other two women were still frozen in place. For a moment no one moved.

Grace couldn't think of anything else to say so she turned and yanked a towel out of the dispenser. She marched toward the trio who stood in her way.

"Excuse me," she said.

She did not stop. Abruptly the three scattered. Grace kept going. She obeyed the little sign on the wall that advised her to use the paper towel to open the door. Tossing the towel aside, she escaped into the hall.

The door closed softly on the still-life-with-bathroom-fixtures in the ladies' room.

Twenty-Five

When he saw Grace coming toward him through the crowd, he knew that something had happened in the short span of time that she had been gone—something unpleasant.

She wore a simple, sleek black gown with a demure neckline, long sleeves and a narrow skirt. Her hair was pulled up in a severe twist. He suspected that she had gone for a look suited to an up-and-coming businesswoman. But he thought she looked more like a sexy little cat burglar weaving her way through the knots of people. When she drew closer he saw the mix of relief and wariness in her eyes.

He took her arm and instinctively checked her back trail. He saw no one who appeared alarming.

"What's wrong?" he asked, keeping his voice low.

She wrinkled her nose. "I'm afraid there was a small scene in the ladies' room a few minutes ago."

That stopped him for a moment.

"What the hell kind of scene could occur in a restroom?" he finally asked.

"I ran into your ex-wife. Or, rather, she ran into me. I think she followed me into the ladies' room."

"Damn."

Grace's mouth tightened. "Brace yourself. It gets worse. There were witnesses."

"All right, let's take this step by step. First, define 'scene.'"

"Diana Hastings cornered me and made some accusations. It was awkward. She's very upset, Julius. Angry and scared. That is not a good mix."

He tried and failed to come up with a reason why Diana might be angry with Grace.

"She can't be jealous of you," he said. He stated that as the blunt fact that he knew it was. "She's the one who left me, remember? So why would she confront you?"

"She's not mad at me," Grace said. Her tone made it clear that she was doing her level best to exert patience. "I was just a placeholder."

"For what?"

He was starting to feel as if he were falling down the rabbit hole. Every man knew that what happened in the ladies' room was supposed to stay in the ladies' room. He was pretty sure there was a rule about it somewhere.

"Diana is harboring a great deal of fear and frustration toward you," Grace said quietly. "She took it out on me—probably because she's terrified to confront you directly. She thinks you're trying to get revenge against her and Edward Hastings by destroying the Hastings family empire."

The pieces of the puzzle finally slipped into place. He allowed himself to relax a few notches.

"I see," he said. "That business."

"An unfortunate turn of phrase, as it happens." Grace narrowed her eyes. "Yes, that business. She wanted me to deliver a message. She said she was aware of what you're doing and that she thinks it's . . . not very nice."

He blinked. "Those were her words?"

"Well, no," Grace said stiffly. "More forceful language was employed. But that's neither here nor there."

"Don't worry. What's going on at Hastings has nothing to do with me. Hastings has been digging its own grave for the past eighteen months."

"I assured Diana that you were not responsible for the company's troubles."

He was strangely gratified by that news.

"You said that?" he asked. "You told her that I wasn't the one undermining Hastings?"

"Naturally. But I don't think that's going to be enough to defuse the situation."

He thought about that for a moment. "No offense, but what the hell do you know about Hastings's financial problems?"

"Nothing," Grace admitted. "I just pointed out the obvious to Diana."

"What, exactly, is the obvious?"

"I reminded her that you are very good at what you do. I told her that if you had been trying to destroy the company for going on eighteen months, Hastings would have crashed and burned by now."

"Huh."

He couldn't think of anything to say to that, so he steered her into the auction room. He was aware that almost every eye in the place followed them to their seats. He could feel the tension vibrating through Grace.

"Ignore them," he said into her ear as he sat down beside her.

"Easy for you to say."

"All we have to do is buy that overpriced chunk of art glass that you picked out earlier and then we're out of here."

"Right. And I would remind you that you were the one who said we had to buy that beautiful piece of art glass."

"I said we had to buy something. I didn't give a damn what we bought."

"It's a really beautiful piece of glass," she said, very earnest now. "I'm sure it will look lovely in your condo."

He started to tell her that the bowl was going to be hers. He had seen the way her eyes glowed with appreciation when she looked at it earlier. But before he could say anything he realized she had gone very quiet. Alarmed, he gave her a quick head-to-toe appraisal.

"Are you okay?" he asked.

"I'm fine," she said softly.

She was focused on the stage. Her calm, serene expression made him suspicious.

"You're doing some kind of breathing thing, aren't you?" he said.

"I'm using one of the Witherspoon affirmations as a mantra, if that's what you mean, yes."

"Which affirmation?"

"Let's just say that I am in my peaceful place where negative energy cannot touch me."

"How is that working for you?"

"Shut up and get ready to bid."

Twenty-Six

Burke Marrick was tall, sexy and gorgeous in the dark, dangerous ways of fictional vampires—all sharp cheekbones and mesmerizing green eyes. Mr. Perfect was too good to be true, Millicent thought, but he was certainly interesting.

She watched him slide gracefully into the booth across from her. She was halfway through her martini but she might as well have been drinking liquid excitement with a twist of nerves. She was, after all, about to make a business proposition to the man who had, in all likelihood, murdered Sprague Witherspoon.

Somehow, knowing that Burke was probably a killer just made the whole thing all the more thrilling.

"I got your message," Burke said. "What is this about?"

His voice suited the rest of him, vampire-soft and seductive. Everything inside her tightened with anticipation. This was the feeling a woman got when she decided to have sex with a devastating stranger, she thought. But Burke wasn't any random pickup. He had a major part in the play she had been scripting for the past few months—ever since he had arrived, unannounced, on the stage. True, the story line had changed from the original version but she was nothing if not adaptable. She had learned the trick early on in life when she had concluded that nothing on the streets could possibly be as bad as life with a violent stepfather and a drug-addicted mother. Her theory had proven correct.

The trendy South Lake Union bar was crowded, just as she had known it would be at this hour. The din of conversation, laughter and background music would provide privacy for the discussion she intended to conduct with Burke.

"Thank you for agreeing to meet me here," she said.

She was about to do something very daring, something she had never done before. But as the Witherspoon affirmation said, *We grow only when we dare to move out of our comfort zone.* She had always considered the affirmations to be downright silly, albeit great marketing tools. But she was willing to admit that this particular affirmation had some truth in it.

One thing was certain, if there was ever a time to take risks, this was it.

"Your message said that you wanted to talk about

something that was of mutual interest," Burke said. "What is it?"

She smiled, satisfied. "Good to know I was right about you, Burke. I pegged you as the sort of man who likes to go straight to the bottom line."

"What is the bottom line in this case?"

"Money," she said. "A lot of it." She paused for emphasis and lowered her voice. "Not as much as you would have had if your own plans had worked out the way you had hoped, but still, a lot of money. And an opportunity to make more."

Wariness sparked in Burke's eyes but his smile was polished and perfect.

"I have absolutely no idea what you're talking about," he said.

"Then you must think I'm as naive as Grace Elland."

The waitress appeared at the table and looked expectantly at Burke.

"What can I get for you?" she asked.

Burke glanced at Millicent's glass and raised a brow.

"Vodka martini," Millicent said. "Dry. Straight up. With an olive."

Burke smiled. "Sounds good."

"Got it," the waitress said. "I'll be right back with your cocktail."

Millicent waited until the woman had vanished into the crowd. Then she idly stirred her drink with the little plastic spear on which the olive was impaled.

"Let me give you some background," she said. "I don't have a CPA degree. I never went to college. But

I am very, very good when it comes to juggling money, and I'm very, very good with computers. I handled Witherspoon's taxes and his investments. I had access to Witherspoon's personal as well as his business accounts. He didn't like to be bothered with the small stuff of daily life. He was a Big Picture guy. I paid his bills—all of them, including those related to Nyla. I'm the one who transferred her allowance into her account on the first of every month."

Mild surprise and a hint of respect gleamed in Burke's eyes but he seemed more amused than alarmed.

"Interesting," he said. "But now you're out of a job."

"Not for long. Witherspoon's chief competition was Larson Rayner."

"So?"

"Larson has concluded that the easiest way to take Witherspoon's place in the motivational guru business is to recruit the very people who turned the Witherspoon Way into a powerhouse operation."

Burke nodded. "Hiring his competitor's people makes sense. I assume Rayner has made you an offer?"

"Yes. I told him I would be delighted to accept a position at Rayner Seminars. And then I thought about you."

"I'm listening."

"I know you were blackmailing Witherspoon for the last few months of his life because I was the one who transferred the money into a certain account earmarked Medical Expenses on the last day of every month."

"I repeat—I have no idea what you're talking about," Burke said.

But there was an edge on the words.

She ignored the interruption. "Witherspoon was very clever about it. When he created the account he told me that the money was being used to pay the costs of hospice care for an elderly relative. I wasn't suspicious at first. Witherspoon, being Witherspoon, wanted the very best private care for his dying aunt, and he could afford to pay for it."

"You should consider writing fiction for your next career, Miss Chartwell."

"Please, call me Millicent. You and I are going to be very close friends soon. To continue with my story, you were smart enough to keep the payments reasonable—just a few thousand dollars a month. Everyone knows that it's easy to spend that kind of money on private nursing care."

Burke's face remained impassive for a few seconds. In the shadowy light his eyes went gem-hard. But before he could say anything the waitress appeared with the martini.

When they were once again alone, Millicent took a sip of her cocktail and lowered the glass. She smiled.

"Let me give you the next chapter," she said. "The money you made with the blackmail scheme was just penny-ante stuff, wasn't it? You were after a much bigger prize—Nyla's inheritance. But that seems to be slipping away, doesn't it? If things don't work out the way you hoped, you may have to pull the plug on your current business plan and move on to another opportunity."

Burke considered that while he drank some of his martini.

"What do you know about my current business objective?" he asked.

"I'm aware of the real value of Witherspoon's estate. But aside from the nice house on Queen Anne, the car and some artwork, the bulk of his fortune has vanished into thin air." Millicent smiled. "The authorities suspect embezzlement but they'll never find the money."

Burke went very still. "Are you going to tell me that you were the one who made it disappear?"

She took another sip of the martini and lowered the glass. "I'm brilliant with money. Just ask Witherspoon. Oh, wait, you can't because he's dead, isn't he? Who knew that he had a secret addiction problem—gambling, to be precise."

"Thanks to you fiddling with his online accounts?"

"Yes." She tried to assume an air of modesty but she was fairly sure she did not succeed.

"You set it up so that it would look like Witherspoon was embezzling from his own company to pay his gambling debts." Burke whistled softly. "You're good, Miss Chartwell. Impressive."

"Thank you. But let me assure you that Sprague left a great deal of money behind, and that money is safe in an offshore account. What's more, I'm good enough to pull off the same operation a second time."

Comprehension lit Burke's eyes. "With Larson Rayner?"

She smiled and munched the olive.

"How?" Burke asked, suddenly intent.

Euphoria zinged through her. The dance of seduction was working. Now the real conversation could take place. She and Burke were two pros talking shop. This was so much more thrilling than seducing a random bar hookup.

"You'd be amazed at the kind of money that starts sloshing around when a successful motivational guru gets real traction," she said. "And there are so many ways to skim off the extra cash."

Burke frowned. "You're saying that Rayner is getting traction?"

"He has been successful all along, but now, with Witherspoon out of the picture, he's set to go into the big time. He's got the looks and the charisma. All he needs is a little fairy dust from Witherspoon's secret source. If everything works out, you and I can ride the gravy train until we decide to get off."

"Who supplies the fairy dust?"

She chuckled. "Grace Elland, of course. She's the one with the magic touch. She took Witherspoon to the top. There's no reason to think she can't perform the same trick again with Larson Rayner. What's more, Larson knows that. When he offered me a job today, he told me he was also making offers to Grace and Kristy. He wants Witherspoon's team."

"But Grace is the one he needs the most. What if she declines the offer?"

"Why would she do that? She needs a job. Larson will pay her double what she earned at Witherspoon and probably include a slice of the pie. She'll take the offer, believe me."

Burke swallowed some more of his martini and lounged into the corner of the booth.

She had him now. The one thing a professional con artist could not resist was the prospect of another big score. Running a successful con created a rush unlike any other.

"One question springs to mind," Burke said. "Why invite me to join you on the new gravy train? What do you want from me?"

"I know how to skim money off the top of any organization," she said. "But laundering the kind of cash that's sitting in that offshore account is more complicated. I need a partner."

"You want me to help you wash that money?"

"And the money we will acquire from Rayner's operation," she said. "He's set to go even higher than Witherspoon. I see our partnership as an ongoing enterprise for the two of us."

"Where does Nyla fit into this plan?"

Millicent waved that aside. "She doesn't."

Burke looked thoughtful. "You're saying I don't need her any longer."

"I know you planned to marry her for the money. Hell, the whole office, including Witherspoon, figured that out. But Nyla's inheritance has vanished, hasn't it? I'm the only one who knows where it is and how to get it. All we have to do is figure out how to bring it home and scrub it clean without making Nyla or the cops suspicious."

"You're stuck, aren't you?" Burke was amused. "You really do need someone to launder the money."

"Either that or I have to go live on some no-name island for the rest of my life. I like it here. Not much in the way of shopping on those no-name islands."

"I'd want a guarantee of a fifty-fifty split."

"Of course." Millicent raised her glass. "Like I said, partners."

Burke tapped one finger on the table. "What makes you think you can trust me?"

"Isn't it obvious? We need each other."

He drank some more of his martini while he considered that. It was time to tighten the leash, she thought.

"Here's the thing, Burke. I've got proof that you were blackmailing Witherspoon because I'm the one who made those monthly payments. I traced them to that account in New York months ago. That evidence will be sent to the police if I were to, say, suffer an unfortunate accident." Millicent used her fingers to make a very precise triangle around the base of her martini glass. "Proof of blackmail will put you right at the top of the suspect list in the Witherspoon murder."

Burke looked impressed. "I do believe that we have a partnership."

"Excellent." She pushed her empty glass aside and reached for her purse. "Would you care to go somewhere more private to celebrate?"

"Where do you suggest?"

"My apartment is within walking distance."

Burke smiled slowly. "That sounds very convenient."

Twenty-Seven

"You can't just give me this gorgeous bowl," Grace said. "It's too much."

"Too much what?" Julius asked.

"Too much of a gift," she shot back.

He drove into the parking space in the condo garage, shut down the engine and turned to look at her. She sat in the passenger seat, cradling the carefully wrapped art glass with both hands as if it were a priceless gem. It wasn't priceless. Granted, he had just paid far too much for a glass bowl that couldn't even be used to serve salad, but it wasn't priceless.

What was priceless was the look on Grace's face when he handed the art glass to her and told her that it was hers. She was still arguing.

"What am I going to do with that bowl?" he asked patiently. "I'm not into art glass. You're the one who picked out the damn thing, so I'm assuming you like it."

"I love it. It's gorgeous. I can see it now displayed under the right light in the right place in a room. It will glow like a big, multicolored diamond."

"Fine. Go ahead and display it any way you want."

She stared at him, shocked. "You mean you don't like it? You should have said something when we were looking at the auction items before the event. I would never have chosen a piece this pricey."

"It's not like there was any cheap art there to bid on. Look, it's a glass bowl. It's nice. But art is not my thing."

"Art is good for you. It stimulates the senses."

He looked at her for a long moment, savoring the sight of her sitting there in his car. In a few minutes she would be standing in the front hall of his condo. It was after midnight and neither of them had wanted to make the hour-long drive back to Cloud Lake. The only question was whether Grace would be sleeping in the guest bedroom or in his bed.

The low-grade fever that had been heating his blood since the night he met her rose a couple more degrees.

"Trust me," he said, "my senses are already running in overload condition. Not sure I could handle any more stimulation."

Her brows snapped together. "What are you talking about?"

He decided not to answer that question. Instead, he got out of the SUV, circled behind the vehicle and opened the door on the passenger side.

Grace handed the package to him with both hands.

"Hold this while I get out," she instructed. "And for goodness' sake, be careful with it."

He tucked the package under one arm. The bowl was surprisingly heavy. He reminded himself that large hunks of thick glass were always weighty objects.

With his free hand, he assisted Grace out of the high front seat. He was learning to enjoy watching her bail out of the vehicle. She never did it the same way twice but it was always interesting. Tonight her stiletto heels made the disembarkation process something of a high-wire balancing act. She negotiated the exit with her customary fluid grace, bouncing a little on the toe of her right foot before she got both feet on the ground.

"You need a ladder for this sucker," she said.

He smiled. "I've been meaning to ask you if you ever studied dance."

"Not unless you count aerobic exercise classes," she said. "Why?"

He closed the door of the SUV. "Just wondered. You move like someone who's had some training."

"Here, give me that bowl." She took the package from him.

He pocketed the keys. "I wasn't going to drop it."

"Maybe not, but it's clear that you are not going to treat this work of art with the proper respect." She held the package in both hands. "Besides, someone has to handle the suitcases."

"This is true."

He opened the cargo bay of the vehicle and smiled a little at the sight of the two bags inside. He liked the way his duffel looked sitting next to Grace's little roll-aboard suitcase. It was as if they belonged together, he decided.

He hauled both bags out of the SUV and closed the rear door.

"Elevator's that way," he said. He angled his jaw to indicate the center of the garage.

She started toward the stairwell and elevator lobby, clutching the package with great care.

"You know, if you really don't want to keep this bowl you could give it to one of your relatives," she said. "Or a close friend."

Her refusal to accept the bowl as a gift was starting to annoy him. "It's yours."

"Okay, okay, you don't have to bite my head off."

"I didn't bite your head off," he said. "I'm just stating a fact. The damn bowl is yours."

"Thank you."

Her excruciatingly polite tone was even more irritating.

"I can't believe we're arguing over a damn bowl," he said.

"It is a little weird, isn't it? The thing is, I've never owned an expensive piece of art."

"Neither have I, at least not as far as I know. The interior designer who did my condo spent a fortune on what she called finishing touches but I don't think any of it qualifies as art. Just expensive stuff."

"You're rich," Grace said. "If you don't collect art, what do you collect?"

"Money, I guess. I've never had the urge to collect anything else."

"Like I said, you're bored."

He was about to tell her that the one thing he had not been lately was bored—not around her—but the sound of rushing footsteps echoing in the stillness of the garage stopped him cold. Shadows shifted in the yellow glare of the fluorescents.

Two men dressed in black clothing exploded out of the dark valley between a car and the concrete wall. One moved toward Grace. The second attacker gripped a length of pipe in both hands. He lunged at Julius.

Julius dropped the duffel and the suitcase and sidestepped the swinging pipe. The length of heavy metal sliced harmlessly through the air at the place his rib cage had been a heartbeat earlier.

The attacker staggered back a step, caught his balance and tried for another swing. Julius rolled once across the floor, slamming into his assailant's legs. There was a solid thud and a grunt when the man hit the ground.

Julius got to his feet, grabbed the pipe and wrenched it out of the attacker's hand. The man on the ground barely noticed. He was too busy clutching at his midsection and trying to get some air into his lungs.

Julius whirled around and saw that the first man had Grace backed up against the wall. He held the point of a knife at her throat.

"Don't move, bitch," the knife man hissed. "We just want to have a little quality time with your boyfriend. It'll all be over real quick."

"It's over now," Grace said. She looked at Julius.

The knife man automatically glanced over his shoulder. He looked stunned when he realized that his companion was groaning on the floor of the garage.

"Don't move another inch," he snarled at Julius. "I'll cut the bitch's throat. I swear I'll do it."

Julius knew that panic and adrenaline were driving the bastard now. The situation on the ground had shifted on him. He and his partner were rapidly losing control.

Grace was still clutching the package that contained the art glass. She rammed it straight up in front of herself, raising it high. The force of the upward momentum pushed the attacker's arm aside, briefly deflecting the blade.

She kicked the knife man in the groin, the toe of her stiletto striking its target with a speed and accuracy that told Julius it was not the first time she had practiced the maneuver.

But she could not keep her balance in the heels. She dropped the package on the concrete floor and went down hard next to it.

The knife man staggered backward, clutching at his privates. Julius kicked his legs out from under him and grabbed his arm, twisting hard.

The knife man screamed. His blade clattered on the concrete floor.

Grace kicked off her shoes, scrambled to her feet and sprinted toward the fire alarm on the wall. She pulled it hard, filling the garage with screeching noise.

The door of the stairwell burst open. Julius saw the familiar face of the night-shift doorman, Steve.

"The cops are on the way," Steve yelled above the shrill sound of the alarm.

The combination of that news and the unrelenting shrieks acted like a tonic on the two assailants. The one who had wielded the pipe staggered to his feet with astonishing alacrity and charged toward the alley door.

The knife man tried to follow but Julius grabbed him and swung him around.

"You pulled a knife on her," Julius said. "That's not allowed."

He delivered two quick, hard chops. The knife man went down again. This time he stayed down.

Julius briefly considered trying to snag the one who had brought the pipe to the party but gave it up as a lost cause. The bastard had a head start.

"We've got the security camera video to give to the cops," Steve shouted over the alarm. "I saw them attack you but it took me a few minutes to get down here."

Julius nodded and looked at Grace. She was bending down to examine the package that contained what was left of the art glass. The lumpy condition of the wrapping paper was mute testimony to the fact that the bowl had not survived in one piece.

She straightened and turned around. Julius opened

his arms. She walked straight to him. He hugged her close.

"It was so beautiful," she said against his chest.

"Yes, it was," he said. "I was wrong about it."

"How is that?"

"I thought that it would never serve any useful purpose."

Sirens sounded in the distance.

Twenty-Eight

You know," Julius said, "I was hoping this evening would end somewhat differently."

Grace met his eyes in the mirror, aware that her emotions were all over the place. Among other things she was experiencing an irrational urge to laugh. It was the adrenaline, she thought, or, rather, the aftereffects. The fierce rush of biochemicals that had flooded her bloodstream during the course of the assault in the garage was fading, leaving her shaky and unnerved.

She was pretty sure that Julius had to be buzzed on similar discordant sensations, but if that was true, he was doing a much better job of concealing it. More practice, maybe.

The camouflage of calm control was not quite perfect, however. She was sure she could detect a little ice and fire in his eyes.

They were standing side by side at the twin sinks in the master bath of Julius's condo. The police had taken their statements, arrested the knife man and departed. They had promised to call with any updates.

She contemplated Julius's reflection in the mirror and wondered why he looked so disturbingly sexy. The last thing she ought to be thinking about at that moment was sex. But she found herself fascinated, not just by the heat in his eyes but by small details—his rumpled hair and the careless way his black tie hung loose around his neck.

En route to the huge bathroom he had removed his tux jacket and tossed it over the back of a chair. His ebony-and-gold cuff links were sitting on the black granite countertop, gleaming in the glow of the bathroom light fixtures. The collar of his crisp white shirt was open, revealing a hint of dark, curling chest hair. There were some smudges here and there, but on the whole he reminded her of James Bond after a tussle with one of the bad guys.

Breathe.

Not that she was having an anxiety attack, not yet, at any rate. That would probably come later, in the middle of the night. Stupid damn nerves. She reminded herself that she had packed her emergency meds.

One decision had just been made—the big decision of the day—the issue of where she would spend the night. She would have to sleep in Julius's guest bedroom. She could not abide the thought of waking up in his bed in the midst of a full-blown panic attack. Not the most romantic scenario. If she was going to succumb to a case of what the Victorians had called shattered nerves, she wanted to be alone when it happened.

But in the meantime, she could not seem to stop thinking about sex. She wanted to hurl herself into Julius's arms again, just as she had following the assault downstairs. But this time she wanted to carry him off into his bedroom and throw herself on top of him.

Breathe.

She exhaled slowly, with some control, and took stock of her own image in the mirror. She did not look at all sexy. She looked like she'd been dragged through a couple of alleys and dumped on a back step.

The hair she had so carefully pinned up into a sophisticated knot had come down in the course of the short, violent struggle in the garage. Her dress was ruined. The skirt had ripped open at the seam and split halfway up one thigh. She figured that had probably happened when she kicked the knife-wielding attacker between the legs. The sides and back of the garment were torn and stained with garage floor dirt. She knew that when she took the dress off she would find bruises on her hip and shoulder. She had scraped one knee on the concrete. It oozed a little blood. The heel of her left palm was raw. The soles of her bare feet were covered in grime.

She was uncomfortable but the real pain from her

bruises and scrapes hadn't struck yet. That would probably come later, like the nightmare and the anxiety attack.

In addition to sex, she longed for a shower. She understood the latter. She needed a shower. It was the desire to ravish Julius that she could not wrap her head around. She had never wanted to be in a man's arms the way she wanted to be in Julius's arms tonight.

Breathe.

She gripped the front of the sink with both hands to steady herself.

"How, exactly, did you expect the evening to end?" she asked.

"Hell, I don't know," Julius said. He considered the question briefly. "Maybe with a nightcap to celebrate the fact that for the first time ever no one fell asleep during the Speech from Hell."

"A nightcap," she repeated without inflection.

She focused on that thought, keenly aware that Julius was watching her in the mirror. His mask of cool control slipped a little more, revealing the stark hunger in his eyes. The stirring sensation deep inside was becoming intense. The atmosphere crackled with tension. She tightened her grip on the sink.

"Don't tell me you couldn't use a drink," Julius said. "I sure as hell need one."

She nodded slowly. "A drink is an excellent suggestion. But I think I need a shower first." She shuddered. "That creep in the garage touched me."

Julius's eyes went stone cold.

"They were waiting for us," he said. "We were not

just a couple of random victims. They were there because of us."

She shivered. "The one with the knife said something about spending a little quality time with my boyfriend."

"Unfortunately, that leaves a lot of room for interpretation. You've got a stalker but I've got a few old enemies of my own." Julius frowned in thought and then shook his head. "Can't see any of them resorting to low-end street talent like that pair in the garage, though. The people I've left on the ground can afford better." He paused. "Or they would do the job themselves."

"I'm sure neither of those two men was my stalker. I've never met either of them."

"Doesn't mean someone didn't hire them to take me out of the picture," Julius said somewhat absently.

She stared at his reflection, shock and horror shifting through her as his meaning sunk in.

"Because of me," she whispered. "I'm the one who brought those two down on us."

He met her stunned eyes in the mirror.

"No," he said. "Not another damn word about being responsible. Those two thugs and whoever hired them—if it turns out that they were hired—are responsible. No one else. Understood?"

The words held the implacable force of a command.

She looked at his reflection. "Julius."

He put his hands on her shoulders and turned her toward him. His mouth came down on hers. He kissed her with a ruthless, driving need that acted like an accelerant on a flame.

She did not try to resist. She did not want to resist.

"Yes," she said against his mouth. "Yes."

She clutched at him, trying to wrap herself around him. She heard the torn seam of her dress rip farther up her thigh.

Julius took the kiss to a deeper, even more explosive level. She felt his hands at her waist and then they went lower. He found the ripped seam, gripped delicate fabric and tore it all the way to the top of her thigh. He pushed the tattered hem of the garment up to her waist, exposing the thin triangle of lace and silk.

The next thing she knew he was cupping her bottom and lifting her up against his erection. She could feel the hard length of him beneath the fabric of his trousers.

She was breathing faster now, in the grip of a rush that was unlike anything she had ever experienced. She needed the release that she knew Julius could give her. A part of her was shocked by her volatile reaction but another part—the part that was in the ascendant at that moment—was thrilled. This was a new side of herself, a side she had always suspected existed, one she had searched for from time to time in the past but never found. This was real passion, the kind that made lovers do mad, crazy, over-the-top stuff in the heat of the moment.

She struggled with the front of Julius's shirt and finally got it open. Fascinated, she spread her fingers across his chest, savoring the warmth of his skin and the contours of the muscles beneath. He held her easily, as if she were weightless.

He set her on her feet again just long enough to lower the zipper at the back of her dress. He peeled the front of the gown down to her waist and tugged the long, narrow sleeves off her arms.

He had her bra unhooked before she realized his intention. His hands closed around her breasts, his palms deliciously rough on her nipples.

She was intensely aware of everything about him. She could tell from the harsh rasp of his breathing that he was fighting for control and she gloried in her own feminine power. But at the same time she was lost in the waves of excitement. She could not wait to see what awaited her at the end of the wild ride.

He got his fingers inside the bikini panties and moved his palms down over her hips, sweeping away the lacy scrap of fabric. He tossed the panties aside and wrapped his hands around her waist.

He lifted her up again and set her on the edge of the counter. The shock of the cool granite against her backside made her take a sharp breath.

"Cold," she said.

"Not for long," he promised.

She heard the whisper of leather against brass and knew that he had just unfastened his belt. The next thing she heard was the slide of his zipper. When she looked down she saw the hard, heavy length of him. For the first time she experienced something that might have constituted a qualm.

"Oh, my," she said.

He opened a nearby drawer and took out a small

foil packet. He got the packet open and quickly sheathed himself.

He put his hands on her knees, parted her legs and moved between her thighs. When he found her melting core she shuddered and clutched his shoulders. He stroked slowly, deliberately, against her clitoris. She strained toward him, trying to capture his fingers inside her. She needed him inside her. He teased her unmercifully until she was so desperate, so sensitized, that she could scarcely breathe.

"You are so wet," he said against her throat. "So ready for me."

"Now," she ordered. She used her grip on his shoulders to urge him closer. "Inside me. Do it now."

She made it an order, not a plea.

He guided himself into her, taking his time so that she was aware of every inch of him. Never had she felt so stretched, so full. She hovered on the brink of a release that she knew would change everything. All the questions she'd had about this secret side of herself were about to be answered.

She tightened around him. Her head tipped back. She closed her eyes against the glare of the bathroom lights and dug her ruined nails into the muscles of his shoulders.

Julius groaned, anchored her rear with his hands and began to piston within her. She fought him when he retreated, closing herself ever more tightly around him in an effort to make him stay deep inside her.

But he was as determined to control the cadence as she was, and he was so much stronger.

Stronger—yes—but she knew that he was also vulnerable. She could feel the rigid tension in the muscles of his shoulders. She knew that every time she strained to hold him he was forced to use more control to master himself.

A moment later the wildfire of her release flashed through her. Julius was pulled into the vortex. She held him close as he drove into her one last time.

The hoarse growl of his exultant satisfaction echoed against the tiled walls. He throbbed heavily inside her for an endless moment.

When it was over he sagged over her, bracing his hands on the counter on either side of her hips. He sucked in deep breaths for a moment. Then he raised his head.

"That," he said, "was how I had hoped the evening would end."

Twenty-Nine

Julius eased out of her body. She winced a little because she was still so sensitive and he was so big. He searched her face and then lifted her gently down off the counter. Her legs felt weak. She grabbed the edge of the sink to steady herself.

"Are you all right?" he asked.

She managed a weak smile. "Aside from the fact that I look like I've been run over by a truck, do you mean? Absolutely."

"Got an affirmation for this?"

"How about *The truck that doesn't kill you only makes you stronger*?"

He nodded with a sage air. "A very uplifting thought." He checked his own reflection, grimaced and started to peel off his rumpled and stained shirt.

"You may have been hit by a truck," he said, "but I look like I was standing on the tracks when the train went past."

The crazy urge to laugh rose up inside her again. She managed to control it but she could not help smiling at Julius's reflection.

"You don't look so bad for a man who caught a bad guy this evening," she said.

"Only after you took him down with that shot to his balls. And in stilettos, no less." For the first time, Julius smiled with icy satisfaction. "I hate to say this because I sure as hell don't want to encourage that kind of exercise, but we made a damn good team tonight."

She smiled, too. "Yes, we did."

Julius's smile vanished. He watched her intently. "Where did you learn those self-defense moves?"

"It was part of the therapy that Mom prescribed after I stumbled into the Trager murder. I was having trouble sleeping. Nightmares."

"Sure," he said, as if sleep that was ripped apart by images of blood and panic were commonplace and only to be expected.

"I saw a shrink for a while but Mom thought the self-defense classes would give me a sense of control. I've kept up with the training."

"It shows," Julius said. "You move like someone who has studied dance or gymnastics or martial arts."

"I'm not the only one who has had some training," she said. "You're good. Very good. The Marines?"

"That's where it started. Afterward I did some martial arts to stay in shape. Like you, I keep up with the exercises." Julius paused. "Back in the day when I was Harley's fixer—"

"You mean when you were his executive administrative assistant," she put in smoothly.

That surprised a short, harsh laugh out of Julius.

"Right," he said. "What I was about to say is that fixing things for Harley Montoya occasionally got complicated. Some of his development projects were located in regions around the world where you could not always count on the support of local law enforcement. In addition, whenever Harley traveled to foreign job sites he was a target for kidnappers. Grabbing foreign executives and holding them for ransom is a big business in a number of places around the globe."

She nodded. "You were Harley's fixer and his bodyguard. That explains a lot."

"First time I've gotten into a fight here in Seattle, though." Julius glanced down at his crumpled shirt. "Can't remember the last time I had trouble in a parking garage."

She smiled faintly. "They do say that parking garages are dangerous places."

"Yeah, I've heard that." He studied her. "Are you sure you're okay?"

She turned back to her image in the mirror. "I need a shower."

"So do I." He glanced at the big, elegantly tiled shower with its array of gleaming faucets, hand sprayers and water jets. "I think there's room enough for two."

"You *think* there's room for two?"

"Never actually conducted an experiment."

She smiled, pleased. "No time like the present."

Thirty

Millicent pulled the tumbled sheets up around her waist and watched the vampire dress. The sex had been every bit as good as she had known it would be, fueled by the knowledge that, even though she controlled him for now, he was still dangerous.

Burke finished fastening his belt and came to stand at the side of the bed.

"That was definitely interesting," he said.

"Yes, it was." She stretched her arms high over her head and yawned. "Maybe we'll do it again sometime."

He smiled. "I'll look forward to it."

She settled herself more comfortably on the pillows, not bothering to cover her breasts. She had, after all, paid a lot of money for them. They were works of art and she liked to display them in the best possible light.

"One last question," she said.

He paused at the door of the bedroom. "What is it?"

"I know that you were blackmailing Witherspoon but I wasn't able to find out what you had on him. Care to satisfy my curiosity? I must admit he always struck me as squeaky clean."

"No one is squeaky clean." Burke smiled. "Least of all Sprague Witherspoon. Shortly before I started dating Nyla, I did my research. I stumbled into the family secret almost by accident."

"Well? What is the Witherspoon family secret?"

"Long before he reinvented himself as Sprague Witherspoon, rising star of the motivational seminar world, Witherspoon was someone else—Nelson Clydemore—small-time con and, eventually, ex-con."

It took a second before the penny dropped. Then she started to laugh.

"Oh, that's rich," she said. "That's just so entertaining. If only Kristy and Grace knew. They both believed that he was the real deal—a true believer in the positive-thinking crap."

"Clydemore did three years for fraud," Burke said. "According to the court records, he ran a pyramid scheme. It all fell apart when some of his clients got suspicious of results that were too good to be true and contacted the Feds. Clydemore went to prison and served his time. When he got out he assumed a new identity. He became Sprague Witherspoon."

"Amazing. Does Nyla know about her father's past?"

"No. She was born after he metamorphosed into

Witherspoon, Motivational Guru. There's no indication that Nyla's mother or Sprague's second wife knew the truth, either."

"That explains why Witherspoon paid blackmail," Millicent said. "You threatened to reveal his past. It would have destroyed his business."

"Sure. But that's not why he paid off on time every month."

Millicent smiled. "He wanted to keep the secret from Nyla."

"He knew that if he was exposed as an ex-con who had once run pyramid schemes, she would have been devastated and publicly humiliated. Their relationship was already tense. He didn't want her to become any more bitter and resentful toward him."

"I see." Millicent made a face. "Family dynamics can get very weird."

"Yes," Burke said, "they can. But sometimes they can be quite profitable."

He disappeared into the living room. A moment later she heard the door close behind him.

Definitely dangerous, she thought. But then, it wouldn't be nearly as much fun if there was not some risk involved.

She pushed aside the covers, rose and went into the bathroom to clean up. When she was finished she put on a robe and slippers and settled down with her laptop. Managing a lot of money in various fake accounts designed to throw the authorities off track was hard work.

The security intercom buzzed some time later. She

smiled. He had come back for more. No surprise there. She was very good at sex, and men got addicted very quickly to good sex.

She closed down the laptop, got to her feet and crossed the room to welcome back the vampire.

Thirty-One

Julius stood beneath one of the showers and watched Grace enjoy the blasts of hot water that were striking her from all directions. She looked sleek and sexy with rivulets running off the points of her delicate breasts and disappearing into the crease that divided her buttocks. Her hair was plastered to her head and her eyes were closed against the force of the water.

He wanted to brace her against the wall and lose himself in her again but he knew that she was exhausted. He should have been exhausted, too. And he would be, eventually, he assured himself. The hard, fast, amazing sex had taken off some of the edge but it would be a while before he could sleep.

He was coming down from the wildfire high generated by the combination of the brutal encounter in the garage and the primal mating act that had followed. But now he was aware of another sensation, one that was equally elemental.

"I'm hungry," he said. "And I'm ready for that drink. What about you?"

Grace opened her eyes. He could see her taking stock of her current status. A trace of surprise crossed her face.

"I'm hungry, too," she said. She wrinkled her nose. "Weird."

"Not when you consider how much energy we expended this evening." He moved out of the shower, allowing himself one last survey of his private mermaid. She looked so good standing there, nude, in the artificial waterfall.

He made himself turn away and finish toweling off. When he was done he wrapped the towel around his waist. Absently, he used his fingers to rake his hair straight back from his forehead. A sense of unfinished business made him pause.

Grace turned off the shower. He handed her a fresh towel and watched while she hastily wrapped it around herself. When she realized he was still looking at her she raised her brows.

"Something wrong?" she asked. "Aside from the fact that we got mugged tonight, that is."

"Not sure yet." He opened a nearby closet and took out the brown, freshly laundered robe inside. "Here, you can use this." He eyed her left knee, which was still oozing blood. "We'd better cover that. Have a seat."

She tugged on the robe. "Thanks, but I can deal with the bandaging."

He was not in a mood to argue. He picked her up and set her on the edge of the counter. She sighed but did not protest.

He eased aside the flap of the robe and examined the raw scrape on her knee.

"It doesn't look too bad," he said. "But I'll bet it hurts like hell."

"A little," she admitted. "But there's no permanent damage."

He opened a drawer and removed a tube of antibiotic cream. She stiffened when he used a cotton swab to dab the cream on her injured knee but she didn't say anything.

He took out a box containing several sizes of bandages and selected one that looked like it would cover the scrape. He plastered it neatly in place.

When he looked up from the task he found her watching him with a very intent expression. The soft, seductive intimacy of the situation stirred his senses. He tried to shake off the rising tide of desire. She had been in a fight. She was hurt and would soon be feeling a lot more pain. She had to be exhausted. The sex would have to wait.

"That should take care of the wound," he said. "You'll probably be bruised tomorrow but I can't do much about that."

"Thank you," she said. There was a husky rasp to her voice and a sultry heat in her eyes.

He had to be strong for both of them, he decided.

He lifted her down off the counter and set her on her feet. "I'm going to make a couple of sandwiches and dig out the whiskey bottle while you're finishing up in here."

"Okay." She fiddled with the sash of the robe, managing to briefly expose one dainty breast. "This robe is . . . big."

"It's mine," he said. "Sorry, I don't have one your size."

She appeared pleased by that information.

"Good," she said.

"Good?"

She smiled and looked a little smug. "Never mind."

Women. Sometimes a man needed a translator.

"I'll go make the sandwiches," he said.

When in doubt, talk about food.

He left the bathroom and crossed the bedroom to the big walk-in closet. He opened a drawer and pulled out a clean black crewneck T-shirt, briefs and a pair of well-worn jeans. He did not bother with a belt.

Barefooted, he went down the hall to the kitchen, turned on some lights and opened the refrigerator. He had alerted his housekeeper that he would be spending the night in town. The Remarkable Renee, who came in once a week to clean, had gone grocery shopping for him. In addition to the wedge of cheddar cheese, dill pickles, bread and mayonnaise there was also a carton of eggs and a few other items.

Making the cheddar-and-dill-pickle sandwiches gave him time to think about something other than the fact that Grace was with him and that they had just had the best sex he'd had in a very long time, possibly in forever. Definitely in forever, he concluded.

By the time Grace came down the hall enveloped in his robe, her feet bare, he had the sandwiches and the whiskey waiting on the long, gleaming sweep of black granite countertop that served as his kitchen table. It also did duty as a lunch and dinner table when he was in the city. He never used the polished teak dining table and chairs in the dining room.

"Check your email," he said.

She stopped, bewildered, for a beat. And then her eyes narrowed a little as understanding hit her.

"Crap," she said. "Do you think . . . ?"

"Check it."

"I had my phone off for your speech and forgot to turn it back on afterward, what with all the excitement."

She went to the table where she had left her evening bag and took out her phone. She powered up the device and studied her messages. When she raised her eyes she looked bemused.

"No email from the stalker," she said. "But what does that tell us?"

"It tells us that the stalker tried to send another kind of message tonight. He or she might not know yet that it didn't get delivered as planned. I doubt if the guy with the pipe called his client to report that there had been a few problems and that his pal is sitting in jail."

Grace took a deep breath and climbed up onto one of the high stools. She watched him pour the whiskey as if she were mesmerized by the action.

"You think that there's a connection between what happened tonight and whoever has been sending me those emails, don't you?" she asked.

He swallowed some whiskey and lowered the glass. "I'm going on that assumption until proven otherwise."

She propped an elbow on the counter and rested her chin in her hand.

"You're in this mess because of me."

"Stop," he ordered. "We've already had this conversation. I'm with you because I want to be with you."

"Yes, but—"

"Shut up and drink your whiskey."

She reached for the glass.

He walked around the edge of the counter, sat down beside her and picked up a sandwich. "There is a slight possibility that tonight was all about me. You met my ex this evening."

Grace paused, her whiskey halfway to her mouth. She stared at him, clearly shocked.

"Surely she wouldn't hire two thugs to beat you up."

"Probably not," he agreed. "Diana has led a rather sheltered life. She wouldn't know how to find that kind of muscle on the street."

Grace gave him an odd look. "Who *would* know how to hire the sort of creeps who attacked us tonight?"

"Good question." He took a bite out of his sandwich. "I'm thinking it's probably the same bastard who isn't afraid to handle a dead rat."

"My stalker."

"Yeah." He took another bite and reflected on the evening's events while he munched.

"Mind if I ask a personal question?" Grace said after a moment.

He shrugged. "Go for it."

"You said earlier that the Hastings family company was digging its own grave. Do you really believe that?"

"Hastings is in bad shape and I'm sure the problems are inside."

"Would Edward Hastings be capable of sending a couple of jerks to punish you with a beating?"

"If Ed blames me for his problems, it's quite possible that he'd take drastic measures. But he and I go back a ways. I'm the one who hired him after he had a falling-out with his father and his uncles. Ed wanted to reboot Hastings and take it into the twenty-first century. But the old guard wouldn't let go. So he walked."

"He left Hastings and went to work for you."

"Yeah, for about two years. Then his father had a heart attack and was forced to retire. The uncles realized they couldn't handle Hastings on their own. They asked Ed to come back and take control of the company. He accepted the offer. Hastings started sailing into troubled waters a few months later. My gut tells me that if Ed was convinced that I was behind his troubles, it's a lot more likely that he would walk into my office and take a swing at me himself."

"He wouldn't hire someone to do that?"

"If he did hire someone to do the job he would have

employed higher quality talent. I taught him that if you do use a fixer, you buy the best."

Grace looked at him, eyes widening. "Wow. That's cold."

He shrugged and finished the sandwich. He refused to pretend to be something other than what he was—not with Grace. He'd tried to be someone else once before with Diana. Things had not gone well.

Grace drank some more whiskey with a meditative air and lowered the glass. "Maybe the police will be able to get some useful information out of the guy with the knife."

Julius ran the scenarios in his head the way he did when he was considering an investment, looking for the stuff that was hiding just out of sight in the shadows.

"My guess is that the guy with the knife won't be able to tell the cops much about who hired him," he said. "The deal would have been a cash transaction. No names. No identities. No good descriptions. What with one thing and another, I think we need to try another angle."

"Such as?"

"We need to find a way to draw the stalker out of hiding."

"How do we do that?" Grace asked.

"I'm not sure yet. But one thing is obvious—the bastard has a reason for stalking you. We have to find out what that reason is."

"Well, if it's Nyla, we know she wants the money she thinks I stole from her father's business. I suppose

I could offer to talk to her about it, but there's not much room for negotiation because I don't have anything to offer."

"What if the stalker's goal isn't the money?"

Grace drank some of her whiskey a little too quickly. She sputtered, coughed and lowered the glass. "What else could it be?"

"You're sure there's no ex in the picture who might have become obsessed with you?"

"Stalkers are by definition delusional and crazy," Grace said. "I suppose it's possible that someone from my past has gone off the rails and decided to fixate on me, but I have to tell you, it's highly unlikely."

"I need a list."

She blinked. "Of all the men I've dated in the past?"

He smiled. "That many?"

She grimaced. "I wish."

"Relax, I don't think we need to go back to your high school prom date."

"That's good because I'm pretty sure Andrew isn't my stalker."

"Andrew?"

"My date for the prom. I told you, he spent the evening whining to me because he had wanted to take Jennifer to the prom but she declined. He was deeply depressed about the situation. He asked my advice on how to attract her attention."

"Did you tell him to think positive?"

"Pretty much," Grace said. "First, I told him that Jennifer was all wrong for him. He didn't want to hear that so I reminded him that he had a genius for computers. I told him to invent an addictive online game, get very rich and then go look up Jennifer."

"Did that advice work?"

"Partially. Andrew did invent a successful social media program. He did an IPO that was valued at a few billion dollars and he did get very rich. But he didn't marry Jennifer, which is a good thing because they would have been very unhappy together. He married someone else, instead—another very nice, very smart geek. It was a much better match."

"What happened to Jennifer?"

"She married well and often. She is now on husband number three, I believe, and living in a mansion on Mercer Island. There is, according to Irene, a very big boat parked in the water in front of the house." Grace frowned at the half-empty glass of whiskey. "I'm rambling, aren't I? Way too chatty. I may crash soon."

"That's a good thing," Julius said.

He drank some more of his own whiskey, letting the heat of the liquor relax him.

Grace made a visible effort to concentrate. "About this list you want me to make."

He put down his glass. "I'm not asking for the names of your old boyfriends. What I want is a list of everyone who was closely connected to Sprague Witherspoon—his business and his family."

"You're convinced that whatever is going on in my world is connected to his murder, aren't you?"

"I think it starts there. The vodka bottle thing can no longer be classified as a coincidence."

"No," she said. "Probably not. Okay, I'll make up a list. But I can't do it tonight. I can't seem to focus."

"Think you can sleep?"

She paused in mid-yawn and looked at him with a considering expression.

"What are my options?" she asked.

"Left side of the bed or the right side of the bed."

"Choices, choices."

Julius was watching from the shadows of the big bed as she emerged from the bathroom in a pretty yellow nightgown. She moved, wraithlike, across the room and climbed under the covers on the left side.

He turned out the lights and moved closer to her. She tensed a little when his arm went around her waist. He kissed her shoulder.

"Sleep," he said.

"Okay," she said.

And she did.

Thirty-Two

The old dream rose out of the depths on a dark tide of panic.

. . . She tried to control her breathing. She did not want the boy to realize that she was terrified. Her heart was pounding so hard she was afraid he might hear it.

The boy seemed frozen with horror. She gripped his thin shoulder with one hand. In her other hand she clutched the neck of the vodka bottle. Together she and the boy listened to the monster come down the stairs. Each thud of the boots sent a tremor through both of them.

The narrow beam of the killer's flashlight lanced through the well of night and splashed across the plastic-shrouded body. Then it probed into a far corner of the basement. He was searching for the boy. As soon as he turned around he would see them hiding in the shadows.

"Run," she said to the boy.

She used her grip on his shoulder to haul him out from under the staircase and propel him toward the stairs. Her stern voice and the physical shove she gave him combined to break through his paralysis.

He charged up the stairs toward the open door.

She followed, taking the steps two at a time. Trager yelled at her. She did not stop.

And then he was on the stairs behind her, moving so fast she knew she could not outrun him. He was so much bigger and stronger.

The boy reached the top of the steps. He paused and looked back.

"Go," she said again. "Don't stop."

The boy disappeared into the gloom that infused the atmosphere beyond the doorway.

Trager caught her jean jacket. She was trapped. She smashed the vodka bottle against the railing, creating a jagged blade. She slashed wildly, felt the resistance when the sharp glass struck skin and bone. Trager screamed. There was blood everywhere.

The crimson rain splashed her clothes, her hands . . .

"Grace. Grace, it's all right. You're safe, I've got you. Just a dream."

It was Julius's voice, pulling her out of the dark fog. She came awake, shivering as she always did after the nightmare. Her eyes snapped open and she gasped for breath. Someone was holding her down—pinning her to the bed.

"No." She struggled, frantic to get free.

Julius released her instantly. She bolted upright, pushed the covers aside and swung her legs over the side of the bed. She tried to go into her breathing routine.

Should have slept in the guest bedroom. Shouldn't have taken the risk. What had she been thinking?

"Sorry," she said. Her voice was tight and thin. "Old dream. Haven't had it in a long time, but ever since I found Sprague's body—"

"I understand," Julius said. "Been there."

His voice was calm and steady, as if he were accustomed to being awakened by a woman who was emerging from a nightmare. No, she thought. He was talking about himself.

"You know something about nightmares," she said.

"Oh, yeah."

The breathing exercises weren't working. She lunged to her feet and grabbed the robe that she had left on the wall hook. She looked out the window. It was still dark, still raining, but the cityscape glittered and sparkled in the night.

Breathe.

She turned and watched Julius climb out of bed. He was wearing the T-shirt and briefs he'd put on after the shower. She was suddenly very conscious of the fact that she was enveloped in his robe.

"I know this sounds weird," she said, "but I need to get some air. I need to move. I need to get *outside*."

"Not a problem." He pulled on the jeans he'd left on a nearby chair. "Got meds?"

He sounded so matter-of-fact she knew that he'd meant it when he said that he'd been there.

"Yes," she whispered. "My purse." Desperate to appear normal, she tried to inject some brittle humor into her voice. "I never leave—"

"You never leave home without them. Neither do I. Haven't had to use them in years but I keep them handy."

That reassured her as nothing else could have done in that moment. He really did understand. But the terrible jittery sensation and the tightness in her chest were not improving.

"I'll use them if I need them," she said, "but I think I'll be okay if I can just get through the door—outside."

She rushed into the vast living room. The light coming through the wall of windows was sufficient to guide her to the balcony slider. Julius got there first. He reached out to open the door. His fingers brushed against hers. She jerked back.

"Sorry," she said.

"It's okay."

He unlocked the slider and pulled it aside.

The door at the top of the stairs was open. She had to get through it. There was no other way to escape.

She stepped out onto the balcony. Julius followed her out into the chilled night.

She gripped the railing and went into the breathing exercises.

Julius stood beside her and waited calmly, as if there were nothing unusual about a date who had panic attacks and needed to go outdoors in the middle of the night.

Slowly she got herself under control.

"Sorry," she whispered again. "Among other things, this is really embarrassing."

"No," he said. "It's not. Are the dreams getting worse?"

"Sprague's body. The stalker. The damn vodka bottle. The rat. The trapped feeling. It's been a very heavy couple of weeks. I should have known better than to think I could get away with sleeping in your bed. I never spend the night with . . . with a date."

Gradually her pulse slowed. Her breathing calmed.

When she was sure she was back under control she released her death grip on the railing and straightened.

"Damn," she said softly. "I hate these crappy panic attacks."

"I know how you feel. I told you, I've been there."

"For me it all goes back to that day in the basement at the asylum," she said.

"Reason enough for an anxiety attack."

"Trager tried to stop me." She sucked in a deep breath. "When I ran up the stairs, he grabbed my jacket. I was trapped. I knew that he was going to kill me."

"But you slashed his face with a broken bottle. You escaped."

"Yes. If I hadn't grabbed that bottle—"

"But you did grab the bottle. You saved yourself and the boy."

She took in another deep, square breath and let it out slowly.

"I've been mildly claustrophobic ever since that day.

But that's not the worst part. I can handle elevators and airplanes so long as they are in motion. The worst part is the dream. The real bad attacks are always linked to it."

"But you never know when it will strike. That's why you never let a date spend the night."

She nodded, mute.

"Nights were always the worst for me, too." Julius gripped the railing beside her. "It's been better in the past few years. I did my time with the shrinks and with meds. But once in a while it all comes roaring back."

She looked at him. "No decent person could go to war and not be changed."

He leaned on the railing and gazed out over the glowing city. "Things looked different to me afterward."

"Because you were different."

He nodded. "But for a while I made the mistake of trying to pretend that nothing had changed. It was time to move forward with my life and all my big plans. And that's just what I did. Got the job with Harley. Learned from him. Started my own business. Got rich. Got married."

"You were determined to be normal," she said.

"Absolutely determined."

"You set an objective and you pursued it," she said. "Is that why your marriage fell apart? Because you were focused on trying to get back to normal?"

"No," he said. "My marriage fell apart because I was not the man Diana wanted me to be. Not her fault.

I had fooled both of us into thinking I could become that man. Diana is a beautiful woman and she is also a very nice person, at least she is when she isn't attacking my dates in the women's room."

Grace managed a weak laugh. "But otherwise—"

"Otherwise, she's a good person. But I think I was attracted to her mostly because she seemed to fit so perfectly into my fantasy of a new life."

"She completed the normal scenario."

"Right. It took me a while to accept that there is no reset button when it comes to normal. And it soon became clear to Diana that I was never going to fit into her definition of normal, either. The more she tried to transform me into the kind of husband she wanted, the harder I worked to build Arkwright Ventures. I used my business the way an addict uses drugs."

"You pushed each other away," Grace said.

"I knew that I was losing her and that it was my fault. Then I started having the nightmares again. Diana was frightened. I think she also found the situation embarrassing."

"Embarrassing?"

"She'd had to overcome a lot of objections from friends and family to marry me. My money got me through the front door of her world but it didn't give me the social polish, the education and the connections required to really fit in. Diana did her best to smooth the transition. I learned a lot from her. She taught me how to dress and how to pretend to enjoy a cocktail party or a reception. But it soon became clear to both of us that I wasn't going to go through some magical transformation."

Grace smiled. "You probably also made it clear that you weren't going to waste a lot of time trying to be someone else."

Julius's mouth kicked up at one corner. "Busted. You're right. I think the fact that I might've been having some post-traumatic stress issues was just one more piece of data confirming that she had made a mistake. She felt she couldn't confide to friends or family. But Edward Hastings was close enough to the situation to see what was happening. She turned to him. It worked out well for both of them."

"What about you?"

"I had to acknowledge that I was a failure in the long-term-relationship department, but the nasty little truth is that another part of me was relieved. I could finally focus on my obsession."

"Right. Your business. It never asked questions. Never tried to change you. Never wondered why you came home late at night. But in the end you found out what every addict learns—there's always a dark side to your drug of choice."

"Yep. The more money I made, the less satisfying it was to make money."

"That's because your life lacked balance."

He smiled. "Is that the problem?"

"I think balance is always the problem. I doubt that anyone ever gets it perfectly right. The trick is to recognize when things are tilting too far in the wrong direction and make course corrections."

"That sounds like one of those dorky Witherspoon Way affirmations."

"I've been told that some people find them annoying," she said.

"Amusing would be more accurate."

Grace took a breath and let it out slowly, with more control this time. The exercises were doing their work.

"You know," she said, "there is a Witherspoon saying that does cover this situation rather nicely."

"Of course there is." Julius looked at her. "What is it?"

"There can be no true definition of normal because life is ever changing."

"What the hell does that mean?" Julius asked.

"Danged if I know, but I thought it sounded rather pithy when I wrote it."

"Very deep," Julius said.

"Thanks. I used it as a tagline for the recipe for Harmony Vegetable Soup in the cookbook." She paused. "The idea was that no two versions of vegetable soup are ever exactly the same."

"Got it." He did not move. "Feeling better?"

She ran an internal check. All the vital signs were once again green. "Yes." She hesitated. "Thanks."

He nodded once and she knew that he did not need an explanation.

"I made it a rule long ago not to discuss the nightmare or the anxiety episodes with my dates," she said.

"What a coincidence," he said. "I made the same rule."

"Did you?"

"I had the same policy that you have when it comes to spending the night. I shelved the policy for a time for marriage and things did not end well. Lesson learned. I went back to that policy after the divorce."

She smiled. "Cinderella Man. Home by midnight."

"No glass slippers, though. I refuse to wear glass slippers."

"Glass slippers are so last year," she said.

"Good to know." He looked out at the glowing cityscape. "So, to sum up recent developments, we have both broken our own rules."

"Yes," she said. "We have."

She moved her palm along the railing until she was touching the edge of his hand. This time she did not flinch. He was warm and strong and rock steady. She relaxed a little more.

After a while Julius tightened his fingers gently around hers.

"Okay now?" he asked.

"Yes, I think so."

He led her back inside and back to bed. This time she fell into a dreamless sleep.

Thirty-Three

I've been thinking about your ex-wife and your former vice president," Grace said.

"Don't think about Diana and Edward," Julius said. "I sure as hell don't want to think about either of them."

"But there are issues here that you can't ignore."

"Watch me."

She was doing just that, watching him from her perch on the other side of the kitchen counter. Julius was cracking eggs into a bowl. He did it with an easy, one-handed action. A man who was in the habit of cooking for himself, she thought. A man who was accustomed to living alone.

"I take it you don't believe in getting closure?" she said.

"There is no such thing as closure as far as I'm concerned." Julius tossed the contents of another egg into the bowl. "Things are what they are. You deal with reality and move on."

"Listen up, Mr. Realist, I'm the one who was confronted by your ex in the ladies' room last night. I've got a right to tell you what I think is going on, and you should listen to me."

"Why?"

"Because we're sleeping together now, that's why," she shot back. "This is a relationship. In a relationship people are supposed to talk to each other."

Julius groaned. "Okay, talk. But talk fast because we've got other to-do items on our agenda today."

"I'm aware of that." She folded her arms on the granite and watched him whisk a little cream into the eggs. "Here's my take on Diana. I think she feels guilty."

"About walking out on me? I doubt it. Hell, she had cause. Just ask her."

"I don't think she feels guilty about walking out on you," Grace said patiently. "I'm sure in her mind she did the right thing—she set you both free from a broken relationship that she knew could not be repaired. And what's more, she had the good sense to figure out that things were not going to work before there were any children to consider."

"I'll give you that point." Julius poured the beaten eggs into the frying pan. "So what's she feeling guilty about?"

"She blames herself for being the reason you are trying to destroy her husband's company."

"Except that I'm not trying to destroy Hastings."

"That is precisely what I told her."

"Fine. You did what you could to straighten her out on that score." Julius picked up a spatula and began dragging it slowly through the eggs. "Can we all move on now?"

"I think you should talk to Edward."

"About moving on? Trust me, he's got enough on his plate at the moment trying to save Hastings. He doesn't have time for therapy."

"I was thinking that you could offer to help him salvage the company."

Julius looked at her as if she'd lost her mind. "In case you haven't noticed, I also have a lot going on right now."

"Yes, I know, and I appreciate what you're doing on my behalf but I think your issues with Edward and Diana are important."

"I just told you, I don't have any issues with either of them," Julius said.

"You said you thought the problems were coming from within the Hastings family empire. If that's true, Edward may be too close to the situation. Couldn't you, perhaps, offer to consult for him?"

"He wouldn't want my help, believe me."

"Do you know that for a fact or are you just assuming that he would turn down an offer from you?"

Julius removed the pan from the burner. "I think it's time we brought closure to this conversation and moved on to another topic."

"What topic is that?"

"Your issues with a certain stalker. You're supposed to make up a list of people in Witherspoon's orbit, remember?"

"I did that for the police," she said.

"The cops are looking for the killer." Julius spooned the scrambled eggs onto two plates. "You and I are going after the stalker."

"What if they're one and the same?"

"That will certainly simplify things," Julius said. "I think there's a connection between the murder and the stalking, but whether we're looking for one or two people is still an open question."

She did a quick little staccato with her fingertips on the granite counter.

"You're not the first person to come up with that theory," she said. "Kristy suggested that Nyla and Mr. Perfect might have conspired to murder Sprague. Millicent agrees with her."

"It's certainly a viable possibility."

She reached for the tablet of lined yellow paper and the pen he had put on the counter. "Okay, I'll see if I can expand the list."

Her phone rang just as she finished writing *Nyla Witherspoon*. She glanced at the screen and saw her sister's name. She picked up the phone.

"Hi, Alison, what's going on?" she said.

"I don't know," Alison said. "You tell me, little sister."

Alison's voice was too cool and a shade too neutral. She was in lawyer mode. Grace went blank.

"I don't understand," she said. "Is something

wrong? Alison, are you okay? Are Ethan and little Harry all right?"

"We're fine. You're the one who showed up on every business and financial blog that covers the Pacific Northwest this morning, to say nothing of social media."

"What?"

"You were Julius Arkwright's date for that Seattle business dinner and charity auction last night." Alison's voice started to rise. "There are pictures, Grace. He kissed you right there in front of half of the movers and shakers in the city. There are rumors of a scene with his ex—in the restroom, no less."

"Oh, jeez."

Grace glanced at Julius. He was sitting right next to her. She could tell from the flash of amusement in his eyes that he could hear Alison.

"Just a second, Alison."

Grace jumped off the stool and hurried across the big living room to the window wall. She did not think that Julius could hear the other side of the conversation from that distance.

"Calm down, Alison," she said softly. "I told you that Irene and her husband set me up with a blind date in Cloud Lake. I said the date's name was Julius."

"You never said his name was Julius *Arkwright*," Alison snapped.

"I didn't think it was important. Besides, you didn't ask."

"Good grief, do you have any idea who you're seeing?"

Grace glanced back at Julius, who was now drinking coffee and putting on a good show of pretending to be oblivious.

"Yes, I'm pretty sure I know who I'm dating," she said, speaking in low tones.

"Why are you whispering? Wait. Where, exactly, are you?"

"I'm still in Seattle."

"You gave up your apartment there," Alison said. "Good grief. You're with him, aren't you?"

"Stop talking as if I'm about to single-handedly launch Armageddon."

"Too late," Alison said. "If you're sleeping with Julius Arkwright, the world as you know it is about to be drastically changed. Listen to me, my naive little sister, there are rumors circulating about Arkwright."

"You mean that gossip about him trying to destroy the Hastings family business? Yes, I know. But they aren't true."

"I heard you defended Arkwright to his ex. And I'm inclined to agree with you. Given his reputation, I have a hunch that Hastings would be in much bigger trouble than it is if Arkwright had decided to take down the company."

"Exactly," Grace said.

"But," Alison continued, "that doesn't mean that there isn't a lot of dangerous drama going on between Hastings, Arkwright and the ex-wife. You do not want to get caught in the middle of a three-way war. Do you hear me? That isn't something you can fix with a couple of dumbass affirmations and the application of positive-thinking principles."

"Dumbass affirmations?"

"Pay attention, Grace. This is your life we're talking about."

"Alison, I appreciate your concern, really I do, but I've got things under control. Trust me."

"Said the bunny rabbit just before the wolf ate her."

Grace smiled. "Little Red Riding Hood."

"What?"

"Never mind. I take it that you didn't hear that Julius and I were attacked by a couple of thugs in the garage after the business affair."

"Good grief." Now Alison sounded stunned. "Are you serious?"

"Yes, but don't worry, Julius and I are fine. A little bruised, but okay. Those self-defense exercises finally came in handy. Unfortunately, the gorgeous piece of art glass that Julius had to buy at the charity auction was smashed to smithereens. But Julius caught one of the assailants. We're hoping the cops will get some information that will lead to the arrest of the guy who got away."

"I can't believe this. I think I may need to lie down and put a cool cloth on my fevered brow. What in the world are you doing?"

"Don't know for sure, yet, but it turns out that Julius is a pretty good bodyguard."

"He is?" Alison sounded bewildered.

"Marines. Then he worked as a fixer for a man who ran construction sites in various parts of the world. Anyhow, I'm in good hands. But don't tell Mom, okay? Not yet. She'll freak."

"I'm freaking."

"My life will calm down as soon as the cops catch the person who murdered Sprague Witherspoon."

There was a short pause on the other end of the connection.

"Are they making progress?" Alison asked in her lawyerly accent.

Grace decided to go for a positive spin. "They're expecting a big break any day now."

"In other words, no progress."

"Look, I've got to go."

"Promise me that you'll be careful," Alison said.

"Promise. Talk to you later. Love you. Bye."

Grace ended the connection and looked at Julius. "My sister."

Julius watched her with an unreadable expression.

"Yeah, I got that much," he said. "I take it she doesn't approve of our relationship?"

"She'll be okay," Grace said. "Alison is just somewhat in shock because she got the news through social media instead of from me. Perfectly understandable. And naturally she's concerned about the lack of progress in the murder investigation."

"So am I," Julius said. "But getting back to the subject of our relationship."

She walked across the room and sat down at the counter. "What about it?"

"You're okay with it?"

The present is the only thing that is certain. Live it fully.

She smiled. "I wouldn't be here if I wasn't okay with our relationship."

Julius did not look entirely satisfied with her response but he went back to his coffee. She reached for the yellow pad and the pen.

Another phone rang. Julius's this time. He glanced at the screen and took the call.

"No problem, Eugene. I told you to call me the minute you came up with anything interesting. What have you got?"

Grace put down her pen and waited.

"Thanks," Julius said. "Yes, this is important. Contact Chief Nakamura at the Cloud Lake PD and give him what you've got. He's coordinating things with Seattle. Good work."

Julius ended the connection. "That was Eugene, one of the wizards I asked to follow the money."

"I remember," Grace asked. "What did he find?"

"I told you I asked the wizards to go deeper into the Witherspoon financial records. They found an interesting item marked Medical Expenses."

"What's unusual about that?"

"Every month for the past few months several thousand dollars have been transferred from Witherspoon's private account to an account in New York. The name on the NYC account is William J. Roper. Eugene says he can't find a William J. Roper at the address on the account."

"That doesn't make sense. Why would Sprague have been paying medical expenses in New York? I don't think he had any East Coast connections." Grace stilled. "Wait, is that Nyla's missing inheritance?"

"No, that's definitely gone, probably sitting offshore. This looks more like a slow bleed."

"What's that mean?"

"Blackmail."

Her email alert chimed, startling her. She froze, the way she always did lately when she heard an alert. Julius went still, too.

They both looked at her phone. Grace picked it up, looked at the screen and sighed in relief.

"It's from Millicent," she said. "Not the stalker."

"Millicent gets star billing on our suspect list," Julius said. He looked grim. "What does she want from you?"

Grace pulled up the email and smiled. *"Life is short. Eat more chocolate."*

Julius frowned. "What the hell is that supposed to mean?"

"It was an office joke. Kristy, Millicent and I used to amuse ourselves thinking up funny affirmations. Millicent came up with that particular slogan. She loves chocolate."

Julius glanced at his watch. "It's eight o'clock in the morning. Why is she sending you that email now?"

"I have no idea."

"Does she make a habit of sending you emails like that?"

"No, she doesn't. The line about eating chocolate was just a little joke around the office but Millicent isn't one of those people who emails things like that." Grace glanced at the email and the time. "It is a little weird, isn't it?"

"Call her," Julius said. "Find out why she sent it."

The cool edge on his words sent a chill through Grace.

"I'm sure it's nothing," she said. She eyed the phone. "But I will admit that a funny email at this hour is a little out of character for Millicent. Unless—"

"What?"

Grace made a face. "I'll bet she heard about that little scene last night at the business banquet."

"The scene between you and Diana?"

Grace cleared her throat. "More likely it was that kiss in front of all those people that got her attention. Alison says there were pictures."

Julius did not look amused. He was very intent. "Why would Millicent email you a jokey affirmation because I kissed you at that damn banquet?"

"Got a hunch she'd think it was . . . entertaining. Millicent was always teasing me about my rather boring social life."

"I'm not seeing a connection with chocolate."

"It's a female thing."

"By all accounts, Millicent is very good with money," Julius said. "A lot of it has recently gone missing. In addition, my financial wizards have uncovered something that looks a lot like blackmail. And now this Millicent, who is so good with money, is sending you funny emails at eight o'clock in the morning. Call her. Find out what's going on."

Grace took a breath. "Okay."

She clicked on Millicent's contact info—and got dumped straight into voice mail.

"Try emailing her," Julius said.

Grace looked at him. "You're very serious about getting in touch with her."

"We know she just sent that email. She's on her phone or computer. Go ahead, hit reply."

Grace tapped out *"Everything okay?"*

She drank some coffee while she waited for a response. When none came, she tried leaving another voice mail message. Then she tried a text message.

"This is important. Please call."

There was no response.

"Do you have her address?" Julius asked.

"Yes, of course. She invited Kristy and me over to her apartment occasionally for cocktails and a movie. She lives in the South Lake Union neighborhood."

Julius got to his feet. "Let's go see if she's home."

"Now?"

"Now."

"I'm not so sure this is a smart idea, Julius. As you keep reminding me, it's still early in the morning. Millicent may not be alone. And even if she does answer the door, what, exactly, are we going to talk to her about?"

"Sprague Witherspoon and the missing money," Julius said. "I've got lots of questions."

Thirty-Four

The apartment building was one of the gleaming towers that had sprung up seemingly overnight in the South Lake Union neighborhood of Seattle. The area between the downtown core and Lake Union—once a sleepy industrial sector—was now a thriving mix of high-rise offices, condos, apartments, trendy restaurants and boutique shops. The sidewalks were filled with upwardly mobile techies and ambitious professionals who liked to live close to where they worked. There were very few suits to be seen. Denim prevailed.

It was only eight thirty but the coffeehouses and cafés were busy. Julius admired the purposeful way everyone in the vicinity moved. The people around him all looked like they were intent on constructing a grand future. There had been a time when he had possessed a similar sense of drive and purpose, he reflected. But somewhere along the line the thrill had faded. Lately he had been running on autopilot. And then Grace had happened.

Grace had changed everything.

He watched her enter Millicent's number into the apartment building's electronic entry system.

"This is an expensive neighborhood," he said.

"Millicent says she likes living here in South Lake Union because everyone is so busy inventing the future no one has any time to pry into other people's business," Grace explained.

"In other words, she likes her privacy."

"Who doesn't?"

There was no response from the entry system. Julius looked through the glass doors. A man sat behind a high desk doing his best to ignore what was happening on the other side of the front door. He was in his twenties. He might have been working on his computer but Julius thought it was more likely the guy was playing games.

Julius took out his wallet and removed some cash. He folded the bills and slipped them into his pocket.

"Contact that guy at the door station," he said.

Grace raised her brows. "You're going to try bribery?"

"Got a better idea?"

"Now that you mention it, no."

She punched in the door station code on the keypad. The doorman responded to the summons. He got up and crossed the lobby to open the door.

"Can I help you?" he said. He looked as if he hoped the answer was no.

"I'm a friend of Millicent Chartwell in apartment twelve-oh-five," Grace said. "I've been trying to get in touch with her this morning. It's very important. She's not answering her phone but I think she's here. I'm afraid she might be ill."

"We're extremely concerned about her well-being," Julius said.

He palmed the folded bills out of his pocket and shook hands with the doorman. When he retrieved his hand, the cash had vanished. The doorman appeared significantly more concerned about Millicent's health.

"You think Miss Chartwell might be too sick to come to the phone?" he asked, brow furrowing.

"Yes," Grace said. "Or perhaps she fell in the shower. She doesn't have any family here in town. There's no one I can call to check on her."

The doorman looked hesitant. "Well, we do insist on a signed PTE from every tenant."

"What's a PTE?" Grace asked.

"Permission-to-enter form." The doorman headed toward the elevators. "I'm authorized to go into the units to perform safety checks. I noticed her car in the garage downstairs this morning when I came on duty but she didn't go out for her usual latte."

The elevator doors slid open. The doorman did not say anything when Grace and Julius followed him inside. On the twelfth floor they all got out and went down the hall to twelve-oh-five.

The doorman knocked loudly several times.

"Miss Chartwell?" he called. "Are you home? A friend of yours is here. She's very concerned about you."

"Something's wrong," Grace said. "I know it. Open the door."

"Or we'll contact the police," Julius added. He unclipped his cell phone from his belt.

"Shit, don't call the cops," the doorman said, clearly alarmed. "She'll be really pissed if you do that. So will my boss. Not a good thing to have cops seen in the building. Gives the place a bad rep. Hang on."

He got the door open with a key card and called out loudly again, "Miss Chartwell?"

Still no response. The inside of the apartment seemed unnaturally hushed. The slice of the living room that Julius could see through the partially open doorway looked as if it had been furnished as a model apartment rather than a home. The color scheme was black and white punctuated with touches of red and gray. There was an empty martini glass sitting on the low black coffee table.

It was all very sleek and modern but it was also impersonal, Julius thought, as if Millicent had simply ordered the entire room from a furniture rental catalog. It reminded him of his own condo, although he was pretty sure his stuff had come with a much higher price tag.

Millicent had not put down roots in Seattle, he decided. It looked as if she was prepared to fold up shop and walk out the door on a moment's notice.

"That does it," Grace said. "You two wait out here. I'll go see if she's in there."

She sailed into the apartment before the doorman could argue. Julius stood in the opening and watched her go through the empty living room and past the kitchen. She vanished down a short hall.

A moment later her voice rang out.

"Call nine-one-one. She's still alive."

Thirty-Five

When I saw her lying there in bed I thought she was dead," Grace whispered. "She was so still. So pale. Barely breathing. Hardly any pulse."

She stood with Julius and the doorman in the hallway outside Millicent's apartment and watched the medics wedge the gurney into the elevator. Several residents from nearby apartments had gathered to witness the solemn process. Millicent was unconscious. There was an oxygen mask on her face.

"I heard one of the medics talking to someone at Harborview," the doorman said quietly. "Something about the situation looking like a deliberate overdose. Man, I would never have guessed she was the type."

There were several murmurs of agreement from the handful of other residents.

Grace shook her head and folded her arms. "I would never have thought so, either. I can't believe it."

Julius looked at the doorman. "How well did you know Miss Chartwell?"

The doorman shrugged. "She was one of the nicer tenants. Friendly. Tipped well. But we didn't have what you would call a personal relationship."

The muffled wail of the ambulance siren rose and then fell in the street outside the building. The small crowd in the hallway broke up as people drifted back to their own apartments.

"I'd better call my boss," the doorman said. He took out his phone. "Sure hope he doesn't get mad."

"For heaven's sake," Grace said, "you just helped rescue Millicent. If she survives it will be because you performed a safety check or whatever it was you called it."

The doorman perked up a little at that and moved a few feet away to talk on his phone.

The thirty-something woman who had emerged from the apartment next to Millicent's shook her head. "I wonder if she was depressed because of that man she brought home last night."

Grace turned quickly. "What man?"

"I don't know who he was but I'm guessing he was married from the way he acted. They came in around nine or so. He wasn't the first hookup she dragged home from a bar but I could tell by the way she laughed that the guy was different. She seemed really excited, as if he was special."

Julius glanced back into the apartment. "What time did he leave?"

"I don't know. It must have been around ten thirty because I was getting ready for bed. He didn't stay gone for long, though."

Grace frowned. "What do you mean?"

"I think I heard someone out in the hallway later. The door opened and closed. I assumed it was the same man. But maybe it was one of her previous hook-ups. Who knows?"

"How long did the second visitor stay?" Julius asked.

"I don't know," the woman said. "I fell asleep."

"Is there anyone on duty at the door station at night?" Julius asked.

"No, just days," the woman said.

"So she had to buzz in the second visitor," Julius said. "She knew who it was."

"Sure," the woman said, a shrug in her voice. "But like I told you, she was always bringing guys home."

Grace went to the doorway of the apartment. From where she stood she could see the empty martini glass on the table. She had to know, she thought. She had to be sure.

"I think I left my cell phone in Millicent's bedroom," she said in a voice pitched loud enough to be overheard by the two or three people who were still hanging around in the corridor. "I'm going to get it. I'll be right back."

Julius gave her a sharp glance. "I'll come with you."

She moved into the apartment and turned to look at him.

"What?" she asked quietly.

"I didn't see any sign of a personal computer," he said. "Never met a numbers person who didn't have one."

"Yes, of course, Millicent had a computer."

"I'm going to take another look around."

He disappeared into the bedroom.

She headed for the small kitchen, dread whispering through her.

She had not imagined it. The liquor bottle stood on the counter. She had caught a glimpse of it earlier, when she'd rushed past on her way to Millicent's bedroom, but she had not had time to take a closer look. Now she could see it clearly. She had been right about the label. A cold sensation washed through her.

"Damn," she said softly.

Julius came up behind her.

"No computer," he said.

She felt him go very still when he saw the bottle.

"The same brand of vodka that the stalker left in your refrigerator," he said. His voice was grim.

"The same brand that I found in Sprague's bedroom." She gestured toward the bottle on the counter. "Millicent drinks vodka martinis but that isn't her favorite brand. Whoever is stalking me tried to murder Millicent last night."

Thirty-Six

"Let me get this straight," Devlin said. "You want me to reopen a very old, very closed murder case?"

"We're not talking about reopening it," Julius said. "The Trager murder was solved. What we're looking for is a connection that links that case to the recent Witherspoon murder and Millicent Chartwell's overdose."

"A connection besides the obvious one," Grace added very deliberately, "which would be me."

"Which is you," Devlin agreed. He contemplated her for a moment. "Interesting."

Irene shot him a warning glare.

"Just making an observation," Devlin said.

The four of them were gathered in Grace's kitchen. It had started raining during the drive back to Cloud Lake. The steady drizzle was still coming down.

There were two large pizza boxes on the table and two bottles of beer. There were also two glasses of white wine.

Irene gave Grace an apologetic look. "You were right. I found out that Devlin did ask Julius to get a read on you the other night when you had dinner with us."

Devlin winced. "Now, honey, I tried to explain—"

"Never mind," Grace said. She gave both men a steely smile. "Old history. Water under the bridge. I'm willing to let bygones be bygones. The applicable Witherspoon affirmation, I believe, is *Never let old storms cloud sunny skies.*"

Julius and Devlin exchanged male-to-male looks.

"In other words," Julius said, "she's never going to let me forget that our first date was supposed to be an undercover sting operation."

Devlin picked up his beer and eyed Grace over the top of the bottle. "But you're prepared to let bygones be bygones, right?"

"Absolutely," Grace said. She gave him another overly polished smile. "However, under the circumstances, I'd say you owe me, don't you agree?"

"Hah," Irene said. "Damn right he owes you. And me."

"I agree, I owe you both," Devlin said. He reached down into a small briefcase and took out a laptop. "After I got Julius's call today I pulled up the old file on the Trager murder again. The brand of vodka was not noted on the evidence inventory but there is a photo of the bottle."

Grace caught her breath. "Same brand as the three bottles I've come across lately?"

"I think so," Devlin said. "But it's a little hard to read the label." He hesitated. "Crime scene photos can be . . . disturbing. Are you sure you want to look at these?"

Images of Trager's bloody mask of a face whispered through Grace's mind. She swallowed hard.

"The only photo I want to see is the picture of the vodka bottle," she said. "I need to be sure."

Devlin nodded. "All right. Just the bottle. No need to look at the bodies."

"Thanks," she said.

He tapped a few more keys and then turned the laptop around so that she could see the screen. She thought she was prepared for the image but she was wrong. The sight of the broken vodka bottle splashed with dried bloodstains sent a shock of horror through her. She had killed a man with that terrible weapon.

"Dear heaven," she whispered.

Devlin looked hard at her. "You saved a little kid's life and your own. Never forget that."

"I won't," Grace said. "I can't."

Julius reached under the table and put his hand on her clenched fingers.

Irene watched Grace closely. "Are you okay?"

Grace took a breath and let it out with control. "Yes."

"Well?" Devlin prompted.

"Yes," Grace said. "It's the same brand that I saw in Sprague's bedroom and in Millicent's kitchen. The same brand of vodka that the stalker left in my refrigerator."

"She's right," Julius added. "Same green-and-gold label." He looked at Devlin. "We are not talking coincidence, Dev."

"I agree," Devlin said. "But just so you know, as of this evening the Seattle authorities are still convinced that Millicent Chartwell tried to commit suicide or accidentally overdosed. They have found no evidence of foul play, and Millicent is still unconscious, so no one has been able to question her."

"Someone tried to murder her," Grace said. "I know it."

"We need to find something else," Julius said.

"Not much to go on here except the bottle," Devlin said. "Both murders and the possible attempt on Millicent's life were carried out in different ways. Mrs. Trager was beaten to death. Witherspoon was shot. Millicent's situation was made to look like an overdose."

Irene studied Grace. "You said you got an email from Millicent this morning but the authorities think she was unconscious hours before you got to her apartment?"

"Yes," Grace said. "When I talked to the police I pointed out that the email was out of character for her but the consensus is that it was Millicent's way of saying good-bye to me. She didn't have any close family and no serious relationships. But she liked me. At least, I think she did. Damn. How can I even be sure of that? Obviously I didn't know her well at all."

"Speaking of relationships," Julius said, "one of her

neighbors said Millicent had a male visitor last night—possibly two male visitors. Or one who left and returned an hour later."

"I told you, Millicent was not averse to the stray bar pickup," Grace said. "She liked adventurous sex but she wasn't stupid about it."

They all looked at her. Neither man said a word. Irene cleared her throat.

"Some people would say that adventurous sex is a working definition of stupid," Irene said. "Maybe Millicent just took the wrong man home. He left, then came back later and murdered her."

"That wouldn't explain the coincidence of the vodka bottle," Julius pointed out. He picked up his beer. "Huh."

They all looked at him.

"What?" Devlin asked.

"The Trager murder was clearly domestic violence," Julius said. "We are assuming that the motive in Witherspoon's death and the attempt on Millicent's life involve money. But there is only one reason why someone would leave the bottles of vodka at the scenes of the crimes."

"To implicate me," Grace said. "Yes, that possibility has not escaped my attention. If the cops ever figure that out—" She broke off and looked at Devlin. "Uh—"

He gave her a humorless smile. "Right. I'm a cop."

"Yes," she said very politely. "I know."

"I am also, believe it or not, your friend," he added.

"Absolutely," Irene said.

Grace gave Devlin a thin smile. "Uh-huh. Right. Thanks."

"Damn, lady, you sure do know how to hold a grudge," Devlin said.

"I never hold grudges," Grace assured him. "They interfere with one's inner balance."

"Good to know," Devlin said. But there was a spark of amusement in his cop eyes.

Julius fixed his attention on Devlin. "Who, besides the Cloud Lake Police, would be likely to have access to the information in the Trager file?"

Devlin shook his head. "No way to tell for sure. It all happened years ago. Before my time here. But anyone who went digging into the records could have found that detail about the bottle. He would have had to look damn hard, though. Like I said, the bottle was entered into evidence but the label was evidently not considered a critical element. At least, no one made a note of it." He gestured toward the image on the screen. "Take a look. You can hardly make it out due to the—"

He stopped. No one finished the sentence out loud. But Grace heard it in her head. *You can hardly make it out due to the bloodstains.*

"As Devlin just told you, he wasn't here at the time," Irene said, interrupting quickly. "It was a huge story locally, of course. Everyone in town knew about the murder and that Grace had used a broken liquor bottle to defend herself. However, I seriously doubt that anyone outside the police would have been aware of the label. I certainly don't remember it, and I was paying close attention because my best friend had nearly been murdered."

"So someone went looking for details of the case," Julius said. He leaned back in his chair and straightened his legs under the table. "There seem to be a lot of pieces here."

"The two thugs who tried to mug you in the parking garage at your condo," Devlin said. "What was that about?"

"Could have been a random thing," Irene ventured.

"No," Julius said. "It wasn't random."

"Someone was trying to frighten you off, Julius." Grace turned abruptly in her chair to look at him. "They were trying to scare you away from me. They intended to put you in the hospital—maybe worse. You're too close to me—practically a bodyguard."

They all looked at her.

"She's right," Devlin said. "Someone wants you out of the picture, Julius. It's the only explanation that fits. I know you're keeping company with Grace now but I ordered extra patrols on this street for the next few nights."

"Thanks," Julius said.

Thirty-Seven

She felt Julius leave the bed shortly before dawn. When she turned her head on the pillow she saw him standing at the window looking out over the lake. She pushed the covers aside, got up and went to join him.

"You're planning something," she said. It wasn't a question. Mentally she braced herself for what she knew was coming. "I can tell that you're working on a strategy."

He put an arm around her shoulders and pulled her close against his side.

"I hate to ask this," he said, "but would you be willing to walk me through the crime scene at the Cloud Lake Inn?"

"Somehow I just knew you were going to suggest that we take a look at the place where it all happened."

"Sorry," he said. "But I think it's something I need to do."

"It's okay," she said. "I'm willing to do it but I doubt that there is anything left to find after all this time. I told you, the place has been abandoned for years. Between the kids who have used it for parties and the transients who have camped out there, any evidence that might have been left at the scene will have disappeared by now."

"I just want to see it for myself. I need to figure out what we're missing."

"All right," she said. "The sun will be coming up soon. Let's do it this morning."

Julius turned her in his arms and drew her close.

"I hate to put you through this," he said. "I know it won't be easy for you."

"Going back into that place can't possibly be any worse than wondering why someone is murdering and attempting to murder people I know and leaving those bottles of vodka at the scenes."

"When morning comes, we'll go to the inn."

"Okay." She looked out the window. Dawn was on the way but it would be a while before real daylight appeared. Nevertheless, she knew she would not be able to go back to sleep, not now that she knew what lay ahead. "There's not much point going back to bed. I'll go take a shower and get dressed."

"That's a plan." Julius cupped her face in his hands. "But I've got a better one."

His kiss was all slow-burn seduction and aching need. She wrapped her arms around his neck and gave herself up to the embrace. He picked her up, carried her across the room and put her down on the rumpled bed.

He straightened long enough to strip off his briefs and then he got in beside her. He leaned over her, caging her with his arms. He brushed his mouth across hers.

The sweet, hot tension built deep inside her. She reached up to touch the side of his face with her fingertips. He turned his head and kissed her palm.

"Julius," she said.

She felt his teeth lightly graze her throat and then he began to work his way down her body. He lingered over her. By the time his mouth reached her breasts, she was twisting beneath his weight. When he reached her belly she sank her nails into his shoulders.

"Julius."

She almost screamed when his tongue touched the inside of her thighs. She did scream when he found her tight, full core. Her release flashed and sparked through her.

Before it was over he shifted. He rolled onto his back and pulled her down on top of him.

And soon it was his low, rumbling growl of satisfaction that echoed in the bedroom.

Thirty-Eight

"This place was a magnet for teenagers back in the day," Grace said. "But not so much anymore. The local kids have found other places to party."

They were standing on the path in front of the old asylum. Julius had a small box of tools in one hand. Grace was surprised at her own inner calm. She felt remarkably steady and absolutely determined. There was still the possibility that the sense of claustrophobia and an accompanying anxiety attack would strike when they entered the boarded-up building. But for now Julius's belief that returning to the scene would provide some answers had a strengthening effect on her resolve.

It would do no good for him to go inside on his own, she told herself. He needed her to give him the visuals. She could do this.

It had stopped raining but the trees still dripped and the surface of the lake mirrored the steel-gray sky. There was another storm on the way.

"I can see why a series of owners tried to turn the asylum into an inn." Julius studied the front of the decaying structure. "Good bones, as they say. Classic Victorian architecture."

"It dates from an era when people believed that the hospital buildings designed for patients with mental health issues should be part of the cure," Grace explained. "The theory was that tall windows, high ceilings and tranquil landscaping would lift the spirits and soothe the nerves."

"Not a bad theory, as theories go. Probably should have built the hospital someplace where there's more sunlight, though."

"Yes," she said. "It is very dark at this end of the lake because of the woods and the hillside." She looked at him. "How do you want to do this?"

Julius considered briefly. "What made you go inside that day?"

"Sheer teenage curiosity. I was on my way to visit Irene that afternoon. I took the lake path, as usual. When I got to this place I stopped to take a look around inside."

"Was that usual, too?"

"I didn't always stop," she assured him. "But there were rumors that some of the A-list kids had held a party in the asylum that week. Sex and drugs were assumed to have been involved. The question of which A-list girl was sleeping with which A-list boy was always a hot topic. I decided to take a look to see if any clues had been left behind. When I saw that the plywood on one of the side doors had been removed, I knew I was onto something. So, I went inside."

"Which door?"

"That one." She pointed toward the sheet of plywood that covered the door. "It's boarded up now."

"Let's go."

Julius led the way alongside the building. When he reached the boarded-up door he stopped and set down the toolbox. She watched him open the box and remove a crowbar.

It didn't take long to pry off the sheet of plywood. Julius set it aside. Grace moved to stand beside him. Together they looked into the deep gloom of what had once been a large kitchen. The door sagged on rusty hinges. All of the old appliances had long since disappeared. The walls were battered and worn.

Julius took two flashlights out of the toolbox. He handed one to Grace.

"Ready?" he asked.

He looked concerned and serious, she realized. But she could see that he did not expect her to lose her nerve. The knowledge that he had faith in her fortitude strengthened her resolve.

"Yes," she said.

She switched on her flashlight and moved into the kitchen.

"All right, you entered here to see if you could find any remnants of the party," Julius said. "Tell me what happened next."

"I walked through the kitchen and into the hall. I remember my footsteps echoed."

She retraced the path she had taken that day. The chill of dark memory and old nightmares raised goose bumps but she kept going. Julius followed close behind.

The basement door was shut. She stopped in front of it.

"I heard thumping sounds," she said.

"Go on," Julius said.

"Something about the thumping sounded urgent—frantic. I opened the door."

"It wasn't locked?"

"No, I suppose there was no way for Trager to lock it that day. But I don't think he was worried that anyone would go into the basement. He knew the boy couldn't escape because he was bound hand and foot with duct tape. Mark's mouth was taped shut, too. I couldn't believe it when I saw the poor kid at the bottom of the stairs. I thought some bully had left him there."

"How did he get your attention?"

"He heard me come into the house. He couldn't scream for help but he used his feet to kick a wooden box that was on the floor. He kept kicking the box until I opened the door."

"Smart kid."

"Yes. He told me later that he made the noise because he could tell my footsteps were different from Trager's."

"Did you know Mark?"

"No. His family lived on the other side of town, next door to the Tragers, as it turned out."

"Let's go down and take a look," Julius said.

I can do this, Grace thought.

She switched on her flashlight and started down the stairs. When she reached the bottom she stopped and looked around.

"I didn't see the body at first. I got Mark out of the tape and he started crying. He clung to me and wouldn't let go. At that point I was still thinking that it was the work of a local bully. But Mark kept saying *Mrs. Trager is hurt. Mrs. Trager is hurt.* I saw what I thought was a sleeping bag. It turned out to be Mrs. Trager's body wrapped in plastic."

"Did Mark understand that Trager had murdered Mrs. Trager?"

"Not exactly. He told me that Mr. Trager had hurt Mrs. Trager and that now she was asleep and wouldn't wake up. I didn't know much about domestic abuse in those days. I'd heard the term but I didn't fully understand. It wasn't something I'd ever had to contend with, thank heavens."

"Where was the body?" Julius asked.

The calm, deliberate way he spoke helped her focus.

"Over there." She walked slowly across the space and stopped again, remembering. "When I got close I could see Mrs. Trager's face through the layers of plastic wrap. Her eyes were open. I will never forget what she looked like. It finally dawned on me that I had stumbled into a murder scene. I started to tell Mark that we had to get out of the house and get help. That's when we heard it."

Julius aimed his flashlight into the shadows. "What did you hear?"

"A truck engine in the yard out front. I told Mark that was a good sign. It meant there was an adult who could help us. But Mark was suddenly paralyzed with fear. He recognized the sound of the truck, you see."

"What happened?"

"He said it was Mr. Trager coming back and that he was going to hurt both of us just like he hurt Mrs. Trager. The kid was so calm about it. I think he was beyond crying at that point. After all, there was a monster coming for him. What could you do when facing a monster?"

"Where was the vodka bottle?" Julius asked.

"Next to the body. I grabbed it because there was nothing else around to use as a weapon."

"Where did you and the boy hide?"

"Over there, under the stairs."

Grace made herself cross the damp concrete floor to the dark shadows alongside the stairs. "I told Mark that we would get away but that for now he must not make a sound. I told him that when I said *run*, he was to head straight up the stairs and get out of the house as fast as he could and keep going until he found an adult."

"He did what you told him?"

"Yes. He was so scared I think he would have obeyed any adult in that moment. It took Trager a few seconds to realize that Mark wasn't where he had left him. Trager evidently assumed the kid was huddling in some corner of the basement and started to search the place with his flashlight. I hauled Mark out of the shadows and told him to go. He dashed up the stairs. I tried to follow him but Trager caught hold of my jacket. I smashed the bottle against the railing and slashed at Trager's face with the broken glass."

"Good girl," Julius said quietly.

"There was suddenly blood everywhere. It was raining blood."

Julius said nothing but he came to stand beside her. He put one arm around her shoulders.

Breathe.

She steadied herself. "Trager screamed when I cut him. He let go of my jacket and toppled backward. I kept going up the stairs. When I reached the top Mark was already outside, running along the lakeside path. I caught up with him. The nearest lakefront houses were empty. They were summer homes in those days and this all happened in winter. My mom and sister weren't at home that day but Mrs. Gilroy was."

"She's the one who called the police?"

"Yes. She locked all the doors to keep us safe from Mr. Trager in case he chased after us. Then she got her big pruning shears out of the closet. I will never forget the sight of her holding those shears, ready to defend us against Trager. But he didn't come after us. Because he was dead at the bottom of the basement stairs."

"You did the world a favor, Grace. But there is always a price to be paid for that kind of thing."

"Yes."

Julius removed his arm and walked slowly around the basement. The beam of his flashlight swept back and forth in a search pattern.

"There isn't any logic to what has been going on when we look at things in terms of the present," he said. "We need to view them from the past."

"How do we do that?"

Julius was silent for a long moment. "You said that Mrs. Trager was watching the boy for her neighbor that day."

"That's right. The poor kid just happened to be in the wrong place at the wrong time. As Devlin said, the police believe that Trager intended to drown Mark and hope the authorities would think the death was just another lake accident."

"What about the family?" Julius said.

"The Ramshaws? I don't know much about them. They moved to California soon after the Trager murder. Mom said they felt they needed to get Mark away from the town where he had been kidnapped. I'm sure he's had a few nightmares over the years, as well."

"Not the Ramshaw family," Julius said. "Trager's family. Did he and his wife have any children?"

"No," Grace said. Then she stopped for a beat, remembering some of the things she had overheard in the past. "But Trager had been married before. I remember my mother talking to Billings, the chief of police at the time. I overheard him saying something about Trager having a history of domestic violence and that his first wife had divorced him. Why?"

"I'm not sure. Just looking for connections."

Grace managed a shaky smile. "Is this how you go about analyzing investments?"

"Pretty much. The trick is to look for the stuff that is hiding in the shadows."

"You know, there's a Witherspoon affirmation that sums up your approach to problem solving."

"What's that?" Julius asked.

"Look deep. The important things are always just beneath the surface."

"I think I'll stick to my rules."

"Trust no one and *Everyone has a hidden agenda."*

"When it comes to words to live by, I believe in simplicity," Julius said.

"Whatever."

"Don't tell me that's a Witherspoon affirmation."

"Sometimes it's the only appropriate response to a situation," Grace said.

Thirty-Nine

Ralph Trager had two children by a previous marriage, a boy and a girl," Grace said. She studied the information she had pulled up on her computer. "The names were Randal and Crystal. The first wife never remarried but she moved in with a series of boyfriends for a while."

"I'll bet that didn't go well," Julius said.

"It looks like she had really bad taste when it came to men. A couple of the boyfriends sold drugs for a living and one was arrested for abusing the daughter." Grace sat back in her chair. "How many times have we heard that sad story?"

Julius picked up the coffeepot and carried it across the kitchen to the table. "What happened to the first wife and kids?"

"Let's see." Grace leaned forward and scrolled

through more data. "Looks like the former Mrs. Trager and the daughter, Crystal, died in a car crash. Randal, the son, went into foster care, moved through a series of homes and then just sort of disappeared for a couple of years."

"Probably decided life was better on the streets. Anything else?"

Grace scrolled through some more data. "Randal held a series of part-time contract jobs, most of them involving computers and programming. Looks like he had an aptitude for that sort of thing."

Julius looked out over the lake. "Go on."

Grace went back to her screen. "He came to a bad end. He was arrested on fraud charges and got six months and probation. He died in a boating accident soon after he was released."

"So it looks like everyone in Trager's family is dead."

"Yes." Grace picked up her mug. "What a tragic scenario."

Julius leaned back in his chair and swallowed some coffee. "It's also a very convenient scenario."

Grace looked at him over the top of the mug. "Are we back to *trust no one*?"

"We are," Julius said. "In light of this new evidence, we need to reevaluate our findings on all of the characters in our little drama."

"What's to reevaluate? We've already checked out everyone involved."

"But now we'll do it from another perspective," Julius said. "We've got a situation that involves fraud, and at least one character in our story did time for fraud."

"Yes, several years ago, but Randal Trager was killed after he got out of jail."

"Maybe."

"Devlin's right, you really do think like a cop. Maybe you missed your calling."

"I don't like guns," Julius said.

"Okay, that might have been a problem for you if you had pursued a career in law enforcement."

A phone rang. Julius's this time. He glanced at the screen and took the call.

"What have you got for me, Eugene?" he said.

He listened attentively for a few minutes.

"That would explain a few things," he said. "Including his career path. Thanks, Eugene. You've done some really fine work on this. Yes, I will let you know how it all comes out. No, you cannot quit to go work for the FBI. It doesn't pay nearly as well as Arkwright Ventures does."

Julius hung up and looked at Grace.

"Well?" she prompted.

"It appears that Sprague Witherspoon may have had a secret past, one he tried to bury a long time ago. It may explain the blackmail."

Grace's heart sank. "Oh, no. Please don't tell me Sprague was a criminal."

"He did time under another name for fraud."

"Damn." Grace closed her eyes. "I really, really admired him, you know."

"I know," Julius said gently.

She opened her eyes. "I'll bet that after he got out of prison he reinvented himself for good and committed himself to helping other people make new lives for themselves. When you think about it, that's a very inspiring story."

"That's definitely one way of interpreting the facts," Julius said.

She beetled her brows. "It's my interpretation of the facts until proven otherwise."

"There is the little issue of his possible gambling addiction and the embezzlement thing."

She glared.

He moved one hand in a dismissive gesture. "Fine. Innocent until proven guilty. Whatever."

The rumble of a vehicle pulling into the drive stopped Grace before she could start asking questions. She got to her feet and went out into the living room. The familiar logo of an overnight package delivery company was emblazoned on the side of the large van parked in front of the house. She watched the uniformed driver climb out. He came up the front steps, a box in one hand.

She opened the door.

"Grace Elland?" he said.

"That would be me."

"Got a package for you."

"Thanks," Grace said. She glanced at the return address and recognized the name of the Seattle chocolatier. "Candy. This is a surprise."

"Sign here, please."

She scrawled her name and took the package. The

deliveryman got back into the truck and rumbled down the drive toward the road.

Grace carried the box of chocolates back into the kitchen and set it down on the table. She tore off the outer wrapping.

"Truffles," she said. "My favorite. Someone knows me well."

Julius eyed the box with narrowed eyes. "Boyfriend?"

"I told you, I don't have one at the moment." She picked up the envelope that had been taped to the top of the box. "Well, except for you, that is."

"Good to know that I count as a boyfriend."

She ignored the sarcasm and ripped open the envelope. For a moment she could only stare at the signature.

"Oh, shit," she said.

"Not what most people say when they open a box of truffles," Julius said. "Don't keep me in suspense. Who sent the candy?"

"Millicent."

Forty

"This is too creepy," Grace said.

She sat at the kitchen table and stared at the rows of elegant chocolates. It might as well have been snakes or scorpions in the box, she thought. All right, maybe not quite that bad. Nevertheless, she was very sure she would not be eating the truffles.

"According to the label, the box was sent yesterday directly from the store," Julius said. He looked down at the chocolates from the opposite side of the table.

"Overnight delivery," Grace said. "But Millicent was unconscious all day yesterday and last night. As far as we know she still isn't awake. She couldn't have sent this box of candy."

"You got an email from her yesterday morning and all indications are that she was unconscious at the time it was sent," Julius said. "If Millicent is the sender, she could have scheduled the email and the chocolates before she was drugged. Probably thought she could cancel both if everything went according to plan."

"But something went wrong, so the email and the chocolates got sent automatically. But why me?"

"Looks like you were her backup plan," Julius said. "Better take a close look at that candy."

"Not the candy." Grace held up the small white card. "It's all right here in the note."

She read it aloud.

Grace, if you're reading this, it's probably because I'm dead. I don't think that there are any good affirmations for this situation. It sucks. Consider this my will. I'm leaving my retirement savings to you even though I know you'll probably hand it over to that ungrateful bitch, Nyla. I can't bring myself to do it, that's for sure. I hope you will at least keep a commission for yourself, but you probably won't do that either. It must be hard always trying to do the right thing. But I will say it was rather entertaining watching you do it. It was fun knowing you for the past year and a half, so at least do me a favor and enjoy the chocolates.

The note was followed by the name of a bank Grace had never heard of and a long string of numbers.

"Offshore account?" Grace asked.

"I think, under the circumstances, we can assume that's the case." Julius sat down at the table and opened his laptop. "Easy enough to find out."

A short time later he had the answer.

"It's an offshore account, all right. And all you need to access it is that number she wrote on the card. There's a sizable sum involved here. A few million."

"So she was embezzling from Sprague." Grace propped her elbows on the table and cupped her chin in both hands. "She seemed—seems—like such a nice person. Always so cheerful. Lots of positive energy."

"I have a hunch that knowing she was raking in a tidy little fortune and setting it aside for her retirement was the reason she was always so cheerful and positive."

"Well, this does answer one question," Grace said. "We now know where the money went. And we know that Sprague wasn't embezzling the funds."

"We know something else, too," Julius said. "Miss Cheerful probably didn't try to kill herself. She was looking forward to an early retirement and the pleasure of spending the cash that she had stashed in that island bank. I wonder how she planned to bring the money back to the States without arousing the interest of the authorities."

"In a suitcase?" Grace suggested.

"Carrying a few million bucks through customs is a high-risk game." Julius shook his head. "This kind of money needs to be scrubbed clean."

"I suppose the next step is to call Devlin," Grace said without much enthusiasm. "And then I'll have to chat with the Seattle cops. Again."

"Dev comes first." Julius took out his phone. "Someone is going to get the credit for what amounts to a very big break in the case. Might as well be him."

"I suppose so," Grace said.

Julius smiled briefly. "Trust me, Dev is on our side."

"I'll take your word for it. But I'm going to call Nyla and tell her that I think we found her inheritance."

"That note and the account number are evidence," Julius pointed out in a neutral tone. "We are going to give both to Dev."

"Fine, whatever," Grace said. She took out her phone. "But Nyla has a right to know that we found her money."

Julius checked his watch. "I've got a meeting in Seattle this afternoon. No sense dragging you along. Can I trust you to stay with Irene at her shop?"

Grace glared. "I'm not a kid. I don't need a babysitter."

"You're a woman with a stalker—a stalker who may be escalating. You need a babysitter."

"Right. Yes, of course, I'll stay at Irene's shop. When will you get back?"

"I should be home by dinner. Just make sure you are with Irene and Dev until I return."

Forty-One

It was all falling apart. The biggest score of his life was crashing and burning around him. If he didn't get out fast he would get crushed in the rubble.

Burke tossed the hand-tailored, neatly laundered and folded shirts into the suitcase and went back to the closet to zip the designer jackets into a carrying bag. He had spent a fortune on the clothes he knew he needed for the job. He was not going to leave them behind.

He had put the plan together with the precision of a military commander preparing for battle. Every detail, from a résumé so solid it could have withstood a high-level government background check—not that the government was that good at background checks—to the dates on his driver's license, had been engineered to perfection.

The timing had been perfect at every step of the way until that first mistake. He had told himself that leaving the vodka bottle at the scene of Witherspoon's death was a harmless whim. It was an error but a survivable one.

Finding out that Nyla's inheritance had vanished had come as a stunning shock, however. He'd almost cut his losses the day he realized that someone else had gotten to the money first. He'd torn the Witherspoon offices apart and then hacked the three computers in a desperate effort to find the key to the cash. He knew the thief had to be a member of the staff. It was the only answer that made sense.

Then Millicent had made him an offer that seemed too good to be true. For a while it looked like it would be possible to salvage the situation.

Now Millicent was in a drug-induced coma and might wake up and start talking at any minute. Another mistake. She should have died. He'd searched her apartment and gone through her computer but he had found no clue to the missing money. Without the account info, there was no way to get at it. It might as well be buried at sea.

The old rage rose out of nowhere, washing through him in a red tide. He had planned so damned carefully.

He dropped the suit carrier on the bed and slammed a fist against the wall of the bedroom. It hurt like hell and it dredged up old memories from his childhood—stuff that he hated remembering—but he felt better almost immediately. His heart rate slowed and his breathing went back to normal. Sometimes a man just had to let off a little steam.

The apartment security intercom buzzed, startling him. He debated whether or not to answer it and then decided to pick up.

"This is Grayson at the door station. Miss Witherspoon is here to see you, sir."

Shit. The last thing he needed was a visit from Nyla. But he survived by adhering to certain rules. The first rule of a well-run con was to stay in the role until you were out of town. With one person dead and another in the hospital, it was very, very important to stick to the rules.

"Please send her up, Grayson," he said. "Thanks."

He ended the call and looked around the bedroom. He had to make certain that Nyla didn't realize he was planning to fly out of Seattle that afternoon.

He left the bedroom, closing the door on the scene of the open suitcases.

The doorbell chimed. He took a breath and focused on channeling Burke Marrick, scion of a wealthy Southern California family that had made its money in real estate.

When he opened the door he saw Nyla's face and knew at once that everything had changed. She was in tears but they were tears of joy.

She threw herself into his arms.

"I just got a call from Grace," Nyla said. "I can hardly believe it, but she says they found my money.

That bitch Millicent Chartwell was the embezzler. I should have known. She handled all of Dad's money. She hid millions in some damn island bank, and more money is going in every day, thanks to the website and blog revenue."

Forty-Two

It was four thirty by the time Julius walked out of the office. An early winter twilight, made even darker by a heavy cloud cover, had settled on the city.

He paused just inside the parking garage and did a quick visual scan. There were a handful of other people heading toward their cars. Office workers, he concluded. Nothing looked or felt wrong.

One little mugging and you start acting like you're back in a war zone every time you walk through a garage. Get a grip, man.

He took a last look around before he opened the driver's-side door of the SUV. Again, nothing appeared out of place. He got behind the wheel, took out his phone and called home.

Home. Where had that thought come from? He

wasn't calling home, he was calling Grace. But somehow it was all one and the same.

She answered on the first ring.

"How did the meeting go?" she asked.

"The meeting went fine," Julius said. "The deal will net a sizable chunk of change within five years. My staff is celebrating at the closest bar."

"But you're bored."

"It was a very dull meeting. I'm on my way back to Cloud Lake now. Should be there in a little over an hour, depending on traffic. I'll stop by my place and change clothes. Then I'll walk to your house. You're still with Irene?"

"Yes, indeed, as promised. We're at her shop. Devlin is going to join us as soon as he leaves his office. We'll pick up some takeout and then go to my place."

"Sounds like a plan. See you soon."

"Drive safe," Grace said. There was a slight catch in her voice, as if she had been about to say something else but she stopped herself. "Good-bye."

"See you soon."

He ended the connection and paused for a moment, wondering what it was that Grace had almost said. *I miss you*, perhaps. Or, maybe, *I'm looking forward to seeing you again*. That was probably it. The chances that she had been about to say *I love you* were slim to none. It was way too soon. And Grace's track record indicated that she was very cautious when it came to relationships. Still, a man could dream.

He hadn't been doing much in the way of dreaming

until Grace arrived on the scene. Grace changed everything.

He fired up the SUV and reversed out of the parking space. He was in a strange mood, one he could not quite define. Whatever it was, it was not connected to closing the Banner deal. The only thing involved there had been money.

By the time he drove out of the garage and into the river of downtown traffic he was pretty sure that the little rush of energy he felt was anticipation. Soon he would be back in Cloud Lake, where Grace was waiting. For now she was safe with friends.

It was full dark by the time the exit sign for Cloud Lake came up in the headlights. Another little rush hit him when he pulled off the freeway. Not much longer.

Coming home.

Fifteen minutes later he cruised slowly through the neat little town and turned off onto Lake Circle Road. He checked the Elland house when he drove past and was satisfied when he caught a glimpse of the windows glowing warmly through the trees. Dev's police vehicle was parked in the drive. Grace was where she was supposed to be. She was safe.

With any luck Devlin would come through with a solid connection between the crimes and Burke Marrick. There had to be one. No con artist was perfect. Theoretically, now that Marrick had the money in sight again he would stop trying to murder people who stood in his way. Theoretically.

Julius turned into his own driveway, parked and

got out. He grabbed his laptop and started toward the front steps.

The door of the neighboring house banged open. Harley appeared. The porch light shone on his bald head.

"Thought I heard you," Harley called a little too loudly. "How'd the Banner deal go?"

"It went the way deals always go. Banner is happy. My investors are happy. My staff is happy."

Harley snorted. "So why aren't you happy?"

"I'm thrilled, can't you tell?"

"You know what your problem is?"

"Grace tells me I'm bored. What's your opinion?"

"You're not building anything. You're just making money. After a while, that's not enough. When I was in business, we built things all over the whole damn world, remember? Water treatment plants. Hospitals. Hotels. Apartments. And it's all still standing. People got clean water and jobs and places to live because we put in the infrastructure you need for those things to happen."

"I'm in a bit of a hurry here, Harley. Your point?"

"I'm thinking maybe Grace is right. All you do these days is make money for yourself and your investors. You're bored."

Julius went up the steps and unlocked his front door. "Now, see, there's where you're wrong. I'm not bored, not any longer."

Harley laughed. "That's because you're heading out to spend the night with Grace."

"I don't want her to be alone until the cops pick up the psycho who's been stalking her."

"Right. You're just a regular Boy Scout doing a good deed." Harley chuckled. "Face it, you're in deep there. The scary part is that she understands you better than you do yourself. That kind of woman can be dangerous."

Julius paused in the doorway and looked at Harley. "Got any advice?"

"Sure. Same advice I always gave you when I sent you out to salvage a job that was in trouble. Don't screw up."

Harley went back inside his house. His front door slammed shut.

Julius went through his own door and switched on some lights. He stood quietly for a moment, listening to the silence. The place felt empty, just like his condo in the city. But that no longer mattered. He would be with Grace soon.

Nevertheless, the yawning emptiness seemed almost eerie this evening. He walked across the front room, his footfalls echoing on the wooden floor.

There had to be a connection to Burke Marrick. What the hell was taking the Seattle police so long to find it?

His imagination was spinning into overdrive. He needed to change clothes and go find Grace and his friends.

He hauled the duffel bag into the bedroom and dropped it on the bed. He was in the process of unzipping it when he heard the faint, muffled *whoosh* of an explosion.

Instinct and old habits took over. Without thinking, he flattened himself against the nearest wall, automatically seeking cover. He crouched and pulled the pistol out of the ankle holster before he even had a chance to consider the possibilities. His pulse kicked up and the battlefield focus infused his senses.

You're probably overreacting. Just someone fooling around with fireworks out on the lake. You're not going to be any good to Grace if you don't stay in control.

Outside the window the night was suddenly lit up with flames. He eased the curtain aside and saw that Harley's boathouse was on fire.

Harley burst out of his kitchen door and charged across the porch. He grabbed the garden hose and dragged it toward the dock.

"Arkwright, get out here and give me a hand. We got a fire."

Julius thought about the fuel, the flares and all the other combustible items that were stored in the boathouse and on board the cruiser.

He shoved the pistol back into the holster and headed for the kitchen door. When he was outside on the back porch he took out his phone to call 911.

"Harley, get away from that damn boathouse," he shouted. "The whole thing could explode at any minute."

Harley continued to haul the hose toward the dock. "It's my boat inside that boathouse, damn it."

"You've got insurance. Besides, we both know you can afford to buy two or three more."

Julius punched in the emergency number.

"Nine-one-one. What is the nature of your emergency?"

"Fire," Julius said. "Twenty-eleven Lake Circle Road. Harley Montoya's place. The boathouse."

"I've got vehicles on the way."

Julius ended the call and started down the steps. "Forget it, Harley. There's nothing you can do. Stay clear. Fire department's on the way."

"You gonna give me a hand or just stand there and tell me the fire department's coming?" Harley shouted.

"Stay away from the boathouse, you stubborn—"

Julius caught the flicker of movement out of the corner of his eye just as he reached the bottom step. A neighbor coming to help, he thought. But the nearest house was some distance away. No one could have run that fast.

The porch light glinted darkly on a metal object in the newcomer's hand.

. . . And Julius was thrown back into a war zone.

He dropped to the ground just as the gun roared. He felt cold talons slash open his right side. The pain, he knew, would come later. At that moment he was riding a wave of adrenaline.

Another shot slammed into the porch boards just above his head. He was flat on his belly on the far side of the steps. It occurred to him that he had made a fine target standing there in the light while he called 911. *Idiot.*

He pulled the gun back out of his ankle holster and watched the dark figure advance cautiously across the yard. When the gunman reached the edge of the porch light he paused, searching for his target in the shadows.

"What the hell are you doing, Julius?" Harley shouted. He started across the gravel lane that separated the two houses. "Are you shooting a damn gun? I've got a problem over here, in case you didn't notice . . . Shit."

"Harley," Julius shouted. "Get down."

Harley finally saw the gunman.

"Son of a bitch," he bellowed. "You set that fire, didn't you?"

The shooter was already swinging around toward Harley, who was clearly silhouetted against the flames.

Julius took a breath, let it out partway and squeezed the trigger.

The force of the shot took the gunman down. He collapsed into the ring of porch light.

Julius got to his knees, his weapon in one hand. He clamped his other hand against his side.

"The gun," he said.

"I've got it." Harley scooped up the weapon the gunman had dropped and hurried toward Julius. "Shit, son, where'd that SOB hit you?"

Julius considered the question closely. It was getting hard to focus, but there was warm liquid spilling over his hand now, he was pretty sure of that.

"Right side. I think. Kind of damp there."

Sirens wailed in the distance.

"Damn, you're bleedin', all right." Harley ripped off his flannel shirt and bunched it into a tight bandage. He pressed it firmly against Julius's side. "The fire trucks will be here in a minute. They'll have some medical supplies."

"Okay." Julius did not take his eyes off the fallen man. "Keep an eye on that bastard."

"Don't worry, I will. You know him? He's not from around here, that's for sure."

"Burke Marrick," Julius said. "Grace . . . Tell her . . ."

"Shut up and concentrate on stayin' right here with me. You can tell Grace whatever it is you want to tell her yourself. Got a hunch she'll be along right quick."

Forty-Three

He drifted in and out of a medication haze, vaguely aware that Grace was somewhere nearby. He tried to focus because he had things to say to her but he kept slipping back into a murky dream world. Machines hummed and beeped endlessly in the shadows. Figures appeared and disappeared, startling him because they moved so quietly. He finally realized what was happening and glared at the nurse who was getting ready to inject another dose of the drug into the IV line.

"No more," he ordered. The words were thick and ragged.

The nurse, a tall, heavyset man with red hair, studied him closely. "You sure?"

"I'm sure."

Grace materialized at the side of the bed. "Don't be an idiot, Julius. Take the pain meds."

"No more," Julius said. "Not now. Need to think."

"Your call," the nurse said. "Let me know if you change your mind."

He left the room. Grace leaned over the railing and touched Julius's hand very gingerly, as if she were afraid he might break. He gripped her fingers and held on tight.

"Marrick?" he croaked.

"He survived but last time I checked he wasn't awake. Devlin has an officer stationed outside his door. His surgery was a lot more extensive than yours. The doctor said that in your case no vital organs were hit. They just had to stitch you up."

"Feels like they did it with red-hot needles."

"You heard the nurse," Grace said. "You can have more pain medication if you want it."

"No, thanks. The meds don't make the pain go away, they just take you to a different place. But everyone around you thinks you're no longer in pain so they feel better."

She smiled. "That's very philosophical."

He pushed himself up against the pillows and groaned when the pain punished him.

"Julius?" Grace looked worried.

He took a cautious breath. "I'm okay."

He surveyed the room and saw a large leather chair. There was a hospital blanket draped over the back. The window glowed with watery morning light.

"Hell, it's tomorrow, isn't it?" he said.

Grace smiled. "It's today. You were shot last night."

"You spent the night here?"

"Of course I did. You scared the daylights out of me. When Devlin got that call saying that two males had been shot at the scene of a fire at Harley's house and that you were one of them—" She broke off and took a breath. "Yes, indeed, I spent the night."

"You didn't have to do that," he said, but he knew it sounded weak. He was thrilled that she had stayed with him. "But thanks."

"You told me you don't like guns," she said.

"I don't. Never said I didn't own one. Used to carry it when I worked for Harley. Dug it out after we got mugged in the garage."

"That turned out to be very farsighted of you." She gave him a misty smile. "How are you feeling?"

"Best not to ask. Does Devlin have any more information?"

"Yes. He'll fill you in on the details but I can give you the short version. Devlin ran Burke's prints and got a hit. They belong to a man named Randal Trager."

"Trager's son by his first wife."

"Right. Randal's prints were in the system because he did time several years ago, remember? I pulled up the details when we researched Trager's family."

"I remember. That fits."

"It gets better. The Seattle police searched Millicent's apartment and found Burke's prints in Millicent's bedroom. He must have been the man she took home that night. Randal, or Burke or whatever his name is, was nailed for his crimes only once long ago but the cops think that he's probably been a successful, mid-level con artist all of his life. Nyla Witherspoon's inheritance would have been a big score for him."

"But only if she got her hands on her money."

"Devlin has been in contact with the Seattle police. It won't be long before Nyla discovers that Mr. Perfect is a scam artist." Grace shook her head. "It's just so sad."

"Now you're feeling sorry for Nyla Witherspoon? Hell, woman. That's right up there with feeling sorry for that dead rat that was in your refrigerator." Julius stopped. "Which reminds me—"

"The mugging, yes, I know. Devlin says the Seattle police picked up the other man who attacked us. Evidently they are violent career criminals with the usual rap sheet. Their main business is drugs but they are available for hire as enforcers. They told the cops that a man paid them to quote, send you a message, unquote."

Julius mulled that over. "Did they run the prints on the vodka bottle we saw in Millicent's apartment?"

"Yes. No prints on the bottle but, as I told you, they did find Burke's prints in her bedroom."

"He wiped the bottle clean of his own prints but forgot about the prints in the bedroom?"

"That's how it looks," Grace said. "The cops think Marrick was very sure that everyone would attribute Millicent's death to an accidental overdose."

"But if they did consider the possibility of murder, the vodka bottle would point toward you," Julius said.

"That's the theory. Millicent is awake, by the way, but she's still disoriented. She told the police that she doesn't remember anything about what happened the night she supposedly took an overdose. Everyone tells me that is not unusual in such situations. But she swears that she never tried to kill herself and that she doesn't do heavy drugs. Beyond that, she's not talking."

"Smart woman. She doesn't want to incriminate herself."

"The cops traced the email about eating chocolate and the online order for the candy delivery. As you guessed, Millicent had scheduled both to go out if, and only if, she did not personally cancel the arrangements every morning before eight o'clock."

"The email and the candy order went out right on time the day we found her in a drug coma."

"Yes," Grace said.

For some reason the thought amused him. "Wonder if she remembers that she sent that email and those chocolates to you and that by now you have the number of that offshore account."

"I don't know. According to Devlin, she's got partial amnesia."

"Or doing a very good job of acting the role of a patient who has lost her memory."

Grace winced. "Just goes to show, you never really know someone. I liked Millicent."

"Don't feel bad. In her own way, she must have liked you, too. That's why she left all the money to you."

"Well, there is that, I suppose," Grace said. She

seemed to brighten a little at the thought. "But I wonder why Millicent got involved with Burke. I always had the impression that she was sure he was a con man."

"That's probably exactly why she did get involved with him," Julius said. He tried to connect dots through the remaining drug fog. "She knew who and what she was dealing with—or thought she did. Looks like they were partners in the scam. They murdered Witherspoon and tried to make you look guilty."

"The vodka bottle at the scene?"

"They knew the cops would be looking for someone close to Witherspoon. If their own alibis didn't hold up they wanted to point the finger at you. Burke Marrick knew the brand of vodka that was in the basement that day because he researched his father's death."

"When I think of how many times I went out for after-work drinks with Millicent—"

Julius ignored that, following the bright red line that connected the dots. "Things must have gone wrong between Millicent and Burke. Maybe he thought she was going to betray him and keep all the money for herself. Whatever the case, he tried to kill her and failed. He took her computer, assuming that he could find the offshore account. But he didn't."

"Millicent was very, very big on encryption," Grace said. "She was obsessive about it. Marrick may be good but I'll bet you Millicent was better when it came to hiding stuff online."

"Marrick must have been ready to pull the plug on

the whole operation. But suddenly Nyla informs him that she has recovered her inheritance and he realizes he's got a second chance."

"But he knew you wouldn't quit turning over rocks," Grace said. "He was afraid that sooner or later you would ask one question too many and expose him for the fake that he was."

Devlin appeared in the doorway. "We'll get more answers out of Marrick when he wakes up. How are you doing, Mr. Venture Capitalist with a gun?"

"Let's just say I'm not focusing on a lot of positive thoughts at the moment," Julius said. "But I do have some negative things I'd like to go over with you."

Grace smiled. "You two spend some quality time together. I'm going home to take a shower and get something to eat. I haven't had any sleep and the hospital cafeteria food is downright hazardous to the health. Wall-to-wall fried things."

"Okay," Julius said. He knew he sounded grudging about it. He couldn't help it. He didn't want her to leave. He still had things to say to her. Not that he could say them in front of Devlin.

She leaned over the bed and kissed him on the forehead. She stepped away before he could figure out how to hang on to her.

"Are you coming back?" he asked before he could stop himself. He was immediately stricken with guilt. The woman had spent the night keeping watch at his bedside. She deserved a shower and a nap, at the very least. It wasn't like he had a right to have her dance attendance on him. It wasn't like he had any rights at all where she was concerned. Still, he did not want her to leave.

Grace paused in the doorway. "Don't worry, I'm going to make up a batch of the Witherspoon Way Harmony Vegetable Soup for your lunch."

"Yikes," he said. But something inside him relaxed. "Will there be an affirmation included?"

"Absolutely. I'll bring you some fresh clothes, too. They're saying you can probably go home later today."

"Home sounds good," he said.

Grace vanished out into the hall.

Devlin waited until she was gone. Then he smiled a beatific smile.

"I knew the two of you were perfect for each other," he said. "Am I born for matchmaking or what?"

"Bullshit." Julius levered himself up a little higher on the stack of pillows. He sucked in a deep breath and waited for the pain to retreat. "You suspected that she might have killed her boss."

"I never actually believed that," Devlin said. "I just wanted to be sure. Now, do you want to hear the details of my big case or not?"

"I want the details," Julius said. "All of them."

Forty-Four

After an hour of tossing and turning, Grace gave up trying to nap. The sleepless night in Julius's hospital room had left her feeling wired. She never had been able to sleep during the day, anyway.

She took a shower instead. It did wonders.

She breakfasted on a high protein meal of scrambled eggs and whole-grain toast and then she set about the task of making up a batch of Harmony Vegetable Soup.

She was slicing the carrots when she heard a car in the driveway.

She put down the knife, grabbed a paper towel to dry her hands and went into the front room. She pulled the curtain aside and watched Nyla get out from behind the wheel of a gray sedan.

She stifled a groan. The last thing she wanted was an extended conversation with Nyla but the woman had been traumatized twice in recent days. The loss of her father followed by the discovery that her fiancé was probably the killer would have been too much for anyone.

If Nyla wanted to talk, it would be unkind to refuse to listen, Grace thought.

She opened the door and stepped out onto the porch.

"Nyla, I'm so sorry," she said.

Nyla came up the steps, her sharp face tight and bleak. She clutched the strap of her purse as though it were a lifeline.

"I'm the one who needs to apologize," she said. "That's why I'm here. I accused you of murder and embezzlement. I'm sorry, Grace. I can't really explain why I was so sure you were the one who killed Dad and stole the money. I think it must have had something to do with the fact that you were the person who had done so much to make the Witherspoon Way successful. Dad was always singing your praises. I guess I was just flat-out jealous. But that's no excuse."

"It's okay, I understand. Please come in. I just made a pot of coffee. Would you like some?"

Nyla blinked, evidently surprised by the offer. Some of the tension went out of her face, exposing the attractive, elfin features that had been concealed all along. Regret and a deep weariness were also revealed.

"Coffee would be very nice," she said. "Thanks."

Agnes's front door banged open.

"Hello," Agnes sang out. She waved her pruning shears. "How are things over there?"

"Just fine," Grace said. "This is Nyla Witherspoon, Sprague's daughter. You remember she visited the other day."

"Yes, of course," Agnes said. She beamed at Nyla. "Your father was a good man, dear. He was all about positive energy. The world needs more of that commodity, doesn't it?"

Nyla flushed. "Yes, it does."

She went up the steps and moved cautiously into the living room. Once there she stopped, clearly uncertain what to do next.

"This way." Grace shut the door and led the way into the kitchen. She gestured toward a chair. "Have a seat."

She had long ago concluded that something about kitchens made it easier for people to relax.

Nyla sank slowly, tentatively, into the nearest chair. "Is Julius Arkwright going to be okay?"

"Julius will be fine. Thanks for asking." Grace set a mug of coffee in front of Nyla. "I just came from the hospital. The doctors expect him to make a full recovery."

There was a short pause. "What about Burke? I was told his condition was listed as serious."

"All I know is that he is out of surgery. I got the impression that he's expected to survive."

Nyla shook her head. "I couldn't believe it when I got the call from the police this morning. Or, maybe I should say I didn't want to believe it. But somewhere deep down inside I knew that Burke was just too good to be true. The perfect man. Dad was right about him all along."

"If it makes you feel any better, I was just as shocked to find out that Millicent Chartwell was embezzling from your father, even though in hindsight, she was the most logical suspect. Frankly, after it was discovered that the money was missing, I thought Millicent was just too obvious. I mean, really, the company bookkeeper skimming off the profits? How ordinary is that?"

"That's probably why she almost got away with it."

"I think you're right," Grace said. She glanced at the colorful heap of vegetables on the kitchen counter. "I was about to make some soup. Do you mind if I continue?"

"No, of course not." Nyla cradled the mug in both hands and looked out the window at the lake. "I suppose my father must have discovered what was going on and confronted her or maybe Burke."

Grace picked up the knife and began slicing the red peppers. "Probably."

"I wonder which one actually killed him?"

"No one knows for sure, not yet. But given the fact that Burke used a gun to try to kill Julius last night, he's probably the one who murdered your father."

"The police implied that Burke was sleeping with Millicent." Nyla's jaw clenched. "How could I have been so blind?"

"A successful sociopath has to be brilliant when it

comes to deceiving others," Grace said gently. She pushed the peppers aside, rinsed her hands and snagged a paper towel off the roll. "The ability to charm you and look you right in the eye while they lie to you and break your heart is their natural camouflage."

"Are you and Kristy going to be okay?" Nyla asked. "I mean, will you be able to find new jobs?"

"We'll both be fine." Grace tossed the carrots and peppers into the simmering broth. "Kristy will probably take a position with Rayner Seminars. Larson Rayner could use her expertise. She's very good with scheduling and she's got excellent relationships with the clients. I expect she could move most of them to Rayner Seminars."

"I don't know how many times Kristy said that Sprague was like a father to her." Nyla sighed. "I can't begin to tell you how much I hated hearing that. Sometimes I got the impression she said it because she knew it upset me."

Grace went to work on the kale, stripping the leaves from the tough stems. "I think she was trying to convince you that she had your father's best interests at heart. She didn't realize how her words would be interpreted."

"It wasn't just the way she talked about Dad. I thought she might be trying to get her hooks into Burke."

Grace paused in mid-rip and considered that comment. Then she shook her head. "That does surprise me. I never saw anything going on between the two of them. She was as suspicious of Burke as Millicent and I were."

"But then, you didn't know that Millicent and Burke were partners in the scam, did you?"

"No," Grace admitted. "What made you think that Kristy was after Burke?"

"I was so worried about losing him. Like I said, deep down, I knew that he was too damned perfect. So I hired a private investigator to watch him for a while. I was told that Burke met another woman on at least one occasion quite recently at a coffee shop on Queen Anne. The PI took a photo of the two."

"Who was the woman?"

"There's no way to be certain. In the shot she's wearing dark glasses and a tracksuit with the hood pulled up over her head. But the investigator followed her back to the apartment complex where Kristy lives. I was sure it was her."

Grace picked up the knife and began chopping the kale. "Well, Kristy did mention running into Burke at a coffee shop on one occasion. It didn't seem to be any big deal. It was after that meeting that she said she thought there was something a little off about him. She said she got the impression he was trying to pump her for information on your father's business affairs."

"That was probably exactly what happened, but at the time I was convinced that she and Burke were sneaking around behind my back. I confronted him about it. He gave me the story about the accidental meeting at the coffee shop, too. At the time, I believed him."

"Kristy was inclined to be chatty. Burke may have hoped to take advantage of that fact."

"Yes, I suppose so."

Grace tossed the kale into the broth and turned to look at Nyla. "I need to ask you again if you're the one who sent me those weird affirmation emails from your father's account. And this time I'd like the truth."

"I never sent you any emails from Dad's account, I swear it. I don't even know the password." Nyla frowned over the rim of the coffee mug. "Why would I do such a thing?"

"I have no idea, but someone sent me emails with Witherspoon affirmations for several nights in a row after your father was murdered. I think they were intended to rattle me."

Nyla's brows scrunched together. "It must have been Burke who sent the emails."

Burke sent the emails for the same reason he left the vodka bottles at the scenes of the crimes, Grace thought. He was after the money but he could not resist stalking her. He would have known about the forty-eight-hour deadline that Nyla had set down. He had wanted to exact some revenge for his father's death at her hands.

"Yes," she said. "That makes sense."

Nyla put down her mug. "I should let you get on with your day. You probably want to return to the hospital to see Arkwright. I just wanted to thank you for letting me know about the money."

"It's yours," Grace said. "Your father wanted you to have it."

"It's strange."

"What is?"

"I thought that if I got my inheritance from Dad, I would feel better. Now all I can think about is that he's gone and there's no way to make up for the disaster of our relationship. I blamed him for my mother's suicide, you see. But it wasn't his fault. It wasn't anyone's fault. I wish I had understood that sooner."

It dawned on Grace that Nyla still did not know about her father's other life as a con man. The truth would probably come out at some point but there was no need to be the one to tell her.

"I can think of a couple of affirmations that might give you some comfort," Grace said.

Nyla turned wary. "What are they?"

"Well, the first one is *You can't go back to change things but you can move forward on a different path.* Your father loved you and regretted the way things were between the two of you. Leaving you that money was his attempt to make amends. The best way to honor his memory is to accept your inheritance and try not to repeat the mistakes of the past as you move into the future."

Nyla's expression was ruefully amused. "That's a very Witherspoon Way thing to say. What's the other affirmation that applies?"

Grace smiled. *"Don't look a gift horse in the mouth."*

Forty-Five

Grace added the rest of the vegetables to the pot and left the soup to simmer gently. She sat down at the kitchen table and opened her laptop. One by one she went through the stalker's emails. They must have been sent by Burke. But he had been after the money and he was evidently a professional con man. The taunting emails didn't seem like something a pro would risk sending.

But in this case, the pro had also wanted revenge. He had left a vodka bottle at the scenes of the crimes to point the police toward her. Sure, he had wanted the money but he also wanted vengeance.

One thing was true of Burke Marrick—he was a professional liar. That meant everything he had told Nyla was false.

Julius's words echoed soundlessly in the kitchen.

Rule Number One: *Trust no one.*

Rule Number Two: *Everyone has a hidden agenda.*

Grace gave up and closed down the laptop. There was no point wasting time on the emails. That was a side issue. The important thing was that Burke and Millicent were both under guard in the hospital.

The soup was starting to smell very good. The ginger, soy and kombu-based broth spiced the atmosphere of the kitchen. Grace got to her feet and went back to the stove. Picking up the big wooden spoon, she stirred gently.

Kristy had told Nyla that Sprague was like a father to her.

But Kristy had the picture of the perfect family on her office desk. She did not need another father figure in her life. Her father was perfect. Just ask her.

And Burke had appeared to be the perfect fiancé. Just ask Nyla. Except that he was a con man and probably a killer.

Just ask Julius and Devlin.

Burke had invented one life story, why not two? He wasn't the kind of guy to do favors—except, perhaps, for someone who was in a position to do *him* a favor. Or someone in the family. Hey, even sociopaths had families, right?

Trust no one.

This was not good, Grace thought. She was starting to think like Julius—the same Julius who was currently in the hospital recovering from a gunshot wound because she had involved him in her positive-thinking world.

Kristy and Burke had met at least once for coffee. But Burke hadn't needed a second source in the Witherspoon offices, not if he had been working with Millicent from the start. Why risk trying to get info from Kristy? He must have known that Nyla would be upset if she found out—which was apparently what had happened.

But Burke hadn't appeared on the scene until about three months ago. Millicent had started skimming Witherspoon money long before that. Burke had, in fact, arrived shortly after Kristy had been installed as the receptionist.

Sprague was like a father to me.

That was a lie. Sprague had been a good employer but he had not tried to be a father figure to any of his employees. He had enough trouble with his real daughter.

Grace took the spoon out of the pot and set it in the small dish on the counter. She went to the table and picked up her phone, intending to call Julius. The sound of heavy footsteps on the back porch stopped her.

. . . And she was sixteen years old again, nearly frozen with panic, listening to the echoing thud-thud-thud of the killer's boots. Trager was returning to the scene of the crime. He had come back to kill the witness.

Breathe.

She looked at the kitchen door, double-checking

to make certain it was still locked. The bolt was in place.

This was ridiculous. It was not yet night. *Don't even think of looking under the beds. Don't go there. You don't want to make the compulsion any worse by firing up a daytime ritual.*

Trager was dead. She had killed him. His son, who may have wanted revenge, was in the hospital. There was no way either of them could be on the back porch today.

That left Kristy but it was not Kristy's footsteps she heard on the back porch.

More solid footfalls shattered the stillness.

She put her back to the wall next to the window and peered out through the crack in the curtain.

Agnes, dressed in her gardening clogs, sunhat, jeans and a loose-fitting flannel shirt, raised her gloved hand to knock.

The wave of relief was so overwhelming Grace started to shiver. She wasn't in the middle of a scene from a horror movie, after all. She lowered the phone and opened the door.

"Agnes," she said. "Are you okay? Is something wrong?"

"I'm so sorry, dear," Agnes said. There was a mix of anger, fear and guilt in her eyes.

"What on earth?" Grace said.

More footsteps sounded—light and quick this time.

Kristy appeared from the far side of the porch where she had been concealed behind the old refrigerator. She had a bottle of vodka in one hand. There was a gun in her other hand.

"Drop the phone," Kristy said. "Do it now or I kill the old lady first and you next."

Grace dropped the phone.

Forty-Six

"It's all coming together," Devlin said. "The Seattle investigators are convinced that Marrick was working the scam with Millicent Chartwell. The partnership went bad."

"No, it's not that simple." Julius paced the small hospital room. The medication and the painkillers had finally worn off. The pain was back but he could think clearly again. "We're overlooking something."

"We'll fill in the missing blanks when Marrick wakes up and starts answering questions."

Julius stopped at the window and looked out at the view of the street. "Marrick is a professional. He should have cut his losses and run a few days ago."

"Everyone has a weak point," Devlin said. "Seems

clear that in Marrick's case, it was the need for revenge."

"No," Julius said. "The timing is off. Millicent was embezzling from the Witherspoon accounts over a year before Burke Marrick showed up."

"Two cons passing in the night, recognize each other and hook up for a score," Devlin said.

"No, this was about revenge from the start," Julius said. "And it only started a few months ago." He went to the nightstand and picked up the phone. "I want Grace where I can see her."

He keyed in her code.

And got tossed into voice mail.

"She's not answering," he said.

"Maybe she's in the shower or taking a nap. She spent the night here at your bedside. She needs some rest."

"I don't like it." Julius opened the tiny closet and discovered that it was empty. "Where the hell are my clothes?"

Devlin raised his brows. "Locked up in evidence bags. Grace is bringing you some clean clothes when she returns with the soup, remember?"

"Screw the clothes. Where's my gun?"

"That's in evidence, too."

Julius swung around. Pain lanced through his side. He ignored it and looked down at Devlin's ankle. "You've got a spare. You always carry an extra."

"Your point?"

"Let's go." Julius headed toward the door, the tails of the hospital gown flapping in the breeze.

Devlin followed. "Do you think it's possible you're overreacting?"

"No," Julius said. "Call Harley. He's closer to the Elland place."

Forty-Seven

Act as if you are in control, especially when you know it's not true. Your mind will clear and you will be able to see opportunities that are veiled by chaos.

"Agnes needs to sit down," Grace said. "Can't you see that she's about to collapse? She has serious health issues, don't you, Agnes?"

She focused on Agnes's eyes, willing her to play along.

Agnes gasped and clutched at her chest. She started to pant.

"My heart," she wheezed. "It's beating so fast. I think I'm going to faint."

Rage flashed across Kristy's face. For an instant she appeared confused. She had not made allowances for small adjustments in her plan—always assuming there was a plan.

Using Agnes as a hostage had been an impulsive decision on Kristy's part, Grace decided, one that had probably been made at the last minute when it became clear that the grand scheme to exact revenge had fallen apart.

Because that was what this was all about, Grace thought. The vodka bottle that Kristy had set on the kitchen table made it clear. This was about vengeance.

"Sit down." Kristy jerked the nose of the gun toward one of the chairs and glared at Agnes as if she were nothing more than a nuisance now that she had served her purpose.

"Move, you stupid old woman," Kristy hissed when Agnes did not move fast enough.

Agnes staggered rather dramatically toward the nearest chair. Grace remained where she was in front of the stove. She watched the gun in Kristy's hand. It was trembling ever so slightly. That was not a good sign.

Kristy was in the grip of an obsession. There was nothing else that could have caused a smart woman to risk two more murders when there was nothing to be gained except revenge. Burke was in the hospital and under guard. He would start talking soon. Millicent was recovering and in time would provide answers to the questions the police were asking. It was all over.

Kristy should have been on the run and hiding under a new identity. Instead, here she was, confronting her target. Vengeance was a harsh taskmaster.

"I'll give you credit for your skill at hiding in plain sight," Grace said. "You and Burke must have spent a long time working on your business plan, so to speak. It went perfectly, at least for a while."

"Burke and I didn't learn the truth about our real father's death until a year ago," Kristy said. Her eyes burned with the fever of her rage. "Mom left Dad while we were still babies. We had no memory of him. She changed our names and our life histories because she was terrified of Dad. Told us he died in a car crash. She never gave us the truth."

"She was probably trying to protect you," Grace said gently.

Kristy giggled. "Sure. She didn't want us to know about the bad genes on that side of the family."

"If your mother was so frightened of Trager, she must have kept an eye on him from afar," Grace said. "She would have been aware of his death."

"Wrong." Kristy smirked. "She never knew what happened to him because she was killed in a car accident herself, shortly before you murdered Dad. Talk about karma, huh? Witherspoon would have loved that. Mom lies to us about Dad's death and then she dies in the exact same way he supposedly died. But his death wasn't an accident, was it? You murdered him."

The gun in Kristy's hand trembled more violently. Grace held her breath. Agnes sat very, very still.

Kristy used both hands to tighten her hold on the gun. She appeared to regain a measure of her control.

"Mother died with her secrets," she said. "Burke and I went into foster care."

"Was it bad?" Grace asked, trying to make the conversation sound normal—reasonable.

Kristy grinned. "Let's just say it was very educational. One of our foster parents taught Burke how to sell drugs, and I learned how to make money in . . . other ways."

"Someone pimped you out?"

"Not for long." Kristy shrugged. "Burke and I gave it a few months and then decided we could manage much better on our own. Burke has a real gift for the tech stuff, and I was the perfect saleswoman. We did pretty well, considering we were a couple of amateurs at the time."

"And then Burke got busted for running a pyramid scheme."

Kristy raised her brows. "You know about that, do you?"

"The cops know everything now."

"Doesn't matter," Kristy said. "This will all be over soon and I will disappear. Yes, Burke did time. He learned a lot inside. First thing we did when he got out was make up some new identities. We've had several over the years. Burke and I die and get reborn on a regular basis. Talk about positive thinking."

"Burke buried your past by changing the records to make it appear that you died as a little girl in the car accident that took your mother's life. He faked his own death after he got out of prison."

"I'm impressed," Kristy said. "You really have done your research."

"What made you come looking for me?" Grace asked.

"Burke discovered the truth when he was preparing the set of identities that we're using now. He got the bright idea of researching Mom's family tree. There's so much ancestry information available online. Amazing, really. Anyhow, that's when he figured out that she had lied to us about our past. Once he started peeling back the layers, it didn't take him long to find the connection to Cloud Lake and our real father."

"How long did it take him to find me?"

"Are you joking?" Kristy smiled. The fever in her eyes rose a couple of degrees. "The girl wonder of Cloud Lake. The young heroine who saved a little boy from a vicious killer. The brave, resourceful teen who killed a man with a liquor bottle. Oh, yeah, your name popped up right away—once we started looking in the right place."

"You started making plans," Grace said. "Nice work landing the receptionist's job at the Witherspoon Way."

"The fact that Sprague needed a new receptionist at the time was just good luck," Kristy said. "But even without that opening, I would have found a way to get close to you, Grace."

"How?"

"Simple. Burke and I would have rented space in the same office tower and set up shop as a pair of investors. It's easy. One way or another I would have become your friend. I wanted to get to know the woman who murdered my father, you see. I wanted time to decide just how I would make you pay for what you did to my family. I wanted to destroy you slowly but surely."

"You intended to start murdering the people around me and leave a bottle of vodka at the scenes?"

"I knew it would take a while for the police to get the significance of the vodka. But that was fine by me. I was sure you would understand immediately that this was all about the past. I wanted to see you suffer and fall apart. I wanted to destroy you."

"Burke was on board with the revenge plan, then?"

Kristy grimaced. "Burke is all about the money. He didn't get excited until he realized how much revenue Sprague Witherspoon was pulling in with his motivational seminar business. That's when he sat up and paid attention."

"He set out to marry Nyla."

Kristy's smile was thin and cold. "I was patient. I gave him the time he required to set up his con, but when I told him I was ready to start putting my plan into action, he got upset. He wanted to ride the Witherspoon Way gravy train for another year or so. He figured the income would double or even triple in that time frame, thanks to you."

"So he didn't want you to take any action that would jeopardize my position at the Witherspoon Way, at least not until he thought that he had maxed out the profits."

"We quarreled."

"Right. That day when you met him at a coffee shop on Queen Anne."

"Shit, you really do know too much." Kristy frowned. "Burke didn't want to meet me but I insisted. I had already waited long enough. I had given him his shot at Nyla. He stood to make a few million. He was getting greedy. He knew that Sprague had to die before Nyla could get the inheritance. It was just a matter of when. He finally agreed."

"Are you the one who murdered Sprague?"

"Yes." Kristy smiled, pleased. "I knew the code to override the household alarm system because I was the one who volunteered to look after Sprague's plants while he was out of town, remember? Sprague also authorized me to buy stuff for him using his credit card."

"That was how you made it look as if he had purchased the vodka that you left in his bedroom."

"Exactly." Kristy beamed. "I let myself into his mansion shortly after midnight and shot him while he slept. He never even woke up."

"The next morning when we all started to wonder why Sprague hadn't come in to the office, you were the one who suggested that someone should check on him," Grace said. "I was the logical one to do that because I lived closest to the office. My car was in my apartment garage, only a few blocks away."

"It was so easy," Kristy said, almost crooning. "Things went exactly as I had planned. Burke was pissed because he figured he'd lost a few million but he was still going to do okay out of the con and he knew it."

"Until he found out that Nyla's inheritance was missing."

Kristy snorted. "I told him, easy come, easy go. He didn't like it but there wasn't much he could do about it. But he called me right after he left Millicent's apartment. Told me the con was back up and running. He said Millicent needed someone to launder her money. She told Burke they could run the same embezzlement scheme at Rayner Seminars."

"So you tried to murder her, too."

"She was next on my list, anyway," Kristy said.

"What went wrong?"

"The bastards I bought the drugs from cheated me." The gun shivered again in Kristy's hands. She took a moment to regain control. "I was in a hurry. I knew I had to move fast. I got to Millicent's about an hour after Burke left. I was in tears. I told her I needed to talk to someone because I had stumbled across some information about Larson Rayner that indicated he was a con. I said we had to talk about it before we agreed to work for him."

"You lied."

"Of course. It's one of my many talents. But Millicent wanted the information she thought I possessed. We had a couple of drinks together. I put the drug in her glass. When she started to pass out, I dragged her into the bedroom and injected her with more of the junk. She should have been dead by morning."

A faint burning odor wafted through the kitchen. The soup was starting to scorch.

"You're the one who sent the late-night emails," Grace said.

Kristy smiled. "Thought those would make you nervous. You knew someone was watching from the shadows but you had no idea where to look. I loved that part."

"Which one of you sent those thugs after Julius?"

Kristy stopped smiling. "That was Burke's idea. We knew Arkwright was getting too close to you. Burke thought a good beating would scare him away. After all, Arkwright was just a businessman. He should have been a soft target."

"A bit of a misjudgment on Burke's part, I'd say. And he certainly didn't hire high-end talent to deliver the message."

Kristy grimaced. "Same bastards who sold me the drugs that were supposed to take care of Millicent. Burke and I were from out of town. We didn't know how to find reliable help here in Seattle. Burke asked around shortly after we arrived. Someone recommended that pair of idiots."

"Were they the ones who put the dead rat and the vodka bottle in my refrigerator?" Grace asked.

"No." Kristy beamed. "That was me. Pretty cool, huh? I had a lot of fun with that bit. Wish I could have seen your face when you opened the refrigerator that day."

"Things really went off the rails after you failed to

kill Millicent," Grace said. "Burke must have been shocked when he realized Millicent had sent me the key to the money and that I had given it to Nyla."

"He said there was still a chance to save the con because Nyla still trusted him. But he had to get rid of Arkwright once and for all because Arkwright was too close to the truth."

"But Burke screwed up last night and now everything is falling apart, isn't it?"

The smell of scorched broth was getting stronger.

"Do you mind if I take the pot off the fire?" Grace asked. "The soup is burning. It might set off the fire alarm."

Kristy hesitated but she obviously wasn't quite ready to pull the trigger. She wanted more time to explain exactly why she had gone to so much trouble.

"Move the damn pot," she said. She gestured with the gun.

Grace turned toward the stove and carefully gripped the heat-proof handle. She lifted the heavy pot off the gas burner and shifted it to the other side of the stove. She did not turn off the burner that she had been using to heat the soup.

Casually she reached for a paper towel to wipe her hands. She pulled the leading edge toward the stove and left it lying on the counter. Then she placed one hand on the counter as if she needed support.

She turned halfway around to look at Kristy.

"You came here today to finish what you started, didn't you?"

"Yes," Kristy said. Hot tears burned in her eyes. "This was about punishing you for what you did to me and my brother."

"What I did to you?"

"If you hadn't murdered my father—my real father—everything would have been different for Burke and me."

"You think your biological father would have taken you in? Cared for you? The guy beat his second wife to death and would have murdered a little boy, just to cover up the crime. Try a reality check, Kristy. What kind of father do you think he would have been to you if he had lived?"

"We would have been a family."

"The perfect family," Grace said softly.

"Yes, damn you."

Grace moved her hand slightly on the counter, guiding the trailing edge of the paper towel into the fire of the gas burner.

The towel burst into flames that raced across the counter, consuming paper towels with stunning speed. The thick roll caught fire. Smoke billowed.

The smoke detector screamed.

Kristy stared at the smoke and the fierce flames. "What did you do? Stop it. *Stop it.*"

Agnes climbed to her feet. She had the heavy pepper mill in one hand.

"Hang on, I'll take care of everything," Grace said.

She looked at Agnes as she spoke. Agnes got the message and hung back.

Grace turned toward the counter as if she were going to try to tamp down the blaze. But she seized the handle of the pot instead, swung back around and hurled the scorching soup straight at Kristy.

Distracted by the smoke and fire, Kristy didn't see the hot soup coming her way until it was too late. Her scream of rage and panic was louder than the shrill squeal of the fire alarm. She fell back, swiping madly at the soup that had splashed across her face and chest.

The gun roared. The shot went wild. Grace sent the heavy pot sailing across the room. It struck Kristy on the shoulder, spinning her sideways.

She was frantic now. In her desperation to get the soup off her skin, she dropped the gun.

Agnes moved quickly and seized the weapon. She aimed it at Kristy with the steady calm of a woman who is accustomed to handling dangerous implements.

"You'd better do something about that fire, dear," Agnes said to Grace. She pitched her voice above the screech of the fire alarm. "Or you'll lose the house. That would be a shame."

"I'm on it," Grace said.

She rushed to the counter, grabbed the long-handled soup spoon and used it to push the blazing roll of paper towels into the sink. She heard the SUV engine in the drive just as she turned on the faucet.

Footsteps thudded on the back porch. She glanced out the window, heart pounding, and saw Harley Montoya. He had a gun in his hand. He kicked open the door before she could get to it and stormed into the kitchen.

Simultaneously, Julius and Devlin arrived through the front door with the ferocity of an invading army. It had clearly been a move the three men had coordinated.

Julius, Devlin and Harley slammed to a halt and took in the situation. They lowered their weapons.

The last of the flames died in the sink. The draft created by the open doors took care of the smoke. The screech of the fire alarm stopped abruptly.

Devlin moved to take charge of the gun Agnes was holding on the sobbing Kristy.

"Thanks, Agnes," Devlin said. "I'll take it from here."

"She's all yours," Agnes said.

She sat down abruptly on the nearest chair. Harley went to stand behind her. His fingers closed around her shoulder. She reached up and touched his big hand.

Julius looked at Grace. His eyes burned. The right side of his hospital gown was wet with fresh blood.

"You might be interested to know that I did a hell of a lot of positive thinking on the ride from the hospital to this house," he said.

She walked straight into his arms. He caught her close with his free arm.

"I told you, it works," she mumbled into the hospital gown.

"Are you okay?" he asked. His voice was raw.

"Yes," she said. "Yes, I think so. I'll probably have

an anxiety attack when this is all over but I'll postpone that for a while."

"Grace."

That was all he said. But it was the only thing that needed saying.

Forty-Eight

"*Trust no one,*" Grace said. "*Everyone has a hidden agenda.*" She shook her head. "I hate to admit it but in this particular case, your affirmations are the ones that seem to fit best."

"You were the target of a carefully planned and executed strategy," Julius said. "It almost worked but it failed because you managed to outmaneuver your opponents."

"Because I had your help."

"Well, it was three against one, if you count Millicent," Julius said. "Seems only fair that in the end you had reinforcements. Even if they did show up late."

They were on the sofa in the living room of her house. Julius was back in jeans and a worn denim shirt that fit loosely around his freshly bandaged side. His sock-clad ankles were stacked on the coffee table.

Grace had her legs curled under her. Earlier Julius had built a fire in the big stone fireplace. Dinner had consisted of takeout and a bottle of wine. It should have been a very cozy, very romantic setting, she thought. There was even an affirmation that suited the scene: *Recognize the good moments and cherish them.* But night had descended on Cloud Lake and in spite of the wine, she was still wired. She did not think that she would sleep. She did not want to sleep.

That afternoon she had worried about Agnes spending the night alone after the disturbing events. But Agnes had declined the offer of the spare bedroom, saying somewhat vaguely that she had a friend who was coming over to stay with her. Grace had understood when she saw Harley's old truck pull up in front of Agnes's house. For the first time in the recorded history of Cloud Lake, Harley had arrived at the Gilroy house with what appeared to be an overnight bag.

"I know Millicent was conspiring with Burke but it was all about the money as far as she was concerned," Grace said. "She had nothing to do with Sprague's murder. I'm sure she had no idea that Kristy is Burke's sister, let alone that Kristy was plotting revenge against me."

"That's certainly Millicent's story," Julius said.

"You don't believe her?"

Julius's smile took a grim twist. "The woman is an embezzler, Grace. Are you sure you want to think of your relationship with her as a friendship?"

"Okay, maybe 'friendship' isn't the right word. But she left all of her ill-gotten gains to me, if you will recall." Grace looked into the fire. "She did that because she literally has no one else in the world. That is just so sad."

"Something tells me she'll make all sorts of friends in prison, assuming she actually ends up doing time."

"You are so cynical." Grace thought for a minute. "Maybe Millicent will become one of those white-collar criminals who gets recruited by the FBI to detect other embezzlers."

"I wouldn't be surprised if she manages to talk her way into a job like that."

"I still can't quite believe that this was all about revenge," Grace said.

"And money," Julius said. "Two of the most compelling forces in the world."

"No." Grace pulled away from the protective embrace of his arm. She knelt on the cushions and caught Julius's face between her palms. "I refuse to believe that revenge and money are the strongest forces in the world."

He watched her with the controlled hunger that always shadowed his eyes.

"Are you going to tell me that positive thinking is the strongest force in the world?" he asked. "Because if you are, I need another drink first."

She smiled. "What I'm going to tell you is that love is the strongest force on the planet and maybe in the entire universe."

"Is that one of your affirmations?"

"Nope. It's just the truth, at least for me. I love you, Julius Arkwright."

He went very still. For a moment he looked at her as if she had spoken in some language that he might have known long ago but had forgotten.

Then he moved. He took his feet off the table and set his glass down with great precision.

"Grace."

He said her name as if he could not quite believe that she existed. As if it could work magic.

She put her own glass on the table and leaned into him—careful not to touch his freshly bandaged side. She brushed her mouth against his.

"I know you've got trust issues and I know that you don't go for the feel-good, positive-thinking stuff," she said. "I get all that because I've got some issues of my own. None of our issues are as important as the fact that I love you."

"Grace."

He kissed her with a desperate passion. It was the kiss of a man who had been thirsting for love for so long he did not know how to ask for it politely. Instead, he seized it with both hands.

"I've been looking for you all of my life," he said simply. "I love you."

The truth was there in the stark wonder that infused his words. The night would be a long one but she would not be alone. Neither would Julius.

"We will hold on to this," she said.

"Yes," he said. "We're both fighters. We know how to hang on to what is important."

. . .

She awoke from a ragged dreamscape that involved darkness, a flight of stairs and an empty doorway.

She sat up, suddenly wide awake but not in the shaky, breathless way that indicated an impending panic attack.

"Julius?" she whispered.

"Over here," he said.

She looked toward the window and saw him. In the glow of the night-light she could tell that he was wearing his T-shirt and jeans.

"Bad dream?" he asked.

"Started out that way." She sat up on the edge of the bed and automatically went into the breathing exercises. "What about you?"

"I couldn't sleep," he said. "Every time I closed my eyes I thought about that damned vodka bottle sitting on your kitchen table."

"Yeah, the vodka thing was creepy. Kristy is creepy. But when I think about what a dreadful childhood she had—"

"Don't," Julius said. It was a command. "Don't go there. I am not going to listen to you make excuses for a psychopath."

She thought about that. "You're right. Sometimes there are no excuses."

"Zero in this case. How's the breathing going?"

She did an internal check. "Okay, I think."

"Need your meds?"

"No. No, I'm fine, really."

"Was your dream the old one that you told me about?"

"At first. I was back in the basement of the asylum, trying to get to the top of the stairs. Trager grabbed my jacket but I broke free. This time I made it through the doorway. I found what I was searching for on the other side."

Julius came toward the bed and took her into his arms. "So, your dream is changing. That's a good thing, right?"

"Yes, I'm sure it is."

Her nerves were still on edge but the sensation—like the dream—was different this time. A great rush of expectation sparkled through her.

"What did you find on the other side of the door?" Julius asked.

She smiled. "You."

"Good," he said. He sounded pleased.

"And my new career path," she added.

"I'm your new career?" He sounded more than pleased now. He sounded exultant. "I can definitely live with that."

"No, no. Sorry for the confusion. You aren't my new career. Well, not exactly. More like my first employee. I'm going to offer you a job."

Julius considered that for a couple of beats.

"You want me to work for you?" he said finally.

"Not full time, of course. I can't afford you full time."

"Honey, you can't afford one hour of my time, at least not in your current financial situation. However, I am willing to negotiate."

"That's good because I'm going to need a first-rate consultant."

"I see." He kissed her forehead and then the tip of her nose. When he got to her mouth he put his hands around her waist. "Why don't you come back to bed and tell me all about this new career of yours?"

"Sure," she said. She wriggled out of his arms and headed for the hallway. "But first I'd better make a few notes. You know what they say, inspiration often strikes in the middle of the night. If you don't write it down, you'll forget it by morning."

"I've never heard that. But as it happens, I'm feeling inspired myself, at the moment. Inspired to go back to bed."

"Wait," she yelped.

He started to scoop her up in his arms. He stopped suddenly, his eyes tightening in a spasm of pain.

"Shit," he said. He took a deep, careful breath. Gingerly he touched his right side. "Okay, let's talk about your new career path."

She told him all about her vision of her glorious new future.

His reaction was swift and certain.

"That'll never work," he said. "Forget it. Find another career path."

"No," she said. "This is what I was born to do. You've got two options, Julius Arkwright. Either you agree to consult for me, or I'll find someone else who will."

His mouth curved faintly. "Is that a threat?"

"Definitely."

He appeared to give that some thought.

"Well?" she said after a moment.

"You do realize that you'll be the first client I've ever had who got away with blackmailing me."

"Really? Others have tried?"

"Sure. Not often, but yes, occasionally one has tried to put me in a corner. And failed."

"Don't think of it as blackmail," she said earnestly. "Think of me as a protégée."

"No, I'm pretty sure this is blackmail. What I'm thinking is that I'm going to let you get away with it."

"Excellent decision," she said.

He kissed her. Then he raised his head and smiled his lion smile.

"Now, let's discuss my fees," he said.

Forty-Nine

Irene poured more coffee into Grace's cup. "You're back on the high-octane stuff today. Are you sure you're okay?"

"Yes, I'm fine, really," Grace said. "Didn't sleep a lot last night but that was only to be expected under the circumstances. I was more concerned with Agnes, to tell you the truth."

They were in Irene's office. On the other side of the window business in Cloud Lake Kitchenware was brisk. The sun had come out and so had the locals and tourists. Customers browsed the elegantly displayed pots and pans and the gleaming kitchen knives with the same pleasure that was usually reserved for art galleries and jewelry stores.

"Agnes is a tough lady," Irene said. "Which reminds

me—word around town this morning is that she did not spend the night alone, either."

Grace smiled. "I can report that for the first time ever, Harley Montoya did not leave before dawn. In fact, he stayed for breakfast. I saw them in the kitchen together."

"About time. Maybe they'll finally get married."

"Don't be so sure of that. I think last night was a special-circumstances thing. Agnes always says that she and Harley like things just the way they are. Gardening club rivals by day, lovers by night. After all these years, I'd say it works for them."

"Each to her own, I suppose." Irene sipped her coffee. "What about you and Julius?"

"Julius needs a home and a career," Grace said. "I plan to help him make that happen."

"He's got both."

"They aren't working for him. I'm going to fix the problem."

"Why would you do that?" Irene asked. "I thought you had decided to get out of the fixing business."

"Turns out, I need some of the same things fixed in my life that Julius needs fixed."

Irene laughed. "I've been aware of that for a long time. Why do you think I went to the trouble of arranging that blind date?"

"You're a good friend. I take back everything I said about blind dates always being a bad idea."

"Next question. Why Julius?"

"Discovering that someone wants to kill you has a

way of focusing the mind," Grace said. "It has become clear to me that I love Julius."

"I see." Irene leaned back in her chair. "And Julius?"

"He loves me, too."

Irene looked pleased. "I knew it. It's in his eyes every time he looks at you. Heck, it was there that first night. Devlin tells me that it's usually like that for men. Hard and fast. So tell me about this new career path of yours and the job you've lined up for Julius."

Grace told her.

Irene laughed. "I can't see Julius going for it, not in a million years."

"It's a done deal. I applied Arkwright's second rule—*Everyone has a hidden agenda*. I found out what Julius really wants and I intend to give it to him."

Fifty

The office of the president and CEO of Hastings, Inc., was located in the southwest corner of the forty-seventh floor of a gleaming office tower. The rain had stopped but it would return soon. The rain always came back in Seattle. But for now the clouds were scattering. Sunlight sparkled on the snow-capped peak of Mount Rainier and flashed on the waters of Elliott Bay.

The wraparound view made for an iconic postcard, Julius thought. This was Seattle at its most spectacular. Sure, Mount Rainier—an active volcano considered one of the world's most dangerous—was only sixty miles away. And the waters of the Puget Sound were cold enough to kill you within half an hour if you fell off one of the picturesque ferries. It was also true that the region was laced with major seismic fault lines. The experts were always warning that it was just a matter of time before the next Big One struck. So what? That just made life all the more interesting.

"What are you doing here?" Edward asked.

"Consulting," Julius said.

"No one asked you to consult for Hastings."

"That is not entirely accurate," Julius said. "Someone did ask me to do just that. My client."

Edward sat forward and clasped his hands on top of his desk. "I hope that your client is paying you because I sure as hell don't intend to. Can't afford you."

"Don't worry about it," Julius said. "My fee will be covered. Now, do you want my advice or not?"

Edward thought that over for a moment and then he sat back in his chair.

"All right, I'll bite," he said. "What's the free advice you're offering?"

"I told you, it's not free."

Edward snorted softly. "There's always a price. I learned that much from you."

"You should have learned something else from me. *Trust no one.*"

Edward's eyes narrowed. "Including you?"

"Your choice, of course. I know there's a theory going around that I somehow sabotaged Hastings in the past eighteen months. But do you really believe I'm the one behind your problems?"

Edward looked at him for a long time.

"No," he said eventually. "I don't. I never did believe it."

"Why not?"

Edward's mouth twisted in a grim smile. "For the same reason your new companion gave Diana—you'd have done a better job of it. I'd be standing in the smoking ruins of the company by now. Instead, I'm being slowly bled to death. That's not your style. You can be cold blooded but you aren't into long-term pain and suffering."

"What security steps have you taken?"

"The usual. I brought in an outside forensic accountant who conducted a full-scale audit. I also had a security firm run new background checks on all employees. Nothing. The clients are just quietly fading away. Contracts aren't being renewed. New ones aren't being signed. I'm in a death spiral. I need financing and I can't get it because of the rumors. Some of my best people are looking for jobs with other firms. You want the truth? I'm starting to think a merger is my only option."

"You're in no position to negotiate one that will be favorable to you and your employees," Julius said.

"Don't you think I know that? But the alternative is to let the company go under, and that would be worse for everyone, including my employees and the family."

"You said you brought in a security firm to investigate your employees."

Edward steepled his fingertips. "They came up with nothing."

"What about your board of directors? Did you have everyone on it investigated?"

Edward did not move. "Are you serious? You know

damn well that every member of the board is a member of the family. Each and every one has a strong, vested interest in the success of the company."

"You know what they say about family feuds. And I can tell you from recent experience that people rarely think logically in situations that present them with an opportunity to punish someone they think deserves punishment."

Edward tapped his fingers together and looked thoughtful.

"Damn," he said very softly.

"People tell you that they operate on logic and reason but that's not how it works," Julius said. "I thought you learned that from me as well. The truth is, most folks make their decisions based on their emotions. After the decision is made, they can always find reasons to justify the action."

"Everyone has a hidden agenda. Arkwright's Rule Number Two." Edward got to his feet. He walked to the window and looked out at the city. "It's true, not everyone on my board likes the idea that I'm in charge now. But it's one thing to be resentful or angry. It's something else altogether to attempt to destroy the whole damn company."

"When it comes to revenge, some people will go to any lengths." Julius gripped the arms of his chair and pushed himself to his feet. "Speaking as your outside consultant, my observations these past few months indicate that the source of your problems is very close to home."

There was a long silence before Edward exhaled slowly.

"Richard," he said.

"Your half brother? I agree. That's where I'd start looking if I were in your shoes."

Edward nodded, more resigned than dismayed. "He has always resented me. Things got worse when the family put me in charge of the company after Dad died. There have been times when I wondered if he was somehow involved in the problems at Hastings but I kept telling myself that he wouldn't do anything that was against his own best financial interests."

"He's probably telling himself that if he can convince the rest of the family that you aren't up to the job of managing Hastings, the others will push you out and put him in charge."

"That's the kind of short-term thinking that can ruin a closely held business like Hastings."

"Yes, it is." Julius crossed the room and joined Edward at the window. "What are you going to do?"

"Have a talk with Richard." Edward rubbed the back of his neck. "I'll make it clear that if he doesn't agree to give up his seat on the board and leave quietly, I'll take the issue to the rest of the family. He'll step down. He won't want the other members of the family to find out that he was trying to sabotage their main source of income—not to mention their social status."

"I think you're right. Richard will leave. But you'd better watch your back from now on."

"A cheerful thought." Edward grimaced. "I can

handle Richard. But it would be good to know that I had someone I could trust on the outside to help me keep an eye on him, someone who always seems to know what's going on in the shark pool."

"Me?"

"You."

"I'll do what I can to watch your back," Julius said.

"Thanks." Edward's expression tightened. "About Diana—"

"Diana and I were mismatched from the start. My fault. I convinced both of us that I could become the kind of man she wanted me to be. That was never going to be true. The two of you belong together."

"I just want you to know that, in spite of what you suspect or the rumors that went around at the time, we were never together—not physically—until after Diana left you and after I handed in my resignation."

"Don't you think I know that?" Julius smiled. "You were the knight in shining armor—for both of us. You saved Diana and me from a marriage that was doomed from the start."

Edward eyed him warily. "That's a very generous way of looking at things."

"I'm in a different place these days. I've had plenty of time to think about the past and put things into perspective." Julius paused a beat and then grinned. "What's the matter? Afraid I'm playing you?"

"No," Edward said. "I think you're telling me the truth. You're trying to close a few doors on the past so that you can move forward into the future, aren't you? That's why you came here today."

"You have to excuse me. I've been hanging out with a positive-thinking expert lately. I'm learning to look for the silver lining. Going with the glass-half-full approach, blah, blah, blah."

Edward raised his brows. "Blah, blah, blah?"

"Don't worry, I haven't completely lost my mind. Just moving in a different direction." Julius started to turn away. He stopped. "One more thing. You're going to need some financing to pull out of the dive."

Edward looked at him. "Are you offering to help arrange a cash infusion?"

"Are you asking?"

Edward thought about it and then nodded. "There's no one else I'd rather deal with at the moment. No one else I can trust. The situation is . . . fragile."

"I know."

"I've got the whole damn family and more than a thousand employees depending on me, Julius."

"You can turn this around."

"With a little help from a friend," Edward said. He smiled. "Thanks."

"Forget it."

"No, I won't forget it. If you ever need anything from me, just ask."

"Thanks. I appreciate that."

They stood there in silence for a time, watching the ferries glide across Elliott Bay.

"That was a good after-dinner talk you gave the other night," Edward said eventually. "Definitely your personal best. I don't think a single person in the audience dozed off."

"I had some coaching."

Edward's mouth twitched at the corners. "Grace Elland?"

"Yes."

"According to the media, the two of you have been living dangerously lately."

"The good news is that the excitement is over," Julius said.

"It wasn't just the after-dinner talk that was different," Edward said. "You seem different."

"Grace changed everything."

Edward smiled. "Diana said she thought that might be the case."

"Did she?"

"You sound surprised." Edward laughed. "Sometimes others see things more clearly from the outside. Your advice to me today would be a prime example."

"You didn't see the truth about the problem on your board because you were unwilling to look in the right places."

"Isn't that always the case?"

"Yes." Julius winced. "Sounds like one of those damn Witherspoon affirmations, doesn't it?"

Edward chuckled. "Yes, it does."

Julius glanced at his watch. "I'd better get going. If I hang around here any longer people will start to think that I'm going for a hostile takeover of Hastings."

"You don't want to swallow my company?"

"No." Julius moved toward the door. "I've got another project in mind."

"Yeah?" Edward watched him. "What is it?"

"Grace is going to establish a foundation. I'm her consultant."

"You? In the do-good business?"

Julius shrugged. "Something a little different for me."

"No offense, but working for a charitable foundation doesn't sound like a good fit for you, Julius. You can't help making money. It's your gift."

"That's what Grace says. She's going to take advantage of my talent to finance her foundation."

"Sounds like she spent too much time working for that positive-thinking guru, Witherspoon."

"You want to know a little secret?" Julius asked. "Grace was the brains of that outfit."

"Yeah?" Edward looked intrigued. "How's that?"

"She wrote the cookbook and the blog. Came up with the affirmations. Figured out the target audiences. Directed the online marketing. She took Witherspoon from a mid-level player straight to the big leagues."

"Grace is that good when it comes to business?"

"She's a natural when it comes to marketing. Unfortunately, she's only interested in a business model that has a feel-good mission."

"Thus your newfound interest in charity work," Edward said. "Got it. What will you be doing, aside from backing her up with funding?"

"Her instincts are great when it comes to marketing, but where people are concerned, she has a bad habit of focusing on the positive. Way too trusting. Tends to see the best in people."

Edward nodded in somber understanding. "That kind of naiveté leads to trouble every damn time."

"Which is why I'll handle the personnel end of things at the foundation. In addition to the hiring, I'll also vet the funding applicants. Grace needs someone to filter out the con artists and the daydreamers."

"What's the goal of Grace's foundation?" Edward asked.

"Lots of people think they want to open their own business."

"Sure, it's one of the big American dreams. Statistically speaking, most entrepreneurs lose their shirts."

"Usually because they don't have someone to teach them the ropes," Julius said. "That's what Grace's foundation is all about. She sees it as a sort of start-up university for people who otherwise wouldn't be able to get a foot in the door because they lack the connections and the financing and the knowledge of how to navigate the system."

Edward laughed. "You mean you actually intend to follow through on that advice you gave in your after-dinner talk? You plan to offer your services as a mentor?"

"Grace says my title will be consultant. I'm clinging to that."

"You, Julius Arkwright, will offer free consulting advice," Edward said neutrally.

"I'm not saying I'd be averse to making a little

money on the side." Julius smiled. "A certain percentage of those proposals that the foundation funds will prove profitable, I'm sure."

"Now that sounds more like the Julius Arkwright I know."

"Wait until I tell Grace," Julius said.

"Tell her what?"

"She says no one ever remembers the details of an after-dinner speech. She claims that all the audience recalls are the emotions they felt during the talk."

"Depends on the speech," Edward said. "By the way, you never told me the name of your client, the one who hired you to consult here at Hastings today."

"Grace."

Edward got a knowing look in his eyes. "I had a feeling that might be the case. Should I ask about your fee?"

Julius opened the door and looked back over his shoulder. "She's buying me lunch today."

Edward laughed. Julius saw heads turn in the outer office. The expression on the receptionist's face and on the faces of the three people waiting to speak with Edward were priceless.

Automatically, he ran the scenario in his head. The news that Arkwright and Hastings were back on good terms would be all over Seattle by the end of the day. Carefully plotted strategies designed to take advantage of the Hastings business situation would collapse. Mergers-and-acquisitions experts would look elsewhere for targets. Headhunters would think twice about trying to lure away some of Hastings's best executives. Employees who had stayed awake at night worrying about their jobs would relax.

Julius crossed the hushed reception room, smiling a little. Grace was right about one thing, the future could be changed. And she was just the woman who could do it.

Fifty-One

She waited for Julius downstairs in the coffee shop. The grande-sized cup of organic, free-trade decaf coffee she had ordered was still nearly full because after ordering it she had concluded that her tightly strung nerves could not handle even decaf.

Like most of the other customers around her, she had her laptop open. She was supposed to be working on the mission statement for the new foundation but she had discovered that she was not yet ready to concentrate on target audiences and marketing strategies. The meeting between Julius and Edward seemed to be taking forever. A good sign, she told herself. Or maybe not a good sign.

She refused to go negative.

The moment she saw Julius walk into the coffee shop, she knew she could stop fretting. His face was as unreadable as ever, but when he got closer, she saw his eyes and knew she could relax.

"I'm hungry," he said. "I'm ready to collect my first paycheck. Where are we going for lunch?"

"I know a nice little place that caters to vegetarians on First Ave. near the Market," she said.

"Oh, joy."

"But first tell me how the meeting went. I want a report."

Julius shrugged. "I doubt if we'll be having Thanksgiving with the Hastings family this year but Ed and I reached an understanding. He knows I'm not after his business and he knows what he has to do to save his family's company. By the time you and I finish lunch, the rumors that Ed and I are doing business together again will have filtered through half of Seattle. The other half will get the gossip before they sit down to dinner this evening."

"Excellent." She smiled, satisfied. "The rumors alone will change the business dynamic of the situation for the Hastings empire."

"Yes, they will, but here's the thing—I don't want to talk about business anymore today," Julius said. "I want to talk about us."

She paused in the act of closing her laptop, a frisson of hope mingled with uncertainty making her go very still. No negative thinking, she told herself. But her future was on the line and she knew it.

"Okay," she said. "Do you want to have this conversation over lunch?"

"No. I want to have it here. Now."

"What, exactly, do you want to discuss?" She felt as if she were walking over quicksand. One false step . . .

He reached across the little table and took her hand in his. "I love you, Grace Elland. I don't think I ever understood what love was until I met you. It changes everything."

It wasn't the first time he had told her he loved her, but she knew she could never hear the words often enough. Her emotions were so dazzled that she feared she might burst into tears, right there in front of the baristas and everyone else. The atmosphere in the busy coffeehouse was suddenly crystalline; pure and perfect.

"Meeting you changed things for me, too," she said, lowering her voice because of the people at the nearby tables. "I love you, Julius."

"I know this is all new for both of us and that we should give ourselves some time. But I don't want to waste any more time." He tightened his grip on her hand. "Will you marry me? Make a home with me? Make a family with me?"

"Yes," she said. "Yes. And yes."

Julius got up and pulled her to her feet. He looked at the baristas and the customers.

"She just said yes," he announced.

Applause broke out.

Grace flushed. She knew she was turning scarlet but she was also aware that she had never been happier in her life.

Julius kissed her, right there in front of the talented baristas and all the people who were drinking coffee and working on computers and phones.

The applause got louder.

Julius released her long enough to pick up her laptop. She grabbed her jacket and bag. The cheers followed them outside into the glittering, rain-polished afternoon. The sidewalks were crowded, as they always were in Seattle when the sun came out to play. Sunglasses were everywhere, appearing as if by magic.

"Got an affirmation for this moment?" Julius asked.

"The one you came up with works for me," Grace said. "Love changes everything."

"That's not an affirmation," Julius said. "That's a promise."

Keep reading for an excerpt from

SECRET SISTERS

by Jayne Ann Krentz.
Available now from Berkley Books.

Tom Lomax was dying. Blood and other matter draining from the terrible head wound soaked the threadbare carpet. His thin, wiry body was crumpled at the foot of the grand staircase that once upon a time had graced the lobby of Aurora Point Hotel.

He looked up at Madeline with faded blue eyes glazed with shock and blood loss.

"Maddie? Is that you?"

"It's me, Tom. You've had a bad fall. Lie still."

"I failed, Maddie. I'm sorry. Edith trusted me to protect you. I failed."

"It's all right, Tom." Madeline held her wadded-up scarf against the terrible gash on Tom's head. "I'm calling nine-one-one. Help will be here soon."

"Too late." Tom struggled to reach out to her with

a clawlike hand that had been weathered and scarred from decades of hard physical labor. "Too late."

The 911 operator was asking for information.

". . . the nature of your emergency?"

"I'm at the Aurora Point Hotel," Madeline said, automatically sliding into her executive take-charge tone. "It's Tom Lomax, the caretaker. He's had a bad fall. He needs an ambulance immediately."

"I've got a vehicle on the way," the operator said. "Is he bleeding?"

"Yes."

"Try to stop the bleeding by applying pressure."

Madeline looked at the blood-soaked scarf she was using to try to stanch the flood pouring from the wound.

"What do you think I'm doing?" she said. "Get someone here. Now."

She tossed the phone down on the floor so that she could apply more pressure to Tom's injury. But she could feel his life force seeping away. His eyes were almost blank.

"The briefcase," he whispered.

Another shock wave crashed through her.

"Tom, what about the briefcase?"

"I failed." Tom closed his eyes. "Sunrise. You always liked my sunrises."

"Tom, please, tell me about the briefcase."

But Tom was beyond speech now. He took one more raspy breath and then everything about him stopped. The utter stillness of death settled on him.

Madeline realized that the blood was no longer

pouring from the wound. She touched bloody fingertips to Tom's throat. There was no pulse.

A terrible silence flooded the lost-in-time lobby of the abandoned hotel. She knew that Tom was gone, but she had read that the first responder was supposed to apply chest compressions until the medics arrived. She positioned her hands over his heart.

Somewhere in the echoing gloom a floorboard creaked. She froze, her gaze fixed on the broken length of balcony railing that lay on the threadbare carpet beside the body. For the first time she noticed the blood and bits of hair clinging to it.

There were probably several scenarios that could explain the blood and hair on the broken railing, but the one that made the most sense was that it had been used to murder Tom.

The floorboards moaned again. As with the blood and hair on the strip of balcony railing, there were a lot of possible explanations for the creaking sounds overhead. But one of them was that Tom had, indeed, been murdered and the killer was still on the scene.

She listened intently, hoping to hear sirens, but the wind was picking up now, cloaking sounds in the distance.

The floorboards overhead groaned again. This time she was almost certain she heard a footstep. Her intuition was screaming at her now.

Instinctively she turned off the phone so that it would not give away her location if the operator called back. She scrambled to her feet.

Somewhere on the floor above, rusty door hinges

squeaked. One of the doors that allowed access to the upstairs veranda had just opened.

She looked down at Tom one last time and knew in her heart that there was nothing more she could do for him.

"I'm sorry, Tom," she whispered.

Her car was parked in the wide, circular driveway in front. She slung the strap of her heavy tote over one shoulder and sprinted toward the lobby doors.

The vast, ornate room was drenched in age and gloom. The dusty chandeliers were suspended from the high ceiling like so many dark, frozen waterfalls. The electricity had been cut off eighteen years earlier. When her grandmother had closed the old hotel she had left all the furnishings behind.

Edith had claimed that the heavy, oversized chairs and end tables; the graceful, claw-footed sofas; and the velvet draperies had been custom designed to suit the Victorian-style architecture and would look out of place anywhere else. But Madeline knew that was not the real reason why they hadn't taken any of the furniture with them. The real reason was that neither of them wanted any reminders of the Aurora Point Hotel.

In its heyday at the dawn of the twentieth century, the hotel had been a glamorous destination, attracting the wealthy travelers and vacationers of the era. Her grandmother had tried to revive the ambience and atmosphere of that earlier time, but in the end it had proved too expensive. In the wake of the violent night eighteen years ago, there had been no way to get rid of the property. Selling the Aurora Point Hotel was never an option after that night. There were too many secrets buried on the grounds.

Madeline was halfway across the cavernous space when she saw the shadows shift beneath the rotting velvet curtains that covered one of the bay windows. It could have been a trick of the light caused by the oncoming storm, but she was not about to take a chance. The shadow had looked too much like a partial silhouette of a figure moving very rapidly toward the front doors. It was possible that she had seen the shadow of the killer. The bastard had used the veranda stairs at the back of the building to get down to the ground and was now moving toward the front lobby entrance to intercept her.

In another moment whoever was out there would come through the lobby doors. She had to assume the worst-case scenario—Tom's killer was hunting her.

Madeline retrieved her keys from her shoulder bag and dropped the tote on the floor. She could hear the muffled thud of running footsteps on the lower veranda now.

She bolted behind the broad staircase and went down a narrow service hall. She had grown up in the Aurora Point. She knew every inch of the place. In the many decades of its existence it had been remodeled and repaired countless times. The gracious, oversized proportions of the public rooms concealed a warren of smaller spaces that made up the back-of-the-house.

There was a large kitchen, a commercial-sized pantry, storage rooms, and the laundry.

There was also the back stairs, which the staff had used to service the guest rooms.

She summoned up a mental diagram of the layout of the sprawling hotel grounds. It was clear that there was no way to get to her car without being seen by whoever was on the veranda.

She heard the lobby door open just as she emerged from the small, dark hallway into the pantry. The silence that followed iced her nerves. Most people who happened to walk in on a dead body would have made some noise. At the very least they would be calling 911.

So much for the fleeting hope that the intruder might be an innocent transient or a high school kid who had stumbled onto the murder scene and was as scared as she was.

She heard more footsteps—long, deliberate strides. Someone was searching the first floor, looking for her. It would be only a matter of time before she was discovered. If the person stalking her was armed, she would not stand a chance of making it to her car.

She tried to think through a workable strategy. On the positive side, help was on the way. She needed the equivalent of a safe room until the authorities arrived.

She went to the doorway of the pantry and looked out into the big kitchen. The old appliances loomed like dinosaurs in the shadows. Beyond lay the service stairs that led to the guest rooms on the upper floors.

She rushed across the kitchen, not even trying to

conceal her movements. Her shoes rang on the old tile floor. She knew her pursuer must have heard her.

Muffled footsteps suddenly pounded across the lobby, heading for the kitchen.

Madeline opened the door of the service staircase and raced up to the next floor, praying that none of the steps gave way beneath her weight.

She reached the first landing, turned, and went down the hall. Most of the room doors were closed. She chose one at the far end of the corridor, opened it, and rushed inside.

Whirling, she slammed the door shut and slid the ancient bolt home. A determined man could kick the door down, but it would take some work.

She could hear the intruder coming up the service stairs. But her pursuer would have to check the rooms one by one to find her.

Heart pounding, her breath tight in her chest, she looked down and was vaguely surprised to see that she was still clutching her phone. She stared at it, oddly numb. Very carefully she switched it on and tapped in the emergency number again. She set the phone on the top of a dusty dresser.

"Don't hang up again," the operator said earnestly. "The ambulance and police should be there any minute. Are you all right?"

"No," Madeline said.

She went to the nearest piece of stout furniture, a heavy armchair, and started to drag it across the room.

"Are you in danger?" the operator demanded.

"Yes," Madeline said. "I'm upstairs in one of the

bedrooms. Someone is coming down the hall. He'll be here any second. I've locked the door but I don't know how long that will stop him."

"Push something in front of the door."

"Great idea," Madeline gasped. She shoved harder on the heavy chair. "Why didn't I think of it?"

The big chair seemed to weigh a ton, but it was moving now. She managed to maneuver it in front of the door.

She heard the footsteps stop outside her room. She grabbed her phone and headed toward the French doors that opened onto the veranda.

The storm struck just as she stepped outside. Wind-driven rain lashed at her. But she could hear the sirens in the distance.

She knew the intruder had heard them, too, because the footsteps were retreating down the hall, heading toward the rear stairs at a run. She knew the killer was headed for the safety of the woods that bordered the rear of the property. She remembered the old service road that wound through the trees.

A short time later she heard a car engine roar to life. The intruder was gone.

She reminded herself that there were not a lot of ways off Cooper Island. A private ferry provided service twice a day. There were also floatplanes and charter boats. The local police might have a shot at catching the killer.

Or not. Most of Cooper Island was undeveloped. A great deal of it was covered in forest. There were plenty of places where a determined murderer could hide until he found a way off the island.

She rushed to meet the emergency vehicles pulling into the drive. Mentally she made a list of what she could—and could not—tell the cops.

She had spent eighteen years keeping secrets. She was good at it.

Perfect menu, perfect party,
perfect crime . . . Perfectly marvelous

JERRILYN FARMER

"One of the authors who makes the amateur sleuth genre work."
Chicago Tribune

"Cooks up delicious mystery you'll savor."
Sue Grafton

"Has raised the bar for the amateur sleuth mystery in a most provocative and exciting way."
Sujata Massey

"No one knows how to serve up a tasty slice of L.A. life like Jerrilyn Farmer."
Jan Burke

Scrumptious praise for JERRILYN FARMER, MADELINE BEAN, and

PERFECT SAX

"An entertaining story . . . [with] precise plotting; appealing, realistic characters; crisp dialogue, and a wry sense of humor . . . *Perfect Sax* shows how a light mystery doesn't have to be be lightweight and why the amateur sleuth mysteries can be endearing."

FORT LAUDERDALE SUN-SENTINEL

"Farmer's seventh breezy culinary mystery smoothly blends all the right ingredients—Beverly Hills money mania, tart humor, romance, and, of course, murder . . . Farmer's menus and decorating descriptions, glimpses into the high-end Hollywood lifestyle, and warmly conversational tone will delight fans of lighter crime capers."

PUBLISHERS WEEKLY

"Madeline Bean is charming, the food is divine, and the Hollywood background is juicy."

JILL CHURCHILL

"Farmer not only folds her heroine's career as a caterer/party planner seamlessly into the plots but also . . . provides a glimpse into the not-always-glamorous world of Los Angeles's wealthy movers and shakers."

CHICAGO TRIBUNE

"Farmer can ham-and-egg her way through a comedic mystery series with ease."

PITTSBURGH TRIBUNE

Books by
Jerrilyn Farmer

THE FLAMING LUAU OF DEATH
PERFECT SAX
MUMBO GUMBO
DIM SUM DEAD
KILLER WEDDING
IMMACULATE RECEPTION
SYMPATHY FOR THE DEVIL

PERFECT SAX

JERRILYN FARMER

AVON BOOKS
An Imprint of HarperCollins*Publishers*

This is a work of fiction. Names, characters, places, and incidents are products of the author's imagination or are used fictitiously and are not to be construed as real. Any resemblance to actual events, locales, organizations, or persons, living or dead, is entirely coincidental.

AVON BOOKS
An Imprint of HarperCollins*Publishers*
10 East 53rd Street
New York, New York 10022-5299

ISBN: 0-380-81720-9
www.avonmystery.com

First Avon Books paperback printing: February 2005
First William Morrow hardcover printing: January 2004

Printed in the U.S.A.

10 9 8 7 6 5 4 3 2 1

For Rick and Julie Klein
who gave Madeline their home and more

Acknowledgments

Snaps for the jazziest people I am blessed to know:

SOLOISTS:

Smokin' Sam Farmer *on sax*
Cookin' Nick Farmer *on drums*
The Fabulous Chris "Daddy-O" Farmer *on lead guitar*

Lyssa "Manhattan Slim" Keusch, *editor*
Evan "The Living End" Marshall, *agent*
Mix-Master Michael Morrison, *publisher*
May "Chops" Chen, *invaluable assistant*
Big Gun Peggy Tataro, *firearms expert*
D. P. "The Doc" Lyle, M.D., *medical expert*
Hot Note Heather Haldeman, *Conrad's expert*
Boogie Woogie Barbara Voron, *first reader*

INSPIRATION BY:

Swingin' Susan Anderson
Jumpin' Jan Burke
Snap-Your-Cap Sally Fellows
Super-Murgitroid Margery Flax
Drivin' Doris Ann Norris
Cool Carol Tager
The Prince of Wails, Mark Tager
and
a great round of applause to all the Buds, baby

PERFECT SAX

"Mood Indigo"

"I love big balls."

Wesley Westcott took his eyes off the road for a moment to glance over at the tall, thin blonde sitting beside him.

"Oh, stop!" Holly caught his look and laughed. "You know what I mean," she said, flushing. "Big *fund-raising* balls. Banquets. *Parties*."

"Uh-huh." He turned back to the road, steering his new white Jaguar S-Type off the freeway and onto Sunset Boulevard as he doused a smirk.

Holly pointed at where the smirk had made its momentary appearance and demanded, "Stop it, Wesley."

"I *am* stopping it," he protested. "Go on, already. Tell me all about your love of balls."

She laughed. "Tonight, for instance. The music blew me away. And the dresses. And the caviar. It was all pretty freakin' faboo."

The Jazz Ball had been a stunning success. Six hundred Los Angelenos had gathered to celebrate the Woodburn School of Music and raise funds to support its prestigious Young Artists Program. The Woodburn, a private institute devoted to tutoring the West Coast's most gifted musical prodigies, liked to suggest it was even more selective than its better-known rival on the other coast, Juilliard.

Once a year, the fund-raising wing of the Woodburn put on a major social event to lure contributions from its well-heeled patrons. The Jazz Ball was famous for the star power of its guest list and the lavishness of the festivities. And this year, the event-planning firm that had won the plum prize of creating this *über*-party was none other than Mad Bean Events, Wes and Holly's own firm.

"I think Madeline outdid herself tonight," Holly said, referring to their friend and leader. "The black-and-white newspaper theme was awesome. She has the coolest ideas."

"That she does. It was a beautiful night." Wes turned the car south on Vine Street and said, "I wish she had come back with us to my house to celebrate."

"I think she's exhausted," Holly said, finger-combing her loose platinum wisps as she ran through the obligatory party postmortem with Wesley. "She doesn't usually leave a party so early."

"I know," Wes said. "But even Maddie needs a break."

Madeline Bean, the head of one of Hollywood's trendiest young event-producing companies, had managed to rise quickly in the world of spectacular parties. She might only be twenty-nine, but she had become a seasoned veteran of the ever rising and falling Hollywood social tide in a short time. And if the clients alone hadn't made her seasick, she'd managed to weather quite a few ups and downs of a dicey economy, too. Running a small business could be treacherous; one way she had found to succeed was simply to work harder than anyone else. A case in point had been the Jazz Ball. Madeline had been indefatigable for the past two weeks. The number of details involved in pulling off a grand party *this* grand was enormous. All the intense attention Maddie had paid to a zillion small concerns—the black linen napkins that arrived were, in actuality, puce; the white peppercorns she had ordered were, at the last minute, unavailable—must, by now, have finally taken its toll.

Wes stopped at a traffic light and looked over at Holly. "When Maddie and I decided to start the company, I don't think either of us realized how much real, honest-to-God work we'd be in for."

"Ah." Holly smiled broadly. "Now I finally understand why it was you so *quickly* hired an assistant."

"We were stunned by your talent." Wes was always a gentleman. And then he added, "You have no idea how hard it is to find a good schlepper."

Holly had begun as their assistant six years ago and worked her way up by mastering just about every party job she encountered. Holly filled in wherever she was needed, as an extra bartender, or the person to make the emergency run for more white asparagus, or the one in full-face clown greasepaint twisting a balloon giraffe for six-year-old birthday twins. Six feet tall, scrappy, and much more likely to wear a Day-Glo orange paisley polyester miniskirt than anyone else you might meet—ever—Holly Nichols was made for parties. And even though she was apt to gaze upon certain celebrity guests with more dogged affection than was entirely suitable for a staff member working a private party, she was in all ways a most valuable asset to the team.

Holly pushed her white-blond bangs off her forehead and six rhinestone-encrusted bangle bracelets clacked as they fell down her wrist.

Wes shot her another glance. "You sure you're up for coming to my place?"

"Absolutely. I'm wide-awake. And I'm starving."

"You're always hungry."

"True. And you always cook so divinely for me."

"True." Wes looked happy with the arrangement. He

loved to cook and, together with Madeline, devised the menus and supervised the chefs at their events.

The traffic was thin at this late hour as they got south of Hollywood. Wes brushed his thick brown hair off of his forehead and eased his new car southwest toward his house in Hancock Park. His black leather jacket, he noticed with the habit of one who takes in every visual detail, looked not at all bad against the custom white leather seats of the Jag. It reminded him again of the Black & White Ball. They'd just pulled off another stunning event. He hummed a riff of "In the Mood."

"Is that jazz?" Holly asked, perking up. "I'm all about jazz now. The band that played at the ball was flat-out awesome. Who knew that kind of music could sound so groovy?"

"Jazz? You mean you don't listen to jazz, Holly?"

"Well, cha! I am major into Eminem. And Radiohead. And Vendetta Red. And, well, Mars Volta. And Clay Aiken. You know me. I dig rap. And rock. And show tunes."

Wes nodded, trying to follow her musical tastes.

"I always thought jazz was just too hard to understand. I mean, before. So I guess I'm evolving. Ya think?"

"I do."

"Tonight was amazing. The horn section! That trumpet drove me wild!"

"The instrument?" Wes knew Holly well. "Or the incredibly beautiful young man playing it?"

Holly had been pulling her light blond hair up on the top of her head and pinned it all there with a sparkly pink clip that she'd rummaged from the bottom of her enormous bag. "Yeah. He was adorable. True."

"Yeah, I thought so."

"Have a little respect here, Wes. That guy turned me on to jazz, you moron!"

"He turned you on, all right."

"Look," Holly said, her dignity clearly in need of defense, "I'm putting on the jazz station. See?" She punched a few of the preset buttons on the radio in Wesley's new car. The sound system boomed and sputtered as Holly rapidly punched in FM station after station, quickly discarding country music, an all-talk format, a string quartet, and an opera, to run out of steam at one that featured all news.

"Sweetie," Wes said, trying to get Holly's attention. "Try KJAZZ at 88.1 FM."

"You always know everything," she replied in a way that didn't sound entirely complimentary. But before Holly could change the frequency, the baritone voice of the news announcer had begun a new story.

"Tonight, organizers at the Woodburn School of Music were unavailable for comment on the apparent theft of a rare and valuable instrument that was the featured auction item at their annual fund-raising ball."

"Hey, it's about us," Holly said, cranking the volume dial.

The newsreader continued, "One of the school's instructors who was present at the gala event, famed jazzman Joe Bernadello, described the instrument as a one-of-a-kind silver tenor saxophone made in the 1950s by the Selmer Company, a top Parisian maker. Bernadello went on to say he was 'shocked and saddened' that the saxophone was stolen from the downtown Tager Auditorium, where the black-tie event was held earlier this evening. Police are looking for anyone who might have information to call the LAPD hot line." The station then began playing a commercial that was mildly persuasive if one had a deep need to buy the cheapest mattress in Los Angeles County.

"Bad news travels fast, huh?" Holly shook her head, her dangling earrings tinkling at the activity. "I was hoping that old sax would just turn up somewhere, misplaced or something." They had heard about the screwup with the missing sax before they left the Woodburn ball. Of course, the auction wasn't something Mad Bean Events was responsible for, so it hadn't been their nightmare.

Wesley frowned. "This is sad. After all our efforts, what will everyone in town be talking about tomorrow? That sax."

"That's the way life is. You plan and you plan. You work and you work. Then something always happens you weren't prepared for. That's Madeline's philosophy."

"She's right," Wes said.

"Something is always going to happen we can't predict and we can't control," Holly said. "But it's not usually something that makes the cops come running."

"Or makes the news," Wes agreed.

"How did they get this story so fast, Wes?" Holly looked at her wrist and shook several of the bangle bracelets until her tiny rhinestone watch was revealed. "It's only two A.M." They had begun breaking down the kitchen before midnight and then spent almost an hour standing around out in the parking structure with their crew overseeing the loading of their equipment and kidding around with the waiters and chefs as they left.

Wes eased the car into his Hancock Park driveway but just sat there, staring at the car radio, turning the sound level down as the commercials rolled on, while Holly pulled a tiny cell phone out of her giant bag and began to dial.

"You calling Maddie?" Wes asked. "Wait a sec, there, Hol."

"Shouldn't we let her know something is going on?"

"Not yet," Wes said, thinking it over. "What can any of us do about the missing sax? Look, Maddie left early. Chances are she doesn't even know about it. Let her sleep."

The newscaster's voice returned to the news after the commercial break and began another story. "With a disturbing report, we hear now from Ken Hernandez, who is out in the Hollywood Hills at the site of a criminal investigation. What is going on out there, Ken?"

"It looks like L.A. has been hit by another shocking crime, Jim. I'm standing in the quiet neighborhood of Whitley Heights, where police have just informed us there has been an apparent home invasion robbery that turned violent."

Sitting in the dark car, Wesley and Holly were once more riveted to the news. Whitley Heights was the tiny section of the Hollywood Hills where Mad Bean Events had its offices and professional kitchen. The company worked out of the lower floor of Madeline's home. Wesley's hand jabbed for the radio knob and turned up the sound.

"We have yet to get the whole story here, Jim, but the police tell us the body of a young woman, age approximately midtwenties, has been found in the house, which is the residence of one of the city's most successful party planners . . ."

"Oh my God. Oh my God." Holly's pale skin turned paler.

The original news anchor spoke up. "We understand it's the home of Madeline Bean. Are the police aware that Bean's catering company was responsible for producing the Jazz Ball at the Woodburn School earlier this evening—the scene, we have just learned, of yet another serious crime? Is there a connection here?"

"I don't know about that, Jim. I'll try to have more information for you in my next report."

Holly stared at Wes. "Oh my God. Oh my God. Oh—"

"Holly." Wes put his hand on her shoulder and she looked up at him, her face going blank with fear, the words dying on her lips.

Wesley Westcott had spent the past several years being the calmest man you'd ever want by your side in a kitchen crisis.

His voice never rose. His cool never faltered. Whether it was because of shock, or habit, or sheer emotional fortitude, his calm voice betrayed almost no strain as he asked his assistant quietly, "Did the idiot on the radio just imply that Maddie's . . . *body* has just been discovered?"

"Nutty"

TWELVE HOURS EARLIER . . .

There are very few things as invigorating as trying to coordinate the efforts of a dozen wacked-out, overly sensitive, testosterone-driven gourmet chefs on the afternoon of a large dinner party. At the moment six of my prep chefs were ready to kill the other six. And I suspect those other six were ready to kill me. What would life be like without its little challenges?

"Philip," I chided, "the soup is supposed to be black and white, not brown and white." We were preparing two soups, a white cheddar cream soup and a black bean soup, which would be simultaneously ladled into the same shallow bowl until the two met in the middle, and then garnished with heirloom tomato salsa and sour cream just before it was served. It was to be the perfect start of our evening's meal, as it fit the black and white and "re(a)d" headline theme of the Jazz Ball.

"I know that," Philip Voron said, looking vexed.

"See what you can do to darken the black bean soup, will you?"

"I told you it was supposed to be blacker! Idiot!" Philip Voron spat out at his neighbor.

I moved on.

Across the room, Wes smiled at me and pointed to his watch. We had to keep moving. We were due at the Tager Auditorium, the site of the evening's party, in a few hours, but I took half a second to appreciate just where I was. On this party day, the day of our final prep for the Woodburn fund-raiser, our industrial-style kitchen could explode the senses of even the most seasoned caterer. The large white-tiled room, with its commercial-grade stainless appliances and high ceiling, was currently filled with the pounding sounds of chopping blocks punished by a dozen chefs' aggressive knives, the intoxicating perfume of freshly crushed garlic and just-picked basil, the heat of gas flames firing high under enormous bubbling stockpots. I love these sounds and scents and sights.

"Mad," called out Holly from near the sinks. She was helping two women who were rolling out our fresh angel-hair pasta. We planned to cook it later when we got to the Tager kitchen, quickly so it would remain al dente, right before serving it to our six hundred guests. The thing that made it interesting was adding the black ink we'd removed from the sacs of ten dozen cuttlefish, which we'd had flown in from the Mediterranean that morning. Cuttlefish are a sort of squid. Sautéed, they taste a lot like softshell crab. My partner, Wes, and I often lament the less than adventurous palates of most banquet planners, but this time, at least, we'd be out on the inky culinary edge. Our hostesses, the women of the Woodburn Guild, were taking the black-and-white theme seriously.

"I'll be right back," I called to Holly. I had to run out to my car, where I'd left a phone number for the ice sculptor who was carving jazz instruments out of black-tinted ice.

I ducked through the butler's pantry, both sides of which were made up of floor-to-ceiling glass-fronted cabinets. There, in the backlit cases, we displayed the hot-turquoise-

and-lemon-yellow vintage pottery collection we often use, the serving platters and bowls we bring to our more informal events. The pantry led from the kitchen to the office that Wes and I share and then out to the front door by way of Holly's reception-area desk.

Outside, I started down the flight of stairs that takes you from my hillside home to the curb. It wasn't until I was halfway down that I noticed something was wrong. The street below, a quiet cul-de-sac where Whitley Avenue dead-ends right up against the retaining wall of the Hollywood Freeway, was covered in trash and papers and the like. What was up with that?

As I began to process the scene, I became angrier with the mess. Dozens of papers had been dumped in my driveway and beyond, like someone had maliciously emptied a wastepaper basket out their car window as they drove by. I had been out front only ten minutes before with Wesley and Holly, and the street had been quiet and neat and clean. Few people come all the way up this street, anyway, since there is no outlet. So whatever was this paper attack about?

I opened up the back of my old Jeep Grand Wagoneer and pulled out an empty carton marked LOUIS ROEDERER 1995 BRUT, removed the inner cardboard partitions that had cushioned and separated the champagne bottles a few months back when I first bought them for a wedding shower, and then, with distaste, began picking up trash off the asphalt. As I tossed handfuls of paperwork into the carton, I was thankful the stuff wasn't filthy. In fact, it was an odd assortment of officelike documents.

Hey, now. Wait a minute. Was that an actual U.S. passport tucked between the sheets of paper I just dumped? I pawed through the pages and fished out the navy blue booklet. Amazing. It looked real. I flipped it open and stared at the two-inch photo of a vital, lean man in his early sixties, judging by his iron-gray buzz cut and allowing for the standard ten years one must always add to the estimated age of anyone one meets in Hollywood. The name on the passport was Albert Grasso. His date of birth proved I could peg ages in this town with the best of them. He would be sixty-three next month. His address was on Iris Circle, the next street up the hill.

I leaned against my Jeep, resting the carton on the hood, and filtered through some of the other items I'd just gathered into the box. There was a handful of framable-size photos that had clearly fallen out of a manila folder marked PHOTOS. I quickly sorted them so they made a neat stack and all faced the same direction, but I could barely finish the task once I caught a glimpse of the glossy side of one of the pictures. It was an eight-by-ten color print, a glamorous studio shot of a seventies icon, autographed *To Albert—singing your praises! With love, Cher.* Cher. I mean, *really*! Whose trash *was* this?

Another photo was signed "Love, Michael," and showed a very young Michael Jackson. A third featured the cast of the Oscar-winning movie musical *Chicago*. Everyone in the cast had signed it to "Albert," offering an assortment of warm thanks and good wishes. Look at that. Richard Gere had mentioned their mutual interest in the Dalai Lama.

I became more enchanted with my trash find by the minute, shuffling through photos of David Bowie, Avril Lavigne, and Charo. The last of the photos proved more intriguing still. It was a shot of two people, one famous, one not. The young, dark-haired girl, maybe twenty or so, was smiling into the camera so hard you could see her back teeth. The older man with his arm around her had a face no one could help but recognize. It was President Clinton. They were standing close together in the Oval Office. The picture had a personal inscription, *To Teresa, with thanks.* And then the initials *B.C.*

Wesley's voice came from far away. I looked up and shaded my eyes against the glare of the sun. He was standing up at the top of the landing by the open front door. "Hey, Mad," he called down. "What's up? You need some help?"

"You've got to see what I found. All this stuff was littered all over the place. It seems to belong to a guy on Iris Circle."

"What is it?"

"Private papers and photos." I picked one item at random from the carton, a letter, and read it aloud.

Dear Mr. Grasso,

Enclosed please find my report on your psychiatric condition. You'll note the diagnosis code represents a diagnosis of anxiety-stress disorder, for which I've been treating you for the past seven years. If you have any questions, or if your insurance carrier requires any further information, please let me know.

Sincerely,
Dr. Stan Bradley, M.D.

"You have some guy's psychiatric files?"

"Apparently," I said, unable to resist paging quickly through a document that was clearly none of my business.

"And you're standing out in the street reading them?"

I looked back at Wes without a trace of guilt. "Hey, how am I supposed to know what all this stuff is? It was littered all over my property. Littering is a crime. I am simply investigating, aren't I?"

"Maybe you can put off your CSI inquiry until after we finish with the party tonight?"

I looked up from the thick psychiatrist's report on the

many issues that had been vexing Mr. Grasso and nodded. Wes was right. I had to get my focus back. "Aye aye," I said, snapping to attention. "Do you think I should try to find this guy's phone number? He'd want his stuff back, I'd imagine."

"Can we do that tomorrow? We are under the gun here, timetable-wise."

"You're right. You're always right." I put the last of the papers back into the carton and hauled it up the stairs. "But, Wes, how do you think all these personal photos and documents ended up on my lawn?"

Wes relieved me of the box as I reached the top of the steps. "I'm sure you'll find out all about it. After the Jazz Ball."

"Between Black & White"

Frankly, fund-raising is social warfare and the gentle ladies who volunteer to run the show are its generals. I had worked on several such events in the past, and I had the battle scars to prove it.

The committee in charge of this year's Jazz Ball was aiming to outdo all other elite L.A. fund-raisers in the cutthroat art of separating dollars from donors. To this end, each party decision was argued over by the Jazz Ball planning committee. Endlessly. Luckily, Wes and I have steady nerves. The theme had been changed up and back and up again a half dozen times. But in the end, the newspaper design theme of black and white, with a touch of red, captured the final vote, and judging simply by the number of guests paying five hundred dollars a ticket, the gala appeared to be a hit. This was the largest turnout in the event's forty-two-year history.

No detail of the party was too small to delight one faction of volunteer women and cause an uproar of seething disapproval in another. Victory in such details took on way too much importance to be healthy, but this was not my call. For instance, one group heavily favored a traditional engraved invitation. Formal. Black on heavy cream stock. However, the chairs of this year's event were bored silly by the memories of too many staid and stuffy charity dinners. They wanted people to talk about this party. In a good way. And despite the disapproval of some of the older members of the committee, the distinctive invitations to the "Headliner's" Jazz Ball had gone out eight weeks ago.

The invitations had been written up in a parody of the style of newspaper articles, printed on authentic newsprint under the banner the *Woodburn Daily Jazz,* rolled up like the morning paper, tied with red grosgrain ribbon, and tossed onto the pool-table-perfect lawns of the city's most generous: those heads of private foundations and leaders of civic-minded corporations and individual donors who kept L.A.'s cultural wheels turning. Naturally, the families of the Woodburn's young musicians and the staff of the school were also invited.

In my role as creative consultant and caterer to the Jazz Ball, I had made many suggestions to Dilly Swinden and Zenya Knight, the cochairs of the fund-raising gala. I have found that timing suggestions is crucial. As an event draws closer, decisions must be made. I have learned to wait for just the right moment to bring up many items in order to prevent committee-itis from draining the energy out of every last creative impulse. It had gotten to the stage where we had to have some final decisions on the look of the event. We were discussing how much of their budget the ladies wished to spend on decorating the Tager Auditorium's grand foyer, where the dinner was to be served. Dilly and Zenya were both savvy to the bottom line. While they wanted to put on a spectacular party, they also wanted to raise the most money for the Woodburn. They asked what we could do that would cut down on costs but make the biggest splash.

We had been sitting in my office, sipping white wine and going over the numbers again. "Can you imagine," I wondered aloud, "if everyone at the ball were to dress up in our color scheme? Hundreds of gowns in black or white, with accents here and there of red?"

Dilly and Zenya glommed on to the idea like the purebred shoppers they were.

"I love it," Dilly said, turning to Zenya.

"Everyone wears black, anyway," Zenya responded. "The men are no problem. Black tie. White shirt. Tux. They're done."

"Who doesn't have a black gown?" Dilly added.

"Who doesn't have two or three?" Zenya asked. "Not to mention something white. Or they could wear a black-and-white print. Or something red. I love this."

Dilly giggled and sipped her Chardonnay. "Oh, please. Who are we kidding? We all buy something new for the ball, anyway. But I just love telling everyone what they must go out and buy."

It was settled just like that. Dilly looked at her watch and shrieked. "Sorry. I have to run."

Zenya, at least fifteen years younger than her cochair, but no less busy, checked her own jeweled wrist and gasped. "Me, too. Let's meet on Tuesday at ten. Will that be all right, Madeline?"

I nodded as the women rushed out. These ladies were always on the go, their Palm Pilots filled with appointments. Dilly had a session with her Pilates trainer across town, and Zenya was running late to meet the manicurist, who was making a house call, so Zenya's second grader's nails could be changed to a new shade of pink. I try very hard not to judge. Very, very hard.

The ball's elegant black-and-white dress code had actually been one of the easier decisions. Dilly had by that time managed to achieve a stranglehold on the rest of the committee. By pairing with a sweet-natured yes-girl like Zenya, she was making all the power decisions. It was they who had approved the gourmet black-and-white menu, daring to move beyond traditional banquet bland. And I had to admire their resolve to make this ball distinctive, both in food and in appearance. Sometimes, clients don't really get it. But these two did.

As I stood in the grand foyer, two hours into their fabulous Jazz Ball, I noticed Dilly Swinden a short distance away. She was standing with her husband; he in a black Armani dinner jacket, with snow-white shirt and a red bow tie; she in a simple, floor-length strapless dress covered in jet-black beads. Her delicate neck was circled in the largest rubies I'd ever seen. The presence of so many couples dressed all in black and white made for a stunning effect, lending the party a more artistic ambience than any amount of swag draping or flower arrangements alone might have done.

Scattered in the crowd, twenty-five young Woodburn kids had volunteered to work at the event. These children left their instruments at home for the evening and were dressed as turn-of-the-century paperboys, wearing black caps with a white sack over one shoulder filled with "newspapers." Guests could purchase a "paper" for twenty-five dollars and take their chance at winning a great prize. The auction ladies had solicited donations from vendors all over the city and each of the "newspapers" in the sacks represented a donated item. One might find their newspaper raffle item was a certificate for a dinner for two at Patina Restaurant, a free eye exam by Dr. Stuart Milliken, or a seven-day Mexican cruise, the grand prize.

The party had been in full swing for more than two hours and I noted that most of our paperboys had done their jobs well. Their sacks were empty and they were ready to go home. They had done their greatest "business" while the guests were arriving and the hors d'oeuvres and cocktails had been served in the grand hall. Then, at seven-thirty, both paperboys and ticket-holding guests found their seats in the

Tager Auditorium for the all-star jazz concert. The event featured twelve of the Woodburn School's very top jazz students, who got to play with some of the country's greatest contemporary jazz musicians. A tremendous silent auction and the black-and-white dinner followed. As my waitstaff moved efficiently among the sixty tables of ten, I kept an eye out for anyone gesturing for more coffee.

Holly joined me. "So far, so fabulous." She was dressed as all our female servers, in black pants and a white lace camisole with a red rosebud pinned to one strap.

"And we're on schedule." I looked at my watch. "In just a minute Dilly and Zenya will start the live auction."

"Are you going to bid on anything?"

I gave Holly an amused smile. "Like I could afford any of this stuff."

"Everyone at Table 23 is talking about the Selmer saxophone," Holly reported. "They say it's priceless."

"Oh, yes?"

"They say there hasn't been one of this type available for years. Something about the year it was made or the registration number. I'm not sure. But two of the guys were getting kind of steamed at each other."

I looked at Holly. She was grinning, adding, "Bidding war. Mark my words."

"That will be good for the Woodburn."

The auction committee had been ruthless in extracting donations to the cause. Every upscale business in town had been solicited and many had come through with splendid items for bid, most of which went into the silent auction. During the first hour of the ball, guests mingled among the overflowing tables and signed their names to bidding sheets, upping the bids on everything from a lavish basket filled with hand-embroidered baby clothes donated by a Brentwood children's boutique, to a certificate for six flying lessons, to a week's stay at Disney World, to four floor seats at a Lakers game along with a ball signed by the entire team.

The full fury of a silent auction is hard to describe. In the final few minutes before the bidding closes, the most competitive bidders hunker down beside the bid sheets of the items they covet most. Earlier this evening, with only sixty seconds to go, I'd seen two elegant women toe-to-toe. They were outbidding each other, back and forth, for a series of twelve facials donated by a hot Beverly Hills aesthetician so in demand, she was unlisted and unbookable. No sooner would one write down $3,600 than the other would fill in the next blank with $3,700 and so on until, battle-weary but determined, they finally called a truce. One suggested they simply split the prize up and each take six sessions. And all would have been settled if at the very last second a man hadn't come up to the bidding sheet and stolen it for $4,000.

I turned to Holly. "If the silent auction is any indication, I expect the live auction to be brutal."

The auction committee saved its most desirable and biggest-ticket items for live bidding. This evening, they had chosen a professional auctioneer from Sotheby's along with a celebrity auctioneer to handle the work. The celeb was Brianna Welk, a sunny-dispositioned news anchor on one of the local channels. I had noticed Brianna paying some serious attention to our martini bar throughout the evening and said a silent prayer for the best.

"I wonder how much money the luncheon we donated will raise?" Holly asked.

"Lunch for twenty women? Maybe five thousand?" I guessed, trying to factor in how much money those two women had been willing to pay for some facials.

"You think?" Holly looked excited. We had been asked if

we would like to make a donation to the auction, and Wes had suggested we offer up a private party. He suggested we provide flowers and vases and he and Holly could give a flower-arranging class for twenty followed by a Mad Bean Events catered lunch.

Wes appeared and we welcomed him to our huddle.

"Wes, how much do you think they'll get for our lunch?" Holly asked.

"Maybe six grand," he predicted, showing more confidence than I had. "Hey. You guys see the smoke? Think I should beef it up?"

We all looked over to the side of the grand foyer, past the sixty white-draped tables filled with black-and-white-dressed guests. Next to one of the entrances we had set up a smoking martini bar that Wes had designed, using enormous glass blocks with hidden wells that provided pools in which he had floated dry ice. Smoke swirled lightly around the bar and the bartender as he worked. I noticed Brianna Welk standing there, wearing a short, flaming red sequined dress, in line with some of the gala's most serious drinkers. They were getting refills of our special concoction, a new drink we discovered in Europe.

The "smoking martini" was a near-lethal mix of Ketel One vodka, dry vermouth, and a splash of Glenlivet. We couldn't help giving in to the drama of pouring bottles of vodka into a crystal tub and adding a large chunk of dry ice. That Ketel One really smoked. And it was quite safe, since the bartender ladled the spirits into long-stemmed martini glasses, carefully avoiding any dry ice. It definitely upped the party's pizzazz quotient.

"Well, for me," Holly said, "you can never have enough smoke."

"Say, did you see the seating chart?" Wes handed me a

sheet. The party organizers had printed them up and placed one at each plate, thoughtfully encouraging guests to locate friends and/or enemies, the better to greet and/or avoid.

I love to see who's who. "The mayor is here," I noted, checking the names quickly. "And Tom Selleck? Table 30." I craned my neck. "Man, I never even saw him. I'll have to saunter by."

"And check out Table 10," Wes suggested.

I put my finger on the table and read the tiny print that offered the names.

"Wait." I reread the name and looked up at Wes. "Albert Grasso?"

Holly looked, too, but the name didn't register with her. "Who's Albert Grasso?"

"He's the guy . . ." Wes answered. "The guy who left all his private papers on Maddie's doorstep."

"That's amazing," I said, dazed to think the man would actually be at my gala. "But, Wesley. Now I feel so guilty. I should have called him. What if he's all worried about his missing paperwork."

"Madeline. We have hardly had a minute to breathe . . ." Wes started, but I didn't wait to hear the rest of his reassurances.

I headed for Table 10. Just then, a spotlight blinked on the small stage at the front of the hall. Dilly Swinden, in her jet-black beads, and her younger cochair, Zenya Knight, wearing a tight white silk gown, approached the microphone and smiled out at the crowd as the guests began to quiet down. The live auction was about to begin. Right on schedule. My eyes swept the room and I saw our crew prepare to serve dessert, black-and-white mini-cheesecakes, formed in the shape of musical notes, the black desert plates decorated with a touch of red—giant strawberries dipped in the darkest dark chocolate, each hand-monogrammed with a swirled white chocolate *W.*

"Ladies and gentlemen, let us welcome you all to . . ."

Squeezing between chairs that had been slipcovered in a black-and-white pinstripe satin, I made my way into the heart of the tight cluster of tables.

"Excuse me. Mr. Grasso?"

The face from the passport photo I'd examined earlier that afternoon looked up at me and smiled a perfect capped-teeth smile. Albert Grasso checked me out and appeared to like what he saw. He took in my slinky halter dress, his eyes lingering on my bare shoulders. I had to bend slightly to be heard over the auctioneers, who had just been introduced. Brianna, I noticed, was sloshed. When I turned my attention back to Table 10, I immediately regretted the deep V of my gown, as it now offered up my cleavage at exactly Albert's eye level. Albert's wife/girlfriend/whatever was on alert. She was a pale woman in her forties with a recently tucked chin and a short blond hairdo.

"I'm so sorry to bother you," I started again, unable to keep from putting my hand up over the deep neckline of my dress. "I wonder if I might have a word with you. It's important."

Albert's date had all she was going to take. She raised her voice and said, "Al doesn't make business appointments at social events, dear."

Another man sitting at the table smiled at me. Clearly a young woman bending over their table was more than most of these tuxedoed old codgers had hoped for when their wives had dragged them out for another fund-raising evening. "Are you a singer?" the second man inquired.

"A singer?" I was not following.

Albert Grasso said, "I might be able to fit you in my

schedule. What's the problem? What's your label? Are you signed?"

"Mr. Grasso, I'm Madeline Bean. I'm an event planner. Actually, I'm surprised to see you here tonight—but you see, this evening's Jazz Ball is an event my company is producing."

"Very nice," Albert said. "Beautiful dinner." And then he leaned closer to my bosom and asked with a wink, "And you sing?"

What was it about singing? And then I remembered the pictures. Cher. David Bowie.

"Are you a singing coach?"

"*A* singing coach?" Albert's date/wife parroted.

"You don't know who I am?" he asked, a twinkle in his eye.

In the background, the auctioneer from Sotheby's was rattling off the first item and was already in high gear. The item up for bid was a week's stay at someone's private castle in Scotland, donated by one of the board members at the Woodburn. The last bid was $8,000, I heard as I turned back to Albert Grasso.

"I'm sorry to bother you here at the party tonight. I probably should have waited until a more appropriate time, but I was so surprised to see your name on the guest list."

"I work in the music business, Ms. Bean. I know many of the musicians who played in the concert tonight. I always try to give back to the community."

"I'm sure you do. I'm sure. It's just that I have a personal matter to discuss with you."

The woman seated beside Albert Grasso had been following the rapid bidding as the price on the Scottish castle week went up to $12,500. She raised a card displaying her bidding number and the auctioneer quickly called her bid of $13,000. Onstage, Brianna Welk put two fingers to her mouth and whistled.

"Yes?" Albert turned to me and waited for more.

"A private matter, Mr. Grasso."

Albert's companion pulled her bidding card down and snapped her head to hear our conversation.

"Private?" Albert again looked at my tight dress and stood up. "Excuse me, Caroline," he said, nodding to the woman and dismissing her as he turned to me. He put his hand on the small of my back as older men like to do, leading me out of the center of the tables and off to the side of the room.

"My girlfriend gets jealous," he muttered with a wink as we found a quieter spot to talk.

"I hope I'm not causing you any trouble."

"A beautiful young woman comes looking for Albert Grasso. That's the kind of trouble I dream of."

"Thank . . . you." I couldn't imagine if that was the correct response. "Mr. Grasso. I know this sounds like none of my business and it's a very unusual question, but are you missing a lot of your private papers?"

"I beg your pardon?"

Just then an eruption of applause drowned out my response. We both looked up at the stage, where the Sotheby's auctioneer was repeating the winning bid. The trip to Scotland with the castle that sleeps twenty-four had just gone for $28,500.

"I live in Whitley Heights," I started again.

"You're kidding! So do I." Albert smiled at me. He thought I was making a pass at him.

"I live on Whitley just below your house on Iris Circle. Somehow, a lot of paperwork and photos and files with your name on them were dumped on my property."

"Holy shit." The gleam went right out of Albert Grasso's eye. "Are you kidding me?"

"No. I can't explain how this mess got on my lawn, Mr. Grasso, but I found your passport and I was planning on calling—"

"My *passport*? What else do you have?"

"Photos of celebrities. Confidential reports. Insurance papers. Bible-study notes."

Albert Grasso stared at me, his face ashen. "Where are they now?"

"At my house. It's also my office. I would have tried to get in touch with you earlier, but of course I had this big job tonight."

"So," he said slowly. "Did you read my papers?"

"Not really. I mean, I was planning on tossing it all out. It was just litter. But then I noticed the passport."

He glowered at me. Didn't he realize I was trying to help him here? How do I get myself into these things?

"How much do you want?" he asked, his voice low.

"Do I want? I don't want anything."

"Yeah. Sure you don't. You better return every single sheet of paper. Every single file. I'll pay two thousand."

Over the loudspeaker, Brianna Welk's high voice came across with the slightest of slurs. She was the lead auctioneer on the next item and told the crowd that the bidding would start at $5,000.

"Mr. Grasso. I'm beginning to feel insulted here. I don't want any reward."

"Do I hear six thousand?" called out Brianna.

"I'll give you six thousand," Albert responded, raising his own bid. What was going on?

"Look, I have your address," I said sternly. "I'll have one of my staff return the box of papers to you tomorrow."

"I want it right now," Albert said, grabbing my wrist. "I don't know what game you're playing. You say you have my personal papers, but just how did you get them? Did you break into my house? Is that how you have my address?"

"No!"

"You must think you're clever. You knew I wouldn't call the police. I'm a big name in Los Angeles, dear. I'm the top vocal coach in town. I have the trust of every singer that gets paid a million just to open his mouth, you understand? I have to protect my privacy and that of my clients. This morning I went into my home office. I saw the file cabinet was open. Obviously, I should have checked more carefully. I looked around and the art was there. The cash was there. But I knew something wasn't right. I didn't get around to opening every drawer, checking every file. I have been distraught, young woman. You think I wanted to come here tonight? Caroline insisted I take her, since she's active on the board and I'd spent a thou on the tickets. Got it? So let's get down to business. I want my files back and you have them."

"You really don't understand."

"Calm down. You will get your payoff, young woman. Just tell me how much."

I pulled my wrist out of his tight grasp as the crowd applauded another winning bid. "Tomorrow," I said, through clenched teeth, "I will turn in all the papers that I found on my property to the police. If you want your things back, I suggest you report what is missing to them. That's what you should have done in the first place. They can sort all this out. I certainly want nothing more from you, Mr. Grasso."

"Ten thousand," he called loudly after me as I pushed through the crowd.

"I have a bid of ten thousand dollars for the private parking space at the Woodburn School," Brianna Welk said with excitement, suddenly pointing to the back of the room, directly at Grasso. "Do I hear anything higher?"

"All or Nothing at All"

"Madeline," Dilly Swinden called out.

I pressed my lips together, quickly changing gears, readjusting my mood. The client deserves a cheerful event planner. "You look stunning, Dilly," I said, admiring her trim figure and the Prada gown covered in jet-black beads.

"No, you do. Look at your long neck. But just wait until next year. I'll look much better after my little trip," she said, winking. "Madeline, have you been watching? They are about to auction off your luncheon." Dilly gestured toward to stage, where Brianna was pulling the microphone out of the hand of the Sotheby's auctioneer.

Ah, yes. Our luncheon. "Thanks, Dilly. I hope we raise a bundle."

"We will," Dilly said, grabbing my hand in a girlfriend-like grasp, the largest stone in her ruby ring bruising my fingers in friendship. "Thanks to your smoking martinis."

Onstage, Brianna began reading the description of our offering, called a Flower and Gourmet Lover's Garden Party for Twenty Ladies, including the flower-arranging lesson (two arrangements would be made and taken home by each of twenty guests; all flowers, vases, and extras were included) and a gourmet luncheon (including a special lobster-and-avocado salad) catered by Mad Bean Events. Brianna's reading was surprisingly flawless, and it made me wonder if she was equally talented at reading her studio TelePrompTer under the influence. I would certainly be watching the local news with a new perspective.

Brianna asked the crowd to open the bidding at $5,000. I, alone, gasped.

Soon, a hand was raised, and although many of the diners were enjoying after-dinner refreshments and greeting their friends, enough guests were following the auction to keep the bidding lively.

Holly brought over a plate filled with chocolate-dipped strawberries about the size of billiard balls. "Schnitzel! It's up to thirteen thousand."

Brianna was getting dramatic, trying to keep the bidding going. "This money is going to the *children*," she pleaded. "Come on, people. Pay attention to me, here. Let's focus! I'm asking for fourteen goddamn thousand now. Do I have fourteen?" She got a bid of $14,000, but the cross-conversations among the happy dinner crowd did not subside.

"Did Brianna Welk just cuss out the guests?" Holly asked, with a whoop of shock.

"One smoking martini too many, I'd say."

"Holy moley."

There seemed to be three women who were still in the bidding for the garden party and gourmet luncheon and I was a little overwhelmed at the money folks were willing to pay. By the time the bids reached $18,000, I began thinking I'd better add caviar to the menu.

Brianna was wrestling to get the crowd to settle down so she could persuade the bidding upward. Just then, Albert Grasso's date, Caroline, approached from out of nowhere.

"You have some nerve," she said, right in my face.

"Hey, whoa!" Holly said, yelping as Caroline trod on her foot.

"Is there something I can do for you?" I asked. "Because right now they are auctioning off—"

"I don't care if they are auctioning off your ass, sweetie," she said, keeping her voice pleasant. "You and me are going to have a nice little talk."

I stared at her. What now?

"Albert wants his papers back and he said you weren't willing to cooperate. He's not going to pay your blackmail money. I'll have you know we have already called our lawyer and the police. Expect to find them at your doorstep with an arrest warrant."

"What?" Holly said, gasping again.

"It's a lucky thing, then," I replied, "that I have over a dozen witnesses to testify I was working in my kitchen on this party all day and an eyewitness to my finding the litter dumped on the lawn."

"You do?" Caroline hesitated for just a minute.

"Do I hear twenty thousand?" Brianna warbled over the PA. *"Please, people, settle down."*

"It is ludicrous for you and Mr. Grasso to come so unglued. But now that I think about it, I can't possibly know to whom all those files actually belong."

"What are you saying?" Caroline said, confused and angrier than ever. "Of course those papers are Al's!"

"Are they?" I asked calmly.

She looked furious, her tight little chin quivering.

The people near us were all laughing and joking loudly, unaware of our spat or the auction, which had reached $21,500.

"I have decided this really is a police matter," I finished. "I am a very close friend of a detective on the LAPD, and I think it's wise to let them handle it, Caroline. And my suggestion to Mr. Grasso is, please keep going to that therapist."

"Everyone . . ." Brianna called from the stage, her high-

pitched voice projecting over the loudspeaker. *"Listen to me now. Everyone . . ."*

"Mad," Holly whispered as Caroline stood there, sputtering, "What the hell?"

"EVERYONE . . ." Brianna tried again, much closer to the mike.

"You are going to regret this!" Caroline shouted at me.

"WHAT?" Holly and I yelled at the same time.

"You leave my Albert alone!" she shouted back.

At which point, Ms. Brianna Welk, up on the stage, had simply had enough. She expected the crowd's respect. She assumed their devotion. And most of all, she demanded their goddamned attention. She screamed into the microphone, "SHUT UP!"

And at that, this assembled group of happily partying arts patrons, parents, and philanthropists, some soused, some flirting, some chatting loudly with friends not seen in weeks, along with Albert Grasso's overwrought lady friend, simultaneously stopped speaking in sheer surprise and alarm.

"That's better," Brianna drawled over the mike, not noticing the stunned glares of disapproval. "I just wanted to say, the flower-thingie luncheon is going . . . going . . . *gone!* Sold to the lady at Table 4 for twenty-six thousand five hundred!"

"Gadzooks!" Holly said, shaking her head, as someone on the auction committee rushed onto the stage and managed to pry the microphone out of Brianna's hand. The Sotheby's auctioneer took over and the party guests went back to a slightly quieter form of chatter. "Say, what happened to that nasty woman?" We both looked around, but Caroline had disappeared. "And why was she so angry?"

"That's a good question. It has to do with the papers I found in front of my house this afternoon. There may be something private among those papers that our neighbors do not want anyone to see. Why else would they get so bent out of shape?"

"Just what you need, Maddie, more crazies."

I smiled.

"And what was that you were telling her about being 'a very close friend of a detective on the LAPD'? Are you speaking to Chuck Honnett again?" Holly asked.

"Well, no. I still hate him, of course. Nothing's changed there. But I was so sick of all her threats and intimidation. I thought it made me sound more substantial to say I have friends in high places."

Holly nodded. "It did."

I smiled back at her. "I know. I wish I still did have one, too."

Honnett and I. Now there was a story. He was this detective with whom I'd had a short, kind of passionate thing. It had started earlier in the year and had ended not that many months later. A pity the whole thing blew up, since we had some great chemistry. Really great. But he hadn't been honest with me. He hadn't told me everything.

"Being hot is not a crime," Holly reminded me, referring to Honnett's long, lean body and stong-jawed, edgy looks.

"We really had nothing in common," I said. I knew it was lame, but there was truth to it. My friends were chefs, artists, bohemians, writers, the unemployed. Honnett was a cop. His buddies were cops. He liked rules. He liked guns. He liked being a macho man, not too many words. I was all talk. This thing would have ended sooner or later. I just hadn't seen the end coming quite as soon as it had.

"What are you talking about?" Holly asked, staring at me. "You and he were cool. So he was a little older than you—"

"Like about fifteen years," I drawled.

"Maybe a real man isn't such a bad thing to have around,"

she countered. "Maybe on him the years looked pretty good."

"It wasn't that. It was the fact that he hadn't gotten around to mentioning that he hadn't completely divorced his wife yet. That kind of got in the way, Hol."

"True. That wasn't good."

I smiled at her. Neither of us had had such good luck with men. Holly had an on-again, off-again relationship with an adorable young screenwriter. In fact, a few months ago they decided to run off to Vegas and elope. We all went out there on a moment's notice, Wes, me, Holly and her Donald, and a dreamy rebound guy I thought I should fall for, John.

Only, when we got to the Venetian Hotel, Holly started getting calls from her mother and her sisters. They wanted to be there when Holly got married. They couldn't believe she'd do it without them. Soon Donald's mother was calling them on their cell phone, too, pleading for them to set a date in a reasonable month and let the family come in from the Midwest for a real wedding. In the end, the impetuous couple gave in. Just goes to show what romantic havoc a cell phone can play. Holly swears if Romeo and Juliet had had a cell, they would never have been lying in bed together when the light from yonder window broke, what with Romeo's mother calling every five minutes looking for him.

Still, we did have a lovely time in Las Vegas. Wes won twelve hundred dollars playing Caribbean stud. Donald got his picture taken with an Elvis impersonator. My new date, John, was a doll and a real gentleman, despite the fact that I kept thinking about Honnett the entire weekend. And Holly was approached about trying out as a showgirl. Poor Holly. Poor me.

"Mad," Holly said, grabbing my arm to get my attention. "This is it. The final auction item."

"Thank God."

"No, it's the saxophone I was telling you about. The priceless one. I bet it goes for a fortune."

The auctioneer from Sotheby's was a dapper man in his later years. With Brianna Welk removed from the stage, he seemed much more at ease. "Ladies and gentlemen, this is the moment many of you have been waiting for. We present the ultimate musical instrument, as is only fitting in this illustrious group of fine music aficionados. May I present the rarest and some say nearly priceless Selmer Mark VI B♭ tenor saxophone in silver, with full engraving."

The folks in the room, table by table, dropped their conversations and stopped clinking their coffee cups. Soon the perfect quiet that Brianna had only dreamed about descended on the room. Two men came forward with a leather saxophone case and unclasped the lock. One opened the lid and they set the sax case on a tilt so the audience could get a look. The bright spotlight caught the highly polished silver of the bell and glinted.

"Ladies and gentlemen. You may never again see its like. This instrument was found in the storeroom of a shop in Milwaukee, Wisconsin. We must assume it has never before been played, since the original cork stops that were used to guard the valves during shipment from the maker in Paris are still in place.

"This exceptional horn really needs no introduction—it's the most famous horn on earth. If you are a professional player or you know a gifted young soul who was born to play the tenor . . ." He paused and looked out at the tables filled with proud parents, then continued, "If you've never played a Selmer Mark VI, you're missing out on the best saxophone ever made."

We all looked at the saxophone and began to dream of

playing the best instrument on earth. Even those of us without any hint of musical ability.

"Ladies and gentlemen. Let me now tell you what has been said about the legendary Mark VI. It is accepted that those made in the 1960s are the best, and those made before 1965 are best of all because they have a better quality of brass and therefore better timbre. The instrument you see before you, and which will soon be going home with one of you, was built in 1961."

There was a palpable thrill running through the crowd. Holly pointed out the table she had waited on, the table with the parents eager to bid on this item. They were sitting quite still.

"Ladies and gentleman," the Sotheby's auctioneer continued, using his cultivated low-key patter to reel the thirsty buyers in even closer. "It is well known that the French-manufactured saxophones, like this beautiful Selmer, have more elaborate engraving, engraving you'll note that stretches to the bow, and it is argued that because of this extra engraving, they sound better and are worth more. For those who may not know such things, the head engraver at Selmer's Paris factory died in 1965, so this Selmer Mark VI before us is simply as impeccable as any instrument gets.

"But before we get to the bidding, ladies and gentlemen, let's talk about the fascinating history of this tenor saxophone. The Mark VI model was introduced by Selmer Paris in 1954 and produced for just the nineteen years. It has been said that no saxophone could equal it. But for those who scoff and suggest that not every Selmer lives up to its reputation, the proof is in the sound. We have come to offer you such proof tonight."

The crowd grew even more riveted.

"I have asked for the assistance of Mr. Sebastian Braniff.

Would you come onstage, sir? Mr. Braniff, as most of you know, is the head of the woodwind department at the Woodburn School, and he is a noted saxophone expert in his own right."

There was a murmur in the crowd as the music teacher rose from a table in the middle of the room. I realized with a start that Mr. Braniff, a small man with a thick mop of dark hair, had been seated at Albert Grasso's table.

What a fiasco that whole Grasso discussion had turned into. Why should such a simple task as returning a man's missing papers cause an eruption of emotion and suspicion? Perhaps Albert and Caroline were simply reacting with shock at the idea that their privacy had been breached. But why would Albert immediately think someone would try to blackmail him for those items' return? What was there of such value? Maybe I should really look more carefully through the documents before I took them to the police in the morning. It might be wise. If I didn't fall dead asleep, perhaps I should just take a quick but thorough peek. After all, possession is nine-tenths of the law, whatever the heck that means.

Onstage, Mr. Braniff began assembling the coveted tenor saxophone. All eyes in the room were on Braniff as the auctioneer continued his refined pimping of the legendary instrument. By the time the sax was ready to play and the auctioneer had finished his spiel, we were all so impressed that I couldn't guarantee Holly wouldn't bid on the thing.

I looked up to see Wesley just making his way toward where we were standing.

"Need some help with the cleanup?" I asked, guilty I'd been standing around for so long.

"Don't worry. All taken care of. Our guys are loading the trucks. We should be ready to depart in an hour or so. The servers are making last rounds with coffee. Things look good. Relax."

"An hour?" I was tired.

"You don't have to wait around," Wes added quickly. "Just leave it to me and Holly."

"I'm wide-awake," Holly agreed.

"Well . . ." I figured if they were okay supervising the teardown, I might get home by midnight. I could take that carton of papers and just sort through it all so I had a rough inventory of what I'd found and what I would be turning over to the police. There was something about those photos that had me thinking. It's not that I wanted to invade Mr. Grasso's privacy . . . exactly. It was just that with all his accusations and threats, I was beginning to think I had better be prepared to defend myself.

Sebastian Braniff, the celebrated music teacher, was standing onstage with the shining silver saxophone now hanging from a strap around his neck. He slowly put the mouthpiece up to his lips. He stood in the spotlight, taking his time as the crowd waited.

"Ladies and gentlemen," the auctioneer whispered into his microphone, "I give you the Selmer Mark VI, serial number 91-023. Until tonight, never before played . . ."

First one long, low edgy note. The tone of the instrument was bright and hot. Nothing soft or mellow there. Then another dirty note ripped the air. "Harlem Nocturne" soared over the top of the hall. Not a word was spoken during the piece. We all listened, as perhaps many of us never had before, to the pure gutsy sounds cutting out from the silver horn.

When Mr. Braniff finished playing the piece, the crowd remained silent. Perhaps we were all in awe of the sheer guts and daring of the auction organizers. What if this fabled instrument had flopped? What if the pads had been dried out?

Or worse. But despite the terrible risk the committee had taken, the instrument seemed to live up to its reputation. The crowd was 100 percent sold. Applause began on one side of the room, and soon all were on their feet, giving a deserved ovation to what might be the best saxophone ever made.

"Mr. Braniff would like our guests to know that he was using a mouthpiece-and-reed setup that would be appropriate for a theater pit band or a big band. These brighter mouthpieces will also usually produce the altissimo notes more easily than very dark-sounding mouthpieces."

I had no idea what he or Braniff was talking about, but still I felt let in on a sly musician's secret. Ah, I thought. A brighter mouthpiece.

The auctioneer, knowing he had us all in the palm of his hand, moved in for the kill. "This amazing Mark VI has been presented to the Woodburn School auction by an anonymous donor. Let's start the bidding at five thousand."

Several hands shot up and in less than ten amazing seconds we were at $25,000.

Holly turned to Wes and me and whispered, "Well, I guess that lets me out."

I laughed.

Wes said, seriously, "I am not sure this instrument is truly worth this kind of money. On eBay, Mark VIs sell in the five thousand–ten thousand range. I realize this one is a better year and in mint condition, but—"

"They sell the sizzle, not the steak," Holly said.

"Hell," I said, "if these people are willing to pay over twenty-six grand for our little lunch with flowers, I figure they aren't exactly hunting for a bargain."

"And they can write off any amount over the fair market value of the saxophone as a charitable contribution," Wes said.

The auctioneer was asking for $30,000 and getting it from

a man near the front. Then, all of a sudden, something going on at one of the tables attracted the attention of the crowd. Two men, from that table where Holly had served food earlier, appeared to be sparring. We heard dishes crash to the floor, perhaps upended during a scuffle. At a table nearer to us, a woman turned and announced, "Two fathers. Both have boys in our jazz band."

"Do you know them?" I asked, addressing her directly. I could see nothing from where I was standing.

"I work in the Woodburn office," she said. "I know them. Ryan Hutson's dad and Kirby Knight's dad. Really."

"Please, gentlemen," the auctioneer said into the mike, trying to get things back on track. "Can I hear a bid, please?"

"Fifty thousand," said one of the fathers.

"Oh my God," Holly said. "Did he say *fifty*?"

"One hundred," said the other father.

Applause ripped through the crowded room. We had it all here, folks. A stellar musical performance. An object beyond price. A fistfight. Insanely competitive fathers with no budget constraints in a battle of testosterone and will. It just doesn't get better than this.

And that's when Ryan's father, or maybe it was Kirby's father, began strangling his rival.

"Party's Over"

Usually, I'm one of the last people to leave a party—I'm supervising, I'm carrying things, I'm working—but not this evening. Holly and Wes had it all well in hand, and I had this nagging urge to get back to my house in Whitley Heights and that carton of documents that Albert Grasso had been so excited about. As soon as the live auction ended, I went to the kitchen to grab my bag and headed out through the main entrance of the Tager Auditorium onto a tranquil, postmidnight, traffic-free Grand Avenue in downtown Los Angeles.

At the curb, a trio of uniformed valets (black pants, cool newsprint T-shirts—okay, we were obsessed with our theme) were running to get cars for departing guests. As they brought up the vehicles, the lineup at the curb displayed the latest in luxury SUVs. Silver was the color du jour, I noted. The lacquered finishes on car after car shone bright as a string of silver beads in the light of the streetlamp. Tired men in tuxes went through the ritual of finding their parking stubs, tipping the valets, and taking their princesses home from the ball. I noticed many couples had been successful in the silent auction, as quite a few were loading giant cellophane-wrapped baskets or other large items into the backs of their SUVs. I handed my ticket to a young man with long sideburns and pulled my silk shawl more firmly around my shoulders.

"Madeline? Are you leaving?"

I looked up to see Connie Hutson, the Woodburn Ball's auction chairwoman. Tall, with a halo of auburn hair and the sort of prominent cheekbones that didn't need quite as much coral-colored blusher as Connie always wore, she was dramatic in white sequined pants. Her matching blazer dipped low, baring lots of tanned chest and a rather amazing diamond pendant.

"Hello, Connie. What a spectacular job you did with the auction!" In speaking to clients after a party, I often gush. Whether it's good PR or just exhaustion on my part, I have yet to determine.

"Ah, it was hell, my dear. Pure hell. But we did raise a staggering amount of money for the Woodburn." She gave me a look, half grimace, half smile.

"Do you have a total?"

"Liz Reed is doing a final tally, but I am simply dead on my feet. I've been here since nine this morning setting up the silent auction tables. Enough is enough."

Of course, I'd been at work even earlier, but it is a rare client who finds that fact compelling. Instead, I expressed my concern for Connie. "You must be so tired. I hope you plan to sleep for a week."

"I wish I could, Madeline. I've simply got too much to do. Ryan comes home from surf camp tomorrow and then he has his sax recital on Thursday, or we would have gone to our Cap Ferrat house and just unwound. Oh, look. Dave is waving at me." She waved back at a handsome man standing farther down the curb who was balancing a neon-yellow splashed, custom-made surfboard, which I remembered seeing on one of the silent auction tables, and turned back to me once more. "Our car isn't here yet, and Dave is not very patient. Well, I just wanted to tell you what a marvelous job you and your firm did for us tonight."

"Thank you."

"And listen, if you see that awful Patsy Stephenson, just whisper to the parking attendants to take their time retrieving her car."

"What? Tell me the scoop," I said, sensing a story.

"Ugh. Patsy. What can I say? She always volunteers to be on my committee and then does absolutely nothing. The rest of us are busting our tails tracking down leads and getting auction items, and she is always too busy or some other excuse. I swear, if her husband didn't give us a check for twenty grand to underwrite the bar, I'd just kick her butt right off the committee."

"Which one is Patsy?" I asked, turning to look at the well-dressed men and women who were continuing to make their way out of the party.

Connie's eyes followed mine and then she turned back. "I don't see her yet. Her daughter plays violin. Actually, the girl is not bad, but the *mother*!" Just then, one of the departing guests caught Connie's attention. "Good night, Mr. Braniff."

"Good night, Mrs. Hutson. Wonderful auction. And say hello to Ryan. Is he practicing?"

"More or less," the mother said, smiling, and then turned back to me. "Sebastian Braniff studied under Marcel Mule. He used to play with Skitch Henderson when he was only a kid in high school. He's my son's private lessons teacher. Wasn't he incredible tonight?"

"Listening to Mr. Braniff play the Selmer was the highlight of this evening."

"Anyway, Patsy," Connie said, easily slipping back to a favorite rant. "Avoid her like the plague."

I count on such insider tips about the private lives of the rich and famous, since I prefer to avoid doing parties and working for the truly beastly. "I'm trying to place her. What does Patsy look like?"

"Let's see. She's blond." Well, that could be almost every woman on the Woodburn Guild. "She's attractive." Ditto. "Her entire manner is off-putting, really. She never made it to even one of our meetings, so I doubt you have seen her. Oh, wait a sec." Connie pulled out the program book for the evening and flipped to one of the opening pages. "How silly of me. Naturally, she did make it to the photo shoot of the committee. There." She pointed to a thin woman in the program picture. "Wearing Gucci. She's so predictable it's galling."

"Oh, Connie. Speaking of off-putting, I had the strangest conversation with one of the Guild ladies. Is a woman named Caroline a good friend of yours? She dates Albert Grasso."

"Caroline Rochette with the terrible plastic surgeon?"

"That could be her. What is she like?"

"She's ghastly, Madeline. Why, what did she do?" Connie Hutson liked to dish the dirt. She enjoyed spit-roasting her friends over the judgmental flames, but she was even more interested in lighting new fires.

"Well, she's threatening to sue me, actually. It's a long story, but I found some papers that may have belonged to Mr. Grasso. He and Caroline went crazy when I told them I want to return the stuff. I can't imagine why."

"Oh, Caroline doesn't need a reason to go crazy, she's already there, my pet." Connie Hutson chuckled.

"What's that story?"

"Albert's not in a hurry to get married for a fourth time, I suspect. He has a wandering eye. Hell, he has even put moves on me, and my dear, I'm too busy raising Ryan and raising money for good causes to raise any hell."

Connie turned to see Dave tipping the valet and she ran down the last two wide-paved steps and slid into their silver Escalade.

I took a minute to scan the incoming valets and the cars they were driving up to the loading zone, but there was no sign yet of my old black Wagoneer with the woody panels.

"Hello," I called to some new arrivals. Hilary and Mike Entemann were just coming down the wide steps. Mike moved on to take care of the valet while Hilary lingered with me.

"Wasn't the live auction spectacular?" Hilary asked. She was smiling. "Could you believe Brianna Welk yelling at everyone to shut up? We have certainly seen the real Brianna tonight, I'm afraid."

"Her judgment may have been . . . impaired," I suggested, smiling back.

"Exactly," Hilary agreed. She was another exceedingly well-groomed woman in her early forties or so. Her pale hair was swept up and held with a diamond clip. Her black gown clung to her athletic body, showing off her muscle tone to the best advantage. "But she kept the bidding rising on your item. Twenty-six five. That must have felt good."

"It's wild." I liked Hilary. The Entemanns' eleven-year-old twins were fine singers and members of the prestigious Woodburn Honor Chorus, a group that regularly won competitions in Europe and New York. "I'm so excited. Did you see who won my garden party? I'm afraid I was distracted at the time."

"It was Dilly Swinden!"

We both laughed. "Really? Dilly bought it?"

"She was absolutely determined. She's going to invite everyone on the committee to the luncheon."

"How generous," I said. It made a lot of sense, really. It would have been equally generous had Dilly and her husband written as large a check when they made their contribution to the Woodburn's annual fund, but in purchasing this party at the auction, she got more. In addition to making an impressive donation, she could provide a wonderful treat to the women who worked hard to support her in planning this event.

"I think Dil was feeling a little guilty," Hilary said in a low voice. "By June, she and Zenya were simply leaving their committee and the board out of everything. They were calling all the shots. I admit, they did a very nice job, but feathers do ruffle. You know how we are. This luncheon will go a long way to smoothing them down again."

"It sounds wonderful to me," I said.

"They'd like to schedule the party just as soon as possible. Next week, if that is okay with you and your partner. I think most of us are going to escape L.A. in August. So let's coordinate by e-mail and set the date."

The Entemanns' silver Mercedes SUV arrived at the curb and Hilary called out good-bye as she departed. I checked my watch. Where was my Jeep?

"Oh, Mad," Holly called, meeting me out on the steps. "I'm glad I caught you. Sara is in a bind. Sara Jackson, remember? The redhead? She's got to meet her boyfriend. It's urgent. And her car battery is dead. I don't have a car or I'd lend it to her. Wesley drove me here, and he's out now, driving one of the trucks back to the rental-company lot. What should we do?"

I looked at Holly. She was so compassionate. One of our servers, a graduate student at USC, I think, had a boyfriend problem and Holly was ever ready to help.

"Can't one of the other servers give her a lift?" I asked.

"That's the trouble. Mostly everyone has already split. She can wait around until Wes gets back, but that could take hours. I thought about calling him. I've got his spare keys and his car is still here. But I'm supposed to supervise the rest of the cleanup and I can't exactly ask him to lend out his brand-new Jag."

"No."

"Right." Holly fixed me with her bright blue eyes. "See, Sara said it was life or death, Maddie. She's got to see her boyfriend right this minute."

I watched as the valet finally pulled up in my old Grand Wagoneer.

I'm afraid I melt for any young woman with boyfriend problems so urgent. "Just ask her to please drive it back over to my house. Tonight."

"Mad, you're the best!" Holly yelled at me, turning to run and tell Sara.

"I mean it, Holly. And she needs to come in and put the keys on my kitchen table. Give her the combination to the kitchen door lock."

"Thanks, Mad. So how will you get home?"

"I'll catch a ride."

In less than a minute, Holly was leading Sara Jackson down to the valet and I met them so I could tip the guy. Sure, it had taken him twenty minutes to find my car, but even parking attendants have to pay their shrink bills in this town.

Sara climbed into the driver's seat and rolled down the window, giving me a sad smile. "Sorry to be such a burden," she said. "You are being so great. I can't thank you enough. Brett is just raging. His dissertation committee met and he's been told he won't get his degree." As she talked, she pulled out the band that was holding her hair up. As she rubbed her head, pulling the ponytail out, her fine red hair fell straight down her back. "I can't explain, but I don't think it was a good idea for me to leave Brett alone. I told him I couldn't bail on this gig tonight. We need the money. And I knew you were counting on me. I mean, Brett knew I couldn't blow off this job. I'd never be able to work your parties again."

I blushed. It was true. I would have been annoyed if any of tonight's crew hadn't shown. Being short-staffed puts an extra burden on all the other waiters. Hell, I hate being a boss sometimes.

"And then my VW stalled out. I mean, what next?" Sara asked, stress making a deep vertical line between her green eyes. "I'm scared. I know it's just a school thing, but you don't know Brett. He's sensitive. I just have to get home. Thank you so much, Madeline."

"No problem," I said. "So you think you can bring the Jeep back tonight?"

"I promise. You'll have it back in less than an hour."

I believe in helping out true love and all that. But I have heard more crisis stories from more temp workers than you can dream up. I'm all for kindness—but I needed my car, too.

"You sure you're gonna be okay?" Holly asked me, and I shooed her away, laughing. I watched her lean, long form trot back up the steps to the entrance, and when I turned back to the cars, I noticed Zenya Knight, one of the evening's cochairs, standing next to a huge, pristinely white Hummer H1, a tanklike, military-style wagon that goes for like $116,000, and that's without the options. The valet was holding the passenger door open, but Zenya was looking back toward the entrance of the Tager.

"Zenya, you leaving?" I asked, walking fast. Here might just be the wheels to get me home.

"Oh, hi, Maddie. How are you? Bill should be here any minute; he's getting the items we bought at the auction. Wasn't it the *best*? I thought you did a spectacular job on the party. We all owe you so much."

"You're welcome. Of course."

"Did you see Bill had the highest bid on the Selmer?" Zenya was enjoying an after-party high. She was younger than most of the Woodburn women, and filled with enthusiasm, even after such a long, draining day.

"Wow. Congratulations." So it was Zenya's table that was so hot to win the Mark VI tenor saxophone.

"Kirby is going to be out of this world with excitement. He's twelve and he's just going to go nuts. Hell, I think my husband, Bill, may even take sax lessons—and he's a guitar player!"

"Oh, Zenya. The bidding was ferocious, wasn't it?"

She shrugged slender shoulders and smiled. "That Dave Hutson. Honestly, we've known them for years, but Dave is just not a very nice guy, now, is he? Imagine him getting so upset over who was going home with that sax. Really."

"This was a wild auction," I said. "What a finish!"

Zenya tossed her long, thick wavy blond hair and grinned. "No one messes with Bill. Bill told me it would be a shame to see that fine instrument go to that Hutson boy. The boy actually writes out all his solos in advance! That's just not jazz." She looked sorry for the boy. "The dad really shouldn't push Ryan so much, you know? It's sad."

See, here is where I think parents really need to get their own life. But that was me. I steered the conversation back to the bidding. "It was such a generous winning bid, Zenya."

"Oh, Bill can afford it," she said, laughing. "My husband collects art, cars, vintage rock guitars. Over the years, I swear he's paid a fortune for his Stratocasters and whatnot. And he tells me the prices just keep climbing up. You know collectors. They want something and they have to have it now. You should have seen the way his eyes were gleaming when they were describing that saxophone. Anyway, the money goes to a good cause. We can't complain."

I shook my head, wondering what life must be like when

one can spend a hundred grand on a whim. My personal reactions moved back and forth between discomfort at how these people seemed to take wealth for granted and gratitude that they supported worthy institutions. The Woodburn School people provide a number of full scholarships to some of the city's least-advantaged kids. And they also donate brand-new instruments to our city's beleaguered public schools. Without the fund-raising work and generosity of supporters such as the Knights, these children would not have such wonderful musical opportunities.

"So you're leaving, Madeline?"

"By any chance, Zenya, are you driving near Hollywood on your way home?"

"We could. Do you need a ride?"

"Actually—"

Just then there was a commotion at the entrance. A man in a tuxedo, one of the guests, was standing at the main door to the Tager Auditorium, yelling.

"What's that?" I asked, interrupting myself.

"It's Bill," Zenya Knight said, her face perplexed. "What's he going on about?"

"Zenya!" Bill was calling to his wife and rushing down the steps toward us. "It's the goddamned sax. It's gone. It's disappeared. Can you believe that? I bet you that asshole Dave Hutson stole Kirby's priceless frigging Selmer!"

"Dear Lord (Breakdowns and Alternate Take)"

Rich guys. There are just not enough bucks out there to convince me to marry one. I get the part about the fabulous home, the fabulous shopping, the fabulous bling-bling. It's just I also see the huge hunk of her soul a girl has to pay in order to catch a rich guy and keep him. My mom used to tell me it's just as easy to fall in love with a rich guy as a poor guy . . . but it really isn't. Not for me. And judging by my father's modest teaching income, not for my mom either. So what the hell was she talking about?

"Saddle up!" yelled Bill Knight as he pulled open the trunk hatch, tossing in a heavy gift basket, and jumped onto the driver's seat of the incredibly large, incredibly white Hummer H1, ready to roll.

"Bill," called his wife breathlessly, "I told Madeline that we'd be happy to drive her—"

"Get in, y'all!" Bill commanded.

Both Zenya and I trotted around the white behemoth and jumped in.

"Are you sure—"

"Come on!"

I was not quite certain catching a ride home with the enraged Texan and his young wife was such a good idea.

Bill was still fuming. "Can you believe it, Zenya? I am

just betting that Dave Hutson took our sax." His short, steely-gray hair seemed to bristle as he punched the gas pedal, jerking the gargantuan tank away from the curb with a burst of pent-up horsepower, nearly mowing down the parking attendant, and then slammed on his brakes at the last second. "Jeeesus!" he yelled. "Get that guy out of my frigging way!"

"Oh, dear." Zenya sighed, mostly to herself.

"If you want to let me off here . . . ?" I had *more* than second thoughts. I was trapped in a mammoth-size luxury vehicle with a madman who had just been robbed of his "precious." Holy cow.

"We'll get you home." Bill Knight's voice was tight and I could guess he didn't really want to hear much more from me in the backseat. I pulled on the seat belt and fastened it just as our tank cranked into a torque-frenzied sharp right turn.

Zenya sat quietly in front. "What did they tell you?" she asked, her voice holding just a hint of quiet concern. "Did they really say Dave took our saxophone?"

"No one knows *what* happened, Zenya," Bill said, frustration and anger making him mock her. "It was just *gone*."

"But the instrument case . . . ?" she asked.

"The case was there. Lucky I insisted they unlock it and show me the sax. And well, looky there, it was gone. Like they thought I'd hand over a hundred-thousand-dollar check and not even look at my sax? Right."

In the well-lit, almost vacant avenues of downtown, the extraordinary stainless-steel-clad Disney Concert Hall, with its massive silvery swoops and flips, loomed over us as Bill slowed before he took another turn.

"I'm sure it'll all get straightened out," Zenya said.

"Like hell it will. I was ticked off that they let Sebastian play the Selmer. That was bad enough. But now, who knows? Maybe that asshole Hutson is going to wake up his boy tonight and let him play it. I bought a sax in pristine, mint, *new* condition. Now that sure ain't what they are delivering, I can tell you."

"Oh, dear," Zenya said again.

I could see her face reflected in the side mirror. Despite her husband's aggressive driving, she remained serene. Zenya Knight was not like the other Woodburn committee women. She was probably only a few years older than me, maybe midthirties, tops. She seemed softer, more passive than some of the Woodburn women I'd dealt with. While the other women were undoubtedly attractive—their beauty was premeditated. These wealthy women had begun to take on an artificial sameness, hair all highlighted to perfection, acrylic nails polished, this body part reduced or that body part enlarged by gifted cosmetic surgeons. Dressed expensively in the same designer labels, they had become more perfect and less individual. In contrast, Zenya had genuinely lovely skin, a naturally youthful face, true beauty. Needless to say, Zenya was a second wife.

"Bill, we need to drop Madeline at her home. She's in the Hollywood Hills," Zenya said.

"I really appreciate this lift," I said, trying to get back to polite small talk.

"Zenya, I'll be damned!" Bill Knight was yelling again. "Who the hell is that in the silver Escalade up ahead."

We were just slowing down for a red light, all the more ridiculous as it was almost one in the morning and there were only two other cars on the entire eight lanes of First Street. These cars were slowing to a stop ahead of us, following traffic laws, despite the fact that there was no cross-traffic whatsoever. "Isn't that Dave Hutson up ahead of that Beemer? I'll be damned. Dave Hutson thinks he's making his getaway!"

"What are you going to do?" Zenya asked.

"Maybe I should just run him down. If that frigging BMW wasn't stopped right between our cars, I think I'd just give it a try. The Hummer could do it, too."

I gulped.

"Did I tell you, Madeline," Bill called back as we waited out the light, "that the Hutson boy, Ryan Hutson, can't play a lick?"

See, I realize Bill Knight is a successful businessman. I get that he's an old rich guy and used to getting his way. Sure, he's a little high-strung. I just wished like hell I wasn't strapped into his car, right about then, as the man envisioned pulling troop maneuvers over another man's Cadillac.

"You hear me okay back there, Madeline?" Bill called.

"Sure thing."

"I say, this Hutson kid isn't really much of a sax player. He got into the jazz band at the Woodburn, but it's pretty clear he doesn't belong there. The boy is a fair sight-reader, I'll give him that. He can read the sheet music a bit. But the thing is, he can't go off the page. He can't improvise. He's got no brain for it. And ear? Hell, that Hutson kid has no damn ear whatsoever, does he, Zenya?"

"Now, Bill. Ryan is a very nice boy," Zenya said, in her soft way. "He really is."

"I'm talking about an ear for jazz now, darling. Not whether we should invite the kid over to swim in our pool. But what I'm telling Madeline here is this Ryan is not like our Kirby. Kirby is a gifted individual and he can play the pants off of that Ryan Hutson."

Mercifully, the light changed. But that was when Bill Knight, fueled by smoking martinis, goaded by the pain of seeing his prize Selmer disappear, and empowered by the heft of a vehicle the likes of which Arnold Schwarzenegger drives, hit the gas.

"Hold on," Zenya called back to me, grabbing the side rail above the passenger door. I gripped the side of the table that is conveniently placed in the middle of the backseat, just in case anyone was in the mood for a picnic. And then to her husband she asked, "Bill, what are you doing?"

"Watch what you say, Zenya," he answered. "I've gotten rid of better wives than you, darling, for saying less."

See? Didn't I tell you the marrying-a-rich-guy thing was wildly overrated? How many vacations in Paris are worth withstanding such contempt? How many Rolexes? How many six-hundred-dollar pairs of heels?

Zenya just laughed a girlish laugh.

Well, perhaps I'm more sensitive than some.

"Here we go!" Bill had managed to shoot out and pass the BMW X5 and gun the Hummer right up behind the Escalade. "Looks like Dave is driving a new car. Let's say hello."

The large Hummer H1 closed in on the back of Dave Hutson's SUV. "They don't know we're here," Bill said, bugged at being ignored. "Can you believe this guy? He's not even worried about driving off with my saxophone. How do you like . . ." At that point, the front of the Hummer made contact with the back of the brand-new Cadillac Escalade. Holy shit. ". . . that?" Bill asked.

The horn blared from the car we'd just struck. Then it pulled into gear and barreled off, turning sharply up a nearly deserted Figueroa.

"Bill . . ." Zenya's voice was light, if slightly agitated.

"Drop me off anyplace here, folks."

"So Hutson believes his Caddy can outrun this cruiser? I don't think so," Bill said, and he gunned the engine, pulling across the double yellow lines and right up beside the Cadillac. We were now driving on the wrong side of the street, side by side, as both vehicles shot down the boulevard with their speeds, as near as I could tell, approaching fifty. Bill Knight pushed the button that rolled the power window down next to Zenya. "Pull over, Dave!"

The tinted window of the Cadillac SUV slid down and a round, red-faced man started yelling. "You're crazy, Knight. You're going to pay for the damage to my car." Connie Hutson, seated beside him, looked as pale as a piece of white bread despite her excess makeup.

"Right. Just subtract it from the hundred thousand dollars you owe me for stealing the goddamned saxophone, moron."

"Screw you!"

Just then, up about a block ahead, from out of nowhere, a lone Toyota Tercel carefully turned the corner. It found itself smack in our lane, aiming straight at us. Never mind that the small red car was in the proper lane and we weren't—we were doing nearly sixty miles per hour and we weighed just over seven thousand pounds. Let's say Mr. Tercel wasn't too proud to launch his car quickly up on the curb in order to avoid certain annihilation.

"Bill, this is getting dangerous."

"Not to us, darling. To that bastard Hutson. He could have pulled his car over anytime, but then he'd have to face arrest charges for stealing our property."

While we were avoiding getting ourselves tangled with the Tercel, Dave Hutson and his shocked wife had made another sharp turn, heading down Ninth Street. Bill cursed. We had already charged through the intersection, missing Ninth, but now Bill put his foot on the break and tried to pull a fast 180-degree turn. Not the H1's best move. Luckily, there was no traffic here, because the Hummer is a hugely wide, hugely tall, hugely heavy vehicle, one big enough and bad enough to strap a missile launcher to its hood, and I, for one, was thanking God Bill Knight hadn't ordered that option. But all that torque or G-force or whatever the hell was now pulling at us hard, swinging us out way too wide. A few seconds of painful tire screeching and we had overshot the street and blasted up on the sidewalk, picking up speed. In a few seconds more I realized we were about to barrel right back into the dazed Tercel, still hanging up on the curb. Hell.

"Excuse me, I hate to be a bother, but . . ." I was sure I could jump out if he would slow down for just a minute.

"Oh, don't worry," Zenya said, waving her hand like you'd dismiss a small indiscretion, like a lunch guest spilling her water glass, "it's just boys having fun with their toys."

"You think I'm having fun?" Bill hollered, and swung down onto the street just a few feet before he would have surely plowed into the stuck Tercel.

Zenya smothered a giggle. I smothered a scream. Bill maneuvered the turn onto Ninth.

"Where is he?" yelled Bill, searching the street.

"It seems he's escaped," Zenya said, also looking for the Cadillac that got away.

Bill began slowing down and turned to his wife. "You got the Woodburn directory?"

"I think so, but—"

"Give me their address. We'll surprise the Hutsons at home."

"Oh, Bill . . ."

"They live in Pasadena. What's the street?" Bill demanded.

"Looks like I have just about enough time to hop out," I said, not waiting for the car to come to a complete halt. I opened the door as Bill said, "Hey, wait. We'll get you home, sweetheart." He actually sounded, despite a touch of maniacal road rage, like a pretty sweet guy.

I was down on the sidewalk before Zenya could add her promise that they would take me home right after Bill "got this out of his system."

"I'll be fine," I assured them, and in a roar of exhaust they were off.

Only when I was standing there in my best high heels, in the still of the night on squalid South Broadway, as a breeze blew some litter into the gutter and swallowed the fading roar of the departing Hummer's engine, did I realize that I'd managed to leave my purse on the cute backseat table. Damn it all. I had no money. I had no cell phone. And I was standing in the middle of a deserted street, in a deserted section of a pretty freaking deserted downtown, way past midnight.

"I Guess I'll Have to Change My Plan"

I considered my options.

I could walk all the way back to the Woodburn. I might still catch Wesley and Holly before they left for the night. But then . . . It could take me half an hour to toddle on over there in my wicked black satin sandals, probably longer. And what if I hiked all that way and they were gone, the lights were out, and the place was locked up for the night? I would be no better off than I was now. I considered the eerie ghost town of silent office towers, giant plazas, and public buildings all around me. Not that I was scared of being out alone at night. I could take care of myself. But I preferred to find the comfort of civilization, or what passes for it in Southern California.

L.A.'s downtown nightlife is spotty. Our party at the Tager Auditorium had been the liveliest thing going for blocks. And that was a couple of miles north and west. Now that the ball was over, there were few vehicles on the street. For instance, this section of Broadway was definitely not hopping. The once stately buildings here are old and decrepit. During the day, this street is jammed—a lively marketplace with a Hispanic flavor, crowded with shoppers—but now storefront upon storefront was locked down tight, metal security shutters covering all windows and doors for blocks.

I really half expected the Knights to return to their senses and come back for me. But as that was not panning out, I began walking as I continued considering my options. I wasn't entirely enthusiastic about the option of ducking into any hole-in-the-wall bar, either, should I happen to stumble across one, because (a) it was too near closing time for comfort, and (b) we were a mere vagrant's throw from the Nickel, the section of Fifth Street that has become L.A.'s skid row.

I could walk to one of the hotels downtown. I could explain my situation and ask to use a phone and call a friend and get saved. But I was more resourceful than that. This was my adopted city and I could take care of myself. And then the fog of possibilities began to clear. I actually said aloud, "The Red Line."

Los Angeles has a rather new if admittedly limited subway system. The best part was, the track ran right under downtown and there was a stop at Hollywood and Highland, easy walking distance to my house. I suppose it is shameful that I hadn't ridden public transportation since I'd moved to L.A., but just stop anyone here and ask if they even know what the Red Line *is*? Anyone except Wesley, I mean. Naturally, Wesley studied the plans, followed the morass of problems with its construction, and rode on the subway on its inaugural day. But that was Wes.

I was giving myself props because I knew all about it and I was just bursting with civic pride about the Red Line now. Simply bursting. And as I was practically on Seventh Street, I took a turn and began trotting toward Flower, where the Red Line station was waiting, saying a silent prayer of thanks to Wes for his long and at the time overly detailed reports. I had purpose in my step. I could take care of myself. I tried to keep my head-swiveling-to-check-if-I-was-being-followed-by-a-homicidal-stalker to a minimum.

Instead, I focused on not twisting an ankle in the enormous cracks in the sidewalk, on how resilient I was feeling about getting myself home in the big, bad city, and on just how I was going to come up with the dollar and change it would take to ride the Red Line train. I had hoped I'd find a few generous folks near the entrance to the metro station who might give a break to a young lady dressed in a thousand-dollar gown, even though I could hardly tell them I got it for 70 percent off. You know, depend on the kindness of strangers. But I began realizing it was pretty late for travelers. In fact, the entrance to the station, still about a block away, seemed fairly deserted.

Focused as I'd been on looking up ahead, scouting out late-night commuters from whom I might borrow the fare, I had not been paying close enough attention to my immediate surroundings. So I was startled—shocked, actually—by some nearby movement.

There, low in the shadows up against the building, something quite close to me had moved. My eyes readjusted to see into the recess of the building's entrance.

It was a man. He appeared to be sitting on the sidewalk. Well, lying was closer to the truth of it. He was semipropped against the building, with a jar on the ground and a rather sweet, if filthy, shepherd mix asleep beside him. The dog looked up as my heels click-clacked closer.

I had the best idea. What if this man might want to lend me the fare? The dog kept his eyes on me, but didn't move. I sort of hated the idea of waking the man, though. By his old clothes and the aroma of alcohol, I figured he could probably use all the sleep he could grab. And then I saw the quarters and dimes in the bottom of the jar.

It's not that I believe in fate exactly, but what are the odds that a desperate woman is walking alone down an empty street in the wee hours of the morning with only one need—

and that would be exactly $1.35—and in almost the very next block she would come across a jar with change, just sitting there? Even I have to bow to a higher power, here.

I slowed and said, "Ahem." The man didn't budge. The dog raised his head and sort of smiled at me.

"Hi there, fella," I said, in my friendly-to-kids-and-dogs voice. "Are you a happy dog or an angry dog?"

I got no response. "Here's my problem," I told the dog just as his companion let out a soft snore. "I need a little money to get on the train that will take me home. It's called the Red Line, you know. We're pretty dang proud of it here in downtown Los Angeles."

The pooch stared at me.

"Well, anyway. I need a little money so I can buy a subway ticket, but the problem I was telling you about is, I lost my purse. Can you believe that? I know where it is, actually, but I can't get to it right now. So, here's my question."

Another soft snore came from the man. The dog was calm, but looking a little bored.

"My question is, do you think I can borrow a dollar thirty-five? I will return it with interest. In fact, I'll come back here tomorrow and give your master a ten-dollar reward for his help. What do you think?"

The dog didn't seem too stressed by the idea. He laid his head back down and I took that to mean, "Go ahead, help yourself."

It wasn't really stealing if you planned all along to give the money back, was it? Under better circumstances, I would certainly have left him my business card, but of course I keep my cards in my purse. And at this precise moment, my purse was in a hundred-thousand-dollar armored vehicle, which, for all I knew, was ramming into a mansion in Pasadena while its crazed driver screamed for his lost Selmer Mark VI.

I reached down for the jar, keeping my eye on the dog.

"This is just a loan. I promise," I promised the dog as I scooped out five quarters and a dime from the dirty glass jar that still had the Clausen's Dill Pickle label semiattached.

I put the jar back quietly and shot a glance at the sleeping man. He hadn't stirred. And, minding my manners, I said, "Thank you, doggy. I'll see you tomorrow, okay?"

I raced up the block to the Red Line station, feeling elated to be on my way home. This had been, admittedly, an odd evening. Not that there wasn't something a little odd about most of the events that our company organizes—parties bring out the oddest behavior imaginable—but tonight was getting to be some kind of record. Not only had the live auction turned ugly, but a priceless saxophone had apparently been stolen. Add to that the bizarre chase scene in the streets between two crazed dads and the fact that I'd just had to roll a drunk to get enough money to take the subway home, and I think even Holly and Wes would agree, this evening deserved a special monument in hell all to itself.

And that was even before the sign on the entrance to the Red Line station had time to sink in. THE LAST TRAIN LEAVES UNION STATION WESTBOUND TO NORTH HOLLYWOOD AT 11:33 P.M. I looked at my watch: 1:38.

Well, no wonder, then, that the street outside the station had seemed so deserted. The last train had left over two hours ago. Damn the Red Line! Damn public transportation!

So okay, I may not know everything there is to know about train schedules, but there is something I do know about. I know every late-night restaurant there is in the 213 area code, and one of the oldest and coolest was just a block west and two blocks south of where I was standing.

It turns out our former Mayor Richard Riordan's legacy wasn't just the Democratic National Convention and the Walt Disney Concert Hall. It's also the landmark diner he owns, a twenty-four-hour T-bone-lover's haven in downtown Los Angeles, the Original Pantry Café. They say it opened in 1924 and it's never closed for an hour since, a legend in a town with less history to boast of than it likes.

I suddenly realized I was starving. It would be kind of nice to slip out of these shoes and order one of the Pantry's famous breakfasts, the #4, which gets you ham, bacon, or sausage, one egg, two pancakes, potatoes, and a cup of joe for only $5.95. I was already humming to myself, my Red Line woes behind me, as I turned down Figueroa, deciding I could use the money I had "borrowed" from the wino to phone Wesley. I liked to be self-reliant, of that there's no doubt. But I wasn't going to make a religion out of it. Maybe Wes and Holly would join me for at the Pantry for breakfast. And bring cash.

There was a whole different vibe on Fig. For one thing, there was some light traffic passing by, which made the scene instantly appear a lot less Twilight Zone surreal. For another, I could see the lit-up Pantry off another block. Dwarfed as it was by the skyscraper office towers around it, it still had the comforting aura of hot food and warm folks inside. In fact, there was actually a line of waiting-to-be-seated patrons coming out the door. At 1:30 A.M. on a Sunday morning. Hot dog! I hurried along, tying my shawl to keep it from flapping.

Just then, I noticed a sporty little car, a dark BMW something, slowing down, pacing me. I hurried some more and the car matched my pace. Good grief. I was so close to people and safety and food!

There was a lone guy inside and in that instant I got it. Look at me. I was wearing a low-cut black gown with a slit up to there and what used to be some pretty spectacular high heels. His window lowered and he said, "Hey, hello."

I probably shouldn't have looked over at him, but I was

curious. And then surprised. He was a nice-looking guy. Quite nice-looking. I kept walking.

"Hi," he said, stopping his car a few feet from me.

I remembered the first time I watched *Pretty Woman* and smiled to myself. This guy wasn't Richard Gere, but he did have an aura of wealth, not to mention amazing great wavy hair, a lean, worked-out kind of body, and great, intelligent eyes. "Sorry," I said, still walking swiftly. I was close enough to the Pantry to yell for help if I had to. "I'm not the kind of girl you're looking for."

"Don't be so sure," the guy in the car said, again keeping pace with me, driving slow.

"Sorry," I said, noticing his hands on the steering wheel, strong hands, and the dimple in his cheek. "You're not my type."

"I can change," he offered. Again, the dimple. Now, what was this fairly cool guy with a laid-back sense of humor doing cruising around downtown at this hour? Didn't he know most of the hookers hung out in Hollywood?

Ever helpful to handsome tourists, I stopped right outside the Pantry and kept talking. "You know, you should try Santa Monica Boulevard, west of Highland."

"Can't do that," he said, smiling up at me. "I'm going to take you home."

The two guys at the tail end of the waiting customer line outside the Pantry turned to listen to our conversation. As I joined the line, my admirer kept his car idling next to the sidewalk.

"And what," I asked, with exaggerated force, perhaps inspired by the fact that I was defending my honor in front of a little audience, "makes you think I would ever put one foot in your car?"

"Well, I'm making the assumption here that you are

Madeline Bean. And if you are, my sister Zenya sent me to take you home. I've been driving all over the upper-class-forsaken streets of this city for at least forty minutes just looking for you."

I stared at him. "What?"

"You must be tired. Want to get in and I'll drive you home?"

"You're *Zenya's* brother?"

"All my life."

"Prove it."

"She's a sweetheart. She's blond."

He had dark blond hair, cut kind of long. I kept looking at him.

"You want more? She's married to a jerk named Bill Knight. I've got a cool nephew named Kirby."

Ah, well. Look here. I was being minded by Zenya's brother.

On the downside, it appeared that my slit skirt hadn't attracted some adorable, random, night-cruising scum. On the bright side, it appeared I hadn't been abandoned after all. Zenya wasn't going to let me wander helplessly in the streets. While that husband of hers might have been out of his gourd with battle-tank fantasies of revenge, still, leave it to Zenya to call her brother and send him out to find me. "What instrument does Kirby play?" I asked.

"Kirby plays the sax," the man said, smiling. "Tenor sax. He's pretty good, too."

"Damn. I thought you were trying to buy my favors," I said.

The two guys who had been openly eavesdropping were told by the Pantry's host to move forward, and they went reluctantly in the door and to their table.

"Want to hop in?" the man asked, gesturing to his passenger seat.

"I don't even know your name. What if you are an extremely clever liar?"

"My name is Dexter Delano Wyatt." He looked out at me from the window of his neat little Z4. "You are something else, Madeline. I've come to rescue you and you won't let me."

Wasn't that about the story of my life? "Well, you look suspicious," I said coyly.

"You are even more paranoid and delusional than the girls I normally date. Which, if you only knew me better, you would find remarkable."

The Pantry's host opened the door once more and this time looked at me. "One?" he asked, brisk and efficient.

"Why don't you join me for breakfast," I suggested, turning to Dexter. "I can use your cell phone to check up on you. And don't try anything funny. I have friends at the LAPD, you know."

"Ah," said Dexter, "that makes you all the more desirable."

I laughed.

"I'll go park the car," he said.

I may have been dumped on the side of the road. And I may have misjudged the Red Line schedule. But my night was beginning to get just a little bit brighter.

"I Want to Talk About You"

And so, eventually, Dexter Wyatt drove me home. But first we'd had a fairly hilarious early-morning breakfast at the Pantry while Dex dialed his family and friends to give me instant character references. "To set Madeline's mind at ease," he explained to all on his cell phone. "she's still squirrelly." I talked to his sister Zenya who was bursting with apologies. She had managed to get Bill calmed down and they were already at home. I talked to Dex's college roommate from Penn, who said Dex was a decent-enough guy except for his habit of waking up East Coast friends at 5:30 A.M. Connecticut time on a Sunday morning. I talked to Dex's high school girlfriend, Mary Kate, who was now married to a Beverly Hills gastroenterologist, and seemed unworried by the call or the late hour, since she was up with her seven-month-old twins. They all agreed that Dexter was an easygoing guy who had a tendency to avoid conflicts, steady work, and marriage.

Over freshly scrambled eggs and refills of hot coffee, Dexter Wyatt and I had one of those weird, off-center, very personal conversations that can only happen between strangers at 2:30 A.M. Dexter admitted he was never going to fall in love completely.

"You may not have met the right person yet," I suggested.

"That's nice of you to say." Dex put his coffee cup down and gave me a slow smile. "But you know I probably have. I've met lots of right women. I've even been involved with a few. But they all figure out I'm not the right person to get involved with."

"Because . . . ?"

"Because," he said carefully, "I am a guy whose mother died when he was eleven. A guy who doesn't have a lot of faith that someone you love will make it until next week. A guy without much trust in life. In a nutshell."

"How did your mother die?"

"Cancer. I can almost remember when she was healthy. Mostly what I remember was that she was sick and then sicker and then she was gone. But things like that happen. Anyway, that was over twenty years ago. It's an old, old scar." Dex took in my concerned expression and began to laugh. "Hey, this is one romantic conversation, isn't it? So tell me why you believe in love."

"Who said I believe in love?"

"You don't?"

"Well, no. I do. But not just because I'm a 'girl' and we're programmed to want to fall in love or anything. I know that's what you think."

"You do?"

"Of course I do. You think there is a conspiracy among womankind to find husbands. To this end, you think we go out at night wearing sexy dresses and strappy sandals scouting out men with nice cars and good hair. And pretty soon everyone thinks they're in love. When they—or I should really say you—are most vulnerable, the woman will demand to be married and have babies and tie you down for the rest of your life, making you work like a dog to pay for private school and braces."

He looked at me across the table, a smile still on his lips. "Pretty impressive."

"Now here is the truly sad part. You need to believe women are out there trying to trap you into serious relationships."

"I do?"

I nodded. "So you avoid finding a steady career. You travel. You knock around. You won't take life or commitments or relationships seriously. But I'm just suggesting here that after you spend like ten years in therapy, you'll see it's all about protecting your heart from another horrible blow, like when your mother left you. In the meantime, these defenses of yours are costing you a real life. They're killing your chance to find a love that could really, truly heal your soul."

"More coffee?" asked Porter, our waiter, with perfect timing.

"So how much do you charge for that wisdom?" Dex asked, meeting my eyes.

"You don't want to know," I said, laughing.

"And what about you?" Dex asked, teasing. "Have you found love to be all that comforting and healing?"

"Me?" I pulled a handful of my reddish curls off my shoulder and smiled up at him. "Of course not. I was only speaking *theoretically*."

"Naturally," Dex said, pouring just the right amount of cream into my cup, stirring in just the right half packet of Sweet 'n Low. Clever boy. He had a gift for observation.

"In my own life, Dexter, I haven't managed the love thing at all well. I was seeing a cop. Honnett. He's married, apparently, and hadn't bothered to tell me the finer points. I guess he was separated, but then she wants to start seeing a shrink. You hear about this kind of thing all the time. So all along I thought we were building up some trust and some caring. I had hoped he and I might be right for each other. I had hoped he would see I made a difference in his life. But I can't ignore his past. The past is a powerful thing."

"That it is."

By the time Dexter Wyatt and I had left the Pantry, our conversation had lightened the heck back up. We were both amused at finding someone who shared a wry sense of humor, underlined as it was by the odd way we'd met. As Dexter transitioned his BMW onto the Hollywood Freeway, I appreciated, as only one who has drunk a few too many cups of coffee can, our strange first encounter, one that only a very jaded and playful fate could concoct.

"I'm glad," Dex said, as if reading my thoughts, "that if my jerk brother-in-law had to kick some chick out of his Hummer, and if I had to be the one called away from a poker game to fix things, that you were the chick that needed help and I found you."

"Thank you."

"Even though I was holding a winning hand at the time."

"Sainted sacrifice."

Dex watched the traffic and changed lanes, heading off at Cahuenga, the freeway exit nearest my house.

"And I'm glad that if I had to lend my car to a waitress in order to be abandoned downtown in order to make my way to the Pantry, in order to be sort of picked up by a virtual stranger, that you were the stranger, and that it could be said I tipped my hat to providence."

"You don't wear a hat."

"Figuratively."

"You are a trouper," Dex said heartily as he slowed and turned up Whitley.

"I hope it could be said of me," I added, filled with a hearty breakfast and comfy on Dexter's leather upholstered seats, "that Madeline enjoyed the journey, no matter how bumpy."

"You know, of course, that you have begun speaking about yourself in the third person."

"Has she?" I smiled at him. "She apologizes."

And then I noticed the police cars. There were three out in front of my house. There were mobile news vans parked in the street, and yellow tape across the gate to my house that read, POLICE LINE—DO NOT CROSS.

"Darkness"

"This can't be good," Dex commented, his eyes shifting up, following a flight of picturesque steps on the hillside. We had been chatting all the way home, but now were struck silent. He found a spot to park as we both studied the strange activity surrounding the small Mediterranean-style house at the end of Whitley Avenue. My house.

The property, featuring beautiful old palm trees and great pots filled with exotic plants, perches snugly on the upslope at the end of the block. There it dead-ends right smack into the side of the Hollywood Freeway. I might like to think of my neighborhood as quaint and "Old Hollywood-y" but in the fifties this lovely area was cut right through by the construction of the 101. My palm-frondy side of Whitley forms a cul-de-sac now, where above us eight lanes of cars, zooming northbound and southbound, are hidden from view by the thirty-foot retaining wall. As for the late-night traffic beyond the wall, what we couldn't see we definitely could hear. It's funny what you can get used to when you don't have a lot of money and you are facing the insanely high prices of Los Angeles real estate.

All this was the usual thing. What wasn't usual were all the police types and media types who were presently milling about in the cul-de-sac and up the steps to my house.

"I don't know what's going on," I said, slamming the car door and walking fast, taking in the entire scene, including a familiar black Mustang convertible parked near the curb, "but I think you're about to meet my cop friend, Honnett."

"You lead an interesting postmidnight life, Madeline."

I nodded.

"Think he brought his wife along?" asked Dex.

"Shut up," I said politely, and pushed past a reporter I recognized from the local news. He didn't seem to know me, but then why should he? On the other hand, and more important, what was he doing out in the street in front of my house at three-thirty in the morning?

There was a uniformed police officer standing at the bottom of the flight of steps that leads up to my front door. When he noticed Dexter and me approaching, he glanced at us sharply, but quickly covered it with expressionless cop cool. "And you are . . . ?" he asked.

"Madeline Bean and a friend. This is my house. What's going on? Have I been robbed?"

"You live here?" he asked slowly.

"Brilliant guess," Dex said.

Oh, terrific. Dex was going to start something, for goodness sake.

"What's your name?" the officer asked Dex, his voice still even. "Let's see some ID on both of you."

Oh, brother.

"Look. This is a friend of mine who is dropping me off." This morning was definitely not going well. "I don't have my driver's license handy right now. In fact, I don't have my purse. I've had a really crappy last few hours and now there is police tape all over my house. What," I asked, my voice getting more heated, "the hell is going on in there? Why are you here? Can you please, please, *please* just tell me so we can get on with this?"

"I'm not letting—"

But before the officer could finish, I shot past him and ran up the stairs. Dexter, right behind me, tried the same move, but with a half second more to react, the cop grabbed him and slammed his body against the stucco retaining wall.

While my neighborhood is filled with lovely older homes built in Hollywood's early heyday, and the palm trees and yucca plants are lush, it is a fact of life that there is crime in these hills. Living on this cul-de-sac could fool anyone into thinking they were safe, but the creeps from Ivar Street and Selma were rather too close for comfort. Druggies looking for valuables to hock were a big problem. And for any felon looking for a quiet block or two of nice homes with a quick escape route only an easy freeway exit away, this area was sometimes a little too attractive.

I was wired on caffeine and weary from a long night and it looked like I had something very wrong going on at the house. I swore out loud as I topped the outside landing and again realized I didn't have my cell phone on me. I couldn't call Wesley yet. I had to get in the house.

The front door was ajar and all the lights were on inside. As I stepped into the entry hall that held Holly's reception desk, I heard the rumble of low voices coming from upstairs, the part of the house where I live, and there were other sounds coming from farther back on the main floor.

I walked quickly through my office and back into the kitchen. Three men and a woman stood around the room working. They were using small brushes to dust black powder over several spots on the white-tiled countertop, and on the wall near my back door, and on the door itself. They had a collection of things in plastic bags. This was too much. I had no time to deal with a break-in. I was too tired.

Near them stood a tall man with his back to me. I could tell from the way his white shirt stretched across his shoulders and then tucked into the narrow waistband of his faded jeans that it was Honnett, even before I noticed that his dark hair looked a little longer and had more gray mixed in than I remembered.

"Chuck, what the hell is going on?" I asked. Okay, I asked it sharply. Maybe I even yelled it.

Honnett turned and looked at me. His face wore an expression I'd never seen on it before.

"Maddie?"

"No one will tell me what happened. The guy downstairs wouldn't even let—"

In three fast strides Honnett was over to me and smothering my mouth with kisses. I put my hands on his chest to push him away, to get my bearings, to adjust to this new angle. "What the hell . . . ?" I said, sputtering.

"Maddie. We thought you were . . . I thought you were dead."

His words had no meaning to me.

"There's a body upstairs."

"A body?" I pulled back from his arms. I simply couldn't understand what language he was speaking. I had no reaction at all as he kept on explaining.

"In your bedroom. Upstairs. In your bed. I thought it was you."

My hand flew up to my mouth and muffled my words. "Oh my God."

"I didn't go into your room," Honnett said, still explaining. "I just thought . . . Can you believe that? I should have gone in, but I couldn't do it yet. The call came in over two hours ago. Gunshots reported. There was a break-in. A woman was shot. She's dead. I thought it was—"

"They found a dead woman in my bedroom? How can this be happening?" I turned away, but couldn't move. I couldn't sort out my thoughts, so fast did they rush one upon another. I was numb to the idea there had been a death in my house. It just couldn't be true. And what was with Honnett? His first reaction was to hold me and kiss me? Hadn't he just a few months back decided to leave me? What was with men, anyhow?

In my confusion and shock, I found myself more worried about what was going on between Honnett and me now than about the awful crime that had gone on in my house. It was easier to grasp, this anger at a man who had hurt me. This shame at realizing I wanted to pause, just push all this other business aside, so I could recall Honnett's exact expression, moments before, when he looked up and saw me, and how warm and safe and fierce it felt when he was kissing me. I shuddered.

It was the murder. In my life, there had been some deaths that had hit me extra hard. It seemed I had another one to deal with. I pushed my heavy hair back and took stock. Here I was, wearing my sexiest black dress with a slit up to my thigh, standing in my kitchen in the early-morning hours, while a woman I'd never set eyes on before, a criminalist, picked up what could have been a single strand of hair from my kitchen drain with a long pair of tweezers, and a man I'd never seen before blew black powder on my huge center island, and a guy I had been hung up on—a man who had walked out on me, but who was back now, big as life—apparently wanted just to hold me. And for all of that, I simply couldn't get myself to concentrate on the big thing. I had yet to experience any reaction to a mystery woman who might be dead in my bed. I mean, it couldn't have seemed less real to me.

"Oh, Maddie," Honnett said, putting his arms around me again, unable to resist touching me. I wanted to relax into him. Why not? I could be angry at him tomorrow. Or I could forgive him tomorrow. Or he could go back to his wife tomorrow. I just wanted to feel better right now. But something in his manner had changed. His voice was tight. "Don't tell me Holly was staying here tonight."

Holly.

I stiffened in his arms and he felt it. All of a sudden the problem about a woman's body upstairs got terribly real. I pushed my way out of the kitchen, heading for the stairs, and began running.

Holly. Oh, that just couldn't be. She had stayed on at the Woodburn and worked on closing the party with Wes. I realized that had to have been hours ago, but she wouldn't be here. She couldn't be. She would have gone off to Wesley's house. Or gone home to Donald. But Donald was out of town for a couple of weeks. I got to the landing and was met by two detectives, both casually dressed with sport jackets thrown over jeans. This was not Honnett's case, apparently.

"And who are *you*?" asked one of the men, the shorter one with the least hair but the best cheekbones. He was soft-spoken and polite and more easygoing than I would have expected.

"I'm Madeline Bean. This is my house."

For a minute, all I received were silent stares.

"Madeline Bean?" the soft-spoken one repeated, looking at the other fellow. They were taking a second or two to digest the news. If *I* was Madeline Bean, who the hell was the body in the bedroom? It's not hard to figure out what detectives are thinking.

"So you came home to a real nightmare, Miss Bean. Sorry about that," said the detective, his eyes watching me thoughtfully. "This is my partner, Detective Hilts. I'm Detective Ed Baronowski."

I nodded. By then, Honnett had joined us on the landing

and shook his head. "Ed, I should have looked at the body. I—"

"Don't worry about it," said Hilts, the taller, muscle-bound guy with the tight, curly brown hair, cut short.

Baronowski kept his eyes on me. "So who's gonna answer the million-dollar question? Who is it in the bed?"

My house is not large. The short hallway upstairs holds just three small bedrooms and a decent-size bathroom. The largest bedroom is actually decorated as a living room, with a sofa in front of the fireplace. The middle room is used as a library/dining room. And the smallest bedroom contains my bed.

They all stared at me, waiting.

"I have no idea. No one is staying with me."

"You married, Madeline?" Baronowski asked softly.

"No."

"What about a boyfriend? You know, maybe he might have brought a friend to the house when you were out?"

I flushed as I realized Honnett was waiting to hear if I had a new boyfriend. "Nothing like that," I said.

The men looked at me.

"How long have you been away from the house? And where have you been?"

"I left about three-thirty this afternoon. My company organizes parties. We were doing a big charity benefit for the Woodburn School last night."

"And you are telling us that you haven't been home in the last twelve hours?"

I shook my head no. But it was a confusing way to phrase a question. Should I have answered yes?

"As you probably noticed, Madeline, there was no sign of forced entry downstairs and the place looks pretty undisturbed. Any girlfriend, then, who might have your key—"

"Look. This body. It's *not* my friend Holly." I was completely firm on this point. Adamant. Why were these cops always thinking the absolute worst thing? "Look, I'm sure it isn't. It can't be. I'm sure—" And that's when I was struck by a totally new and horrible thought.

"Oh no," I said, my voice coming out much lower now, so low I didn't think I'd said it out loud.

"What?" Honnett and Baronowski asked almost in unison.

I walked the five steps to the bedroom door and noticed more black powder on the doorknob, on the wall. "May I . . . ?"

"You ever see a gunshot wound before?" Baronowski asked, in his low-key way.

I turned back to him. "No."

"You gonna faint or something?" he asked, studying me.

I couldn't stand to be coddled and insulted in my own damn house. I opened the door and stepped into my bedroom. My electricity bill was not a concern to the police employees of the City of Angels. The lights were all on in there as well.

At first, I didn't even see the woman's body. I was dazzled by the sight of all the blood. The red-soaked sheets. The red-stained quilts. The red-blotched rug. The red-splattered walls. The smell of fresh blood, that slightly ironlike smell of a butcher shop, was everywhere. But then I saw her. And it was just as I'd feared.

The young woman who was lying in all that blood was half on her side, half on her stomach, one arm stretched up over her head, like she had been swimming and was caught midstroke. She was wearing slim black slacks and what had once been a pure-white lace camisole. The red of the rosebud pinned to one strap was drowned in the red of three open wounds.

I could see the side of her face clearly. Sara Jackson's green eyes were half open. Her skin seemed sickly white beneath the disheveled strands of her long red hair. Her freckles stood out in relief.

"You know her?" Baronowski was at the doorway, looking at my face, gauging my reaction. His voice was still soft. Maybe he was trying to be sensitive. My house. A huge blood-soaked mess. Maybe he was trying to soothe me into confessing something. He suspected me of being involved in this. He was watching to see if I was faking, lying, deceiving.

"She worked for me." For some reason, I was startled to hear my own voice. It sounded almost normal. How could anything about me be normal after seeing this? I knew the police were wondering why I was pausing. Every one of my actions and reactions was being measured. If I hesitated, would they think I was reacting to the traumatic sight of my bedroom awash in blood and murder, or would they suppose I was taking some time to come up with a plausible lie? I rushed on. "Her name is Sara Jackson. She sometimes works as a server at the parties we cater. She was working on the Woodburn School dinner downtown. I just saw her. I mean, the last time I saw her it was around midnight. She asked to borrow my car, which I lent her. She said she'd bring it back here before morning."

When I mentioned the Woodburn, Baronowski and his partner, Hilts, exchanged looks.

"Can you account for your time between midnight and now, Ms. Bean?" asked Baronowski, flipping open a small spiral-topped notepad.

"I . . ." I looked at the room, the dead woman, my trembling hands. "I had a little trouble getting home from the Woodburn, actually. It's a long story. I was sort of stranded downtown, but I ended up having breakfast at the Pantry on Figueroa with a friend. His name is Wyatt. Dexter Wyatt. He may still be downstairs. Anyway, he brought me home."

Honnett had been standing close to me as I took in the scene. Now he put his arm around my shoulders, a move that was far from lost on the other police detectives. But I needed space. I shrugged it off. There was a dead woman in my bed. The police thought I was connected to her death. I didn't need to melt into anyone's arms. I needed to think.

"The Chill of Death"

We stood in the little bedroom, which was really getting claustrophobic, what with three men and myself and Sara Jackson's lifeless body. The morgue guys were running behind, I had been told. It was barely 4 A.M. The phone on the bedside table rang loudly.

"You expecting anyone to call?" Detective Baronowski asked, making me suddenly feel guilty about the phone.

"No," I replied. It rang a second time, and I felt I was somehow being viewed with even more suspicion. "But then I wasn't expecting any of this." I didn't have to gesture at the body in the bed. "Should I answer it?" I asked, confused, as it rang out again. "Or I could leave it. My machine picks up after four rings."

"Why not take it?" asked Baronowski quietly. "We're done fingerprinting in here."

I reached out for the phone, disturbed that I had to walk a step closer to the bed to reach it, a step closer to Sara Jackson's corpse. I was keenly aware of being observed.

"Hello."

"Madeline?" It was Holly's voice, very screechy and breathless. And before I could reply, I heard her continue to shout, but she wasn't talking to me anymore. "Oh my God, Wes! She's okay. I got her. She's home!" And then back to me: "Maddie! We heard on the news you were dead. And then we both kind of fell apart. But then we just heard on the news you were *not* dead."

"They already have that I'm not dead on the news?" I asked, realizing the news reporters down in the street must have talked to Dex or something.

"Maddie. Did you hear me? Wes and I thought you had been shot. We heard about it on the radio when we got home to Wes's house. And we have been just *falling apart.*"

"Not that we believed it," I heard Wes say in the background, trying to manage Holly's end of the phone conversation.

"And hell, Mad," Holly said, "at first, Wes just kept calling the police, but all they would do was take messages. No one would call us back. They said it was too soon. And then, when we heard you were *not* dead, *you didn't answer your cell phone*. I've been calling your cell every five minutes until I thought I'd go insane. And we just can't believe you're, well, like, *okay*. I mean, really okay and not dead!" She was melting down. I could hear the tears. It might be the first time, too. Holly believed in the song "Big Girls Don't Cry."

I looked up and saw that Honnett, Baronowski, and the other detective were actively listening. And waiting.

"It's my friends. Wesley and Holly. They thought I was dead. And . . . and you can imagine their reaction now. I love them so much. They are just so . . ."

Honnett gave me a look. Yes, I knew he had felt it, too. He had panicked and I knew it. And that was something I would surely have to think over when I had the time. Even now, I could tell he was beginning to feel a twinge of jealousy over my relationship with Hol and Wes. Like he was a little left out. Like maybe now my real friends would show up and I'd turn him out.

"Well, that's pretty fucked up," said Hilts, who as a rule hadn't said much all night.

I had to know what the cops were thinking. "What's that?" I asked.

"The damn TV reporters."

Baronowski looked at Honnett for a second and spoke directly to him. "You gonna look after her? Maybe it's not a good idea for her to stay alone tonight, you know."

"What's this all about?" I insisted. "Lieutenant Honnett is not a close friend of mine anymore. So this is not his problem, okay?"

Baronowski turned back to me, assessing me anew. "I guess I didn't realize how the situation stood. My apologies. See, the thing is, Madeline, we do not know squat about what happened here, do we? Some girl was killed. Now it is possible that she was followed here. Maybe she was killed by someone that knew her. That's one scenario, and believe me, we will look into that carefully. But it is also possible the gunman was some random bad guy looking to break into this house that maybe startled her as she was returning your car. She might have been a witness to a lousy break-in who got into the wrong guy's way. Right?"

I nodded.

"Or maybe you yourself, Madeline, have an enemy. After all, this is your house and your bed."

I looked down at the bed reflexively. I had to get out of this room. Why were we all standing there? The harder I puzzled and demanded rational thought, the dizzier and more detached I felt. Enemies? I hadn't any enemies. It was ridiculous. But then so was the entire night. So was this awful, awful death. I began shaking a little. If I couldn't begin to figure any of it out, all I could think to do was to force myself to stay conscious. I tried again to focus on Detective

Baronowski's soft voice and to concentrate on what he was saying.

"You and the victim both have red hair. You're both young and attractive. This whole thing could have been a case of mistaken identity, and your life may very well have been saved by a mistake, have you thought of that?"

I shook my head, passive. This was too much now. I looked very little like Sara Jackson. True, we were of a similar build and size. But the way we were put together was different. She had a thinner, athletic look. I have a lot of curves. My hair was more strawberry blond, and thick and super curly, while Sara had that lovely fine, straight hair, and it was much more red than blond. No one who knew me could confuse the two of us. But I was shaken by the thought just the same.

"And if that is the right scenario," he continued, sounding even kinder, "it might have been better if those newspeople could have just shut the hell up so the world hadn't learned you are officially 'not dead' so soon."

"Oh," I said.

"Oh," I could hear Holly's voice faintly say from the receiver of the phone, which was still gripped in my dangling hand.

"Now I'm not saying that's the case. I don't want to spook you any more than you are already spooked."

I nodded my head, probably looking like the poster child for "spooked." At that, Baronowski's partner, Hilts, laughed out loud. I noticed Honnett, standing back in the corner, looking like he'd like to punch the guy. He'd clearly been agitated all night and needed an outlet. Let a guy laugh at me, even, and Honnett was ready to knock him down. Baronowski noticed it, too.

"Look," he said, "I apologize if I misinterpreted your

friendship with Detective Honnett. He's not officially on this case, as I think you know. He asked to come in on the basis of having worked with you in the past, so we may have assumed too much."

I looked at Baronowski steadily, not having the heart to meet Honnett's eyes. Here Honnett had rushed over to my house, presuming like all get-out that I had been murdered in my bed, telling his associates on the force that he and I had been close. Hell, he'd been so stricken he hadn't even been able to bring himself to identify my dead body. And these cops had respected him for it. And now here I was, acting like we were barely acquaintances. I could almost believe that I was, indeed, a horrible, ungrateful bitch if I didn't also remember that Chuck Honnett had been my lover for several months before he ever bothered to tell me he hadn't actually gotten all the way divorced from his last wife.

"Mad!" It was Holly, yelling at me through the receiver. I put the phone back up to my ear.

"Sorry, Hol. I'm here with Honnett and a few detectives."

"Wes says we'll come right over to get you. You're staying with him, he says."

"Thanks," I told her, and I almost burst into tears as the pent-up tension of the night seemed to explode at just the thought of escape and comfort and friends. "But I have my car here." I hadn't seen it parked down in the cul-de-sac when I had arrived with Dexter Wyatt, but Sara must have left it down the street.

"Oh. Okay, you sure?" Holly asked.

"I'll drive you over to Wes's," Honnett said, his deep voice sounding awfully warm and protective.

"Or maybe Honnett will drive me," I told Holly.

"O-kay," she drawled, with significance.

"Yo!" We turned and the cop who had been manning the outside stairs came to the door of the room. "This joker downstairs, Wyatt, won't leave until he finds out if the lady here needs a ride anywhere. He is a huge pain in the ass, and I'd like to tell him to take a hike, but he insists he's driving her around."

"Dex?" I asked, having lost track of the guy who was detained outside for so long.

"Right," the young uniformed cop said, his eyes now fastened on the body of the dead woman in the bed. "And the coroner's van is out front. They're here for the body."

Just the way fate does things, I guess. Only four hours earlier, I couldn't get a ride if my life depended on it. Just now, I had four offers of transportation, not to mention a chance to hitch a lift with the coroner's wagon.

"You stay put," I told Holly firmly. "I'll get to Wes's by five."

"Sure thing," she said, sounding more and more like the bubbly Holly and less and less like the shrieking fiend who might have just lost her best friend. "Wes said to tell you he's baking you something special and he doesn't even want to *hear* about you saying you have no appetite. He just doesn't care."

I smiled and said good-bye. And then it hit me.

Four rides. Had there been such a surfeit of transportation around midnight and had I come directly home, as I had originally planned, what might have actually occurred this evening? Would all be calm? Would all be well? Would Sara Jackson still be alive?

Would I?

"Little Things You Used to Do"

Before I left the house, I made photocopies of the personnel file we had on Sara Jackson and handed it to Detective Baronowski, as he had requested. And following his instructions, I made a quick survey of the house. I did not find anything obvious missing. Honnett had stayed in the background. He had offered to wait for me outside, and by his tone, I knew I'd have to spend some time talking it out with the guy before I could leave. I owed him that, I supposed. And I had to admit I was still amazed he had gotten emotional over me. Of course, it had taken me getting murdered for him to do so.

The police let me pack a bag and take all my essentials from the bathroom since they had finished examining the upstairs section of my house long before I had arrived. I caught sight of myself in the bathroom's full-length mirror as I scooped up my makeup and stopped to take stock: Clear skin. Fairly straight nose. Full lips. Overdressed. I had to change out of this gown. I pulled it off in one quick movement and dropped it in a wicker basket.

Nice enough body, I thought, looking in the mirror critically. Well, first let me qualify that. No one is allowed to like his or her body in L.A.—it's like a secret sick law that keeps us going to gyms and shunning carbohydrates—but I'm not an actress or model and I guess my standards are a little more realistic. I figured until gravity did its dirty work, I couldn't complain. Having a real bosom was a novelty in this town. I remembered, suddenly, a time I'd spent in this very room with Honnett. The steam from the shower had fogged this full-length mirror, but not so foggy that I couldn't still see us together as we explored a new use for the old claw-foot bathtub.

I knew this was a dangerous way to be thinking since I had to face the man in just a few minutes. I kicked off my high-heeled sandals. I was longing for a shower, but simply didn't have the time or the stomach for it right there, right then. As I heard the men from the coroner's office bump down the narrow staircase, carrying Sara Jackson out of the house, I stood in the center of the bathroom and shivered. I dressed quickly in a pair of old jeans with a black top and flats. Since it had gotten chilly overnight, I tied a gray cashmere sweater around my shoulders for warmth and went down to see Honnett.

He was waiting outside by the front door, where I found him eyeing Dexter Wyatt. Again, I had forgotten Dex was still around and I felt pretty guilty for letting him hang out all this time.

I put my suitcase down. "Dexter, did you meet Lieutenant Chuck Honnett?" It wasn't the timeliest introduction, since the two men had been standing around together for some time. But that's me, Miss Manners. I had these party habits so firmly embedded I would probably still be introducing folks when I got to heaven. Or wherever.

"Sort of," Dex said. "What the hell happened in there? The coroner came out with a body bag. Who the hell was it?"

"A college girl who worked for me," I said. "She borrowed my car tonight and—"

"Can we stop reporting the news for a minute," Honnett interrupted, "and just tell your friend here to shove off now.

He's on the verge of getting arrested for interfering with an investigation." Honnett never used to get hostile. I think this whole scene was getting to him, too.

Dex, for his part, didn't seem too exercised by Honnett's attitude. He just kept his laid-back charm going, no matter how many bodies might have to be loaded and taken off to the morgue before we could have a moment to chat.

"Maddie, can you ditch the cops now?" Dex asked, meaning not just the detectives still upstairs in the house, but also the one hulking around my front door. Not exactly diplomatic, but to the point.

"They said I could leave," I answered. "I gave them the number where I could be reached. I'm going to stay at my friend Wesley's house for a while. Maybe for a long while."

Honnett just leaned against the wall, waiting for me to finish with Dex, but clearly not enjoying that I had a guy hanging around, interested.

"Good," Dex said, and smiled. "I'll take you over there. It's like my job, you know?"

I smiled back at him.

"Not that I mind," Dex said, "but you don't seem an easy girl to get home. You're a challenge. I like that."

"I aim to drive men crazy," I said, not bothering to check Honnett's reaction. "But the thing is, I'll have to take a rain check on that. I need to have my car with me at Wes's. You understand."

"Okay." Dex kept his voice kind of gravelly low. It must have been driving Honnett nuts trying to hear. "So you won't let me rescue you again?"

"Once a night is certainly enough," I said. "But I do appreciate it. Oh, and could you do me a favor? Could you tell Zenya I think I left my purse in her car?"

Dexter agreed, and then left, taking the number at Wesley's house and saying he would call me, maybe bring my bag by tomorrow. I thanked him again, he glowered at Honnett, and he was out of there.

Honnett and I were finally alone. "We really need to talk, Maddie. We've needed to talk for a long time, but you weren't that interested in hearing from me."

"I found the key to my Jeep that Sara left on the kitchen counter. It's probably parked up the street."

He sighed. "I'll walk with you."

Just as we turned toward the stairs, Detective Hilts stuck his head out the front door and stopped us. "Hey," he said, calling to me. "Wait up. We're going to need to impound that vehicle of yours. The one the vic was driving."

"Can you please refer to Sara by her name?" I asked, weary almost beyond words.

"Sure. Anyway, no one touches that truck until we get our lab boys to take it in and give it the works. So I'm going to need the key."

I walked back up the steps and handed Hilts the damned key, giving him the plate number and where he might find it parked.

"Thanks."

"But what am I supposed to drive?" I asked, suddenly worried that the entire tide of transportation was turning against me once more.

"Beats me. I can ask Baronowski if we can give you a lift, but we're not going to be leaving anytime soon."

"That's okay, Hilts," Honnett said. "My car is right here."

"Good, then," he said, and ducked back into my house.

Honnett grabbed my suitcase and waited for me to lead him down the front steps to the street.

That was when it hit me. What I had intended to do before all the bizarre activities of the past few hours began to twist and turn.

"Wait here," I said, and turned back to the house. I walked

quickly through the entry and into the office I share with Wes. Below my side of the partner's desk, where the chair was pushed neatly into the kneehole, I bent to retrieve a cardboard box. Inside were the papers and assorted pictures and files I'd cleaned up much earlier in the day—Albert Grasso's paperwork.

I grabbed my backup diskettes from my computer and a few other necessary office folders and scooted out the door into the cool air. It was almost five and I realized Wes and Holly might start to worry again if I didn't show up at Wesley's place soon.

"You ready?" Honnett asked quietly.

"Let's go."

We got down to the street and I noticed that the cop guarding the house and the news vans were gone. Once the body had been taken away, they must have figured they were out of luck for any more dirt. It was late, they had deadlines. Thank goodness for that. The last thing I could handle at the moment was an array of microphones shoved in my face.

We got to Honnett's Mustang and he unlocked the trunk for me, placing my suitcase inside and holding out his hand to store the cardboard carton there as well. I gave it to him and settled myself on the passenger side of the car.

"You want me to drive or you want to sit here and talk?" he asked, when he was in the driver's seat.

"Drive and talk," I answered.

"Fine." He got the car in gear and did a neat 180-degree turn, heading back up Whitley. "Where does Wes live these days?"

My partner, Wesley Westcott, is constantly on the move. He's had eight addresses in the past five years. He has a side business of fixing up historic old houses and selling them. Each time he buys a new house, he moves into the wreck-in-progress and lives among the carpenters and the dust and the electricians. Every time he finishes one of his masterpieces, he moves in all his fine furniture and puts the house on the market. These past ten years, L.A. has been in a nonstop real estate boom and these top-of-the-line properties, fixed up to the hilt, sell very well. As it turns out, Wes spends about 90 percent of his time living in a gutted mess or a construction site, 5 percent of his time in a great mansion, and the other 5 percent boxing or unboxing all of his belongings and moving.

"He's in Hancock Park," I directed. "On Hudson. On the Wilshire Country Club side."

"Near Beverly?"

"Near Third."

Honnett nodded and steered his car out of the Hollywood foothills and into the flats, heading first south and then west.

"Look," he said finally. "You going to be okay? This is pretty tough, finding that young woman in your house."

"I can't believe it." It had yet to really sink in. Hadn't I just been talking to Sara? Hadn't we just put our heads together, Holly and I, to see if we could get her out of a jam? That boyfriend of hers. I just remembered him.

"Chuck," I said quickly. "I forgot to tell Baronowski and Hilts about Sara's boyfriend."

"You know him?" he asked, interested.

"No. See, Sara was just a temporary employee. She worked parties when it fit into her school schedule, that kind of thing. But tonight, the reason I loaned her my old car was because she was worried about her boyfriend. He goes to 'SC, I think. Grad student. Anyway, he was having a rough time with his Ph.D. Sara was sorry she left him alone tonight."

"Why?"

"Who knows?" I was frustrated. When you manage a constantly changing staff of young servers and bartenders, you don't always listen to every little detail of their lives. If you did, you would be more into soap opera and less into event planning. "I didn't pay the closest attention, but she was really worried. She thought he might be suicidal . . ."

Honnett shot me a look.

". . . but I'm sure she was just getting dramatic. Anyway, she was supposed to go home and then come right over and drop off my Jeep. I specifically made her promise to return the car to me tonight. I . . ."

Honnett stopped at a red light on Santa Monica and looked at me. He could see me thinking it over. He could see it sinking in.

"Maybe if I hadn't been such a hard case, she would still be alive," I said softly. "If I hadn't forced Sara Jackson to drive out to my place so late at night, maybe she wouldn't have been killed."

"We don't know what happened," Honnett reminded me. But kindly. "Until we do, this could have happened anywhere. Don't beat yourself up, Maddie."

"Right." Like I could ever let anything like this go.

"Tell me, why didn't Sara just drive her own car home from that party tonight?"

"Some mechanical thing," I said absently, thinking about the role I might have played in that young woman's death.

"So blame that. Blame her bad luck with her car. Don't blame yourself, Maddie. You were trying to help the poor kid."

"I know," I said. "Some help."

The light changed and Honnett accelerated through the intersection.

"Did you really think I had been killed?" I asked Honnett.

He didn't answer right away. And then he didn't answer directly. He said, "I know you don't trust me. I get that. But you should believe me when I tell you this. I never meant to hurt you, Maddie. I never intended to make you miserable. You are the last person in the world I would want to be unhappy."

That sounded okay, but I was leery of Honnett. I waited to hear it all.

The fact is, a few months ago Honnett dropped the bomb on me that he was going back to his wife. His *wife*. The wife, I should point out, he *never* told me he still had hanging around. He delivered this news flash at a big party I was putting on at one of the studios and I just about flipped out. There we had been, getting closer and closer, and I had thought we were actually making a sort of good start. Then he tells me there's a wife still in the picture. It was so classic. I couldn't stand that I had been tricked or deceived or played. The guy I was falling for had a wife, damn it! I don't know. I suppose there might have been a reasonable, rational way to continue such a conversation that night. For my part, I just told him to get the hell out of my life and ran off for a weekend in Vegas with a new male friend. Call me communicationally challenged. Whatever.

"You are so young," Honnett said, with affection in his voice. I loved that voice, so masculine and deep. When it held any softness at all, it made me melt.

"I am not," I argued. I knew Honnett had qualms about our age difference from the start. I'm twenty-nine. He's forty-four. Big deal. He had a thing about it, though. And here he was bringing it up again, like that was the problem. Like the fact that he was hiding a wife in the wings had nothing to do with it.

"I am not putting you down," he said. "Don't get so defensive. I just mean that you haven't had as many years to screw up your life as I have. You don't have as many ghosts from the past, I'm betting."

"I've got my share," I said huffily.

"Yeah, sure you do," he said, chuckling. "And so do I.

Since you are such an experienced old woman, I know you'll understand how a person's history can sometimes catch up with him."

"You mean past relationships?"

"Well, in my case I think I told you I had been married before."

"Right. What a convenient way for you to have put it. Not too specific, were you? And I thought you meant it was all over. You were divorced. You were free to start something new with me."

"You want clear? Here it is. I've been married twice," he said. "Once to a gal I met in college. In Texas."

"Were you some big football hero?"

"I believe I was," he said, laughing at me. "We Texas boys love to play ball. Anyway, she was a sorority girl. A pretty sorority girl from a nice Dallas family. She liked having a good time. She liked to buy nice clothes. You can picture the type. She wasn't too wild about me joining the PD. Things had never been too good between us. We were too young. You hear that a lot, right? But I was working all the time anyway, so I didn't get how unhappy we really were. After about seven years, she left me for a guy who owned a plane."

"A plane guy?"

"Yep. His daddy owned a furniture warehouse in San Antonio, I believe. Anyway, we hadn't had any kids. She didn't want any, she told me. I tried to change her mind about the plane guy, but . . ." He smiled and shook his head. "I was young then. Maybe about your age."

"Shut up."

"Some time went by and I moved to Los Angeles, and a couple years later I met Sherrie. She worked for the LAPD, too."

I looked up, surprised. "She's a cop?"

He nodded. "She's a cop. Anyway, she had just gone

through a rough divorce herself. We hooked up and just sort of fell together. I figured she was more my kind of person, you know? She loved being a cop and she was proud of how well I was doing, moving up, that sort of thing. We got married and thought we'd have a family."

"You have kids?"

"We weren't successful. Sherrie wanted to do the fertility things. We spent a lot of money and she really suffered, taking hormones and whatnot, trying to get pregnant."

"Well, now you've done it," I said. "Now you've managed to get me feeling sorry for this wife of yours. Thanks."

"Anyway, we were not successful in other ways. We had grown apart. She and I had never had that much magic. I began to realize how it really was with Sherrie. She was more interested in having a kid and being someone's mom than in being my wife."

"Oh."

"So we separated. This was maybe two years back. We should have gotten the whole divorce thing settled, but I couldn't afford it and she knew it. I'd used up all of my savings on fertility clinics and things like that. We'd even signed up for private adoption and that cost money, too."

"So why did you go back to her?" I asked. "Why did you leave me?"

"I am still tied to this woman, Maddie. I still care for her. I still feel guilty I wasn't committed enough to our marriage to make it work."

"Guilt!" I was tired of the concept, tired of its grasp. I knew it well. Hadn't I just insisted that some poor, overworked girl rearrange her evening so she could drive my filthy old car home? Hadn't that led to her death? I buried my head in my hands.

"Sherrie called me out of the blue. I honestly hadn't heard a word from her in several months, Maddie. She called me to say she had just been diagnosed with breast cancer." I stared at him as he drove in the dark night. "She was scared to go through it alone."

"But your marriage was over . . ."

"She made promises that we could go to see a counselor together. She wanted me to move back into our old house and . . . and to take care of her while she went through the chemo."

I shook my head. No words would come.

He drove on, waiting for me to catch up.

"Do you still love her?"

He took a while to answer. "Maddie, it's complicated."

What had I expected? An unequivocal no? He was still attached to his ailing wife. And really, in the light of this other woman's anguish, how could I think he wouldn't be? I was ashamed of myself. "Of course you should help her, Chuck. Of course."

"This isn't the way I wanted to tell you," he said, sounded frustrated.

"Honnett," I said, "I can't think anymore about you and me. Not tonight. I'm just not—"

"Shh. That's okay," he said. "You have every right to hate me, Maddie. I know it."

We turned onto Hudson and traveled silently to Wesley's block. I showed Honnett where to pull over. He helped me carry my luggage and carton up the drive. Wesley's new project was a large two-story English stone manor house, currently deep in the demolition stage. There was a Porta Potti out at the curb for the construction crew, and a large Dumpster next to the driveway, filled with debris.

"How are you going to stay here?" Honnett asked, looking at the state of the place.

"Wesley is living out back in the guest house. He's leaving it alone until he finishes up restoring the front house. I'll stay with him back there." I led Honnett along a path that wound around and behind the three-car garage.

"Is his guest house going to be big enough?"

We crossed the patio behind the garage and then the lawn that led up to the pool. The sky seemed to be lightening from black to navy blue.

"That's where you're staying?" Honnett asked, taking in the perfect miniature mansion beyond the pool. "It's larger than my condo."

"It's got two bedrooms. Wes has been using the second bedroom for storage, but I guess we'll figure it all out. I just don't want to think about any of this right now."

"Don't worry," he said, putting down my things and putting his hands on my head, brushing back my hair. "I know you are completely wasted. I won't try to kiss you again or anything."

"Oh, really?" It must just the perverseness of my nature that I couldn't let him leave like that. At the door of the guest house, I leaned into Honnett's arms and lifted my face.

As he bent down and gave me a tentative kiss, the door opened and Holly and Wesley started screaming with relief.

For better or worse, I was home.

"Living Space"

I staggered to the love seat in the living room of Wesley's charming guest house and just sighed. "I am too tired to talk, too tired to stand, too tired to . . . itch," I said, collapsing onto the down-filled cushions. The white linen slipcover made an almost noiseless whoosh.

"Of course you are!" Holly took my heavy suitcase and the rest of my things and disappeared into the second bedroom. I closed my eyelids and felt my tired eyes burn, and then gently the tension began to ease. When I opened them again, Holly popped out of the bedroom on tiptoe.

"She's still awake," Wes whispered to Holly, ever alert to the flicker of my lids.

"We cleaned out the extra room," Holly whispered to me.

"I moved in that old Philadelphia spindle bed, the one you love," Wes whispered to me.

"Thanks," I said, trying to smile through my grogginess.

"Want to go to bed?" Holly asked, still talking low.

"I do," I said, but didn't budge. They waited. A few moments more and I had to ask, "Something smells wonderful. What did you bake?"

"Mandelbrot," Wes said. "I know you don't want to eat. I just needed to get it out of my system."

"Did you use my auntie Evelyn's recipe?" I closed my

eyes again, breathing in the warm scent of bitter orange and walnuts and sugar. I knew he had. Wes loves authentic ethnic cuisine and had miraculously seduced several well-kept family secrets out of my eighty-year-old great-aunt. Mandelbrot is a dry, semisweet cookie, sort of like Jewish biscotti. My mother was Polish Jewish, my dad was Italian English. It makes for a schizoid culinary heritage.

"Yes, I did, but don't feel like you are obliged to taste them right now. You know they will keep. Do you want to go to bed?"

"I don't know," I announced, and then opened my eyes once more. "I seem to be stuck." There sat my two best friends, so concerned about me that they were willing to leave all questions and curiosity and worries about the events of the past evening for later.

"Just say the first thing that comes into your mind," Holly advised. "Maybe you don't know what you want, but something will pop out."

"Shower."

"See, there!" Holly chirped. "I should have my own cable show. It works."

Wesley's guest house has only one bathroom, but it was huge. Built in the thirties as a sort of folly, the guest house has ridiculously grand twelve-foot ceilings, which not only add a slightly surreal touch to the dimensions of the cottage, but also permit the extensive use of large crystal chandeliers—even in the loo. The vintage bathroom was tiled in the style of its Art Deco period, all sea-foam green six-inch squares on the floor and about eight feet up the walls. Border tiles were of forest green and here and there were Art Deco accent tiles featuring geometrical pink lilies with dark leaves on a sea-foam ground. All the porcelain fixtures, the toilet, sink, and tub, were a matching shade of pale green.

It was like stepping back in time as I stepped into the

green tub, turned the hot and cold faucets until I got the right mix, and pulled the lever to switch on the shower. Under sharp spikes of hot water, I just drifted away to a time where none of the present evening's troubles could intrude. Steam filled the room as I stood there, thinking of nothing more disturbing than which of the five trendy shampoos Wes had neatly lined up on the built-in tile shelf might work for my tangle of wet curls.

When I emerged from the bathroom, clean and warm, with a pale green towel wrapped around my head, I was wearing a freshly pressed pair of Wesley's pajamas, soft white cotton, which he had kindly left out for me on the small chair in the bathroom. I had rolled up the waistband, and was doing the same with the long sleeves, but I felt so much better I almost couldn't believe it.

It is funny how tired you can be one minute, and then somehow you get that extra energy, that second wind. I know I missed an entire night of sleep, but I can do that sometimes, and just keep going.

"You look pretty good," Holly said, checking me out.

"I brewed you some tea," Wes said, also checking me out. "Darjeeling."

"I put it in the bedroom," Holly said, "on a tray with some mandelbrot."

"Well, what are you waiting for?" I asked, leading the way. "Wesley, bring that cardboard box. We have a lot to talk over."

Holly went to fetch extra teacups and then we all settled on the high bed Wes had made up for me in the guest room, each finding a comfortable perch. I started combing through my long hair, gently detangling it, and began to talk it out.

"Look, you guys. You are being so patient with me. But this evening—last night—is hard for me to deal with. So much has happened . . . And I have this feeling I'm missing some important connections. Like some of the answers are right here in front of me, but I haven't put it all together yet." I rubbed my head where my comb had pulled too hard. "Only I don't know which parts go together. It's like sorting through a pile of jigsaw-puzzle pieces and suspecting you may have a few pieces from another puzzle mixed into the wrong box. But you can't tell which belongs to which. And the whole pile is overwhelming." I looked up at my friends.

"Just start wherever you want," Wes said calmly. "We can help you sort."

"It's hard to start," I said, "because every time I think it over, I feel like I'm getting it wrong. Like it really must have started earlier. And then when I go back, it seems like it started even earlier."

"Then don't start at what happened at your house," Holly suggested gently. "Start earlier. Like right after the party tonight?"

I shook my head. "Earlier. Remember the rubbish I found outside my house yesterday? I thought it was just a case of teenage vandalism or littering. Then, when I glanced at the stuff, I began to see the papers made sense—they belonged to a man and it didn't seem like he would want to lose all that stuff."

"Right," Wes agreed.

"But then I discovered that the man, Albert Grasso, was at the party last night. And he and his woman friend were livid. Remember, Holly? They were angry at me because they thought I'd stolen those papers. So what really happened? Maybe there was a crime up on Iris Circle yesterday and maybe those papers were taken from Grasso's office. Not by me, of course. But maybe they were stolen. As to why they were then dumped on our doorstep, I have no idea."

"I'm going to take notes," Holly said, and then left to find her notebook. She returned a few minutes later as Wes and I tried to make sense out of it all, and frankly couldn't.

"That's the first crime," I said to Holly, and she marked it down in her notebook.

"Saturday morning or early afternoon. Private papers taken from Grasso office on Iris Circle. Saturday afternoon. Private papers dumped one block below on Whitley. Saturday night. Albert Grasso learns his papers have been found and goes ballistic," she read. "That right?"

"Yes. So then there is that tenor saxophone from the Woodburn. You guys may not have heard, but—"

"We know!" said Holly. "We were there when they called 911. One of the auction chairladies nearly fainted."

"The cops showed up and searched the hall," Wes added. "Whoever took it left the sax case. They were fingerprinting and such."

"I hoped maybe it had just been misplaced or something," I said, remembering Bill Knight's rage. "You know Zenya Knight's husband won the sax in the auction and he was convinced that another Woodburn dad took it out of spite. But I thought he was just venting. He didn't have any proof. What do the cops think really happened?"

They filled me in. The Selmer saxophone case, along with all the other items, had been left in an unsecured storeroom right off the stage, where items were kept both before and after the auction. Lots of people had been milling about near the storeroom, and certainly several fund-raising volunteers had nipped in and out during the closing minutes of the auction, but with all that activity and so many people hustling here and there, no one saw anything out of the ordinary.

"I have to say, this maybe fits in with what Bill Knight was suggesting. I mean, how could this have been a premeditated crime?" I asked. "I realize a lot of people had knowledge that the Selmer had been donated to the Woodburn auction, so I get how it might have been the target of a theft, but who could have anticipated having any privacy in that storage area? Not even somebody with insider knowledge—"

"Like someone who worked on the auction committee!" Holly suggested.

"Right, someone on the committee might know there were no plans for armed guards, or locks or anything, but they *still* couldn't predict in a crowd of hundreds of people that they could get to the sax and not be observed."

"That's true," Wes said. "And if it *was* someone working as a volunteer, it would have been easier to steal the sax sometime before the ball. Fewer witnesses."

"So you're saying," Holly said, picking up Wes's line of thought, "it must have been done on impulse. Someone must have seen a few seconds of opportunity and pounced."

We all thought it over. I couldn't buy that some wealthy dad would risk his reputation in order to get his hands on that sax. It wasn't as if his son could ever play it in public, after this. What would be the point? Whoever stole the sax didn't give a damn that the Woodburn would end up losing a hundred-thousand-dollar donation, and Dave Hutson's wife was the chairwoman of the whole freaking auction committee. It made no sense.

"What sort of person would be likely to do it?" I asked.

"A crime like that. It takes real balls." Holly Nichols, criminal profiler.

Wes said, "Holly has been into a whole 'balls' theme this evening. Don't ask."

"But it's true," Holly said, defending her point. "They had to unlock the case when no one was looking, grab the horn, and just waltz out—who could have managed that?"

Wes picked up the heavy pot of tea and began to pour. "It's

like one of those old locked-room mysteries where you'd swear it couldn't have happened. There were dozens of helpers milling about. Even if a disgruntled bidder suddenly went insane and was seized with an overpowering urge to snatch his rival's prize, how the heck could he get it out? Believe me, no one left the storeroom with a bulky, heavy, shiny, curvy, three-foot-long, fully engraved, sterling-silver tenor saxophone under his dinner jacket. *That* would have been noticed."

"Maybe you're right," Holly said thoughtfully. "But maybe no one realized what was going on. Just wait. Someone will remember something. Or no! I bet somebody saw something and just isn't talking."

We both eyed Holly, considering this.

I nibbled on the crunchy, crispy mandelbrot and tasted the fine tea, which was incredibly mellow and flavorful. Wesley had become a student of the subtle art of tea brewing and was a connoisseur of estate-grown Indian teas. Of course.

Holly took a piece of mandelbrot and considered motivations. "These Woodburn dads can get nuts."

"It's like they are secretly insane," I agreed, taking my second piece of mandelbrot.

"It's like Darwin," Wes suggested. "In more primitive times, these two dads would be clubbing each other to get dominance over their tribe. Today, they use their checkbooks to clobber their sons' musical competition."

Holly finished scribbling notes and then read: "Saturday night. Ten-thirty, tenor sax sold at auction for one hundred thousand dollars. Midnight, B. Knight goes to pay and finds the case is empty. Lots of witnesses report they saw nothing suspicious near the storeroom. Stolen sax may have been taken by D. Hutson out of primitive urge."

We shared a what-a-world, what-a-world look as we each sipped our tea. "This is fantastic," I said, breathing in the steam.

"Darjeeling, of course," Wes explained, our font of all things arcane. "Grown in the foothills of the Himalayan Mountains in northeastern India between Nepal and Bhutan."

"I knew that," Holly said.

We looked at her.

"Sort of."

Wes smiled. "You can tell, Hol, by its characteristic dryness and muscat overtones." He gazed into the rich golden amber liquid in his cup. "The Champagne of Teas, it's called."

"First flush?" I inquired nonchalantly.

Wes looked at me.

I took another small sip. I like to keep Wesley on his toes by throwing out the odd esoteric fact.

"Naturally." He raised an eyebrow in deference to my knowledge.

"What's *first flush* mean?" Holly asked, playing right into my hands.

"Tea plants hibernate during the winter months, Hol," I explained. "As March approaches, the warm sun stimulates the growth of the leaves, but the cool temperatures keep the growth rate slow. This first new growth of leaves is full of flavor and it's referred to as the *first flush.* It's considered the ideal time to pluck the classic 'two leaves and a bud.' "

"Wow." Holly looked into her cup.

I smiled. I had read all about it when I was working temporarily as a writer on a culinary game show. Who says TV rots one's mind?

"Chamling Estate?" I asked Wes. I knew I was pushing my luck, but whenever else would this sort of trivia come up in conversation?

"It's Thurbo Estate, actually."

"Go on," I urged.

"The Thurbo Tea Estate is located in the Mirik Valley of Darjeeling at an altitude ranging from 980 meters to 2,440 meters. It has a planted area of 485.11 hectares and produces 263,600 kilograms of tea per year."

"You are good," I said. You had to hand it to Wesley. He knew his stuff. "Too bad I'm not still working on *Food Freak*. I could have used all that."

Somehow, the camaraderie of my pals and this tea break had brought me back to myself. After all, with Holly taking notes, and Wes to puzzle it through, we had already gotten somewhere. I was fortified to deliver the rest of my story.

I approached the next part gingerly. I explained to Wes and Holly how I had been practically hijacked in Bill Knight's Hummer and raced around the streets and abandoned downtown and the hour it took me to finally find civilization. Naturally, I expected a reaction from my best friends. I got it.

"That's the funniest thing I ever heard," Holly said, cracking up.

"Well, not at the time it wasn't," I said.

"But you've got to love the part where it ends up with Maddie thinking she attracted a 'john,' " Wes said, grinning at Holly.

"Yeah, real funny," I chimed in with less enthusiasm.

"Well, at least you liked this guy Dexter Wyatt who came to rescue you. Is he cute?"

"Yeah. Too cute. It's just that I don't have the bandwidth to deal with cute at the moment," I said, feeling my energy ebb.

"So do you want me to write it all down in my notes about the Knights hijacking you and the guy picking you up?" Holly asked, with belated sensitivity. She held up her pen, a fuzzy-topped purple glitter Gelly Roll, showing me she was taking my pain seriously. Now.

"Not necessary," I said. "I can't blame anyone but myself for getting into trouble downtown. Remind me never again to ride home with one of our party guests."

"So what happened when you finally got to your house?" Wes asked, staring at me. He had been patient, holding on to this question as long as anyone could. But Wes and Holly had been up all night, too, worrying about me. They needed to be told.

"It was a total disaster," I said, suddenly sober.

Holly bit her lip. She also seemed to be coming down from her Darjeeling high.

"Was there a break-in at the house like they originally reported?" Wes asked. "And why did they think you were . . . dead?"

"They found someone else. It was a woman's body," I said. And the light mood we had just enjoyed vanished in an instant.

"We didn't know that . . ." Holly looked at both of us. "We were hoping it couldn't be true. That it was a mistake, too."

"We heard about the break-in, but when they announced that you were really alive . . ." Wes quickly picked up my nervous reaction. "I guess we didn't pay close enough attention."

"But how could there have been a body?" Holly asked, truly perplexed. "Was someone killed in your house?"

I nodded, tears springing up out of nowhere. Apparently the news reports had been sketchy. And Wes and Holly had been frantic. And I suddenly realized they really had no idea what I had just gone through.

"It's someone we all know. It was Sara Jackson."

"I'm Beginning to See the Light"

"I've been thinking," I said, walking back into the living room of the guest house. All the wooden blinds had been shut and the room, even in midday, was dim. Holly was trying to sleep on an inflatable mattress that Wes had put out for her. Her lean frame was much too long to fit comfortably on the love seat, even curled up. I noticed she was also wearing a pair of Wesley's white cotton pajamas. Even on her, the sleeves had to be rolled up.

"Aren't you sleeping?" Holly asked, pushing up on one elbow.

"No. Can't. Sorry, did I wake you up?"

"Not really. I didn't want to go home because I would just be alone and I don't want to be alone after hearing about what happened to Sara."

"I know." I sat down next to her and put an arm around her. "You must be missing Donald."

She nodded. "I wish we really had eloped. If we make it to our wedding day, I'll be an old lady."

"When's he coming home from visiting his sister?"

"Nine more days."

"At least you can dream about your wedding."

"I guess I could, if I could get to sleep. What have you been thinking?" she asked.

"I've been so overwhelmed, I forgot about Albert Grasso."

"What a geek! He and his friend Caroline went psycho last night. I hate it when people get so bent out of shape."

"That's what I mean. Look, he doesn't have to love me, but I am a young businesswoman. I have a reputation. Why would he jump to the hysterical conclusion I had stolen his papers?"

Holly sat up and wrapped her long, slender arms around her knees. "Look at how everyone runs around ranting and venting! All these people need a good massage therapist and some meditation."

She did have a point there. It seems like all the people we know keep themselves going on some secret recipe of adrenaline, deadline pressure, and Starbucks. A little too much of any one of those ingredients and they could explode from all the stress.

"Well . . ." Holly rubbed her white-blond topknot, a little droopy now after a few hours against a pillow. "How the heck did this guy Grasso's junk get dumped out on your lawn, anyway?"

"I don't know," I admitted. "But what if he had some very private things in his office, papers or photos that he thought no one would ever see?"

Holly nodded.

"And then I came waltzing up to him at the party, right there out in public, and started telling him I had a whole pile of his most secret, private papers."

Holly nodded. "That would screw up his night."

"He got incredibly defensive, you know? And then went on the attack. Like he assumed I would be blackmailing him. I didn't get it at first, because I was so blown away by his hostility. But maybe he was scared out of his head."

"O-kay . . ."

"This just feels right to me," I said, warming up to this new idea. "I would bet you a doughnut that there is something among those papers that Albert Grasso would hate to have discovered by anyone."

"Well, that's pretty scary," Holly said. "Do you remember seeing anything really suspicious when you looked through the junk yesterday?"

"Not really. Maybe that photograph of the president with a young babe, but—"

"Like there aren't a million Clinton pics floating around." Holly dismissed that idea and went on. "Perhaps something is buried in among all the bills and invoices? There might be something incriminating there—like showing he overbilled some celebrity or something."

"Or worse," I said, thinking it through.

I suddenly noticed Wes standing at the door to the master bedroom, fully awake, wearing the same white cotton pajamas as Holly and I.

"Very interesting," he said, joining the conversation. "Presuming Grasso had some secret papers, he would naturally be looking for your motivation, Maddie, for telling him you found them. You must have caught him completely off guard. But then you didn't act smug or menacing. You didn't appear to know anything worth blackmailing him over. You didn't act like you wanted his money and he must have been shocked."

We all nodded. As Wes, Holly, and I picked up this new thread, we carefully avoided the promise we'd made to one another that we would get some sleep and put all thoughts of theft and murder and littering out of our heads.

Wes continued, "What if he realized he and his lady friend had overreacted, and in doing so, they must have gotten you nervous. He would have to be afraid that you would run back home and look through the papers more thoroughly when you had some time."

"That makes sense," I agreed. "That is exactly what I intended to do. You think he might have gone over to my house last night to get the papers and photos back?" I was getting creeped out.

"Oh my God," Holly said, her hands flying to her mouth.

Wes picked up the story. "What if he found Sara there, coming over to return your car? And she saw him and what he was doing. He was afraid she would get him arrested for breaking and entering, not to mention the cops would have to look at the papers and might discover what terrible secret Grasso was trying to hide."

"So the singing teacher might have shot Sara. Just to cover up what he was doing?" Holly seemed to be getting paler. "That's horrible."

I spoke up. "What sort of paper could be worth killing an innocent girl?"

"Maddie, where is the carton with all of Grasso's trash now?" Holly asked.

"Was it gone? Did Grasso get to it?" Wesley's voice was alert. "It would look very suspicious if that box of papers is gone now. The police could make something of that."

"No, no, no," I quickly replied. "The box was still under my desk. I had such a difficult time getting home last night, I wasn't going to leave that box behind."

Wes and Holly just stared at me.

"You mean it's here?" Wes asked.

"Yes!" Holly yelled, suddenly remembering. "I brought it into Mad's room when I took in her suitcase."

"I've been weeding through the documents for the past few hours, reading every paper, checking out every receipt. But for the life of me, I couldn't find anything there that is truly shocking or juicy. Just a lot of private junk."

"Wait now," Wes said, his posture perfect, as always. "That would make Grasso even more clever, wouldn't it? What if he did break in, but he was careful to just pick out the one folder or photo that was the most sensitive and then left the rest? It would be much less suspicious. See? You would notice if the box was missing. Of course you would mention it to the police. But how would you ever notice if one slip of trash was gone?"

"To be honest, Wes, it didn't look like anyone had been in our office. And the box was exactly where I left it." I bit my lip, trying to remember.

"Maybe we should all go through the papers, Maddie," Holly suggested, her voice still subdued. Holly had taken the news about Sara Jackson terribly hard. Naturally. Like me, she felt responsible for Sara ending up at my house. After all, if not for Holly and me, that young woman would not have been at that very wrong place at that very wrong time.

"I think we need to turn it over to the police," I said. "I wouldn't mind having a copy of everything in case Grasso claims I stole anything. But otherwise—"

"Why don't I run over to Kinko's?" Holly offered, jumping up from her mattress on the floor. "There's one near the Grove.

"I'll just copy every damn thing in the box and we can go over them more thoroughly, later."

"Well . . ." It didn't sound like a bad idea to me at all. "And I guess I could call Honnett and tell him about our theory."

Wesley gave me a look, like he had heard this sort of thing from me before, and more important, he remembered, even if I didn't, the "high" regard Honnett held for my impressions of his cases. It was true. In the past, Honnett and I had had our share of encounters over his work. He was usually kind, but pretty unimpressed with my little notions of crime and punishment in the City of Angels.

"I'll get him to listen," I said, sounding defensive even to my own ears. "And this isn't even his case. I would just feel a little safer if a cop was hearing this and taking over the evidence."

"Fine," Wesley said. "But you might get further if you called the detective you told us about. The one who is in charge."

Holly returned from the bathroom, changed back into her black pants and white camisole, the outfit she'd been wearing the previous night. It reminded me of Sara Jackson and I suddenly felt queasy.

Luckily, Holly hadn't seen what I had seen. I went and retrieved the carton of papers from the guest bedroom and Holly left, taking the keys to Wesley's new Jaguar.

"What's wrong?" Wes asked.

"Nothing. Just . . . Wesley, the last girl wearing that exact outfit who borrowed a car, she ended up . . ." I shook away the memory. He came over and joined me on the love seat.

Wes was nothing short of six-foot-three, and he was thin and sinewy, with not an ounce of extra fat as far as I could tell. Still, when he held me in his arms, I found a spot on his shoulder that wasn't entirely bony. And I let a tear dampen the collar of his snowy pajama top.

"We look like twins," he said, changing the subject.

"Where on earth did you get so many identical pairs of pajamas?" I asked, my voice not sounding entirely natural.

"Oh, Lord! My mother sends me a new pair each Christmas," he said. "And they're all still practically brand-new. I never wear them."

"Do you sleep in the—"

"Maddie! No. I wear a pair of knit boxers or something."

I giggled, letting another tear escape. "I can't believe we are sitting here talking about your underwear."

Wes stood up and said, "All the better to get those other scary images out of your head, my dear."

"Why don't you just tell your mom not to send them anymore?"

"It would break her heart. She somehow got this notion that I love them."

"Somehow," I chided. I knew Wes was a big softie and I could imagine he thanked his mother profusely that first Christmas. This was typical Wesley.

There was a knock at the door.

"Holly? Back so soon?" I walked over and opened the door.

But it wasn't Holly at all. It was a tiny blonde with a tight face-lift. Caroline Rochette, Albert Grasso's lady friend, stood in the glare of the sun, smiling. "May I come in?" she asked.

I looked back at Wes, who was just finishing folding up the deflated inflatable mattress.

"Sure," I said, so surprised I automatically went into my default "gracious" mode when I had every right to be flat-out pissed off at this absurd woman.

"Thank God," said Caroline. "I just simply have to talk to you. I'm in terrible trouble."

"Hello, Goodbye, Forget It"

Caroline Rochette suggested we take a walk around the grounds of Wesley's fixer estate so we could have a little privacy for girl talk. I was stunned she had found me there. Who could have told her where I'd be?

But then, I was dying to question her about Albert Grasso. To see if my theories might be substantiated. How could it hurt to walk around Wesley's backyard, in broad daylight, as long as he kept an eye out the bay window of his guest cottage? I quickly changed into my old faded jeans and a black T-shirt from my little suitcase and met her in the garden.

It didn't seem an enormous risk, after all. We were not exactly in some abandoned alley, and we were hardly alone. Noisily performing demolition work on the main house were two Hispanic men I'd gotten to know on some of Wes's other projects. They were now pulling rotting shingles off the roof.

"Hi, Cesar!" I waved.

Caroline shaded her eyes with one hand and looked up. I think she got the point. I had men all over this property who were keeping their eyes open. Not that I was frightened of her. Aside from a nasty tendency to wear false eyelashes in the daytime, Caroline Rochette didn't scare me. Much. But naturally, I was a little jumpy with all the horrible things that had happened.

"I'm so sorry for all the . . . fuss last night," Caroline said, jumping right into the end of the conversational pool in which I most wanted to paddle around with her.

"Fuss?" I almost spit the word out. "You and Mr. Grasso behaved horribly." I looked her right in the eye. She was balanced upon four-inch heels, and still I had to look down a little. "You both made terrible accusations. None of it was true. And all I had wanted to do was to be helpful."

"It was an odd . . . thing," Caroline said, with a friendly chirp to her voice. She had a distinctive speech pattern, where she picked and chose odd words and gave each a separate inflection. Sort of like someone who is not terribly talented at conversation. Or lying.

"Odd. Yes. What sort of trouble have you come here to discuss?"

"It's as you . . . guessed. About the papers."

We had stopped walking in front of a stone garden bench at the far end of the yard, well away from the large formal pool. Beyond the far fence stretched an incredibly green fairway and one of the holes of the Wilshire Country Club golf course. The day had been warm and the shade of a jacaranda tree, just bursting with pale blue flowers, gave us a bit of a break.

I waited for the story and she went on.

"About Albert's . . . files." She batted ultrablack eyelashes against sharp little cheekbones. "Well . . . I know who took them."

"It wasn't me!" I said, staring her down.

"No, no. I know that. It was actually me."

"You?"

"Oh, damn." In an outburst of fluttering lashes Caroline sat down hard on the bench.

Now this was pretty interesting stuff.

"Look," she said, "you *have* to give me all of Al's papers. Please." She searched her tiny designer bag for a cigarette. Then a lighter.

"Well, excuse me for pointing this out, Caroline, but those papers don't belong to you."

"But . . . that's . . . just . . . I mean, you can't . . ." Eyelashes went ballistic. Cigarette waved in one hand, remaining unlit.

I stood there, waiting for her mouth to coordinate with the quick-excuse centers of her brain, but she was clearly not up to the fast retort, so I swooped in with a question of my own. "Why on earth did you take Mr. Grasso's personal papers, Caroline?"

Perhaps the shock of my flat-out accusation got her going. In any event, she began speaking rapidly. "It was nothing like you must think. It was simply . . . innocent. I was planning a surprise for Albert's birthday." As she explained, she lit her cigarette and took a sharp drag. "He is a hard man to shop for. Someone gave me this terrific idea. I was going to get him a new . . . briefcase to replace the horrible old one he's been lugging around for years. He likes a certain kind of leather case and I didn't want to get it . . . wrong. I was told I could simply bring in the old one and let the luggage store order one just like it."

"You wanted to buy him a briefcase," I repeated. I stood there on the flagstone path, looking down on her. She was dressed in a tiny St. John knit suit. Pink, white, and baby blue. Size 0.

"So yesterday morning, Saturday, I borrowed the briefcase and walked on down to my car, which I had left parked . . . on Whitley. Your street."

Parking could be very problematic in my neighborhood. She'd had to park down the hill.

She took another quick puff on her cigarette, leaving a

cotton-candy-colored lipstick print around the filter end, and went on. "I got to the luggage store and thought I would . . . die. I wanted to die. I couldn't find Al's briefcase. I searched through my Mercedes and it just . . . wasn't . . . there."

"Imagine that," I said.

"I drove back. I swore at myself. Really, over and over. I retraced my route. I finally got back to Whitley Avenue. You can't imagine how I was . . . cursing. Yes, cursing. And then I got to Whitley, and half a block from where I had parked my car earlier I saw Albert's briefcase." She tossed her cigarette to the stone walk and crushed it with a jab of her pointy-toed shoe. "It was lying against the curb, almost under a parked car, cracked open. And then I remembered. I had rested the briefcase . . . on the top of the car. I placed it there while I was opening my car door. I must have left the damn thing there, right on the roof, and driven off. And then . . . it must have fallen off into the gutter and cracked open. I can only imagine that the papers inside were scattered about. That must have been near your house."

"You mean you took Mr. Grasso's briefcase without his knowledge and then accidentally drove off, causing the case to crash open in the street?"

"Basically . . ." she said, looking terribly upset. "Yes."

"Then—forgive me for speaking bluntly, Caroline, but what was all the bullshit last night at the Woodburn gala about calling the police and accusing me of theft?"

"Oh, I would never have called the police," she said, putting her gold lighter up to the tip of a second slender cigarette. She inhaled deeply and continued: "You're a woman, Madeline. You know men! I couldn't tell Albert what had happened to his papers. Believe me, I was reeling from shock to discover they had been . . . found, after all." She took another puff of nicotine. "Albert told me all about the little talk the two of you had, when he got back to our table.

He was much more upset about all the missing papers than I had even imagined. So you see, I just couldn't go into the whole ghastly story right then. Of course I plan to . . . tell him. Someday. When the timing is right. But he was really amazingly angry." She exhaled a tight, white stream of smoke.

I was willing to put aside how easily Ms. Rochette had served me to the lions, the night before, to save her own surgically enhanced neck, if I could get her to reveal a little information about the contents of that briefcase. "That's the part of your story that concerns me the most. Why do you think Mr. Grasso was so very *unhinged*? Did he say anything to you about what exactly he thought might be missing among those papers?"

"No, dear. Not a word. But he was so angry and worried he insisted we leave the gala almost at once."

I hadn't noticed them leaving. "Did you go directly back to Mr. Grasso's house on Iris Circle?"

"I had left my . . . car parked there, yes. I wanted to make him a drink, put on some music. Albert loves to listen to his stars, as he calls them. He has coached the world's best voices, you know. He has CDs by everyone you can imagine and he deserves much more credit than he ever gets."

"I'm sure. But he didn't relax last night?"

"I've seen him upset before, but never like this. He refused to let me console him. Can you imagine? I was willing to do anything to make him feel better, but no."

"He told you to leave?"

Caroline's short blond bob was sprayed so stiffly that not a hair moved as she nodded her head. "Al said he planned to go over his office with a fine-tooth comb. He needed to figure out exactly what was missing. He said if the computer had been taken, he could live with that. He had a system to back up his hard drive or something and he kept the backed-up discs off-site. But he said if the briefcase was gone he was as good as *dead*."

That got my attention. I was certain I was on the right track. Albert Grasso must have suspected some very important, very incriminating document was missing. That was the only explanation for his extraordinary overreaction.

Caroline noticed my interest. "See what I mean? I just couldn't tell my sweetie I had done such a dizzy thing. Anyway, I'm sure he'll calm down when he gets his papers back. But in the meantime, last night at the ball I was in a pinch. I had to play along with him, you know? I had to pretend *you* were the . . . scoundrel. But I just knew you would understand it all when I told you what happened. We chicks have to hang on to our men, don't we?"

"I don't have a man," I admitted, meeting her eye. "And I don't think I would value one who required lying to."

Caroline laughed a pretty laugh and tossed her spent cigarette down on the flagstones next to its mate, crushing it with the pointed toe of her pink pump. "That is simply because you are so young and so pretty. You think you will remain this way forever. I know. I thought that, too. Just wait." She winked at me with one extra-thick artificial lash. "But I want to make up for last night. I think you do deserve a reward, dear. And I've brought . . ." She looked in the tiny pink bag she had hanging from her shoulder and brought out a stack of green. "Here. A thousand-dollar reward. For the return of Albert's papers and files. That should make up for the unpleasantness last night, right?" Caroline held up the crisply folded bills, which I ignored.

"I would like some information."

"Like what?" She looked at me shrewdly, her sweet-thing mask slipping.

"Does your friend Albert have a gun?"

"A what?"

I waited.

"Where is this coming from?" she asked. "Are you afraid he might come after you? Oh, no, no. That's absurd."

"He has a gun, then."

"There is one in the house, if that's what you mean. For protection. Everyone has a gun, don't they?"

"I don't."

Caroline Rochette squinted at me as I stood there with the sun behind me. "You don't? You should. This is Los Angeles, for heaven's sake. You never know when you're safe or when you're in danger here."

"I don't think I'm a gun sort of person," I replied.

"No? Well, you must be the only one in this town who isn't. How do you feel safe at night? No man. No gun. Do you have a dog?"

I gave my head a defiant shake.

"Foolish things happen to foolish girls," she said.

Was she threatening me? And why had I just admitted to this infuriating woman that I didn't have a prayer of a chance to defend myself? I just had to show off how self-reliant I was. Damn. I made a mental note to get a boyfriend, a dog, and a gun. Soon. I covered up my annoyance at myself by asking another question: "Do you know if Mr. Grasso went out again last night, after you left him?"

"Well, how would I know that? I didn't speak to him later, if that's what you're asking. What's this all about?"

"Perhaps I'm trying to judge how sincere you are. You admit to lying last night, so why should I trust you now?"

"Okay. But no more questions about Albert."

"I'm curious to know how you found me here," I said.

"Oh, that was just so easy. I went to your home on Whitley first. But there were policemen on the street and they wouldn't let me drive up. I figured you called the cops about

Albert's missing paperwork. Naturally, I didn't want to have to explain anything to any nosy cops. But I saw Nelson Piffer, one of your neighbors. He was out walking his weimaraner."

"You know *Nelson*?" He was a dear man who lived two doors down from me. Nelson was a retired studio art director and I had heard he resented William Wegman deeply for getting the idea of photographing weimaraners posed in human clothes first.

"Oh, yes. Nelson walks Teuksbury up on Iris Circle. Albert and I like to take walks around the neighborhood, too, and we always comment on the fact that Nelson has taken to dressing up the dog in short-sleeve sweatshirts. He loves that dog. And he's worried she gets cold now that she's getting older."

I hadn't known that. I made a mental note to get Teuksbury a sweater next Christmas. "Okay, so you know Nelson Piffer."

"Yes. And Nelson didn't know what was going on at your house, but he said if you weren't home I should try calling your partner. Well, I made a few calls among the Woodburn women and got Wesley's name and it was very familiar. I'm a realtor, you know."

"No, I didn't."

"Oh yes. And I . . . recognized . . . the name Wesley Westcott. He has a favorite agent at my office on Sunset who keeps her eye out for special properties for him. I knew your Wesley bought and sold, of course." Caroline Rochette batted her thick lashes. After staring at her for the past half hour, I was startled to find I was beginning to like the look on her. "It was a quick search of my multiple-listing recent-home-sales database and . . . I found the address of this house."

Just like that. If I had any illusion that I was hidden or safe, I had just lost it.

"Now I'm through playing twenty questions," she said, standing. She swayed slightly, her narrow high heels finding the flagstone path uneven. "Give me Albert's papers and I'll return them to him with all my apologies. Then we can be done with it."

"I can't do that," I said.

"You what?"

"I don't have them here, for one thing."

"Then let's go back to your house."

"No."

Caroline dropped the girlfriend act fast. "Bitch. You think you can shake Al down for more than the thousand, you are just dreaming."

"This isn't about money, Caroline." I turned and began walking back toward the guest house. Our conversation was at an end.

"Oh, come on! Everyone can use some extra cash. Be real." She followed me on the trot. "Who pays for your nails? Your shoes? Your hair?"

"We're finished talking. Get out."

"Don't walk away from me!" she screeched, frustration making her small voice climb to the upper registers. She lunged for me, and, by some instinct, I quickly stepped to the side.

A small splash accompanied her yelp.

"Oh my God!" I couldn't believe my eyes as Caroline Rochette, dainty knit suit, taffy blond hair, face-lift, and all, sank to the bottom of the pool. Before I could react, Cesar and Rolando came on the run. Cesar threw off his hard hat and Rolando pulled off his shoes.

Caroline was not bobbing to the surface. Perhaps the shock of hitting the cold water had temporarily struck her senseless. Perhaps she couldn't swim.

One two three, we all jumped into the pool to rescue her.

The last thing I saw before I hit the cold water was Wesley running toward us.

I got to her first, and with the faint memory of some Red Cross certification training from a long, long distant summer camp in Wisconsin, I hooked an arm under Caroline's chest and dragged the small, sopping woman to the surface, kicking and sputtering. She swore at us all as she was pulled to the shallow end, but adrenaline was working its magic and I wouldn't let go of her until I had her up on the steps and out of the pool. Frankly, I doubted I could remember CPR, and after watching her smoke all those cigarettes, I was determined to avoid experiments in mouth-to-mouth resuscitation.

"Don't squirm," I told her. "You might have drowned." Holding on to her, I got a close look at her tight little face and its expression of shock and fear.

"I must get," she panted out, "insurance."

Cesar had recovered Caroline's tiny handbag and Rolando fished around and captured one of her pale pink leather pumps. They handed the dripping accessories to her as she continued to curse at us all.

My soaking jeans weighed a ton as I slogged out of the pool. Wesley came over to me and put his arm around my shoulder. "Are you okay? I saw the entire thing. That woman just ran into the pool. I think she meant to push you in."

With what little dignity she could muster, Caroline stood up straight and stepped into the shoe Rolando had rescued. "This has been an absolutely horrific couple of days," she said. "I don't know what has gotten into me. I just don't know. No man is worth this, honey," she said, giving me a disgusted look. "No man. You can quote me."

I don't know if the dunk in the pool had cooled off her temper, or if she was going on pure realtor instincts. In the presence of a great client like Wes, a man who bought and sold a lot of expensive properties, she was probably trying to undo any professional damage she could. In any event, she seemed to revert to the "polite" social manners that were the mainstay of her trade. She opened her bag with a snap, sending off a small cascade of droplets, and pulled out the cash. I noticed the bills were fairly dry. She handed a hundred each to Cesar and Rolando, who both said, "No, no, señora." Eventually, they were persuaded to take their tips and went on back to the roofing job.

"Everyone in L.A. needs a little extra. Call me," Caroline said, with a wink. She was trying to pull off good-natured and jaunty, but there was definitely something uneasy about that wink. Then she turned and, dripping wet, left the property.

"Can you believe that woman? I mean, can you *believe* her?" I was staring after the spot where she had disappeared around the main house, noticing the wet footprints she had left on the path.

Wesley just shook his head. That's when Holly came through the back gate, holding the carton full of Albert Grasso's papers that she had just taken to be copied, missing running into Caroline Rochette by seconds.

Holly checked out my wet face, my wet hair, my wet clothes. "What's going on? Why is Madeline soaking wet?" she asked, looking from Wes to me.

"It's a long story," Wes said, "which Mad is about to tell us."

"Ew," Holly said, pointing into the pool.

But when examined more closely, the big, black bug that had grabbed Holly's attention turned out to be nothing more menacing than one of Caroline Rochette's eyelashes, gone dismally astray.

And while we found it easy to laugh at the bizarre woman and her bizarre visit, I began to wonder if she wasn't really more of a threat than I gave her credit for. Had any of the things she told me this afternoon been true? The birthday-gift plans? The briefcase accident? Her real reason for coming to see me, even? Was it to get Grasso's papers or to find out what I knew and how well guarded I was here? Damn.

The breeze blew against my wet jeans and shirt. I began to shiver. I am not one to make enemies if I can help it. But for the first time in my life, and over a discarded pile of junk, I realized I had just made a few serious ones.

I looked at Holly holding the cardboard box of paperwork that seemed to be at the center of my troubles. I would turn it all over to the police. We would look through the copies and see what we could see. But what then? My home was a crime scene and it appeared anyone who knew a real estate agent could track me down at Wesley's place in a matter of minutes. Plus Caroline Rochette had actually been here, scoping out the lay of the land. I began to wonder again why Sara Jackson had been killed at my house. Had she seen something that put her in danger?

Holly said, "You should get out of those clothes, Mad. It's getting cooler out."

"You're right," I said, trying to return her smile.

But as I followed her back to the guest house, I remembered Caroline's warnings and couldn't stop shaking. What should I do? I was away from home too often to keep a dog. I seemed unable to keep a boyfriend. But a gun . . .

"Who's Sorry Now?"

Wes and Holly and I had spent hours in Wesley's guesthouse living room examining Grasso's private papers. We pored over the copies Holly had made of what had once been, if we were to believe the scheming Caroline Rochette, the contents of Albert Grasso's briefcase, but understood no more than before. As for the originals, I had left a message for Honnett. I wanted his advice on what to do with Grasso's junk. The police, it turned out, didn't want to take custody of it. When I called my local station, they politely suggested I toss it all out.

The pathetic fact was: Nothing new leaped to our attention. If there was something in the papers that warranted the sort of apoplectic reaction that Grasso had displayed, we were missing it. There were no notes of dirty deeds, no confessions of criminal activity, no admissions of illicit love. Nada.

"Okay, here are the pictures," Holly said, having neatly reorganized the Xerox copies of the fifty-some documents and photos once again.

Wesley was typing a master list into his laptop. He swiftly keyed in the names and inscriptions he found scrawled across a dozen autographed eight-by-tens, all from grateful Albert Grasso celebrity clients. Among others, the five-member boy band that made ten-year-olds swoon. The aging

Vegas diva, a woman who was certainly due a free liposuction if her plastic surgeon gave an incentive gift for every dozen nips or tucks. The airbrushed faces of several young hopefuls who had become recent celebrities on *American Idol.* The legendary screen star from the fifties, Catherine Hill. Her face brought a smile to my lips. This glamorous old MGM superstar had become a "close personal friend" of mine, as Wes and I liked to joke. Catherine Hill and I had actually met several times. And in Hollywood, Wes and I had learned, any slight acquaintance (Phil Collins's plumber? Charlize Theron's optometrist?) seemed to be all it took to claim intimate relationships with the stars. And then there was the photo of the former president with the smiling young woman.

"I'm guessing that's Albert's niece or daughter," I said, rechecking the image. "Damn, I should have thought to ask Caroline if Albert had a daughter while I had her here, answering questions."

Wes pushed a few keys and was soon deep into a Web search on Albert Grasso. Duh. I mean, why hadn't I thought of that?

"Here he is," Wes said, his eyes scanning the screen. "I've pulled up his biography."

"What's it say?" Holly asked.

"Usual sort of things. He was born in Oklahoma City. He studied voice at the University of Oklahoma on scholarship. Opera. Broadway. Yadda yadda."

We waited. "Says he arranged music and did vocal work with Sonny and Cher way back when. And worked on their show."

"All these people," I said, "who surround the stars. They all manage to make a living, don't they?"

"As do we," Wes pointed out. That got all of us thinking for a minute. Then he said, "Here's all it says about his personal life. 'Albert Grasso lives in the Hollywood Hills. His daughter, Gracie, is a recent graduate of Georgetown University and attends Harvard Law School.' "

"Bingo!" I said, feeling rather pleased with myself. "She must be the intern in the picture with Clinton."

"Ew," said Holly. I was surprised at her reaction. Frankly, Holly still had a crush on the former president. I looked at her and raised a brow. She asked, "How can you name a kid Gracie Grasso?"

That was something to think about another day. "Can we look through the documents one more time?" I asked.

"I have just about finished logging them," Wes said. "There are seven letters of thanks or recommendation from various celebs and academies. There are four requests for donations to charities or thank-you notes from foundations. There are six receipts for various items."

"Can we go over those again?" I asked.

"Sure. One from CreateTech for an item called Digital Performer—"

"That's recording software," Holly commented. "You know, so you can turn your Mac into a recording studio sort of thing."

"One for clothing, specifically two Armani Collezioni suits and various shirts from Boutique Giorgio Armani Beverly Hills; one five-page itemized account from the Four Seasons in Las Vegas for a ten-day trip last October; one from a place called Art-4-Less for an oil painting entitled *Dog Living in Luxury with Cigar*; one sales slip for Grasso's Audi A6; and the deed to a luxury condo on Prince Edward Island."

"So what does that tell us?" I asked. "Nothing."

"Maybe Grasso has a love nest in Canada," Holly tried.

"Holly, don't blame our neighbors to the north," Wes said.

"He's dressing up in the new Armani," Holly continued,

"driving his Audi out to Vegas, setting up private recording sessions—"

I finished, "And hooking up with the cigar-smoking dog?"

Wes laughed. "If Albert Grasso was sticking up a gas station one day, and one of these receipts proves he was in the area and busts his alibi—we're never going to know that."

"Maybe Albert had to buy those suits to replace two identical models that he ruined by spilling someone's blood all over them."

Context. Any little thing could be innocent or much more dangerous if one knew the context.

"So we agree," Holly concluded, stacking the papers up again, "we definitely don't know what we know."

"Comforting," Wes said, looking over at me, concerned.

"I left a message for Detective Baronowski. Since this carton of Grasso's things had been stored at my house at the time of the break-in, maybe he'll take a look."

"Good," Wes agreed.

I picked up the phone and dialed the number to get the messages off of my home voice mail. I was ready to handle the accumulation of work and backlog of messages that had piled up since yesterday. We often get called on the weekend. Party anxiety can hit our clients at the oddest times.

There were several events-related items: a couple who were picking dates for a September engagement party, a public relations agent who wanted to make sure we had allowed extra space for the paparazzi at her beach barbeque soiree, and already a call about the Woodburn flower-arrangement class/luncheon we'd been asked to schedule so soon. A flurry of short, sweet messages came in from Zenya Knight, Connie Hutson, Dilly Swinden, and four other Woodburn ladies, with praise for the Black & White Ball and thanks for putting on such a fabulous party. These women may have suffered a drunken celebrity auctioneer, a major robbery, and a hundred-thousand-dollar loss to their auction revenues, but you couldn't tell it by their warm thank-you calls. Had their mothers beaten these manners into them as small children, or was such graciousness genetic?

Surprisingly, there was only one message about the police activity at our house. My neighbor Nelson Piffer was wondering what all the fuss on the street was about. He'd heard a terrible rumor from another neighbor—a woman he detests with a yippy dachshund—who said the coroner's van had been spied on Whitley Avenue around 4 A.M. It sounded like Nelson was angling for some details, although he was much too well mannered to ask directly. He signed off by reminding me the Whitley Heights Homeowners Association meeting had been canceled for the month, and that, as always, Teuksbury sent her love.

The most intriguing message came last. "Hello, Miss Bean. It is Albert Grasso calling with deep and very sincere apologies. I seem to have made a royal ass out of myself last night. I was extremely upset, as I don't need to remind you. But, clearly, I was taking out my anger on the messenger, and what a charming and beautiful messenger you were, too.

"As for the terrible misunderstanding, all has been explained to me by Caroline. She came over this afternoon and told me everything. What the hell can I say? She begged for my forgiveness and she begs your forgiveness, too, of course, and whatever Caroline did, she meant well. I am so sorry our foolish little drama has impacted you in such a nasty way. Look, the point of this call. I'd like to apologize in person. You've been a trouper through this whole fiasco. If it is at all possible, I would love to get my papers back. Please drop them off at your earliest convenience."

I played that one back twice and then hung up.

"Million messages?" Holly inquired.

"Always," I answered. "The Woodburn ladies loved the party, despite the several glitches in their fund-raising efforts. Not our responsibility, of course."

"Thank goodness," Wes said.

"And a few other calls. Zenya Knight wants to talk to me. It's sure to be about her weird husband. I wouldn't be surprised if he was in jail after the way he was driving last night. And there was a call from their auction-bidding rivals, the Hutsons."

Wes looked up. "What did they want?"

"They'd like to plan a birthday party for their twelve-year-old sax genius. They suggest holding a 'battle of the jazz players' kind of competition."

"Oy," Holly said, and giggled.

"And then I got a call from Mr. Albert Grasso, very sorry and all that."

"Really?" Holly looked shocked.

"So maybe he's just a blowhard kind of guy. Big blowup last night, and apologies today."

"Men are weird," Holly said.

"Hey," Wes said.

"I think I better give him back his junk."

"Really?" Wes was surprised.

"Well, I realize Grasso was rude as hell to me last night. Unfortunately, that crime is not yet recognized in the state of California."

"Your problem is you are too forgiving," Holly said.

"If Grasso and Caroline are apologizing for their craziness, that's more than you usually get from the assorted loonies we work with."

"But—"

"And look at this stuff." I tapped the box that was piled with the man's items. "We have his passport and his therapist's report and his detailed Bible-study notes and his book proposal for *How to Sing Like a Bird.* There are three handwritten letters from his mother from like thirty-five years ago. Those have to be precious to him."

"True," Holly agreed reluctantly.

"And we've got all that other stuff he'll need, like the copies of his divorce papers. And the detailed inventory of his coin collection and those papers from Mid-Pacific Insurance and North American Home Insurance and every other legal document he's going to need in his life."

We all sat and thought about it.

"But, Maddie, what about Sara . . . ?" Holly said, shaking her head.

"We don't know what happened to Sara, Holly. Maybe it was just a junkie looking for something to steal, something he could hock for drug money. And then Sara showed up and she . . . If someone was breaking into the house and got scared, they might have followed her up to my room. Maybe she ran . . ."

Holly's eyes were beginning to tear up and I knew if I let myself go there, in a minute or two, mine would, too. It was funny how emotion could suddenly wash over you, like waves. And if a swell caught you unprepared, it could knock you down. I steadied myself and went on: "Look. This Grasso business needs to be cleaned up."

"I know," Holly said, tears running down her cheeks. Wes kindly handed her a box of tissues.

"I wanted to believe I could figure everything out," I said, sitting down next to Holly. "I thought I could make sense of Sara's murder and Grasso's anger. I was looking for one neat solution. But they just don't seem connected."

Holly wiped her eyes and nodded.

"We checked it out as best as we could," Wes said. "Holding on to Grasso's papers isn't going to help Sara."

"No." Holly blew her nose. "Maddie is right. I think we're all freaked out and twitchy. I know I am."

"That's right, Holly." I gave her a little hug. "And we just have to get past it. I've got to get back to normal. And I'm going to start by returning Albert Grasso's papers."

Okay. I wasn't 100 percent sure that Grasso was an innocent, if rage-challenged, jerk. I just had no real proof to the contrary.

"And just in case," I said, "I'll let Grasso know that I've already shown the papers to lots of people."

"Good idea." Holly sniffled.

"And tell him copies of everything in his files are going to the police," Wes added.

"Fine," I agreed. "Look, I've got to get out of here already. I'm going a little stir-crazy. I'll drop off the copies at Baronowski's office and give Grasso back his precious junk. And I've been thinking I should pay a condolence call on Sara Jackson's boyfriend. Sara said he was depressed. I can't imagine how he's getting through all this."

"I forgot about him," Holly said, in a hushed voice. "So do you think maybe he's a suspect?"

"I'm sure that's how the police view him. But he could just be a grieving grad student who needs some help. So, can you get me Sara's address?"

"That's okay, Hol," Wes said. "I've got it in my PC. And I am going to go along with Madeline."

"What?" I swung around and faced him. "Like I can't walk around without an escort?"

"Honey, we thought we lost you."

I quieted down. Of course they had. Why was I so defensive?

"Look, you've been dumped in the middle of downtown, dunked in an unheated swimming pool, and there's been a murder in your bedroom. At this point, I'd think you might appreciate a little company."

Wesley Westcott was a great guy.

"Big Nick"

After the heat of the day, the early-evening air was refreshingly cool. I brushed off my white jeans and smoothed the tan silk sleeveless shirt as I waited on the front walk outside Wesley's house, right next to a mammoth-size demolition Dumpster, in leafy old Hancock Park. From around back, I could hear Wes as he opened the garage door. But before he could pull his new Jag down the driveway, another car pulled up the street and turned into it.

Dexter Wyatt. Ah.

I was seriously annoyed to notice how raggedy my breath got as vast quantities of adrenaline, or something like it, began pumping up my senses.

Dex stepped out of the car in one languid movement and smiled at me. His hair tumbled over his forehead. His shorts showed off tanned legs, great calf muscles. His boyishness was extremely sexy.

"Impressive," he said as he walked behind his car and over to me at the curb. "You been standing out here next to a Dumpster all day hoping to catch a glimpse of me?"

"Maybe." Eye contact made me intensely aware of how warm the evening was, after all.

Dexter handed me a large sequin-dusted Hawaiian-print shoulder bag, the one I usually bring to our events because it can hold everything and it's hard to miss. "Yours, I take it. Properly returned, with apologies from my sister."

"Thanks." I took the bag and opened it to find my cell phone. I wasn't too surprised to discover the battery was dead.

"Nothing disturbed, I hope. No loose change missing. Never can trust that brother-in-law of mine."

I giggled. "It's fine, I'm sure."

"So you want to go somewhere?" Dex asked, gesturing a playful finger toward himself, and then me, and then hitching his thumb over to his cute sports car, laying on the charm. "Grab a bite, maybe? Seeing as you are looking so hot."

"Thanks. Now don't get me wrong. Normally, I would love to be picked up on the street by a passing guy. Really."

"I know." Dex had a great smile and he used it. "I remember last night with fondness."

"But things are just a little messed up right now . . ."

The red taillights of Wesley's Jaguar came suddenly into view, backing down the long driveway, until it stopped, blocked by Dex's car.

Dexter reassessed the situation. "Boyfriend?" He actually sounded crestfallen. My solar plexus did a little flip.

"Not exactly. Best friend. Partner."

"Gay?"

I mock-scowled at Dexter. "Look, I have a few errands to run and I better get going. Thanks so much for driving this by." I gestured to my purse. "You didn't have to go to all that trouble."

"Trouble? I wanted to see you again, Madeline. I have been thinking about you all day. Did you ever get to sleep?"

"No."

"Me neither. I kept thinking about you."

"Oh, man." I giggled. "What a line."

"Women," Dex said philosophically. "They never believe you when you are telling the truth."

"Maybe, but that puts us in an excellent position to *not* believe you when you are telling us big lies, you see." I leaned a little closer to him, catching his scent. He smelled yummy. I stepped back.

"You lack trust," he said, shaking his head sadly.

"I've got to go."

"How about later?"

"Why?"

"You seem like a complicated woman," he said. "Moth to the flame."

"I am so going to cure you of that," I said, laughing.

"Good." Dexter took a few seconds to look me over. "I take even the slightest scolding as encouragement. So when will you be free? Nine?"

"Make it ten o'clock. I'll meet you somewhere. I'll have Wesley drop me off."

"Where?"

"How about Fabiolus on Melrose?" I suggested a charming little Italian place in an odd part of Hollywood, right behind Paramount Studios. It seemed to fit us, as we had already set a precedent of eating off the beaten path.

"I'll be there." He walked me over to Wesley's car. "So it's a date, then." As he bent down to open the door, his lips almost brushed against my hair.

"Fine." I sat. "Wesley, this is Dexter Wyatt. Dex, Wes."

"Hi there," Wes said amiably.

"Good to meet you. And, Madeline, I'll see you later." Dexter Wyatt shut the car door, hopped into his own vehicle, and drove smoothly off, heading south. Wes pulled out of the driveway and turned north.

As we glided up the street, he cast a look over at me. "So I leave you for three minutes and you pick up a guy?"

"That was Zenya's brother, the guy I told you about. He was returning my bag."

"And what does he do?" Wes asked.

"I don't think he does much. Trust funds, I assume."

"Oh ho."

On our rounds, we dropped by the police station, where I left the copies of Grasso's paperwork for Detective Baronowski. He wasn't in. Next, I asked Wes to drive me downtown, where we scouted around the quiet Sunday streets looking for my loan officer. He wasn't in front of the building near Flower, but about two blocks over I spotted his dog. When I approached the dog, sitting alone on the sidewalk in front of a closed office tower, the owner came out from the shadow.

"I borrowed some money from your dog last night," I told the man, trying to remember if he was the same guy. It was the same dog, all right. His tail beat the sidewalk in happy recognition.

"Big Nick shouldn't be giving nobody no money," the man muttered, eyeing me. "What you want?"

"I owe Big Nick a dollar thirty-five, plus a bonus of ten dollars." I had the money in my hand and held it out.

"So give it to 'im," the man said, watching me like I must be a cop and he wasn't about to get pinched.

I could see no sign of the man's collection jar, so I just bent down and put a ten and a one and a quarter and a dime on the pavement.

Big Nick stood up and sniffed the money then sat back down, tail thumping.

"Big Nick don't like most people. So if he bite you, don't be blaming me. Big Nick is a mean mother."

"Thanks for the tip." Big Nick looked at me with love in his eyes.

"Don't I get nothing?" the man asked.

"Sure. Sorry. You have a jar?"

He kept staring at me.

So I opened my bag and took out another ten-dollar bill. I handed it to the man and he snatched it before I let go, almost ripping it.

There was no thank you involved, but I didn't mind. I had repaid a debt and gotten to see Big Nick again. Sometimes, low expectations help in life.

Wes had pulled his white S-Type into a no-parking zone on Seventh, just around the corner. When I got back, he was smiling.

"You always amaze me, Mad. The people you know, the friends you meet."

"I own this town," I said, and then asked nicely to be driven over to Iris Circle. As it turned out, no one was home at Albert Grasso's house. I decided to leave the cardboard carton of papers at the front door, and then I second-guessed that decision. After all the commotion, I hated to leave the stuff there unattended. But I hated even worse the idea I would still be stuck with them. I tucked the box behind a shrub to one side of the door and hopped back into Wesley's Jaguar. I must say I could get used to such service.

After that, I felt a lot better. I needed to pick up some vitamins and Wes was uncomplaining as we ran a few other errands. Even though he was a dear, I longed for my own wheels. I needed some independence to get back to normal.

We stopped back at my house on Whitley to pick up a few items I'd forgotten to pack. I was pleased to see the crime-scene tape had been removed. Wes and I discussed what to do about the house and where I should stay. We agreed that it was best for me to hang at his place for a while. We'd open the office tomorrow, as usual, and work out of the downstairs rooms. Wesley had already called a cleaning service, which would arrive in the morning, and he insisted he'd deal with the upstairs rooms. He suggested we take this opportunity to remodel a bit, maybe push out a wall and expand the bedrooms. I was unfocused, unwilling to think about my bedroom the last time I stood in it. Unable to avoid it. And the awful memory of Sara Jackson.

Before we left the neighborhood, I asked Wes to swing around to Iris Circle again. I hoped the cardboard carton I had left by the door earlier had been taken in. But when we drove up to Albert Grasso's house, I could plainly see the box sitting half hidden by the shrub where I had left it.

"Wes, hang on half a second while I go up and ring the doorbell again. Maybe Grasso was doing laundry or giving a late singing lesson when we stopped by before. Maybe he didn't hear me knock. I'd feel better if I didn't have to worry about that box all night."

"Sure."

But again, no one answered.

"Enough. Let's get out of here," I suggested when I was back in the Jag. "I have a date for dinner."

Fifteen minutes later, Wes dropped me off at the Fabiolus Café. Dexter Wyatt was already seated at a table and I joined him.

"Am I late?" I asked.

"I was early," he said. "Hope you don't mind, but I already ordered for us."

That caught my attention.

I should explain. In most of my recent relationships, I'd had the upper hand in the foodie arts. It isn't surprising. I am, after all, a graduate of the Culinary Institute. A professional. I'd worked as a chef in Northern California and down in L.A. before Wes and I started our catering/event-planning firm. I love exotic cuisines and complex, demanding recipes.

The men I had dated tended to be less food involved. In fact, my longest-lasting boyfriend of record, Arlo Zar, was a certified food wimp. He was a Big Mac kind of guy. Among other oddities, Arlo eschewed vegetables outright. He refused to eat anything green, on principle, except for iceberg lettuce. And only iceberg when it was cut into a wedge and served with Thousand Island. Arlo was a comedy writer and sitcom producer and considered his food quirks charming. I had been amused, as I always was, by Arlo and his ways. At least, for the first couple of years.

Honnett and I only lasted a few months, and even then our romance had been on the erratic side. After Arlo, Honnett was amazingly open to trying new foods. But he was at heart a steak-and-potatoes kind of guy. I can always tell what people like to eat best, what flavors comfort them most. Holly says I have EFP—Extra-Foodery Perception. I claim no alien gifts, but I will admit this sensitivity to others' tastes and desires has served me well in my business, planning menus for so many clients. And I have relied on it, knowing I have an edge in evaluating new people.

I looked across the linen-draped table at Dex and smiled. What a guy ordered from a menu was a most revealing right of passage in a new relationship. I prolonged the delicious suspense a moment longer as I sipped my glass of cool white wine. The bottle of Valpolicella Classico Superiore "Villa Novare" 1997 sat on the table. Dex had good taste in wine. Very good taste. Extra points.

"Great wine." I looked up at him and found everything I saw appealing. This was dangerous. "What did you order?"

"For you," he said, "the goat-cheese-and-blackened-chicken salad to start. Balsamic dressing on the side."

I smiled.

"Okay so far? Followed by penne ai calamari—penne pasta made with sautéed calamari and a fresh sauce of cherry tomatoes, garlic, basil, and white wine."

"And for you?"

"I'm having polenta e poccio—cornmeal and prosciutto

covered with a Gorgonzola sauce, and also the lonza di maiale al provolone e asparagi, which is the—"

"Pork loin in white wine and asparagus sauce," I interrupted, "covered with provolone cheese and served with sautéed spinach."

"Exactly," he said. "And I figured we could share if you found anything more appealing on my plate."

I eyed the menu quickly and discovered I couldn't have ordered any better myself. What a pleasure.

Another memory surfaced. Xavier Jones had been a true culinary genius. He was a boy I met in culinary school, the top of our class. He and I planned to open our own auberge in the wine country of Northern California together someday. That was all just a dream, of course. We never did anything like that. We didn't even get married. But it had only been with Xavier and, later, with my friend Wesley that I had found such extreme-sport cuisine compatibility.

"You judging me?" Dex asked, amused.

"A-plus. But don't let it go to your head."

"So," Dex asked me, refilling my wineglass, "how come you don't look tired? I look like shit and you look beautiful."

"Thanks." I remembered flirting. I liked flirting. I tried to remember how. "I can go without sleep. One of my few true talents."

"Too modest," he said. "If we're going to be friends, and I insist we are going to be, then you have to tell me the three best things about yourself. No, five."

"Oh, come on! I am much too demure. Too shy. Too—"

"Full of it. Come on. You must. And I'll tell you the five best things about me. You go first."

Our first course was delivered, which gave me a moment to think. It's not that I'm really demure and shy. It's just that I don't think about myself very often. I realized, too, that not many men had seemed all that interested in my view of myself. Which was interesting, really.

"You've had enough wine and you've missed enough sleep, so be totally frank," Dex said, looking at me over his wineglass.

"I'm a pretty good speller."

Dexter laughed loudly. A deep, handsome, masculine laugh. "More personal stuff, Madeline, or I'll have to raise your number to ten."

"No, no! Okay . . . I'm honest. Not everyone agrees that's a good trait, however. But I am really truthful. And I'm curious about everything, so I read a lot and tend to ask a lot of questions."

"Again, all your good traits seem to have two edges."

"Ain't that the truth? Let me think. How many is that?"

"You have given me two—you're honest and curious. I'm throwing out the good-spelling confession."

"Okay, but you must count how good I am without much sleep. I have great energy. That's three. And I'm a great cook. I love to cook," I added. "And I like sex."

Well, there. That got Dexter's attention. I couldn't believe I said it, but it was true.

Dexter said, "Well, well, well. We have a good trait in common, then. Count that as my first. Then as to the other four: I am loyal. I love my sister. I don't do drugs. Anymore. And I'm pretty talented at starting fires in fireplaces."

"That must come in handy," I said with admiration.

"It does. I also played tennis sort of professionally."

"So that's six things you are good at," I said, adding them up.

"Well, if I'd been *really* good at tennis, I might have done a little better on the circuit, but I can hit the ball around."

My salad was wonderful, and Dexter insisted we taste each other's dish. His polenta was very good, but not, I thought secretly to myself, as good as my own. I would have to cook it for him someday.

"Now your worst traits," Dex said, unable to hold back a grin.

"No way."

"You must. You said you're honest. Prove it. I want your three worst qualities."

I tried not to blush as he made a great show of refilling my wineglass yet again, the better to loosen my tongue, I gathered.

The waiter removed our plates and brought on the main courses. The aroma of garlic and basil and white wine rose from my steamy plate of pasta. It looked wonderful and I suddenly realized how hungry I had been. Dexter declared his pork loin to be perfectly cooked and the waiter retreated.

"Okay," Dex said, getting back on topic. "I'll show you what a good sport I am. I'll go first. My three worst traits."

I paused with a forkful of short, hollow penne noodles almost to my lips.

"First, I don't have a job." Dex spoke lightly, but I suspected not much escaped his notice as he confessed his sins. "Second, despite my extremely prestigious education, I don't have any skills with which to acquire a job."

"Where did you go to school?"

"Yale. Philosophy major. Played tennis and skied."

"Minored in girls?"

"You apparently know me much too well," he said, putting down his fork and meeting my eyes. "Alas, no great job market there."

"No. And what else?"

"And third, and worst of all, my trust fund is almost completely obliterated. I could blame the market, which as you know has been terrible, but against all the good advice in the world, I've been leaning rather hard on the principle. Eventually, it will run out. My family had money at one time, or so they tell me, but at present, they are pretty much broke. All except Zenya, thanks to her jerk husband, Bill. He's got bucks. But not me. In other words, Maddie, I don't have any money, or ambition, or goals."

"That's sad," I said, filled with wine and sympathy. "Isn't there anything in life that appeals to you?"

"I don't know," he said. "I like sports. I like photography. I like you." He smiled.

"Have you ever done anything with your photographs?"

"What do you mean?"

"Have you ever tried to sell them?"

"No. I used to take lots of pictures when I was playing tennis. I haven't done much recently."

"Okay. If I was in charge of your life, I'd suggest you call a few of your friends who are still playing professional sports and get passes to their events. You take some pictures, and if you like how they turn out, you sell them. Simple, huh?"

He gazed at me across the table. "So I guess your three worst traits are, you have no problem with meddling in sensitive areas, you can get a little bossy, and you have the extremely annoying habit of being right."

"That pretty much sums me up," I said, wondering if I had offended him.

"No wonder my sister was so keen on my meeting you," Dexter said. "Say, not to be nosy . . ."

"Nosy? You?" I laughed. "After demanding to know my best and worst traits. That's ridiculous."

"Well, thanks. I have been kind of curious about what was going on at your house last night. The cops. The body in the bedroom. Can you fill me in?"

"It's a long story," I said. "Long. And I don't understand most of it. Just a sad event. Remember, when you rescued me last night I told you I had lent my car to a young woman who worked for me? She came to my house to return my car. We don't know exactly what happened, but while she was there she got shot. The police are thinking she may have interrupted a burglar. It's all just horrible."

"That is tough," he said, putting his large hand over my hand.

"I want to help in some way, but I can't figure out what to do. I'm thinking, maybe her boyfriend could use a little help. I've never met him. I was going to see him this evening, but that was before I ran into you." I put my hand to my temple. I was getting a headache.

"This wasn't something I should have brought up. I'm sorry, Madeline," Dex said quietly.

"No, no. It's okay. I am suddenly feeling exhausted," I said. "I need to get some sleep, if you don't mind driving me back to Wesley's."

Dexter Wyatt didn't even ask for the bill. He just casually threw two hundred dollars onto the table and stood up. "Let's go."

"Sorry to spoil your night," I said as we walked to his car, parked out front.

"No, I understand," he said. "You have a lot on your mind."

"I do. I have to go see this dead girl's boyfriend tomorrow. And then, I am still hung up on old boyfriend."

"The cop?"

"Yeah.

"And I have a bad feeling about some papers I dropped off today. No one was home, so I decided to leave them at the door. Now I'm thinking that wasn't the best idea."

Dex touched a button on his key chain that unlocked the doors to his car. But before he reached down to open the passenger door for me, he turned and put his hands on my shoulders. "You need some sleep. In the morning, everything will look a lot better."

"I hope so."

"You'll see. The problem with the girl and her boyfriend. The papers. Me."

"You have been great. I mean it. You've been fun."

"I get that a lot," he said, with a sly smile. And then, standing out on Melrose Avenue with very little traffic, he pulled me gently toward him and kissed me. His lips were soft and light. I was tense but his body felt good, holding me close. By the second kiss, I had sort of given up much resistance. Why struggle to understand things that were beyond me? If I could just stay in the moment, I was fine. More than fine. I was hoping for a third kiss, but Dex pulled back and kissed me on the forehead instead.

"So when you get this cop out of your system," he said, "can I see you again?"

I had the strangest thought. I suddenly wondered if Big Nick would approve of this new guy in my life. More, I figured, than he'd approve of a married cop.

"The Shoes of the Fisherman's Wife Are Some Jive-Ass Slippers"

I looked at the small clock on the bedside table. Seven-thirty. Eight hours of sleep, I calculated. Quite decent.

After a quick shower, I decided to let my hair dry naturally to save time. I'd deal with the wild, electric-socket ringlets later. I pulled on some khaki capris and a clean, white T-shirt, and found my way out to the tiny kitchen. Wes was preparing French toast.

"One or two?" he asked me as he began dipping thin slices of his home-baked bread into the egg mixture.

"Just one, thanks." I picked up the kettle of boiling water from the range and poured it into a mug over a humble tea bag. Wesley had already brewed himself a cup of estate-grown English Breakfast tea, but he kept a stash of Lipton's just for me, knowing I often preferred my morning cup of tea plain and simple and familiar. "I had a big dinner."

"How'd that go?" Wes asked, raising his voice slightly to be heard above the sizzle as he put rich, egg-soaked slices of bread onto the hot griddle.

"Fine," I said. "Okay. Pretty good."

Wes adjusted the gas burners, using just one-hundredth of his conscious brainpower, keeping the other ninety-nine hundredths focused on me, an expectant look on his even features, waiting for more.

"He's terribly cute. But I'm not sure I can take another mistake in the boyfriend department."

"Mistake? What's wrong with him? You know, Mad, my mother used to tell us, you can just as easily fall in love with a rich man as a poor man."

"My mother said the same thing!" We smiled at each other. "Only problem—the horrible sledgehammer of power I observe some rich men wielding over their women."

"Oh. Good point."

"Some of these women, Wes. It's like they are always worried they aren't cute enough, or thin enough, or young enough, or whatever. And I think the money does that to them. They realize their rich old husbands can always go out and get younger, cuter women."

"Well, then. Down with rich men," Wes said, amused.

"But on the other hand, it turns out that Dexter isn't rich."

"Really? Score one for him, then. So what's the problem?"

"I may still be in love with Honnett. I don't know."

"It will all sort itself out," Wes said, serving me a perfectly cooked slice of French toast. I sprinkled a quarter of a teaspoon of powdered sugar over it and joined him at the tiny table for two in the corner.

"Glad you aren't trying to stay thin to please some rich guy." Wes eyed my meager plate and smiled.

I got his point. "I think this is different. I'm single. I may not know what the hell I'm doing in the ocean of romance, but I still need to keep the bait fresh." I forked another small bite of French toast. "Mark my words. Someday, when I'm happily married to my soul mate, who loves me for all the right reasons, I may just let this whole body of mine go straight to hell."

"I'll rejoice in your happy fatness."

"But until then . . ." I pushed the plate away.

Over our breakfast, Wes informed me that while I had

been out, Detective Baronowski had returned my many calls. He'd thanked us for dropping off the copies we'd made of Grasso's paperwork but didn't act like it was some great big lead. Wes sensed the detective didn't think there was much to go on there. We'd done our duty, at least. And while Baronowski had remained tight-lipped about his investigation into Sara Jackson's death, he had asked Wes for more information on Sara's boyfriend. Unfortunately, we knew very little about most of our temporary waitstaff, so Wes couldn't be much help. Baronowski did confirm that we could get back into my house on Whitley, as their investigation there was complete. That was a good thing, since we'd already been back there last night. On the disappointing side, the cops would need to keep my car for a few more days. Their forensics people were pretty backed up.

When we'd cleaned up the dishes, Wes agreed to drive me to the Enterprise rent-a-car office up on Sunset. Now that my purse had been returned, I had my driver's license and my credit cards and I could finally get myself a rental. After driving my very old Jeep Grand Wagoneer for years, I discovered I was in for a treat. Renting a new car is fun. I decided to try a Chevy Trailblazer. I selected a red one and was thrilled to realize I now temporarily possessed more cup holders than had ever been featured in my wildest dreams. I couldn't wait to zip into the nearest In-N-Out Burger and try out every size cup of Diet Coke.

Out on the street, I felt a sudden uplift in my spirits. As I rode Sunset east, I heard a familiar beeping. My cell phone, all charged up overnight, was once again in working shape. One by one, the pieces of my world were coming back to order. I smiled.

"Hello."

"It's me." Honnett's voice sounded calm. He'd experienced his one evening of strong, barely controlled emotion the other night. I doubted I'd see that side of him again. Something to consider.

"I'm on my way to my office," I said. "You know, back to my house. I have got to face it, don't I?"

"It's still pretty soon, isn't it, Maddie? You can't rush things if you are feeling overwhelmed."

"Overwhelmed, get out of town. But it's sad. I'll never feel good about that house again." I was glad to be saying it out loud. I didn't want to let Wesley down, but I was nervous. Post-traumatic stress. "I don't feel safe there, Chuck. But it's where I work. I need to get back to work."

"You'll get through it. You're tough. Can I meet you there?"

I hesitated.

"Something wrong, Maddie?"

"Actually, I have a few loose ends," I said. "I need to visit a couple of people. Maybe I should do that first. What's this about, Honnett? Official business or—"

"No. I just need to see you. Things were said the other night. We haven't talked in months. We still haven't cleared the air, have we?"

"You mean," I suggested into my small cell phone, stopped at the red light at Laurel Canyon, "I still haven't forgiven you for being married."

"Now that you put it so clearly, yes." Honnett sounded amused. He could handle sarcasm. I liked that in a man. "Will you see me?"

"Why don't you stop by the house around lunchtime?"

"Great."

Great, I said to myself when he had clicked off. I looked over at the note I'd written with Sara Jackson's address. She had lived in the Promenade Towers on South Figueroa, in downtown L.A., just a mile from the Woodburn. If I'd realized she lived so close to the party, I'd have offered to drive her home the other night. If I'd bothered to ask her. I thought about how I had managed to know so little about my employees.

I turned onto the Hollywood Freeway and drove south, enjoying the horsepower and unfamiliar ride of the rental, then transitioned slowly to the 110, and finally pulled off on Third Street. I spotted the high-rise complex of the Promenade Towers located in the Bunker Hill section of downtown, and turned the Trailblazer into its underground parking lot.

The elevator took me to the large lobby, an impressive, two-story, marble-floored space. Beyond the lobby, through glass doors, I could see a water wonderland. Fountains and pools filled a courtyard that was sheltered by the many residential towers of the complex. There was a sign posted on the glass announcing that good apartments were still available for rent. A sign nearby boasted about the excellence of the building's swimming pool. Another claimed THE BEST FITNESS CENTER IN DOWNTOWN! ASK US ABOUT OUR STUDENT SPECIALS! FURNISHED STUDIOS—$775! PETS! LAUNDRY FACILITY!

I wondered what exactly I would say to him, to Sara's boyfriend. I knew Sara was carrying him financially. Maybe I could offer him a small gift. He might need a helping hand with the rent.

In the lobby, I went over to the courtesy desk and spoke to the guard.

"Apartment 4-2029," I said.

"You're here to see . . . ?"

"I'm here to see . . ." It was damned awkward. I stood there for a second or two, and the guard, a tall, heavy African-American guy in his forties, began to look at me suspiciously.

"Yeah?"

"Sara Jackson in Apartment 4-2029, please." It was fairly creepy. I had just asked for a dead woman.

"And you are . . . ?"

"Madeline Bean."

"You asking for Ms. Jackson?" He stared at me.

"Yes. Or her roommate. Sara's fiancé. I don't have his name."

"No one going to be home there," the man said. "You family or something?"

"No. I'm Sara's employer. She worked for me."

"So, you're her boss?"

"Yes."

"Hold on," he said. He didn't pick up the courtesy phone. Instead, he lumbered away, down the hall marked EMPLOYEES ONLY.

I took the opportunity to peek over the high counter. There was a well-worn three-inch black binder. The label on the cover was peeling. It said MASTER. I figured it was the current listing of tenants and grabbed it while the lobby was still deserted.

The listings were alphabetical. I had been hoping I could just look up the apartment number and get the name of Sara's boyfriend quickly. Instead, I might have to page through hundreds of listings. I started at the beginning. Amber Alviera, Daniel Anderson, Diego Arroya . . . As I zipped through the index, I noticed several tenants shared the same apartment numbers. I tried to imagine three grad students sharing a studio apartment and shuddered. Maybe I was looking too quickly, nerves getting the best of me, but I couldn't find another name that listed apartment 4-2029 aside from the listing for Sara Jackson herself.

A group of young tenants entered the lobby from the elevator that comes from the parking garage. One young woman called to her friends that she was just going to check her mailbox as she disappeared into a room off the main lobby. The rest of them used their key cards to access the large glass door that led to the courtyard with the pool and fitness room.

At about the same time, a young man came in from the street entrance, with a small beagle-ish dog on a leash. I walked over to the glass door to the courtyard, absentmindedly rooting around in my purse.

"Cool dog," I said, still rooting in my bag.

"Yeah. His name is Waldo."

I smiled. "Where's Waldo?"

"He's right here," the guy-without-an-ounce-of-humor said, looking blank.

I giggled. "No, it's a joke . . ." I began to explain.

He stared at me, the pain of hearing a thousand "Where's Waldo?" comments coming to the surface.

"Oh, I'm so sorry. I'm so brilliant this morning. Duh."

Waldo's owner had long, unruly brown hair and troubled skin. He smiled at me, though, and found his own key card in his pocket "first."

"Here," he said, holding the heavy glass door open for me. "What building do you live in?"

"Four." I took a guess. Sara's apartment number was 4-2029.

"Yeah? Me, too. I wonder why I haven't seen you around here. I check out all the cute chicks."

"Aw, that's sweet," I said, walking with my escort across the landscaped courtyard. A large waterfall tumbled into a pool behind a forest of ferns. The ferns looked a little brown at the tips.

"What floor are you on?" he asked.

"What floor are *you* on?" I countered, flirting just a little.

"Nineteen," he said. "I get a great view, but it costs extra. I am on a waiting list to get a lower floor. You?"

"I'm staying in a friend's apartment," I said. "On twenty."

"So that's probably why I don't know you," he said. We had reached building four and he pushed the button to call the elevator. "Who's your friend?"

"Sara Jackson."

"Oh, Sara."

I couldn't read his expression. "You know her?"

"Pretty redhead about this tall?" He held his hand up. "I know her."

"Didn't you two get along?"

"Oh, I like Sara just fine. She's just out of my price range, if you know what I mean."

"No, I don't." We traveled up the elevator together as I thought how best to handle Waldo's buddy. "Look, my name is Madeline. Sara and I used to work together."

"That figures," he said. "That makes you out of my league, too."

"Huh?"

The elevator stopped at nineteen, but I got out and followed my new friend and his dog down the hall. He seemed embarrassed by something.

I persisted. "Aren't you going to tell me your name?"

"Arnie Creski. But what are you wasting your time talking to me for?"

"Arnie, I have a confession to make. I am really here to see Sara's roommate—her boyfriend, in fact. Do you know him?"

"Her boyfriend? I don't know who you mean. Sara had a lot of boyfriends, didn't she? Don't you?"

"What?"

We had gotten down to Arnie's apartment door, and he seemed to be on the retreat. I had only a few questions more and I was pretty sure he would disappear behind his door with his little dog.

"What are you saying, Arnie? Sara was a hooker?"

"Duh."

"Really? I can't believe that. She worked with me as a waitress."

Arnie gave me a look like the young man had seen all that the world had to offer, and if Sara Jackson was a waitress, then he was the queen of France. "She works at celebrity-type parties. With rich men. Right?"

"Wasn't she a student at USC?" I asked, feeling the rug had been tugged a little too hard and I was in peril of slipping.

"I guess," he said, trying to end our conversation. "I saw her with books. Now, could you just let it go? I don't want to get the girl in trouble. I like her."

"Arnie, you must not have heard the news. Sara Jackson died the other night. She was shot."

Arnie's little beagle mix, Waldo, had had enough of standing out in the hall. He wanted inside and whimpered in front of the door.

"I've gotta go," Arnie said apologetically. "I didn't know about Sara. I'm sorry to hear it. But that girl didn't have any time for me, I can tell you that. I didn't have any money and she just wasn't interested."

"And you're sure she didn't live with another grad student? A young man?"

"No. She lived alone. I know that for sure. But I saw her bring a lot of guys around, let me tell you. Suits, I would call them. Johns, probably." And then Arnie let Waldo into his apartment and quietly shut the door.

"Sing Sing Sing"

"I'm parked in front of Albert Grasso's house," I told Wes. I was calling in from my cell phone. I had meant to simply drive by on Iris Circle to assure that the blasted box of papers had been safely found and brought inside. "The box is still sitting there."

"That's not a bad thing," Wes suggested. "No one has stolen them."

"Yes. I suppose."

"And if you were concerned that Grasso was going nuts trying to get his hands on them again, this should reassure you that they are just, simply, a box of old papers. Nothing very pressing about them."

"Yes."

"But?"

"I found a good parking spot," I said to Wes, getting out of the red rental SUV. "So I'm just going to look around the property."

"MAD!"

"Wesley, I'm right up the street. The sun is shining. This will take ten minutes, tops. If you want, just walk up here and join me." I pressed the end button on my cell phone before hearing his reply.

There was a short brick path to the front door of Albert

Grasso's large stucco house. As on so many of the upscale residential streets in the Hollywood Hills, space was at a premium. The tightly packed homes on Iris Circle were set right on the street, all hugging the curb. While these homes lacked much in the way of front yards, there was a trade-off. Sloping hillside lots, such as these, provided wonderful rearward-facing views of the local canyons. Neighbors looked down upon scattered red-tile rooftops and aquamarine swimming pools, partially hidden by the feathery greens and grays of bushy palms and yucca trees and thick, spiky century plants.

Albert Grasso's home was a large, English affair in the Tudor Revival style so popular in Southern California in the twenties and thirties. Wes had educated me on all the charming "faux" architectural details of that period, since older L.A. homes are his passion. The fanciful, storybook style of Grasso's house, with its steep, complex roofline and small-paned windows, was a version of Tudor Revival called the Cotswold cottage. His was quite a terrific specimen, although it looked in need of a serious rehab.

I approached the front entrance and rang the bell, hearing its muffled ring echo in the quiet interior. No one came to the door. I put my hands up to shield the sun from reflecting off the leaded-glass pane in the door. The old glass caused the image to blur, but I could see only the dark entry hall.

The floor plan of these Cotswold cottages tends to include numerous small, irregularly shaped rooms, and the upper rooms have sloping walls with dormers. I looked up but all was quiet. I checked more closely around the front of the house, walking to the side. There, I found the low gate had no lock. I unlatched it easily and followed the path around the corner to the backyard. I admired the home's cedar-shingle roof, even though I knew it wasn't considered fire-safe anymore for hillside homes to have them. Fires could spread too easily, cinders flying from roof to roof. But Wes had told me those who owned these older houses were exempt from the new ordinances, at least until it was time to reroof. I guessed that Albert Grasso had been in this house a long time.

I was soon standing on the back patio, checking out Albert's dusty potted garden, admiring the huge hot-pink-flowered bougainvillea bush growing all over the back of his garage, noting his pavers could use some sweeping, taking in his fabulous canyon view. All was quiet, save the swishing sound of a neighbor's sprinklers. All was perfectly peaceful. As long as I was there, I thought I might as well knock on the back door. Perhaps Albert was working in a quieter part of the house and hadn't yet heard me.

On the back door was a note in fine printing. It read: ENTER—STUDIO DOWN THE HALL.

I knocked. No response. And then I tried the door handle. The doorknob turned easily in my hand. Without thinking, I entered Albert Grasso's dark kitchen.

Grasso must expect his students to let themselves in. I had an idea. Perhaps I should just go get that carton of papers and photos and leave them here, inside the kitchen door. Much safer.

I strode outside and rounded the corner, around front where the massive stucco chimney dominated the right side of the house. I grabbed the cardboard box that had once held champagne bottles and trotted back to the kitchen door. Once inside, I felt better. Surely Grasso would appreciate that I'd done my best to protect his bloody files. I could detect faint sounds now, coming from deeper in the house. Music. Singing. He'd find it all when his session was over.

But after I'd put up with Grasso's extreme drama at the Black & White Ball, not to mention suffering a visit from Caroline on Albert Grasso's behalf, to let this incident go without giving the man a chance to apologize in person felt, well, unfinished. As the music continued in the background, I stood there, considering.

Grasso was down the hall in some almost-soundproof studio, working on his music, no doubt. Why shouldn't I let him know I was here? I called out, "Mr. Grasso!"

There was no reply, so I stepped a little farther into the kitchen. A thin shaft of sun shone through the curtains and lit up a slice of the fairly nice-size room, although it was one that had not been remodeled since the fifties, if I was to guess. This was the sort of fixer house that would get Wesley's creative juices flowing. Perhaps when all this business was settled and behind us, Albert Grasso would give Wes a tour.

I stepped into the back hall, calling more loudly: "Excuse me! Mr. Grasso! It's Madeline Bean. Are you here?"

The music I heard was coming from this rear hallway. One of the rooms at the far end had its door closed. That must be the room Grasso used as his recording studio. Here, I could more clearly hear the music. It was the sound of a young woman's voice going over the same musical phrase. The song was familiar. "Dancing Queen." I had seen the musical version of *Mamma Mia!* in Las Vegas with Holly and Wesley. We'd loved it. Maybe Grasso was coaching a performer from one of the road companies.

I was just outside the door now, and it was fascinating how Grasso would give an instruction and the singer would repeat the phrase. In fact, now that I was just outside the door, I realized she was singing the word *li-i-i-fe,* over and over. She had a rich clear voice. And then I saw that the door wasn't completely shut. I knocked, gently so as not to startle them, but the door swung open.

It was then that I realized my mistake. There was no vocal student in Albert Grasso's recording studio. It was only a voice on his Mac, playing and replaying a digital file. Her voice sang out again, "Li-i-i-fe." And yet the room was not entirely empty.

Albert Grasso was sitting in an easy chair, his headphones askew. His eyes were open. His posture was slumped. A dark red stain ran down his forehead. A bullet had gone straight through his head.

"Something to Remember You By"

The rest of the day went by in a blur.

Wesley had arrived almost immediately. He had already been on his way to Grasso's house to see what was keeping me. Together, we called Honnett and then he took care of the rest.

I spoke to the homicide detectives, Baronowski and Hilts, again, as they had been assigned to investigate the new Grasso murder. The police department couldn't ignore the possible connection between two deaths within two blocks in the same quiet neighborhood. The media were making a big stink. Our homeowners association was on the warpath, asking men in Whitley Heights to patrol the streets.

I tried to read between the lines as the investigators told Wes and me we could leave Grasso's house, but we were not to leave the city. As we walked down to my house, I worried to Wesley about how the cops had reacted. There I was, somehow connected to two deaths of people I barely knew. I had felt their eyes on me, reassessing. Wesley told me I was imagining things, but he is not to be counted on for the harsh truth when there is the least temptation to sugarcoat something.

Wes had made a few good points. It helped some that I had been up front with the cops all along, telling Detective

Baronowski what I was up to. I had left several messages about my theories, about my visit from Caroline Rochette and her plunge into the pool, and I had dropped off copies of Grasso's papers. I had frankly told the cops everything. Everything, that is, except my penchant for spur-of-the-moment breaking and entering.

I smiled feebly at Wesley. "I haven't been arrested yet."

"Mad," he said, facing me seriously, giving my problems his full attention. "Don't worry."

"Don't worry," I repeated.

"Be happy."

"Don't worry. Be happy. I'm working on those."

Wes and Holly and I spent what was left of the day in the office, returning phone calls and paying bills. We were not our usual joking selves. Honnett came by to check up on me after spending most of the day on the periphery of the new investigation on Iris Circle. He couldn't or wouldn't tell us much about what was going on there. Wes took the cue to grab Holly and run out to do some errands, leaving me alone with Honnett on the back patio.

"You hate me," I said to Honnett. "I keep getting mixed up with dead people. This has got to hurt you with your coworkers, you knowing a girl like me."

When he sat down next to me on a teak bench, he sat closer than I would have expected, what with our relationship in suspended animation.

"How could I hate you?" he asked, watching me, checking me out closely. "You look like hell."

"Ah." I laughed. Not the complimentary sort, my guy Honnett. But observant. "The pity vote. And the sad thing is, I am grateful for it."

He laughed at that.

"But now, Honnett, I have to ask a big favor. As you know,

two people have ended up dead. Shot. And as hard as I've tried, I can't figure out what's happening."

"It will get itself sorted out," he said.

"Someday. Maybe." I chewed my lip and then caught myself acting anxious and stopped it. "Maybe it's this house. Maybe it's some instinct. But I don't feel safe anymore."

"You're not staying here, are you?"

"No, but anyone who is looking for me can find me at Wesley's house." I shivered, even though the late afternoon was still warm. "Why are all these people dying? I feel like some shadow is following me, something I should see, and I'm just too dense to figure it out. I'm . . . nervous about staying at Wesley's house," I admitted. "What if I bring this trouble to him?"

We sat there quietly, Honnett and me. He looked deeply into my eyes and took a breath. "Move in with me."

"What?"

"I am not staying with Sherrie anymore."

"Since when?"

"I moved out the other night. We are not going to make it. She understands."

I nodded, but was more confused than before. He had left his wife again, he was telling me. But I wasn't happy. He left his sick wife. That made me feel like dancing all right.

"Maddie, I think you should stay with me."

"I can't."

He stared at me. "Why not?"

"Where can I start here?"

We looked at each other, both a little wounded. I found it hard to stay focused, sitting there beside him. The physical closeness reminded me of our short time together as a couple. It had only been a few months, but we had gotten to that point of comfort with our bodies, comfort in knowing each other's points of pleasure, and the electricity between us was even now still hot. It was dangerous sitting so close to a former boyfriend. So many doors, previously opened, seemed to beckon. One step, one easy step. Back in his life, back in his arms, back in his bed.

"Why not?" he persisted, putting his arm around my shoulder. "I'd take care of you."

I shook my head.

"Why not?"

"It's not right. I wouldn't be comfortable. You are married. I'm dating someone new. Pick one."

Honnett pulled away and put his hand in the pocket of his jacket. Then he lifted his head and met my eyes. "So you want me to back off?"

"I don't know what I want to do with you," I said.

His eyes stayed on mine.

"You had your reasons for doing what you did. You were worried about your wife's health. That's honorable, Honnett."

He smiled a sad smile. "Honorable."

Our situation had become irreparably complicated and he seemed to be asking me for simple answers. I tried again. "Look, it's nice of you to offer to share your apartment. It's nice you want to look out for me. But don't you know me better than that? Don't you know how important it is for me to be strong on my own?"

He shook his head. "You *are* strong, Maddie. But do you have to think so damned much all the time? Can't you go with your gut, here?"

"My gut?"

He nodded.

"My gut tells me stay away from you."

He exhaled. I thought he had run out of things to say, but then he finally asked, "Why?"

I looked at his intelligent blue eyes, his long legs tucked

under the bench, and exhaled. "I've already been hurt enough, Honnett. It's enough. You say you've left your wife again. You've moved out for good. But what does that really mean? We can't just start up again like before. You're not really free. These entanglements have a nasty habit of hanging on to us. They take time to resolve. And your wife, she's been sick, right? And she probably hasn't been working. So whose medical insurance is she on?"

He looked at me, but didn't answer.

Health insurance ruled the universe. No one asks a woman in chemo to give up her husband *and* her medical coverage. That's inhuman. And then, there was the real state of Honnett's feelings to consider. Right now he wanted to protect me, but he had also wanted to take care of her. The time had come to call him on it.

"You may have moved out, but I know you still have feelings for her," I said slowly. "You do. So stop pretending you are here for me. You aren't. That's the truth."

He nodded and we sat there for a while, the sun moving far to the west and behind the house next door, leaving us in that perfect late-afternoon light.

"You look sad, Maddie," he said, brushing my hair off my face.

"I've been sad about us for a long time," I said softly. "First, I was pretty angry. Did some foolish things. That passed." He didn't comment and I went on. "So in a lot of ways, you are the last person I want to turn to for help right now, but the truth is, I do need you."

"Anything."

"I have given this a lot of thought. I want you to believe me, Chuck."

"Okay." He waited.

"Two people died. I don't know why. And now I don't believe I am safe."

He didn't challenge me or try to talk me out of my fears. He simply asked, "What can I do?"

I stood up and walked to the edge of my patio, grabbing a couple of bottles of water from a cooler, before I turned back to him. "I need a gun."

"What?"

"A gun. You know." I handed him one of the bottles of water. "A gun."

"Do you know how to shoot one?"

"No."

"Maddie, you aren't making any sense. First, you can never get a concealed carry permit. You will probably end up getting yourself into trouble. If you aren't going—"

"Hey. Stop. Time out."

He stopped, but gave me a very concerned look.

"I need to be able to protect myself. Just in case. Look, I'm staying out at Wesley's guest house. What if someone tries to get in? I mean, look what happened to Sara Jackson and Albert Grasso. They were inside houses and they were both shot to death."

He didn't answer. He didn't want to believe I was in danger.

"You told me to listen to my gut earlier; well, this is what my gut is telling me to do. I can't get through this night and the next night and the next. I won't be able to stand it. I need protection."

"You want me to come over to Wesley's every night and guard you? Because I will."

"I need to protect myself, Honnett."

"You want a gun? You?" Honnett looked upset.

"Why not me? I can go to the shooting range and practice. It can't be that hard."

"No, it's not hard. It's just so not you."

"Don't bet on it. I need a gun, Honnett."

"You can buy one, I guess," he said, not convinced.

"That takes weeks, doesn't it?"

"You go in and pick out your gun and do the paperwork. The state just passed a bill that requires you to take a safety course and pass an exam. And then California has a two-week waiting period."

I looked at him, frustrated. "That's what I'm saying. Maybe I don't have two weeks. Maybe someone will be knocking down my bedroom door tomorrow night, Honnett. I want a gun now."

He looked down to see my hands clenched around the seat of the bench. I loosened them immediately, trying to appear less worked up and insane.

"Look," I said, "can't you lend me a gun? Until I can get my own. Maybe I'll like what you give me and I can buy one just like it."

He looked at me.

"See, I don't know who else to turn to. I don't know that many people who might have a gun. We're kind of a peaceful crowd. And I figured you would understand about weapons."

"In case you haven't noticed, I'm not a real 'gunnie,' Madeline. I don't have dozens of firearms stored in my basement bunker, whatever you may think of me."

"Can you lend me a gun or not?" I asked, staring at him, waiting. He had let me down before, so I was just thinking about what I would do if he refused to help me now.

"All right. I'll bring you a gun. But only on the condition that you let me show you how to clean it and store it and that you really do take that safety course and go out to a pistol range and get some serious, professional instruction."

"Thank you, Chuck," I said, burying my face into his shoulder, hugging him hard. "I'll be fine. I'll practice. I'll just have it for an emergency, you know?"

"Okay," he said, hugging me back, but I could feel he wasn't as happy about the gun as I was.

"Can we go get it now?" I asked.

He looked at me, uneasy. "I'll bring it to you at Wesley's."

"When?"

"How about an hour, an hour and a half?"

"No later, okay?"

He kept looking at me. "And you promise you won't take risks. You won't take it out with you. You won't—"

"Honnett! I won't get you in trouble. I'll be good."

We stood up. Honnett looked apprehensive. Me, I practiced looking like an angel. An angel who would soon have a gun.

"I Get a Kick Out of You"

I got down to the Brea Indoor Shooting Range by 7 P.M. The box that held my first pistol, my loaner from Honnett, was beside me on the passenger seat of the rental Trailblazer. I had looked at it at Wes's guest house. It was pretty darn cool.

There were many reasons why I had never thought of owning a pistol before. I don't come from gun people. My parents didn't hunt or shoot. No one in my extended family did. My friends and I were not into guns and ammo. Before this, my weapon of choice had been my Cuisinart. But I had never doubted for a second that pulling a trigger and trying to hit a target might be fun. I have played my share of Tomb Raider. I enjoy games of precision, of cat-and-mouse intrigue, and to be truthful, a certain amount of animated destruction. I'm the first one to suggest we rent *Terminator* again. And in my present situation, I was certainly not immune to the lure of the power of a handgun. Hell, it was the very urgency of my situation, my powerlessness, that had propelled me to this northern section of Orange County in search of a shooting range and my appointment with Andy Abfel, my as-yet-unmet shooting instructor.

As he had promised, Honnett had brought the gun to Wesley's house by six o'clock. I had already been on the phone with the Brea Indoor Shooting Range to book a private lesson. The range closed at ten, but I offered a bonus if my instructor could stay even later and show me everything I needed to know. This would present no problem at all, I was told. And I'd end up with a certificate that would satisfy the state of California. Excellent.

I eventually pulled off the 57 Freeway at Lambert Road, as I'd been advised, and headed west a mile and then turned right on Berry. The indoor shooting range was located among the complex of commercial buildings on the east side of Berry Avenue.

In the reception area, I got my first surprise. Andy turned out to be Andi. Her black hair was pulled into a ponytail that reached almost to her waist. She was about my height, but about ten years older than I am, if I had to guess. Her dark brows were full and expressive and her dark brown eyes gave me a kind look. She wasn't as annoyed as I would have been to have her gender misguessed by a name. Just when you think there is no one on the planet more liberal-minded than you are, you get a wake-up call. Thanks, universe.

Andi asked to look at my handgun. I put the box on the counter and she opened it. Inside was a very clean, very shiny revolver. It was a .38-caliber Smith & Wesson Lady Smith with special custom engraving.

"This yours?" She couldn't have sounded more skeptical.

I became nervous they wouldn't teach me if I didn't own the gun. "A friend gave it to me." Which was, you know, technically true. "Why?"

"Must be a pretty good friend," she said, checking me out. "You know how much a gun like this is worth?"

"No."

She eyed me carefully.

"It must be a lot," I said. "So why would I come here with an expensive custom gun and not know the first thing about shooting it? you're wondering."

"Well, that's not a bad question," Andi encouraged me. "Go on."

"My friend is a cop. Lieutenant Chuck Honnett of the LAPD. He thinks I need to have something at home for protection. He just brought it over. I had no idea he would bring something valuable. Tell me about it."

Andi relaxed at the mention of a friend in the department, and I relaxed when she relaxed. I might know nothing about guns, but I do know people. I run parties, I plan major events. I deal with people all day long. I know what buttons need to be pushed to smooth away resistance.

Andi lifted the gun out of the satin-lined case. "It's beautiful," she said. "This is the 65LS, a thirty-eight-caliber revolver. You know about guns at all?"

"No."

"I didn't think you did. Well, a revolver is a good choice for a beginner. They're the simplest to clean and take care of. That what your cop uses?"

I had no idea what kind of gun Honnett carried. I was ashamed to realize I had never taken enough of an interest to find out. "I'm not sure."

"Well, standard issue for LAPD are the Beretta 92 nine-millimeter, Kimber 1911-style forty-five, or Smith & Wesson in either forty caliber or nine-millimeter."

"Oh." I wondered if she could tell I hadn't understood a word she had said.

"Let's take it slowly," she suggested kindly. "The caliber of the ammunition—like a police-issue forty-five?—describes the size of the bullet. The larger the caliber, say a forty-five versus a twenty-two, the more stopping power. Got it?"

I nodded. "So bigger is better."

"Well, some folks think so. But then the bigger guns are heavier and bulkier to carry, right? And they have serious recoil." She laughed. "They kick like hell. So there are always trade-offs. Everyone has a theory on what is best. But your cop friend's duty gun is going to be a pretty large piece of equipment in a serious caliber."

"So this isn't like that," I said, knowing I was a fool.

"Well, this is a *Lady* Smith. It's marketed for us women." She smirked. "But if that doesn't offend your feminist sensibilities, it's a fine gun."

"And thirty-eight caliber is . . . enough?"

"I'd say so. It's a pretty popular size. You find a lot of folks take to them. Not as hard to handle as a forty-five, although I love my forty-five."

I nodded, just like I knew what she was talking about.

Andi continued: "You should be very happy with it. This model is really an evolution of the famous Smith & Wesson Chief's Special, a revolver that cops have carried for years. No wonder your friend bought it for you. And then, she's a beauty. Look at that scrollwork. He must like you very much." Andi touched the fanciful etching on the stainless-steel barrel. And I had to admit, none of my girlfriends had ever before gauged the depth of my boyfriend's affection by the coolness of the gun he'd given me. The life lessons I had yet to learn were staggering.

"It's a revolver," I said. "Is that good?"

"Revolvers are easy to use. The mechanics of this type of gun are simpler and it has fewer parts than a semiautomatic, making maintenance—even very minimal maintenance—easier. It is also less likely to have firing problems—you know, jams—because of its design. And, assuming a clean gun using the correct ammunition, most such problems can be fairly easily cleared by the owner. For this reason alone, revolvers are often recommended to new shooters."

"Okay. That sounds fine."

"Revolvers are also easier to load," she continued, opening a box of ammunition as she instructed me on the gun. "The cartridges go into the cylinder, which is part of the gun. See? Like this. You put the rest in."

I did as she had done. The weapon felt good in my hands, I had to admit. Weighty and smooth and cool.

"Very good," she said, watching me. "Now unload the chambers. Like this." I did. Pretty simple, really. I began to believe I could get all this down and relaxed a little.

Andi nodded approval. "Okay, with the ammo back in the box, the gun is now safe, got it?" She made eye contact to check that I was staying with her.

"You a former cop?" I asked.

"Ex-army," she said softly. "My husband and I both."

"I was expecting I'd get one of those modern-looking guns," I told her, looking at a chart on the wall that showed a line of sleek black handguns. I read a bit of the ad copy. "A semiautomatic. Are they better?"

"Different," she said. "Some folks like them better, but a semiautomatic has a separate magazine and they can be a little more finicky mechanically. If you don't know about guns, you may not want to take on that learning curve right away."

I was only the lowest-rank novice, and already I was having gun envy.

Andi smiled at me. "Frankly, lots of folks like their looks. High tech and all. More *Matrix* than Bat Masterson."

I nodded. "But a revolver works. Right?"

"Yep. You've got a terrific handgun here. See, she's large enough to give stability and that means much less recoil. You'll get a chance to feel what I'm talking about in a few minutes."

I smiled, reassured.

"Really, the main drawback to a revolver for home defense is capacity."

"I beg your pardon?"

"Capacity. Most revolvers hold only six rounds. In many situations—one or even two attackers—this is plenty. In some situations, however, the gun owner might find herself in a fight that requires more than six shots."

I swallowed. "More?"

"A home invasion that ranges over a wide area, with no one immediately incapacitated, for example. Or if a second or third attacker was revealed after the first few shots were fired . . ." Andi turned her hands up, showing just how lame that would make one feel with one's revolver plum out of bullets.

Nice. Real nice. As if my nightmares hadn't been graphic enough before.

"But you'll be just fine," she said, and went back to instructing. "She's short-barreled, see? She comes with a pinned black-ramp front sight and fixed rear sight." As she talked, she pointed out the features. "Well balanced with the help of a full-lug three-inch barrel, and this rosewood grip feels great in your hand. And I have to say, the engraving here is as fine as it gets. Look at the scrollwork on the cylinder and all over the side plates?"

"Yes. It's pretty." Did people say that about guns? I was so lost.

"Have you ever shot a gun before?"

I shook my head no.

"We'll get you out in the range in just a few minutes. You'll have some fun then." Andi smiled.

Seven hours later I arrived back in Hancock Park, with enough training on handgun safety and cleaning and loading and aiming and squeezing the trigger to give me a little confidence. For one thing, I wasn't too bad out on the range. Not bad at all. Give Nintendo credit. For another, Andi told me that most defensive home handgun situations do not require you to hit a tiny circle on a target twenty yards away. Closer and larger targets are easier to hit. I found that comforting. Somewhat. Considering I was limited to six shots.

When I got to my room in the guest house, I found Wes and Holly were still out. They'd been working a small dinner party in Calabasas. I undressed, and then brought my gun case with me to the bathroom as I took a quick, hot shower. I pinned up my hair, put some cream on my face, and put on a fresh tank top and boxers, then, carting my gun case with me, I turned down my covers. I thought it over and then knelt down and put my new gun, case and all, under my bed. I turned out all the lights and then slid between the cool white sheets.

The house was quiet and very, very dark. I was exhausted. And yet I heard the ticking of Wesley's grandfather clock coming from the living room. *Tick-tock-tick-tock.* It was extraordinarily loud. And then I heard the creaking of footsteps, or maybe that was just wind in the floorboards?

I flicked on the light, climbed out of bed, and pulled the case with the revolver—my revolver—my Lady Smith .38—out from under the bed and opened it up.

I knelt at the bed and prepared to load the gun just the way Andi taught me to. The filigreed, engraved satin finish gleamed. I checked out the patterns, which covered the barrel and other metal parts. It was then, for the first time, I saw a variation in one of the scrolls. What I had taken for a flourish on one of the curlicues on one of the side plates was actually a fanciful letter. It was an *L* or possibly an *S*. I stared. It quite possibly could have been a *Q*. How intriguing. I opened the box of bullets and began placing them in the six chambers.

Andi had warned me that revolvers don't have safeties. She had advised me to be extremely careful with a loaded weapon. But there were no children in this household. And a gun was no good to me if it wasn't close and convenient and loaded.

I fought the strong urge to put the gun under my pillow. Instead, I placed it on top of the nightstand and again turned out the bedside lamp.

I tossed a bit under the covers. The night was still warm enough to require only a sheet. I kept imagining outrageous calamities. Wesley's maid comes in early and tiptoes into my room and inadvertently jostles the nightstand and . . . Impossible. Or, an early A.M. earthquake, one strong enough to knock the gun off the nightstand, then it hits the floor and discharges. In which direction would the bullet go?

I reached for the lamp switch. I climbed out of bed. I opened the drawer of the nightstand and moved my tangle of little thong underwear to one side. I carefully rested the Lady Smith in the drawer. Worst-case scenario, I'd grab the gun and have a pair of panties hanging from my fist.

That done, lights out, sheet perfectly arranged, I found I was finally able to get a good night's sleep.

"I Got It Bad (and That Ain't Good)"

It's funny how a good night's sleep can change everything. I got up early and, first thing, unloaded my gun and stored it in its case, which, like a responsible adult, I then tucked into the nightstand drawer. The forceful wave of the previous evening's paranoia was now spent and gone. I pulled on a fresh pair of yoga shorts and a white sleeveless top, thinking the usual, normal things—like wondering when I might find time to do my laundry, rather than worrisome things—like why my life had become enmeshed in so many crimes.

I left Wesley a note. He had been out late the previous night, so instead of cooking myself breakfast in the smart little guest-house kitchen and maybe waking him, I decided to walk up to the old Farmers Market, only three miles away.

The early-morning air was fresh, cool. I pushed myself, moving fast, getting my heart pumping. I strode down Hudson until I came to the first major thoroughfare and then jogged west along Third, admiring the stately old mansions in the neighborhood: the gray mock French Normandy; the lilac Gothic Revival; the ubiquitous Mediterraneans in white or pink or tan, each with exquisite landscaping and perfectly trimmed trees. The majestic corner homes shared an edge of their upscale property with modern, car-clogged Third Street. City life. Say hello to the honking reality of L.A. real estate.

I stepped up my pace. In a little while, I was going to meet with Dilly Swinden and Zenya Knight to firm up our plans for the flower-arranging luncheon Dilly had bought at the Woodburn auction. I'd ask them about the menu and their choice of wine. We'd discuss decor and I'd offer a selection of invitations. They had settled on next Monday for their party, and since the event was to be held in just six days, we would construct the invitations ourselves; then a few of our regular staff would hand-deliver the them later this afternoon. I was to receive the final guest list at our meeting.

Maybe I might find out more about Zenya's brother as well. Maybe she and I would discover a quiet moment to chat. A sister could be a wonderful resource. Wait. What was I thinking? What was with me? I wished I would stop all this adolescent mooning. Somehow, Dex had wormed himself into my brain. I was, like, Dexified. Disgusting. Even as I drove home from the shooting range last night, it was Dexter Wyatt who filled my thoughts. Last night, just before I drifted off to sleep, it was Dexter Wyatt. Man!

It wasn't just his great laugh, or that he so completely got my sense of humor, or his unflappability among late-night escapades and odd restaurants. It wasn't simply the rush of his obvious interest in me either. He just seemed so free and unencumbered. Not only did Dex not have a *wife,* he hardly seemed to have had a serious girlfriend in his past. And yet, beneath his charm, I suspected he was serious about me. My stomach fluttered at the thought. And let's face facts, he did have a perfectly sexy smile with perfectly straight, very white teeth. And he had this disarming quality that was both sophisticated and antiestablishment funky. And his hair . . .

Snap! I told myself. Snap out of it!

I crossed a street, continuing west, nervous I was beginning to daydream about this new guy in my life like some thirteen-year-old staring at her Chris Martin poster. I swear,

I didn't recognize myself. But as soon as I told myself, No more fantasies, I felt awash with a sudden sadness, a loneliness. Arlo had been the wrong guy for me, I was sure of that. And then Honnett . . . Honnett had seemed right, but he was still entangled with . . . I simply refused to think about his wife one more time.

I shook my head, crossing another small side street, and then looked back again. I was not only obsessed with a cute guy, I still couldn't shake the feeling that someone was watching me. But I stopped and checked again, thoroughly, and there was no one paying me the least attention at 8 A.M. on that busy street as rush-hour traffic honked by.

In just a few blocks, the older quality of the neighborhood had begun to brighten, freshen, become more fabulous. Everywhere I looked, I saw new buildings where old ones used to be. On my left were amazing, glamorous new apartments. On my right was the Grove, a brand-new shopping mall along with its huge new parking structure. I sighed.

All these new buildings make me sad. I love L.A.'s history, short and tacky and tasteless though it often is. I love to learn about the movie studios and neighborhoods. I collect stories of old-time residents. L.A. was never very "real" to start with. And each twentieth-century building that is leveled to make way for some brand-new "twentieth-century-*style*" building just messes with my head. How can they destroy all that authentic fakeness for this newer and more glam fakeness?

Anyway, I walked more quickly, happier pondering architectural philosophy than where I stood with my boyfriends, and headed for an actual relic of the old Los Angeles I admire.

To get a feel for L.A.'s history, one doesn't need to go back very far in time. In 1870, a guy named A. F. Gilmore drew straws with a partner and ended up owning a 256-acre dairy farm. It was just his luck that by the turn of the century, while drilling for water for his herd of dairy cows, Gilmore hit oil. By 1905, the dairy was gone and the Gilmore Oil Company was on its way to becoming the largest independent oil company in the West. Isn't L.A. grand?

By 1934, farmers were doing what they could to fight the Depression. They pulled their trucks onto empty land at the corner of Third and Fairfax, and displayed their produce on the tailgates of their vehicles. It was suggested that Gilmore could make some money by charging the farmers fifty cents a day to sell their produce out of wooden stalls. The original farmers' market was born. I read all about it in a book Holly gave me for my birthday.

Today, this ancient relic of a tourist site was almost overshadowed by its glamorous neighbor, the Grove, an upscale, open-air mall modeled after some grand old fantasy downtown with architectural facades inspired by L.A.'s Art Deco era. But why, I ask, would anyone prefer to wander through yet another Gap when she could, instead, explore old-time Farmers Market establishments with names like the Gift Nook? And the Gift and Gadget Nook! And the Gadget Nook Gourmet? This is incredibly authentic tourist-trap chic, people. To get into early-twentieth-century L.A., one can't be allergic to kitsch.

I turned into the old wooden complex, feeling perkier than I had in a week, as I observed the stands of fresh produce, where avocados were the size of grapefruits, and grapefruits the size of small planets. I would pick up a couple of gargantuan cantaloupes to bring back to Wesley—a little gift for his breakfast. And maybe I'd find a few special things and cook a dinner for Dex.

L.A.'s old Farmers Market is made up of a series of fifteen large, white wooden buildings with green roofs and brown shutters. They encircle an open-air quad, which is filled with at least thirty smaller, freestanding stalls, creating a maze of narrow, sunny walkways. I had entered at Gate 12—no grand entrance covered in limestone in sight—happily walking in through this modest side door between two sections of Mr. Marcel Gourmet Grocery. A small sign by their register announced they do local deliveries. How cool. I'd have to tell Wes.

Food. It was the central idea of Farmers Market, its core, perhaps the greatest reason I love this indoor/outdoor bazaar so much. Everywhere you turn, your eye is offered dazzling displays. In addition to dozens of shops and grocery vendors, there were all sorts of delicious things on display. There were three produce stands, two meat markets, a homemade-candy shop, two nut shops, two poultry marts, two bakeries, a flower shop, and two ice-cream parlors. I loved to smell fresh peanut butter being churned at Magee's Kitchen. Or to taste fresh horseradish ground from giant, gnarled roots. Everything edible is here. You can watch apples being dunked in caramel at Little John's, and over at Du-Par's restaurant a plate-glass window lets you observe their bakers rolling dough for their pies.

And there were dozens of cafés and open-air food stands. Cajun gumbo, Japanese sushi, Belgian waffles, Italian pasta, and on and on. Sometimes, Wes and I select a different item at three different stands, often finishing up by sharing a magnificent crepe. But today I was looking for a place to think.

I turned left and walked halfway down the lane until I reached Kokomo Café, a truly great breakfast place tucked among the Farmers Market's fruits and nuts. Think modern California cuisine in a diner setting. Salads, soups, sandwiches, shakes, and the best thick-sliced bacon in town. In a serve-yourself kind of environment, I found the funky sit-down atmosphere and the quirky waiters at Kokomo's a bit of self-indulgence I could afford.

My waiter, a dreamboat actually, came for my drink order.

"A large iced tea, please."

"Coolio." He made eye contact.

"Say, I can't help it, but you look so damn much like James Dean."

He smiled. "I get that all the time." And then he told me a story I hadn't heard before, about how James Dean ate his last breakfast here at Farmers Market just before embarking on his final, fatal auto trip. "Not at Kokomo," he quickly added.

"Wow."

"But if you're in the mood for a current celebrity sighting," he said, leaning his head to the right. "Drew Barrymore. Be cool now." And he went off to fetch my tea.

I took a brief, California-cool peek. It's not polite to disturb the stars. But a peek? No problem.

I checked the menu briefly. I know it pretty well. I considered their famous red flannel turkey hash, and then their special huevos rancheros—eggs prepared with smoked-tomato salsa—but life had been freaking me out. I needed the carbs of comfort offered by Kokomo's fluffy pancakes.

"What can I get you?" asked the James Dean guy.

"Pancakes." I sighed, giving in.

"With a side of bacon?"

"Naturally."

The star spotting and breakfast ordering accomplished, I knew I needed to get my head together. I pulled a notepad out of my bag and uncapped a pen. I enjoyed the sounds of big-band music piped over their stereo system. Benny Goodman. By the time my pancakes arrived, steamy and hot, I had covered three pages in notes. Most were regarding the upcoming Woodburn-ladies luncheon, but the last page veered off, of its own accord, in the direction of the missing saxophone. I guess it was all the big-band music in the background, but I began to wonder if anyone at the Woodburn had ever found out what happened.

By nine-thirty that morning, I had made it back to Wesley's place. I showered and changed into my meet-the-clients clothes. In the ranking of my casual wardrobe, this higher level of formality required a snappier top and a pair of designer khakis. I chose a black rayon blouse worn open over a white tank tee, and high-heeled sandals to complete the ensemble. My hair was pulled into a high ponytail, as the day was getting hot.

I had been ignoring the pile of messages Wes had left for me, the topmost announcing I could pick up my Jeep from the police lot, and walked out to my waiting SUV. I liked the new-car smell and the extra cup holders in the Trailblazer. My old Grand Wagoneer could wait another day. At eleven o'clock, I climbed the steps to Zenya Knight's house in Beverly Hills, down the street from her neighbor and benefit cochair, Dilly.

In Zenya's living room, I found Dilly had already arrived and was sipping from a bottle of Arrowhead water. The three of us moved to the magnificently furnished dining room and put our heads together. In short order we nailed down all the details that needed to be nailed regarding the upcoming Monday luncheon, all of us very conscious of how rushed the event planning would need to be. It was fun to see Dilly and Zenya again, as we had spent a lot of time together over the past months working on the Woodburn affair. This time, we had no committee approval to get past or benefit to run. The flower party would be a relaxed and happy occasion.

"Are you traveling in August?" I asked them both, making polite conversation.

Dilly was a gorgeous dark-haired former model with long graceful legs and dancing eyes. Although probably around fifty, she dressed in an aggressive young fashion. Like a twenty-year-old with a $200,000 clothes budget. She gave Zenya a knowing look and asked, "Should I tell her?"

"Oh, Dilly!" Zenya giggled, flipping her long hair back, and opened a bottle of Chardonnay.

"What?" I asked.

"I'm telling everyone I'm going to Tahiti, but I'm not."

"Where are you going?"

"To the Desert Palms Clinic." She waited breathlessly, but I had no idea what she meant. "To get a lift."

"Really?"

"Just a partial. Not the eyes. I'm so excited. I shouldn't tell anyone, but I can't wait."

"You're getting a face-lift?" I thought Dilly Swinden was one of the most beautiful women I'd seen. She was tall and fine-boned and had barely any signs of age to notice, besides which I like people who look like they have had a life. "You look so young."

"No, I don't." She put the tips of her index fingers on her two cheekbones and tugged ever so slightly up. Then she let it go slack for a moment and again pulled upward. She repeated the demonstration a third time. "See?"

"Really, Dilly. It barely makes a difference."

"I can see it," she said.

Zenya, only thirty-five or so, looked down at her hands.

It was rarely talked about openly in these circles, but successful older men, the ones who could afford such fantastic homes as these and attracted such beautiful wives, did occasionally trade them in for younger models, a fact of which both Dilly Swinden and Zenya Knight were intimately aware. After all, they were both second wives themselves. Dilly had married her husband, Gerard, when he was in his midforties and she was just twenty-five. She must realize that at the time of his hurried divorce years back, Gerard's old discarded first wife had been younger than Dilly was today.

Gerard Swinden was the chairman of the board of a savings and loan and was also on the board of the Woodburn. He and Dilly had no children, but he had a family by his first marriage, and his oldest daughter had been an excellent cellist, I'd heard. At the time of his divorce, all those years ago, his first wife was literally shut out of her old life. She'd had to leave her friends at the Woodburn Guild since she couldn't stand to watch Dilly, the new Mrs. Swinden, take her seat on the board. Dilly found those early committee meetings chilly. It was hard to be accepted into this crowd of do-gooding women, each one eyeing the next young wife who made her entrance with the sick expectation that her own place could be taken . . . in time.

So here was Dilly today, agitated enough about her looks that she was obsessing in the mirror over almost nonexistent wrinkles.

These men. They come to believe they should always have the best. Always have something perfect. What pressure their wives were under. It wasn't for me. If I ever found the right guy, he wouldn't be the kind who was looking for the best he could buy, always on alert for the latest upgrade. While I thought my thoughts, Dilly and Zenya caught up on the latest gossip, discussing who in their crowd was having what "done." Plastic surgery. It was more of a lifestyle than I had realized. Then they turned back to me.

"Wasn't the Black and White Ball fabulous?" Dilly asked, unable to resist reliving the past glory. "We couldn't have done any better."

"It was gorgeous," Zenya agreed. It was an interesting dynamic between these two women. Dilly seemed to be the natural leader and Zenya always deferred to her opinion.

"Darius really came through for us," I said, referring to the most outrageous florist on the west side.

"Incredible. Those big arrangements with the masses of white roses! And I had never before seen *black* hollyhocks." Zenya smoothed her long blond hair off her shoulder with a swish.

"Alcea rosea nigra," I murmured, pleased.

"Oh, and then the dozens and dozens of Queen of the Night black tulips," Zenya continued. "Gorgeous. Didn't you think so, Dilly?"

Dilly nodded and picked up her wineglass. "There is nothing as sophisticated and simple as black and white. Like that etching, Zenya. Who's that by?" She referred to the artwork on the wall of the Knight dining room, a naked Madonna held aloft by putti. As we finished a lunch of cold artichoke salad, the two fund-raising cochairs nursed large glasses of Chardonnay and I sipped my Diet Coke.

"Oh, that one is called *Magdelena and Her Travel in Heaven* by Raffaello Schiaminossi. Sixteen-twelve. Bill has a thing for old etchings. His collection was borrowed by LACMA, remember, Dilly?"

Dilly shot her friend a quick glance, clearly remembering something she didn't want to mention while I was around. I wondered what that was.

The picture on the wall was large and impressive. Sixteen-twelve. Wow. The little boy angels looked like they were tasked by a heavy load, however. Seems this Schiaminossi fellow liked his female models in the Raphaelesque tradition—hefty.

"The L.A. County Museum of Art borrowed this piece?" I was impressed.

"This and a dozen others," Zenya said. "We had a bit of bad luck with three of the best works, though. Dilly knows."

Dilly looked like this was the very thing she had been avoiding mentioning. "Zenya was so distraught," she said. "I didn't want to bring up something that would upset her."

"No, I'm fine," Zenya said quietly. "I know we can never truly possess anything. I'm making my peace with the theft."

Theft? I looked up from my artichoke, alarmed.

"What happened? If you don't feel terrible talking about it."

"I'm okay now," Zenya said, refilling her tall wineglass with the last of the Chardonnay and opening another bottle. "We had just lent the best pieces Bill had in his collection. Most of them were Renaissance-period etchings. This one here is by a relatively unknown artist, although he is rare and therefore more valuable each year. Bill collects with a passion. The thieves knew exactly what they were doing. Only his prize pieces were taken."

"They had a very nice 1502 etching of Adam and Eve by the German genius Albrecht Dürer," Dilly said sadly. "There is one like it in the Rijksmuseum in Amsterdam."

"Oh no." I was troubled. Was theft just a part of the rich person's life? "How horrible. Were they stolen from the County Art Museum while they were on loan?"

"No," Zenya said. "It was several months after they were returned. They were hanging in the living room again, but we were out of town. Bill and I had taken Kirby to our condo on Maui for a few weeks. We got a call one night. There had been a break-in here at the house. Three of our best pieces were gone. That was three years ago, and to this day they have never been recovered."

"Did your alarm go off?" Dilly asked her.

Zenya shook her head.

"Oh, that's right," Dilly said, remembering. "Your brother was staying here at the time, wasn't he? House-sitting?"

I looked up, alarmed. *Dexter?* Wait, now. Had Dilly just said Dexter had been here, watching his sister's house, while millions of dollars' worth of artwork up and walked out the door?

"Money Jungle"

It was the season for last-minute parties. In addition to rushing to bring off the Woodburn flower luncheon on Monday, we had been asked if we could possibly do a teen's birthday brunch on the Saturday two days earlier. Connie Hutson, the tireless organizer who had helmed the Woodburn auction committee, was determined to throw a battle-of-the-bands-style affair for her son Ryan's thirteenth. Our business was enjoying a summer boom, and coming as it did after a particularly slow winter, we hated to say no to anything. Feast or famine—our business as well as our finances.

I pulled into the driveway of the Hutson house after briefly stopping by the office to give the invitation specs to Wesley and Holly. They were now busy producing the invites, glue-gunning dried, pressed flowers to vellum, while I took this last-minute client call. The Hutsons lived in Pasadena, a twenty-minute drive out of Hollywood.

"Come on in, Madeline," Connie called from the sunroom of her genuine Arts-and-Crafts-period home. She was seated on a dark settee, a Mission oak beauty that I would swear was an authentic Stickley. Connie's bright summer dress, a turquoise silk jungle print, perfectly set off her thick auburn curls, which she wore, as always, neat and short. Her makeup appeared pronounced in the natural light of the bright sunroom. Her full lips were painted dark coral, her cheeks set ablaze with blusher. And a funny thing: I began surreptitiously checking for any signs of plastic surgery. See how suggestible I am? I remembered Dilly and Zenya mentioning Connie's name and I couldn't help but check her out, up and down. Her boobs may or may not have been real, but they were awesome.

Before we could begin our discussion of the birthday party she wished to host, a quiet young Hispanic woman brought in a large pitcher of lemonade and left.

"Thank you, Graciela," Connie said before she called out for her son to join us.

Ryan appeared at the sunroom door, looking awkward and skinny and just about thirteen. Surf camp had bleached his long stringy hair blond. Adolescence had left his skin in a muddle. "My birthday is not until August twentieth," Ryan said in a sort of a whine.

"But we're going to France in August," Connie said to him.

"That's what you keep saying," Ryan replied. "I don't want to go to stinking France."

"You'll love it," she answered patiently.

"So my mom wants me to have my party now." Ryan Hutson's hands found the pockets in his long, baggy shorts and settled there.

"You're inviting all your musician friends?" I asked him, opening my notebook.

"Sure. The kids who are still in town. I told my mom we should wait until school starts and more of my friends are here," he began again, addressing his mother.

"I need to get this *over with,*" she said, in a measured way.

Ryan's eyes darted down and I bit my lip. I'm sure Connie didn't hear how it sounded. And I had learned never to jump to judgment with parents of teenagers. Never.

"We want you to have something nice," Connie coaxed.

"And this is our last open weekend in three months, sweetheart."

"Right," Ryan said under his breath.

His mother gave him a penetrating look and he sulked back to her. Oh, lovely. Another happy family.

"I'd love to help plan Ryan's party," I said. "But you do realize we are limited in what we can provide with such little time to prep. What sort of food did you want?"

"Nothing dorky, Mom."

"How about In-N-Out?" I suggested to him. He smiled at me, suddenly a kid again, and happy. "We can get a truck to come to your house."

"Awesome."

"That sounds fine," Connie said, easily agreeing to the fast-food burgers the kids all loved. The popular restaurant chain had a few mobile lunch trucks in which their cooks grilled up fresh fries and cheeseburgers to order.

"I just have to see what strings I need to pull to get a truck here this Saturday. They book up at least six months in advance. We may be asked to pay a fairly steep premium, if it's available at all."

"Mom?" Ryan was now on board. "Please."

"Oh, fine," she said, happy to see her son get into the party spirit. "Don't worry about the money."

"I can't promise," I said to Ryan, "but I usually get what I'm after."

"Cool."

"Entertainment?" I asked.

"Wynton Marsalis is coming," Connie informed me. I was stunned to hear her casually drop the name of one of the world's most famous jazz greats. "Dave invited him and he had a day free. That's why Saturday is the date we must have, you see."

"Wynton Marsalis is going to play for Ryan's party?"

"And his jazz ensemble. Oh, yes. Dave took care of it."

"So you'll need a sound system and chairs set up for . . . how many?"

"Just a hundred," Connie said firmly. "We're calling friends and doing it all very impromptu and fun. Don't worry about invitations."

"Can I get a contact number for Mr. Marsalis's people?" I asked, scribbling notes quickly. "We'll want to arrange to have everything he needs."

"Oh, wonderful," Connie said.

"And for the adults," I asked, "would you like us to do a small buffet? A few salads, some fresh fruit, desserts, coffee?"

"Yes, whatever you think would be appropriate is fine with me," Connie said, looking pleased.

"Or we could bring in sushi?" I said, thinking aloud.

"That's perfect," she said. "Absolutely perfect. My husband, Dave, loves sushi."

I wrote more notes. In-N-Out burgers and sushi. Ah, yes. Another eclectic kids party. However, this was all doable. We'd get my favorite sushi restaurant to deliver on Saturday. I'd pull in a big favor with the burger people and get the truck to cook up fresh Double-Doubles right in the driveway out front. The biggest challenge would be getting the staging and audience section set up. I needed to get a plan of their backyard. I asked and Connie Hutson agreed to have it faxed to my office.

"What about the cake?" I asked Ryan.

His mother answered. "We'd like a large cake, Madeline. One that will serve all the teens, so make it for a hundred and fifty, just to be on the safe side."

"Chocolate," Ryan said. "With whipped cream."

"Sounds great," I said, writing.

"And how about in the shape of a saxophone, Ry?"

He wrinkled his nose. "A tenor?"

"Sure," his mom said. "Ryan has been begging to move up to a tenor sax. He currently plays alto. We're trying to get the Woodburn to let him change instruments, but his instructor there, Mr. Braniff, has been reluctant."

That was interesting. I thought again about all the fuss that had been made over the great Selmer Mark VI saxophone that had disappeared from the Woodburn after the live auction on Saturday night. I couldn't help but wonder if the wealthy dad who had arranged for Wynton Marsalis to play at his boy's party hadn't also thought a spectacular instrument like the Selmer might make the perfect birthday gift.

We talked over a few more essential details, and although I knew Mad Bean Events was cutting things close on too many events, I said we'd do it.

Ryan quickly slipped out of the room, relieved to escape the grown-ups, to get back to his waiting Xbox.

Connie walked me to the door.

"Thanks, Madeline. This is going to be fun."

"I'll fax the budget to you later," I said. "We need approval and a deposit before we can start renting chairs and ordering food. I'll begin lining up vendors and contact the Marsalis people, but we have to move quickly."

"No problem. I'll have Dave run a check over to you tonight, if that's okay."

"Fine." I looked at Connie, who was taller than me, even standing in her flats. "By the way, I've been curious about the Woodburn auction. Did it do well?"

"Well! We did *fabulously* well," she said, her face all smiles. "We outearned every damn benefit ever thrown for the school in forty-two years of fund-raising. We surpassed our goal of four hundred and fifty thousand dollars."

"Wow." That was an incredible amount of money.

She nodded happily.

"Even after losing the money for the sax?"

"We didn't lose any money," Connie said.

"Bill Knight still paid you the money?" Stranger and stranger!

"Uh, *no*." We both chuckled at the idea. "It was insured, sweetie. We wouldn't have risked bringing such a priceless instrument to the event without insurance."

"That's so lucky."

She winked at me. "It's smart. One of our members took care of it for us." And in an instant, Connie's face changed from sunny to cloudy. "Oh, dear. It was Al Grasso who took care of it. You know about what happened to him?"

I stared at her. Grasso was connected to the stolen saxophone. He'd arranged for the insurance. How did this add up?

"Connie, I have to ask you a question. Was your husband terribly disappointed to have lost out on the bidding for the sax?"

"Of course not," she said, her face completely composed. "He didn't really want it at all."

I looked at her. She had to be the best liar I'd ever met. Or perhaps what she was saying was true. "Really? I thought he was bidding it up against Bill Knight."

"Yes, well . . ." She winked at me.

"What?"

"We were doing it for a good cause, you understand. That made it all right."

"What made what all right?"

"Before the auction, Bill Knight asked Dave to keep the bidding going on the sax."

"No way!" I looked at her, but she was grinning. Not a sign of guilt on her.

"We wanted to raise the pot, you see? Bill said he was going to buy it, but he wanted to get the price high, make a big donation, and get a big write-off. He thought it would make for good drama, and we wanted to inspire other bidders on other objects to be really generous. We thought it was a sweet idea. So Dave played the game."

"Played the game?"

"Well, okay. It got way out of hand. Bill was hamming it up, scuffling with Dave at the table during the bidding. That was outrageous, but that's Bill Knight. He's larger than life, sometimes."

"Excuse me, Connie, but are you absolutely sure about all this? I was in Bill and Zenya's car the night of the Black and White Ball. Bill was screaming about Dave. My goodness, he actually rammed into your car. You and your husband looked appropriately horrified. What was that all about?"

"Bill can be a real asshole when he's drunk," she said flatly. "What we have to put up with from our men, sometimes. If I knew Zenya better, I'd tell her to watch that guy."

"So you forgave him for plowing into your car?"

"We were shocked when he hit our car. But Bill can be a cowboy. Dave says Bill is going through a midlife crisis to end all. I mean, you've seen it yourself. Bill's been drinking too much. He's been loud. He chased us after the party. He's even been seen with . . . Well, that's not important. We realize Bill can get a little unstable at times. He sent us an apology the next morning, along with a case of Dom Pérignon and a large check to fix our car. It's in the shop right now."

I shook my head. "Then why was Bill saying Dave stole the Mark VI?"

"What?" Connie put her hand on my arm, looked in my eyes. Her face drained of color, leaving only dark coral lips and red-stained cheeks. "He said Dave *stole* the sax? He's insane."

I looked at her, not knowing what to think.

"Maddie, who do you think donated that saxophone in the first place?"

Oh ho.

"Dave found it in a bankruptcy auction in Milwaukee. He bought it for under five thousand dollars. We didn't think such a fine instrument should go to a child, or we would have kept it for our Ryan. We were hoping to make this auction the best one ever and we did. The rest of this is all ridiculous."

"I'm sorry. I'm a fool. I should have known. It was such a shock to be in Bill Knight's Hummer and watch him attack you like that. He was just raging."

"Well, Zenya must be used to it," she said, quieting down. "Between you and me, no one would blame her if she took the kids and left him."

"I see."

"But I refuse to get dragged down by the Knights or anyone else, Maddie, and you shouldn't either. The important thing to remember is we raised a good deal of money for the Woodburn last week, and that means many more children will have a chance to study music and develop their art."

"You're right."

"I'm sorry Bill Knight had a tantrum, I'm sorry the saxophone has been misplaced or whatever happened to it, but the insurance covered that and the Woodburn will get its money."

I looked at her, suddenly curious. "Did you insure the Selmer for five thousand dollars?"

"No. As a matter of fact, the policy was written to insure each item for its full auction value, and since we had already held the bidding, we had the current auction value on the Selmer Mark IV established."

"You mean the Woodburn gets a *hundred* thousand for a five-thousand-dollar instrument?"

She nodded.

"Boy, that was lucky," I said.

"Smart," Connie corrected, her natural color coming back once more.

"Jeeps Blues"

A few days passed as Holly, Wes, and I got down to work, planning the two parties we had squeezed into our already well-booked lineup. Frankly, it was hard to concentrate on burger trucks and flowerpots. I had begun to believe that someone was watching me. I was convinced that the chain of shootings hadn't ended.

Each night I lay in Wesley's spare bedroom, thinking of the loaded revolver I had put in the nightstand drawer, getting up several times to check on it, eventually leaving the drawer open all night, fearful that someone was out there in the dark, waiting to catch me off guard. Each morning, I closed the drawer again, wondering if any of this effort was necessary or if I was going nuts, wondering if I would ever feel completely safe again.

By Friday, the police were no closer to naming a suspect, as far as we knew, in any of the crimes that had plagued us. There were no breaks on the murder of Sara Jackson. No breaks on the murder of Albert Grasso. After three days of empty dramatic announcements that there were "still no arrests in the linked murders in Whitley Heights," even our local news channels had let the story cool down. And no one but me seemed to give much thought, any longer, to the theft of the vintage tenor saxophone, even though I had dutifully called Detective Baronowski and reported what I had learned from Connie Hutson about the insurance. The policy had been obtained properly, high premiums had been paid, and the Woodburn didn't seem to be out a dime on that one, so perhaps no one was still upset over it. No one except Bill Knight, I thought.

So life went on in that way it always does. After the police allowed us back into my house, it was only a matter of hours before Wes had his crew over there, tearing out the upstairs rooms. I knew I could never sleep in my bedroom again. I didn't even want to climb the stairs. Demolition, Wes had often maintained, was good for the soul. It fulfilled the classic cycle, he said. Death and rebirth. Destruction and rebuilding. He could get pretty Zen over the demo stage of his projects.

Wes had drawn up plans several years ago when I first purchased the property. At the time, we went ahead with construction on the commercial kitchen and office area downstairs but put a hold on spending any more money. Now, however, I was seriously thinking about selling my home. Despite all of Wesley's good intentions, it had been violated in a way no remodel could fix.

I couldn't talk about it. I couldn't even think about it. Wes and Holly didn't know what was going on with me, but the truth was I felt guilty for grieving. My pain was nothing compared with the real suffering around me, of the people who had died and the people who had lost them. Of course I knew that. But this had been my first house. I had thought I'd stay here forever. I had loved this house.

So the demolition stage went on with Wes leading the assault. And the odd thing was, it got a little better after that. Like Wes, I am a fixer and a salvager. It felt like the right thing to do, to repair the house. All this looking over my shoulder and worry was definitely not like me. A redesigned second story, rebuilt from the studs out, might help me to recover my equilibrium. It was possible. And if not, the remodel would make it easier to sell the house quickly and move on.

And then, sometimes, I couldn't even believe the murder of Sara Jackson was real. As I worked with my friends in the large, white-tiled kitchen, the violence that had occurred upstairs six nights before seemed utterly impossible. We had hardly known Sara. How had she come to die in my room?

My mind would wander like that. Off to the unknown and the deadly. And then I snapped back to the present. Holly was laughing about how her hair had turned out. Her straight white-blond hair was gelled back off her forehead with magenta-colored gel. She hadn't intended to get the streaked look, she was saying, but she was philosophical. Holly was always willing to sacrifice herself in the exploration of a new fashion edge.

Wes looked up at me. "You thinking about what happened here?"

"I can't help it," I said. "I'm becoming obsessed. I feel responsible for Sara being here Sunday morning. And yet . . ."

They had that patient look. It wasn't the first time I had made them listen to this.

"And yet, what am I doing now to help? There must be something I can do." I trusted my instincts. I could see connections. I had a great track record for spotting liars and understanding motives. None of these alleged gifts had helped me this time.

"Did the police ever find her boyfriend?" Holly asked as we unpacked the vases we had selected for the Woodburn luncheon. They were fluted cement urns, heavy, classically designed, with a ten-inch diameter.

"I am not getting regular updates," I answered. "The detectives on the case don't return my calls. And Honnett may know something, but he and I are in a transitional period."

Wes looked up at me across the center island where we were working. "Transitioning in or out?"

"I can't tell," I said, opening several large boxes with my box cutter. "It's a mess. His wife is going through a rough time. He's had to help her more than he was expecting, I have been told."

Holly looked up at me. She was on her knees, pulling planters out of the boxes and lining them up on the floor. "A rough time?"

"Mastectomy. Chemo."

"Oh," Wes said.

"I mean, if she really needs him, how can he abandon her?"

No one, it seemed, could argue with cancer. My friends looked worried but said nothing and I began to open boxes of oasis foam and other floral supplies.

"So you never found Sara's boyfriend," Holly prompted again. "Did she just make that up? I can't believe she was lying to me on Saturday night about having to get home to him. She had this whole story down, you know? How he was at home waiting for her. How he was freaking over his Ph. bloody D. What was up with that?"

"I'm not sure," I said. But I had learned that if one is not expecting to be lied to, one often misses a whopper.

"Oh, Mad. I picked up your Wagoneer," Wes said, suddenly remembering. "You know they were bugging us to come and get it." He sounded apologetic.

"Thanks, Wes. I couldn't face it. The bedroom. The Jeep. All my things have been ruined."

Holly quickly sprang up and gave me a hug, a jumble of long arms surrounding me in friendship. She was wearing very short shorts and flip-flops.

"I want to get rid of the Jeep," I told Wes. I waited for him to try to talk me out of it. Wes is sensible. He didn't give in to fear. He was still talking to me every day about giving Honnett back the damned gun.

"That's probably not a bad idea," he said slowly.

I met his eyes. "Why? Did they find something?"

"They had to cut out some of the rear-seat upholstery fabric," he said.

"What?" I stood there, with Holly's arm still draped lightly on my shoulder.

"They found some stains and they had to check them out," he said.

"Ew." Holly got grossed out easily.

"What kind of stains? Blood?" My head raced to the most horrible things these days.

"They wouldn't tell me," Wes answered. "I called that guy at the forensics lab who likes you. Sanchez. Remember? I got nada."

I picked up the phone and dialed the number for Detective Baronowski. To my surprise, he answered his own phone on the first ring.

"Detective, this is Madeline Bean."

"Hello."

"I have just been hearing from my partner that you found stains in my truck."

He didn't answer at once. After a long pause he said, "And?"

"What kind of stains? What's going on?"

"I was planning to call you, Ms. Bean. I've got paperwork stacked up like you can't believe. My partner came down with the flu, by the way. Great timing."

"About my truck . . ."

"I'm getting to that. Give me a second to find my notes."

I waited.

"Okay," he said, and I waited a few more seconds. "Several samples were taken from the rear seat. You understand, when we find anything in your truck, we're going to have to be pretty clear on what was there before you loaned the Jeep to the victim and what may have been brought to the vehicle by Sara or possibly someone who was accompanying Sara. That's where we need your help. We've got to determine if any of the forensics evidence that has been removed from your vehicle belongs to you and your friends. You understand?"

"Sure," I said.

"Right. And this may strike you as a delicate question, Ms. Bean, but I'm going to ask if you can think of anyone who might have left a semen stain in the backseat of your Jeep."

He had to be joking.

When I didn't answer, he spoke up. "I don't make this stuff up. We found fresh—"

"Listen, Lieutenant, it's not that I'm squeamish. I'm not the shockable type. But this is a conversation I never expected to have, in my entire life, with the police or anyone else."

"I don't doubt that."

"Let me just say, for the record, that I have done nothing more horrible than lend my truck to an employee who told me she needed to get home fast."

"We know that."

"As my reward, my home was broken into, a young woman was shot to death in my bed, my Jeep was confiscated, a neighbor was killed, and now you're asking me which of my friends might have left his semen on the upholstery. Is that right?"

"Yes."

Could it, I wondered, get any more freaking odd than this? I had to smile. What gives with this crazy world?

Baronowski couldn't keep the chuckle in now. "If you don't mind," he said. "You know, for the record."

"I know of no one who would fit that description."

"No boyfriend, perhaps. Think back."

"I hate you," I said, beginning to laugh. "No. No one. Not my style, Detective."

"I realize this may seem strange, but we need to rule out any possiblc, uh, legitimate stains."

The absurdity. The complete absurdity of my life began to crash in on me. I think he was waiting for me to confirm I had no knowledge of a backseat stain.

"I'm twenty-nine years old, Lieutenant. My friends are old enough to ride in my car without spilling anything."

"Okay, good," he said. I had passed some test, apparently, because his voice sounded more inclusive than it ever had. I took the opportunity to ask a question of my own.

"Look, did you ever track down Sara Jackson's boyfriend?"

"Why?"

"If you stop laughing at me, and start sharing some information, I might do the same. I've learned a few more things about Sara myself."

"Such as?"

"You first. Did you find her boyfriend, the grad student?"

"We did."

"What? Who is he? Does he live in her apartment downtown?" I was shocked. I had decided Sara was a nutcase, and dismissed her as a terrific liar. But if she really had a boyfriend, perhaps I had misjudged her again.

"His name is Brett Hurley. Lives in Silverlake. They shared an older cottage there. I can't tell you any more."

"Is he a suspect?"

I received silence for my answer. "So do you have anything to tell me, Ms. Bean?"

"I tried to find Sara's boyfriend myself, but struck out. Last Monday. I wanted to offer him my help, if he needed it. I felt terrible and was trying to do the right thing."

"And?"

"I went to the address Sara had given us on her employee application. It was an apartment downtown."

"We checked it out. Didn't look like she stayed there a lot. Maybe she rented it, but she seemed to live out in Silverlake with Hurley the last six months at least."

"I see. Well, I got to talking to one of her neighbors."

"We canvassed her floor, Ms. Bean. No one knew her very well. Lot of folks move in and out of those kinds of buildings. Lot of foreign students, that kind of thing."

"I met a guy who lives on another floor. He had the impression Sara was a call girl."

"A hooker? How'd he get that idea?"

Wesley and Holly were watching me, listening to my side of the conversation. They were stunned.

"This guy tried to come on to Sara, but she shined him on."

"So that makes her a hooker?" Baronowski seemed skeptical.

"He saw Sara going into the elevator with a lot of different guys."

Detective Baronowski asked for the name of the man I talked with and I gave it to him, along with his apartment location.

"Thanks," he said. "I'll check into it."

"And I'd like to talk to Brett Hurley. Come on, Detective. Can't you give me his phone number?"

I received silence.

"Then would you call him and give him mine?" I gave Baronowski my cell number as well.

"I'll see what I can do," he said.

"Good. You know, 'cause I'm thinking about those traces of semen that were found in my truck."

"They don't belong to the boyfriend. We checked. But you're thinking Sara had a 'date' in the backseat? Anything is possible."

I looked from Holly to Wesley as I hung up the phone.

"From what we just overheard," Wes said sagely, "you are definitely selling that Jeep."

"Frisky"

It was the rare Friday night when I didn't have to work an event. Weekends get booked up early, but not this Friday. Wes and I had been careful to keep our schedule clear in the aftermath of the big Black & White Ball. We had figured we might need downtime. It was with true relief I found I only had to do minimal prep for Saturday's birthday party for Ryan Swinden and then I could actually go out on a Friday night date.

Dexter Wyatt had tried to see me every day that week. He had left charming messages on my answering machine. He had called my cell phone a few times, too. He stopped by the office on Thursday afternoon, unannounced, and when it appeared I wouldn't be back anytime soon, he took Holly out to a late lunch and pumped her for insider information about me. She claims it only took a ride in his BMW Z4 with the top down, two mimosas, and a grilled-shrimp Caesar to get her to divulge all my darkest secrets. Those included the fact that I was free on Friday night.

I liked Dex. I liked him all too well. But he interfered with my thought processes. I needed to keep my brain focused. I had to sort out our problems. Things were still terribly wrong. I could feel it but I still couldn't figure it out in my head. Sara had been in trouble. Grasso had been in trouble. And now maybe I was in trouble.

I could hardly get to sleep at night, thinking about all that had happened in the last week. I had a hard enough time giving myself a break on the best of weeks. On the worst, such as this one, it was unthinkable. In the meantime, I busied myself with my work while my brain took on tangents of its own, spinning away, trying to solve all the world's problems and my own nasty ones in particular.

After cleaning up the kitchen, I was ready to put the last flourishes on Ryan's birthday cake. Wes had baked the cake that morning and frosted it that afternoon. It turned out great. The enormous, three-layer masterpiece in the shape of a tenor saxophone now rested on the kitchen counter. It had been a challenge for Wesley, the swoop of the bell, the detail of every valve, the fine edge of the narrow, graceful neck and mouthpiece, but he has exquisite pattern-cutting skills. Wes is an artist. Holly looked at it earlier and exclaimed, as she does after every cake he produces, "This is your finest work, man."

Both Holly and Wes had been at the house all day, but left to run additional errands. Soon after they departed, the upstairs construction crew stopped by to tell me they were knocking off for the weekend. I checked the clock: 5:25. I said thanks and good-bye. It wasn't until after they took off that I realized I was now all alone. Alone in my house for the very first time since the break-in. I went about my tasks, self-conscious and alert. Overall, I was surprised at how fine I was. I would work another fifteen minutes and then drive back to Wesley's place and get ready for my date.

I looked down at the cake, set out on the counter, and concentrated. It had been smoothly frosted in cream frosting tinted the color of pale brass. Using my most steady hand, I laid down the final frosting details, applying gentle even pressure on the pastry bag. Before me, a thin and perfect trail of black piping outlined each perfectly shaped brass saxophone key. I finished up in a tour de force of outlining technique, edging the entire instrument in one perfect unbroken line of icing. It was complete.

Wes had constructed the cake on a huge cardboard platter covered in black foil. The platter rested inside a flat, unfolded bakery box. I quickly folded the thin pink cardboard to construct the box's sides and top and closed the lid, carefully moving the box to the walk-in refrigerator to keep it cool until the next day.

I then roamed through my house, turning off lights, feeling remarkably good. Perhaps the prospect of seeing Dex again was keeping my mind off other troubles. Perhaps I'm just sickeningly upbeat. Either way, I was pretty happy.

I turned to lock my front door and descended the flight of stairs to the street. I was still driving the rental SUV, and as I turned the ignition, I thought about what sort of car I should buy to replace my old Jeep Grand Wagoneer. Car shopping would be fun. Maybe Dexter would have some suggestions on what I should test-drive.

The traffic was what one expects here, considering it was a Friday during rush hour, which only added to the usual summer crowds of Hollywood tourists. I made my way south and west, looking for side streets that would help me avoid the worst intersections. I turned right on red on Franklin and noticed a black sedan on my tail. I had remembered seeing the same sort of car when I had pulled out of Whitley onto Cahuenga, but I was determined not to give in to my low-simmering, weeklong hysteria. I checked the mirror again. The sedan continued to follow my path as I zigzagged right and left around Highland, staying on Franklin. Nothing unusual about that, but I kept my eyes on my rearview mirror.

Sometimes I get nervous like that. I'll become aware of a certain car. I'll become alarmed if it seems to be taking all the same turns as I do. You live in the city, you should notice these things. I am not going to drive straight to my house, when I'm driving alone, if I'm suspicious. Most of the time, before I can really get spooked, the car that's making me nervous will turn off and be gone. I'm not the best at identifying cars in my rearview mirror, but I was pretty sure the dark sedan was a Honda Accord. I tried to check the license plate but none was displayed in front.

Normally, I'd take Franklin west to La Brea, where almost everyone makes a sort of swing left onto the major southbound street. But I decided to test my nerves. I got in the left-turn lane, just like I always do, and put on my signal. The dark Accord was two cars behind me, also waiting for the left-turn arrow. This is a popular place to turn, as going straight onto Franklin Place leads nowhere. Besides, it gets dark and quiet on Franklin just past this intersection. As the green arrow lit up, permitting left turns, I pulled forward and then veered sharply to the right, changing lanes at the last second to go straight through the intersection. The woman who was driving the Volkswagen Jetta to my right looked scared out of her wits as she careened out of my way.

In my rearview, I saw the car that had been behind me complete his left turn. However, just as the light was changing to red, the dark Accord behind him jutted over to the right, pulling the same boneheaded traffic stunt as I had just done, coming right up behind me on dark and quiet Franklin Place.

Bad driving was a given in L.A. But my senses were now on hyperalert. I was looking into my mirror more than I was looking where I was going. I tried to see into the windshield of the car behind me, but I was driving directly into the setting sun and the combination of the glare the sun produced and the dark tint on the Accord's windshield kept me from seeing much. It looked like there wasn't a passenger, just the driver. But I couldn't see more.

I turned left on the first small street I could, Fuller, and gunned my engine. The Trailblazer took off, so I had to get on the brakes fast or risk smashing into the Camry ahead of me. I glanced at my rearview mirror. There was no car at all behind me. The dark Accord hadn't turned. It wasn't following me.

Oh, man. It can give me a knot in my stomach every time. But the relief to find it had only been my stupid imagination was immense.

I zigged and zagged across Hollywood, keeping an occasional eye on my mirror. I had one brief scare, one missed heartbeat, when I thought I saw the same Accord. Dark color. Tinted windshield. No front plates. But I was mistaken. It's a popular model and not everyone has his or her front plates on. This black Accord suddenly came into view as it turned the corner from Larchmont, going east onto Beverly, but it was heading in the opposite direction I was. When it passed me, I admit I was startled. But I got a pretty good look at the driver. It was just a woman in her midforties. Thick red hair, cut in layers. Pretty. She didn't even look my way. I relaxed a bit more after that.

By the time I pulled into the driveway of Wesley's house on Hudson, I was sure no one was paying attention to me. I loved feeling anonymous in the big city. And there was Wesley's new Jaguar, parked in the garage, so I was safe. More or less.

"You going out?" Wes asked, an hour later, sitting on the sofa in the small living room. He looked up and watched me as I stepped into my high heels, freshly showered, changed and made up like I cared how I looked.

I hadn't been sure Wesley would approve of my date with Dexter. Normally, the idea of Wes passing judgment was not an issue between us. But it felt different now that I was living in his house.

"I told Dex I would come over to his place and cook him dinner."

Wes looked impressed. In our line of work, that was shorthand for seduction.

"Are you sure about this?"

"Wes."

"Hey, I'm just asking," he said conversationally. His eyes took in my tight little white linen skirt and low-cut black shirt. "This is the guy you said lacks a little life direction, right? The guy who is too cool for prep school. The one who got mixed up in some art theft you were telling me about?"

I finished putting gold hoops onto my ears and gave Wesley a pained look. "I have enough 'life direction' for ten people. I might like to play with cool prep school boys. And I am going there tonight to find out more about the art theft. This is purely investigational."

"Uh-huh." Wes looked at me thoughtfully. "What are you cooking?"

Now, that was a leading question and Wes knew it. I got a little defensive. "I've made a lot of the dishes in advance," I said, waving nonchalantly to the packed bags I had waiting on the kitchen counter.

"Menu," Wes requested.

"Chilled avocado soup with lime cream, pork carnitas tacos, black-bean-and-corn salad, cilantro-lime rice, Mexican chocolate cake."

"So you're going to bed with him?" Wes knew I meant business when I took the time to bake a flourless chocolate cake.

"I'm not making any comment on that," I said. "If he turns out not to be a con artist or a thief or a murderer, why not?"

"Will you at least do me one favor?" Wes asked, looking more concerned than I would have thought.

"What? Call you at midnight? Let you know I'm safe?"

"No, I was going to say when you make the lime cream, would you *please* thin the sour cream down with some heavy cream first?"

Cooks! It's amazing the two of us could live under the same roof for this long. I threw my little beaded bag over my shoulder and picked up my satchels of groceries and precooked items.

Wes watched me, but couldn't leave well enough alone. "And did you make up fresh salsa?"

"Wes. Of course. Now make up your mind. Do you want to save me from the clutches of a tomcat or do you want to advise me on how much jalapeño I should have used?"

"Both," he said, smiling. "And I'll leave the light on for you tonight."

"Thanks, Dad." That would get him. I smiled as I closed the door behind me.

It took me about twenty minutes to drive to Dexter's house, which was located up on Stone Canyon Road in the hills of Bel Air north of Sunset. He had given me clear directions because it's easy to get lost up on those winding streets. I parked in his driveway, up off the street, and checked out his home.

Some folks really hate the kind of boxy-room, low-ceiling, ranch-style homes that were built by the thousands around Los Angeles in the fifties. Others now call it "Mid-century" design and boast about it in their real estate listings. I wasn't sure where I stood on the debate, but I found I really liked Dexter's relaxed, uncluttered environment.

He met me at the door and smiled his laid-back smile. "Hey, you made it," he said. "Here, let me take those bags. Want a tour?"

He had bought the place a little less than three years ago, he said. His house had four bedrooms, two fireplaces, and the requisite white cabinet/black granite kitchen. As he pointed out this and that, I noticed that he was neat or had a very well-trained housekeeper. His furniture was authentic fifties stuff, with a lot of white upholstered pieces and those cool black leather chairs.

In one hallway, I was struck by a series of black-and-white photos along the wall. Dirty faces of very poor children. Groups of boys playing soccer in a Mexican village square. A heartbreakingly beautiful close-up of a mother holding a small girl.

"Did you take these?" I asked.

He looked embarrassed. "I forgot I told you I liked to take pictures."

"They are amazing, Dex."

"You can't take a bad shot of those kids."

He slid open a large glass door, and I walked outside onto the crosshatched used brick of his rear deck. A top realtor would call the scene from his pool patio "all-around endless views" and I was impressed.

"I'm actually out here most of the time," he said.

"I can understand why."

The sun was just setting and the sky was tangerine and orange and deeper rust. "Pretty," I said, admiring the peaceful dusk.

"I agree," he said.

I looked over at him, a little surprised. "Most people feel compelled to tell me it's really smog."

"Those who choose to be so freaking literal often miss the beauty of life entirely," Dex said.

"That's true."

"We should pity them." He looked at me, expressing equanimity.

"I do." The in-the-treetops perch of his patio made me feel like I was on top of the world. I reluctantly turned back to the house. "I'd better get our dinner started."

"Can I help?" he asked.

"Can you cook?"

"Nope."

"Then, sure, if you don't mind a few helpful hints."

Dex had dropped the bags off earlier on the granite counter of his open kitchen. He followed me back into the kitchen.

"I can open a bottle of wine," he said, acting a little more like a host than I had expected.

"How about I mix something fresh for us to drink?" I offered. "You have a blender?"

"I knew there was a reason I bought one of those." He smiled and led me to a shelf of appliances stored neatly in his pantry. I found a brand-new blender and plugged it into a socket next to the sink.

"This is cool," he said, walking back to the pantry and returning with a new black chef's apron. He held it up and I smiled, so he looped it over my head and then slowly smoothed it over my body. He let his hands linger there just a few moments longer than were absolutely necessary, then efficiently pulled the string tight in the back and, circling his arms around front, tied it neatly at my waist.

"You're good at that," I said, turning to look at him. His hands on my body had felt great and he could tell I had liked it, the bastard. He let me go slowly and then leaned back against the counter, standing close to me, watching as I washed my hands thoroughly. He was about six feet tall, maybe a little taller, and had clearly spent some time working out. He was dressed casually, wearing jeans with a tan shirt.

I pulled some of the ingredients out of the bags I'd brought and set them up on the counter, including a small, perfectly ripe watermelon,

"What's this for?" he asked, grinning.

"Summertime drink, I thought." I opened the drawer most likely to contain utensils and found the knife drawer on my first try. I pulled out a long serrated knife and, using his cutting board, began rapidly chopping the fresh fruit into about one-inch dice, removing the seeds. Then I asked him to puree it up in the blender.

"This is so cool," he said, showing no fear with an unfamiliar tool.

I found a crystal pitcher in one of his upper cabinets and measured in two cups each of bottled water and Grey Goose vodka.

Dex picked up the Grey Goose bottle and read the label. "You can get just about any man you want with this routine of yours, isn't that right?"

"Any man who drinks too much," I agreed. "So that's something I've got going for me."

I had brought a container filled with fresh-squeezed lemon juice and poured in two cups of that along with a cup of sugar. Then I asked Dex to measure out four cups of the fresh-pureed watermelon, and when he had, I stirred it well.

"What do you call this?" Dex asked, awe in his voice.

"Spiked watermelon lemonade à la Dex." I filled two tall glasses with ice from his icemaker and poured us each a glass, which I garnished with lemon wheels and sprigs of mint. It's in my DNA. Can't help it.

Dex held up his glass and clinked it to mine. The corners of his warm hazel eyes wrinkled when he smiled. "To you, Madeline."

"Aw." I tried the drink. Sweet, sour, and lots of punch. I took another sip. It went down easily, very easily.

"And now that we have our liquid refreshments," he said, taking a sip and smiling, "why don't you ask me what you are dying to ask me?"

"What?"

"Think about it."

"Why the world is round?" I joked, sipping my drink. "Why chickens cross the road?" I'd have to pace myself on the old spiked lemonade if I didn't want to be too dizzy to cook dinner.

He put down his glass and looked at me thoughtfully. "I'm not worried about your ex-boyfriends, Madeline. And I'm giving this thing my best shot. But I think you want to know what really happened that night three years ago when the three best pieces in my brother-in-law's art collection were stolen."

I stopped midsip. Zenya must tell her brother every little thing.

"Or am I wrong about that?" Dex had a very direct gaze.

So, pow! There went my little idea of tiptoeing up to the subject ever so gingerly. A perfect time to take another tiny sip of spiked watermelon lemonade à la Dex.

"Look of Love"

Hold that thought," Dex said, toying with me.

So sly. He knew I was interested in the art theft. Though he might play for laughs most of the time, there was no doubt in my mind the man was extremely smart.

So I went along with the flow, allowing the question of crime to sink below the surface, biding my time, and I set about prepping our little Mexican meal. Dex placed oversize aqua plates on the glass-and-chrome table in the open dining room while I whipped up some fresh tomatillo salsa and served the chilled avocado soup.

We talked all through dinner. He had many questions, and I ended up telling Dexter about my childhood in the suburbs of Chicago. How tame it had been growing up in middle-class Lincolnwood, but how equal parts exhilarating and devastating my childhood had been, even there. It's funny, those getting-acquainted stories we tell to a new person in our life. We reveal ourselves in shades, depending on our mood. The mood moved me to share the story of how I shocked the nay-saying Mrs. Applebaum and won the fifth-grade spelling bee by spelling the word *culinary,* thus foretelling my future career, as well as the horrible time my best friend Debra and I were escorted into the manager's office at Walgreen's. I had been sobbing, totally shocked, until Debra, with a pout, pulled several bottles of frosted nail polish out of her Levi's pocket.

"What happened?" Dex asked.

"My mom told me, 'Be careful the friends you pick.' "

"A story with a moral." Dex had an easy smile. "So did you dump Debra?"

"Of course not. She was my best friend." I ignored good sense and poured each of us another drink. "That episode did answer one burning question, though."

Dex looked interested. "You mean about integrity?"

"I mean how Debra, with the same exact allowance as I had, managed to have the coolest nails in Lincoln Hall Junior High."

Dexter told me more about his life, too. He and Zenya had grown up in L.A. in the well-off west side of town, the "good" side. Their parents sent them to the right private schools and belonged to the right country club. But after his mother had died, Dex was mostly left to raise himself.

"Did your father ever remarry?"

He cocked an eyebrow. "I was twelve and Zenya was fifteen," he said, serving himself seconds of every dish I'd made from the colorful platters and bowls I'd brought to the table, pausing his story to comment, "This corn salad is amazing."

"Thanks."

"Anyway, Georgia—that was our new stepmother—was twenty-one."

"Oh. That can be tricky. Was it bad?"

"I didn't *hate* her."

"Okay."

"I didn't love her, obviously. Hey, I was in like seventh grade. I maybe had a crush on her. She was definitely hot."

"Boys," I said.

"But in any case, Georgia was sent packing after a few

years. My dad kept busy, though. He managed to marry two other women after that. I think. I didn't actually go to the last wedding."

"Really?"

"I'm not even sure what their names were," he said pleasantly.

"Not too bitter, though," I commented. "Which is healthy."

He gave me his best smile.

"Then one thing and another," he continued, putting his fork down, "and my dad made the usual bad business decisions and bye-bye fortune."

"Had it been your mother's money?" I asked.

"Of course it had," he said. "And all we were left with, Zenya and me, was the trust fund our mom's mother had set up. Oh, Dad worked with the lawyers for years to get his hands on that. But it was pretty well set up."

"And that's what you live on," I said, wondering how different my life would have been if I'd had such an inheritance.

"Well, I would if I could," he said. "The market is down. I have needs. Let's just say it's going to be gone soon."

"But you still have this house?" I was in the man's three-million-dollar pad, the twinkling lights from the hillside homes beneath us glowing beyond the walls of glass.

"Sure. As long as I can keep it. But I might have to sell. Need the cash."

Rich folks have different problems from the rest of us. I couldn't imagine anything better than the life he was letting slip away. Or perhaps I had it better than I realized. I needed to work. I loved to work. I had achieved a great deal. Dex hadn't been raised to know the joy in such things. No wonder he seemed adrift.

"Oh, you poor little rich boy."

"I like sympathy," he said. "More, please."

"And Zenya?"

"Zenya got a rotten deal. My grandmother left her much less money than she left me. I guess she was expecting Zenya to make a rich marriage and thought she wouldn't need it. I don't know. And Zen is so sweet she did what was expected. She married Bill. What a deal, huh? I only hope she's happy with it."

"Isn't she?"

He spoke quietly. "I don't think so. No."

So all this time, Dex had had to watch his sister wrestle with a difficult marriage and he'd felt guilty because he'd inherited more than she had. I thought it was sad and noble that he wanted to protect her. To Dex, his sister's rich life had too steep a price and he would rather sacrifice his own safety net to get her out of there. He looked at me across the glass table and reached for my hand. "I never talk about this stuff. Not to anyone. My last girlfriend didn't even know I *had* a sister, and here I am, telling you . . . everything. I don't open up to people. But there's something going on here, Madeline. You're killing me."

The one thing you never expect from a self-confident guy is an admission of weakness.

"I was only trying to maim you. My aim must be off."

"It's like I'm fourteen again and I like this girl too much." He held on to my hand and laughed at himself.

My breathing became shallower and I could feel myself get jittery. You know, like when you want a certain guy to like you and you get the signal that maybe he really does.

"I don't know anyone like you," he went on. "You're so calm when things are going crazy. You have this goofy smartness. I never know what you're going to say. I'm scared I'm not worthy of you. You are something else."

"Ah, that's just the spiked watermelon talking," I said, smiling a little.

"I have fallen for you. So watch out what you do with my heart, okay?"

I burst out laughing.

"I'm not joking." But then he smiled, unable to maintain such a serious tone for too long. "Ah, crap. I am suddenly thinking of all the girls I've left along the way. Karma. What a horrible thought. So, are you going to pay me back for those women I was a bastard to?"

I looked at him. His eyes were teasing, but I thought I saw something more there. He was clearly a man who had spent a lot of his life avoiding any dependence on a woman. Since he was a kid. Since his mother had left him so young. I'm no Sigmund Freud, but anyone watching a month's worth of Lifetime movies could make such a simple connection. For all of that, I was so attracted to him.

"Anyway," he said, after a significant pause in which I did not tell him to get lost but on the other hand did not confess I was falling for him, too, "*any*way, that's why I'm going to have to sell this place. I want to offer the money to my sister. So she can leave that asshole. She deserves so much better than that."

"Has she told you she wants to leave?"

"No. She doesn't get it all yet. But she will."

"Does this have anything to do with the art that was stolen?"

"So." Dexter played with his napkin, a linen weave in oatmeal colors. "We're back to that already."

Without my realizing it, something had shifted, so that solving a puzzle and sorting out a crime seemed so much less important than getting to the heart of this man. But I was not ready to let this topic alone. I had to remember my mother's sensible advice and make a good choice here. I had to consider what he was capable of.

Dexter rose and began clearing dishes and I joined him, picking up two empty serving bowls. His tone was light but resolute. "You want to know anything, Madeline, I will tell you the truth. It will always be that way with us, okay? Let's make it a rule."

"Like you enjoy following the rules," I joked.

"I'll start now. Zenya's husband, Bill," Dexter said, walking around the glass-topped table, but stopping to make eye contact. "What a bastard. He knew I needed money."

Oh no. My stomach sank.

"Anyway, he and Zen and the kid were going to Maui and they asked me to stay at their house." We walked together to the kitchen as he talked. "Bill said they'd pay me for my time. That was before I had this place, so I was like Uncle House-sitter for a few weeks." Dexter began rinsing the dishes. I opened the dishwasher.

"And then what?"

"And then I came home from a concert with a date and the front door was standing wide open. The alarm company was already there and so were the cops. It had been a simple heist. The only things missing were the three most precious etchings from Bill's coveted collection."

"They didn't take anything else? His guitars? Any other art? Zenya's jewelry?"

He shook his head.

"Didn't the cops think that was sort of odd?"

"Look, the artwork had been displayed a few months earlier at the friggin' art museum. Any good crook could read Bill's name on the donor plaque and wait until the exhibit had ended. They must have found out where Bill and Zenya lived and waited until the house was empty. That was that."

I looked at him. For once, the easygoing manner was gone.

"What?" he asked, looking more closed down than I'd

seen him before. "You wondering if I had something to do with the theft?"

"Well, did you?"

"Of course not."

"Okay. Whew. That's good." I smiled up at him.

He grabbed me and looked at me for a minute. I felt the rush of too many spiked watermelon lemonades à la Dex. After the strength of his grasp I was unprepared for the softness of his mouth on mine. We stood in the kitchen kissing for so long my knees really did go weak. I had missed being with a man, missed being held. I wanted him to go on kissing me.

He ripped my shirt open, popping the tiny buttons, which I heard hit the polished hardwood floor.

"Dexter," I said, breathless. "Dex, you have no curtains in this entire house."

"I know," he whispered. "Too much money." He began to nibble my ear.

"And the whole place is made of glass. All windows," I pleaded as he slipped my blouse off and cupped my breasts in his hands.

"Are you worried about the neighbors?" he asked, touching me in a way that made me want to pull him down on the floor right there, beg him to stop talking.

"I am feeling," I said as he pulled my skirt to the floor, "a little exposed."

I stood in my tiny white silk thong panties and high heels and nothing else. His hands brushed over me, caressing my skin, touching me all over.

"Do you want me to?" he asked, nuzzling my neck, his hands slipping into my panties and twisting them, touching me, making me gasp.

"The lights," I said, looking to see where the switch was,

hoping it was close by because I was so turned on I couldn't have left him for even a moment.

"Leave them on, Madeline," he said, playfully pulling off my last garment. He was now fully clothed and I was fully not.

"Dex, I can't," I protested. But he knew I could. I wanted him. He could feel it between my legs.

"Does it turn you on more thinking I'm a villain?" he whispered as he kissed my hair, my ears, my throat.

"I . . . don't know." I was shocking myself. "Right this minute, I don't care about that at—" He pulled my hand and I followed him, naked, to the nearby living room. On the floor was a bright yellow shag rug.

"Oh no," I said, giggling. "Not on the shag."

"Come on," he said, teasing. "I'll treat you so well, Madeline."

I realized I couldn't stop myself. I wanted him. Even suspecting that he might very well be involved in a crime didn't seem to matter to me. He'd admitted he needed money three years ago. He admitted the "burglars" only took a few very specific items. He bought this amazing house right after the theft. I was beyond wanting to add it all up.

"Look," I said, my breath coming fast, almost losing my nerve as I realized we were standing, entwined, in front of an inch-thick wall of glass. The canyons of Bel Air were just beyond.

He kissed me again. "What? L.A. is at our feet." But then he pulled back and looked at me with such sweetness. "Just tell me you want me, Madeline. It's up to you. We don't have to do this."

While I tried to think it over, I leaned in to kiss him one more time, and the warmth of his mouth on mine made my brain go fuzzy again. It had been such a long time since I had managed to let myself go, to turn off my mind. His hands were experienced and knew exactly the right places to caress and to stroke.

That was the moment I realized I wouldn't stop him. I opened my eyes just as he began to slowly take off his shirt, his broad shoulders backed against the wall of windows. He was gorgeous, so cool and tanned. I don't know what it was that drew my eye away from him and outside. Perhaps some tiny flicker of movement.

In the dim patio light I could just make out a silhouette on the other side of the glass. A woman. Oh my God! A woman was standing right there on his deck. She was watching us through the glass from just a few feet away.

And then I recognized her. The light picked up the red color of her hair. It was the woman I had seen in the Honda Accord. The woman who had been following me.

I screamed.

Dex whipped around, beyond stunned. Then he saw her, too, before she was gone. He bolted for the sliding-glass door, fiddled with the lock, and then tore it open. The cold night air rushed in on me.

"Stay here," he said, his voice sharp with anger at what was happening. An intruder was ruining our night, he must have thought.

"Dex!"

He ran out into the dark yard and I scrambled to get back into my clothes, which I found scattered around here and there. I was shaking, and tears were streaking down my face.

I was thinking a hundred crazy things. Jumbled among the thoughts were my fears of the past week, my sense that I had been a target all along. And then my anxieties mushroomed. Perhaps there was a greater power at work here. How had I so easily become attached to a man about whom I knew so little? Was there anything rational about Ping-Ponging from the cop who lied to me to a crook who swore he'd always tell me the truth? Tonight's bizarre events suddenly seemed to be my punishment for giving in to pleasure, for wanting to start fresh with a new man who might love me. Things have a purpose. Everything was connected. Damn it, I didn't believe in random. I didn't believe in accidents. I always needed to know *why*.

I was sitting in a heap on one of the black leather chairs when Dex came back in the house. He was breathing hard.

"She's gone. I lost her. I heard the sound of a car engine."

I continued crying, not able to talk.

"Look, Madeline. I'm so sorry. I have no idea who she was. You have to believe that. I've never seen that woman before in my life."

"That's okay. It's not your fault," I finally managed to say between sobs. "I've seen her before. Earlier today. I think she's been following me."

Dex's whole manner changed. "Who is she?" He looked at me seriously now. Perhaps he had thought it was some outraged neighbor lady coming to complain about our indecent show. But he suddenly realized something more sinister was happening to me.

"I don't know." I stopped crying and tried hard to think it through. "At first, because of her age, I thought maybe she could be one of the women who worked on the Woodburn gala. Maybe I should recognize her. But I just don't."

And while I was still coming down from this enormous shock, racking my sorry brain for answers, Dex suddenly smiled at me. "Man."

"What?"

He shook his head, still smiling. That smile made all the difference. He had an interesting effect on me. He didn't let pathos boil over very long, which was a great relief. I looked at his grin and made the obvious guess. "You can't believe how much trouble I can get myself into, right?"

"No. I can easily believe that."

I might have been on the ragged side of drunk and lovelorn and completely freaked out, but I could still take a joke. I grinned.

"It's just that until that lady came along," Dex continued, holding his thumb about an inch away from his forefinger, "I was about this close to having the best sex in my entire sorry life."

"Of that," I answered, "you should have no damn doubt."

"Blues in the Night"

Dexter insisted on following me back to Wesley's house. I complained it was too much trouble; it was late; I was fine. He just stared at me. His car stayed right behind mine all the way home.

My eyes swept across the midnight streets, some residential and dark, some Friday-night raucous, scouring each lane, looking for the Honda Accord. Naturally, I didn't see it.

"You okay?" Dex asked, talking to me by cell phone as we drove down a jamming Sunset Strip.

"Stop calling me," I said, laughing. "I'm fine." I disconnected and waved in my rearview mirror as we inched past the giant billboards.

But I had to think about how fine I really was. Who was that woman? Why had she followed me? And more disturbing, if she meant to harm me, she knew where to find me. I was sure of it. She must have been tailing me better than I realized. I had to assume she'd followed me from Wesley's place in Hancock Park up to Dexter's house earlier that evening, so I had no doubt she knew where I was staying.

On Hudson, Wesley's street, I slowed down and examined every parked car. No Accord with a missing front plate. With Dexter following behind in his Z4, I drove right past Wesley's house and then proceeded slowly up and down the quiet streets in all directions, scouting the curbs for dark Hondas. This is a neighborhood that doesn't encourage street parking for its residents. The few scattered cars parked in the area were more than likely partygoers'. I strained to keep vigilant and yet I spied no Hondas that matched my stalker anywhere within a one-mile radius of Wes's place.

Dexter's and my two-car convoy slowly cruised by the Canadian consulate general's English-style mansion, then past the official, but uninhabited mayoral mansion, the Getty House, on South Irving. By then I was blocks away from Wesley's house, but I wanted to be sure.

My cell phone, thrown on the passenger seat of the Trailblazer, chirped.

I fumbled for it and hit the on button. "Okay," I said, looking in my rearview mirror. "I'm fine. I'm heading to Wesley's right now."

"Just checking." Dex's voice sounded calm over the phone.

I drove back to Third Street and over to Hudson. Then I pulled into the long driveway and Dex pulled his car in right behind me. Before I could unfasten my seat belt and gather my bag and phone, he had walked up to my door and opened it. We didn't talk as we walked together back to the guest house behind the empty main house. The porch light was on outside the door of the cottage. Thanks, Wes.

I turned to say good night.

"You sure you don't want me to come in for a little while?" Dex tilted his head, watching my face in the porch light. He seemed concerned with what he saw. "You know, check that everything's all right." He reached out and softly stroked my arm in a friendly gesture, but I didn't move closer to him and he let his hand drop.

"No. Thanks. I've got to be up early tomorrow morning."

"Right." He looked like he was about to say something more, but then thought better of it.

"I had better go in. Don't want to disturb Wes."

"So Wesley's home," Dex said, sounding reassured. "Good."

With an evening that had wound up resembling some new X-rated extreme sport more than a good, old-fashioned date, there seemed no correct way to end it. "Sorry about tonight," I said. Lame but true.

"Say, don't be. It was an incredible meal. You are amazingly beautiful. I am swooning for you." I laughed as he gently brushed my long, curly hair back with both hands, resting them on my shoulders. "Things could be worse, you know?"

"Sure."

Dex gave me a short, tentative kiss. I kept my eyes open this time.

"You are completely freaked," he assessed sadly.

"Yeah. I know. Let's talk later."

"Tomorrow?"

"I'm working during the day, but maybe later in the afternoon."

"Where are you working?"

"At a kid's party in Pasadena. Say, you want to hear Wynton Marsalis play live?"

I gave Dexter the address and we said good night.

Wesley was still up, reading the latest Harry Potter. He put the heavy book down the moment I entered the living room. That's when I noticed Honnett was sitting in one of the club chairs, ankle resting on knee, foot tapping.

"I called Honnett," Wes said. It was an unnecessary explanation. I had phoned Wes to tell him about the stalker woman turning up at Dexter's house. Now I was sure she'd been following me earlier in the day. It had taken Wes maybe four seconds after I hung up to get Honnett over to the guest house. It was sickening. I was relieved.

"Maddie, sorry to intrude here," he said, looking uncomfortable. How much could he have heard through the front door when I was kissing Dexter good-bye? "Wes was worried about you."

"I'm worried, too," I said.

"Yeah? Well, add me to the list. I wanted to go pick you up, drive you back here, but Wes wouldn't give me the address of your . . . friend. I guess you got back okay." Honnett was doing an impressive job of holding on to some serious rage, keeping his expressions in check, but his voice showed the strain. I couldn't tell what was at play here, the idea that I was in danger or the fact that I was dating someone new, and he wasn't allowed to come rescue me.

"But she's fine now," Wesley said, doing his best to settle us all down.

"Look, you need to call Baronowski and bring him up to speed on what's going on here. Give him a description. It was a woman, right?"

I nodded.

He thought it over—a woman—and appeared to be as stumped as I was. "Did she have a weapon?"

I shook my head no.

"You sure? Because the only crime we have here is maybe trespassing. And if there was no weapon in sight and she left immediately after you spotted her, it's kind of hard to make anything of it. That is assuming we can find her. Do you think your friend wants to press charges?"

"I don't know. She didn't really do anything to us. She just sort of watched us for a while, through the window."

"What were you doing?" he asked, following the trail of the story.

"We . . ." I simply could not think of an appropriate response.

Wesley coughed, and then asked brightly, "Would anyone care for a cup of coffee?" And without waiting for a response, he took himself off to the tiny guest-house kitchen and gave us some room to fight in privacy. I love Wes.

Honnett smiled a little and shook his head. There were clearly secrets separating us now. Things I wouldn't go into. Things about me and another man. Maybe he got the irony of our situation. I don't know. But he looked ill, that was for sure. I considered it. Maybe even as ill as I had felt when I discovered he wasn't all mine.

"You trying to hurt me, Maddie?" he asked softly, still smiling at me.

I thought about it. I can't talk about my unconscious or subconscious or id or whatever, but I didn't *think* I had gotten myself involved with Dexter on purpose to hurt Honnett. On the other hand, I could see the power of his reaction. And it did feel awfully good, I'm ashamed to admit, to see he still cared about me this way. I could see why a woman would do something like that, to provoke a man who dumped her, to make him jealous, just to get a little of her own back. I looked up at him. Any momentary pained expression I might have observed was now replaced by the trusty Honnett mask of calm.

I recovered and picked up my point. "But I'm sure this person has been following me. I've had the creepiest feeling all week that I'm a target. First Sara, then Grasso, and now me."

"Look, Maddie," he said gently, "you've been under a lot of strain. Your house is ripped apart. You're living over here. You told me you're not sleeping much. Your nerves must be shot."

"I'm not mistaken, Chuck. I'm not."

"Well, I'm just saying it's easy to get jumpy. It was dark out. A woman startled you and she may have looked like someone else you barely got a glimpse of."

"I'm not seeing things," I said, my teeth clenched.

"Okay, but I'm going to talk to you like a cop now, okay? I have to say this. What do you know about this guy you were just seeing? You've known him how long? How do you know this woman wasn't an old friend of his, maybe even an ex?"

I stared at Honnett hard. "You mean," I said quietly, "maybe he has another girl he's not telling me about?"

Even Honnett got the real point I was trying to make.

"I just hope," he said, looking at his hands, "this guy of yours is good enough for you. I hope he's a right guy. At least I could live with that. I could be happy for you. I don't want to think about you getting mixed up with some creep. And don't yell at me. I know it's none of my damn business who you go out with now. I'm just saying."

"And that's just you talking like a 'cop'?" I smiled at him. For a bastard with a wife still attached, he did care about me. He did.

"Anyway, the point I'm making is, you are tired. And we have to face it. There isn't any hard evidence anyone is after you."

I tilted my chin down and gave him the eye. "Yeah, right. You know I don't believe in coincidences, Honnett." I waved my hand in front of my face, dismissing the topic. "This is not making me feel better. What I want to know is what the hell is going on? Why would someone want to follow me? How does this connect to the murders?"

Wes returned and put a tray on the coffee table. There were fresh-baked round chocolate wafers, which had been half dipped into white chocolate, along with a carafe of coffee and a pot of tea.

"Thanks, Wes," Honnett said, and then he looked back at me. "Okay. Tell us what you think is happening."

What I wanted was Honnett's cop head, not his ex-boyfriend head, and he was finally getting there. I moved to the sofa across from him and crossed my legs.

"I keep thinking that this must have something to do with Albert Grasso's papers."

"But how?" Honnett asked.

"We looked through them," Wes said, doubtful like Honnett. "There was nothing there."

"But let's say someone thought there was something to worry about in those papers," I persisted. "Grasso knew I had seen them. Maybe others did, too. Maybe they want me dead."

"So, you figure they came to your house on Whitley to kill you last Saturday night?" Honnett seemed detached now and ready to lay it all out. And it's funny. It had annoyed me when he kept insisting I was wrong, but now it spooked me just as bad to realize he might think I was right. "And the shooter made a mistake."

"Right. Let's say that was Grasso. And he mixed up Sara Jackson for me. That doesn't make a lot of sense, I know. Sara and I don't . . . *didn't* really look that much alike."

"But wait, Mad . . ." Wes picked up a teacup, reconsidering this scenario. "Albert Grasso didn't know you very well. Maybe in the dark. She's alone in your house late at night. She has long red hair. Maybe he got confused."

"We're both about the same size . . ." I looked at Honnett to see if he was buying any of it.

"Okay. Keep on telling your story. For now, let's say Grasso killed her."

"Right. Then the people he was scared about, the ones his files may have incriminated in some way, they came by his place and killed *him*."

"Okay," Honnett said, sounding neutral.

I spun out the rest. "Those people who killed Grasso had more cleaning up to do. They see the news and realize Grasso killed the wrong girl. I'm still a threat. So they are sending some hit woman out after me."

"Maddie. Honey. You think anyone outside of the movies uses hit women?" Honnett had gone about as far as he could go.

"I don't know! Okay, not a professional killer." We all laughed. "But this woman . . . She was *attractive,* regular-looking. Hey, what about this? Maybe she was a friend of Caroline Rochette's. She looked about Caroline's age."

"And what would that be?" Wes asked. "Somewhere north of forty and south of death?" He looked pleased to see me smile, and continued: "I suppose there could be some wacked-out posse of killer real estate ladies after your property . . ."

"It doesn't fit," Honnett observed, looking at me. I followed his eyes down. My blouse was held together by paper clips. Dex didn't have a sewing kit. Figures.

"Why not?" I asked, ignoring his gaze. "Leaving aside the killer-realtor theory, what's wrong with the first part of my story?"

Honnett sighed, and poured himself a cup of coffee. "You're talking like 'the Mob,' right? This is not their style, Madeline. But putting that aside . . ." He stirred in a spoon of sugar and looked back at me, getting serious. "First, if Albert Grasso and/or whoever else was part of some scheme was willing to kill to make sure no one read those files, they'd have to kill a hell of a lot more people than you. They would have to kill his gal pal, Caroline Rochette, not to mention Wes and Holly." He waited for my reaction.

"True."

"And now it gets even more complicated. The police detectives in the case have copies of the papers, which was a very smart move on your part. So assuming those papers of Albert Grasso's really do contain something very hot, we all missed it. The people who care about it gotta realize by now we're too frigging dense to find it."

I listened to his logic as it tumbled my theories like the proverbial dominoes.

"So, if there *was* something explosive among Grasso's box of junk and none of us geniuses have discovered it, they'd be fools not to leave it all the hell alone now, wouldn't they? At this point, coming after a little caterer makes no sense."

He was right. Why would they?

Honnett spoke kindly, but he didn't let up until he got me to see it his way. "Honey, killing you is the opposite of what they would want right now. It would only direct suspicion to those papers, which right now no one is really focused on, don't you see? If I were them, assuming there *is* a 'them,' I'd lie low now or get out of town. You know, fly to Belize. I wouldn't keep kicking up dust, Maddie."

"Right," I said slowly.

"And then let's face another fact. There's a good chance there was nothing important among those papers in the first place." Honnett was not averse to rubbing in a little salt.

It stung, but he was right. I had become completely insane, fearing the world was trying to kill me. He made sense. Hell, I had used the same arguments to talk myself down from the ledge of my paranoia all week. Each night, as I rechecked the chambers of the Lady Smith .38, just to reassure myself that she was ready, I thought about how ridiculous it was for anyone to still be after me.

"Thanks for coming out here tonight, Honnett."

He met my eyes, held the contact. I was startled by the emotion I saw there.

"Look," I said, "I'm . . . Well, I'm tired. I need sleep. Obviously. Wesley is here. You should go home."

"I'll stay," he said, looking surprised I'd kick him out.

"That's okay. I'm fine now."

Honnett looked over at Wesley, waiting for support, but Wes didn't insist he stay either.

"If you're sure," Honnett said, sounding tired of fighting me. "Walk me to the door, then?"

The room was small, and Wes took the hint, excusing himself and disappearing into the back bedroom.

"You'll be okay?" he asked.

I looked at Honnett. He seemed older somehow. He still had the great rugged face, the strong cheekbones and jawline of a cowboy. But his clear blue eyes looked a little vague, like he had a lot on his mind.

"How's everything with you?" I asked, standing with him near the door.

"It goes on. The usual. Sherrie has been doing a little better. She's getting out a little more."

"Good."

"So, Maddie. You like this other guy a lot, huh?"

"This is not a good time to go into this, Chuck," I said. I had had enough drama for one evening. I wanted a bath and bed. My own.

"Okay. Sorry. Look, I have to ask for the thirty-eight back, if you don't mind."

The what? I looked at him like he had suddenly slapped me. Now, I could stand a lot of things. I could stand to watch my romantic evening destroyed in an instant. I could stand to find my old boyfriend waiting up for me at home. And I could probably get through a teenager's birthday party in a few hours. But I simply could not part with the gun.

"No."

"I'm sorry?"

"You can't have it back now. You can't. I haven't had time to buy one of my own. And—"

"Maddie—"

"NO! Look, if you're worried I don't know anything about guns, you don't have to worry. I found an instructor. She's really kick-ass. And I've been out on the range, shooting real bullets. I can shoot, too. That is not a worry. But the whole idea," I rattled on quickly, "is to provide me with a little goddamned sense of security in the crazy world, Honnett. And if you take that revolver away from me now, while who knows what freakin' forces of evil are gathering to get me, I'll completely, *completely* wig out. I will. So this isn't even a question, okay? You can't have it back right now. Understand?"

"Bad timing, I get it," he said, taking me and my paranoid outburst with measured calm.

"Okay. So good night. And thanks for coming by."

"Good night," he said, searching my eyes for something. I think he wanted to kiss me. It wasn't going to happen. Access to my lips was closed to all, perhaps forever. Didn't these guys realize that despite the logic and the scenarios, despite their theories and all the cops in the world working on the case, I knew without reason that someone was maybe trying to kill me?

"I'm going to drive around awhile," Honnett said, opening the door to leave. "What sort of car should I be looking for?"

"Honda Accord. Black. No front plate."

He stopped in the doorway, and looked back at me, thinking it all through, I guess. How we had gone from where we were a few months ago to where we were now was a hard journey to map. I was sure he was going to say something more about the time we had been together. But instead, he simply asked again, "An Accord, you say?"

I stood there, exhausted, nodding. And then he left.

"Look Beyond"

Jacked up on Double-Double Animal-Style burgers and third helpings of Chocolate Madness Saxophone cake, three dozen twelve- and thirteen-year-old boys raced through the Hutson backyard, whooping at one another that they could beat anyone at Starcraft.

I was happy to see the party had come off so well. Sometimes ''impromptu" works. Wes was pouring Holly and me glasses of champagne to celebrate the fact that our crew had cleaned up and was ready to move on.

Wynton Marsalis had been brilliant, charmed the audience, and cut out about an hour earlier. Even in this wealthy crowd, guests were whispering about how much money Mr. Hutson had spent for this treat. The much-touted battle of the bands, or more specifically, young musicians, was yet to come. But it wasn't our responsibility to get all those carbo-crazed boys and their instruments up onstage. Thank God.

We had leased the tables, risers, and audience chairs, as well as the sound equipment and soundboard. The truck would come to collect it all tomorrow. I raised a flute of sparkling, straw-colored wine and clinked glasses with Holly.

"To more easy gigs," she said, taking a sip of the tiny bubbles that gave joy to this particular vintage of Louis Roederer Brut Premier.

"Amen," I said.

"And no shocking surprises after," Wes said, taking a drink.

"Hey," Holly said, looking over my shoulder. "Someone here for you."

I turned. Dex Wyatt had appeared. He was coming down the path in the Hutson's huge backyard. When he missed the Marsalis concert, I had briefly wondered what was up, but then I got busy as I always do and sort of lost track of time. Suddenly a commotion broke out not ten feet away from where Dex was walking.

"Hey, Uncle Dex!" A fully clothed young man had decided it would be hilarious to sit in the Jacuzzi. He held his alto sax above the bubbling hot water and began playing. Several other young party guests and their instruments followed his lead. You had to love kids.

"Hey, Kirby," Dex called to the boy, saluting him back, and then he walked over to us. "Wes. Madeline." Dex stopped by my side and I could swear the sun got brighter. I'm not making this up. "You okay?" he asked me.

"Fine. You missed the concert."

"Stuff came up I couldn't get out of."

"That's okay."

"Hey, I didn't realize my nephew, Kirby, would be at this thing. How wild."

"You know Holly Nichols, Dex."

"Holly," he said, with a devilish grin. "I've been dying to see you again. And you look stunning."

Holly, standing in full daylight in a proper Pasadena garden, was currently wearing a tiny red Paul Frank muscle tee with the famous image of Julius, the puzzled monkey, on her chest. The shirt ended way above her navel, and it was only after many inches of bare, tanned stomach that her pink hip huggers began. I won't even go into the belly-button ring, or the sprinkle of glitter in her blond hair.

"Thanks," said Holly, dimpling.

"So what has Madeline told you two about me, then?" Dex asked.

"Everything," Holly said.

"Everything?" Dex looked at me, voice squeaking in mock shock.

"I cook with these guys all day long," I confessed to him. "The hot stoves. The bright lights. They get every detail out of me. I should have warned you."

"I'm cool with that," Dex said.

"Great attitude," Holly commented, admiring my new man and giving me a nod. "Mad is like some supernaturally gifted pitcher. When you're at the plate, you never know what she's going to throw at you. So, my advice would be, stay alert."

"You a baseball fan, Holly?" Dex was a sports guy, so he sounded intrigued.

"Well, not really," she admitted.

"She just likes the metaphors," Wesley explained.

Connie Hutson walked up to our group and I turned on my party-planner personality. "Connie, we're just ready to leave. Is there anything else you need?"

"I was coming over to congratulate your group. It's a terrific party. Ryan has had the best time. Despite himself."

"I noticed some of the guests are in the whirlpool," Wes said helpfully.

"Oh, these boys! We've brought out towels and they will just have to play in the contest in soggy clothes. We're about to get started. Anyway, thanks so much for taking us on at the very last minute."

"You're welcome," Wesley said, smiling.

We all began to depart. When we got to the front of the house, I hugged Wes and Holly good-bye and we separated to go to our own cars. Dex had walked out with me and asked if I had time for a private word. I wanted to talk with him, too. We stopped in front of my parked Trailblazer.

"Dex," I said, "I've got to ask you something and I need you to be completely honest with me. Okay? This is serious."

"Sure. What?"

"The woman. Are you telling me you never saw her before? Or is she someone you dated or something. It's important. I need the truth."

"What are you talking about?" Dex sounded genuinely insulted. "I told you the truth last night. I don't know who she was or what she was doing there. What is this, Madeline?"

"I think I'm in some serious trouble, Dex. I need to know what is going on now. A cop warned me I might be being naive. He thought it was likely that woman was connected to you. I just had to make sure."

Dexter stared at me, putting it together. "So your boyfriend, the cop, is getting you all worked up over me, right?"

"I'm not usually like this," I said.

"Madeline, you think I'd lie to you?"

My eyes stung with sudden tears, which I fought to hold back. "Men lie," I said, with more force than I had intended. "I'm not saying you are, right now, but it happens."

"That's a great attitude you've got. What the hell did I do? We are just getting started. Why are you suddenly so suspicious?"

"Don't sound so self-righteous," I said, snapping back. Fearing for my life for the past week had done a number on my legendary self-control. And the last person in the world I wanted to take it out on was Dexter. He stood there in the dappled sunlight of the lush trees, looking angered by my attack. Like he wasn't going to take on the burden of all the men who had done me wrong. But before I could begin to trust him, I had to know what was real to him. In the daylight, I doubted everything about everyone.

"You are hard work, Maddie," he said with a half smile, defusing my anger with the sudden shift of tone.

"Oh, hell."

"That's part of the attraction for me, no doubt. I've had it pretty easy my whole damn life, as I'm sure you have figured out. But I want to work this out, you and me. Did you hear what I said? I said the word *work.* Several times."

I smiled. "Only twice."

"And I know deep down you can't entirely approve of me, can you? But I feel like we have a connection. And if I get my act together, we could be awesome. I've never felt that before."

"Really?"

"Really. And if you want honest, I'll be honest. The girls in my life . . . Well, the girls have been kind of easy to get. You know, I'm lucky like that. But they never last with me. I can't get that attached. I'm like a Velcro guy, but all the girls don't have the right loops or whatever it is that makes Velcro stick together."

I nodded, smiling more.

"No one reaches me. We've talked about this before. But it's different with you. You've got the right kind of loops for me, Madeline."

"Oh, Dex."

"You are completely odd." He touched my cheek.

"Odd." I smiled.

"Odd, but I like it."

"I like you, too, Dex. I do. But there's something very wrong. I know there is. I just feel it."

His smile faded a tiny bit and he finally nodded.

"And until I can figure all of this out, we can't work as a couple."

"Do you have to make some big decision about us today? Why can't we just keep on? Get to know each other a little better."

I shook my head, working hard to resist him. It made my words come out hotter than I intended. "You haven't been completely honest with me. You know it. There's something more going on between you and the art collection that was ripped off than you are willing to tell me. I felt it last night when you were avoiding the questions. Tell me if I'm wrong about that."

We stood near my red rent-a-car, our voices suddenly heated.

"What do you want from me?" He didn't look away from my eyes. "If you wanted a saint, you wouldn't have been hanging out with me this long, Madeline."

"You're not a saint. What exactly does that mean?" I was unable to hold back all my frustration and anger. How dare he make me fall for him! I was no longer content to wait for answers. I had to know where we really stood. "Did you have something to do with the art theft, Dex? Is that it?"

He stared at me, hurt and surprised.

"And what about the tenor saxophone at the Woodburn auction? Did you have something to do with that theft as well? You showed up downtown that night and everything around me started falling apart. And that woman in your yard. Did she really follow me to your place, or did you set me up, Dex? Did you have something to do with these murders that have haunted me?"

"Sweetie . . ." He sounded honestly shocked. "Maddie,

this is too much. Are you accusing me of murdering someone? We have to talk. You can't be for real."

"I need the truth, Dex."

"The truth . . ." Dex shook his head. "The truth is tricky, Madeline. The truth can hurt people. I'm not always sure the truth is such a good idea."

It wasn't the answer I was looking for, but it worked. Here I'd been ranting about how I was afraid to trust him, and I suddenly saw clear as day that all along he had been afraid to trust me. Somehow, the sadness of his voice and honesty of his concern woke me up out of my anxious spell.

I loved his face, even now, showing some strain. He may have perfected his charming facade and fooled everyone with the happy-playboy act, but I saw another man. Dex seemed so lonely to me despite his great humor and easy smiles. So much more real. Maybe I was one of the very few who saw the real Dexter Wyatt. And then my anger seemed to dissolve. I knew he wouldn't lie to me. I couldn't believe he would hurt me. His character may have many flaws, but I believed he wanted to play straight with me. And I realized I was willing to risk being a fool rather than give up on this man.

"Tell me," I said softly.

From behind the large Arts-and-Crafts-style home we heard faint sounds of many instruments tuning up. The battle of the young jazz musicians was about to begin.

"Okay," he said. "We'll do it your way."

I took his hand and we leaned against the car and he began to tell me his story.

"Three years ago, Zenya's husband, Bill, asked me to house-sit. Four weeks. I said no problem, plus he offered to pay me. So you know what happened. There was a break-in and three etchings were stolen. The cops always thought it might be me behind it, but they never recovered the artwork and that was that."

"And?"

"And I didn't do it. I didn't. But I think I know who did."

I looked at him and stroked his arm, waiting for more.

"Zenya called me from Maui the day before the theft. She never calls when she's away, so it was kind of unusual. Anyway, she told me that months before they'd planned the Maui trip, she bought tickets to a Stones concert in L.A. They were for the next night. She'd forgotten about them until just then, she said. She told me where I could find them in her desk and told me to use them. She hated to think they'd go to waste."

"And that's the night you went out and that's when the etchings were taken."

He nodded.

"But that could have easily been a coincidence," I said.

He looked at me. "It was funny. Odd. She never bought tickets to concerts. And Zenya doesn't really go for the Rolling Stones. And she actually called me the day of the concert to make sure I was going. I thought it was all very strange even before the break-in."

That did sound suspicious.

"And that's not all. About a month after the theft, Zenya called to tell me she had gotten lucky with some investment and she was buying me a house."

"What? I thought you said Zenya didn't have a lot of her own money."

His eyes looked pained. "She doesn't. And she told me a big story about how Bill had given her a little money to invest. Anyway, she had a friend who was a real estate agent find a great place for me. Zenya always hated that I lived in an apartment. So she told me she found me a place and she put the down payment into escrow. It was up to me to pay the rest of it."

"And you did?"

"I needed some permanence. I thought it was the only way I'd grow up and settle, you know? I wanted to pay her back, but she wouldn't let me."

"And you think Zenya was involved with the art being stolen? She needed money and kind of paid you your share for not telling the police about the circumstances that got you out of the house that night?"

"I try not to think about the whole thing very much. Pretty weak of me, isn't it? Well, you knew there was some outside thing about me, Madeline. You have always known I don't have the highest moral fiber. I think it's what attracts you to me and pulls you away. Even your mother warned you about hanging out with the wrong crowd."

"My mother was proud of me for forgiving my friends their mistakes," I said. "And Debra turned out great. She outgrew her bad-girl phase and overcompensated. She's an attorney in Chicago now."

"Is that so?"

"But explain more. What happened after those etchings were stolen? What's the bottom line?"

"Just ask Mid-Pacific and North American Insurance. They were insured for twenty million dollars."

Oh my God.

"Sisters"

After Dexter departed, I sat in my rented SUV, engine idling, thinking too hard about everything. My usual bad habit. The In-N-Out Burger truck backed slowly out of the driveway of the Hutsons' beautiful Craftsman-style home. I watched the guy navigate the turn into the street when I noticed Zenya Knight's Range Rover coming into view. She pulled up across the street and found a parking space. That's right. She was coming to pick up her son, Kirby, from Ryan Hutson's party. I cut my engine and thought hard about what to do.

I'd confront her. I'd find out what I needed to know about Dexter. I flipped my rearview mirror down and looked at myself, taking stock. I was reduced to living by impulses lately. I said aloud, "Get a grip, Bean."

If only I had been able to go back to my own home and take a shower, like I was used to doing after a long event, I'd cool down, rethink, take it slow. But going home had lost its power to comfort. In just one night's time, that sanctuary was lost to me.

I watched Zenya through my windshield as she stepped down from her Range Rover, oblivious to me sitting in my parked car, and crossed the road to the Hutson house. She was beautiful as always, dressed this afternoon in tight tan cropped jeans and a pink top. I detected some slight family resemblance between Dex and her that I hadn't noticed before—the same big hazel eyes, the same fair coloring.

I needed to figure out what was going on between her brother and me. I could prolong my anxiety or I could talk to Zenya Knight. That meant I'd be stepping right over the line of good family-of-the-boyfriend relations and on into hell. I took a breath and reached for the door handle.

My cell phone rang and I wrestled it out from the depths of my bag.

"Hello."

"Is this Madeline Bean?" The male voice mispronounced my name slightly. He said the last syllable like "lin" while I pronounce it "line." I never correct people, though. Let them call me what they like.

"Who's this?"

"My name is Brett Hurley. You don't know me."

I'd heard the name Brett recently. Where?

"Anyway, I got your cell-phone number from a police detective. I hope that's okay."

Brett Hurley. Sara Jackson's troubled boyfriend. I remembered it all now.

"I'm glad you called," I said. "I'm sorry about your loss. Do you think you're up to talking about Sara?"

"Kind of. Yes. Do you think we could meet somewhere?"

On a normal day, I'd ask him to meet me at my office. But I wasn't keen on being there at the house alone on a Saturday. My house had become the enemy. Besides, how could I ask Sara Jackson's boyfriend to go to the site of her murder?

"I'm not sure. Where are you?"

"I'm just driving," he said. "I can meet you anywhere."

I thought it over as I watched Zenya walk to the front door of the Hutson home and then correct herself and follow the walkway to the side and around to the back, where the party was just ending. The muted sounds of several jazz solos had ceased, as had the applause that had followed. Now all seemed quiet and guests began departing.

"I'm parked in Pasadena," I said. I was out of ideas for meeting spots. "Why don't you drive over here and we can talk."

He hesitated a second or two, but then agreed and asked for the street address. He said he could be there in less than twenty minutes. It was as good a spot as anyplace for me. I was homeless. I couldn't keep bringing folks over to Wesley's little house. We both needed our space, and Wes had given up too much of his privacy out of friendship for me. I felt horrible about putting him out. If it meant I would take up working out of the trunk of a rental car, so be it.

By the time I had disconnected with Brett Hurley, Zenya was coming back out through the gate, accompanied by her twelve-year-old son, Kirby. He was a sturdy-looking boy who had not yet hit his growth phase, still about six inches shorter than his mom. Kirby's cargo shorts were damp from his lark in the Jacuzzi, and he carried a large instrument case, his gait awkward as he swung the heavy case across the front lawn.

I stepped out of my SUV and called Zenya's name. She shaded her eyes in the afternoon sunlight and saw me.

"Madeline? Hi! I was looking for you inside. Connie told me you left already. And Kirby just told me Dex was here, too. I'm sorry I missed him." She walked across the grass and joined me on the wide sidewalk that edged the huge homes in this leafy neighborhood. Kirby trudged behind.

"Zenya. I wonder if I could talk to you for a minute."

"Sure. Of course." She turned to her son and gave him permission to go back into the party. She said to leave his saxophone case with her. Kirby looked put out in that way teens have when their parents continue to make boneheaded decisions that end up ruining a kid's perfectly good life. But he was happy enough to go back and join his friends. Other parents were arriving and departing with their boys as Zenya turned back to me.

"What's up?"

"I wanted to talk to you about your brother."

"Dex?" She looked so happy. "You two falling in love?"

When I didn't light up in that expected girlfriend way, she quickly apologized. "Oh, wow. Did I say the wrong thing? Madeline, I was just kidding. I'm sorry."

"Dex is a great guy," I said carefully. "It's me. I'm having 'issues.' " Then I laughed at myself, so absurd was this conversation.

"What sort of issues?" Zenya asked, concerned.

"Trust, mainly. I was recently involved with a man I thought I could trust. But then it turned out I couldn't. Or I shouldn't have. Anyway, I'm just telling you this so you understand. I need a lot of real, pure, uncomplicated honesty right now."

"And Dex isn't someone you can rely on for that," she finished, thinking about it.

"There have been a lot of very strange things going on in my life," I explained, trying not to sound like a witch who was condemning this woman's brother's integrity to her face. But of course, that was exactly what I was doing.

"I know. The girl who was killed at your house. I have been worried about that."

"You have?"

"I want Dexter to find someone to care about, Maddie. He needs the right sort of woman to set his life back on track. He's been lost, I think. For a long time, really. And I was so happy to hear he liked you. I thought the two of you could be so good together. But when I heard about what happened the other night at your house, that girl who worked for you, I began to think again. Maybe Dex needs someone who is a little less . . ."

So it goes. Here was me, worried that Dex was less than reputable. Here was Zenya, worried the same thing about me. There was Dex, scared his sister had done something horrible. Go figure.

"I had nothing to do with that poor girl," I said, "except that she did work for me. And she had borrowed my car and was returning it. The police haven't discovered why she died. But I am trying to find out myself."

"What can you do?"

"I don't know, Zenya. But I am worried about Dex, too. I can't help but think he might be mixed up in some funny things."

"Dex? Oh, no."

"Okay. Here I go." I took a breath and rushed on with it all. "You mentioned there had been an art theft at your house."

She looked up at me, a hardness settling in around her hazel eyes. "What are you talking about?"

"I'm worried Dex was involved in it in some way." At last, I'd spoken the truth out loud to another person. I had heard Dexter's story. Now I had to know Zenya's. "Look, I'm sure you don't want to dredge that mess back up, but I have this very bad feeling. After all, Dex was taking care of your house at the time. I keep asking myself, Why wasn't there an alarm? Why didn't it go off?"

"Oh, Madeline. You have to believe me. None of that was Dex's fault at all."

"I need to be reassured here, Zenya. Please tell me about it."

"It was a combination of things that just got fouled up. The alarm had been acting up a lot. For a month, it just kept triggering by itself and we'd had several false alarms. The police hate that, of course. They had sent us a warning notice saying they wouldn't respond to our address any longer if we didn't take care of our false-alarm problem. One more and we'd be shut off.

"Bill tried to troubleshoot it, but the alarm company did nothing to help. We couldn't risk another crossed wire setting the alarm off. That's why Bill insisted we have Dex stay at the house."

"I see."

"We were leaving for Maui, but Bill wasn't comfortable relying on that faulty alarm system. We told Dex not to even set it, in case another rash of false alarms were to occur. Listening to this now with hindsight, knowing we had a theft, the whole thing seems stupid, I know. But we told all this to the police at the time and they checked the records of those past false alarms with the Westec people, and they checked our notice from the local police station warning us against any further false alarms—"

"Oh."

"Maddie." She looked hurt. "How can you be suspicious of Dexter? Why are you digging up all this garbage?"

"I think it was the down payment for his house. Dex told me."

Zenya looked exasperated. "What's wrong with that? He would never have settled down. I was helping him."

I shook my head. "But what if Dexter arranged to have those etchings stolen. He loves you, Zenya. What if he was doing it for you? When the insurance money came, you might have given him a little gift back."

"Maddie, what's going on here? This doesn't sound like you at all. Is it all the stress about that young lady who died? I can understand how her death must have upset you."

I shook my head, yet wondered if she was right.

"You have no need to worry about this," Zenya said, her soft voice back to its normal reassuring tone. "We lost our art. We can't get it back. And that's what insurance is for. As for the money we received from the insurance company, we could have sold our art pieces and received the same amount of money or more! There was just no reason for any of us, including Dex, to steal anything."

I couldn't think of an answer to that. How freaking obsessed must I have sounded? I simply said, "I'm beginning to fall for Dex, Zenya."

She finally smiled. "Look, I love my brother. And I think he has very strong feelings for you. I know I'm the last person on earth to give romantic advice, but if this thing is going to work out between the two of you, you can't let yourself get so worked up over things that are ancient history. Dex isn't squeaky-clean. I'm sure he has enough things in his glorious past to concern any new girlfriend. *But our etchings?* Come on now." She smiled again. "There is nothing there. Leave it alone. That's my advice."

I probably should have. But I had one more question. "Connie Hutson told me her husband never really wanted to bid on the Selmer sax at the Woodburn auction. She said Bill had arranged that little charade with Dave in advance. Were you aware of that?"

"That's not possible." Zenya, always the most agreeable person on any committee, flushed. I don't think she'd ever raised her voice in her life, but she looked like she was getting closer to it every second. I had the most amazing effect on people. "Maddie, what on earth is going on with you?"

"With me? I am asking myself every day what's going on with your family. I want to believe you. I want to believe Dex. But there is too much here that doesn't make sense."

"Well, good luck to you, then," she said, in a tone that

could only be described as curt. Maybe this was the first time she'd been pushed to it, but she did "curt" pretty damn well for a beginner. "I hope you make it all work out, no matter what other people might get hurt."

"I can't help that," I said softly.

Zenya, her lovely golden hair pulled back in a clip, folded her arms under her chest and looked at me with disappointment. "I had a different impression of you, Maddie. You, with your super career and your great sense of style and your friends. You seemed to have everything. You're so independent. So strong. So in control. Bill always warns me not to meddle in matchmaking, but even he saw how cool it could be to get you and Dex together. He's the one who suggested I send Dex out to find you last Saturday night."

"You're kidding."

"Please don't be mad at us because we tried to set the two of you up. I thought you could be good for Dex the way Bill is good for me. Sure, Bill kind of runs things in our household, but you know what? There needs to be a leader and a follower. And what's wrong with that?"

"I'm sorry," I said. "I don't agree. I think both people have to do both those things for a real relationship to work."

"Maybe you should leave things alone, Maddie. All those questions you feel you need answers to. Will any of this make a difference? Really?"

"It's a question of trust, Zenya."

"Yes. I get it. But in love, doesn't trust always call on us to make a leap of faith?"

Kirby appeared again, rejoining us at the sidewalk under the huge California live-oak trees, having grabbed another slice of birthday cake. Despite the crumbs on the corner of his mouth, you could tell by his expression he was so ready to leave now.

"Sorry, I've got to go," Zenya said, smiling at me tentatively. "I want us to be friends, Madeline. Dexter means that much to me. I hope you can find it in your heart to give him a chance."

Kirby picked up his heavy sax case and walked across the street to his mom's car. As he was loading it into the backseat of the Range Rover, I noticed a young man was standing a few feet away from me on the sidewalk. Probably one of the departing party guests.

I was suddenly overwhelmed by what Zenya had said. Was it ever possible to get enough proof that a man was trustworthy? Had my past relationship problems pushed me so far I had begun terrorizing admirers, looking for skeletons in every closet like a crazy woman?

"Are you Madeline?" He said it like Mad-a-lin.

It was Brett Hurley. I turned and looked at him more carefully. He was so thin and pale he was either seriously ill or in a rock band. His long black hair was swept straight back and he wore a pointy little beard.

"I'm so sorry about what happened to Sara," I said, feeling awkward. "Say, do you want to sit in my car?"

"That's okay. Let's walk."

It was a beautiful late afternoon. We started off down the pavement, under a bower of shady trees, walking side by side.

"The police detective told me you were looking for me," Hurley said.

"It's true. I was so upset about everything."

Hurley kept his head down, not reacting at all.

"I must admit . . ." I looked over at him. "I hardly knew Sara. She had worked several of the large parties over about six months' time. I wish I had known her better."

"She wasn't easy to get to know. Don't feel bad."

Was it my imagination, or was this guy not too broken up about the death of his girlfriend? "Well, Sara had been trying to get home to you that night and I thought the two of you were close. I worried that you might need some help. That's all."

"What are you talking about?" Brett Hurley stopped at the corner and looked confused.

"That last night after the Woodburn ball. Sara was very upset. She said she had to get back to you. You were on her mind. I thought you would want to know that."

"*I* was on her mind?" he asked, surprised.

"Yes. Didn't you have some disappointing news that day? Something about your dissertation, she said."

"Look, I didn't tell this to the cops, for obvious reasons, but Sara wasn't all she appeared to be. She looked sweet, but looks can fool ya."

"What do you mean?"

"Sara had a lot of schemes going on. She was always working an angle. She didn't look like it, but she was a real operator. Like how she put herself through school. She hooked. Did you know that?"

I shook my head, feigning surprise. Well, I hadn't had a clue before I did a little checking around after her death.

"I'm sorry to tell you this," Brett said, rubbing his little goatee, "but the reason she worked for you was to line up dates. She was sort of freelance. She wasn't a streetwalker, you know? But if a guy had money, she was willing."

"And you knew about this?"

He nodded. "I told her she was crazy to do it. It wasn't safe. And she just laughed at me and asked if I knew of a better way to lay my hands on five hundred dollars for an hour's work."

Certainly more than the two hundred a night I paid my waitstaff, I mused. How was it I had no idea this sort of thing was going on at my own events? Damn it. Wes and I needed to review our files of temp workers and figure out if we had any other parasites.

"So do you think that's why she wanted my Jeep? To hook up with some guy from the Woodburn party?"

"I don't think so," he said, and began walking again, turning the corner and starting up the block.

"Then why?"

"Look, I'll deny any of this. So don't think you can tell anyone, right?"

I nodded, shocked.

"Sara was running a scam. I'm sure of it. She had found out some rich old geezer was a con man and she figured he'd pay her some money to keep the information from the police."

"Wait. You think Sara was blackmailing some man at the Woodburn?"

"Yeah. She wouldn't tell me about it. But I knew."

"Who?"

"She wouldn't tell me who it was, but the guy was loaded, she said. She was going to meet him after the party that night, that's all I know. Maybe when her car broke down, she thought she'd blow her meeting. So she put on some sad story about having to get home quick to me. She was a great little actress. You know that was her major—theater arts?"

"No, I didn't."

Brett Hurley grunted.

It was taking a moment for me to get my head around this news. "So you're saying Sara wasn't in a rush to get home to you?"

"Sara? Worried to death about me? Like that isn't a laugh. She and I were not doing all that well. I'd tried to leave her a few times, but with Sara, she'd show up at my house and have all this money on her and . . . Hey, I'm an artist. I'm broke. She knew how to reach me. I kept breaking it off with her, but it wasn't sticking. She said she'd have a really big score that night. She told me to wait up."

"You didn't tell the police all this?"

"Are you crazy? That my nasty hooker ex-girlfriend was shaking down some fat cat at the Woodburn ball? Get real. But that's why, when I heard what happened that night, I wasn't so shocked that she wound up dead. I mean, she was kind of asking for it. She didn't think of the consequences. I told her, but she never listened."

"Don't you want to see some justice for Sara?" I couldn't believe he would let the scum who had killed his girlfriend get away with it.

"Justice is funny," he said, looking over at me as we walked together around the block. "It's not black and white, like your fancy ball. Maybe Sara was just one of those girls who was going down the wrong side of the street. Sooner or later she was going to get creamed, know what I mean?"

I shook my head. No one should be written off. I didn't care if this woman was a scam artist or a prostitute or whatever. "No one had a right to take her life."

"So that's your opinion. I don't feel like getting into the middle of this mess, okay? What if the guy who got to Sara decides to come after me?"

"Right." I couldn't believe this guy. "But in the meantime, other people might be in danger."

We had come around a full block. Party guests were still leaving the Hutsons' house, pulling out of parking spaces along the street.

"Like I said, everyone has to look out for himself, Madeline. When this detective told me you were poking around, looking for me, I figured you were maybe getting yourself in over your head. You don't want to go near Sara's trouble, miss. You just don't."

"I'll think that over," I said, trying to sound less judgmental than I felt. "But can't you tell me anything about who Sara was trying to blackmail?"

"Nope. Don't know and don't want to know. But I can tell you this. She said a guy worth twenty million dollars should be willing to pay big."

"Twenty million?" I turned my head and focused on Brett Hurley.

"Yeah. And I think she came onto his scam when I told her some old stories about the time I worked part-time for the County Art Museum."

"What did you say?"

"I was a clerk there three years ago, just part-time while I went to school. You know, low-level typing and filing."

"Did you work with their donated collections and special exhibitions?"

"Say, how did you know that?"

"It's a Sin to Tell a Lie"

Twenty million dollars had a tragically familiar sound to it. Just when I was working myself up to giving the whole Knight/Wyatt clan a break, the news just kept getting weirder.

"Baronowski here." I had dialed the detective as I drove across town.

"Did you ever find out who left that semen stain on the backseat of my old Jeep?"

"Not yet. We're DNA testing the boyfriend."

"You might want to widen your search to anyone with five hundred dollars handy."

"Yeah, we followed the lead at her apartment complex with that guy, Creski. Maybe Sara was doing a little part-time hooking. If so, and if she picked up a john last Saturday night, we may finally get a handle on this case. Problem is, we have no witnesses yet that saw Sara in that car that night, alone or with a man. But we might get lucky."

"What did her boyfriend tell you?"

"Hurley? Nothing. Pain in the ass. He's an artist with a capital *A*. Maybe a druggie. He's the type who hates anyone in authority, so naturally we got along great. Still, he seemed pretty harmless, the little twerp. We fingerprinted the guy, by the way, and we didn't match him to any prints found at your house, in case you're wondering."

"Good."

"I gave him your number, like you asked, and figured he'd be hitting you up for money."

"Men," I lamented gently.

"We're adorable. Call me if you learn anything meaningful, Ms. Bean."

Next I dialed Holly.

"Say, don't you have a friend who works at the L.A. County Museum of Art?"

"Megan Grossbard?"

"Right. Doesn't she work in the costume department?"

"Yep."

"Think she knows anyone in security over there? In the area of art fraud?" I gave Holly a quick rundown of what I had learned.

She promised to track down Megan and then called back five minutes later. We could meet Megan at the museum in an hour. The museum didn't close to the public until eight on Saturday night, and Megan and her friend were both going to come in and talk to us.

I called for messages and found one from Honnett. He stressed how important it was for me to phone him back immediately.

"Honnett. It's me, Mad."

"Where are you?" he asked.

"I'm driving home from my gig in Pasadena. And I'm cutting across town to stop and meet Holly first. What's up?"

"I've got to see you."

"Can you tell me on the phone?"

"No. Where are you meeting Holly?"

"LACMA. I'll be there a little early. Look for me outside, in front of the main entrance."

"Right. I'll be there in ten minutes."

All this urgency. What couldn't he tell me over the phone?

The main buildings at LACMA are located in the Miracle Mile area of the city between Fairfax and La Brea, on Wilshire Boulevard. I had made good time, so I drove around the block searching for the ever-elusive street parking. After all, it was nearly five in the afternoon. But it was Saturday and it was Los Angeles and who was I kidding? I paid the steep rate and pulled into the parking lot, and then waited forever while an Astrovan loaded with kids finally pulled out of a spot.

Honnett was already there, waiting, when I walked up to the entrance of the museum.

"Can we sit somewhere?" he asked me.

"What's the matter? You seem nervous."

"Let me buy you a Diet Coke," he offered, avoiding my comment.

I didn't want to sit, so I ended up steering him past the Plaza Café near the courtyard. I checked my watch and warned him I'd have to meet Holly in thirty minutes.

"No problem. I can say this in ten."

"Come with me," I said, and led him down to the art rental and sales gallery, located on the lower level of the Leo S. Bing Center.

"Go ahead and talk," I said, leading him through the exhibit rooms filled with artwork by contemporary young Angelino artists. This was not part of the official museum exhibition space. Each of these works was available for sale or rental. We walked among the paintings.

"I have some difficult things to tell you, Maddie. About this guy Wyatt you've been seeing."

I looked at him, caught off guard. Honnett had been a busy investigator. "So. You know his name."

"The guy hasn't been straight with you. I ran a check on him. And I've had a friend of mine, an ex-cop, do some digging around."

"You did *what*? I can't believe this! Do you realize how completely *jealous* you are behaving, Honnett?"

"I knew you'd react like this. Just hear me out."

I glared at him and he stopped. Okay. I probably deserved some of this. It's true. I had felt some satisfaction over Honnett's jealousy for a little while there. I knew it was immature of me, of course. It is unforgivable that I felt any empowerment from the pain of another, even if that person had hurt me really bad first. How could I? And now here was that jealousy, running amok, ultimately causing us all more pain. Honnett had come to see me this afternoon to share some horrible news about Dexter. How fitting was this retribution. Fate really had that irony thing down.

Honnett saw my face.

"Never mind," he said. "If you don't want to hear it, I'm not going to go on. I can see this was a mistake. I apologize."

So here it was. I was being offered the information I had really wanted all along: evidence that would prove if I should dare to trust Dexter Wyatt. And here was Honnett, the least impartial investigator on the planet, offering it up.

"Tell me what you know," I said, weariness setting in my throat. "Just don't make this about you and me, Honnett. Please. If you have something, I'll listen. But first know this. I really care about Dexter Wyatt. I like him. I am hoping to have a relationship with him. And even if you found out something completely sickening, like he was a criminal in the past, I'm not sure it would matter to me."

Honnett met my eyes, looking like I'd kicked him, which I guess I had. He didn't know what to say.

"So, there it is," I said, a little more gently. "Knowing how I feel about Dexter, do you still want to tell me what you found?"

"Can I help you?" A tall, thin Asian-American woman materialized out of nowhere. "Have you chosen that one?"

She referred to a small abstract acrylic painting nearby, a challenging piece with thick blue streaks and black.

"How much to rent it?" I asked, not having noticed it before.

"Only twenty-seven dollars every two months. Very reasonable. And the rental payments go toward purchase."

"The artist gets seventy-five percent of the money," I told Honnett, who couldn't have cared less about art.

"I'll take it," Honnett told the woman, and handed her his credit card. She praised his great aesthetic taste and hurried off to ring up the rental and work on the rental-agreement papers. He would have to become a member of the museum, she informed him as she glided off. But she would take care to include that amount in his total.

"You didn't have to do that," I said, surprised at him.

"I do what I want, Maddie. Don't worry about me."

"So tell me what you found out about Dex," I said, calmer now. "What can it be? Fraud? Theft? What?"

His eyes told me what he thought about any man about whom I could so casually ask such extraordinary questions. "No, he doesn't have that kind of record. A drunk-and-disorderly. A bar fight back when he was younger. But it's his personal life that worries me."

"Because . . . ?"

"This guy used to date Sara Jackson, Maddie."

The art on the walls swam and then settled down.

"Here's your painting, Mr. Honnett," the salesclerk said cheerfully, bringing a large bag over along with Honnett's charge slip and the rental agreement. He signed them all and took his copies. As she explained again how the art rental program worked, I thought about this shocking new development. Could it be possible? Had Dexter known Sara? And why hadn't he mentioned that fact to me after all this time?

The clerk smiled at the two of us and left.

"How do you know this, Honnett?"

"One of Wyatt's friends told my pal. And then there is Sara Jackson's cell-phone log. She had called Wyatt earlier on the night she died."

"My God, Honnett. Is Dex a suspect in the murder?"

"You know the department doesn't announce their suspects. But off the record, I can tell you he's being looked at. Among others, so that's something."

I hadn't thought I could feel anything like friendship for Honnett, so wrapped in anger had I been over the past few months, but when I heard him try to make the news about Dex sound a little less threatening, I began to unravel some.

"You'll be okay, Maddie. I just wanted you to have all the facts. If that means you have to go on hating me, I know I deserve it."

"I can't hate you."

"So what do you think of it?" Honnett asked, pulling the small painting out for me to view once again.

"At least it's not *Dog Living in Luxury with Cigar,* I said and then, suddenly, I remembered something from the inventory of Grasso's paperwork.

"I'm late," I said, with a start. "I've got to meet Holly and her friend."

Honnett looked up at me as I rushed off to find the elevators.

"Three years ago, Bill and Zenya Knight lent some of their etchings to the museum for a temporary show. Would there be any paperwork on it?"

"Of course." The young woman sitting before us was tapping on the keyboard of her computer. "Only three years ago, it should be here."

Holly's friend Megan had introduced us to Divinia Denove, one of the museum's investigators. Both Megan and Divinia had come in on their day off to answer our questions.

"I should have realized it when Caroline Rochette fell into the pool," I told Holly quietly so as not to disturb Divinia, who was searching her computer files.

"Why?" Holly whispered.

"She said something about getting insurance."

"I wasn't there," Holly reminded me. "What exactly did she say?"

I thought back to that day in Wesley's backyard. "She said she must get insurance."

"Like accident insurance?"

"I thought she was making a joke. It didn't make a lot of sense at the time, but then the woman had just tripped into the pool, for heaven's sake, wearing at least sixty dollars' worth of makeup. But now I think she must have meant something else entirely. I think she had come there that day to get her hands on some insurance paperwork that was among that junk from Albert Grasso. There were policies there from Mid-Pacific Insurance and North American Home Insurance."

"Here it is," Divinia said. She had found the file she had been searching for. "We had an exhibit a little over three years ago. 'Black and White: The Genius of the Etchings of the Sixteenth and Seventh Centuries.' The Knights lent us thirteen works." She read over the file, clicking through multiple pages. "It looks fairly routine. Was there a problem?"

I was sitting with Holly and Megan in chairs in front of Divinia's desk.

"They were insured?"

"Of course. We have a blanket policy that covers all the art in the museum. But according to our notes, these pieces were undamaged and returned to the Knights," she said. She scrolled down the screen and looked back at us. "The museum's receipt was scanned into the file. The date of delivery to an address in Beverly Hills is marked and Mr. Knight himself signed upon receiving the works back in good condition."

"Do your records list the appraisal value of the etchings?"

"Well, it's not really our appraisal," Divinia said, smiling. "It's sort of a formality. When the owners fill out the paperwork, they mark down what value they want placed on the works."

That sounded odd.

Divinia noticed my expression. "It's never been taken advantage of. But, as I said, the museum carries insurance against all the artwork we own or borrow. In the case of works on loan, the actual dollar amount is filled in for each individual piece by the lending party. We pay extraordinary insurance premiums, as you might imagine, so we have taken pains to make sure no owner feels their work is undervalued."

"Oh, I just had an amazing idea," I said, wheels turning ever so quickly now. "Would you mind taking a look at the values placed on the Knight etchings?"

"Well," she said, "it is pretty typical for our patrons to undervalue their artworks a little. Most aren't up on the current market value since the pieces were often acquired so long ago. Then we have others who fudge a little on the upside. Let's see." She read through several electronic documents. "Wait now. This is strange."

We looked at her.

"One etching from the Knight collection is a true masterpiece. A Dürer of exceptional quality. Nothing like it has been at auction in years. Who can say what its value might be today? Maybe three million. Maybe six. On this form, Mr. Knight listed it at ten million."

"Wow." Holly looked impressed.

"The Dürer is an extraordinary piece, and in the art world, one can never tell what a truly great work might bring," Divinia said. "So that valuation, in and of itself, is not terribly out of line. But here's the amazing thing. Look at the other etchings in their collection! The other twelve pieces were nowhere near that value. There's a Madonna listed by Raffaello Schiaminossi and Luca Ciamberlano. It is valued by the Knights at five million."

"And its real value?"

"About five hundred."

We stared at Divinia.

"Only five hundred thousand? That's one tenth what they claimed."

"Actually, Madeline, this Schiaminossi is only worth about five hundred *dollars*."

"And they claimed it was worth ten thousand times more?" Holly asked. "Holy schnitzel."

"I can see that the five-million-dollar value they claimed was absurd." Holly's friend Megan spoke up for the first time. "But what harm could it do?"

"I have an idea about that," I told Megan. "And the other works?" I asked Divinia. "The same overinflation of value?" I finally figured out what had happened.

"Yes," Divinia said, laughing. "It's much the same. The greatest real value is two thousand dollars, but all of them are self-appraised in the millions. What does this mean, Madeline?"

"These forms the owner fills out, do they get signed by an official here at the museum?"

"Of course. Several of our people, from the show's curator to the director of the exhibition, in fact. We must be very careful with the artwork that is lent to us."

"And then the forms are used as riders to the museum's own insurance policy?"

"Exactly. But no claim was ever made to our insurer, so what can this mean?"

"I think that Bill Knight had a much cleverer scheme. He used those official documents, the riders from LACMA's insurance carrier with their insanely inflated valuations, to scam his own insurance company. Your paperwork established the worth of his collection, complete with a prestigious museum's curator's signature on the bottom. Knight must have gone out and increased his own art-insurance coverage with his private insurance company to these massively inflated prices after the LACMA show."

"I suppose that's possible. Although I would think any insurance underwriter would look a little closer at something like that."

"I'm not sure about that," I said. "They aren't art experts themselves. They rely on documentation. And the L.A. County Museum of Art documents clearly substantiate these numbers."

She nodded. "And as long as the customer is willing to pay the high premiums, I can see why an insurance salesman would be happy for the business."

I nodded.

"Incredible," Megan said.

"This is fascinating speculation, ladies," Divinia said. "And if it were actually true, it's insurance fraud."

"With the museum as an unwitting collaborator," I pointed out.

"So what do you know?" she asked me, looking worried.

"Three of those art etchings were stolen from the house in Beverly Hills about three years ago, the Dürer and two others. Mr. Knight collected twenty million dollars from his own insurance carriers for their loss. If the Dürer was really worth three million and the other two were only worth a few thousand, I'm beginning to believe he scammed his insurance company out of nearly seventeen million, thanks to some clever paperwork."

And that's why Bill Knight couldn't just sell the etchings to get all the money, as Zenya had suggested. Those pieces were worth seven times more to him vanished than they'd ever be on some gallery wall for sale.

"Come on-a My House"

Sunday morning. Wesley went out to hang with an old college buddy who was down from Palo Alto for the weekend, but not before fretting for an hour over leaving me alone. He urged me to join them, but all I wanted was a little private time, and I was grateful, finally, that he understood and didn't cancel his plans because of me.

I did all the normal things I had been meaning to get to. I went back to bed and grabbed a few more hours of missed sleep. I did laundry. I had fun in the kitchen. From Wesley's well-stocked pantry, I mixed together rolled oats, peanuts, and sunflower seeds, sweetened the mix with plenty of brown sugar, and then enriched the flavor with natural vanilla, tasting and adjusting until I got the blend just right. My eyes roved Wesley's counters and cabinets until I had that "aha!" moment, and chuckled. A few seconds of grinding and soon chopped espresso beans joined the party. Voilà! I'm calling it cappuccino granola. A batch of this private blend was now displayed in a pretty stoppered jar, waiting as a treat for Wes.

I poured milk over a small bowl of cappuccino granola, and stood at the counter reading the Target ads in the Sunday *Los Angeles Times.* It was criminal to have back-to-school sales in July. I checked the book-review section, hoping to find a review written by Dick Lochte. I flipped through the car ads. Would I look good in a Porsche Boxter? I read the real estate listings, wondering if I was in the market for a new house or if I would be able to salvage my wonderful Mediterranean on Whitley. As a potential seller, it rocked to see the real estate market was way up. As a potential buyer, it sucked.

I thought about visiting a few open houses. Wes would love to go with me, but I expected his day with the Stanford buddy would stretch out. I reviewed the hundreds of listings, spanning so many neighborhoods. The euphemisms used to describe any house I might barely be able to afford were heavy with double meanings. *Loads of potential* (tear down). *Maintenance-free backyard* (there was none). I sighed over descriptions of wondrous homes that were way beyond my reach. And then a house listed for almost five million dollars caught my eye. Not simply because the house was located just blocks away from Dexter's, although the proximity did cross my mind.

I reread the no-euphemism-necessary description. *Magnificent Italian-style villa by Bob Ray Offenhauser on a prestigious cul-de-sac in Bel Air. Gated motor courtyard. 2-story entry, large open rooms with high ceilings. Screening room and gym. Magical gardens, sun-drenched pool with indoor/outdoor flow. Ideal for lavish or intimate entertaining. Very private.* Well, that privacy angle certainly had a new appeal.

This was so out of my league, it wasn't even funny, and certainly not the sort of property I was looking for, but I was extremely interested in talking with the broker. The house was a Caroline Rochette listing. Albert Grasso's ladyfriend. She would be sitting in the house all afternoon waiting for potential buyers, like a spider ready to spring on some tasty flies. However, she was now also a ridiculously easy target for me to trap. I wondered how a natural predator such as Caroline would react to finding the tables turned. I showered, daydreaming about past episodes of *Wild Kingdom,* and then dressed, deciding to wear boots in case any metaphorical bug stomping might become necessary.

Outside, I looked at the clear, cloudless sky. It was another hot and sunny day, which does a lot to perk many of us locals up. In case you are wondering why anyone is crazy enough to live in Southern California: the weather. Obvious as this is, it cannot be repeated too many times. It's addictive. And with a little extra rest and some time puttering in the kitchen, I was feeling pretty good again.

I jumped in the SUV and made use of one of the Trailblazer's zillion cup holders. Ah, the simple pleasures. Like the giddy freedom of driving a honking-big Chevy while swigging from a can of Diet Coke, combined with the virtuous certainty one is minimizing the chance of spillage. This was the life, I thought as I drove past the UCLA campus in Westwood and turned north into the Bel Air gates, eyeing real estate that is considered as good as it gets in Southern California.

The Trailblazer easily took me up Bel Air's winding, hilly streets. It was rare to find one of these high-end properties held open at all. It spoke of either desperate sellers or a broker who used every house on her list as bait to catch newbie buyers, most often to sell them some other property. As the road wound upward into the foothills of the Santa Monica Mountains, there were occasional roadside signs bearing balloons, markers that pointed the way to the open house ahead. I steered up to the 10500 block of Mocca Road and pulled into the cul-de-sac, admiring what five million bucks can buy you.

The doorbell played a classical melody. Charming. While

waiting, I tried the elaborate brass handles on the double front doors. They were, of course, locked. In a few minutes, one of the heavy doors swung open and Caroline Rochette, appearing much drier than the last time I'd seen her, greeted me, her blond bob sprayed stiff, her pointy chin well powdered, her welcoming expression instantly falling.

"You!"

"Nice 'gated motor courtyard,' " I said, quoting from her house ad as I walked past her into the "2-story formal entry."

"Are you looking for a house?" Caroline was thrown. Should she have on the *salesman* face? Or the *bitch.*

I smiled. "I might be. But I'm actually here to talk to you."

She looked unhappy. "Well, sign in."

I realized she meant for me to sign the guest register displayed on the large entry table in the center of the rounded foyer. No matter that I was bringing all sorts of unpleasant memories to Caroline Rochette's doorstep, she would make sure to show her homeowner clients that she had at least one interested buyer come through the house today. My name was the only one on the register.

"What do you want?" she asked, uncertain.

"Would you show me around the property?" I smiled at her again.

"Oh, all right. Come this way. We'll start with the kitchen. It's in the east wing."

Caroline's sling-back high heels clicked on the limestone floor as she led the way.

She went into her spiel, but didn't give it any oomph. "Wolf restaurant range, Sub-Zero refrigerators, Miele dishwashers, Grohe . . . faucets, custom-built cabinets in maple, granite countertops." Caroline stopped when she reached the far end of the enormous gourmet kitchen.

"Navaho white," I added.

"What's that?"

"This is the lightest-color granite commercially available." The stone used for the counters was a pointillist mix of small white, gray, and black flecks.

"Really?"

"Sure, the white mineral grains are feldspar. It's the most abundant mineral found in granite. The light gray, glasslike grains are quartz, and the black, flakelike grains are biotite or black mica."

Caroline stared at me, trying to figure me out. I silently wished her luck.

"I know about kitchens," I explained. She was definitely not sure what to make of me.

"Did you come here to upset me about Albert?" she asked, point-blank. I had weirded her into submission. I have that talent.

"Upset? That's not the word I would have chosen, no."

"Look, dear, you and I have had our problems. But I want to clear the air, here. You found Albert's . . . body," she said, "and for that I must be grateful to you. Oh, dear Jesus in heaven! What if it had been me? I was coming over to Albert's house that very afternoon. What if I had let myself in with my key . . . and gone back to his studio . . ." She didn't finish that thought, but moved on. "So you saved me from that, anyway, Madeline. I could never have stood seeing that. I am so utterly and completely devastated by Albert's death, I cannot begin to describe it."

"I'm sorry for your loss," I said quietly. "But then I'm glad to see it hasn't interfered with your work."

She gave me an evil look.

"So," I continued, "you're carrying on." I noticed Caroline had the Capresso coffeemaker brewing and a plate of bakery cookies set out on a silver tray. She did not offer me any refreshments.

"Why are you really here?" she asked, vexed.

"You told me there was a problem with Mr. Grasso's insurance papers. How much did you know about it?"

She gasped.

I waited.

"I didn't tell you a thing!"

"Yes, you did. That afternoon when I helped scoop you out of the pool. Look, Caroline, Albert is gone now. Tell me what he was up to."

"I don't know. I really don't know."

"But it was the insurance papers he was frantic about. Wasn't it?"

"I think so. I mean, he was livid about having mislaid them. I told him not to worry. I would get them back. But, of course, I didn't. You prevented that. But then I told him you had no idea there was any reason to look closely at those documents. And even if you did, they wouldn't tell you much."

"There was a rider to his regular policy to cover his coin collection," I said, recalling what I could about the pages I'd skimmed through last week. I mean, who even reads their *own* insurance policy—let alone someone else's boring paperwork?

"He had overvalued the collection," she said. "That was all. I couldn't imagine that it was really the end of the world. He stated a far greater appraised value, and the insurer accepted some receipts as the true value."

"What kind of receipts?"

"Albert bought a little extra insurance for his coins when he traveled to London for a big coin show. For travel insurance, you just mark in the values and pay the premium. Because it's only in case his luggage was lost or stolen, the insurer doesn't care much about the actual value. Whatever you pay to cover is covered. Anyway, it turns out Al used that temporary insurance policy as documentation of value for his collection. Then he bought a new rider to his homeowner's policy for his coins using this inflated amount."

This scam was becoming familiar. "How do you know about it?"

"Al told me. He was screaming at me. He couldn't believe I had been so stupid as to take his private papers out of his house and, on top of that, to lose them."

"So what happened? Were his collectible coins stolen? Did he get paid off by the insurance company?"

"Oh my, no! He wasn't trying to do anything funny. He was just a proud old man. He liked to show people the 'value' of his coin collection. He liked people believing he was worth serious money. What's wrong with that? It was a quirk."

I could imagine Albert Grasso, living in that outdated house, needing to boost his ego by showing off his "worth" to his multimillionaire buddies. He could have told fellow Woodburn board member Bill Knight about his priceless coins. After all, Knight was a collector of precious objects, too. And perhaps they shared insurance concerns. Perhaps Albert even let Bill in on a few little secrets.

"Do you know who sold him the insurance?"

"Oh, of course. It was Al's half brother."

"It was?"

"Yes. He's some wealthy Oklahoma businessman who never understood what Al was doing out here in Hollywood, coaching singers. That was the reason Al embellished the coin collection's value in the first place. To show off to his brother, to impress him. Aren't men so predictable?"

My mind raced with this new knowledge.

"And Mr. Grasso's brother worked for Mid-Pacific Insurance? Or for North American?"

"He was a broker for both those companies, I believe. They both specialize in covering fine art and other treasures."

"I've got to go," I said, thinking a mile a minute. I turned abruptly and headed for the front door.

"Wait!" Caroline followed me through the large house, straining to catch up. "What is going on?"

I got to the door and turned on her. "Tell me the truth, Caroline. It could help both of us. Who was the man who suggested you buy Albert Grasso a new briefcase?"

"What?"

"There is no way to keep this a secret anymore. You've got someone on the side. He'd probably seen Albert pull those insurance papers out of his old briefcase—you said Grasso liked to show them off. This friend of yours said he'd help you shop for the new briefcase; just bring Albert's old one to the luggage store. A handy time for him to grab the documents he was after."

"But I was going to be there, too!"

"Your friend was counting on you to keep your mouth shut. Of course, what he hadn't counted on was your ability to drop the case and lose all the files before you made it across town."

"This is ridiculous."

"I think what's really ridiculous is why any woman would get herself mixed up with Bill Knight." I supposed when a financially needy woman's sole criterion for landing a fellow was that he have multiple millions, she pretty much had to accept whatever damaged goods presented himself.

Her blue eyes were glassy. Her voice was desperately low. "How do you know about Bill?"

"Secret Love"

Caroline Rochette's eyes widened in what could have been a horrified expression, that is, if her Botox injections had left her with any discernible facial expressions left to give. Instead, I received a blank, if wrinkle-free, stare as she groaned, "How could you know? Have you been following Bill and me?"

Ah! Freaking! Ha! So it *was* Bill Knight at the center of this scam, cheating on his wife, Zenya, cheating the insurance company, and trying to manipulate Caroline Rochette.

Caroline seemed ever more alarmed when I didn't respond. "Damn it to blazes. I need a cigarette." Her mouth twisted in anxiety, finding an expression at last, undoing all the smoothing that careful plastic surgery had done.

In this whole wacked-out scenario, Bill Knight was the only name that made sense. Sara Jackson's boyfriend had said she was blackmailing some rich guy. It had to have been Bill Knight.

Spending those days typing up the boring insurance valuations at LACMA three years back, an art student like Brett Hurley must have understood just how bizarrely high Knight had hiked up the values on his pieces—it was the sort of thing he might recall again years later and jeer at. While Hurley laughed at the deception, Sara probably saw its criminal potential. Clever Sara. She took an idle comment by her boyfriend and found a way to squeeze money out of it. But to find out if Bill Knight had cashed in on his lies, she had to do research. She would have needed to make sure there was a big illegal score, or what good was her hunch?

Honnett had told me that Dex had dated Sara. Maybe Sara made a play for Dexter, scouting for info. That's the way I wanted to think about it right now. Sara Jackson using Dex. If she put her knowledge of the inflated art prices together with stories she'd coaxed from Dexter about the theft and insurance score made by his brother-in-law, she knew that Knight had twenty million reasons to pay her to keep quiet.

Maybe that's what happened the evening of the Black & White Ball. Bill paid Sara. That could have happened right before we left the building. Then Sara found her car had stalled and begged Holly for a ride. It could explain why Bill Knight was really raging as he drove like a mad bombardier out on the streets of downtown—maybe he was letting off steam after paying blackmail money to Sara Jackson. That's a hell of a better reason to go nuts than freaking out over an old saxophone.

And with a large roll of cash in her bag, it also explained why Sara didn't want to stand around some parking garage waiting for AAA to come start her car. She made up the story about her boyfriend needing her, but her worry that night had seemed pretty genuine.

And maybe there was another stage to Sara's plan. If she double-crossed Bill Knight, she stood to make even more money. Insurance companies pay big rewards to informants.

But while I stood in the elegant foyer, unraveling this puzzle of art and fraud and blackmail, Caroline Rochette had major worries of her own. Among other things, her secret affair with Knight had now slipped out.

"I know you're close with Zenya," Caroline said, her body

language all squirmy, like a rat that had been cornered. Well, a petite rat wearing Manolo Blahniks, batting thick eyelashes that curled aggressively.

"Caroline, you're in trouble. Bill Knight was using you. You better look out or you're going down, too. So if you are thinking about calling and warning him—"

"I won't." Right. Like I believed her.

"Pay attention, Caroline. If things get ugly, you'll be losing a lot. Your friends. Your position at the Woodburn. Your job. You'll be lucky to get off with a humungous attorney's bill, a trillion hours of community service, and a record. And that means you lose your real estate license and folks who own houses like this one won't even let you wipe your shoes on their doormat."

She sobbed, but no tears fell from those heavily lashed blue eyes.

"The police are already on to Bill Knight, so be smart. You don't want them coming after you next."

"I didn't do anything," she wailed.

Divinia Denove had phoned the LAPD the previous night, as well as the insurance carriers who had paid off on the twenty-million-dollar claims. Even without evidence pinning the art heist on Knight, they had a clear case of insurance fraud since the etchings had been grossly overvalued.

"Clear the air here, Caroline. It's not just about the insurance anymore. It's about murder."

"Oh my God." Caroline looked ill. "This doesn't have to do with that girl who was killed in your house, does it?"

I felt like dipping Caroline into the swimming pool, one more time, just to jar her awake. "Sara was blackmailing Knight," I explained patiently. "She may have planned to double-cross him on top of that. Knight could have decided to end all his problems."

"I had nothing to do with any of this," she said, shifting into defensive overdrive.

"Here's some advice. Barter. If you know anything else about these crimes, you had better get yourself over to the police and tell them immediately. While it can still do you some good."

Caroline Rochette's eyes darted to the window, but there was not a looky-loo in sight; no one coming up the drive to look at the five-million-dollar home this sunny Sunday.

"Did you know," she whispered, "Sara Jackson had been taking voice lessons from Al?"

"What?"

"She had only been to the studio a few times. She paid cash. She wasn't on his books, so we didn't tell the police about it. Al didn't want us dragged into that murder at your place."

"Let me get this straight. Sara Jackson knew Albert Grasso?"

"She started coming to the house about two weeks before the Woodburn gala. I didn't like her. She was common."

"You mean she was coming on to him."

Caroline Rochette nodded.

"And he responded?"

Caroline made a face. "Men like young girls."

I had to think all of this through. Sara Jackson was using her body to get closer to Albert Grasso. Caroline Rochette was having an affair with Bill Knight. Who knew such things went on in my quiet little neighborhood?

What had Sara been up to with Albert Grasso? Perhaps she was tying up loose ends, digging around for more details behind the fraud, somehow connecting Grasso's insurance-selling brother into the mix, scouting out a couple more potential blackmail victims. She might have hinted about Grasso and his brother to Bill Knight, like she was getting more proof, so he better pay up.

I'd bet money that was what spooked Knight into sending Caroline after Grasso's briefcase, to remove those insurance documents. The papers would have given Sara the name of the insurance carriers, and Knight probably feared that a besotted Albert might admit to fudging with his coin-collection values if Sara pressed the right buttons.

Bill Knight's crime had gone so flawlessly for so long. He'd have no choice now but to plug up these disastrous leaks. When the scheme to grab Grasso's briefcase and papers began to unspool, Knight must have completely flipped out. Did that lust for self-preservation change the man? He'd been content to do a little diddling with paper numbers before, but had he now been pushed over the edge? Did Bill Knight kill both Sara and Grasso?

I looked back at Caroline, who by now had dropped several real tears over her predicament. Her heavy mascara had left two smoky tracks down either side of her tight little face, and one eyelash was coming loose at the corner of her eye. I reached for the doorknob.

"Please! *Please!* DON'T LEAVE YET!" she yelled after me, desperate, as I opened the massive front doors, only to find an elderly African-American man with a thin young blonde standing on the front step.

"Very devoted realtor," I said to them as I walked swiftly down the drive.

Outside the house, I turned on my cell phone to make a quick call to Detective Baronowski. I told him what I had learned and was reassured to hear that all the wheels had been turning properly. They were working on Bill Knight's arrest warrant and would soon have the man in custody on suspicion of insurance fraud.

I disconnected, and then instantly received an incoming call. From the number displayed on my cell phone, the caller was Dex. My heart skipped in a completely annoying manner.

"Dexter?"

"Madeline. Where are you?"

"I'm running around solving shit. It's exhausting—you've got to believe me. I am trying *very hard* to find a way to trust you, Dexter."

"I know, honey. You're like making this your life's work."

"I'm dogged. And I'm right in your neighborhood."

"Come over."

And in five minutes I was at his house.

He wanted to kiss me. I wanted to talk. This pretty much sums up my view of male/female needs.

"What's up?" he asked, his arms around my waist.

"Here's the thing. I need to hear about you and an old girlfriend of yours."

"Now?"

"Yes. Tell me about Sara Jackson."

He turned so I couldn't see his face. He didn't answer.

"Dex?"

He turned back and took my hand. "You know about me. You know I've had a lousy track record with women. I'm not a model of virtue. But, Madeline, do we have to go *there*?"

"Where?"

He smiled. "To a place where you drag up every horrible mistake I've ever made with a woman and throw it at me? Because I just want to say, if we're going *there*—we will be there awhile."

"Dexter." I looked deeply into his eyes, seeing only affection and some chagrin amid the mysterious multicolor of his shade of hazel. I could detect no trace of deception. I sighed. It was official. I couldn't read this man at all. "Dexter, you don't have to tell me about any other woman from your past, ever. But I have to know about Sara."

He looked at me. "You can't leave this one alone?"

"Dex, it's things like this here that break down the trust. You know?"

"I know," he said.

"Why didn't you tell me you had been dating the girl who was killed at my house?"

"At first, I didn't know. Really. That first night I drove you home, no one ever mentioned who was dead there. You never said her name. The next day, when I watched the news, I pretty much freaked out. Sara had been a psycho, but no one deserves what happened to her. I was stunned that this girl I used to know could have died at your house. Then I took Holly out to lunch, remember? Holly told me that Sara worked for your company. One of those insane coincidences. What are the chances of that? I started thinking this city *really* isn't big enough. When the girls with whom I've had flings start working for the ones I'm just getting to know, I may have used up a town. That sort of thing."

"And then . . . ?"

"And then you and I were having such a rocky time of it, Madeline. The more I wanted you the more I could tell you were scared of me. So when was the right time to tell you I had spent a lousy month going to bed with a chick that I ended up finding out was a *hooker,* for Christ's sake, and one who was no doubt using me? If I told you that, how likely was it that you would have jumped into my arms?"

If he was lying to me, he was just too good. "Using you?" Did Dex know that Sara was blackmailing his brother-in-law? "In what way?"

"That girl liked to smoke dope."

"Dexter Wyatt, do you sell drugs?"

"No! No. But she thought I was rich or something and that I'd have druggie pals . . ."

So this was the answer. Dexter Wyatt was afraid to tell me he had once slept with the dead hooker in my bedroom because he thought I'd be bugged to learn my new boyfriend hung out with prostitutes and potheads.

And you know what, he was right.

"So we're over now?" Dex asked, his voice low.

"I'm not sure how we ever got started," I said, rubbing the sting out of my eyes.

"Aw, Madeline." He looked so sad. "But tell me this at least. Do you trust me, sweetie? Do you know I'm telling you the truth?"

"I think I do."

"But it doesn't help much, does it?"

"The idea of dating a bad boy had a lot of appeal . . ." A tear escaped, damn it.

"But the reality bites," Dex finished for me, and, putting a gentle arm around me, added, "I know."

"Consequences"

What the hell are we doing here?" I whispered to Wesley as he let me into the kitchen entrance at Zenya and Bill Knight's luxurious home in Beverly Hills on Monday morning. All the previous day and night, I had expected to get a late call canceling today's flower luncheon. After all, hadn't Zenya's husband been arrested? Wouldn't she call off this gathering of Woodburn ladies on a morning like this? "Is it still on?"

"Apparently." Wes shrugged, looking mystified. "Zenya just left to take the little girl to a friend's house for the day. The boy, Kirby, is around. And the husband . . ."

I stared at Wes, not believing this.

"He's in his study," Wes finished, keeping his voice low.

"Oh my God, Wes." It wasn't every day I turned a guy in to the police while I puttered around in his kitchen and threw a party for his wife. I was on the edge of freaking.

Meanwhile, Wes filled me in on where we were with the event: "Holly is out on the covered patio with Annie and Kara, finishing decorating and setting up."

We had planned to do our flower-arranging lesson outdoors. Three rows had been made of rented tables, which Holly and our other helpers were draping in dark green canvas and presetting with the vases and flowers and greens. The floral foam was being presoaked and placed in each vase, to make everything easy, and a pair of good florist scissors was placed at each setting so that each of our twenty ladies would have her own workstation from which to trim stems and weave vines and play with the flowers.

"Any word from Detective B?" Wes asked.

"Nothing. He never called me back yesterday and I've left two messages this morning." I'd left long overanxious recitals of all my fears, all the way up to the speculation that Knight may have been behind the murders of Sara Jackson and Albert Grasso. Even though I had no evidence, I was sure I was on the right track. The logic of it. The motivation of all the players. It just gelled. But still Bill Knight was free! And what was worse, he was right here. And what was worse than that, so was *I*. I felt flushed with concern.

"What do you want to do?" Wes asked.

"Let's just keep going," I said. "What else can we do?"

The Woodburn Ladies Flower Lunch, donated by our firm in the auction and hosted by Dilly Swinden and her cochair Zenya Knight at the Knight home, went down in the short history of Mad Bean Events as the most surreal event we had ever produced. Every time the doorbell rang with the arrival of a new guest, I was sure it would be the police coming to drag away the man of the house.

The Woodburn women, in blissful ignorance of the drama behind the scenes, displayed the completely opposite attitude on this day. They were relaxed, cheerful, and beautiful as always. They wore their version of casual clothes, summer-weight pants and capris in bright colors, little backless sandals with high heels, expensive ankle chains and earrings. Their adorable tiny designer bags rested on a table we'd set out for that purpose. The collection of these ladies' purses alone must have been worth over fifteen grand, and that wasn't counting the contents of their Louis Vuitton wallets.

Everyone was having a grand time. All the committee women I had met over the months while planning the Woodburn fund-raiser were there. Connie Hutson, Dilly and Zenya, even Caroline Rochette had the nerve to show up, soaking up the shock and sympathy of her many friends over the death of Albert Grasso. It was almost too much social facade for me to bear. As they laughed and complimented one another on a new pair of shoes or a belt, I was overburdened with knowing too much of what was going on beneath the surface. Behind the smiles, many of these women were anything but carefree. They were women desperate to hang on to their youth, women worried about money, women who had affairs with other women's husbands they must hide. I found it difficult to put on a friendly face and be as shallow as the situation demanded—which was really a disability for a party planner.

While I got lost in my thoughts, Wes and Holly stood in front of the flower tables and passed out six stems each of alstromeria and snapdragons and demonstrated how to use the number three to design a simple and elegant formal flower arrangement. By making a triangular pattern in the deep floral foam with your three most important flowers, like the large white casa blanca lilies we'd provided in this case, you next fill in with two each of the other flowers around that triangle and form a symmetrical and appealing shape. All the while, as they quickly learned to remove the pollen sticks from the lilies, or artistically arranged their ferns, or daintily sipped on tall glasses of iced tea, or playfully commented on others' flowers, the Woodburn ladies looked relaxed and pleased. The only ones in the entire house who were tense appeared to be Wes, Holly, and me.

Zenya pulled me aside as the group was about to start on their second flower arrangement, a simple design with roses and hydrangea that Wesley would show them how to place into tall, square-shaped vases.

"We're still friends, right?" she asked me, smiling sweetly.

What could I say? Yes, right. I have managed to break your brother's heart while at the same time working to put your no-good husband in prison, but of course we are buds.

I worked on my faux-happy skills a little harder and tried to smile back at her. "Why would you ask that?" It sounded lame, even to my own ears. "Are you having a good time?"

Zenya squeezed my hand and went back to her guests. They were all having a ball. Clearly, they'd all aced the honors course in keeping their secret worries hidden, while I'd forgotten to sign up for that class at all.

After the two very different flower arrangements had been completed and excessively admired, the beautifully filled vases were set in a cool spot where they'd stay until it was time for the ladies to take them home. The party moved on to the pavilion on the far side of the swimming pool, where we had set up lunch. Dilly Swinden made a little speech before the lunch of lobster salad, thanking her committee for all their hard work. She asked Zenya to take a bow and say a few words. As I walked back into the house to find the extra corkscrew, I heard the faint tinkling of the front doorbell.

I walked quietly into the dark hallway and listened.

"What is this?" Bill Knight asked, his voice loud and surly. He had answered the doorbell himself, his wife and everyone else seeming to be in the backyard.

"Bill Knight. You are under arrest for suspicion of—"

Knight tried to slam the front door, but one of the uniformed officers in the group pushed it open, hard, and then another grabbed Bill. While Bill was a big man, he would never have been able to shake them all off. I saw four officers and Detectives Baronowski and Hilts.

More scuffling and swearing ensued as the officers struggled to get a pair of handcuffs on Bill. Handcuffs! In his own home in Beverly Hills. I had expected this. I had. But I was shocked, anyway, to be right there and see the end of this drama unfolding. The officer read Bill his rights, but Bill was cursing through most of it and threatening so many horrible repercussions on these policemen that I doubt he heard a word they were saying.

"Dad!" Kirby Knight darted out of a bedroom and into the fray.

"Kirby," Knight yelled out to his son. "Go get your mother. Get her to call our attorney. Tell her to get those idiot women out of this house right now."

"But, Dad!" Kirby's eyes showed the kind of raw pain a twelve-year-old's face can still show, before life teaches him how to bury it away completely and the man he becomes grows accomplished at never revealing it again.

No one saw me standing with my back flat against the dark hall wall, thank goodness, and I ducked quickly into the kitchen before Kirby ran past me and out into the garden party.

Wesley was coming toward the house as I emerged.

"Kirby just made the announcement," he said, but I could tell that by the reaction among the party guests.

There had been a sudden hush followed by furious movement around the lunch tables. In a few seconds, the casual luncheon had turned into an emergency military retreat. Many of the Woodburn ladies must have suddenly discovered immediate engagements that had to be tended. The flower arrangements were collected and departures were rapid.

Zenya saw me coming out on the lawn and separated from the friend or two who had stayed behind to soothe her. Two other women were on their cell phones, speaking to their attorney husbands, lining up representation for Bill Knight before he even had a chance to make it to the police station.

"Madeline," she said, her face as beautiful as ever, but shocked and disbelieving. "Did you hear? It's awful. Everyone is leaving. I don't know what to do."

"We'll clean up here," I said, feeling so sorry for this woman. For this family. But I wasn't responsible for the crimes her husband had committed. I looked away, as more guests made speedy exits. Even so, I felt a sort of tangential guilt at having tracked the insurance plot down to her husband and delivering his head on a platter to the cops. Could she really care about Bill Knight? Dex might not know anything about her feelings at all.

"What am I going to do, Maddie?"

"You'll do fine," I said. "I think your husband may have been capable of some very unpleasant things, Zenya. You may not know him as well as you thought."

"Bad things? Like what? You think he stole the etchings?"

I nodded.

Zenya thought it over. "I had a long talk with Dexter last night and he agrees with you. I told him I couldn't believe it, but now . . . But now even if it's true, Maddie, what can I do? He's still my husband. The father of my children. He may have gotten some things mixed up with our insurance and found some loopholes, like Dexter explained, but I have benefited from it, too, haven't I? I live in this house. I spend our money. I may not have known about what happened to those etchings, but I guess I share the blame. I have to stand by him, don't I?"

"It's worse than simply insurance fraud, Zenya," I said, catching sight of Caroline Rochette as she got ready to leave. "Please tell me something. That night after the Woodburn ball, when Bill was driving like a crazy man, did you go straight home? Did he stay with you all night?"

Zenya looked like it was hard for her to focus on anything but the past ten minutes, but she tried. "He went out again."

"Please, Zenya. Please tell me what happened that night. Just how you remember it."

"He left you in the middle of the street downtown, which was so horrible. Then he told me to call Dexter to find you and round you up. He was very specific that I had to get Dex to go. He thought the two of you might make a cute couple. Fancy that. Then he cooled down a bit and decided he wouldn't go chasing over to Pasadena for a showdown with the Hutsons. So we came home."

"About what time?"

"I don't know. Maybe one."

"And after you came home?"

"He was restless. He went to his study and was on the phone, I think. Pretty late, but that's not unusual for Bill. I went to bed at one-thirty and Bill said he thought he'd go take a drive. I don't know what time he got back home. He was out late, though. I awoke around three-ten A.M. and he still hadn't returned. What is this, Madeline?"

It was exactly as I had feared. Bill Knight did not have an alibi for the time Sara Jackson was getting shot at my house. I tried to work out the timetable in my head. Perhaps Zenya had mentioned to Bill the reason I had needed a ride home that night—that I had lent my own wheels to one of my waitresses, Sara Jackson. She probably told Bill how Sara was going to return my car that night. Bill could have seized the opportunity to get rid of Sara Jackson as a threat for good.

"What is going on?" Zenya was as anxious as I'd ever seen her. She had just witnessed her lovely party be turned to shambles by the arrest of her husband. And I was standing there on her grass telling her it was much worse than simple insurance scams.

"That woman who was shot at my house," I said, my throat dry. "She knew your husband."

"Don't tell me this," Zenya whispered, shaking her head. "Were they having an affair?"

"I don't think so," I said. "But . . . your husband wasn't being faithful to you, Zenya. I can't believe I'm the one who is telling you this, but I just found out yesterday."

"What are you talking about?" She looked completely perplexed, her hazel eyes wide.

Caroline Rochette walked by us and stopped. Oh no.

"I took your advice, Madeline," Caroline said to me. "Just in time. I am through with all the lies."

"Good," I barely whispered. Zenya and Caroline were standing together. I was seriously concerned about spontaneous combustion.

Caroline turned to Zenya. "I'm sorry, Zenya. I had no desire to hurt anyone. You simply have got to believe that. I'm afraid it all spun out of control so fast, I got a little lost."

"What are you talking about?" Zenya asked her. And then her eyes focused and she knew. "You were sleeping with my husband."

"I was worried about Albert. He seemed to be growing a little tired of us. I couldn't lose him . . . I know it makes no sense."

Zenya Knight, the sweet flower child of the fund-raising crowd, spun and slapped Caroline Rochette's face so hard the crack of it silenced the few remaining departing guests.

Caroline Rochette, after a lifetime of delusion, denial, and dermabrasion, had finally resolved to confess her sins. She needed to, once and for all, get the whole story out, and a dizzying right hand to her cheek wasn't going to keep her quiet.

"Please understand," she begged Zenya, "Bill came to me and said he was leaving you anyway. I believed him, Zenya. How was I to know he was such a liar? He came to me at a vulnerable time in my life. I'm just telling you all of this so you know the real man those police just arrested. I didn't want you ruining your life supporting him without knowing this."

Zenya raised her right hand again and Caroline, her cheek blazing red, didn't flinch. But Zenya lowered it, her anger directed in too many other directions to take it all out on poor Caroline Rochette.

Wesley signaled to me that our truck had been loaded and we needed to split. I had never been so grateful to leave one of my own parties in my life. I told the women I had to go.

Caroline Rochette did not stick around an instant longer. Zenya stood in the middle of her empty backyard, almost alone. Her son, Kirby, walked up to his mom, hanging his head as he hugged her.

"Things always work out, Kirby my boy," I heard her saying to him as I walked away. Whether from a natural talent for bouncing back up, or a lifelong habit of putting a sunny spin on every bad turn in life, Zenya had her soft smile back in place, ready to cheer up her son.

"I called Uncle Dex," Kirby said. "He's coming right over."

"Good boy," she said, rubbing his hair.

"Mom. What are we going to do?" Kirby's strained voice could be heard even as I walked across the lawn.

"We'll improvise, sweetheart," I heard Zenya say to her

jazz-playing son. "You're so good at that. You'll teach your mom."

When I reached Wesley at the front of the house, he looked grim. It had been an unprecedented party. We'd never had a hostess lose her husband in the middle of the meal before. First time for everything.

"It's okay," I said to Wes. "I think Zenya is ready to hear the truth about Bill now. She has some big shocks ahead. But I think she'll be able to roll with them."

"Mad," Wes said, ignoring my words. "I just got off the cell. They're letting Bill Knight go."

"What?"

"Rich men get a different kind of justice, right? Bill Knight's lawyers have already raised the roof. Since this is just a suspicion-of-insurance-fraud arrest, with no priors, they're letting him go on his own recognizance."

"But, Wes! The murders of Sara Jackson and—"

"I know, Mad. The cops don't have any evidence to make that sort of charge right now. I just talked to Honnett, who was calling for you, by the way. They didn't find Knight's fingerprints in your house or in Grasso's house. They have no witnesses that place him at the scene. He said he was home with his wife on the night of Sara Jackson's murder."

"But he *wasn't*!"

"I'm just telling you what Honnett told me. The police don't have any real evidence."

"Shit. This is all taking too long. I can't stand it. Zenya said Bill went out early Sunday morning, after the Woodburn ball. And now the cops are going to need more time to pin down everything that asshole has done."

"You're right," Wes said. "Look, I need to return the rental tables. What are you doing?"

That was an extremely good question. I felt that too-familiar clawing of fear in the pit of my stomach. What was I going to do now? A murderer was very likely going to be out on the street in a few hours and I was pretty sure who he would come after.

Me.

"Surprise"

I was in serious trouble. I ran all the way up the path to Wesley's guest house and used my key to enter. Bill Knight was about to be released. My name would have been mentioned a lot. Tracking down the valuations from LACMA and talking to the cops. Telling his mistress, Caroline, about his ulterior motives. Letting his wife know about his affair with Caroline. Sticking my nose into every horrid secret the jerk had tried to get away with. Bill Knight might figure that if he eliminated me, he would be home free. Or he might just want payback.

It was maddening. There wasn't much evidence tying him to the murders of Sara Jackson and Grasso and they wouldn't lock him up for good until they had some. I had to find more proof fast. If I waited for the cops to do it, I might be dead first. It was only a few strides to get to the guest bedroom.

Inside, I stepped out of my shoes and changed into a clean pair of shorts. Then I pulled open the nightstand drawer and touched the Lady Smith .38. I had no holster or other method of carrying it safely, but I didn't care. I grabbed the loaded gun, shoved it into my big Hawaiian-print bag, and slung it over my shoulder, trying to calm myself down. Trying to chill.

When I got back out into the main section of the guest house, I noticed something odd. I must have missed it earlier when I raced to my room. Holly's shoes were kicked off in the corner of the kitchen. The silver open-toe wedgies she'd been wearing at today's party. It wasn't unusual for Holly to stop by Wesley's after a gig. It was a tradition, really. But where had she gone?

"Holly?" I walked through the little cottage. The bathroom door was open. It was empty. The other rooms were silent.

I opened the front door of the guest house and looked across the pool to the main house. The chandelier light was on in the empty living room, but I hadn't seen Rolando's truck outside today. Holly must have gone over. While I knew Wes could be delayed returning the rentals, I would feel much safer hanging with Holly.

Outside, I barefooted it across the warm grass. The French door that led to the sunroom was unlocked. Wes had told the crew to lock up when they left the site for the day, but maybe Holly let herself in with the key and forgot to relock it.

I had the sudden high-school-girl urge to surprise Holly and scare the heck out of her. I crept along the sunroom and into the main hall. The house was a shambles of dust and drop cloths. A ladder leaned against one wall. I edged along the hall to the front foyer. I was about to yell, "Surprise," when I heard a voice. Holly was talking. Maybe I shouldn't give her a heart attack while she was talking on the cell phone. Maybe it was Donald. She'd been missing him a lot since he'd been out of town. The good angel won out over the bad. I would eavesdrop before I pounced, hiding in the entry closet. Inside the tiny space, I couldn't hear a thing.

So I gave it up. I came out of the closet and headed for the arched doorway that led into the step-down living room. The large empty space was covered in hideous cranberry-colored deep-pile carpet. Wes planned to tear it out and refinish the hardwood floor underneath. With my bare feet, I noiselessly entered the room.

When I turned the corner, I froze.

Standing in front of the gigantic fireplace in the middle of the room, facing me, was Holly. Standing with her back to me was the woman with the red shag haircut. The one who had followed me in her Honda Accord through Hollywood, and shown up to spy on me on Dexter's deck. She was now pointing a hand at Holly, a hand holding a 9mm semiautomatic handgun. I remembered it from the charts.

I ducked back out of sight, my heart pounding out of my chest. Holly had seen me. I was certain she must have. But she hadn't reacted at all. Oh my God. What did that woman want with Holly?

I tried to move silently as I rushed out to the back sunroom. Who was that woman, anyway? *Who was she?* I had to do something to rescue Holly. I opened my shoulder bag and saw the .38, heavy at the bottom. I blanched, frozen for a moment, unable to think clearly. I reached past it and grabbed my cell phone, quickly dialing Honnett's number, resenting the sounds of the little beep tones as I hit each number. Several rings, and then his machine. I despaired. I left him voice mail. I called 911 and waited for the second ring. They would pick up. They would—

"Drop it!" a woman's voice said.

I jerked around. The red-haired woman stood in the doorway of the sunroom, her gun pointed at me.

"Drop it right now or you are dead."

I let the cell phone hit the tile floor.

"Kick it over here. Now!" she yelled.

I had a frantic panic that she had killed Holly, but I tried hard to control the fear. I hadn't heard a gunshot and her weapon didn't seem to have noise-suppression equipment. I prayed Hol was all right. The woman snapped off the power button on my cell phone and dropped it back onto the floor.

"What did you do to Holly? Who are you?" I stared at her. She had fair skin and faded looks, like she had been pretty at one time. Close up, I could see that despite her good bone structure, her skin looked worn, covered with many fine lines. She would have looked a lot better if she had been wearing some makeup. With her sparkless looks, it was hard to see a resemblance, but her coloring was similar to Sara Jackson's—the same dark red hair and freckles.

"You really have no idea who I am," she said, amazed.

"Are you related to Sara Jackson?"

She shook her head, amused.

I couldn't help staring at the gun in her hand. She held it firmly and capably, two-handed for support. I had the fleeting thought that Andi, my gun trainer, would be impressed.

"Why have you been following me?" I asked, trying to stay calm. "Do you know Dexter Wyatt?"

"I have the gun, so I'll lead this conversation, okay?"

She acted like a pissed-off cop.

"Which reminds me," she continued, "I want my thirty-eight back."

Her .38? The gun Honnett had lent to me, the engraving had included an initial. *S* perhaps. And a former cop. Sherrie? Sherrie Honnett. Oh my God.

"This can't be happening," I said, my brain swimming. Honnett's wife. The age was right. As a cop, she'd be familiar with firearms. But what the hell was she doing pointing a Beretta 9mm at my heart? "Sherrie, put the gun away."

"Finally," she yelled at me. "I've known about you for a long time, and now you finally know me. Perfect."

"What are you doing here?" We stood in the empty sunroom and I was becoming more alarmed by the minute. "What did you do to Holly? Did you hurt her?"

"Your girlfriend is sleeping in the other room."

Sleeping! My stomach jumped. I steadied myself and tried to follow what she was saying.

"I let myself into that little cottage where you live, looking for my revolver, and I found your friend instead. She began yelling and getting hysterical, so I brought her to this house, where I could leave her for a while. My plan was to come back and wait for you. But I took too long, didn't I? And here you are."

"I don't know why you've been following me, Sherrie. Or why on earth you think you're entitled to break into my house or hurt my friends. But you have got to wake up now. You can't get away with this behavior."

"I don't intend to," she said, in disgust. "I'll take responsibility for it all. You don't know me very well, but you'll see."

The woman was completely irrational. I kept the anger out of my voice this time. "You must be very upset, Sherrie," I said, making eye contact with her. "You've been sick. You need your husband by your side. I know that now. I'm aware of everything now."

"You, little girl, know nothing. You have no idea what you are talking about." Sherrie Honnett looked like she would like to spit on me. Or shoot me. "Sit down on the floor," she ordered. "Over in the corner. Now. Move."

I sat down where she told me to, and she followed my actions with the gun, carefully settling herself on the floor ten feet away from me, resting the Beretta on her knee, pointing it right at my chest.

"I know you must love your husband," I said, trying again.

"You have no idea what I feel," she said, still gravely annoyed. "He is the most honorable, exceptional man you have ever met, Madeline Bean. You don't appreciate that, of course, because you are a class-one bitch. But that man is the best there is."

Her eyes were gleaming. Her voice was harsh.

I kept quiet, trying not to obsess over the opening of the unblinking gun barrel as it stared at me.

"I met him ten years ago when I was working at the Hollenbeck Division," she said. "Chuck served his probationary period there, but he wanted more excitement, so he moved to the Seventy-seventh Street Division in South Central. Did you know any of this?"

I shook my head.

"Figures. You take up with a man and know absolutely nothing about him. What do you care, right?" Her eyes challenged me.

"I do care," I said, wondering if this was what she wanted to hear, trying not to piss her off any further.

"Then you'll be delighted to learn that Chuck was a favorite out there. He tried new things. I was so damned proud of him in those days. They would always pick Chuck first to work the dangerous undercover assignments. He did good work."

I had no idea how I was going to get out of the corner of this dusty sunroom alive. I had no choice but to keep Sherrie talking, and she clearly had a lot more she wanted to tell me.

"Is this cop stuff boring you, honey?"

I shook my head no. "What happened next?"

"He worked the South Bureau Narcotics Task Force and was part of some amazing busts. In time, the department knew how much trust they could place in Chuck. He was given the 'problem probationers' ready to be fired for various things in their performance as cops. Chuck would turn these cops around and keep them from being fired. Do you have any idea what sort of man this is, Madeline, this man you have treated like crap?"

Wait. Was Sherrie angry with me for getting involved with her husband or for treating him like crap? Hold on. "What about your career?" I asked, trying to get it just right. "You were a great cop."

"My own career with the PD was minor league. I always worked hard, but Chuck was the star in the family. He was on the gang task force until June 1998, when he was hand-picked to be the senior officer in the Robbery Homicide Division. Do you understand what sort of man he is?"

The level of hero worship combined with the intensity of her feelings were enough to frighten anyone. The unwavering gun barrel scared me even more. "Sherrie. Please, let me talk. When I first met Honnett, I had no idea he was still married."

She actually laughed at me. And why shouldn't she? "You saying he lied to you, like some common scumbag? You're talking about Lieutenant Charles W. Honnett of the Los Angeles Police Department," she said. "This man doesn't lie, kid. Do you actually think you're going to sell that story? He doesn't lie."

She was right. Technically, he hadn't lied to me. He just never went into the details. And to be 100 percent fair, I had never asked for a detailed review of his previous relationships. I thought men hated to be quizzed. I had been trying to be a free spirit. For all the good it did me.

"Sherrie, he said he had been married before. That was all. Married before. And this was a long time ago, at a time when the two of you were separated. How could I know? Then, later, when he told me more about you, about how he was getting back together with you, of course he and I split up. That was it. I know he loves you, Sherrie."

A tear fell from her eye. I was shocked I had gotten through. I kept talking. "There is no need for you to get into bigger trouble over a . . . a misunderstanding, really. No need for guns or any of this. Men sometimes make mistakes with women, no matter how good the guy might be. The important thing is that Honnett loves you and he went back to you when you needed him."

"Shut up," she said. The gun never wavered in her hands. She had years of training on pistols, I realized. And this was, after all, her service gun.

I thought of her other gun, the expensive .38 Honnett brought to me after I'd begged him for his help. He never told Sherrie, of course. Probably hoped she wouldn't notice it missing. That was Honnett's style of honesty. Never say too much. Never explain. Right.

"He came back to you, Sherrie," I said, trying to convince her she had nothing to fear from me.

"Chuck never would have come back to me if I hadn't told him about being sick. He said . . ." Her calm monotone became ragged and she sobbed once, then pulled it together. "He told me he'd met someone. He said you weren't like us. You were different. Some sort of cook. Young and liberal and all of that. Kind of like some arty bohemian. I asked him if this new girl had any idea what kind of hero he was. And do you know what he told me? He said you didn't pay much attention to what he did on the job." She shook her head, remembering. "This great cop, but what do you care about any of that? It was all wrong. I worshiped that man, but he wanted you. I didn't know what else to do. I had to get him to pay attention to me again, so I told him about the cancer."

"I heard you've been sick."

She shook her head. "You heard wrong."

"You don't have cancer?"

With one hand she pulled off the red wig she had been wearing, keeping the other hand, the one holding the Beretta 9mm, steady on me. Beneath the thick shag wig, her own brown hair was pinned up under a net.

"We'd been living apart for over a year. He kept drifting farther away. I had to tell Chuck something. So I bought a wig and told him I'd been going through chemo."

This woman was so seriously nuts.

"That's when he paid attention. He realized we needed to work out our troubles," she said. " 'Cause he thought I was dying. Not because he wanted me."

I stared at her.

"It was no good, you see? You had ruined him by then. He wasn't mine anymore. Nothing I tried made any difference. He asked the therapist we were seeing how long she felt I would need his support. She told me that one night after a session. I knew he would be leaving me any day to go back to you."

"I'm sorry. I swear I never knew."

"So you can see why I'd want to check you out."

"You started following me."

"Chuck told me you were a party girl and came home late at night. I knew about your Grand Wagoneer and I got your address on Whitley off of your driver's license. I went to your house one night. I watched you come home. That first time I saw you I had such pain. Like fire. You were so young. You were so young and thin and vibrant—that's the right word. I hadn't expected that. And I watched you go into the house and turn on some lights."

"When was this?" Some creepy strange woman had been stalking me. I had felt it. I had known it. But I had always managed to push it out of my thoughts. It was creepier by far to hear about it from the point of view of the stalker.

"A week ago Saturday night. Or I should really say early Sunday morning."

And it all clicked into place. This jealous/crazy woman had been staking out my house on the night Sara Jackson had returned my Jeep Grand Wagoneer. Sherrie Honnett had not known what I looked like then. She mistook Sara for me.

"You'll Never Go to Heaven"

"It was Sara," I said, my voice dead.

"I thought it was *you*. So young. So pretty. She let herself into the house by the kitchen door. She left the door ajar and I entered behind her. She was already walking up the stairs when I entered the kitchen."

I was shocked. Why had Sara Jackson gone up to my room? I had never figured that out.

"She was standing in your bedroom, opening drawers, playing with your jewelry box."

I was astonished. "My what?"

"She was holding up a pair of emerald earrings. Now, why would I imagine that that young woman fooling with your earrings was anyone else but you?"

"Sara was ripping me off?" Of course she was. Alone in my house, she had to investigate to see if there was anything around worth stealing. From what I knew now about Sara Jackson's character, I should never have given her the combination to my back-door lock. But at that time I was careless, trusting. A fool.

"When I realized I'd killed the wrong person, I had to think it over," Sherrie said. "The girl was going through your pathetic little jewelry box. When you think about it, you owe me some thanks. I shot a burglar in the middle of the act. If only I had known, I might have spun the story correctly at the time. I'd be wearing a medal today."

"You shot her."

"With the Lady Smith, as a matter of fact." I remembered the revolver that was currently loaded and resting at the bottom of my shoulder bag. Sherrie was smiling, recalling that night with a chillingly inappropriate, matter-of-fact calmness. "It was an odd scene now that I recall it. I told her to leave my husband alone. I told her I had cancer. I told her she could fall in love with any man in the world and he would fall in love with her back."

Oh my God. What had Sara Jackson, the sometime prostitute, made of this bizarre woman begging her to leave her man alone?

"She laughed at me, Miss Madeline Bean," Sherrie said calmly. "The little bitch told me that it was cold old women like *me* who made her work easy. She said I deserved to lose my man. She showed not one single ounce of remorse, do you understand?"

I nodded, getting the picture.

"And to shut the smug bitch up, I told her to sit on the bed. She ignored me and turned back to the jewelry case. So I had to take my gun out and tell her again."

I was about to be sick.

"And that wasn't smart, I know," Sherrie said, sounding almost apologetic. "Chuck would be angry. And I didn't want him to be angry, even though he had just that very day broken my heart into a million pieces. He said he loved you. In our therapy session on Saturday afternoon. He said he needed to be honest with me."

My head couldn't take in everything she said. Like this last bit. Honnett had never used the word *love* with me. Ever. So there I was, for months holding a grudge against this man for his betrayal. I had convinced myself that I had read him wrong, that he had never really cared about me. While for months, Honnett was painfully extricating himself from his entanglement with a sad and sick wife, telling her he loved me before he would ever say those words to me.

"So I had to make a decision." Sherrie picked up the story, enjoying my captive attention. "Chuck would never understand why I had gone over to your house to meet you, Madeline Bean. He'd be angry with me for going inside. I had to think very quickly, but there was no way I could get out of it. And all the time, this girl that I thought was you kept berating me. She had a filthy gutter mouth. No God in her at all. She kept swearing at me. I was holding the gun on her and she didn't care. She kept calling me disgusting names."

I shook my head, unable to imagine Sara's foolish toughness.

"I was horrified," Sherrie whispered, "horrified to see whom my Chuck had given his heart to. Madeline Bean was a stupid, foulmouthed whore," Sherrie said, still in that eerie casual tone of voice like she was talking about a recipe. "And I had to shoot her to shut her up."

I swallowed down my sudden feeling of nausea.

"And it gets better," Sherrie said. "The irony. You'll like this part. When I was leaving your house, I realized I had been observed. I almost peed in my pants when I spotted him out there in the dark. At one-thirty in the morning, when no one should have been anywhere near your house. Some nasty old man was hiding in the bushes. Probably some Peeping Tom, but that pervert picked the wrong night to peep. When I came out of the house, he ran away like a scared squirrel."

"Who was it?"

"Some man who lived up on the next street. I had to track him to his house," she said, remembering back. "I'm sure he heard the gunshots. It was dark, but he may have seen me. I couldn't take the chance."

Albert Grasso must have come down to my house early Sunday A.M., perhaps looking for a way to get his briefcase papers back. And during his late-night prowling, he'd had the bad fortune to witness Sherrie's spur-of-the-moment burst of terrorism. Grasso fled, but not before Sherrie was able to discover where to find him. She must have come after him later and killed him, just to cover her tracks.

"You are the one to blame for all of this," Sherrie said adamantly. "You backed me into a corner, and when you wouldn't listen to reason, I had to kill you."

"Sherrie. That wasn't me, remember? I *would* have listened to you. But you were talking to some twisted hooker who was in my room to steal my things. It was Sara Jackson who taunted you, not me."

"Shut up! That's not what this is all about. I don't care about myself. Not at all. I am just a vessel for justice, which is exactly as it should be. I prayed to God for years over my marriage. I asked God for babies, but He didn't have that blessing for me. I was confused about that, I'll admit it. I was lost for a little while. But I prayed and I found God again. God didn't see fit to give me children, but he does have a job for me, Madeline Bean, and I'm doing it the best I know how."

This was not going to end well. She had a job to do. I wanted to scream.

How had Honnett managed to put up with her for so long? Or did her mind unravel so slowly that her quirks and moods might go unrecognized as they shrank further from the bounds of sane behavior? Perhaps Sherrie had the gift of hiding her inner turmoil from her husband, her mental illness progressing to a state where she had nothing left but vengeance and fury, without Honnett seeing into the depths of her despair.

"I know what I have to do," she continued. "I have to

leave this earth. I have taken two lives, and although they were hateful lives, I can't stay. I know I have broken the law. So I'm not crazy. But then there's Chuck. Do you think he could forgive me?"

"You're still his wife, Sherrie," I answered carefully. "There's always hope."

She shook her head sadly. "No. He's too good. He'd have to send me away. But I had one more task to perform before I go to God. I had to look after my dear husband. I had to find the real Madeline Bean and decide if you were honorable enough for this man."

"But, Sherrie, Chuck and I broke it off months ago. We haven't even kept in touch."

Sherrie ignored me. Her voice held utter contempt. "And I discovered your true moral character."

I thought about the night she was standing out on Dexter Wyatt's deck in the moonlight, looking in. "But, Sherrie," I said, worried. "Chuck and I were not even seeing each other then. We were over."

"Didn't take you long, did it? You were already catting around with another man. No better than that insulting hooker I killed in your bed. You never loved Chuck like he deserves. And he loves you, don't you see?"

I stared at the barrel of the Beretta. "You're going to kill me because I'm . . ." How could I say it so she'd wake up? "Because I'm not a good-enough person. Why don't you just tell Honnett. Tell him."

"I noticed my favorite gun was missing the other day, and I can tell you, it worried me. It worried me greatly. Did you know that pistol had been a gift to me from Chuck on our first wedding anniversary? I love that gun."

Oh God.

"And as it happens, that thirty-eight can be tied to those two shootings, can't it? I couldn't very well have this weapon traced to the killings. I just came here to retrieve my own property. So where is it?"

"It's in the trunk of my car." I wanted to get out of this empty house. I wanted to be outdoors.

"You're lying."

Something else occurred to me. The other night I told Honnett the stalker woman drove a Honda Accord with a missing front plate. He had to have known right then it was Sherrie who had been following me. He'd gone kind of quiet and I'd put it off to his mooning over the wreck of our relationship. But no. He had more to worry him that night. He had to have noticed Sherrie's ever-more-disturbing behavior, realized she was unstable, and then discovered she had been acting out against me, but he never mentioned a word of it to me.

"Where's the gun?" Sherrie shouted at me.

"In my car. If I was lying, I'd have said I don't have your gun anymore."

"Well, we'll see. Get up now, missy," Sherrie said, gesturing with the barrel of the black 9mm semiautomatic. "Up with you. I want you to sit over on this bed here." There was an old paint-splattered daybed over in the corner of the sunroom that the guys used as a platform to paint the high moldings.

She was going to shoot me here in Wesley's empty estate, just as she had shot Sara. Just the same, on the bed.

"Stand up!" she yelled.

There was a tap at the front door. We both heard it.

"Don't make a sound," she said, walking up to me and putting the barrel of the gun up to my neck as I got to my feet.

The tapping at the door continued. We heard a heavily accented man's voice call, "Miss Maddie?"

"Who is that?" Sherrie whispered in my ear. She held

me by the back of my waistband, still keeping the gun on my neck.

"I think it's Rolando," I answered. "He works here on the property."

"Miss Maddie, I need the garage opener."

"Rolando has the key to this house," I lied to Sherrie. "If I don't answer the door, he's going to let himself in."

Her breathing became more rapid. "Don't screw this up," she said to me, holding me by the waistband of my khaki shorts and pushing toward the door. "Just tell him through the door that he should go home. No work today."

"He won't believe me," I said. "He works for—"

Sherrie struck me on the side of my head with the gun. I almost dropped from the sudden crash of black light and pain. "Tell him to go or I'll kill two people today."

"Rolando," I said through the door.

"Miss Maddie? I need to put some things in the garage."

"Not today, Rolando."

"¿Que?"

"He doesn't understand a lot of English," I explained to Sherrie, worried she was going to shoot both of us for my freaking inability to remember one word I learned in high school Spanish.

"Tell him to go," she insisted.

"Go, Rolando. Go home."

"What, miss?"

"Damn it," Sherrie said. "Open the door slowly and tell the idiot to get out now. You have ten seconds or I'm shooting you both."

Sherrie slowly opened the door inward and pushed me forward, two feet away from the barrel of the 9mm and a step closer to fresh open air.

The man standing at the door grabbed my arm. He yanked

me so hard I lost my balance. Before I could tell what was happening, I was falling, tumbling to the ground, pulled out of the line of fire.

Some villains are all punk talk; they intimidate their victims by making grandiose threats. When put to the ultimate test, they can't pull the trigger. But that couldn't be said for Sherrie. Sherrie had never been bluffing. She had been a police officer too long. She was calm in the face of sudden danger. She had been trained to shoot in situations that were going down wrong, and ask questions later. And now, here, in the bright Hancock Park afternoon, something was seriously going wrong.

As I began falling away, she pulled the trigger of her semiautomatic, squeezing off two shots in rapid succession. Stunned by my sudden fall, Sherrie hadn't fully adjusted her aim as I barreled downward. The slugs whizzed by, much too close to my head. I watched in slow motion as her bullets did, however, find a home. They struck down the man standing on the front step, my savior. Only it wasn't some innocent, startled Mexican-American construction worker who went down. It had never been Rolando at the door. It was Sherrie's beloved husband.

Chuck Honnett fell backward, his face expressing shock, pain, clutching at his chest.

What the hell had he been thinking, just walking up to the front door and pulling me out like that? *My God!* I saw his face for a second after he was hit. He never figured Sherrie would hurt him. But he hadn't counted on what kind of a wreck she had become, how the sudden confusion of the moment and her cop instincts and her tortured brain might propel her to make a deadly mistake. Or maybe he hadn't cared about his own safety at all. This wild and rash action was the way he'd chosen to clean up after his disaster of a wife. That's what men like Honnett did.

I pulled myself to my feet and tripped my way across the front of the house, then dropped again and rolled into the thicket of overgrown bushes, thankful that Wesley had not yet relandscaped. I'd have been shot before I ever made my way to this cover, no question, had not the horror of recognition as Sherrie saw her own man fall to the ground stunned her into a momentary trance. Her husband lay unconscious not six feet in front of her, having taken what I figured were both shots at extremely close range to the chest. I had not chanced another look back to check on him as I clawed my way to shelter, propelled by some force of survival instinct I'd never felt before. When I was deep into the shrubbery, I tried to get into a position where I could see what was going on.

"Chuck?" Sherrie could hardly focus her eyes on Honnett's fallen body. "Chuck, honey? What did you make me do?"

I had no idea if Honnett lay dead or dying, but I crawled up against the house, pulling myself back through the shrubbery, leaving bloody scratch marks on my face and down both arms as I scraped through the brambles to find shelter.

I was alive. Chuck was dead. Sherrie was armed. My brain could only think in sentences of three short words as I tried to get a grip. I almost laughed, so strung out was I into shock. I owed my life to voice mail, whose inventor I now owed the best dinner of his life.

I tried hard to focus. Think slowly. And the giddiness subsided. My message. It must have jolted Honnett out of his denial. Sherrie, his disturbed wife, had been tracking me. And now she had Holly and me trapped in a big empty house.

Honnett knew that Sherrie had been tailing me and maybe he had hoped that would be as far as it went. A small, sad matter—his sick wife pathetically watching his girlfriend—something he could make right somehow before it escalated out of control. But my message had been short and clear. Sherrie had a gun. At last, Honnett had to face the truth. And so he came to my rescue.

Sirens were faintly perceptible in the far distance now. Maybe Honnett had called for backup before he approached the house. Maybe the neighbors were cowering in their mansions, hearing gunshots on their quiet streets, frantically dialing 911.

Sherrie fell to the stone-paved sidewalk to get closer to the man she had just shot down. She was talking to him softly, telling him he would be all right. Not to worry.

It was unnerving to hear her coo at his unconscious form, gun still in her hand, while he bled to death on the front walk. The tension as Sherrie dithered on about love and God and the pain she endured, as she threatened the peace in leafy Hancock Park, was unbearable. But as long as Sherrie held a loaded weapon, she could rant about whatever she wanted. That was her power now.

I prayed the police would show up in time. I prayed hard. Sherrie had momentarily forgotten to track where I had gone. But upon hearing the faint sounds of sirens, she snapped back to the here and now.

She stood up and yelled, "Where did you go, bitch? Come out here and see what you did to Chuck! You whore!"

I don't think she saw me, but she guessed the general direction in which I'd fled. I was sitting, masked by a thicket of camellia bushes and other greenery, up against the exterior wall right below the bay window of the living room, trying not to move, not to make a sound, as the explosive crack of two shots rang out. The bullets had been fired in my direction. One hit the stucco not three feet from where I sat cowering against the house, hugging my knees. The other struck slightly higher and shattered a pane in the multipaned bay window. Shards of glass blew out, a few falling on me.

The last time I saw her, Holly had been in that room, I thought, desperate. Please, God, I begged. Let Holly be all right. Let her be all right.

Sherrie screamed in rage. The sirens grew louder, maybe now only three blocks away.

They'd never make it in time. Sherrie had a semiautomatic weapon with a clip. She was not limited to six bullets. She could keep sniping away and pretty soon I'd be dead.

She crouched down again, just outside the front door, stooping over Honnett's motionless body. I could hear her crying as she called to me and begged me to come out so she could finish her job.

I slowly pulled my Hawaiian-print bag off my shoulder with as few movements as was possible so as not to set the bushes shivering, and I pulled out the Lady Smith .38 revolver with the custom-engraved *S*.

Two more shots spat out in my direction. The cops had not arrived yet, maybe never would. Holly and I were going to die. I peeked between the foliage and could see Sherrie pretty clearly. The front entry of the house was only about thirty feet from where I was hiding. She was bending low and leaning close to Honnett.

It was impossible. Even if I was an excellent markswoman, I would never be able to hit her with only six shots. I was using a short-barreled revolver and was in a horrible position. And I wasn't a sharpshooter. I'd miss her. I'd give away my position. And I'd probably end up shooting Honnett.

Two more shots hit the windows above me, raining down a hailstorm of glass, as the police sirens blasted much more loudly, hiccupping as they turned onto Hudson.

Sherrie was frantic now. She stood up and planted her feet shoulder-width apart, just the stance Andi had instructed me for best positioning during a firefight.

Sherrie's 9mm pistol shot out again, and this time the lead

came within inches of finding me on the ground. She was aiming lower now. Two more bullets bit into the dirt near my hand. I was pinned, afraid to scramble away, fearing the movement in the shrubs would give away my position, knowing I was about to die.

I looked up through the branches as Sherrie peered in my direction. She didn't want to leave Honnett, or she could easily have walked over and finished the job. Then behind Sherrie, inside the house in the open doorway, I saw Holly Nichols, swaying slightly. Blood dripped down the side of her face. Holly was a tall woman, an athlete in high school. I knew with sick certainty she would try to save me. She looked determined to grab Sherrie from behind.

The two police cars were screeching to a stop in the middle of Hudson, distracting Sherrie from noticing Holly coming at her from behind. But then she must have realized something was wrong. She swung 180 degrees, facing Holly, gun ready.

"Holly!" I screamed, standing up in front of the blown-out bay window and planting my feet shoulder-width apart. "Get away!"

What happened next went by in a blur. Holly fell back into the house, slamming the heavy door. Sherrie snapped her head toward the sound of my voice. She didn't even waste a shot in Holly's direction. Sherrie turned and pointed her Beretta directly at my chest. At about the same time the cops were jumping out of their cars, drawing their guns, screaming for everyone to put down their weapons, I was pointing my gun at the center of Sherrie Honnett's body, steadying myself to fire. It was odd—in the middle of that escalating melee, I felt no fear. I heard a dozen lead bees whiz by my head as I pulled the trigger on the Smith & Wesson .38 six times.

Sherrie crumpled on the front steps of the house as three more patrol cars tore up Hudson and screeched to a halt.

The four officers who were already in position in the street, barricaded behind their cars, were joined by six others. All of them immediately turned their service guns on me. One screamed, "*Drop your weapon right now or we will fire.* DO IT!"

I threw my gun out on Wesley's front lawn.

"Put your hands on your head," a voice yelled.

I did it. "That man," I yelled back as they swarmed forward with guns still out. "That man is Lieutenant Chuck Honnett. Sherrie shot him. She shot him. I was trapped."

I was pushed facedown on the front lawn. A uniformed female officer stepped on my shoulders and put all her weight on me, holding me hard with my face in the grass, her gun pointed at my back.

"Maddie," Holly shrieked, opening the front door. Then she yelled at the cops, pointing at me, "Don't hurt that woman!" More sirens screamed up the quiet upscale street as Holly pleaded, "She's the good guy."

"Lotta Sax Appeal"

Two days passed. I hadn't been sleeping well. Nightmares. Which was pretty understandable, I suppose.

I was still living out of suitcases in Hancock Park while my own house remained ripped open, under construction. Between Wesley and me, neither of us had a residence that hadn't been the recent scene of some terrible, violent, bloody action. We desperately, giddily contemplated an escape, maybe to Holly's one-bedroom apartment in West Hollywood, but then Donald was coming home any day. The pair had big plans for a climactic reunion. Neither Wes nor I needed to witness that.

So Wesley supervised the cleanup of the blood and damaged stucco and blown-out glass, and each time I walked past the main house, I tried not to stare at that spot near the bay window where I had almost been killed. It was enough to make taking a Xanax or two sound almost interesting.

Former police officer Sherrie Honnett survived the firefight in the front yard on Hudson, barely. But despite the efforts of the paramedics as her ambulance screamed up to the emergency entrance of Queen of Angels–Hollywood Presbyterian Medical Center, she was pronounced dead on arrival. I learned later that one of the three bullets that hit her was a .38. I had been the only one there carrying that caliber.

It was kind of a miracle that I came through the ordeal unharmed, save in the most trivial way—several dozen deep scratches down my arms and legs from the bushes—and the more profound—the shudder in my soul from the unrelenting horror that I had shot someone. I realize my pain is nothing compared to the shocking finality of death, but it stung almost unbearably hard just the same. I knew I would have to learn to live with my wounds, and as for Sherrie, I would hope that she had found some peace.

Chuck Honnett had been relatively lucky, if the word *luck* can even be used when describing a gunshot wound to the chest. It turned out one bullet grazed his arm. He had only been hit seriously by one of Sherrie's shots. But at point-blank range, even one blast of a 9mm bullet can do a severe amount of damage. Sirens wailing, Honnett also had been transported to Queen of Angels and then rushed into surgery. One lung had been damaged and he lost a lot of blood. I'd been told by his doctor that Honnett's wounds were relatively minor considering just how close he'd come to death. Sherrie had missed Honnett's heart by an inch. Ironic, no?

On Wednesday morning, I awoke from a vivid dream, another nightmare. A man very much like Honnett was sitting with me at an old-fashioned saloon and he was forcing me to drink shot glasses of whiskey. I had a horrible pain in my chest, which I somehow figured was from drinking too much, but he kept smiling and making me take another shot.

Since dreams often use puns, this was not the most ambiguous image on the planet. Me and Honnett. Heartache. Shots. You can see why I don't need a shrink just yet to analyze my dreams.

It was only six-ten but I woke myself up fully to shake the

fear of my dream away. What had I been trying to tell myself? Was my subconscious still in turmoil because I took those "shots" at Sherrie? Undoubtedly. Or maybe it was more than that. I wanted to blame Honnett for getting me into this mess. He had put me in a position where I had to take shots at his wife. But in the light of day I knew it hadn't been his fault. From the first day we met, Honnett had tried to avoid getting too involved with me. I had been the impulsive one, the one who insisted we get together, so innocent of any consequences or danger.

No matter my nightmares and their true meanings, I could always find a way to blame myself. Here I was again, back to that. And I knew what Wes would say and what Holly would say. All this self-pity wasn't doing me much good. I sat up in bed. I needed something to distract me from my own emotional devils. And just at that moment, a new idea popped into my head. It was so irresistible, I immediately grabbed for the phone.

Maybe I should have been more mindful of who I telephoned at six twenty-three on a Wednesday morning, but I dialed the number of Connie Hutson anyway.

"Hello?" It was Connie's voice. She'd picked up on the second ring.

"This is Madeline Bean. Sorry, Connie. Did I wake you?"

"No, of course not. I'm just going to the gym to work out. I've been meaning to call you," she said. Many of the Woodburn ladies had avoided me since Bill Knight was arrested in the middle of the flower party, followed by the latest round of shoot-outs, which all made screaming headlines. It was one thing to have a caterer with a colorful past, but it seemed I'd stepped over the line from colorful to notorious. These were all sensible, conservative women. It was human nature to be wary of associating with anyone who seemed to attract gunfire as much as I had lately.

"I understand," I said. "Listen, I have a quick question. Do you have just one minute?"

There was a slight hesitation and then Connie said, "Just one."

"Do you remember back on the night of the Woodburn gala, exactly what all did Bill Knight buy at the auction?"

"You mean the Selmer Mark VI? He had the winning bid on that."

"I know. But did he or Zenya get anything else? Anything from the silent-auction tables, maybe?"

"Yes," Connie said, sounding surer of it now. "Everyone lines up after the affair to find out what bids they won and pay for their items. We had different lines, set up alphabetically by last names, so letters *A* to *F* lined up in one line and so on. I was supervising that process and it's terribly hard. Everyone is in a hurry to pay and go home. No one has any patience at that time of night. And our volunteers were also tired. They had just been processing the silent auction bid sheets for an hour and also wanted to go home. Anyway, I remember Bill insisting he check out his items before he paid."

"Was that unusual?"

"Well, yes. You understand, all the money raised at the silent auction goes to a good cause. Most bidders are aware that they get no real guarantees with anything they purchase. Besides, they can look everything over carefully before they bid. No one has ever tried to return anything in all my years working on these auctions."

"But Bill wanted to check out his items?"

"Yes. But then he did spend a lot of money to get that saxophone. I didn't think that much of it at the time."

"So what did he do?"

"The Knights also had the highest bid on the Baby Bundle Basket in the silent auction. Bill took that and the Selmer case back to the little office and checked them over, I suppose. It was a good thing he did, since he discovered that the saxophone was not in the case. Now, Maddie, I really have to run."

"I know and I really appreciate this, Connie. Just one more question: What exactly was in that Baby Bundle Basket?"

"It was a lovely item donated by Haute Baby on Beverly. Know them? They sent in a huge Moses basket filled with their designer baby bedding and clothes. If I were ever crazy enough to have another baby, I'd have wanted to bid on that myself."

"Isn't it odd that the Knights would buy baby clothes?"

"Maybe they planned to give it as a gift."

"Perhaps. Do you remember how much they paid for it?"

"Nineteen hundred dollars, which was well over the retail value. Very generous of them, especially—since now that we're talking about it—I remember one of the gals mentioned that she found the baby clothes left out in the office."

"What?"

"Apparently, when Liz Reed was closing up the little office, she noticed a stack of baby clothes left on the desk chair. We figured Bill had looked through his basket and then forgot to repack it in all the fuss about the saxophone."

"But he took the basket," I asked, "and the baby blanket?"

"Yes."

And the Selmer Mark VI! I had figured it out. Bill Knight had stolen his own freaking saxophone.

"Thanks, Connie. Sorry to keep you so long."

Bill Knight had gone into the little office and was alone with the sax. That had to be how he pulled it off. He tossed the baby clothes aside, put the Mark VI into the basket, and covered it all up with the baby blanket, leaving it behind for the moment in the office. Then he brought the empty sax case out and made a huge fuss. While all the auction volunteer women were in shock about this unprecedented theft and also trying to handle the huge lines of party guests impatient to check out and get their auction items, he must have swooped back into the office, grabbed his baby basket, and stormed out of the Tager Auditorium.

I remembered it now. I was standing at the bottom of the steps with Zenya. Bill had roared down the stairs holding a large something, which he threw into the back of the Hummer H1 while he yelled at us to jump into the vehicle.

Bill Knight stole his own bloody vintage saxophone. Damn. It had to be. It fit his freaking MO. Why not pull the stunt again? The Woodburn wouldn't lose a cent. In fact, they'd get a lot more than they would if the sax had been sold to a reasonable bidder for a reasonable price. He'd known that the tenor was insured. He was on the Woodburn board, so he knew Albert Grasso was taking care of insurance on all the big items. He figured he could bid up high and look like a very big man indeed. And then, he simply stole his own sax. That way, he got the collectible instrument he coveted, wiggled out of paying for it, and helped the Woodburn get a whopping $100,000. He must have figured himself to be some modern-day Robin Hood. I was startled to realize it all made sense. In fact, I was surprised Bill Knight hadn't bid $200,000 for the sax. Or a million.

And then I had another brilliant zing of recognition. What had Zenya said? Bill left her at home that night of the ball and went out to take a drive. More loose threads were beginning to tie up.

Bill must have been surprised, that stressful night, to find his wife had invited an unexpected guest along for the ride home. As I imagined it, Bill had paid off his blackmailer, Sara Jackson, and then gone through the charade of discovering that his precious saxophone had been stolen. When he finally emerged out of the Tager Auditorium, with his baby-blanket-wrapped Selmer resting in a designer baby basket, he must have made a few last-minute alterations to his plan.

Bill's fake rampage through the streets, up on curbs, ramming cars, must have been to impress this impartial witness with the authenticity of his anger. He put on a good rousing reaction scene. He'd been "ripped off." Then he ditched me. What was that about?

I thought about what he did next and realized he told his wife to call her brother, Dex, to come to my rescue. For a last-second plan, it hadn't been bad. Bill Knight had deflected suspicion from his own involvement in the missing Selmer and drawn Dexter out of his house. Now why would Bill Knight want to involve Dexter in this late-night farce? Of course, to make sure Dex wasn't at home late that night. As I recalled, at about the time Dex and I were just sitting down to breakfast at the Original Pantry Café, Bill Knight had gone out again. Taking a drive, Zenya said. I suspected he drove directly to Dexter's house in Bel Air and—oh my God!—found a way to ditch the Selmer *there*.

And if that was true, Bill Knight was going to use his brother-in-law as his patsy. He must have always had a backup plan, just in case any investigators got a little too close for comfort. He intended to blame his brother-in-law for the Mark VI heist if the shit hit the fan. And I had a horrible hunch that just such an unsavory object was about to do just such a messy thing. I jumped up out of bed and got dressed fast.

An hour later I was standing at Dexter's front door.

"The Bean Stalks Again"

The morning sunlight picked at the golden highlights in his hair as Dex stood there, looking down at me. His expression was friendly, if a little subdued. "You've caught me off guard, Madeline. I didn't think I'd get to see you again. I've been leaving you messages, but when you didn't call me back, I pretty much knew where we stood."

"Dex . . ."

"You don't need to explain. You didn't want me bothering you anymore. I knew."

"That's not it," I said, feeling incredibly awkward. I had been so attracted to Dexter Wyatt that I don't think the analytical centers of my brain had registered just how physically handsome he was. No wonder I had fallen under his spell. So much beauty is kind of dangerous. "Look, I haven't been fair to you, Dex. I've had a lot of things going on that have nothing to do with us. But still, they kind of took over my life. You know how that can happen."

"I know."

"I'm really sorry."

"No. You don't have to be sorry. Look, I watch the news. I get it. Anyway, I've been worried about you. Say, come in." He suddenly remembered we were just standing in his open doorway. I followed him to his living room, the glass walls presenting their magnificent canyon views.

Dex waited for me to begin talking, but when I couldn't get started, he took the lead like an accomplished host. "That woman who interrupted us the other night. She's the one who was killed at Wesley's house, wasn't she? Shit, Madeline. A cop."

"I know." We both shook our heads.

"The police were out here twice with questions. I tried to remember all I could about that night she was trespassing. They seemed pretty pissed off I never filed any sort of report about it, but who the hell knew she was so off her rocker?"

"You couldn't have known."

Dex shook his head, still working it through. "You were totally wigged out that night, which was completely understandable, but even when you thought you recognized her, I wasn't sure. I'm sorry I doubted you."

"That's okay. The whole thing was too weird, wasn't it?"

Dex grinned. "It seemed more likely she was some old lady here in the hills who got a little cranked up over my love life, such as it is."

Dex had a way of defusing my tension like no one else. "On the contrary. By now I'll bet all your neighbors have bought themselves binoculars and telescopes. Bet they can't wait until Dex Wyatt brings home a date." I meant to laugh at myself and lighten up the mood. But he was serious now.

"I'm so sorry for everything, Madeline. That's all I can say. I'm sorry."

"I know. So am I."

"And that woman was your cop boyfriend's *wife,* it turns out. I can't get over it. Usually *I'm* the one with the messed-up lovers. Kind of a relief for me that it was all about you, this time."

I smiled in a rueful way, acknowledging his efforts to joke me out of my mood. He could be very sweet, could Dexter Wyatt.

"The reason I'm here," I said, "is I'm suddenly positive your brother-in-law, Bill, is planning to damage you. I'm afraid he's planning to trade secrets with the cops to save his own skin. Maybe he can deal down the indictment on insurance fraud if he gives them evidence for a robbery conviction, I don't know, but I'm sure it is bad bad news for you, Dex."

"What are you talking about, Madeline? What robbery? The etchings three years ago?"

"Maybe. But I'm also worried about the Woodburn's Mark VI."

"The sax Bill bought at the auction," Dex said, just catching on.

"Well, he never paid for it. But I do think he stole it."

I spent five minutes reviewing all my suspicions with Dexter and he followed it all. He was surprised to learn that Bill had been behind the call he got from Zenya, begging Dex to drop everything and find this poor, lost party planner in big, bad downtown L.A. He was angered to hear that Bill had gone out later that night, leaving Zenya alone to, according to my theory, hide the stolen saxophone.

"We have to search your house," I told him. "Then we can call the police. Bill has made you his fall guy, Dex. If Bill gets to them first with a clever story, and leads them to where 'you' hid the stolen goods, you could wind up in jail doing your brother-in-law's time."

"Well, it was no big trick getting into my house," Dex said, furious. "Zenya has a copy of my front-door key. If Bill took it, she'd never have known." He stood up with the kind of energy a man has when he'd like to punch someone. "Where do you think we should look?"

"You know your house," I said. "Is there any storage area that you don't use very often? A location you might be expected to ignore?"

"No. I can't . . ." As he spoke, Dexter's expression changed. "Wait a minute. I have a wine cellar. Down a flight of stairs, built into the rock foundation. I've never used it and one day last winter I realized the key doesn't even work in the lock anymore. I was meaning to get the lock replaced, but since I don't collect wine, it wasn't much of a priority."

"Where is it?" I was sure he must be right. Bill had Dexter's house key. Perhaps Bill had the locks replaced sometime when Dex was out of town. If the wine room was in a location that was out of the way, Dex might never have noticed.

Dex led me through his kitchen. At the far end was the pantry, and inside of the pantry was a small door. Dex opened it and showed me a short flight of cement steps that led down.

"This is it. There's a small room at the bottom of the steps. But the key that used to work when I first bought this house doesn't unlock the door anymore. It's kind of a shame, because the previous owner told me he had the room specially climate-controlled to preserve fine wine."

"Dex. We have to get in there. Do you have an ax?"

"An ax?" He looked at me, startled. "Well, I've got a small ax out in the garage. I use it for firewood."

One of Dexter's self-admitted best qualities, I recalled, was his ability to start a wood fire. I smiled at the unlikely Boy Scout and encouraged him to go get his ax.

In a few minutes, he came back and descended the staircase to the wine-cellar room below. He swung the ax at the wooden door and splinters began to fly. It was only a few minutes before he'd hacked the frame and door to something that looked like it had been attacked by a grizzly, but the metal lock still held. I waited as he continued his assault. Five minutes more and the job was complete.

Dexter brushed away the shredded door frame and pushed open the door. I rushed down the steps to join him.

The small room was lined with shelves. It was cool and dry, which I suspected was due to the separate climate system and air conditioner, which we could hear humming away. On the floor in front of us sat a lovely basket covered in pink toile fabric, white satin, and rose-colored grosgrain ribbons. In it was a long bulky bundle wrapped up and completely covered in a pink-and-white velvet baby blanket. I stepped into the small room, careful to avoid all the wood splinters, and lifted the corner of the blanket.

"Now that's a beautiful baby," Dex said.

We stared at the world's most perfect silver tenor saxophone.

But that was not all we found in the wine cellar. On the shelves were three large works of art. The missing etchings. The three pieces that had been stolen from the Knights' home three years back.

"That bastard was going to turn me in to the cops," Dex said, his voice hoarse. "He was planning this all along. He set me up. I'll bet he was behind the rash of 'false' alarms three years ago, setting the stage so he could arrange to have me stay at his house that night. I'm sure he told Zenya to call me and insist I take those concert tickets, too. And he probably encouraged her to help me buy this house, just to make me look good and guilty. And to seal the deal, he planted the stolen art in my cellar."

"He was only after the insurance money," I said. "He didn't care about the art at all. It was more useful for him to use it to frame you. Just in case he needed it."

Dexter grabbed me and for a moment I thought he was going to kiss me. He looked deeply into my eyes and then recovered himself and let me go. "I've got to call the police."

"That's good."

"But what if they don't believe me?" he asked.

"They can find out who changed the lock on this door. Maybe the locksmith can identify Bill."

Dex knelt down and found the door lock amid the pile of wood shavings on the floor. "This is a common lock, Maddie. Something he could have bought at Home Depot. Bill may have changed it himself."

"We'll think of something," I said. And then I did actually think of something. "Come on," I told him, grabbing him by the hand. "Come with me."

Dexter drove as I used my cell phone to get the right location. We pulled up to a small parking lot on Sunset. Jon David Realtors. They were one of the most successful brokers in Los Angeles. This office mostly served the Hollywood Hills and West Hollywood.

"You!" Caroline Rochette sat in her work cubicle. Her voice carried the edge of such honest alarm that several other agents sitting nearby looked up to see what could possibly have caused one of their own to express a true feeling.

"I want to list my house for sale," I said loudly, causing the other workers to settle down and mind their own business. I noticed them turn back to their phones and their PC monitors.

"Is this some sort of joke?" she asked me, but her eyes were now on Dexter. "I'm sorry," she said, batting heavy lashes, her mood and tone of voice changing. "We haven't met. I'm Caroline Rochette." She had a business card in Dex's hand before he had a chance to know what had hit him. "Can I help you?"

"I'm serious," I said to Caroline. "If you want my home's listing, there's a price."

She dragged her eyes back to me for an instant. A new listing or a gorgeous young man. It was really the acid test for Caroline. Her eyes came back to rest on me.

"What do I have to do?"

"Tell me about the theft of the etchings from Bill Knight's house."

"I have no idea what you are talking about!" Caroline stood up and picked up her purse, a cunning little black lizard bag. "Come outside, won't you?" she asked in an overly pleasant tone, more for the cube farm, I imagined, than just Dex and me. We followed her out a side exit and stood in the parking lot.

"Look," she hissed at me. "I am telling you this because I don't want to have any part of any of this ever again."

"Good," I said.

"But you were telling the truth? You want me to sell your house?"

"Yes."

"Good, then this is what you are waiting to hear."

Dexter looked at me and then back at the little blonde who was pulling a cigarette out of her purse and lighting it.

"Albert needed a favor. His daughter, Gracie, wanted to work at the White House as an intern before that was a dirty word. But Al just didn't have contacts high enough up. I think Bill Knight knew someone. Anyway, Gracie got her job. So when Bill asked Albert to do him a favor back, of course Al wanted to show his gratitude."

She took a long puff of the cigarette and exhaled smoke as she talked.

"Bill told Albert to go to his house in Beverly Hills and pick up a few art pieces, then hold on to them until Bill got back with his family from Maui. You know what happened.

It made the papers that there had been a theft. Albert got nervous, naturally. He wasn't sure what was going on. Bill had sent him the door key. He'd assured Al there wouldn't be an alarm set, so Al would have no trouble doing the favor. Al was set to go to the police and explain the mistake, but Bill called him from Hawaii. He told Al not to worry, Bill would take care of the cops. When he got back to town, Bill came and picked up the pieces. That's all Al ever knew about it."

"So Albert never called the police and told them?"

"No. As time went on, Al figured out what must have happened. But by then, he was afraid he might be arrested for the theft himself, if Bill didn't back up his story. And the police were more likely to believe Bill. He could be a charming bastard when he wanted to be. Just ask me."

"So Grasso said *nothing*?" Dex was pissed.

I was, too. "Even though it was Albert's half brother who was taking the fall with the insurance company?" I asked. After all, Grasso had to know his brother would lose a lot of clout if one of the policies he had sold ended up costing the insurance companies millions and millions in settlement money.

"I think that was the part that Albert actually liked," Caroline said, taking another deep drag on her cigarette. "Anyway, no one ever came around to Al to ask about it. It all just died down. And now that he's dead, poor man, I don't ever want any of this to be dragged up again."

"Think again, lady," Dexter said. "We're all going to the police right now."

"What? No," Caroline said, shaking her head. "No, I won't go."

Dexter caught the look I was throwing him and changed his approach. "Caroline," he said, pulling her a step away from me. "How did an attractive woman like you ever get mixed up with difficult men like them, anyway?"

"Rotten, rotten luck," Caroline said with feeling.

"You deserve better than that," he said, looking deeply into her thickly fringed eyes. "I know you want to do the right thing."

When Dexter Wyatt fixes a woman with his undivided attention, she feels it down to her designer T-straps. Take my word for it. I could see Ms. Rochette melting right before my eyes.

"Hell!" Caroline said. "I want to do the right thing."

She threw down her cigarette, and before she could make a move, I put my own boot down and stomped it out.

"Just One More Chance"

I joined the rest of the audience in the Tager Auditorium in applause. All around me people were coming to their feet, giving a standing ovation to the seventeen young musicians of the Woodburn Jazz Band after their hard-swinging version of Freddie Hubbard's "Little Sunflower."

Each soloist got a chance to take a separate bow. Ryan Hutson, newly promoted to the rank of tenor sax player, stepped forward, beaming. Hanging from a thick strap around his neck was his shiny silver horn, the exquisite Selmer Mark VI, which had been returned to the Hutson family in due course. This boy had done a fine job on his solos, improvising like a champ. Ryan bowed to the cheering audience and then stepped back.

Another boy took his turn in the spotlight, and soon Kirby Knight stepped forward. Met by applause, he smiled shyly out to the crowd. I admired this young man, the night's star performer, for carrying on despite his family's turmoil. Dark and raw emotions seemed to shine through his music. Artists are lucky that way. They have an outlet for their feelings, even the painful ones.

My eyes searched the audience for the hot spot from which the loudest burst of applause could be heard. There, across the aisle and several rows closer to the stage, I saw

Zenya Knight and her little girl. And right beside them was Dexter, clapping away for Kirby.

I was thankful that Kirby's father wasn't present. Bill Knight was awaiting trial on several new and serious charges. He wouldn't be able to avoid jail time on all they had against him, or so I'd been told. Zenya had already taken steps to get her life back. She'd filed for divorce and put their Beverly Hills house on the market. With just a little prompting from her brother, Zenya had decided to use Caroline Rochette to handle the sale. I'd heard they had already received a purchase offer. So it goes.

"You ready to go?" my date for the evening asked.

I looked up at Honnett and nodded.

"This was great, Maddie."

"Talented kids amaze me," I said. "Where does musical genius come from?"

"I wonder if they realize how lucky they are," Honnett said, "to have this school and parents that support them."

"Are you kidding? They're teenagers."

Many of those in the audience had ties to the young folks in the band, and so they milled about the lobby, talking excitedly, waiting for their sons, siblings, nieces, or other loved ones to be allowed to leave after the concert. Honnett and I walked toward the parking garage alone.

Honnett smiled. "You know, I want to thank you for inviting me tonight. This was inspiring."

"I'm glad you could come," I said. "I was afraid you might not be comfortable sitting for so long."

"I'm doing fine." He'd stayed in the hospital for only a week and then had spent several more on pain meds resting at home. Honnett had proven remarkably resilient. He'd taken to punishing workouts, pushing his physical therapist to a frazzle, seeing improvement every week.

At the elevator to the parking structure under the Woodburn, Honnett turned to me. "Please, Maddie. Can we stop and talk? I've got something I'd like to say to you."

"Wait until we're downstairs," I said. I was so lame.

In all the weeks that had passed since I had been attacked and he had been shot and his wife had been killed, Chuck and I had not been able to talk about what had happened. When I first visited him in the hospital, with his tubes and IV lines dangling, I didn't want to worry him any more than he obviously was. Then later, after he'd been released from the hospital, I kept in the background. I cooked him a dozen gourmet dinners but always managed to get Holly or Wes to deliver them. Honnett called me, of course, but I let the phone machine collect his thank yous. The few times we talked, I cut the conversations very short. Eventually he stopped bringing it up, this painful event we had between us.

Over the past few weeks, instead of dealing with Honnett, I kept busy working out, catching up with friends, straightening up my disordered life. I put a lot of time into the business, throwing myself into a dozen parties. We got an official wedding date from Holly and Donald, on top of everything else, so we were hip-deep in planning-a-wedding details. This spoke volumes about the success of Donald and Holly weathering their long time apart and even more about the restorative powers of a climactic reunion. We were so relieved to have some good news upon which to focus, we let the wedding discussions take up a lot of our free time. In addition, the construction on the upstairs of my house was almost complete and the remodel looked fabulous. Soon I would have to decide whether I could bear to move back in or whether Caroline Rochette would earn another commission.

And then last week, Honnett began leaving messages asking if we could get together. I was as confused as ever, but I knew he couldn't be put off much longer. It was so hard to separate what I felt about the man from the disaster that had been brought into our lives by Sherrie.

I looked over at Honnett as we rode down the elevator in the parking garage in silence. He had driven to the Tager Auditorium in his own car and I'd met him there, having borrowed Wesley's Jag. Our cars were parked side by side on the lowest level. Down there, the air had the acrid odor of gas fumes, so I tried not to breathe in too much of it as we made our way to our cars.

"Maddie . . ." Honnett began, sounding very serious.

"Did you hear that I'm getting a reward?" I asked him, keeping the conversation anything but personal. "The companies that insured the Knights' etchings pay a ten percent finder's fee to anyone who recovers stolen objects. So anyway, they estimate that the true value of the Dürer and the other etchings are close to four million dollars, can you believe that? So they are offering Dexter Wyatt and me four hundred thousand. Of course, they will only pay us if they can recover the money they paid out to Bill Knight, and that means Zenya will lose any chance of getting a decent settlement in her divorce, so it's not all roses and chips. But I thought it was kind of hilarious, you know, in a sick sort of way—"

"Maddie," Honnett said, interrupting, "are you going to let me tell you that I love you?"

I stopped talking, of course.

"It isn't going to change your mind about me. I know that. I just needed to say it to you. I needed for you to hear it. Think of this as your way of relieving a guy of a terrible burden, okay? No need to answer. There."

You'd have thought it would melt my heart to hear those sweet words from this man about whom I cared so much. But I couldn't let myself melt. Maybe the reason for all my nightmares and sleepless nights and avoiding his calls was this: I suspected, deep down, Honnett and I were relieved his wife was finally out of the picture now. How vile was that? To be relieved a woman was dead.

I turned to Honnett. "You really can't know how you feel. Neither can I. There has been such a lot of extreme stress and anxiety. We need time to let things settle down."

"*I* don't."

"But Sherrie—"

"This isn't about Sherrie," he said. "I've loved you for almost as long as I've known you. But I didn't have any right. I knew that."

"Oh, Honnett."

"When I told you at the beginning that I was too old for you, you laughed at me. Remember that? You thought I was putting you off. Like I thought you were too young for me to take seriously."

"I'm not that young. You're not that old." His age had never mattered to me.

"I just meant I was old enough to know better. I'd lived enough life to know I had screwed mine up. I had problems at home. How could I abandon my own mess and start with someone as bright and new as you were? Life doesn't work like that. You just don't get a free pass to start over that easily."

"I didn't understand."

Honnett nodded. "Before I met you, Sherrie was getting out of control, more and more. The department asked her to take a medical leave, but they were more concerned about her state of mind than any other health issues. Her behavior . . . I was worried about her, but I was angry, too. We'd never been the greatest match, Sherrie and I, but now nothing she did or said made any sense. We split up, which was the direction we were heading in all along, and she just got worse."

I put my hand on Chuck's arm and he paused, his eyes meeting mine. "When she came to me after I'd been moved out for a year and told me she had cancer, I didn't know what to think anymore. Maybe her suicidal moods were due to the chemotherapy or maybe just the cancer itself, working on her nerves, making her act crazy. I saw her moods were getting worse. When she told me she needed me back, that she wanted us to start seeing a therapist together, I knew it was the right thing to do. It was the only way to get Sherrie to see someone who could help her. Of course, I should have known better than to believe anything she told me. Hell, she never listened to the shrink. She didn't have cancer. The chemo was just a made-up story. More of her lies and games."

"I know."

"That's why I had to leave you, Maddie. I had to go back and try. I wanted to do things right, to see if I could help her get squared away. I couldn't move forward with you and me until I had."

"But you never told me," I said. "How could I understand what you were going through if you were keeping all these secrets? We had this relationship going, but you didn't trust me. You didn't want me to know the truth. Or to really know you."

He thought it over and I could tell he didn't like what he was thinking. "Maybe you're right." He shook his head. "At the time, I wanted to protect you."

I sighed.

"It really worked well, didn't it?" he asked, his voice almost light. "Instead of keeping you safe, I brought unholy hell down on top of you. I put you in danger. I caused you unbelievable pain, Maddie. That's what damned good my love is to you."

We had been standing by our cars, and I asked if Honnett wanted to sit down in Wesley's S-Type so we could get out of the musty air. He shook his head and said he should be going, anyway.

"Then just give me one more minute and hear this," I said. "I don't hold you responsible for anything that happened. I don't even blame Sherrie, really. Maybe it's natural to hate the people who try to hurt us, but that's not how it works with me. After all these weeks and all this thinking, I don't have any anger left in me. I just feel very sorry about how much pain Sherrie was in. And very sorry for what she must have put you through. So really, Honnett, you may as well give up this guilt you are carrying around. I don't blame you at all."

"Maddie." Honnett looked at me for another long moment, and then said, "I better get going."

I met his clear blue eyes, not sure there was any more we could say, and nodded.

"I guess I should I leave you alone for a while," he said.

"Or not," I said softly.

"Sure. Then I'll call you." He smiled then, a regular Honnett-style smile. "And thanks for bringing me here tonight. It was the perfect evening out for a man feeling his age while he's recovering from surgery, all those kids blowing their horns, full of talent and life. I love jazz. It's cool you remembered that."

Standing in the parking garage, watching Honnett climb into his Mustang and lower the convertible top, I realized I had become a different person since the day the two of us met. I don't know if the changes are good or bad, but given enough time and bumps, I suppose growth is inevitable. Can't stay in Neverland forever. Damn it.

Honnett waved at me as he pulled away. I stared after him as more families now entered the parking structure. He was a different man in my eyes as well. Maybe a little less the iconic hero, a little more human. Sherrie had been right. He was an honorable man.

I drove off and thought again about Honnett and me and

the difficult subject of how his life with Sherrie had hurt us. Can we ever escape the past lives of the person we get involved with? I sped over to my old house and parked the Jag S-Type on Whitley, stopping to pick up my mail before heading back to Hancock Park. As I stepped out of the car, I saw two familiar friends out walking in the evening.

"Hi, Teuksbury," I said, bending to scratch the weimaraner on the head. "Hi, Nelson."

"Well, hello, Maddie. We see the construction crew is gone. So is your house finally done?"

"Just about. There's some finish work needed inside, but they have done an incredible job. And how are you and Miss Teuks?"

"We're doing pretty well," the old man said, bending to pat her on the side.

"I just came by to pick up my mail."

"Oh, Maddie," Nelson Piffer said diffidently. "I have a little confession to make. I've been meaning to tell you but . . ."

"But what?" I looked at my elderly neighbor and wondered whatever could he be talking about.

"It's about your old car. You know, the old Jeep. This is a very indelicate subject to bring up, so I hate to be the one to tell you this."

I was more than intrigued. "Tell me."

"Teuksbury and I were taking a walk a couple of months ago. It was a dark night, but right here in the middle of Whitley, we could see a bitch was getting it on with a stray, a Dobie mix, looked like."

"Dogs? Dogs *making love*?" I covered my smile, as I could tell Nelson took such subjects a little more seriously than I ever could.

"Yes. It was the little lurcher from two houses down. Trixie. God only knows what she was doing running out in the street, but when those bitches are in season, it's a good job keeping them in."

"I would imagine," I answered, a little too circumspectly considering my own intemperate past.

"The point is, it is also a good job trying to separate a breeding pair once they're in the act."

Poor Trixie. I could relate.

"And I knew Ms. Fellows would go mental if she found her little Trixie knocked up by some rogue stray. Well, this is a long way around, Maddie, but the point is I did finally detach the rascals. Of course, then the male was quite aggressive."

I could well imagine.

"I had to think fast. Your car was unlocked, so I put my Teuksbury and Trixie in the backseat of your Jeep, just to keep them out of harm's way until I could chase off the Dobie mix."

That semen stain on my backseat. I laughed out loud. Good luck to the LAPD crime lab on matching that sample.

And then it all suddenly struck me. Standing out in the cul-de-sac at night with Nelson Piffer and his sweet Teuksbury, I got a glimpse of the impossible challenge of my need to problem-solve, made simple and clear and hopeful for a brief second. Like a pile of a thousand spiky pieces that might make up several finished jigsaw puzzles, it's anyone's guess most of the time which pieces in life fit into any given puzzle. The key to order was proper sorting.

And over the past few months I'd watched so many jigsaw pieces pile up: the trash left on my doorstep, the disappearance of a priceless saxophone, the theft of three etchings, the death of a waitress, the murder of a music teacher, and add another piece named Dexter Wyatt, and then another named Chuck Honnett—all needing proper sorting before any puzzles could be solved.

It was my nature to tackle that pile, impossible though it might seem, but what made it worthwhile was an instant like this: this rare and sudden joy—this one sharp, simple moment of seeing the puzzles truly sorted out. The deaths, the thefts, the men . . . and even the mysterious stain on the backseat of my old car.

An hour later, I was back at Wesley's place. What had followed that gleeful moment of clarity—the belief I finally *got* it—was the natural onset of gloom over all the things I, in fact, *didn't* get. I had come no closer, for instance, to understanding my own heart. I couldn't even sort out what feelings I still had for Chuck Honnett. Even though I was over my anger and my hurt. Even after he said he loved me. Still, we could never erase what had happened. He hadn't trusted me. I hadn't trusted him. I had shot his wife. How could we move forward? It was too damned complicated.

At the guest house, I found a large manila envelope leaning up against the door. It said TO MADELINE on the front. It must have been hand-delivered because there was no postage attached or even a full address.

As I let myself in, I began to rip open the envelope.

"What's that?" Wes asked, looking up as I entered the door.

I pulled out the contents and showed them to Wesley. In my hands were a dozen black-and-white photographs, size eight-by-ten. They were amazingly well focused and beautifully composed. The subject of one of the photos was Serena Williams as she accepted a special award at the U.S. Open in New York. Other photos were candids of the tennis star and others on the court swinging rackets, and backstage at the awards, and at the after party. A note slipped out, attached by paper clip to a ticket.

Wesley looked even more curious.

"It's from Dexter," I said, reading the note. "He sold two of his pictures to *Sports Illustrated*."

"You have got to be kidding!"

"Isn't that great? He says they are asking him to shoot some stuff in color in Bangkok in a few weeks, an international tennis tournament. He sent me a ticket. Said he'd like me to come."

"Oh, Mad."

"Oh, Wes." We both stood there shaking our heads. "It's a lucky thing that men do not tempt me anymore."

"Well, that *is* a lucky thing," Wes said. "I hadn't heard that news yet."

"Late-breaking update," I said, smiling, "hot off the presses. I have finally learned my lesson about men."

"Impressive," Wes said, offering me support. "I can see you are a changed woman. Mature. Sensible. Strangely calm in the eye of the storm."

I smiled at him.

"And your enlightenment . . . from where did this deep well of wisdom spring?" he asked.

"From a sadder but wiser little lurcher named Trixie."

Wes enjoyed his laugh.

"No. I'm serious here."

"So where are you off to?" Wes asked.

"To go call Dexter."

Wes laughed again.

"Well," I said, "I've got to congratulate him, don't I? *Sports Illustrated.* Wow. That boy takes direction."

Pour yourself a mai-tai, sit back, and join Madeline Bean and her cohorts on a vacation in paradise that suddenly takes a deadly turn . . .

When her beloved assistant Holly Nichols sets her wedding date, Madeline Bean throws the hippest bachelorette luau ever—a destination bridal shower on the big island of Hawaii. The moonlight hula lessons! The coconut grilled shrimp! The dead man floating in the surf!

Suddenly, the bride has a case of the jitters. To smooth the matrimonial path, Maddie must track down the mystery man Holly may have married a decade ago . . . and forgot to divorce. With the luau guests enjoying one passion fruit martini too many, Maddie catching the eye of a suspiciously laid-back beach boy, a murderer in their midst, and a freaking volcano erupting, it looks like anything but fun in the sun for Maddie and company.

The Flaming Luau of Death

Available Winter 2005
in hardcover from William Morrow

Wahine Male
(Married Woman)

A tall, willowy blonde stood silently in the doorway to my office. She was wrapped, all six-feet of her, in one striking color. Bright pink flip-flops with matching toenail polish. Hot pink jeans and jacket over a tiny pink bandeau. Shocking pink sailor's cap tipped at an angle above her white-blonde bangs. How long had this vision of raspberry sherbet been standing there?

"Holly." My voice sounded calm. Good. I remembered to smile. "Wow. You're early today."

"Um," she said. "I was actually kind of hoping I could maybe talk to you. Just for a minute. You know, if you have time."

I straightened a few papers absently, and in the process, scuttled the ocean-turquoise travel brochure for Hawaii beneath the pile of chef's catalogs and order forms on my desk, where it had been sticking out like a Britney Spears fan at a Julie Andrews concert.

"Hey, then," I said to my assistant, intoning just the right casual, cheerful note. "Sit down."

"Where's Wesley?" she asked, arranging her lean legs in a puzzle of twists as she took the chair opposite my desk.

"Kitchen." I casually swept aside the pile of papers on my desk. "Doing Friday morning stuff."

Wesley Westcott and I own an event planning company in Los Angeles, going on eight years, which we operate out of my house. Holly has been with us almost from the start. Our firm does every kind of way-out party. Every kind. From the killer "Mock" Mitzvah we threw for the thirteen-year-old daughter of a millionaire rapper—never mind the family is Southern Baptist—to a series of small dinners for a hip mah-jongg club of Hollywood Hills gamblers, we just kind of elevate the celebratory insanity to meet our town's taste for the lavish. For each event, Wes and Holly and I work out every detail, plan every menu option, spend a ton of our clients' cash to achieve, as close as we ever can, a perfect party.

"Look, I know you're busy," Holly said, her manner much more subdued than her outfit. "But . . ."

"What's up?"

Holly fiddled with the enormous pink diamond on her third finger. "You know how I am, right?" She squunched her nose.

I began to pay closer attention. Aside from the standard-for-Holly outrageous wardrobe—the blinding garb and the neon-hued lipstick—I was beginning to perceive that this didn't look entirely like my usual Holly. My usual Holly was a million smiles, a pedal-to-the-metal talker. But now she was quiet. And I noticed her twisting her ring around and around. "Is something wrong, sweetie? Are you having some . . ." (There had to be a kinder word than "doubts") ". . . some thoughts about your wedding, Holl?"

"Yeah. How'd you . . . ?" She looked up at me. "Well, yeah."

"Is it Donald?"

"Donald? No, no. Donald is great. He's fine."

"Okay, then. Cool." The way she was acting had me worried, there.

"Donald?" she said, laughing. "He's fantastic. What a guy!"

In only two weeks time, Holly Nichols is to have her big

dream wedding and become Mrs. Donald Lake. There ha been all the usual plans and festivities. I thought they were extremely cute together. But truthfully, as a couple, they'd been through more than their share of ups and downs. On any given month, frankly, it was difficult to remember if they were on or off. But for most of the past six months, they'd been on. Way on. I looked at my watch. 8:34. We had twenty-six minutes, but I really should have been in the kitchen already working with Wes, so . . . "Okay, talk."

"Maddie, you know how you help people sometimes? Not just with planning the parties. I mean how you can solve problems for people. Like you look into things and figure them out."

"I like to get to the bottom of things. Yes."

"Take a look at this." Holly unzipped her hot pink purse, a narrow leather roll hardly large enough to hold a tube of lipstick and a pack of mints. She pulled out a piece of white copier paper that had been folded, fanlike, into a tiny slip, and handed it across the desk to me.

I unpleated the paper. It held a printed message and appeared to be a printout from Holly's e-mail account. Netscape, I noticed right away, and in the Subject field, it read: Ugly Trouble Coming. The e-mail was from: nmfhot@gotmail.com, but that meant nothing. Anyone could set up a gotmail account, they were free and untraceable, and hide their true identity. The date field said 5:02 this morning. It was addressed to Holly Dubinsky at holly@madbeanevents.com, her company e-mail account. The note read:

Mrs. Dubinsky,

Your husband won't be able to hide forever. And if we can't find him, we'll come and do our dirty business with you. Be smart. Give us Marvin and we'll leave you alone.

It was not signed.

"But," I said, rereading the note, "it's a mistake. You're Holly Nichols. Your husband-to-be is a screenwriter named Donald Lake. This is not you."

"Well . . ."

I looked up. Holly repositioned herself, rewrapping, right over left, long thin pink denim legs.

"There's this other thing. And I was meaning to get to this other thing, Mad. I was meaning to. But time just sort of slipped away from me."

"This *other* thing?"

Holly tipped her jaunty cap at a slightly different angle and chewed her lip.

I waited as patiently as I could, considering Wes was presently in the kitchen just down the hall at the back of the house, receiving our secret guests all alone, and probably wondering why I was taking so long. Finally I could hold it in no longer. "Holly? This other thing?"

"This other thing," Holly said, "is kind of a goofy thing. Look, you know me. I have all the best intentions. Right? I want to help my fellow man. Women, too." She stopped and looked up.

"You're a helper," I prompted.

"Thanks. And then, sometimes I can get distracted. I mean, I don't have anything like A.D.D. or that, but you know I've never been tested for it, either, and . . ."

"Holly," I said, with a little snap to my voice. "Please. This century."

"Okay. I think I got married when I was eighteen to a guy named Marvin. Frankly, I could hardly remember his last name."

I stared at her.

She continued. "I guess it could have been Dubinsky."

"You got married?"

"I'm not totally sure about that part. It was Vegas, Mac die. We were kids. It was after the prom."

"The prom? You got married after your high school prom?"

"Hey." She looked thoroughly miserable. "I can't remember everything I ever did, can I? I thought it was a joke."

Okay. I'm a professional problem solver. I get paid to do this—although usually the problem has to do with how to feed thirty hungry nine-year-olds when the parents told us they were only inviting ten. But still, I guess you could say I know a problem when I come across one. Holly, whose wedding to Donald Lake was only fourteen days away, was already married to another guy. A guy named Marvin. I tried to get my dear young friend to focus. "Holly!"

Under the jaunty hot pink cap, beneath the fringe of blonde hair, her bright blue eyes were on me, intense. "This is bad."

No, no, no. This had to be a joke. I smiled at her. "Are you telling me that all this time we've known each other, you have really been Mrs. Marvin Dubinsky?"

Unfortunately, Holly didn't smile back. "Possibly."

"Oh, man. So you never got it annulled? Or filed for a divorce? Or talked to an attorney?"

"My bad." She raised her eyebrows, waiting for me to yell at her or something.

"Holl. You know that motto they have now: 'What happens in Vegas stays in Vegas'? You can't really count on that."

"I'm an idiot. I know." Her eyes burned bright with anger, directed inward. "I just didn't think about it. It didn't seem for real."

She was my friend and she was in pain. Holly's lovely

e crumpled, showing that awkward, it's-my-own-damned-ult kind of pain—the pain of consequences slowly and finally catching up.

Holly. Always so wonderfully carefree. No worries. But me, I am the yin to Holly's yang. I see the potential for danger everywhere. I check things out ahead of time. I research. I plan. I prepare. I wouldn't go to the corner 7-11 without thinking it through, let alone go out on a date with a guy whose last name I couldn't recall. Or to the prom. *Or to a wedding chapel in the middle of the night with a fresh marriage license in my hot little hand.* Now that, no matter where you stand on the control-freak scale, was totally flipping nuts.

But my way, the tiptoe through life way, was not the right recipe for everyone. And I loved Holly and the way she could charge ahead in life without worrying herself to death over six zillion things that could go wrong.

In the end, I had to laugh. "Honey, who the hell is Marvin Dubinsky?" Holly was twenty-six and yet, in all the time we'd been buds, I had never heard that name.

"He was just some guy from high school. He was in a band," Holly said, relaxing back in her seat, smiling back at me. "The Roots. He played bass."

"Sounds like your type."

"He was the shortest guy in our senior class."

"It figures." I got a great mental picture of teenage Holly, Amazonian-tall wild child that she must have been, attending her senior prom with the most vertically-challenged boy in school.

"He was really, really smart. He took all APs and had a freaking enormous brain. He ended up going to some supergeek college, I think. University of the Insanely Gifted, or something."

Holly has a certain flare for picking men. Always had. "So you married a diminutive, bass-playing genius?"

"He was a sweet guy. I think he was going to go into some agro-techy field, you know, study plants. Like Aquaponics, or I don't know what."

"Botany?"

"He grew orchids and bromeliads and stuff like that."

"Holly, you are like a magnet for weird males."

"I can't help it. It's like a gift."

"So what happened?"

"Well, he was like my tutor for senior Bio. That's how we met. Without Marvin I'm sure I would have flunked the damned course, but he got me through. At the end of senior year, after all those Tuesdays and Thursdays in the science room after school, he finally told me he was in love with me, which, you know . . ." Holly became a bit dreamy-eyed at the memory. "Well, he was sorta sweet. So, anyway, one day he admitted to me his darkest secret; that he hadn't been able to get a date."

"To the prom?"

"*Ever.*" She shook her head, awed. "Isn't that, like, sad?"

I thought about high school. What a minefield of pain it could be for the short, smart guy. I sighed.

"So you know me," Holly continued. "I'm all heart. I just felt it was my duty to help the poor kid out. He was really a pretty funny guy when he wasn't getting all giggly. I think I made him nervous."

I nodded, picturing it all, and bit my lip.

"And I think he was gonna have a nice smile someday, you know, when he got his braces off."

"The poor boy was still wearing braces in 12th grade?"

Holly nodded, grinning. "He had what we might call 'appearance issues', Maddie. And he was shy. So I just got it into my head and asked him to our prom."

"You have always been very sweet."

"My friends thought I dated him just because he gave me

all the answers to the Bio final, but that wasn't it at all. I mean, I was really grateful for the help with those answers, but I had always kind of liked him. He used to write me poems, Maddie. I used to go home and actually look up some of the words. They were always flattering, too. Like he called me 'serene'."

"Okay. You asked him to your prom. This is all fine. Generous even. But then you married him?"

"I honestly don't know how that happened. One thing led to another. I was pretty wasted, actually. Everyone gets too drunk on prom night; you know how that is. And we were having fun, Marvin and I. And I didn't have to get home right away because my parents already thought I was going to stay overnight with my girlfriends."

"So after your prom, you went to Vegas?"

"Right. He told the limo driver to keep driving. He'd been joking with me all night about how I was wearing this white gown and he was in a tux and we looked like we were getting married. When we got to Vegas he told the chauffeur-guy to drive to the Marriage Bureau over on 3rd Street and see if they were still open. It was something like four in the morning."

"And they were open, I'm guessing."

"Did you know that that city office stays open until midnight most every night of the week and 24-hours on holidays, Maddie?"

"Incredible service," I said, and wondered why my local library couldn't stay open on Saturdays.

"So I guess we got a marriage license. I wish I could remember that night more clearly, but I do seem to recall I had to find my driver's license for some reason. I just don't know! I mean, we were having a great time and I was smashed."

"Okay, Holly. But think hard. Did it all end in a ceremony at some chapel and then move on to the traditional wedding night . . . event?"

"I swear. It's all a hazy blur." Holly just widened her al- ready wide eyes. "I wish I could remember."

"My God, Holly."

"I know," she said.

"Correction," I said, in awe of Holly's entire romantic history, but this chapter taking the prize. "Make that: my God, Mrs. Dubinsky."

"It's totally twisted, for sure." Holly shook her head slowly.

"So how did it end?"

"It was my fault, no doubt," she said, with a guilty look. "I mean, it had all been a lark. We were just having fun. And then I guess I kind of flaked on poor Marvin."

"You broke his heart?"

"I never meant to hurt his feelings in a million years, but I think that's what happened. The next day, I remember I was mega-hungover. We drove back to L.A. in the limo and I called my mom to kind of update my cover story, and to check for messages. I guess I shouldn't have squealed so loudly right in front of Marvin, but my mom told me I'd gotten a call from Griffin Potecky."

I looked at her, not understanding this turn of events.

"Griffin Potecky was a teen god, Maddie. I'd had a crush on Griffin since middle school. I'd been trying to get him to notice me forever. And he was finally calling me! But I probably shouldn't have squealed in front of Marvin, huh?"

"Hm."

"And then I got dropped off at home. Next thing I heard, my sister told me Marvin had gone right off to college, early, just like that. And I never heard another word from him."

"Wow."

"But, Mad, this was all so long ago. I haven't really thought about Marvin or the prom or any of it in years."

"Does Donald know about this?"

"No. Heck, I don't even really know."

Just then, a muffled sound made its way from the back of the house, from the direction of the kitchen. We both looked up.

"What's that?" Holly asked. "Wes?"

"Must be," I said, and quickly went back to Holly's urgent matter. "But, now, about your present crisis."

"Can you help me?"

"Of course. It looks like you have three main problems, Holl."

"You are always so organized," she said, exhaling. "Thanks, Maddie. Thanks."

"First, if I had to place a bet, I'd say you probably *are* married to this Dubinsky person, because how else would these anonymous e-mailers get your name unless it was off of some official marriage record somewhere, right? Which means you need to get out of that fluky old marriage immediately in order to marry your Donald."

"Right."

"Second, you are going to have to tell Donald about your past."

Holly nodded, her face serious. "Okay. I can do all that."

"Good."

"And third?" Holly asked.

"But then, third, clearly," I said, looking back at the creased paper, "since you actually knew a Marvin Dubinsky, and you actually *married* a Marvin Dubinsky, then you are actually the Holly these jerks are threatening by anonymous e-mail, after all."

"That's the part," Holly said, "that I sort of already *got*, Mad."

"And I hate to see anyone I love being bullied. So just don't worry about this anymore, okay? Some idiots using scare tactics. We'll get to the bottom of it."

"I knew you could help me."

"Do you have any idea where Marvin Dubinsky is toda

"I have absolutely no idea in the world," she said. "Na none, zilch."

"Well, that's something we need to find out. Because this Marvin dude seems to be dragging you into some kind of trouble and we have to clear that up."

"Cool."

"And we're going to need to get you clear of that marriage, too, if it was legal and you really got hitched."

"Right."

"So we'll just have to do a little digging around and find Marvin Dubinsky. I mean, how hard can that be?"

A feast of funny, savory, and delectable murder

JERRILYN FARMER

The Madeline Bean Novels

PERFECT SAX

0-380-81720-9
$6.99 US/$9.99 Can

Just as Madeline is wondering what else can go wrong at the prestigious Jazz Ball, the hip event planner arrives home to discover a dead body in her bedroom.

MUMBO GUMBO

0-380-81719-5
$6.99 US/$9.99 Can

When Madeline fills in as a writer for a hot TV game show featuring a dishy celebrity chef she finds herself face-to-face with a murderer.

DIM SUM DEAD

0-380-81718-7
$5.99 US/$7.99 Can

Madeline and her charming partner Wesley are determined to throw a gonzo Chinese New Year banquet. Until one of the mah-jongg players turns up dead.

A KILLER WEDDING

0-380-79598-1
$6.99 US/$9.99 Can

When a corpse turns up at a glittering wedding party in the Nature Museum's Hall of Dinosaurs, Maddie just may be the next species to become extinct...

IMMACULATE RECEPTION

0-380-79597-3
$6.50 US/$8.99 Can

Things quickly go from serene to sinister when a young priest turns up dead in the bed of an uninhibited Hollywood star.

SYMPATHY FOR THE DEVIL

0-380-79596-5
$5.99 US/$7.99 Can

Madeline and her partner Wesley have successfully pulled off Hollywood's most outrageous A-list Halloween party when a notorious producer is poisoned to death.

And coming soon in hardcover

THE FLAMING LUAU OF DEATH

0-06-058729-6 • $23.95 US/$33.95 Can

Available wherever books are sold or please call 1-800-331-3761 to order.

AuthorTracker

www.AuthorTracker.com JF 1104

AGATHA AWARD-WINNING AUTHOR
JILL CHURCHILL

The Jane Jeffry Mysteries

BELL, BOOK, AND SCANDAL

0-06-009900-3/$6.99 US/$9.99 Can

When a famous ego-squashing editor is undone by an anonymous poisoner at a mystery convention, suburban homemaker Jane Jeffry and her best friend Shelley Nowack jump right in, ready to snoop, eavesdrop and gossip their way to a solution.

THE HOUSE OF SEVEN MABELS

0-380-80492-1/$6.99 US/$9.99 Can

While helping to restore and redecorate a decrepit old mansion, one of their fellow workwomen ends up dead, leaving Jane and Shelley to try and nail the assassin.

MULCH ADO ABOUT NOTHING

0-380-80491-3/$6.50 US/$8.99 Can

Jane and Shelley's scheme to improve themselves dies on the vine when the celebrated botanist slated to teach a class at the Community Center is mysteriously beaten into a coma.

A GROOM WITH A VIEW

0-380-79450-0/$6.99 US/$9.99 Can

While Jane plans a wedding for the daughter of a prominent, wealthy businessman, someone suspiciously slips down the stairs to her death.